HEARTSTOPPER

VOLUME 3

All rights reserved. Published by Graphix, an imprint of Scholastic Inc.,
Publishers since 1920. SCHOLASTIC, GRAPHIX, and associated logos are
trademarks and/or registered trademarks of Scholastic Inc.

The publisher does not have any control over and does not assume any
responsibility for author or third-party websites or their content.

Heartstopper: Volume 3 was originally published in England
by Hachette Children's Group in 2020.

This book is a work of fiction. Names, characters, places, and incidents
are either the product of the author's imagination or are used fictitiously,
and any resemblance to actual persons, living or dead, business
establishments, events, or locales is entirely coincidental.

Library of Congress Control Number: 2019957497

ISBN 978-1-338-61753-5 (hardcover)
ISBN 978-1-338-61752-8 (paperback)

10 9 8 7 6 5 4 3 2 1   21 22 23 24 25

Printed in China 167
This edition first printing, May 2021

ALICE OSEMAN

HEARTSTOPPER

VOLUME 3

graphix
An Imprint of
■SCHOLASTIC

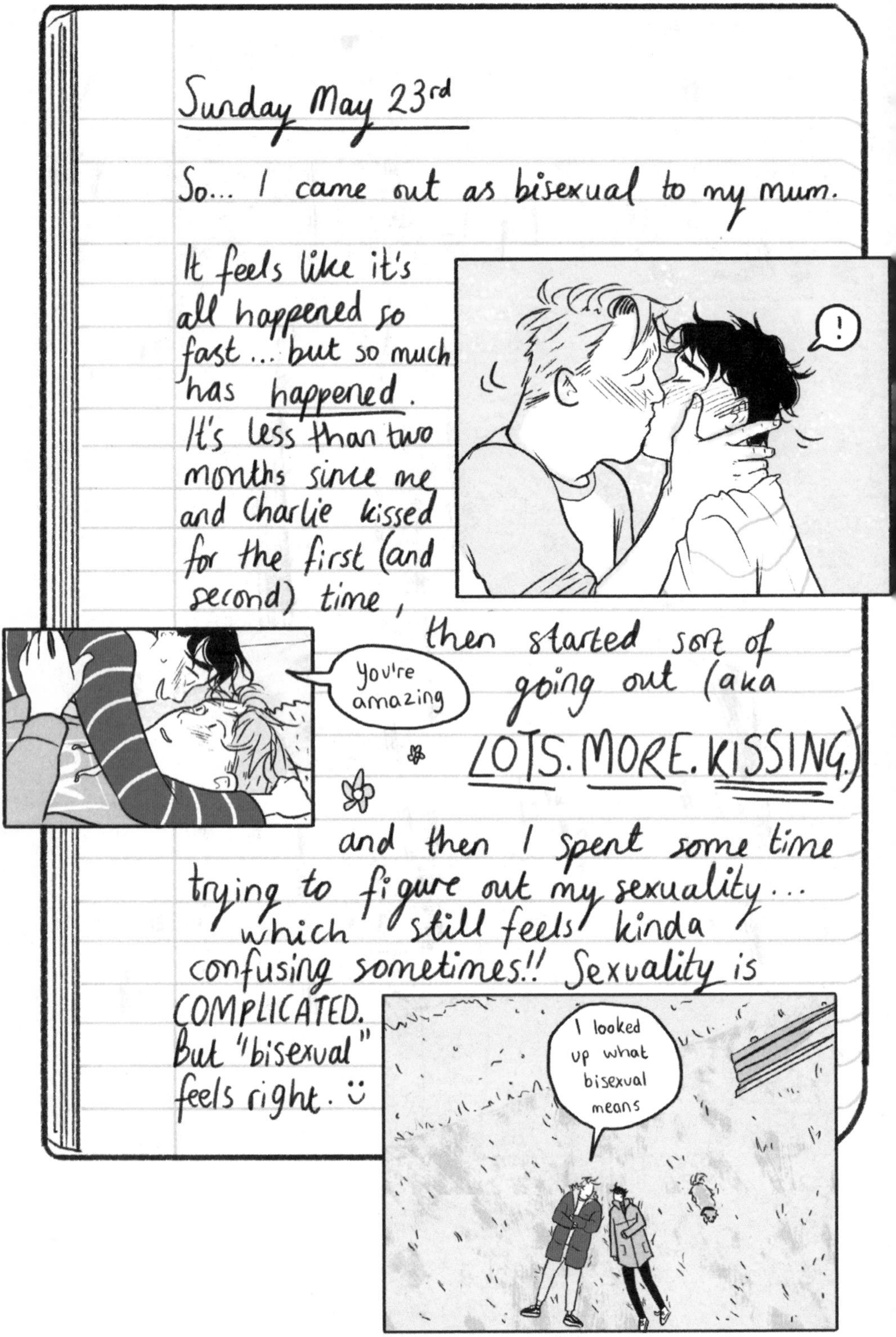
Sunday May 23rd
So... I came out as bisexual to my mum.
It feels like it's all happened so fast... but so much has happened. It's less than two months since me and Charlie kissed for the first (and second) time,
!
then started sort of going out (aka LOTS. MORE. KISSING.)
You're amazing
and then I spent some time trying to figure out my sexuality... which still feels kinda confusing sometimes!! Sexuality is COMPLICATED. But "bisexual" feels right. :)
I looked up what bisexual means

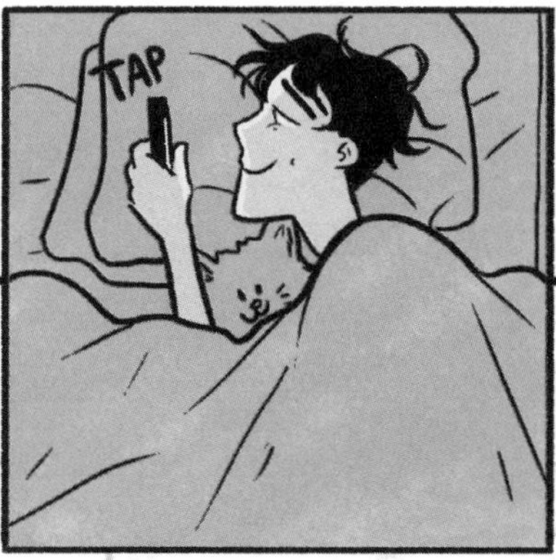
TAP

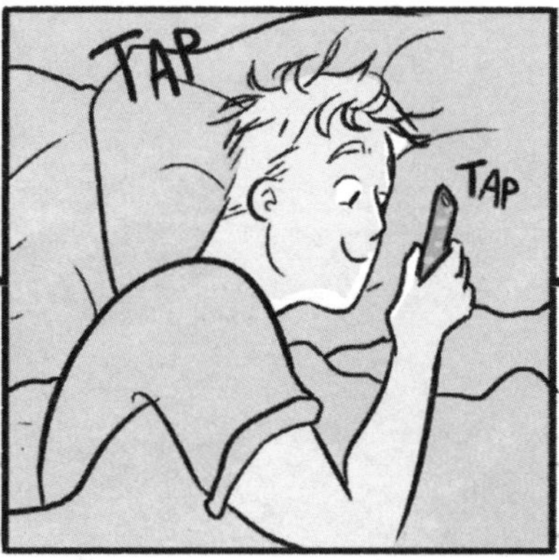
TAP
TAP

And now we're officially boyfriends. That feels so awesome to say.

I HAVE A BOYFRIEND!!!!

(and he's amazing ♥)

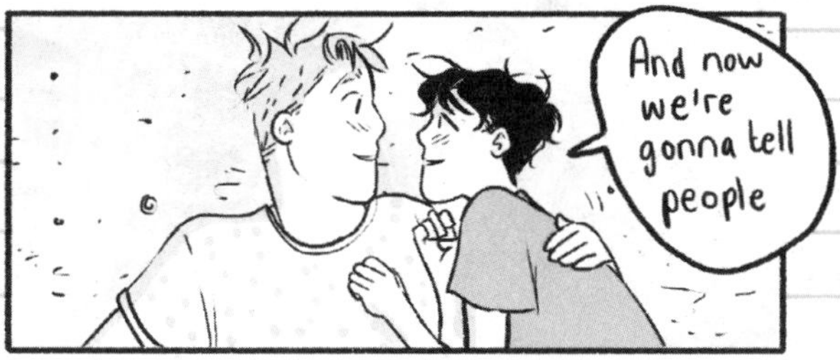
And now we're gonna tell people

We said we might start telling our friends and people at school, but... how would we do that?? No one even knows I like guys. And Charlie got bullied pretty badly when he was outed last year.

Maybe it'd be better to keep it a secret for a bit longer...

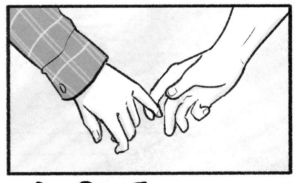

4.OUT

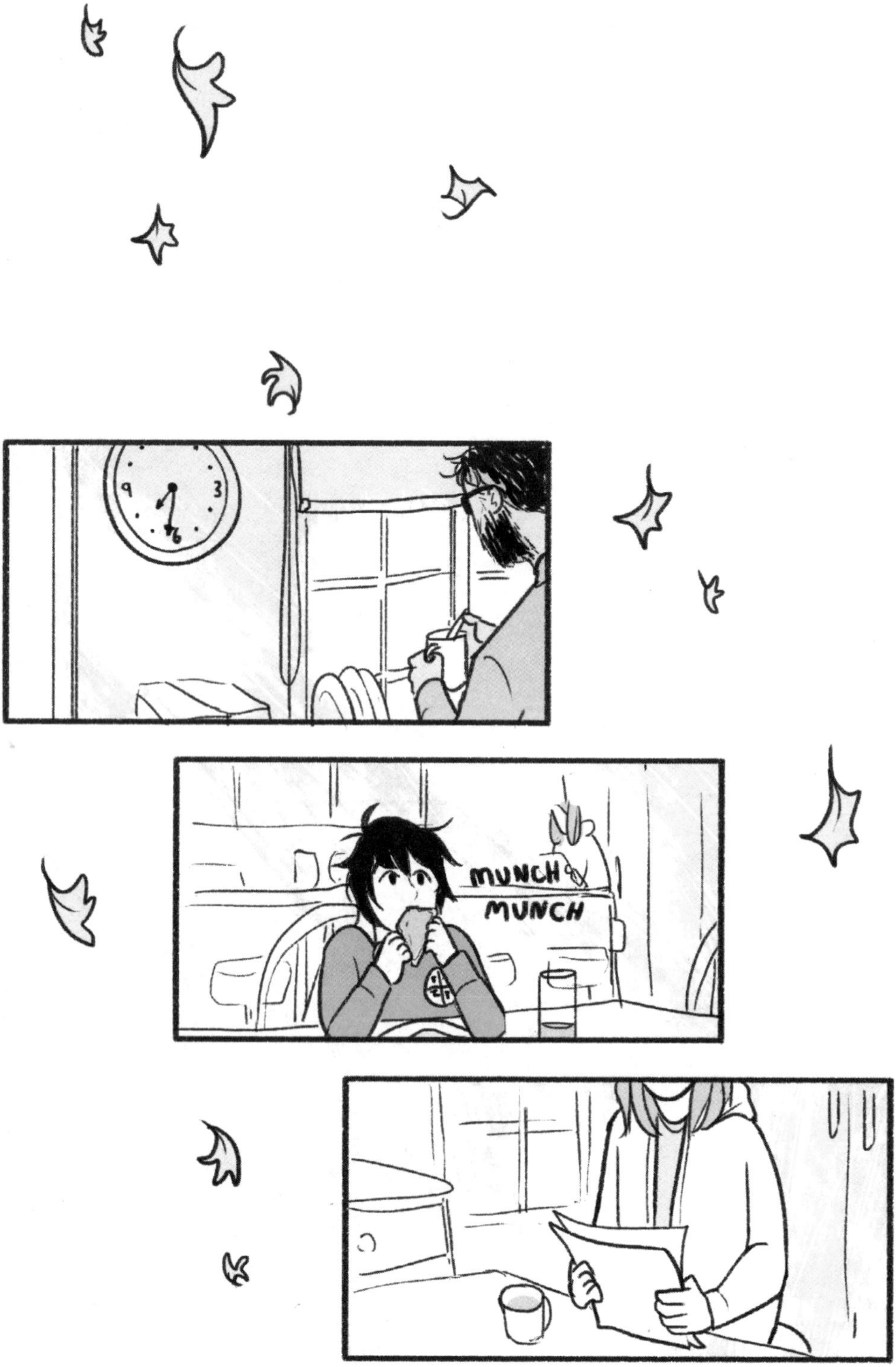
MUNCH
MUNCH

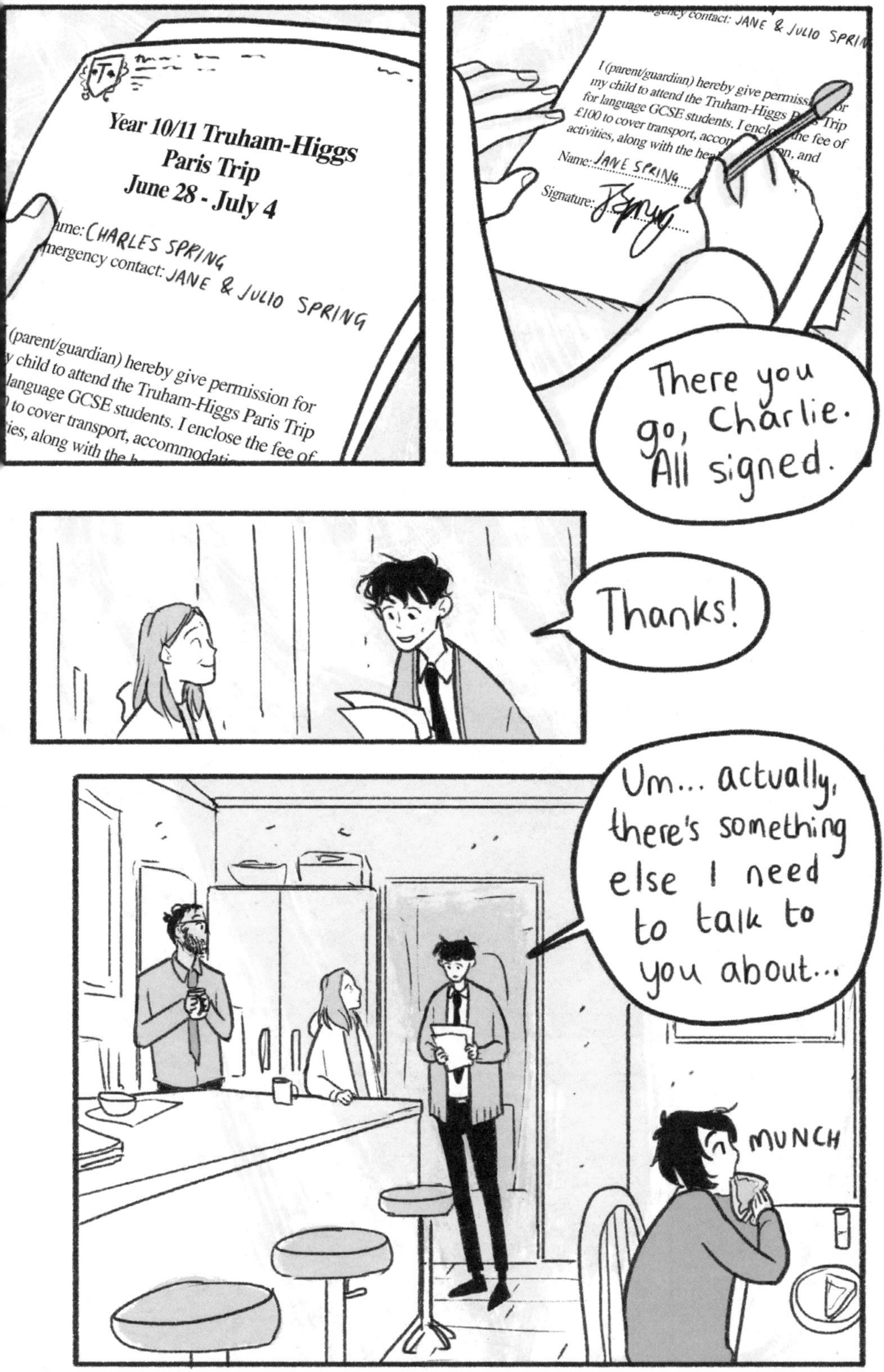

Year 10/11 Truham-Higgs Paris Trip June 28 - July 4
CHARLES SPRING
JANE & JULIO SPRING
(parent/guardian) hereby give permission for
child to attend the Truham-Higgs Paris Trip
language GCSE students. I enclose the fee of
to cover transport, accommodati
I (parent/guardian) hereby give permiss
for language GCSE students. I enclo
Name: JANE SPRING
Signature:
There you go, Charlie. All signed.
Thanks!
Um... actually, there's something else I need to talk to you about...
MUNCH

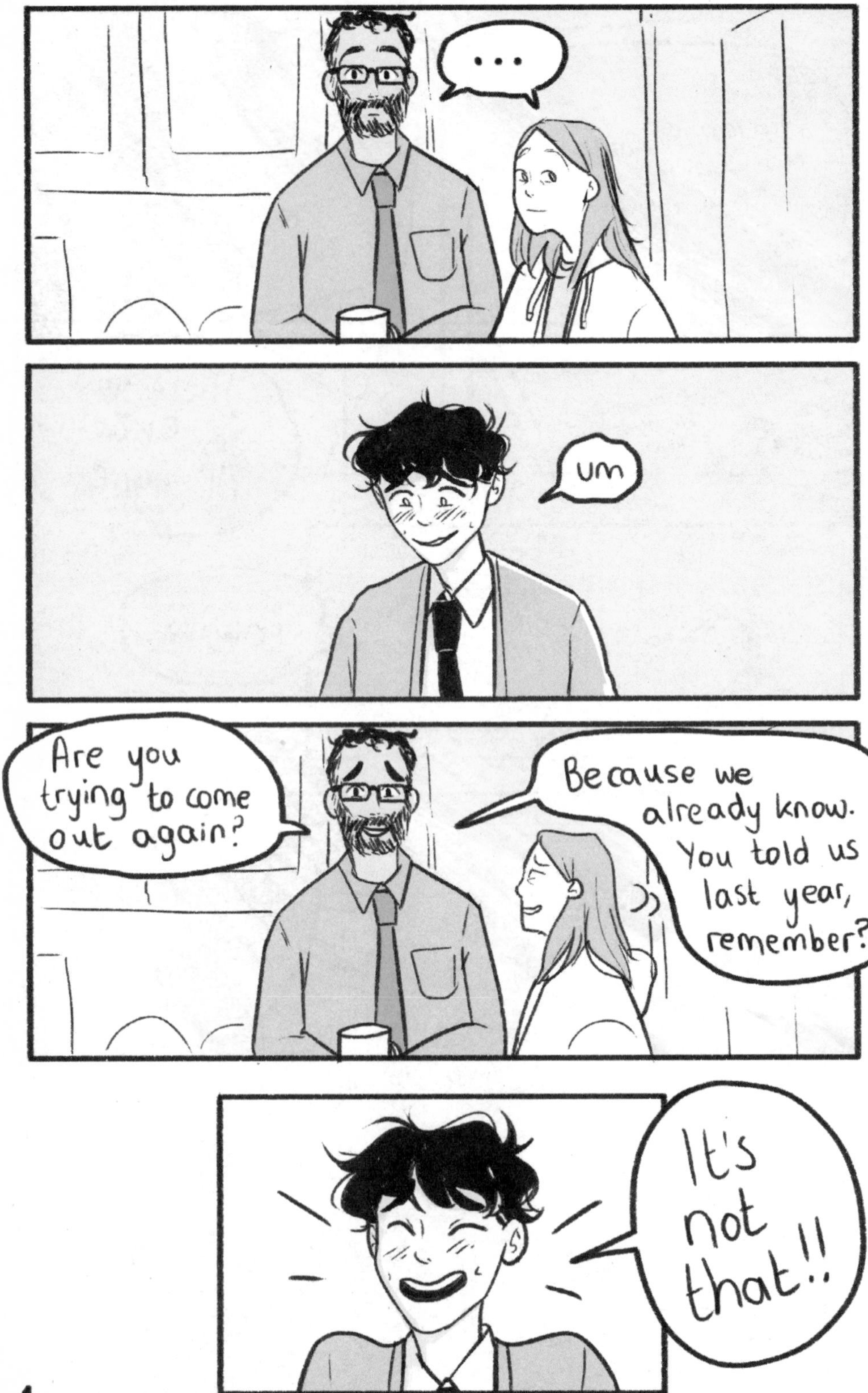
...
um
Are you trying to come out again?
Because we already know. You told us last year, remember?
It's not that!!

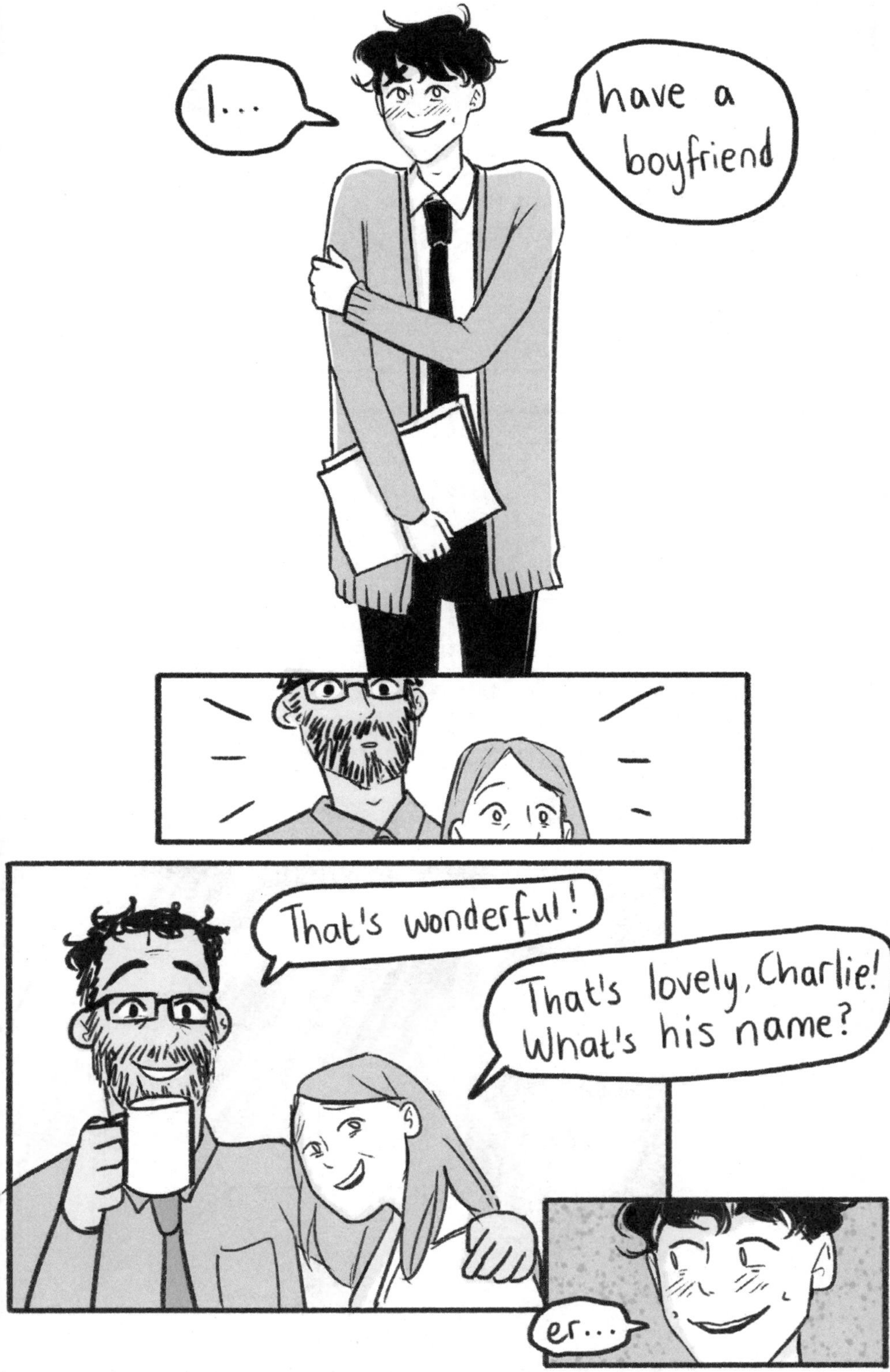
I...
have a boyfriend
That's wonderful!
That's lovely, Charlie! What's his name?
er...

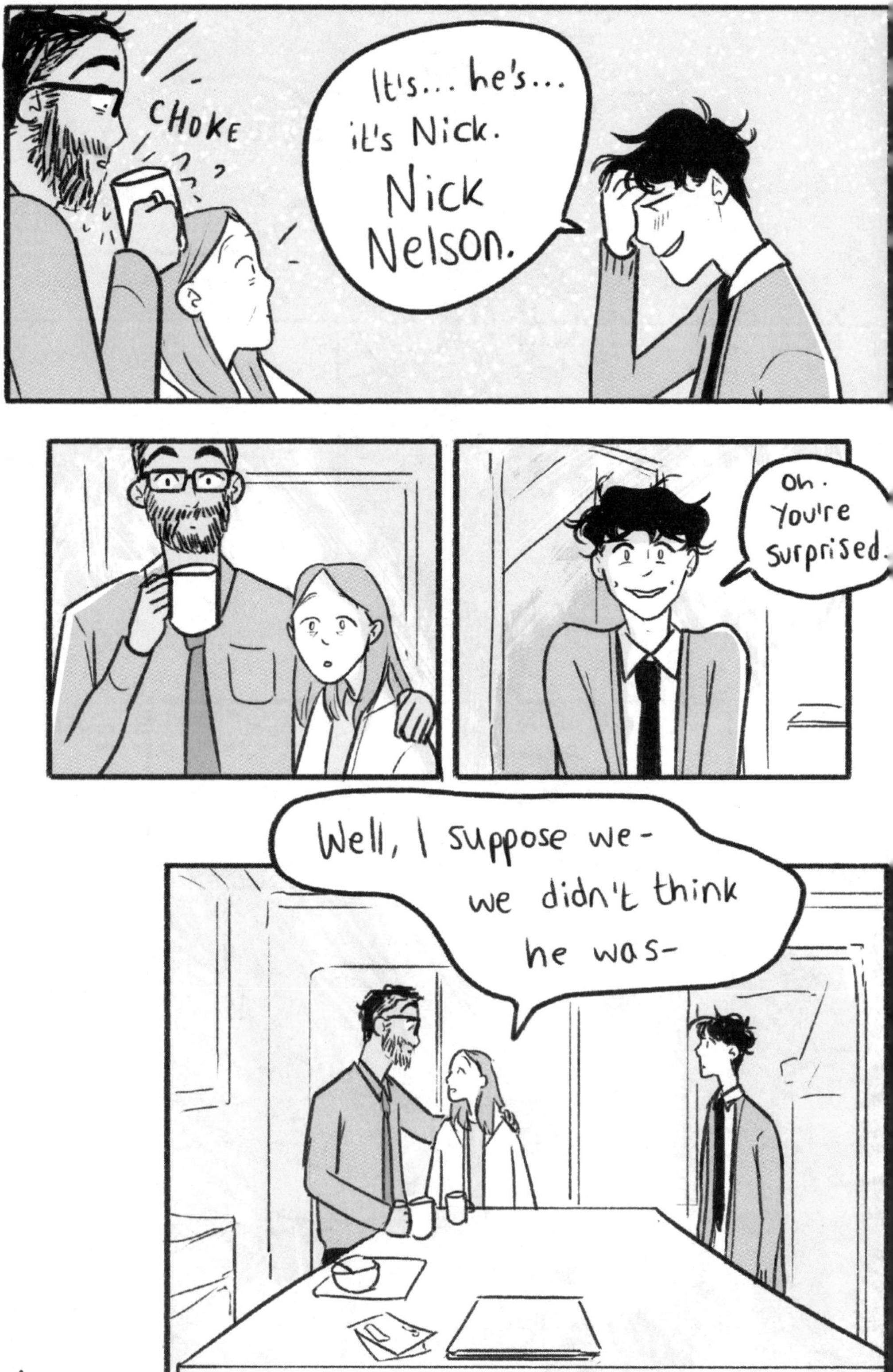
CHOKE
It's... he's...
it's Nick.
Nick
Nelson.
Oh.
You're
surprised.
Well, I suppose we-
we didn't think
he was-

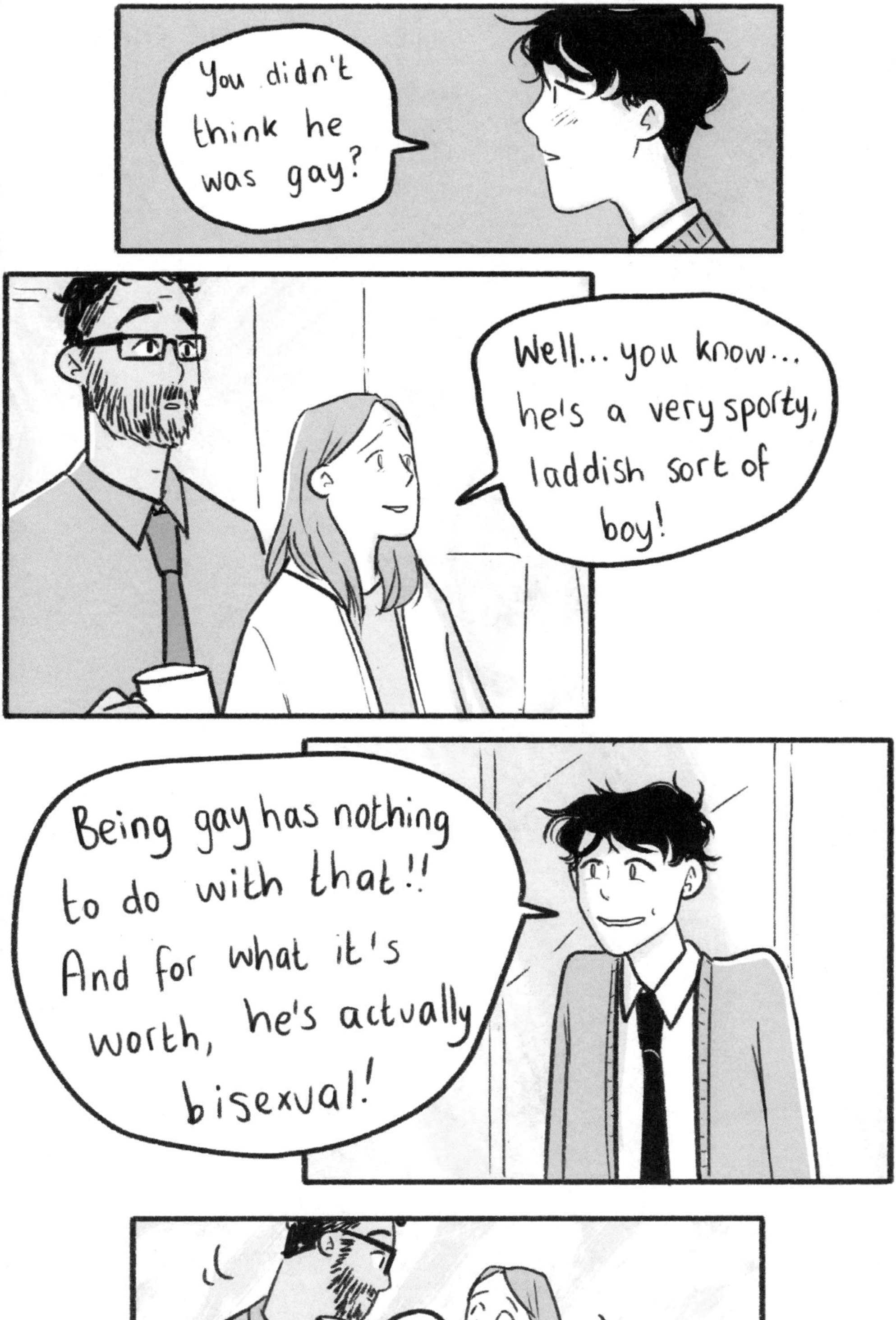
You didn't think he was gay?
Well... you know... he's a very sporty, laddish sort of boy!
Being gay has nothing to do with that!! And for what it's worth, he's actually bisexual!
...

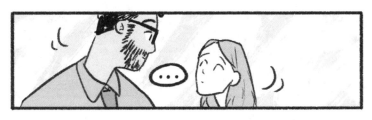

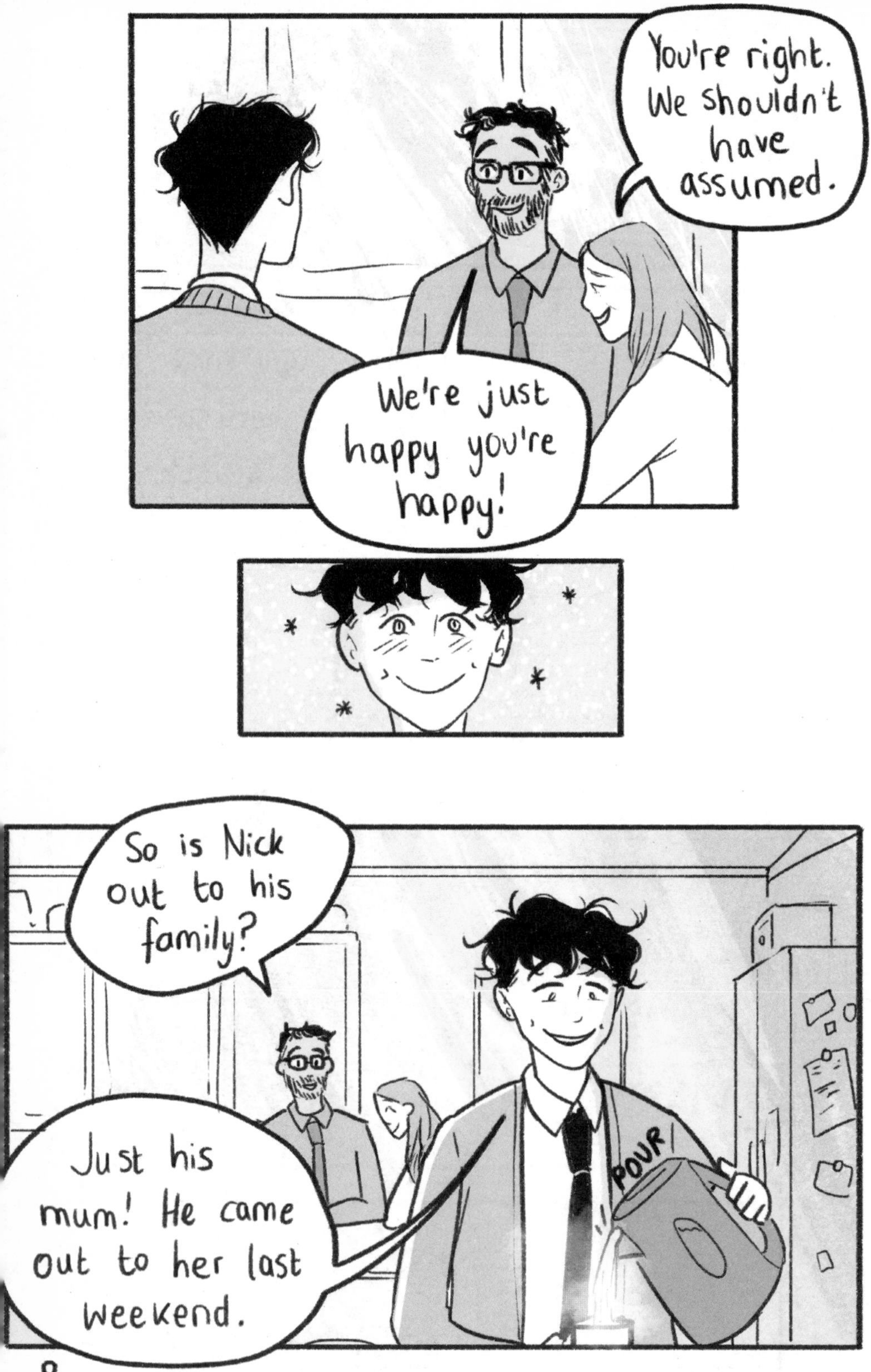
You're right. We shouldn't have assumed.
We're just happy you're happy!
So is Nick out to his family?
Just his mum! He came out to her last weekend.
POUR

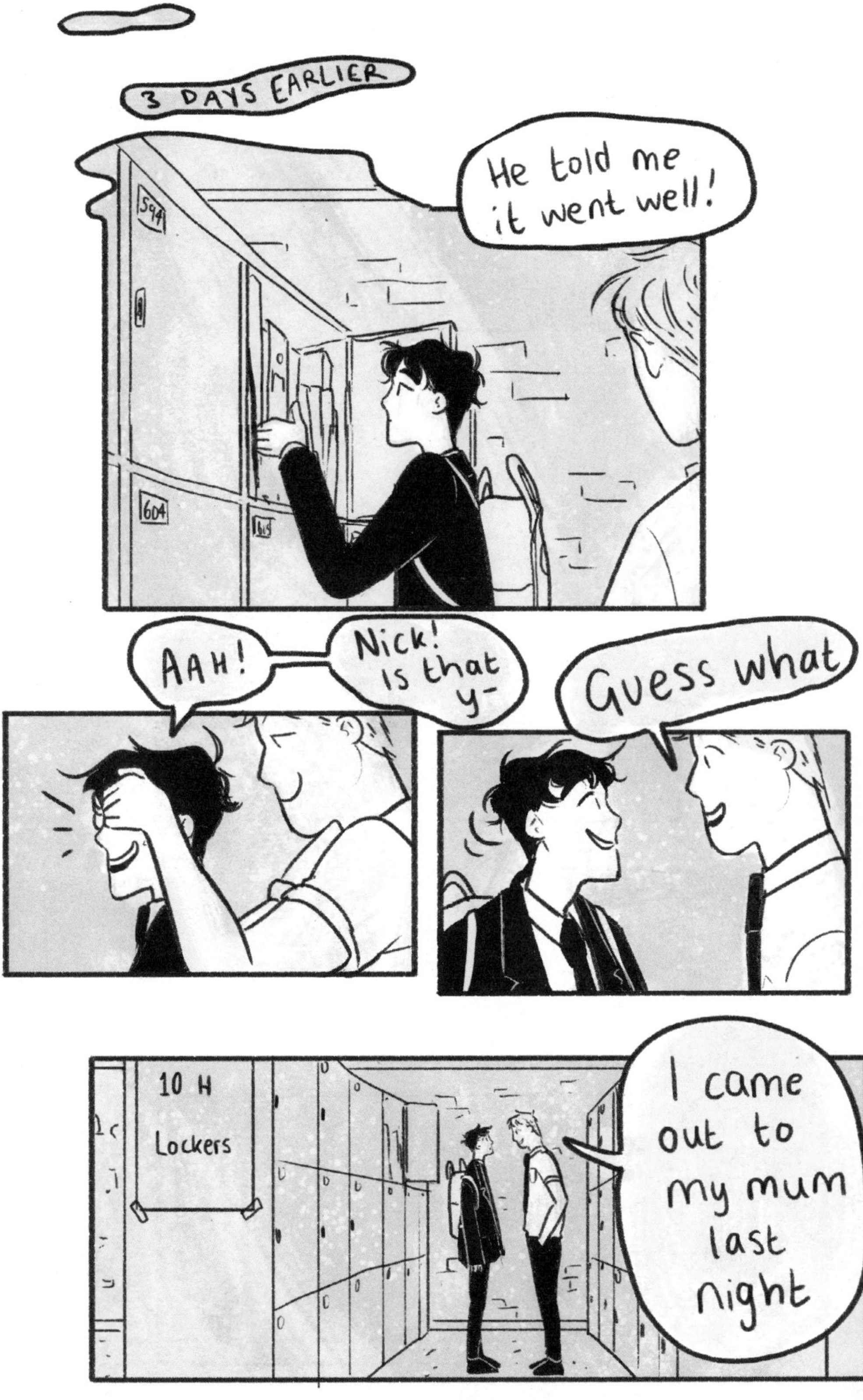
3 DAYS EARLIER
He told me it went well!
594
604
AAH!
Nick! is that y-
Guess what
10 H
Lockers
I came out to my mum last night

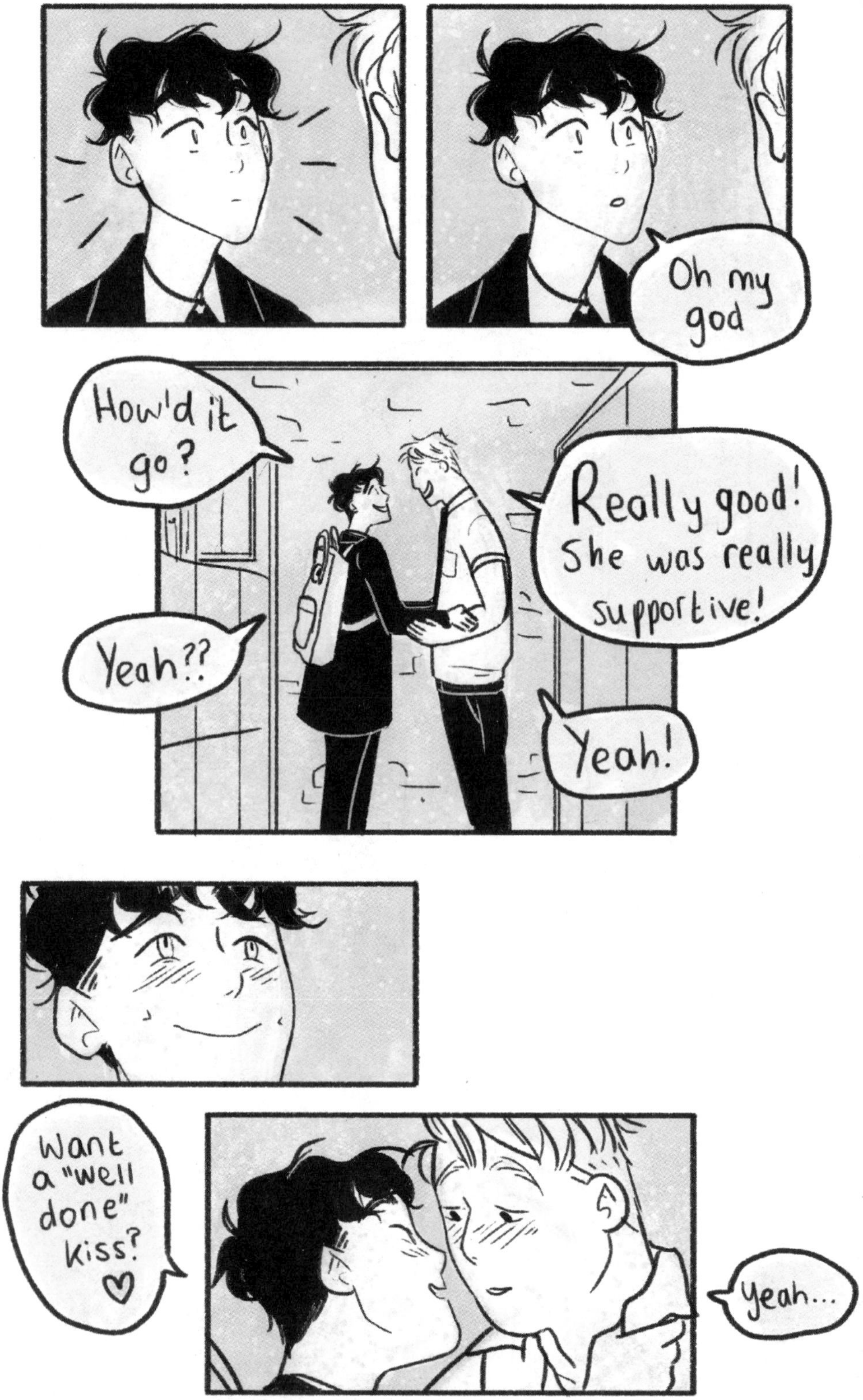

Oh my god
How'd it go?
Really good! She was really supportive!
Yeah??
Yeah!
Want a "well done" kiss? ♡
Yeah...

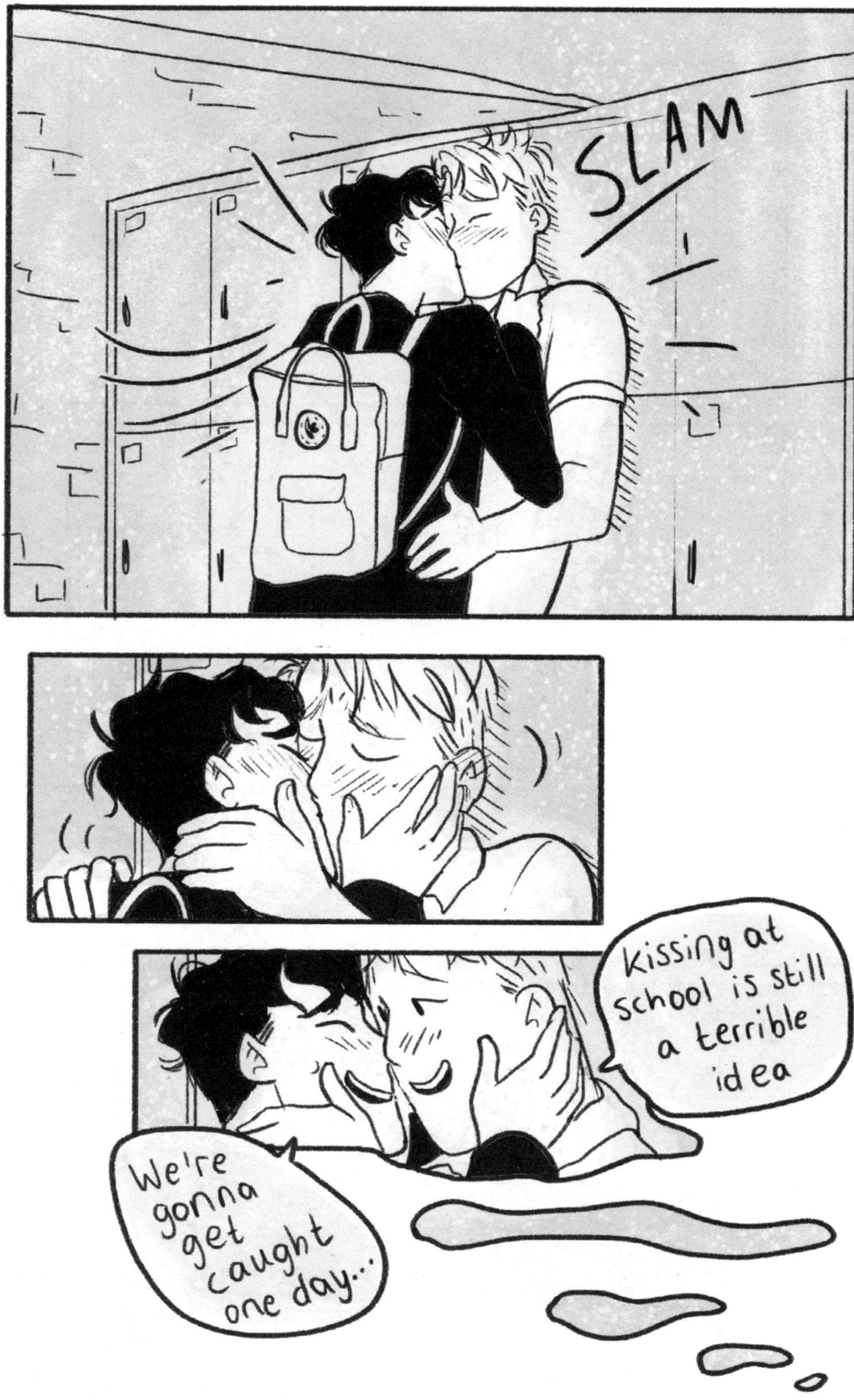
SLAM
Kissing at school is still a terrible idea
We're gonna get caught one day...

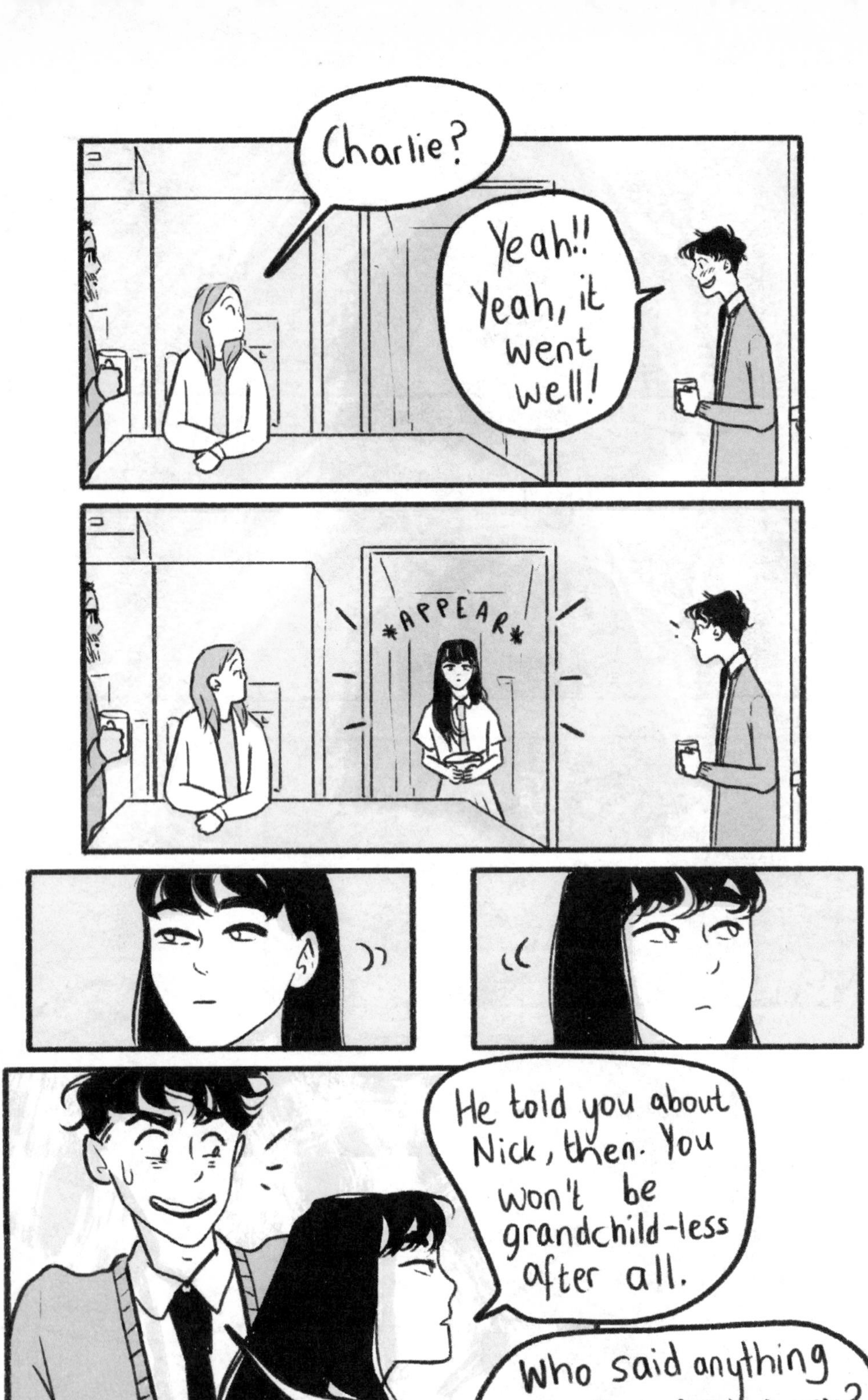
Charlie?
Yeah!! Yeah, it went well!
APPEAR
He told you about Nick, then. You won't be grandchild-less after all.
Who said anything about GRANDCHILDREN?

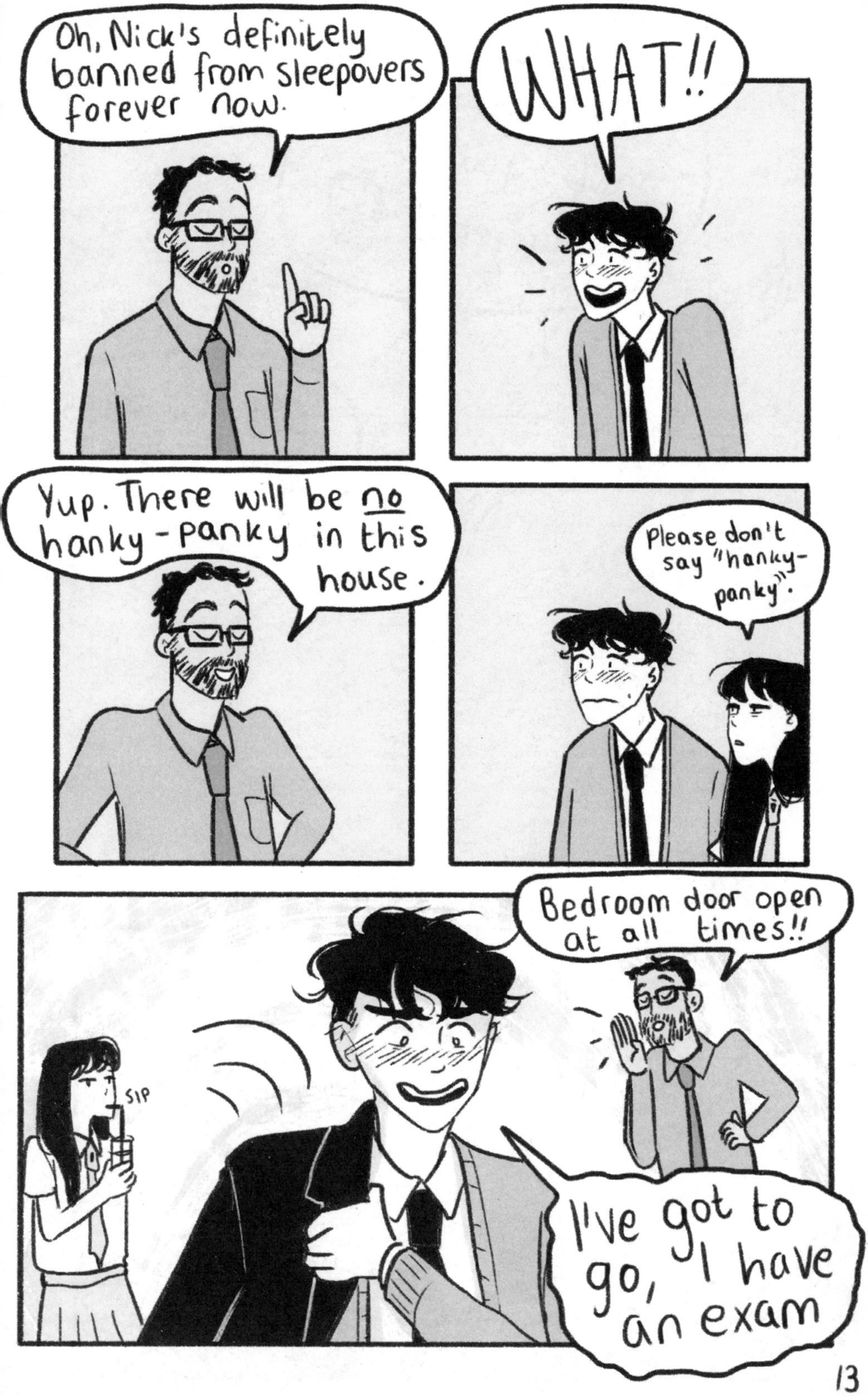
Oh, Nick's definitely banned from sleepovers forever now.
WHAT!!
Yup. There will be no hanky-panky in this house.
Please don't say "hanky-panky".
Bedroom door open at all times!!
SIP
I've got to go, I have an exam

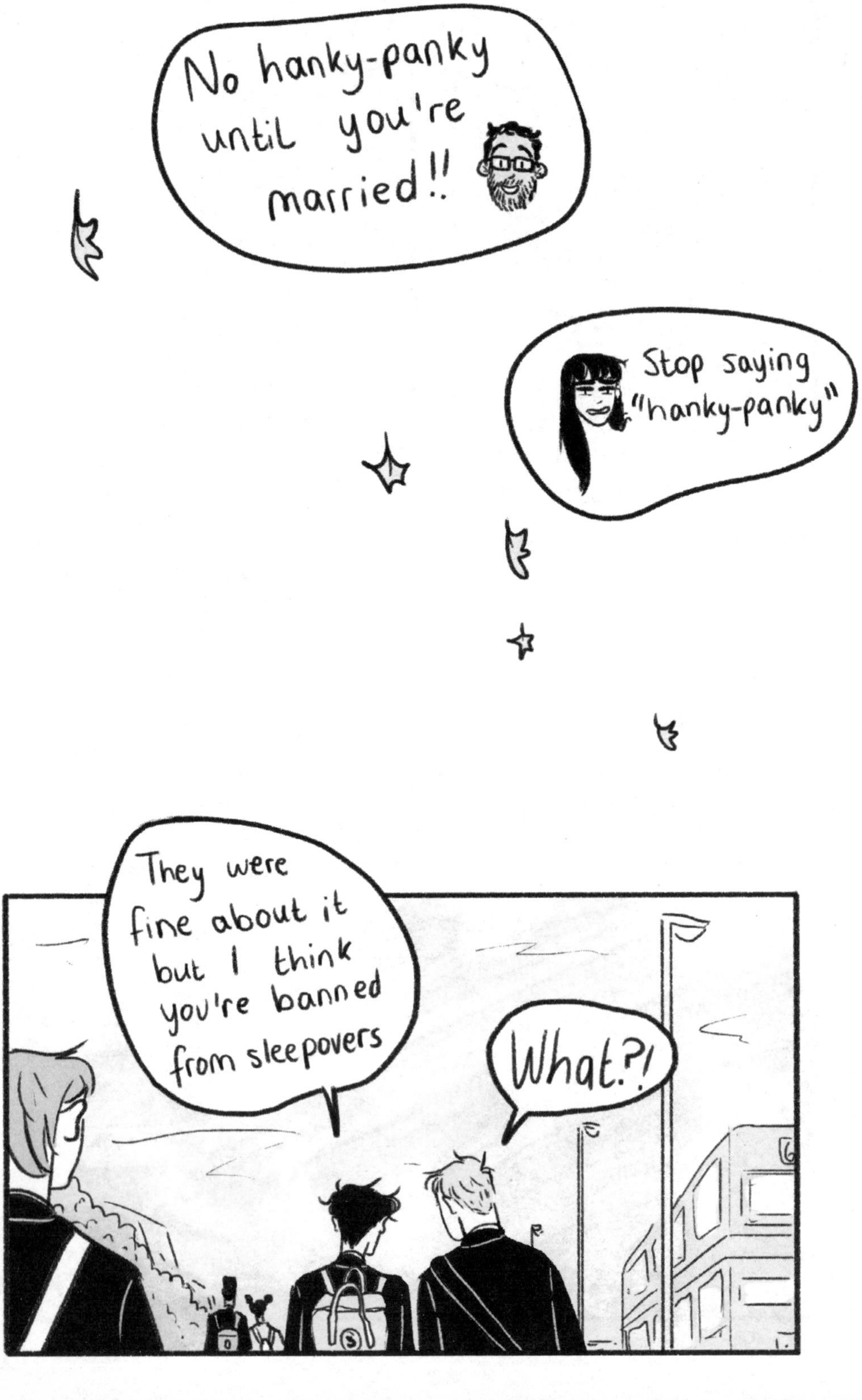
No hanky-panky until you're married!!
Stop saying "hanky-panky"
They were fine about it but I think you're banned from sleepovers
What?!

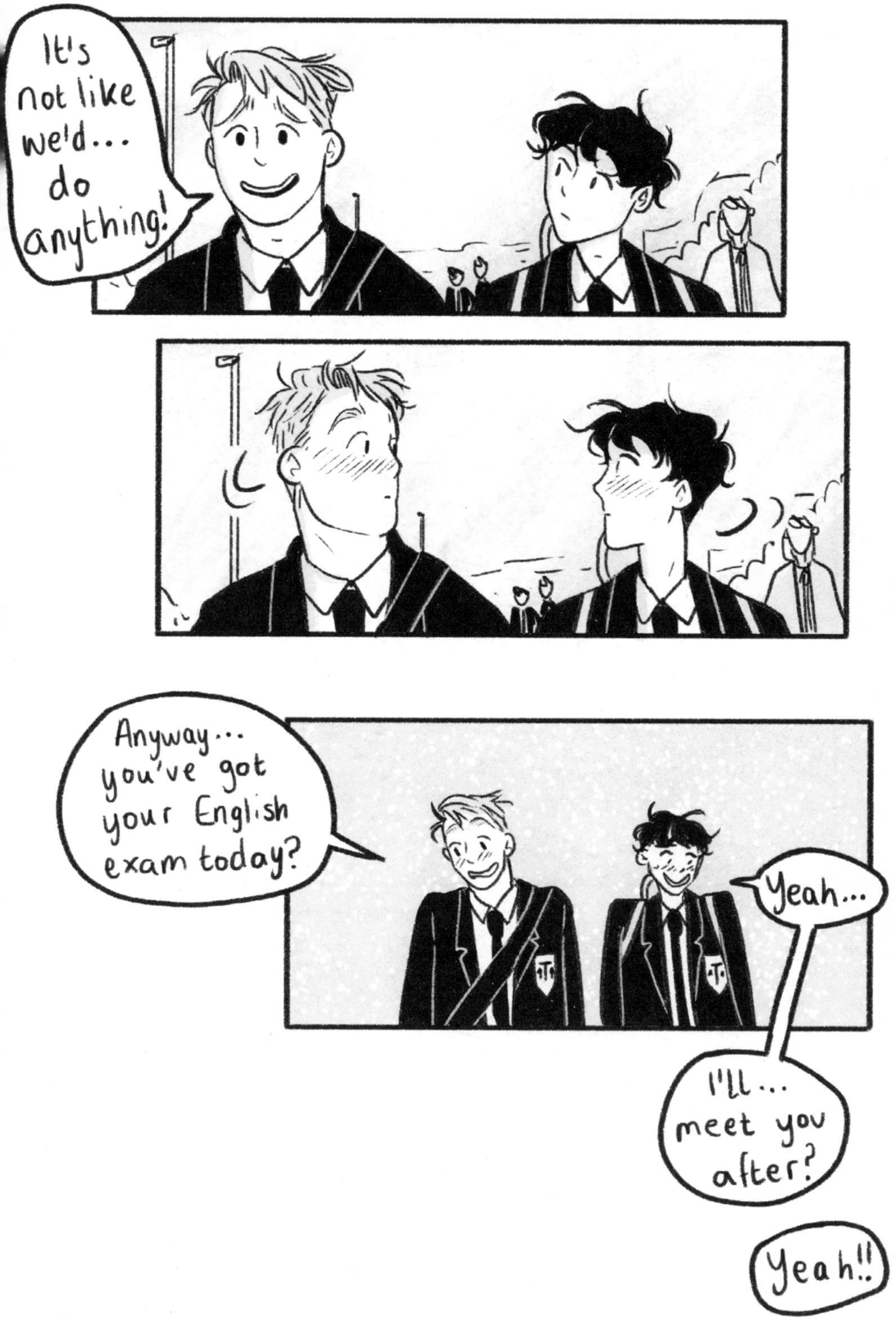
It's not like we'd... do anything!
Anyway... you've got your English exam today?
Yeah...
I'll... meet you after?
Yeah!!

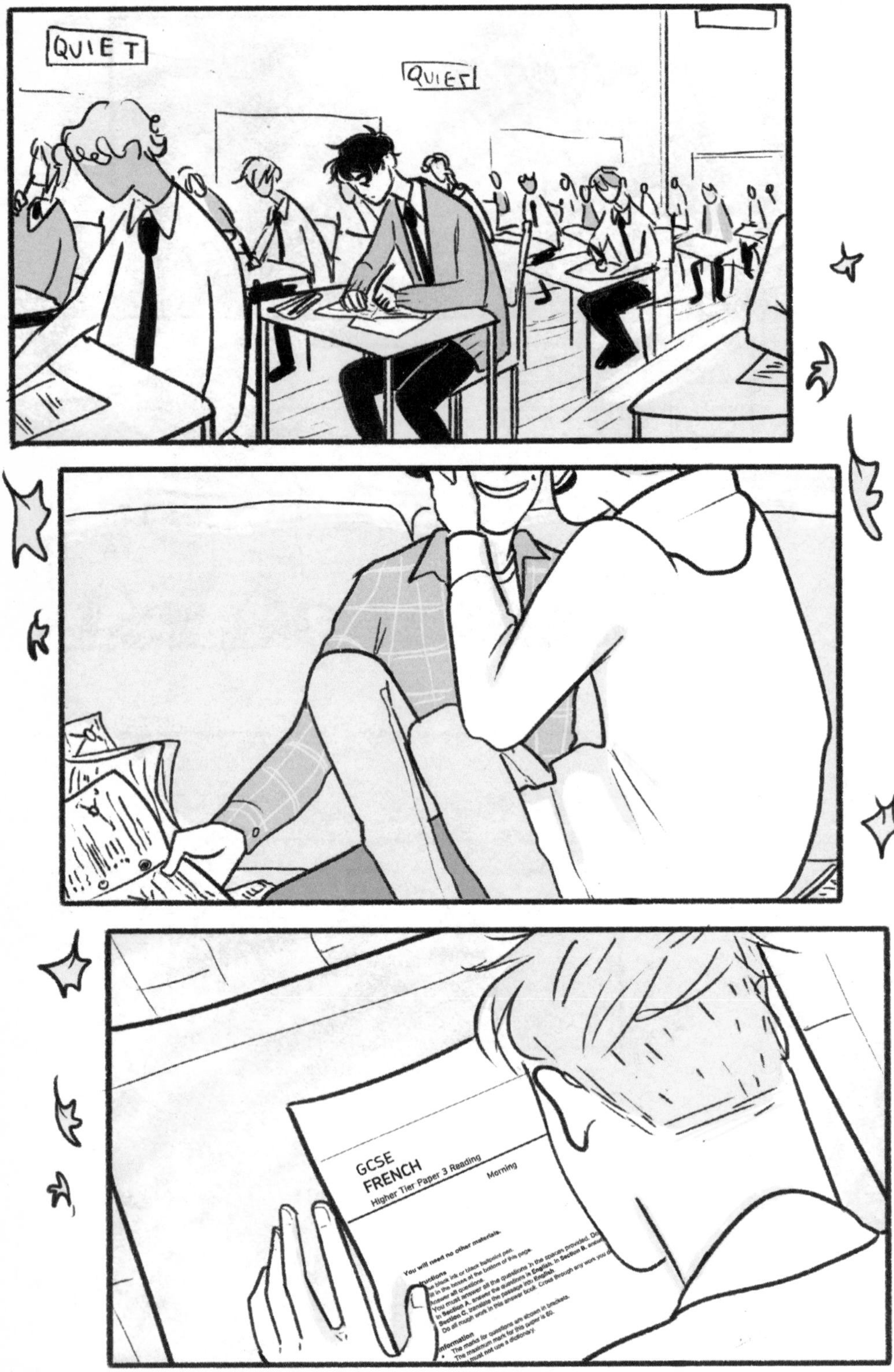

QUIET
QUIET
GCSE
FRENCH
Higher Tier Paper 3 Reading
Morning
You will need no other materials.
Answer all questions.
Do all rough work in this answer book.
Information
The marks for questions are shown in brackets.
The maximum mark for this paper is 60.

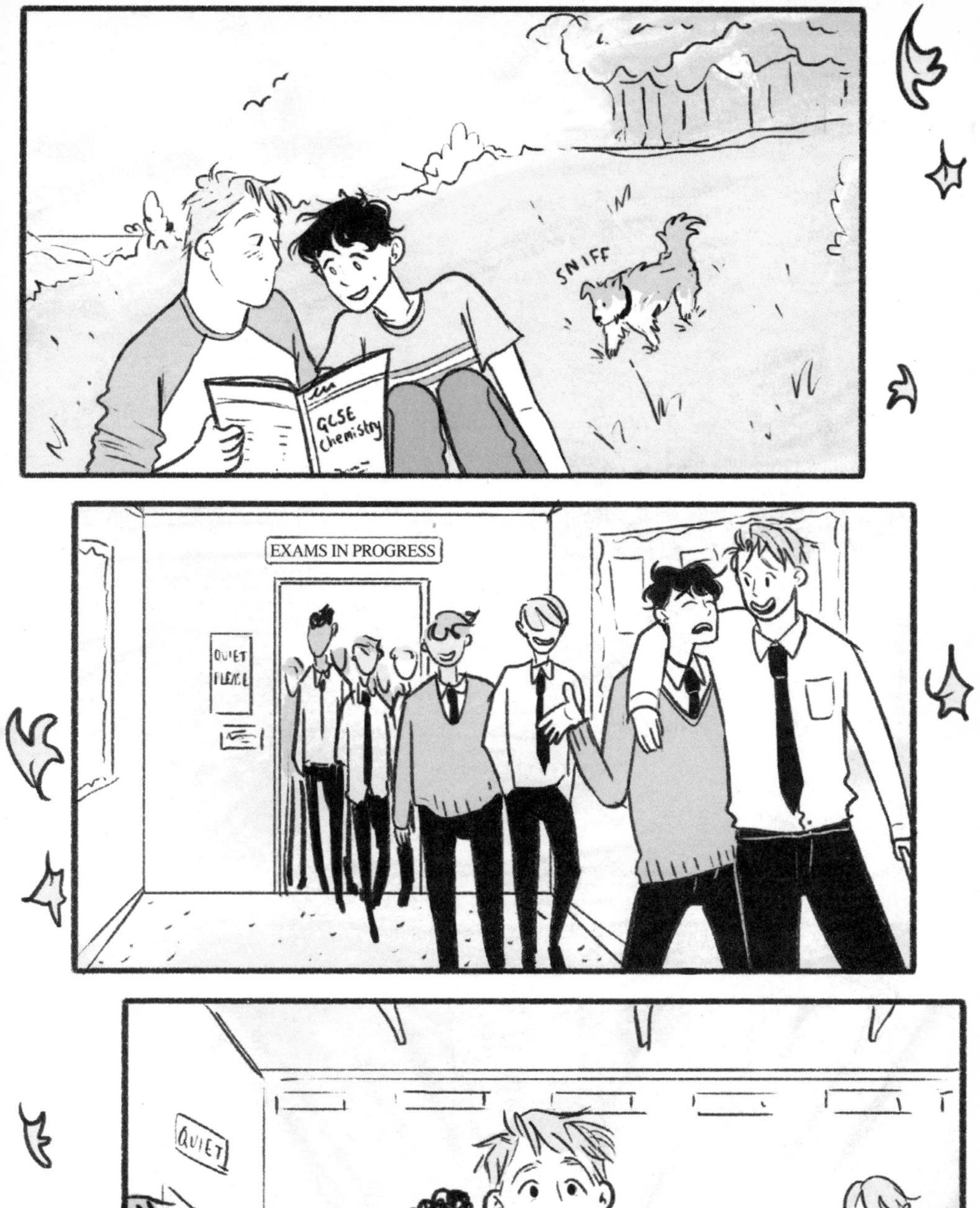
GCSE Chemistry
SNIFF
EXAMS IN PROGRESS
QUIET PLEASE
QUIET

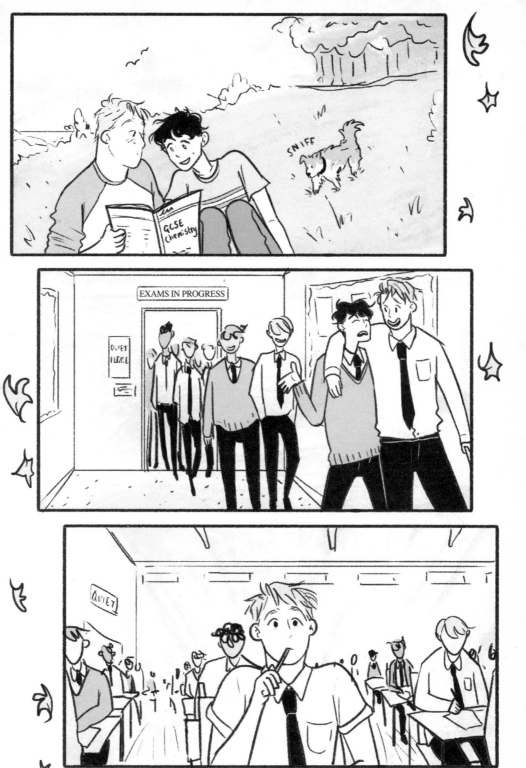

JUNE

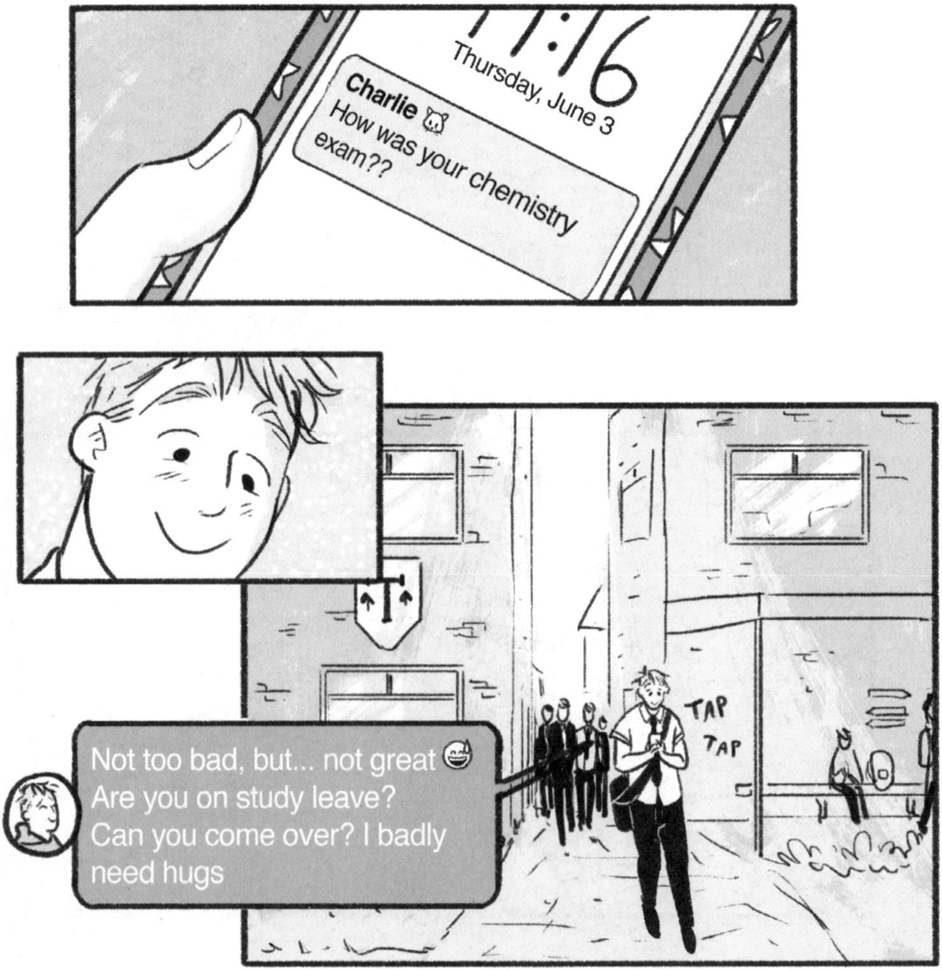

Thursday, June 3
Charlie
How was your chemistry exam??
Not too bad, but... not great
Are you on study leave?
Can you come over? I badly need hugs
TAP
TAP

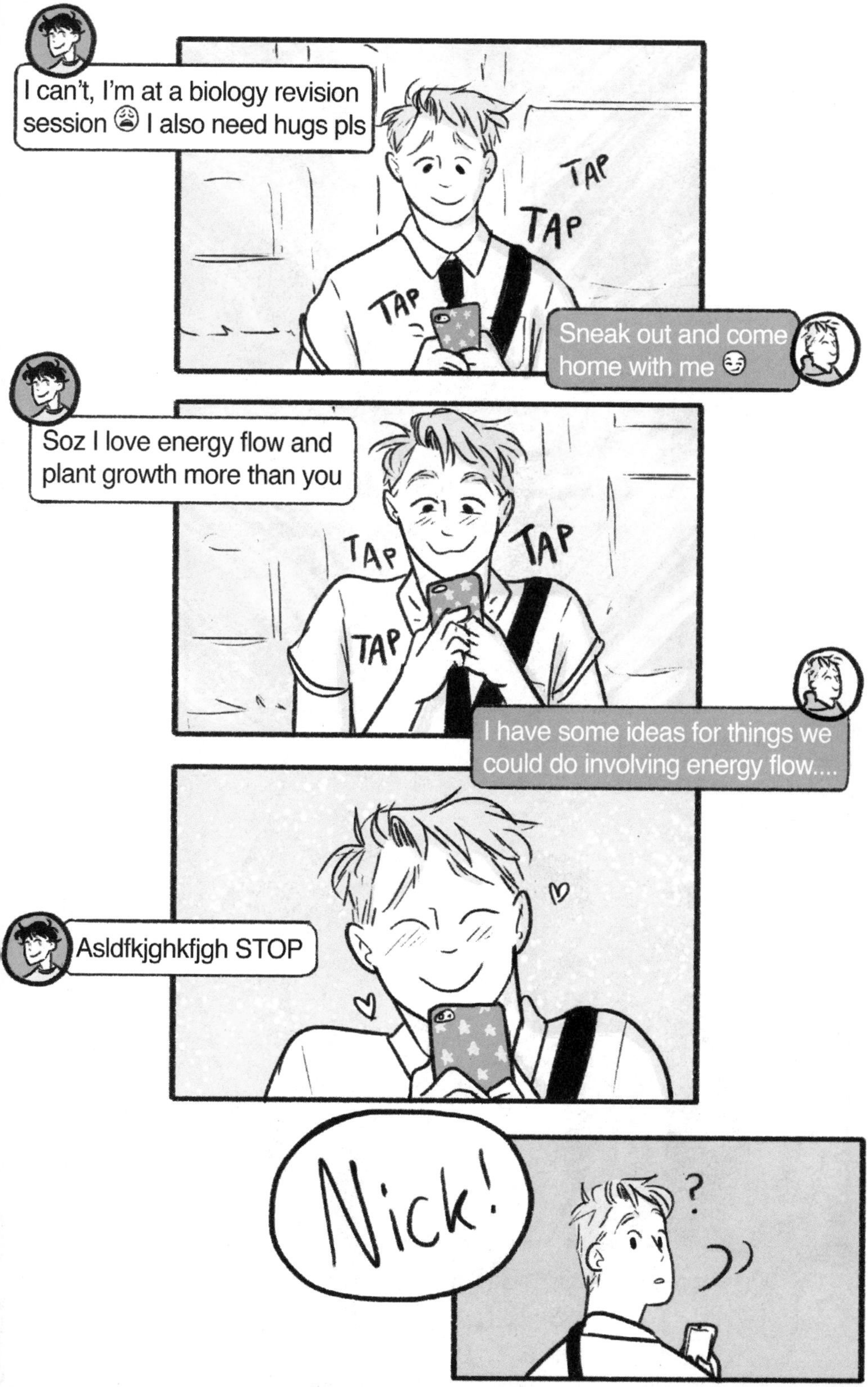

I can't, I'm at a biology revision session 😩 I also need hugs pls
TAP
TAP
TAP
Sneak out and come home with me 😏
Soz I love energy flow and plant growth more than you
TAP
TAP
TAP
I have some ideas for things we could do involving energy flow....
Asldfkjghkfjgh STOP
Nick!
?

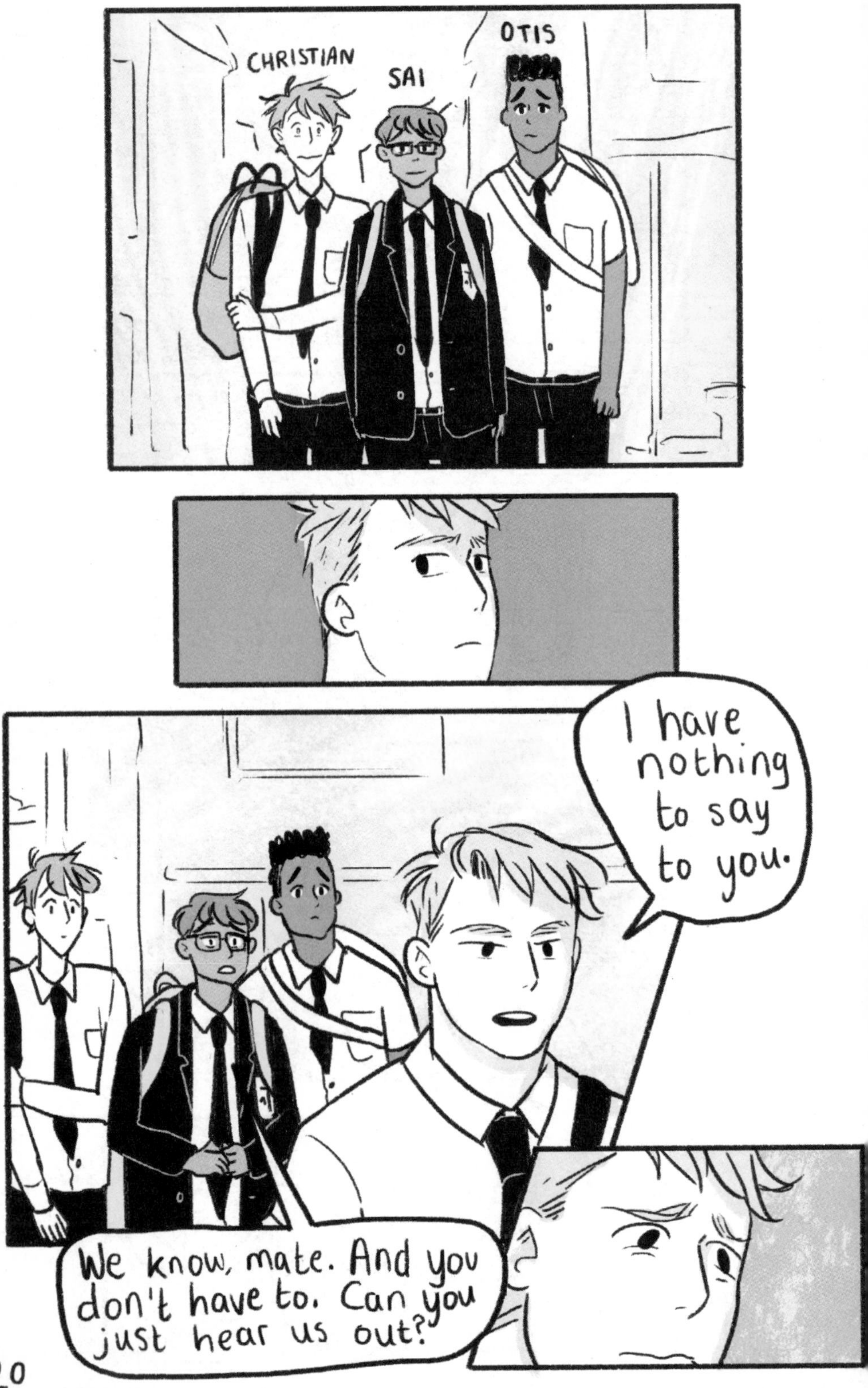
CHRISTIAN
SAI
OTIS
I have nothing to say to you.
We know, mate. And you don't have to. Can you just hear us out?

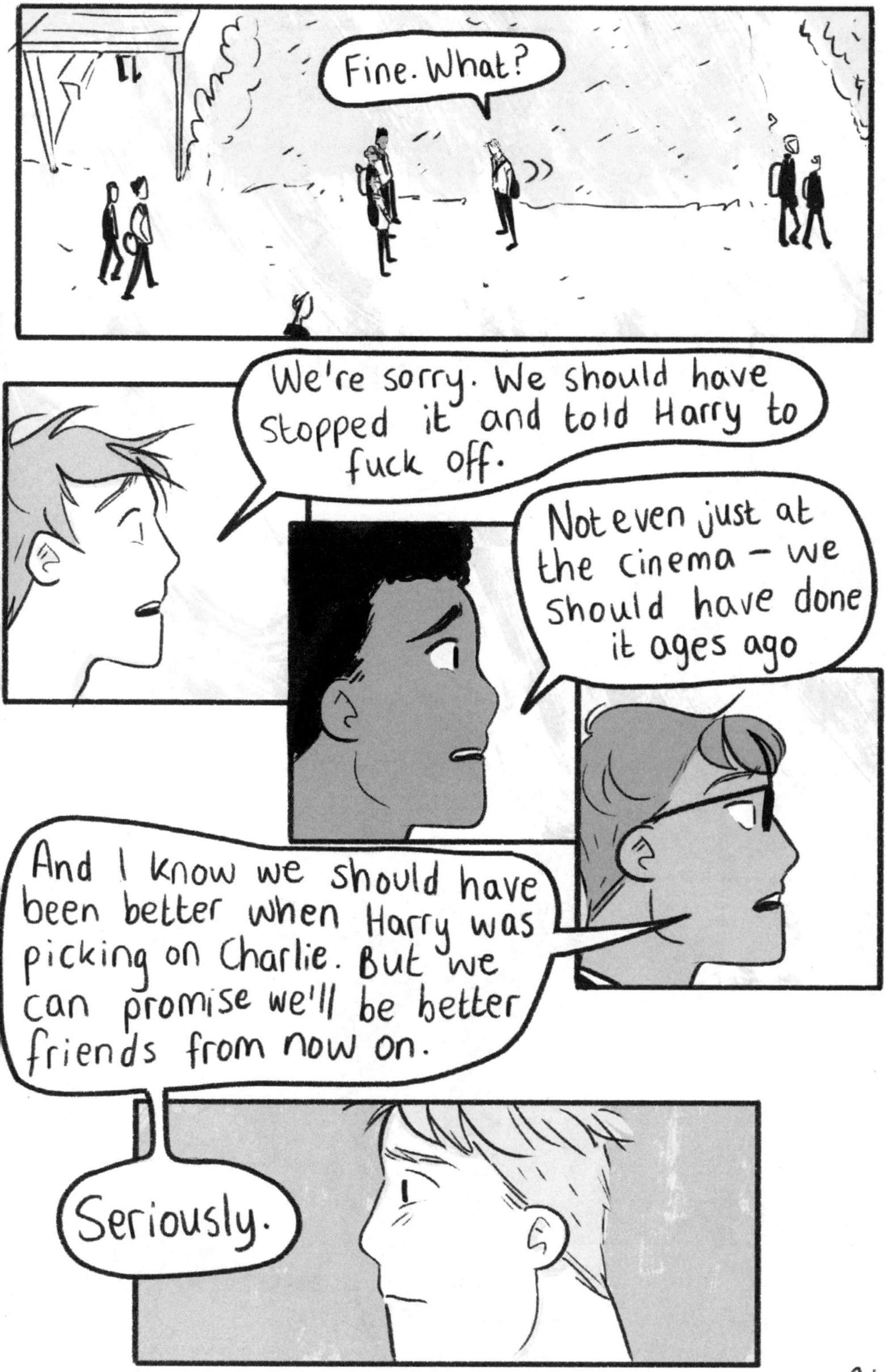
Fine. What?
We're sorry. We should have stopped it and told Harry to fuck off.
Not even just at the cinema - we should have done it ages ago
And I know we should have been better when Harry was picking on Charlie. But we can promise we'll be better friends from now on.
Seriously.

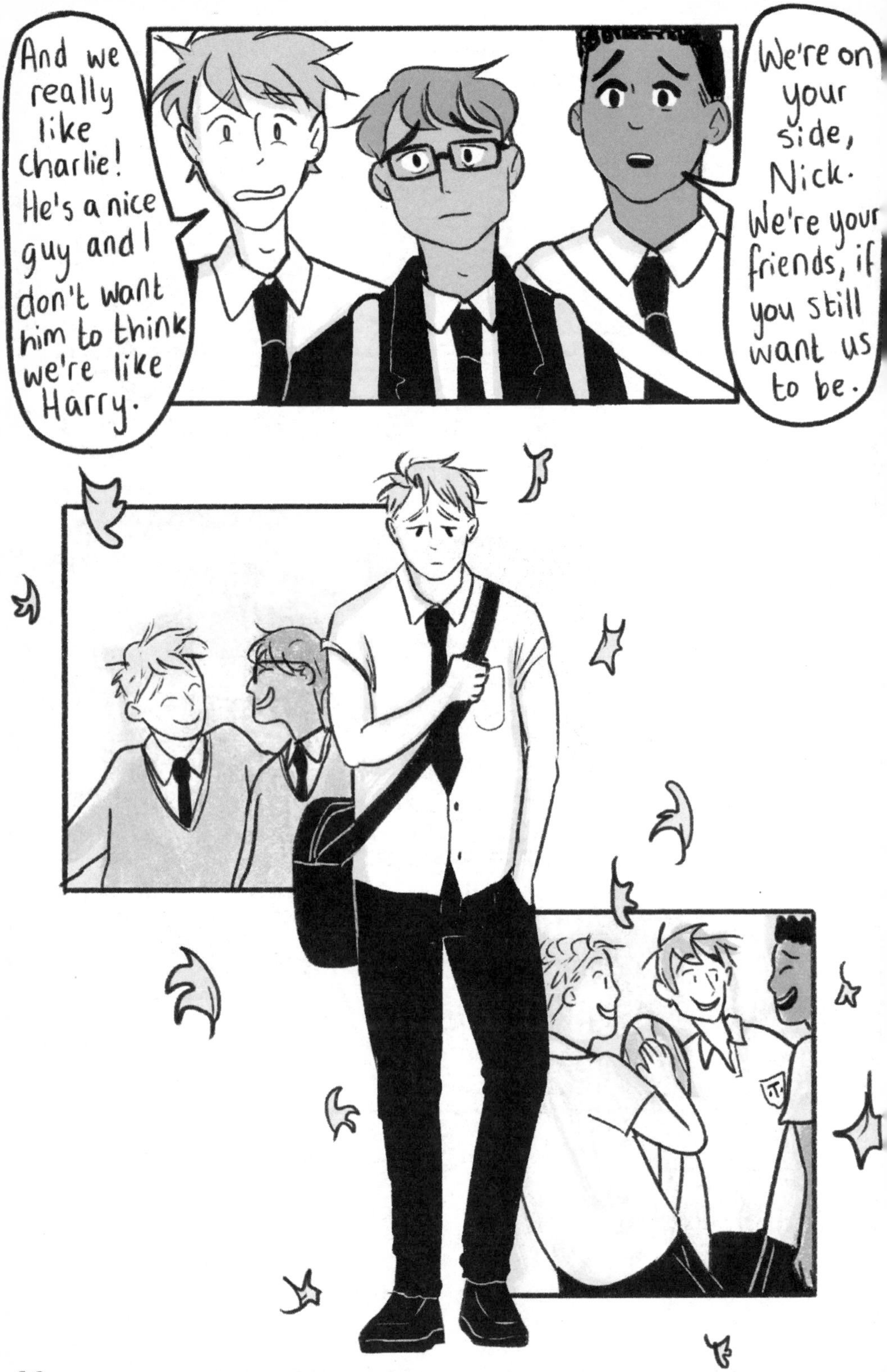
And we really like Charlie! He's a nice guy and I don't want him to think we're like Harry.
We're on your side, Nick. We're your friends, if you still want us to be.

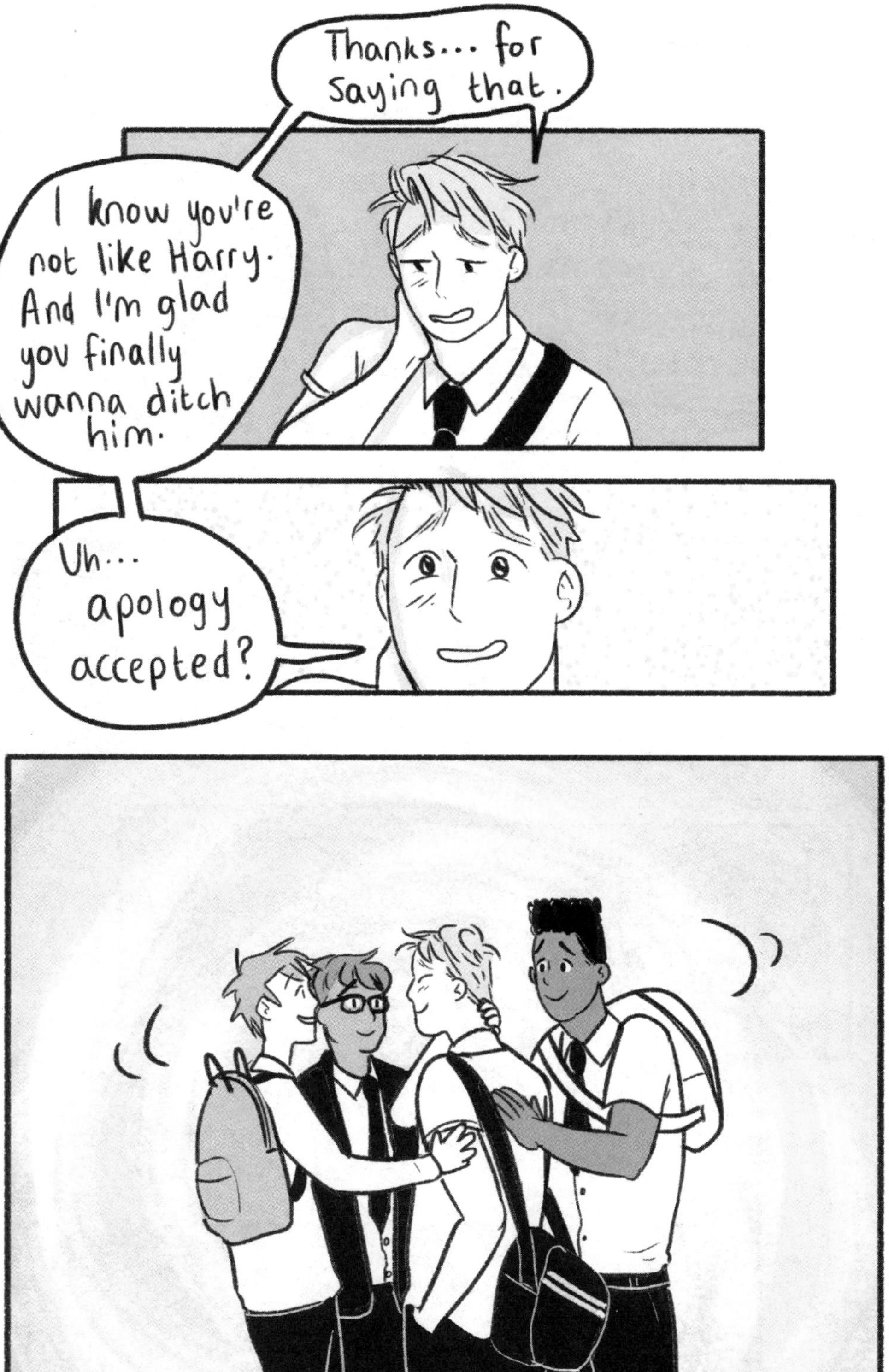
Thanks... for saying that.
I know you're not like Harry. And I'm glad you finally wanna ditch him.
Uh... apology accepted?

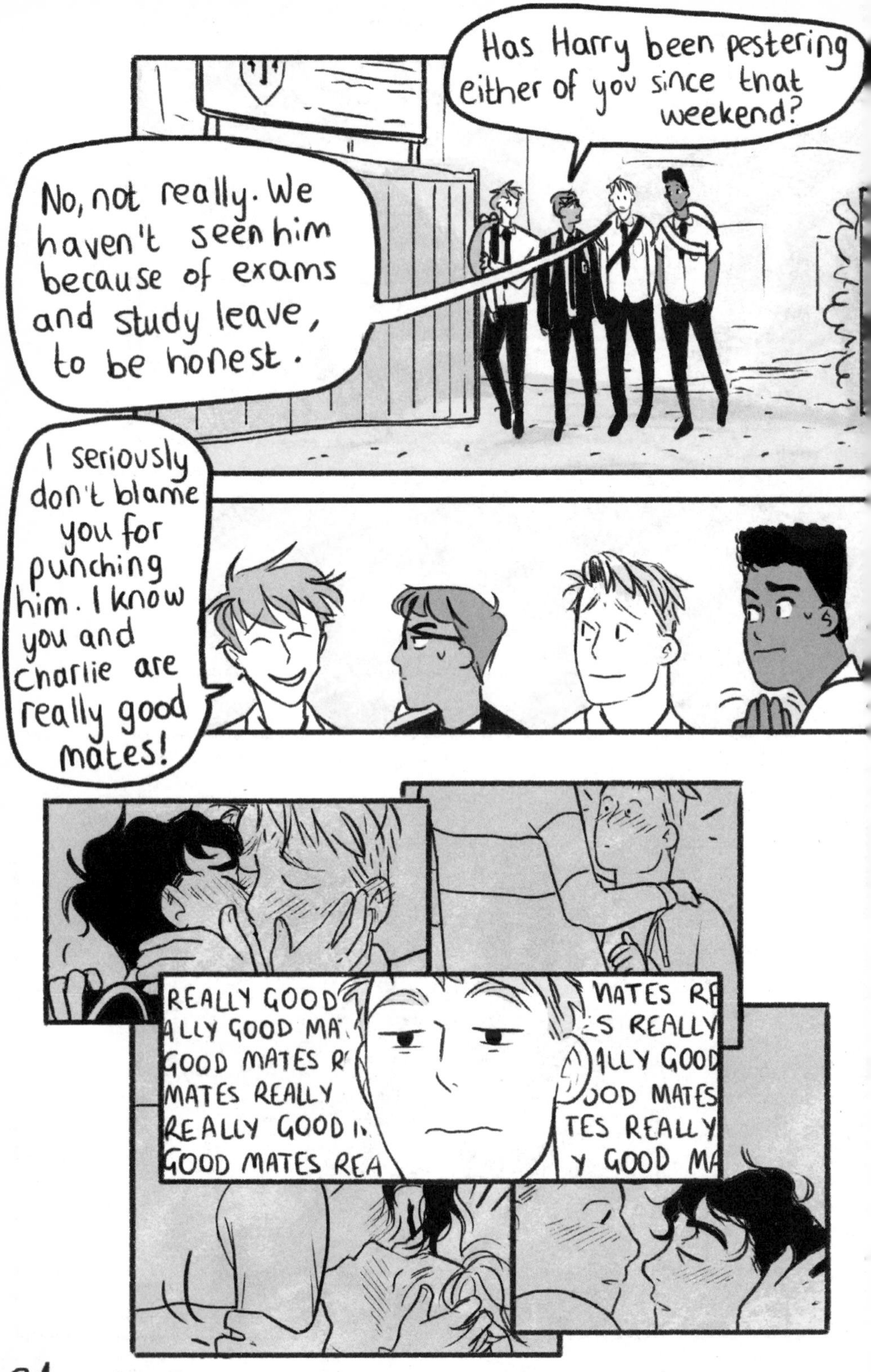
Has Harry been pestering either of you since that weekend?
No, not really. We haven't seen him because of exams and study leave, to be honest.
I seriously don't blame you for punching him. I know you and Charlie are really good mates!
REALLY GOOD
ALLY GOOD MA
GOOD MATES R
MATES REALLY
REALLY GOOD
GOOD MATES REA
MATES RE
ES REALLY
ALLY GOOD
OOD MATES
TES REALLY
Y GOOD MA

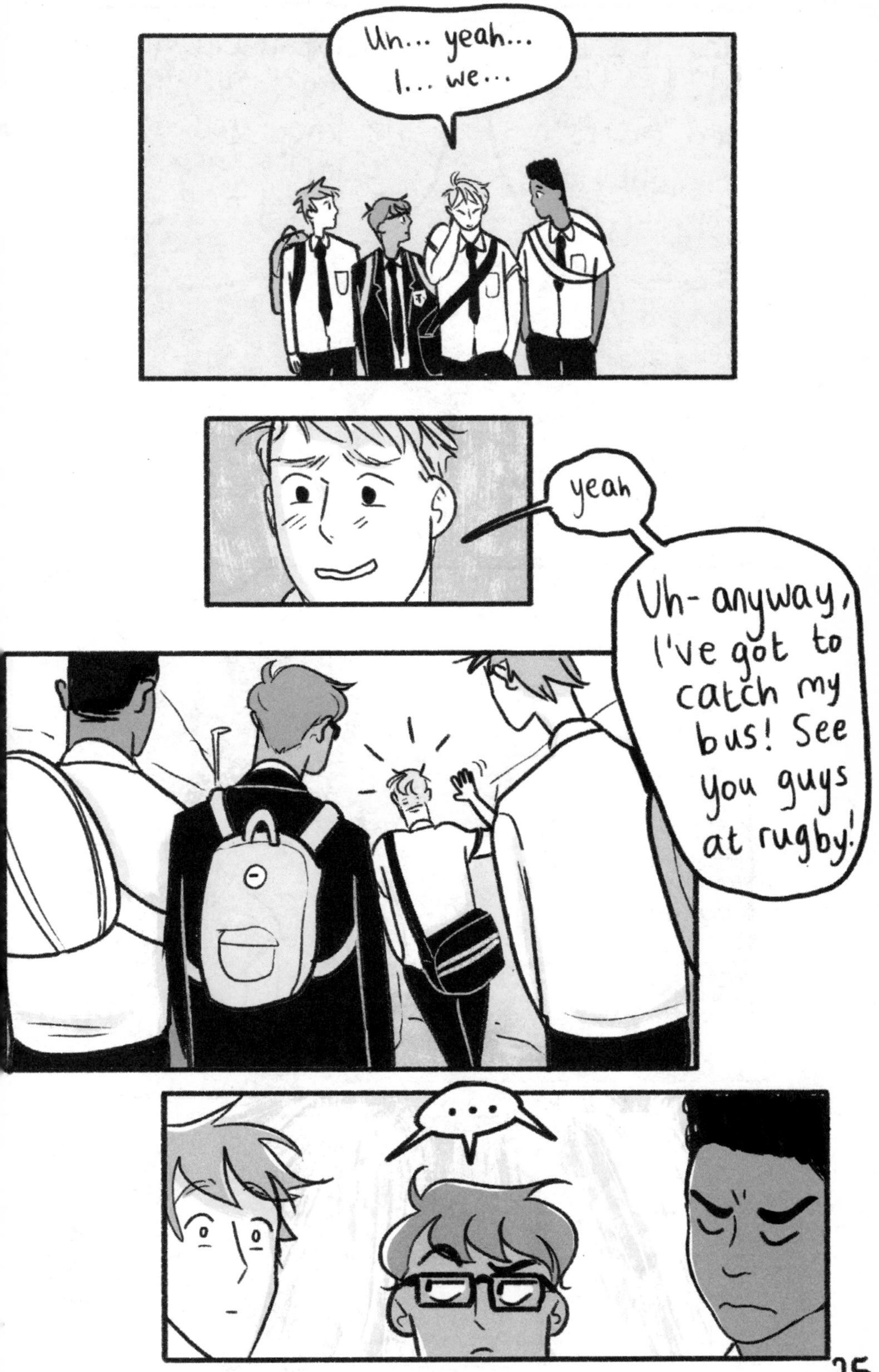
Uh... yeah...
I... we...
yeah
Uh- anyway, I've got to catch my bus! See you guys at rugby!
...

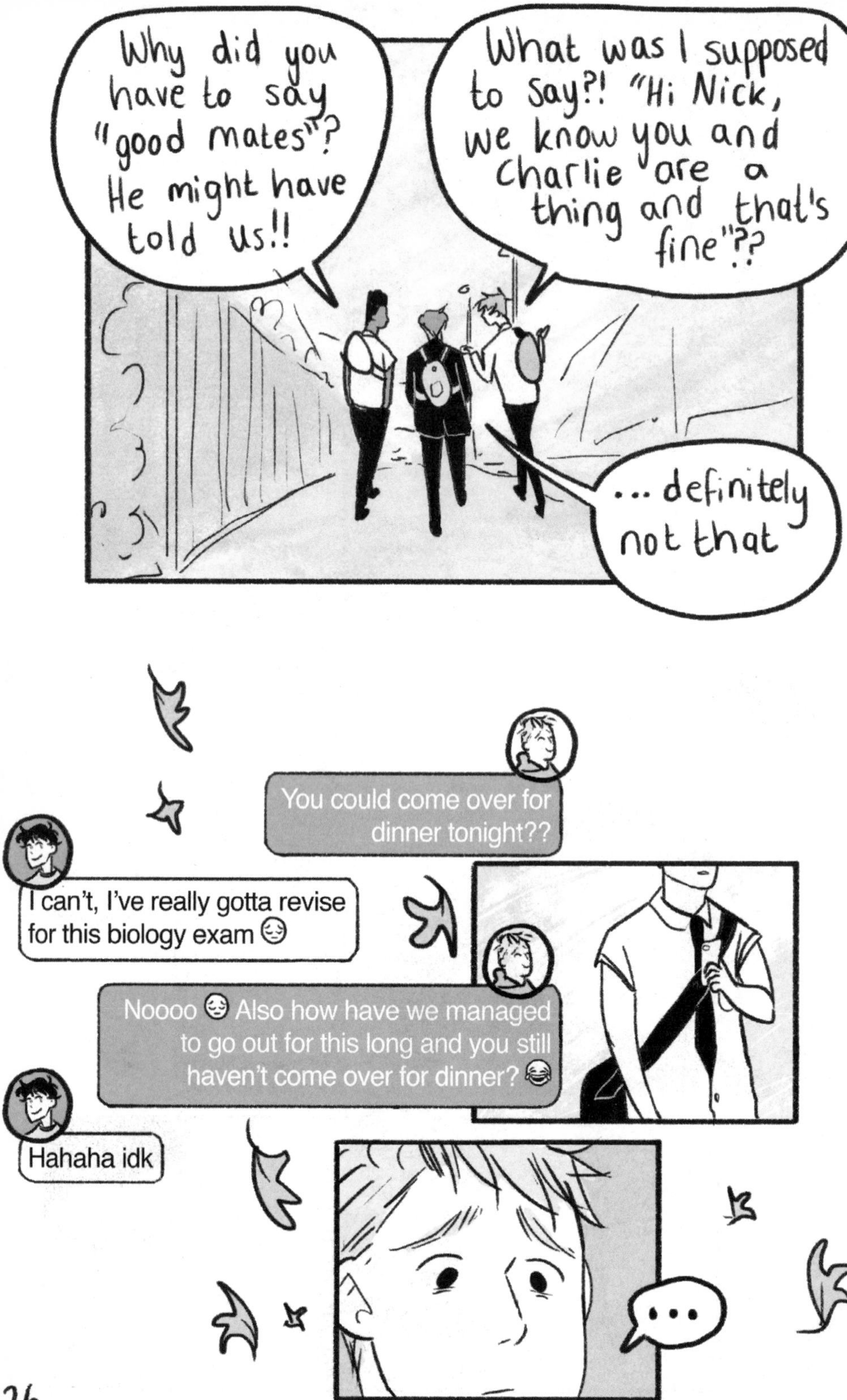
Why did you have to say "good mates"? He might have told us!!
What was I supposed to say?! "Hi Nick, we know you and Charlie are a thing and that's fine"??
... definitely not that
You could come over for dinner tonight??
I can't, I've really gotta revise for this biology exam 😔
Noooo 😔 Also how have we managed to go out for this long and you still haven't come over for dinner? 😂
Hahaha idk
...

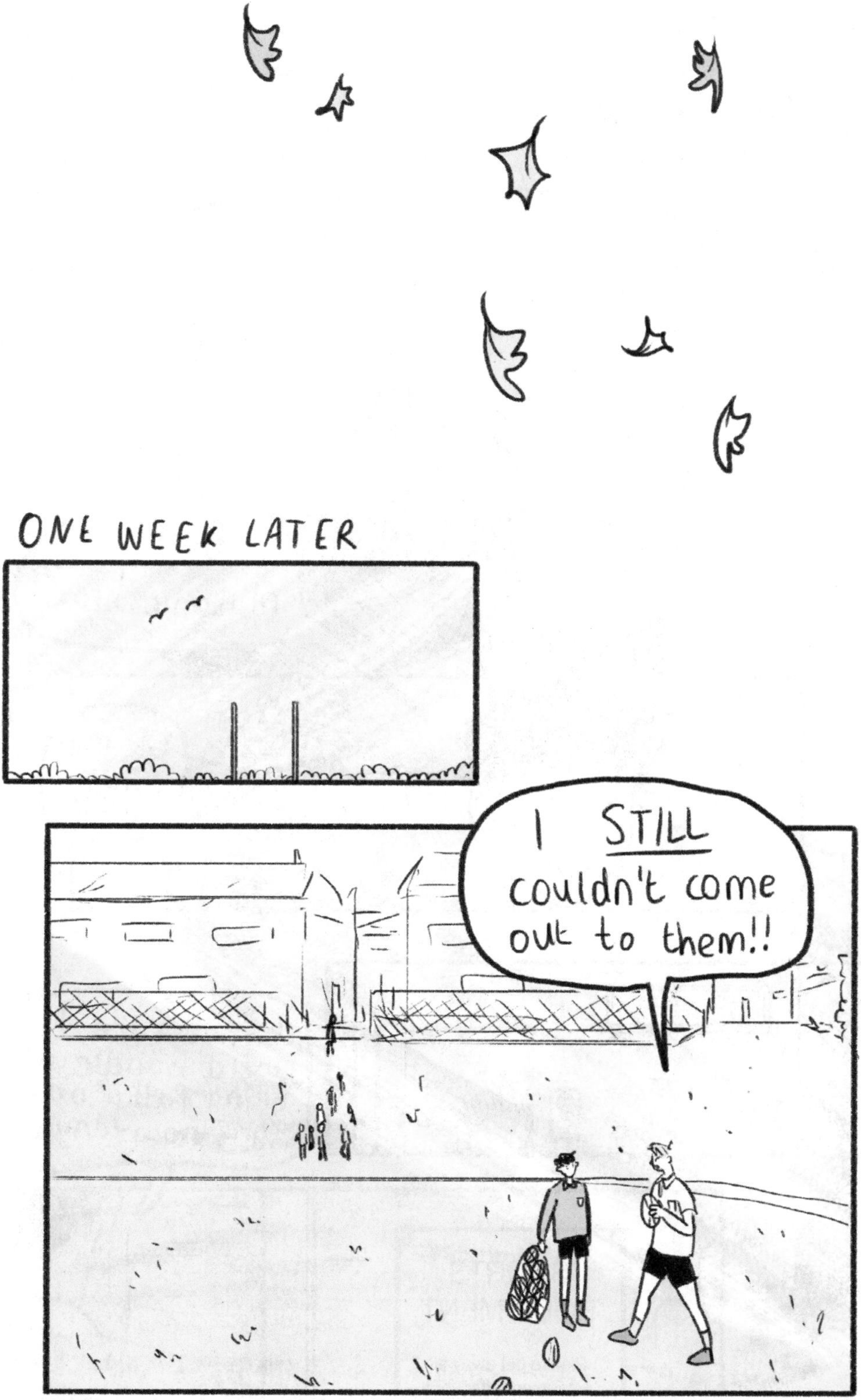
ONE WEEK LATER
I STILL couldn't come out to them!!

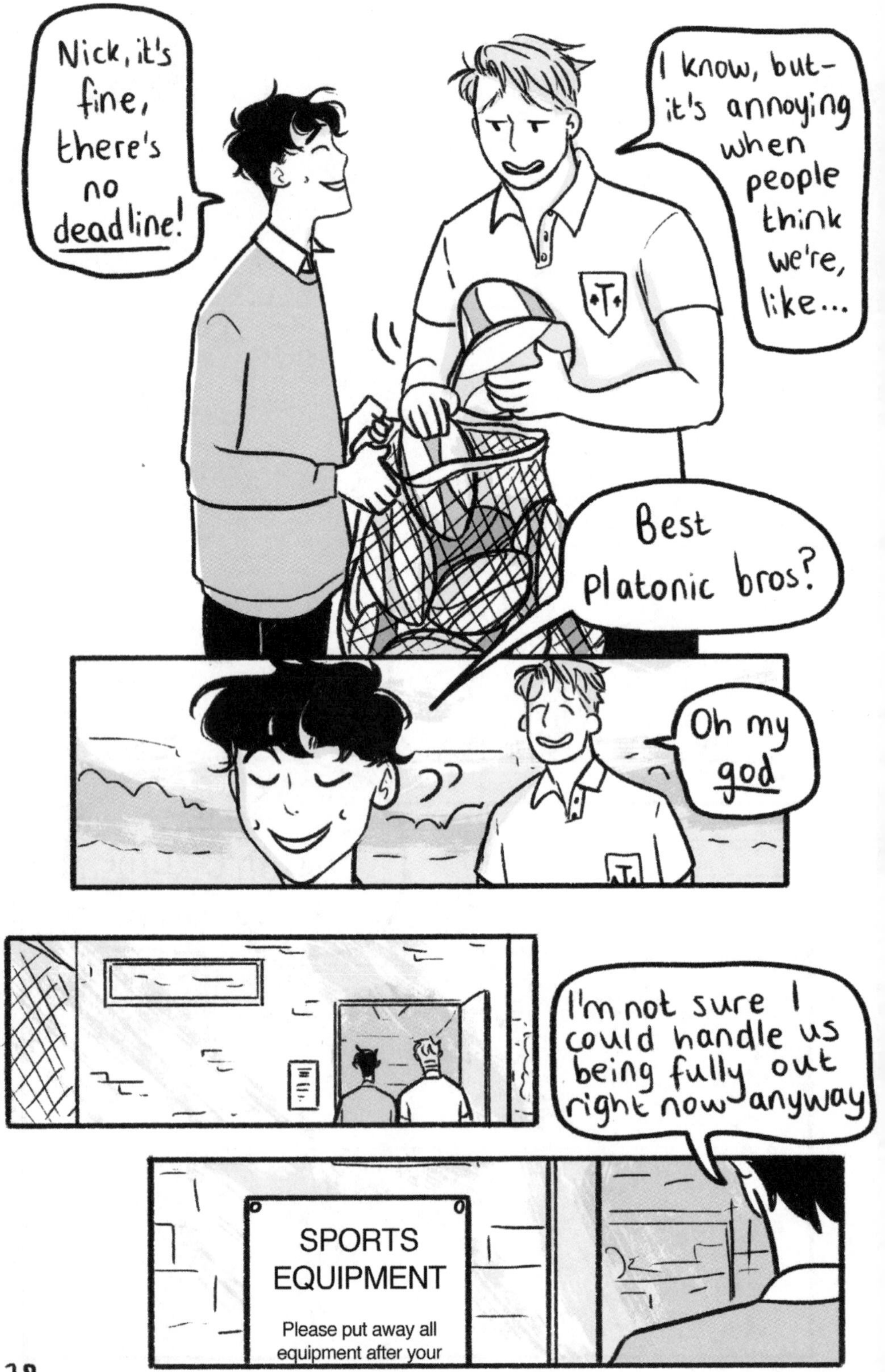
Nick, it's fine, there's no deadline!
I know, but- it's annoying when people think we're, like...
Best platonic bros?
Oh my god
I'm not sure I could handle us being fully out right now anyway
SPORTS EQUIPMENT
Please put away all equipment after your

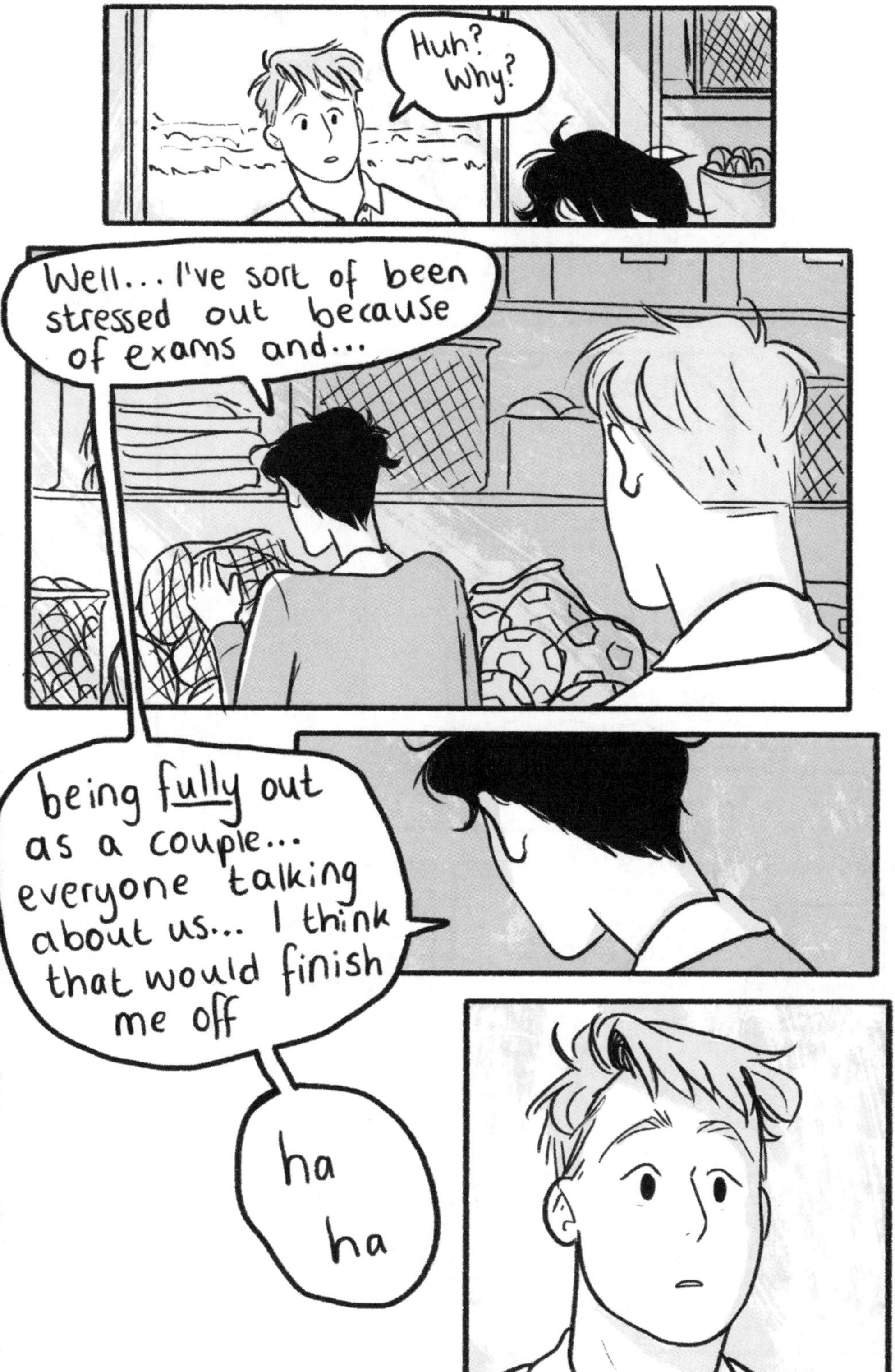
Huh? Why?
Well... I've sort of been stressed out because of exams and...
being fully out as a couple... everyone talking about us... I think that would finish me off
ha ha

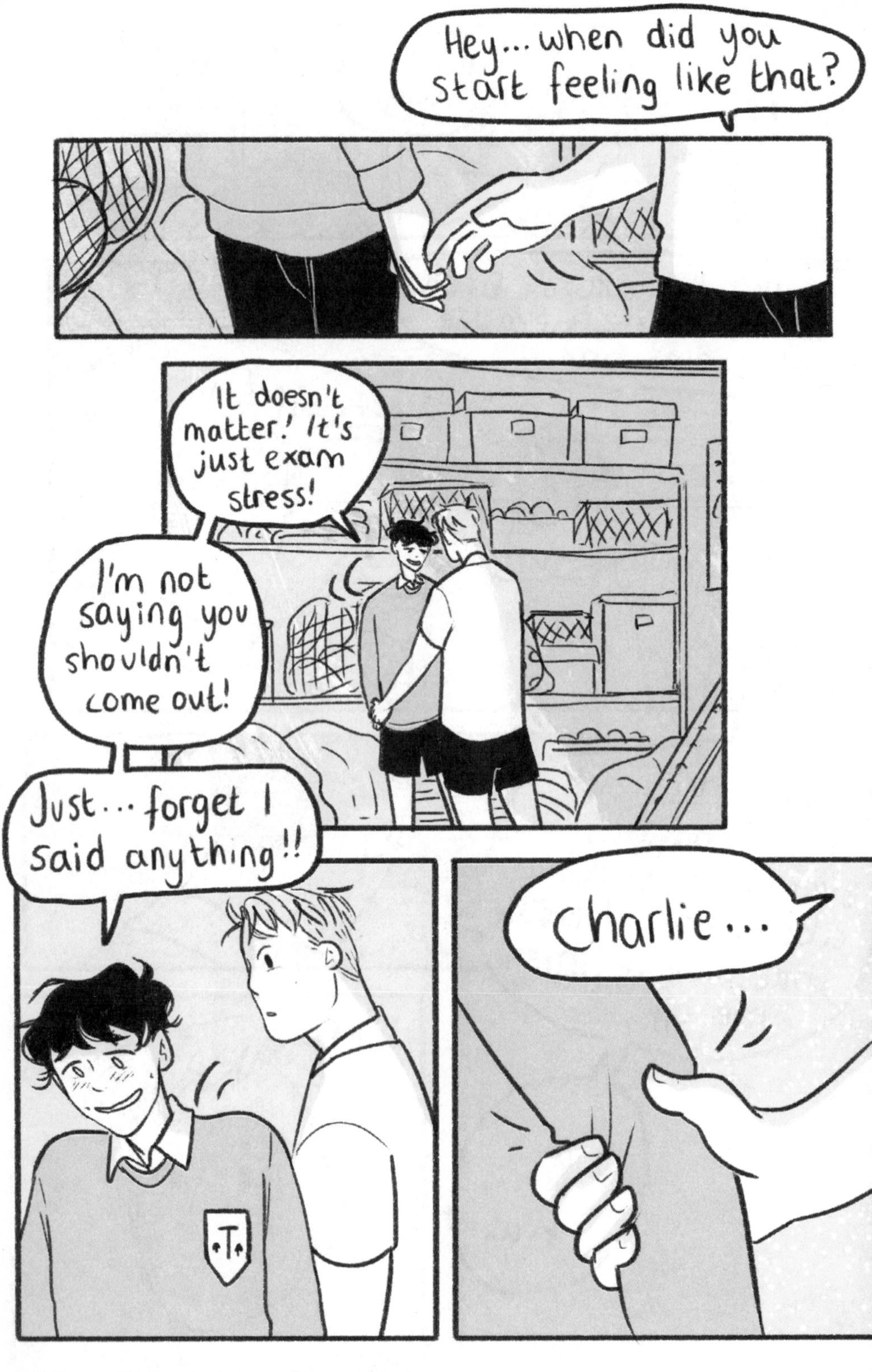
Hey... when did you start feeling like that?
It doesn't matter! It's just exam stress!
I'm not saying you shouldn't come out!
Just... forget I said anything!!
Charlie...

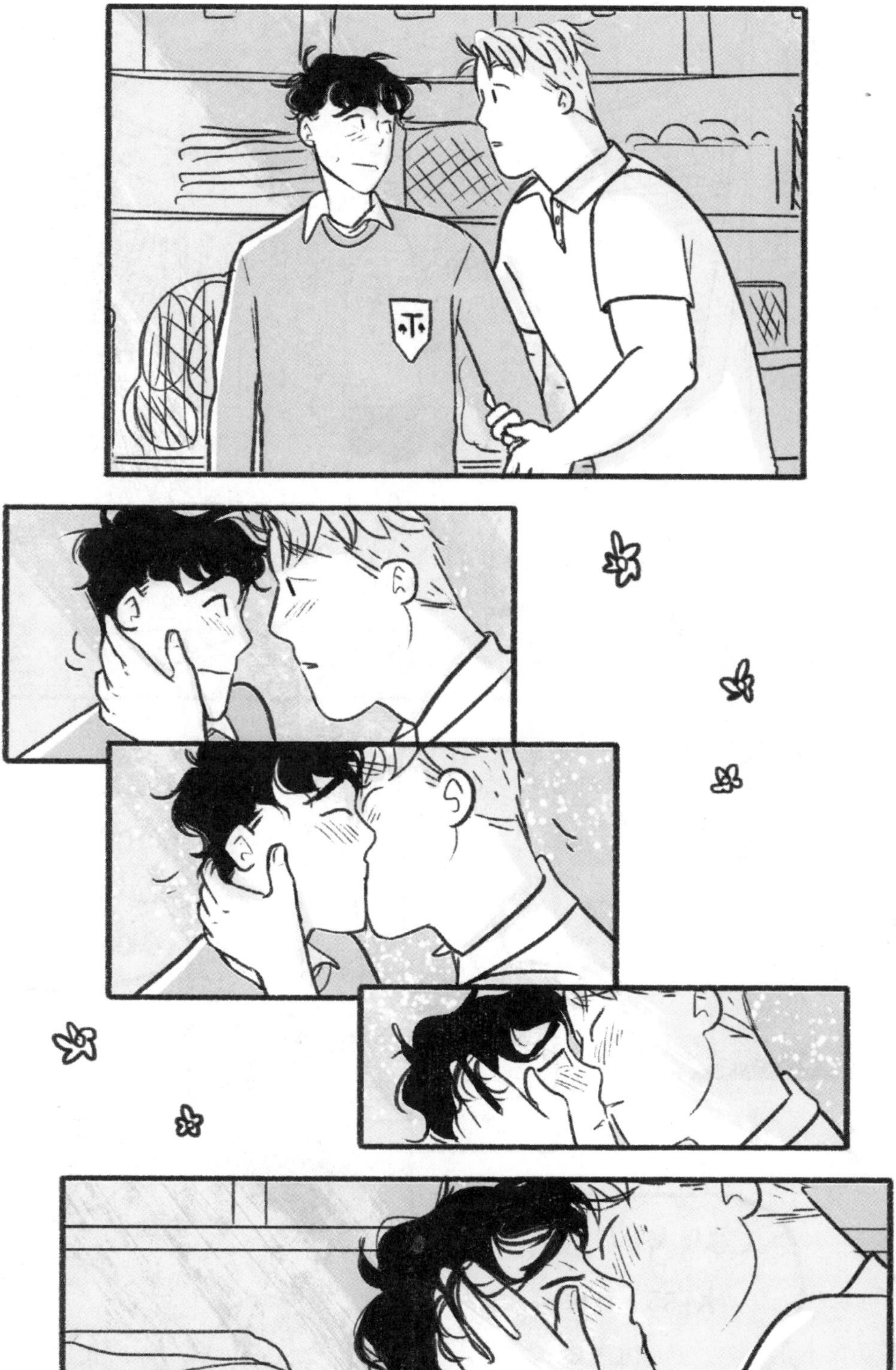

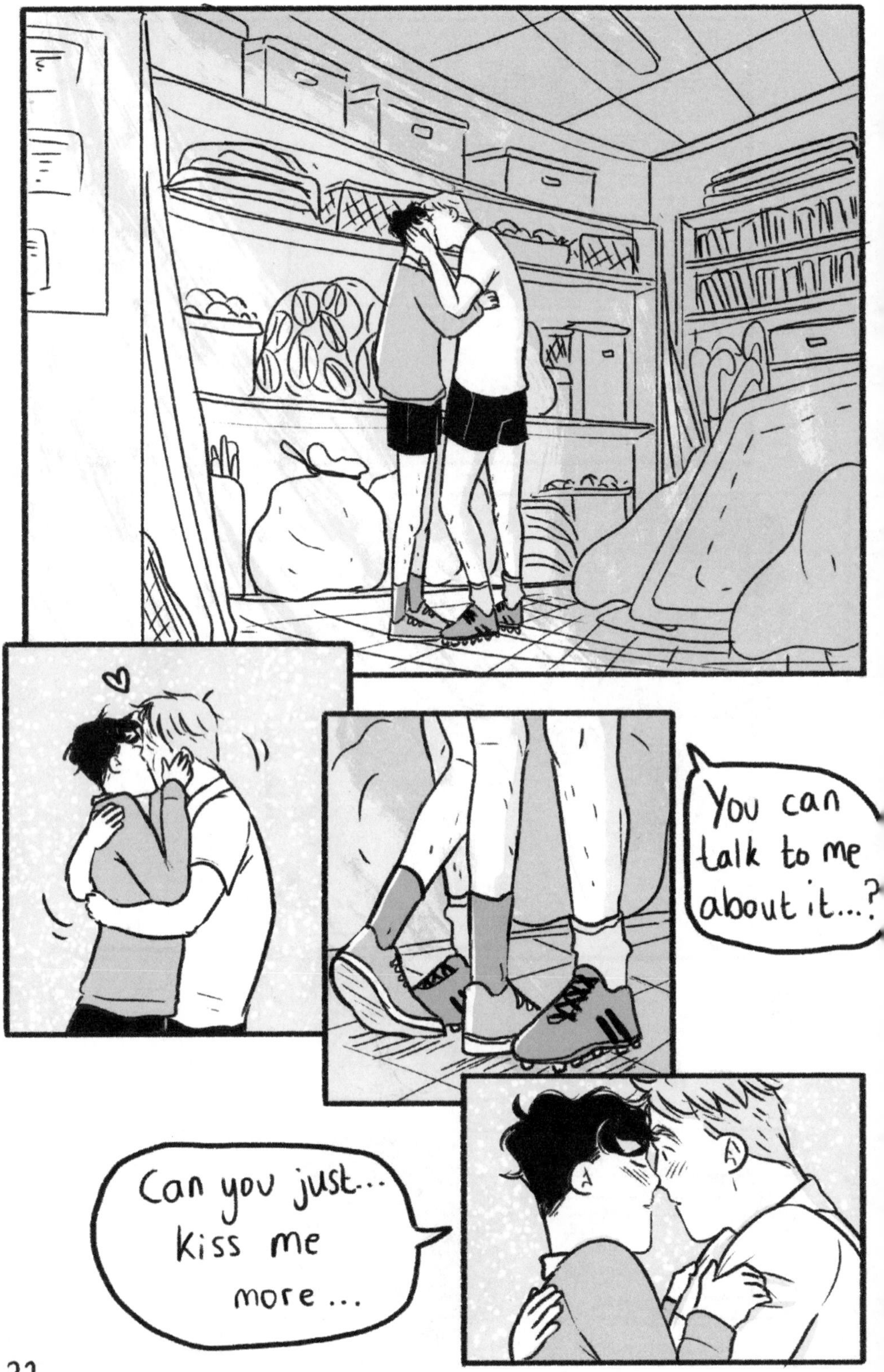
You can talk to me about it...?
Can you just... kiss me more...

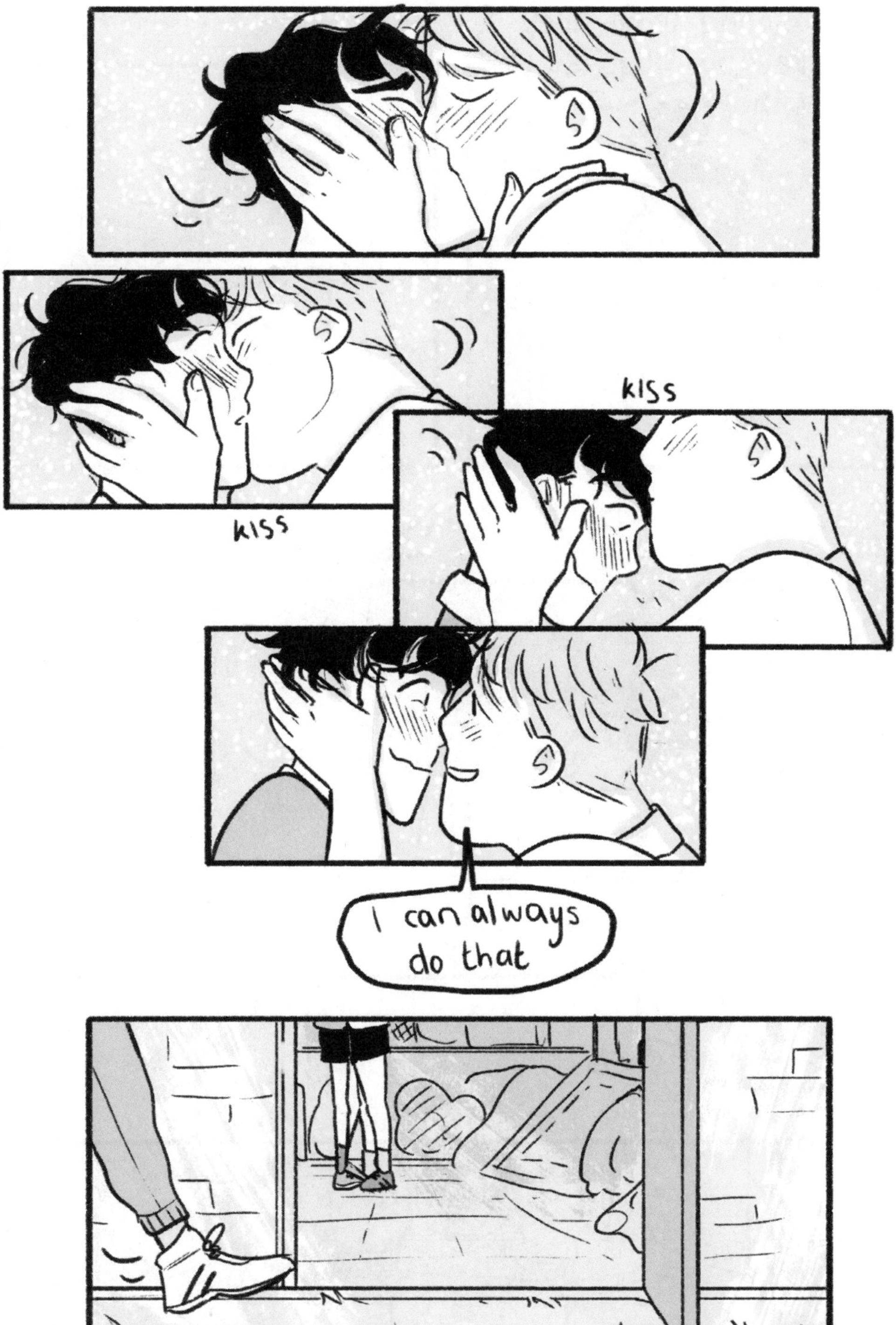
kiss
kiss
I can always do that

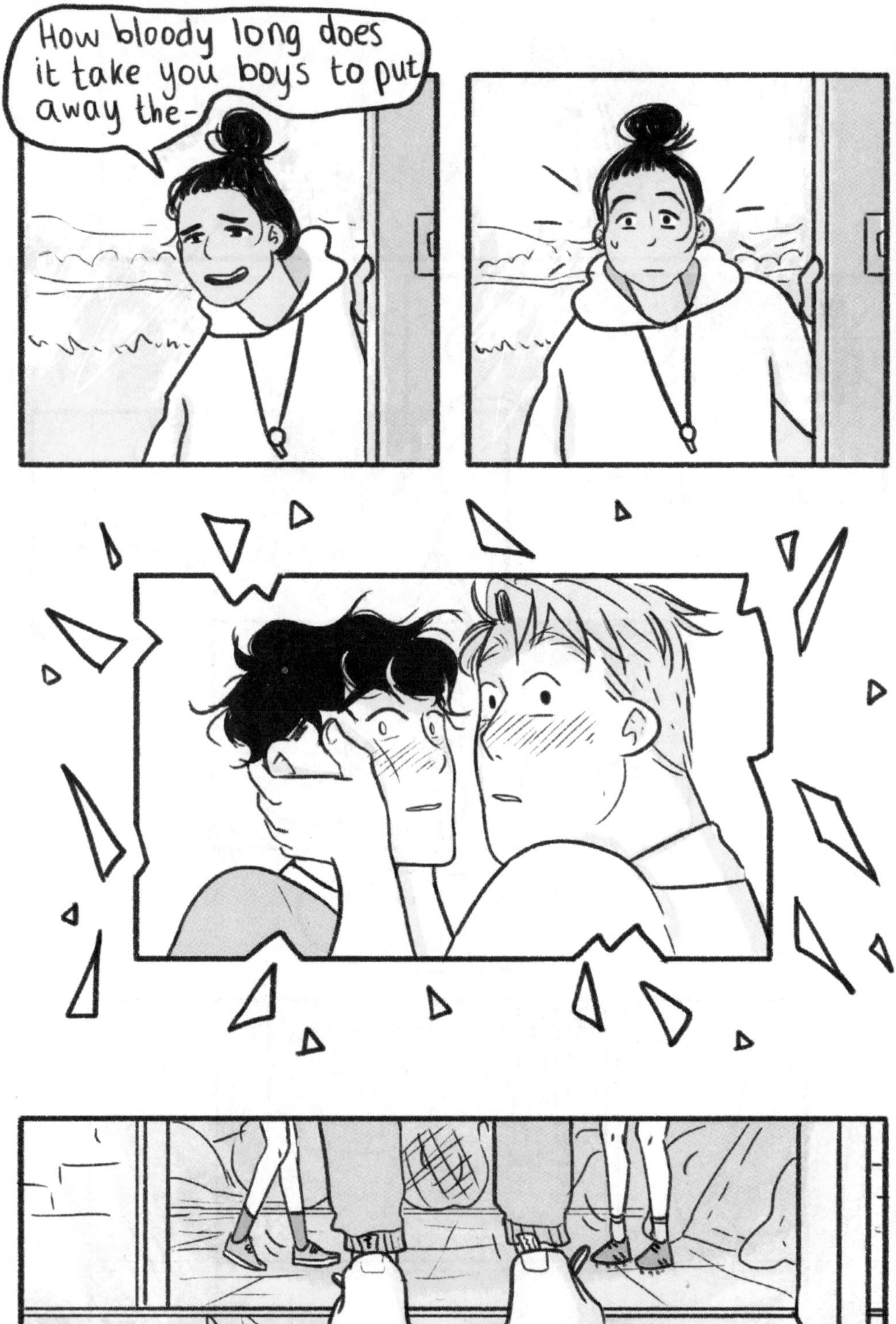
How bloody long does it take you boys to put away the-

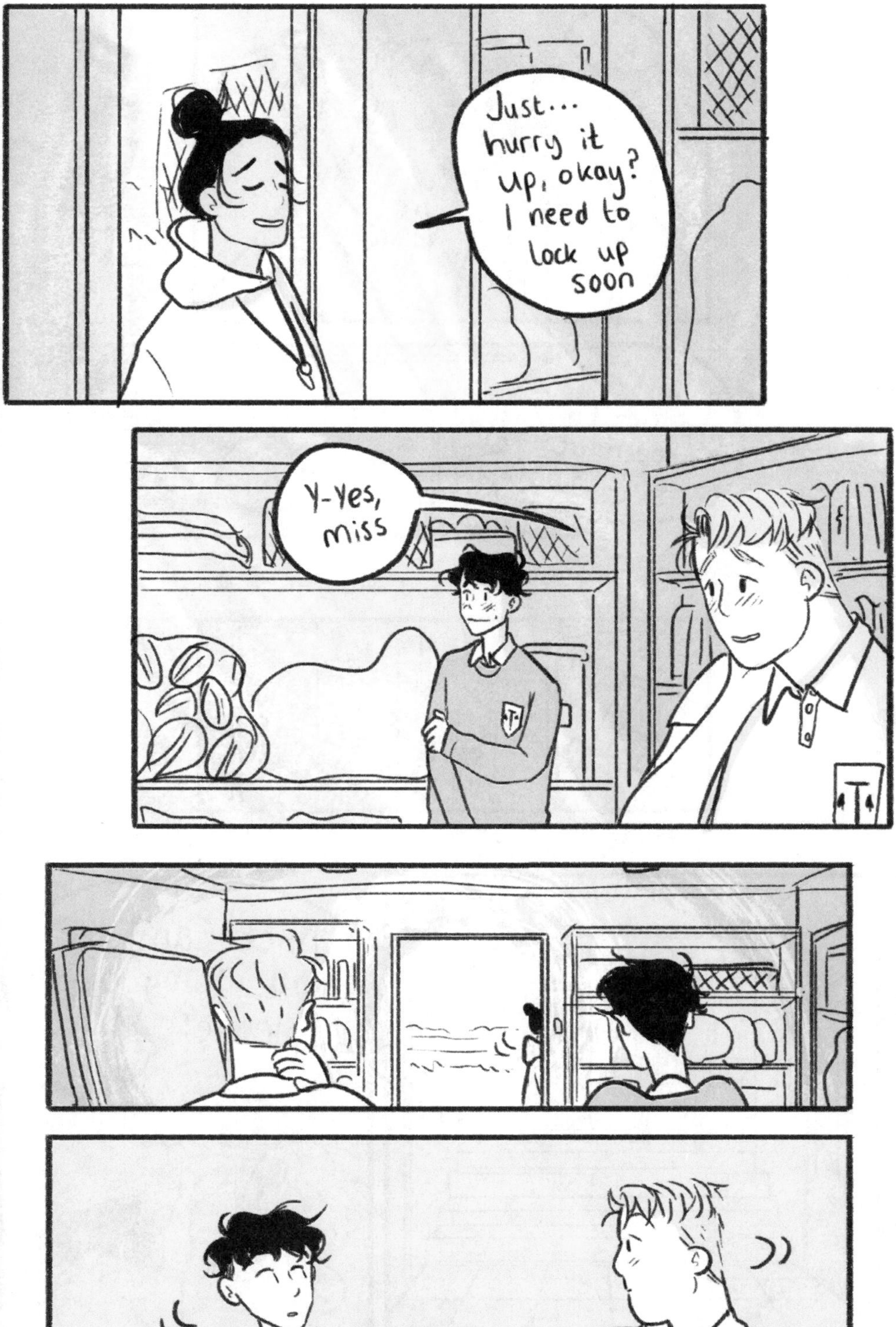
Just... hurry it up, okay? I need to lock up soon
Y-Yes, miss

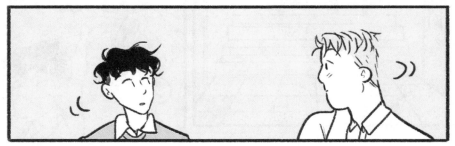

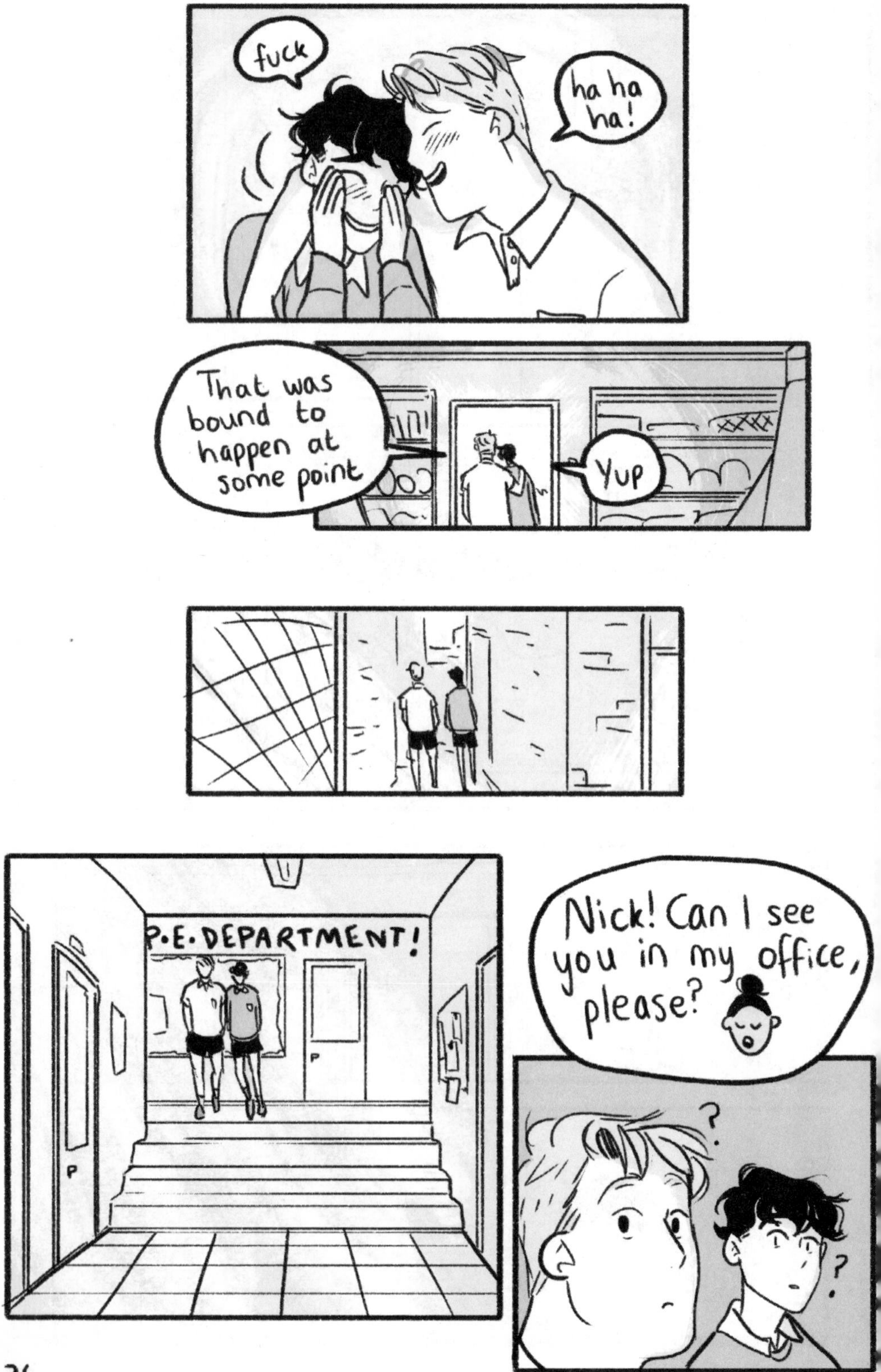
fuck
ha ha ha!
That was bound to happen at some point
Yup
P.E. DEPARTMENT!
Nick! Can I see you in my office, please?
?
?

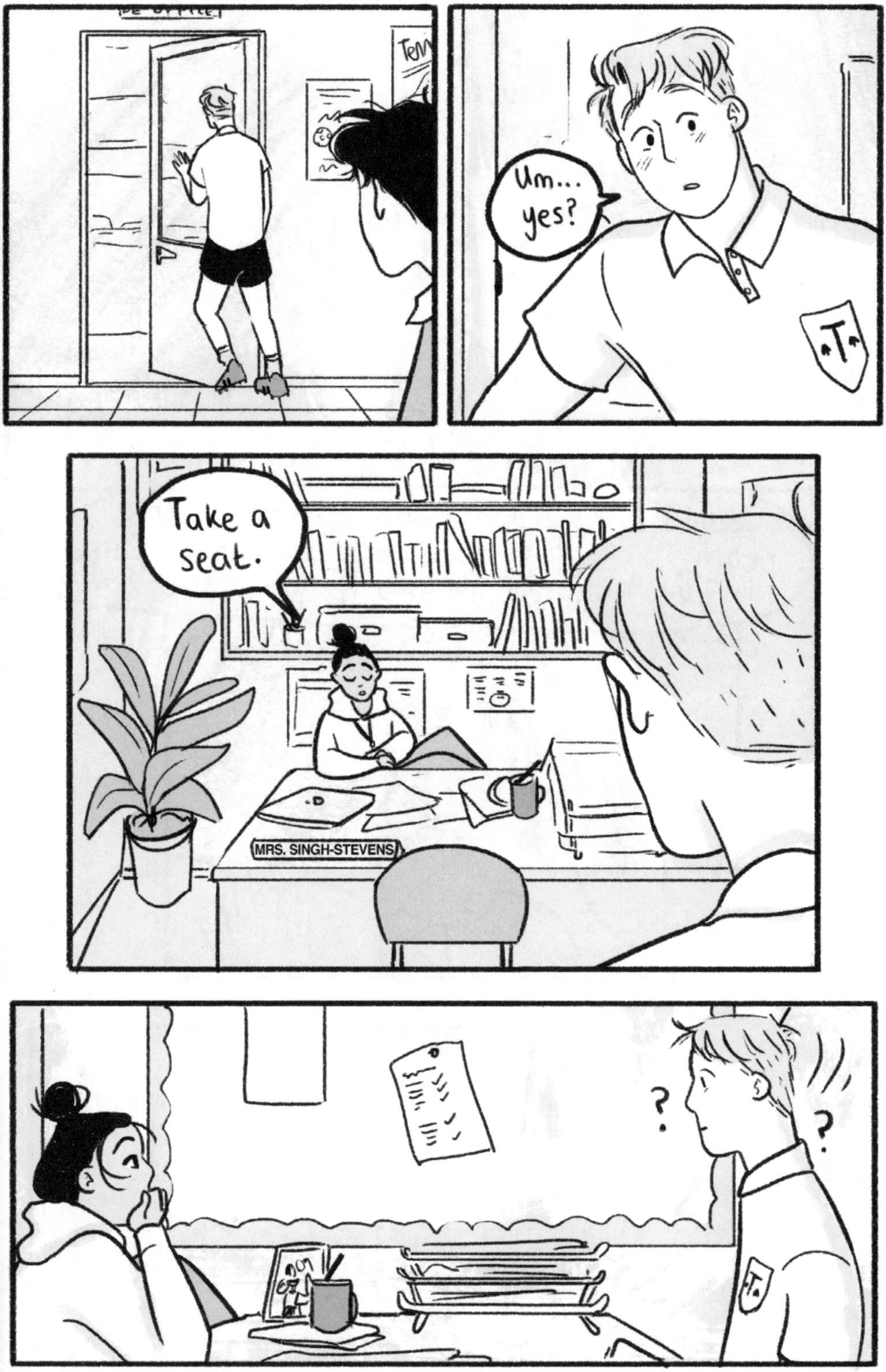
Um... yes?
Take a seat.
MRS. SINGH-STEVENS

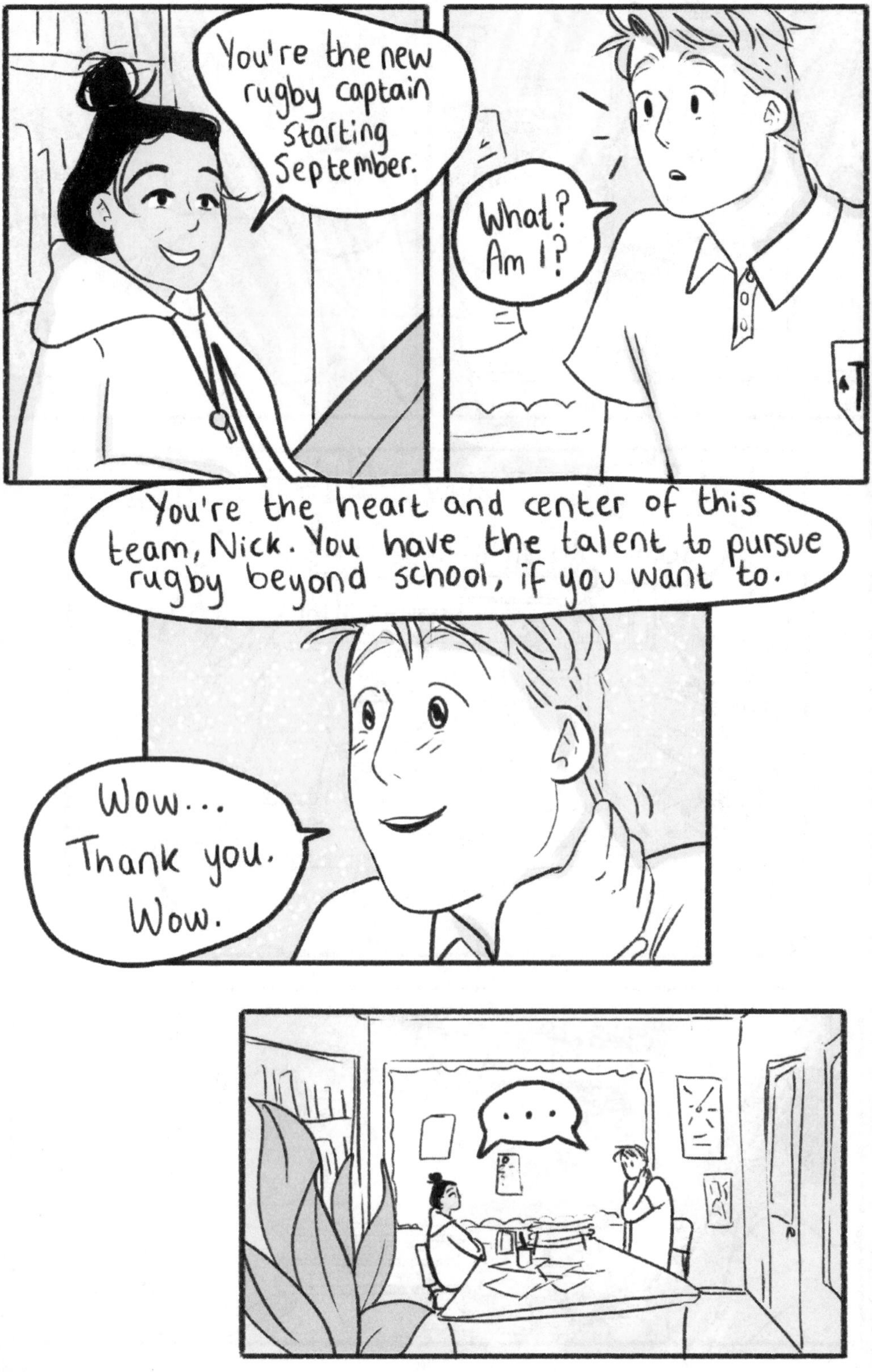
You're the new rugby captain starting September.
What? Am I?
You're the heart and center of this team, Nick. You have the talent to pursue rugby beyond school, if you want to.
Wow... Thank you. Wow.
...

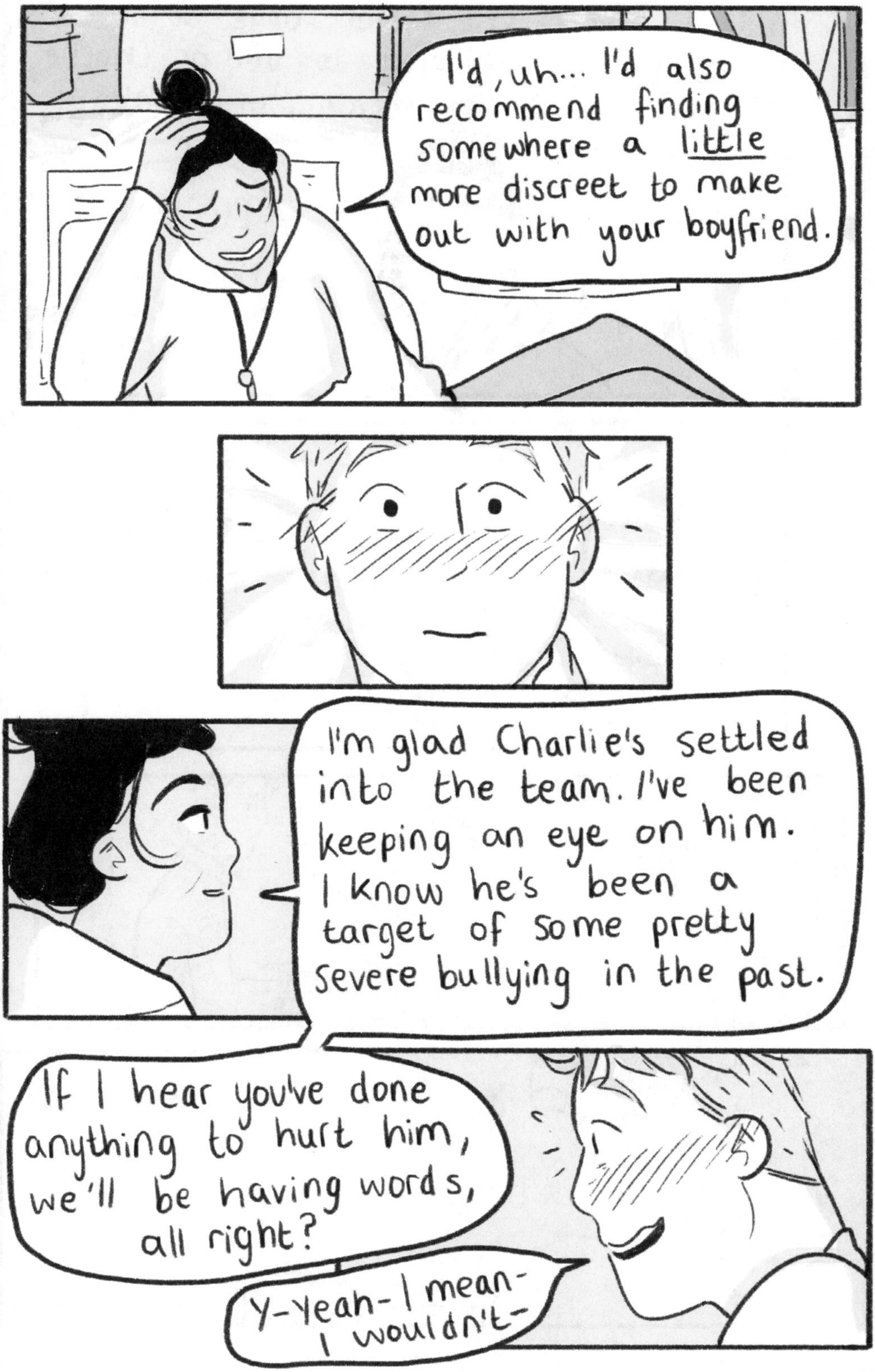
I'd, uh... I'd also recommend finding somewhere a little more discreet to make out with your boyfriend.
I'm glad Charlie's settled into the team. I've been keeping an eye on him. I know he's been a target of some pretty severe bullying in the past.
If I hear you've done anything to hurt him, we'll be having words, all right?
Y-Yeah- I mean- I wouldn't-

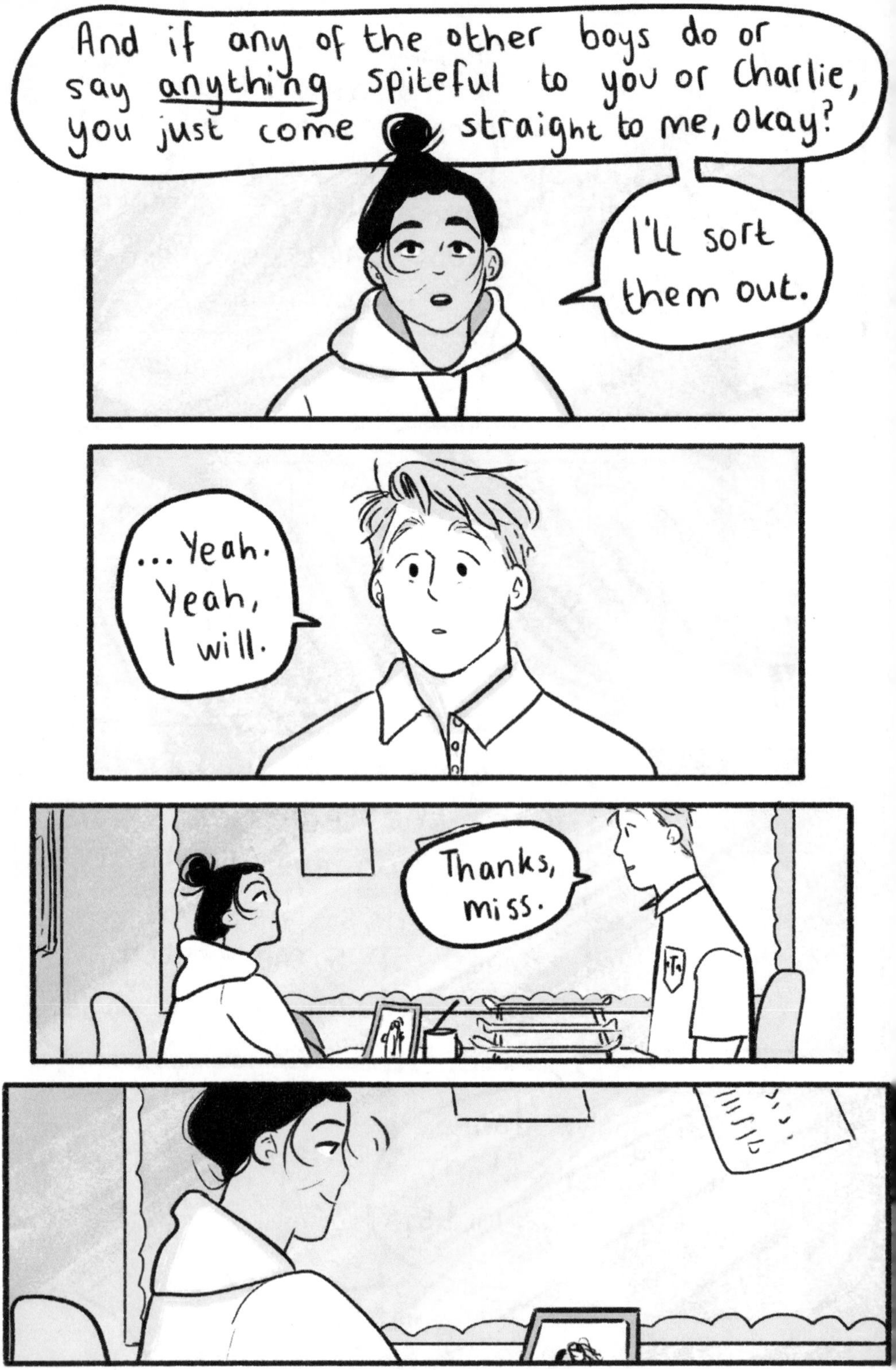
And if any of the other boys do or say anything spiteful to you or Charlie, you just come straight to me, okay?
I'll sort them out.
...Yeah. Yeah, I will.
Thanks, miss.

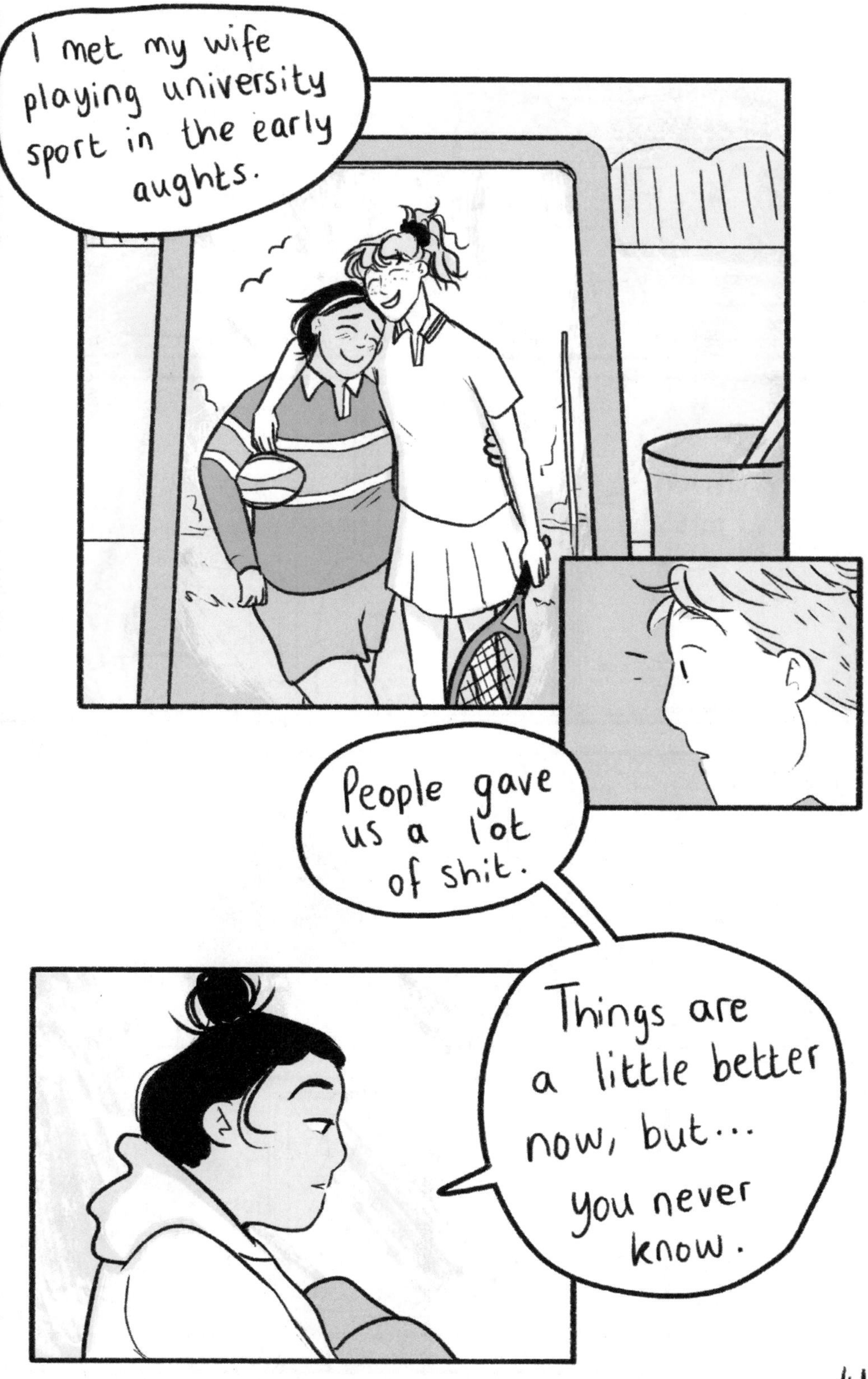
I met my wife playing university sport in the early aughts.
People gave us a lot of shit.
Things are a little better now, but... you never know.

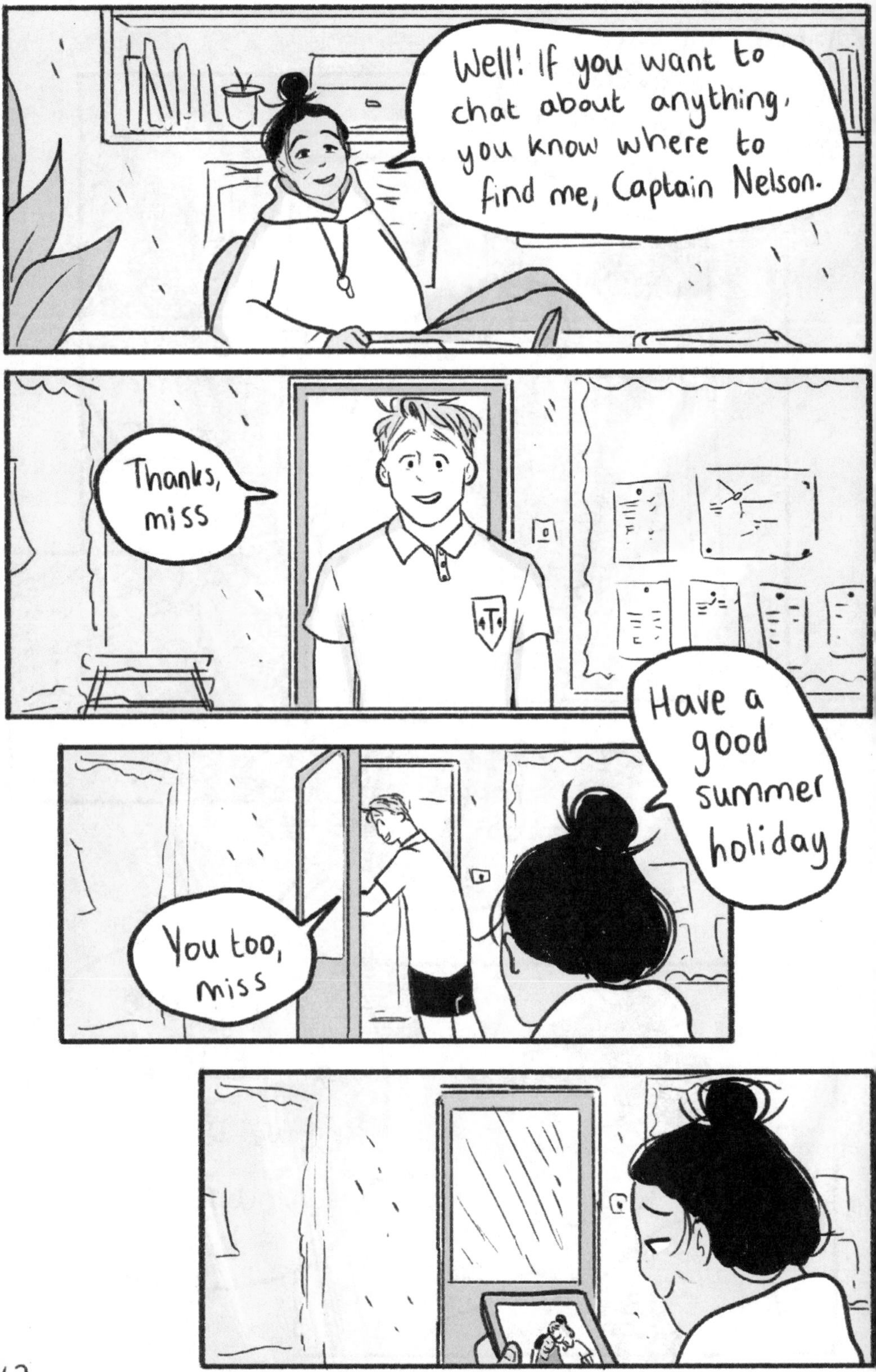
Well! If you want to chat about anything, you know where to find me, Captain Nelson.
Thanks, miss
Have a good summer holiday
You too, miss

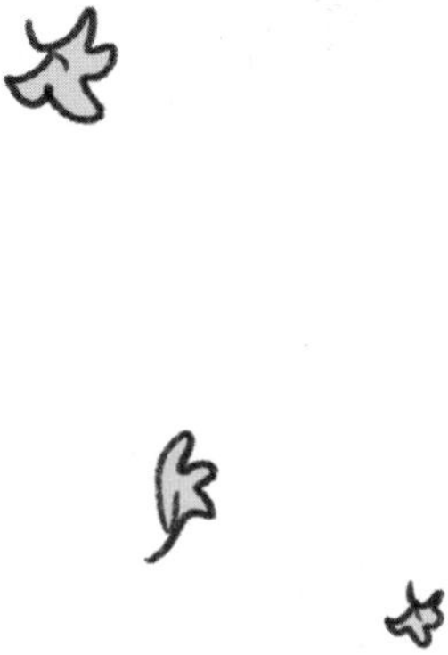

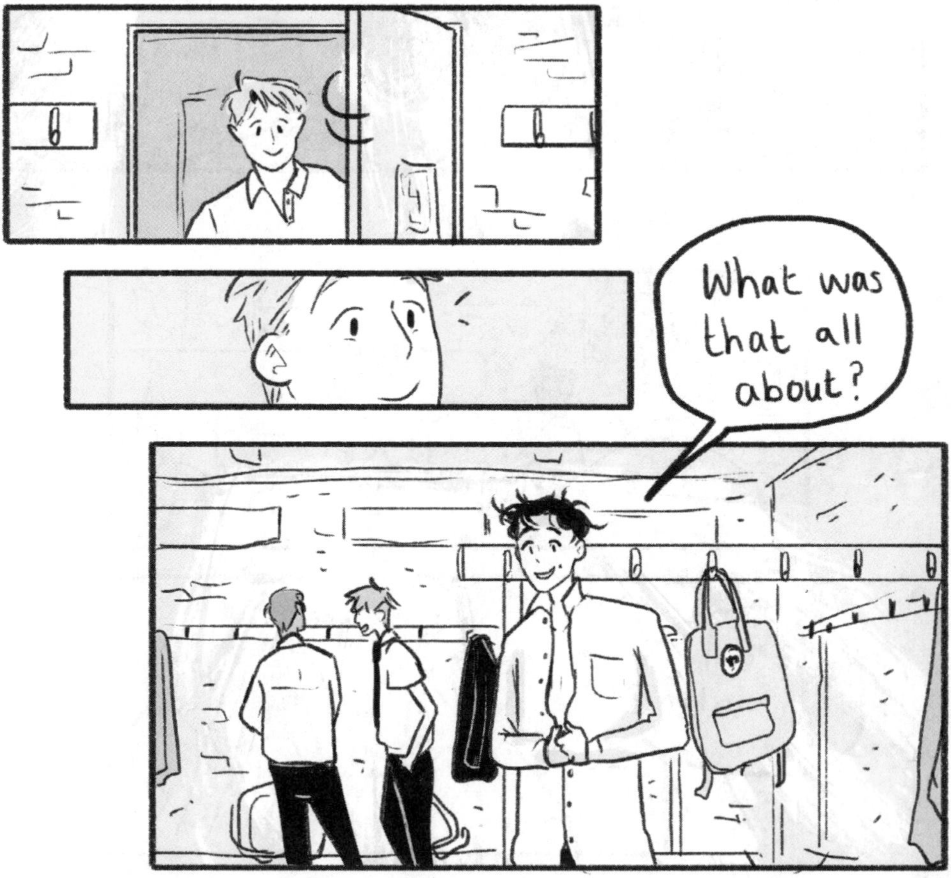
What was that all about?

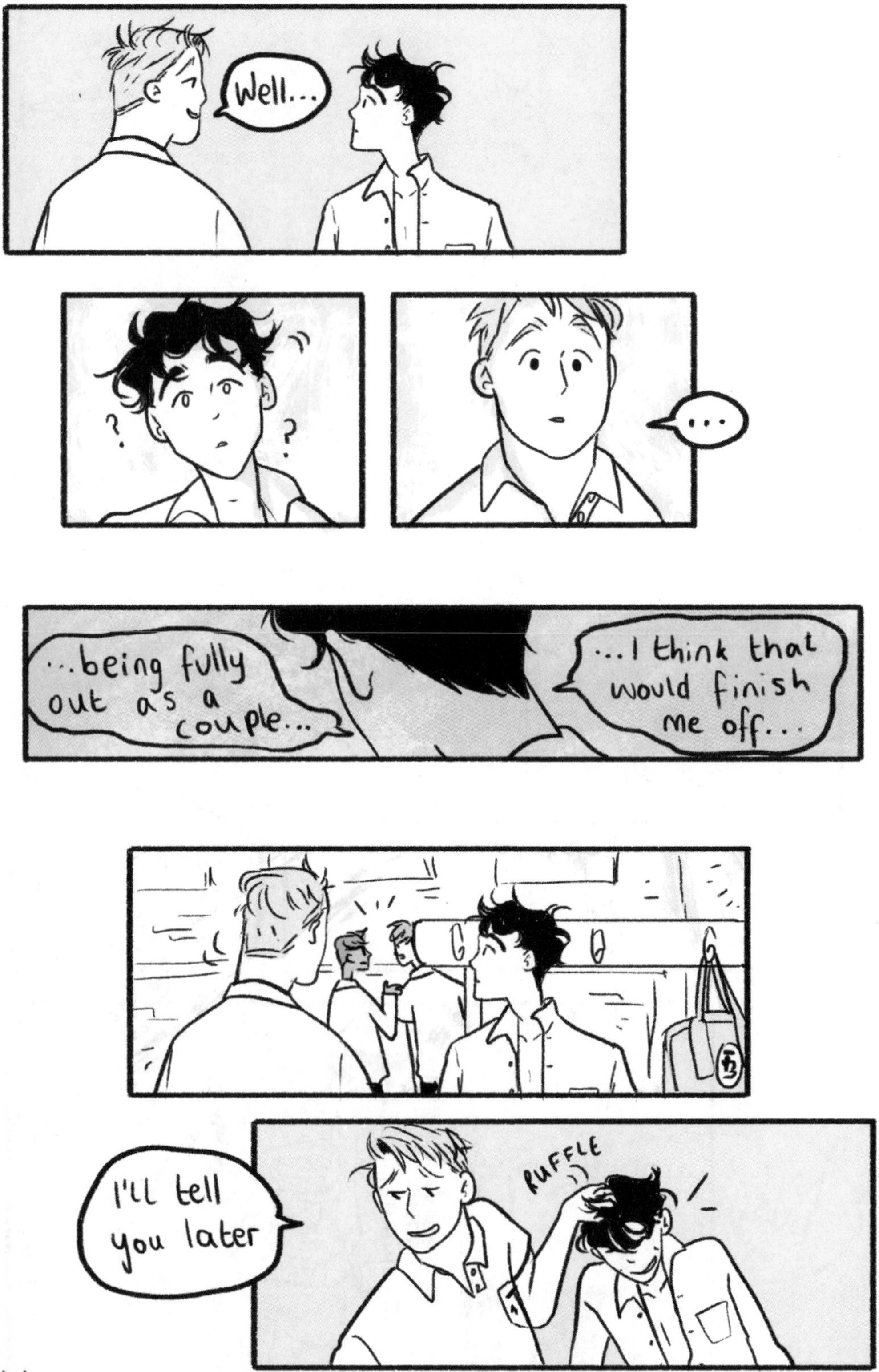
Well...
...
...being fully out as a couple...
...I think that would finish me off...
I'll tell you later
RUFFLE

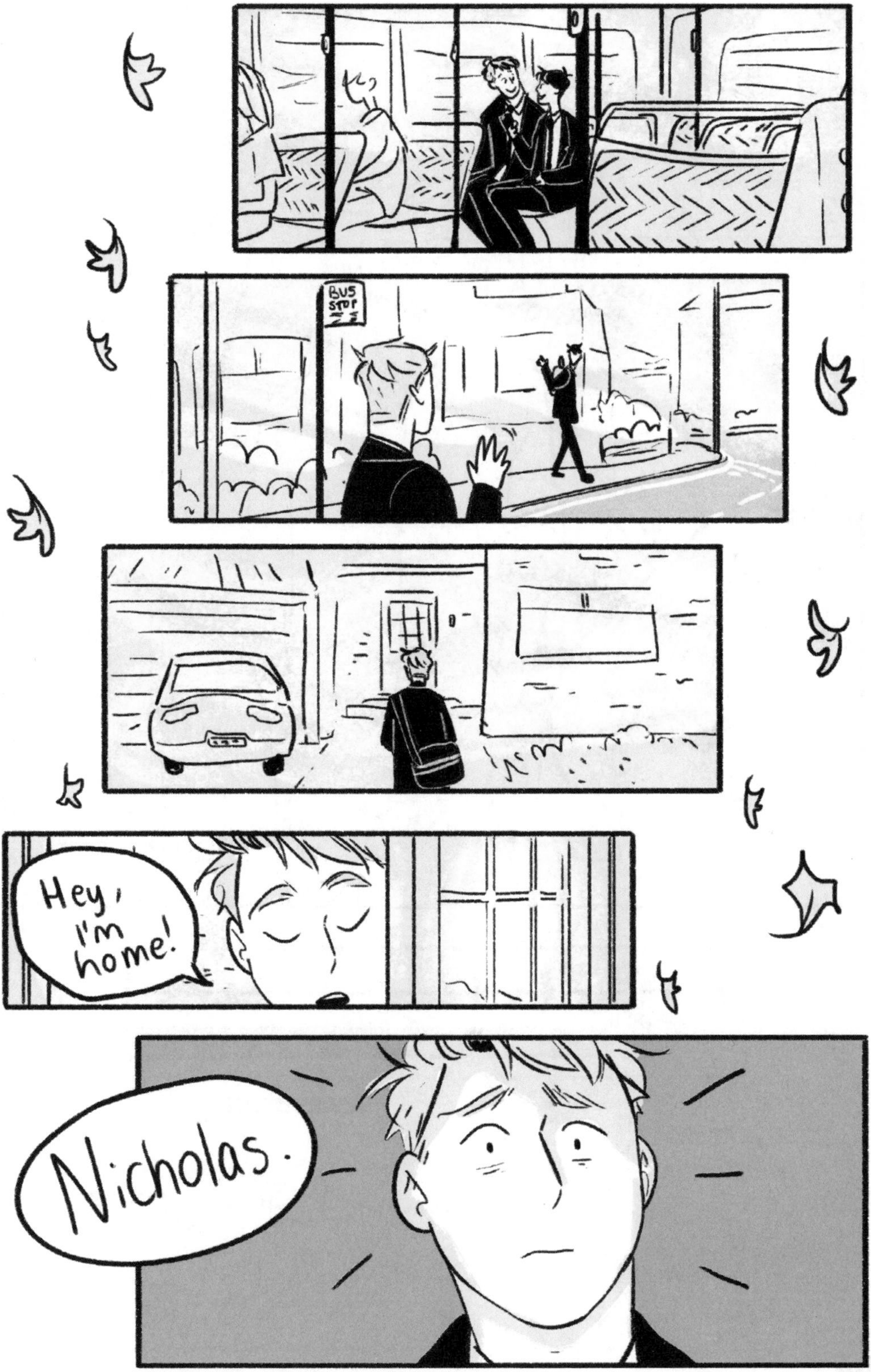
BUS STOP
Hey, I'm home!
Nicholas.

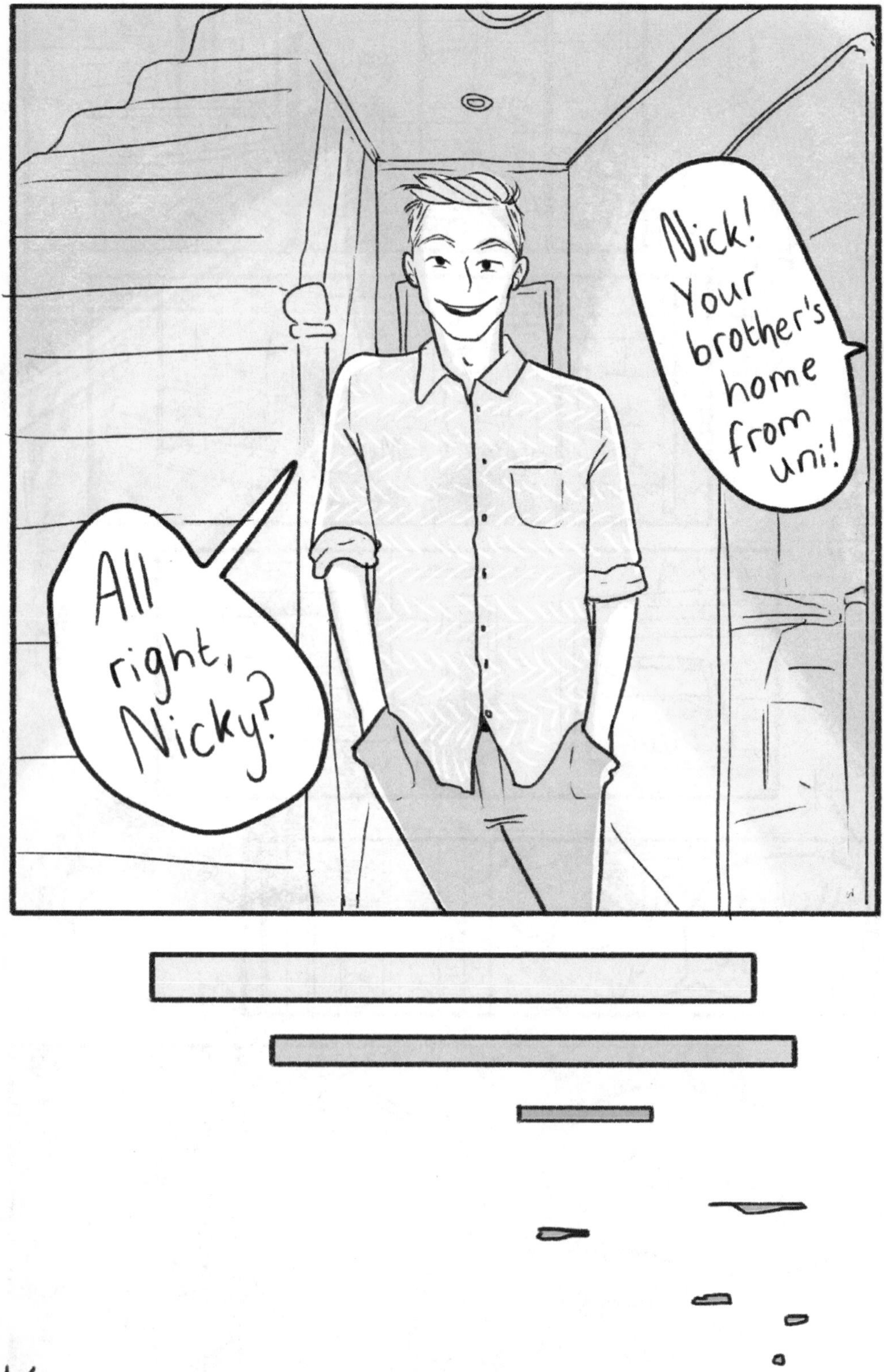
Nick! Your brother's home from uni!
All right, Nicky?

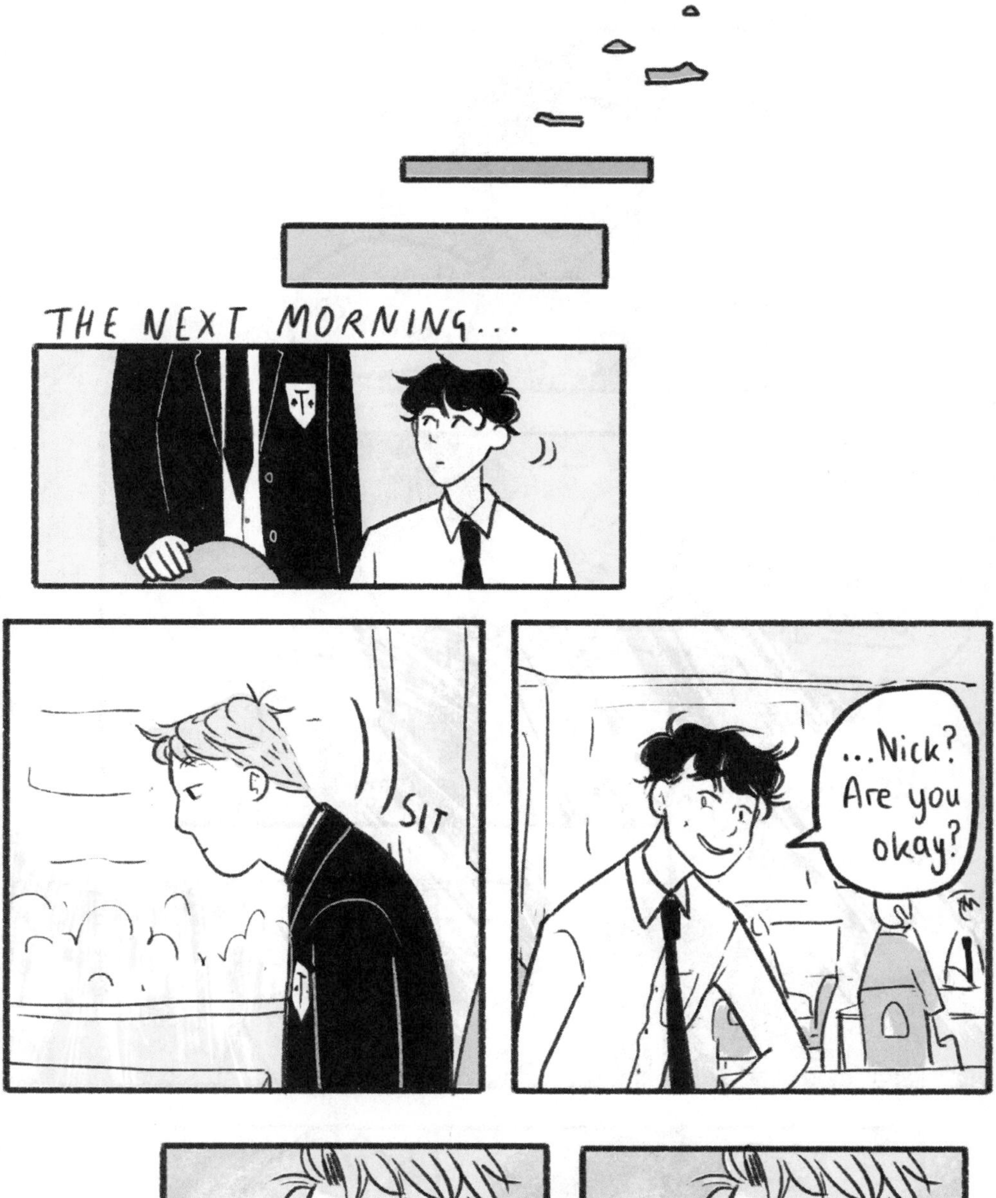
THE NEXT MORNING...
SIT
...Nick? Are you okay?
Late night

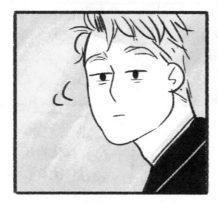

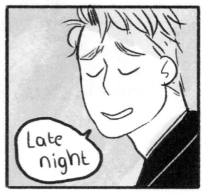

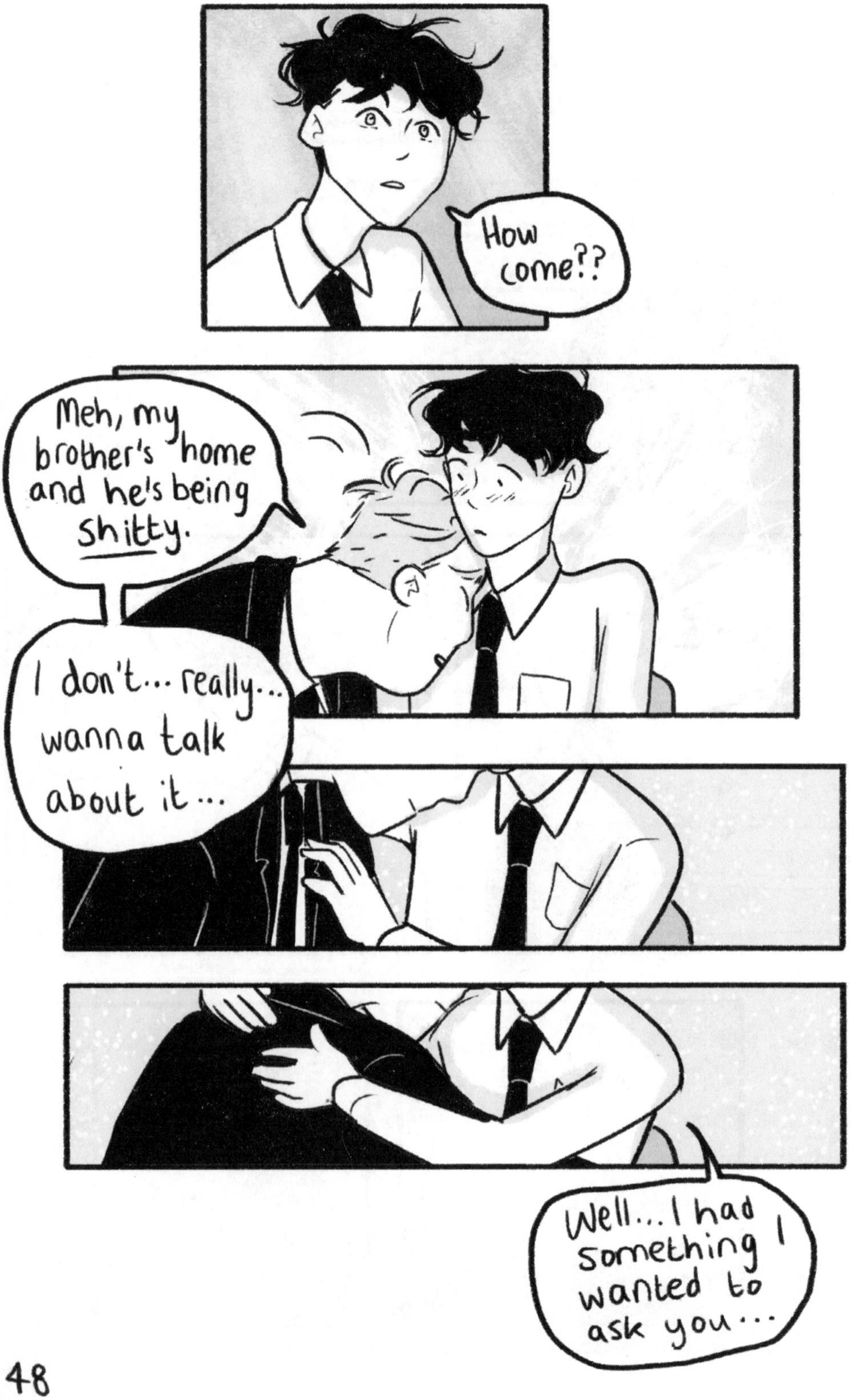
How come??
Meh, my brother's home and he's being shitty.
I don't... really... wanna talk about it...
Well... I had something I wanted to ask you...

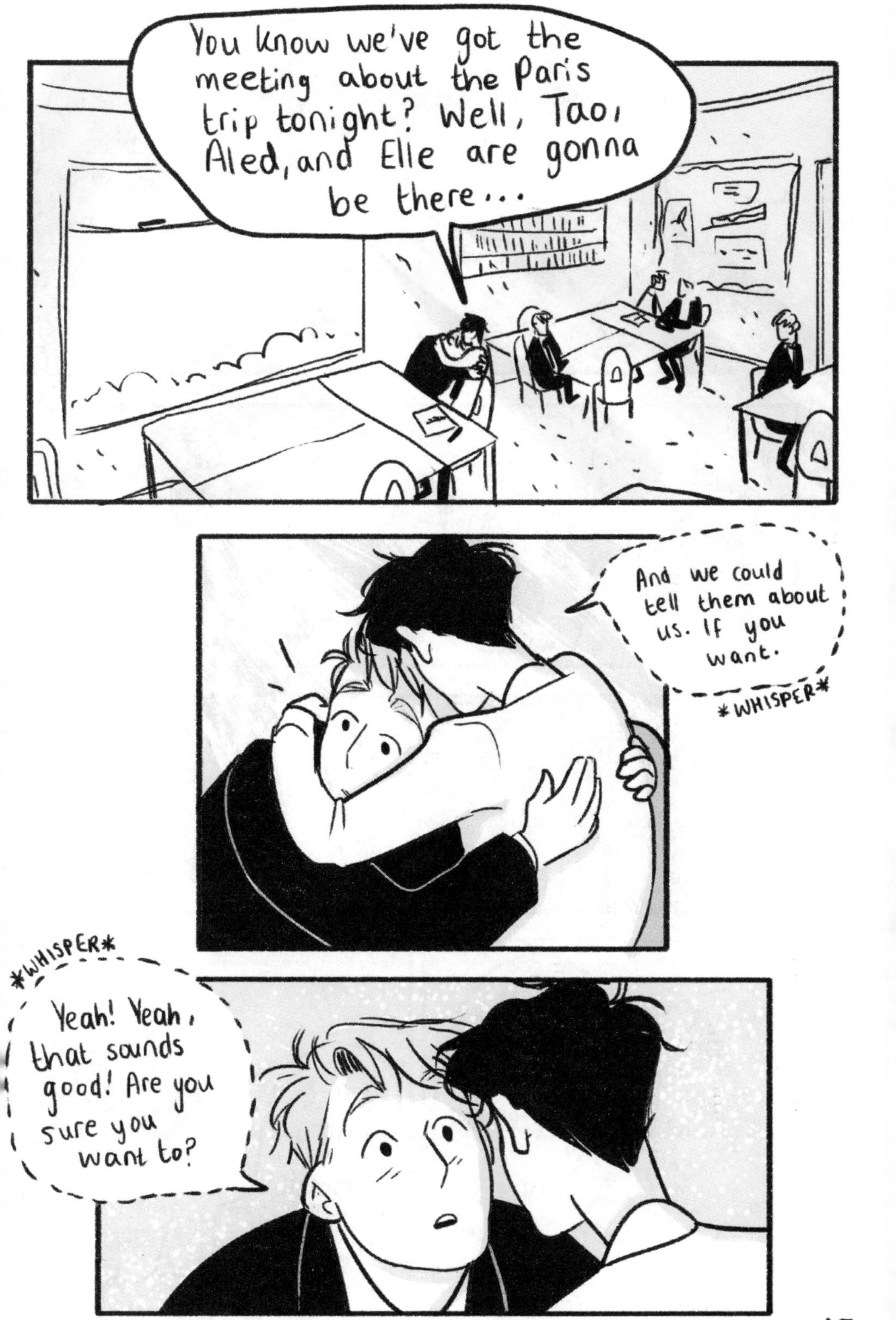
You know we've got the meeting about the Paris trip tonight? Well, Tao, Aled, and Elle are gonna be there...
And we could tell them about us. If you want.
WHISPER
WHISPER
Yeah! Yeah, that sounds good! Are you sure you want to?

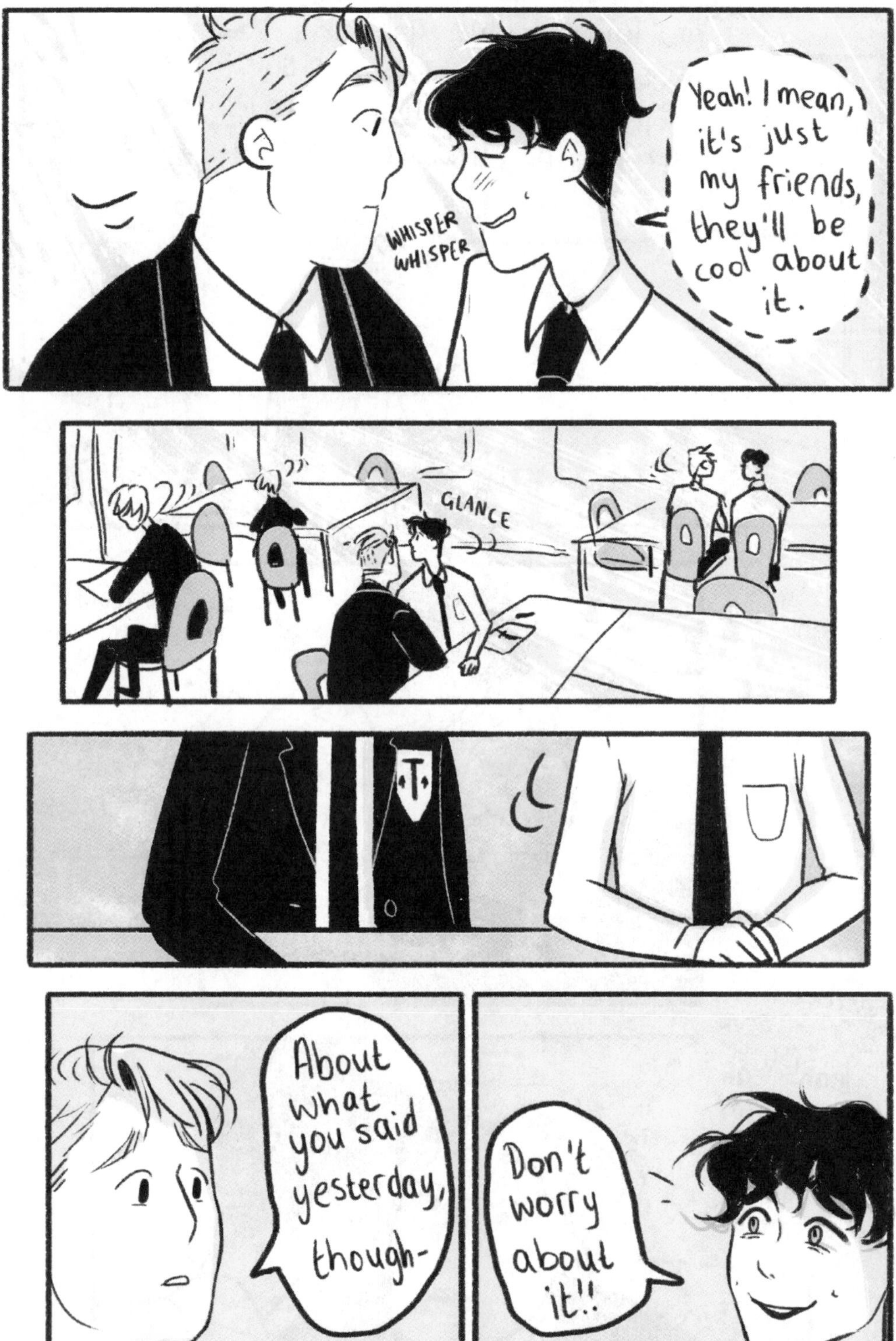

Yeah! I mean, it's just my friends, they'll be cool about it.
WHISPER WHISPER
GLANCE
About what you said yesterday, though-
Don't worry about it!!

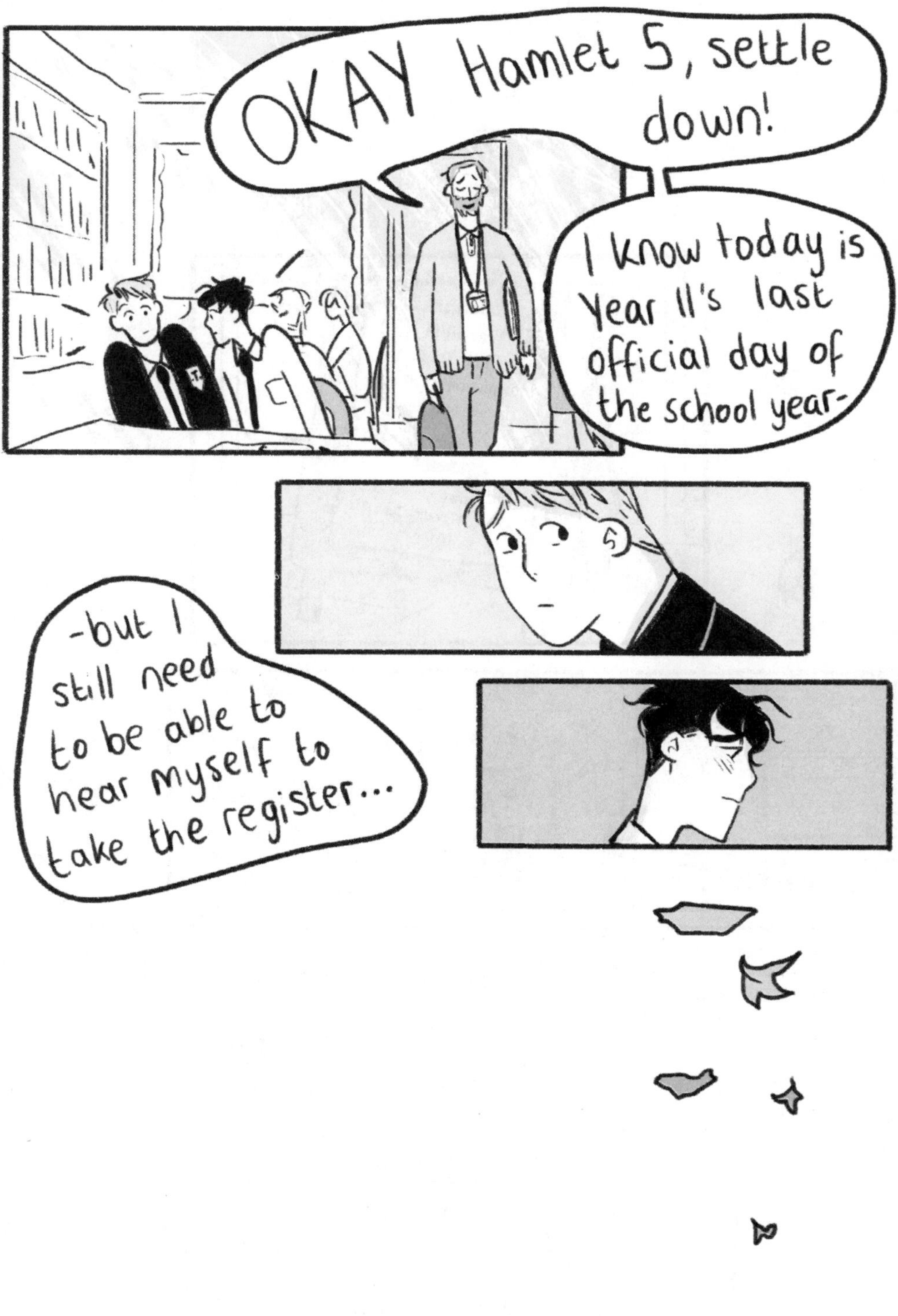
OKAY Hamlet 5, settle down!
I know today is Year 11's last official day of the school year-
-but I still need to be able to hear myself to take the register...

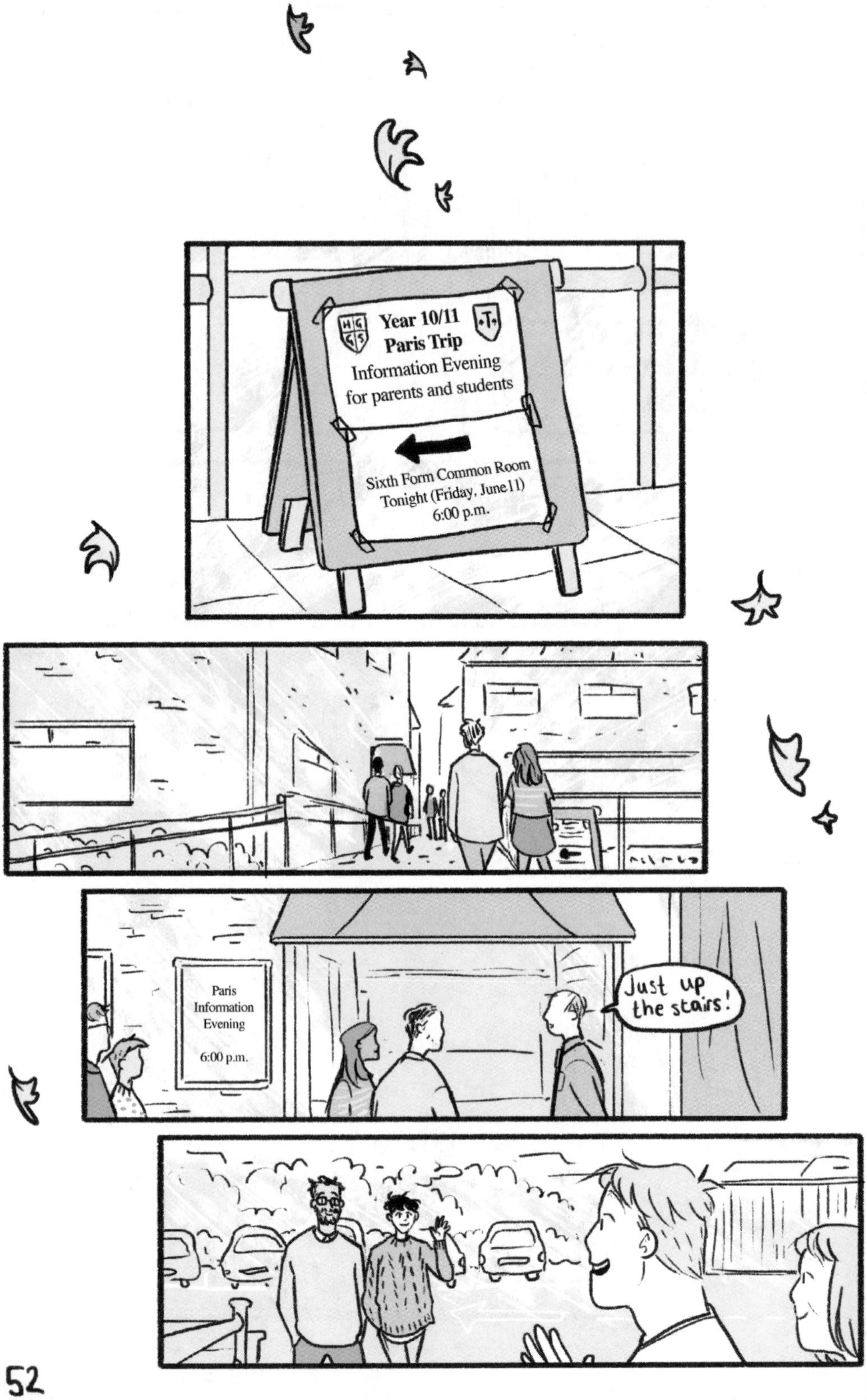
Year 10/11
Paris Trip
Information Evening
for parents and students
Sixth Form Common Room
Tonight (Friday, June 11)
6:00 p.m.
Paris
Information
Evening
6:00 p.m.
Just up the stairs!

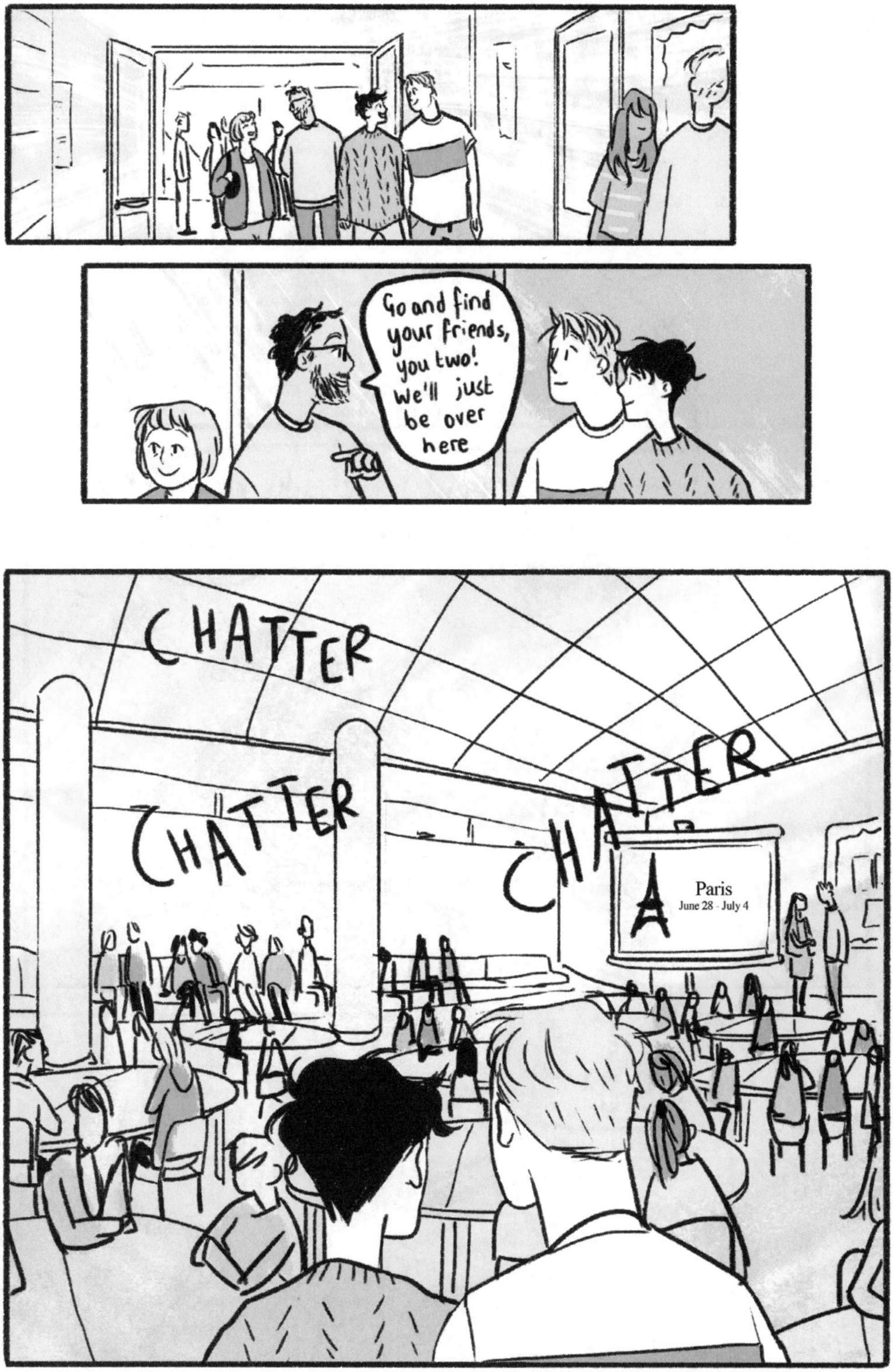
Go and find your friends, you two! We'll just be over here
CHATTER
CHATTER
CHATTER
Paris
June 28 - July 4

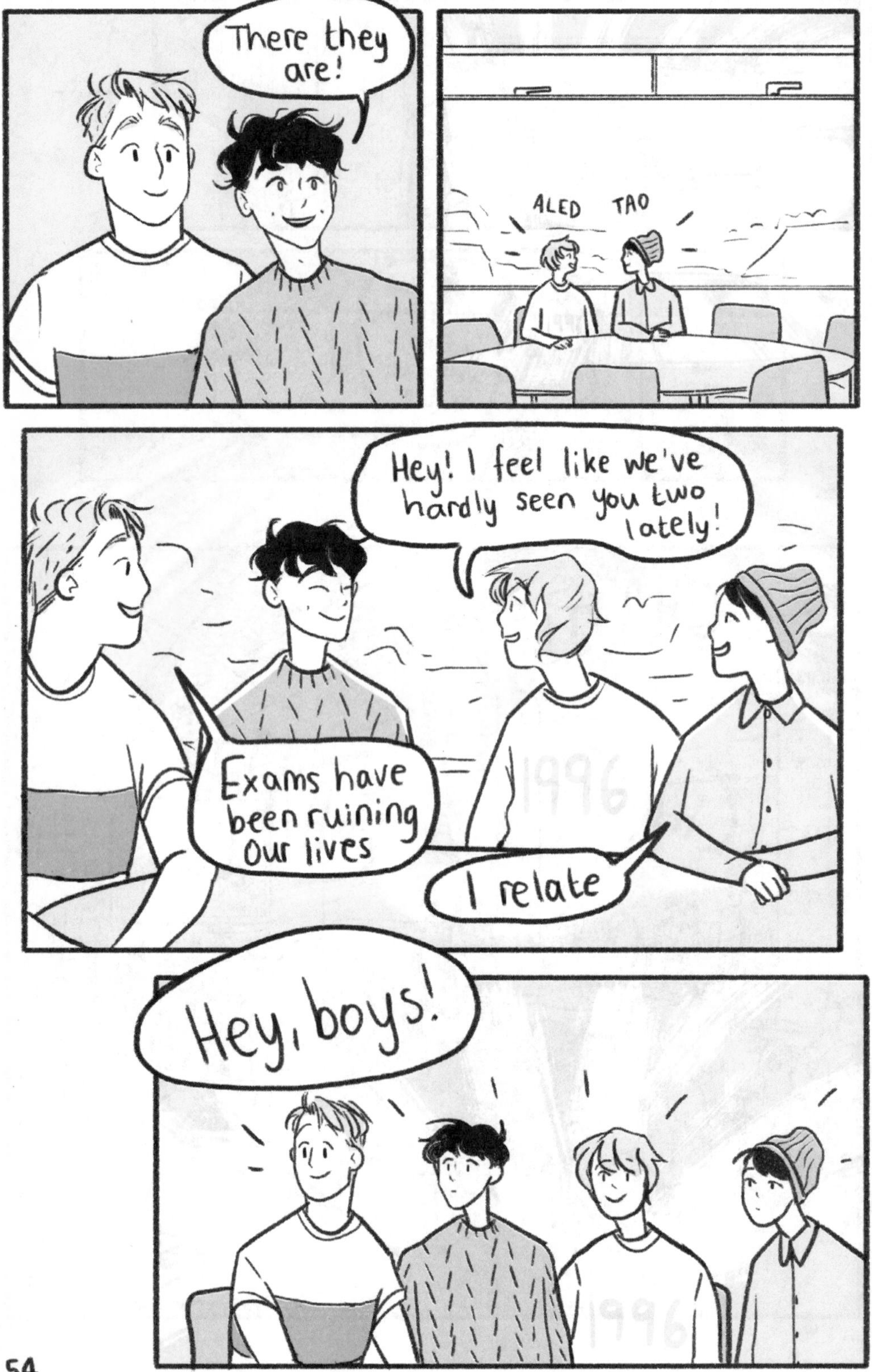
There they are!
ALED
TAO
Hey! I feel like we've hardly seen you two lately!
Exams have been ruining our lives
I relate
Hey, boys!

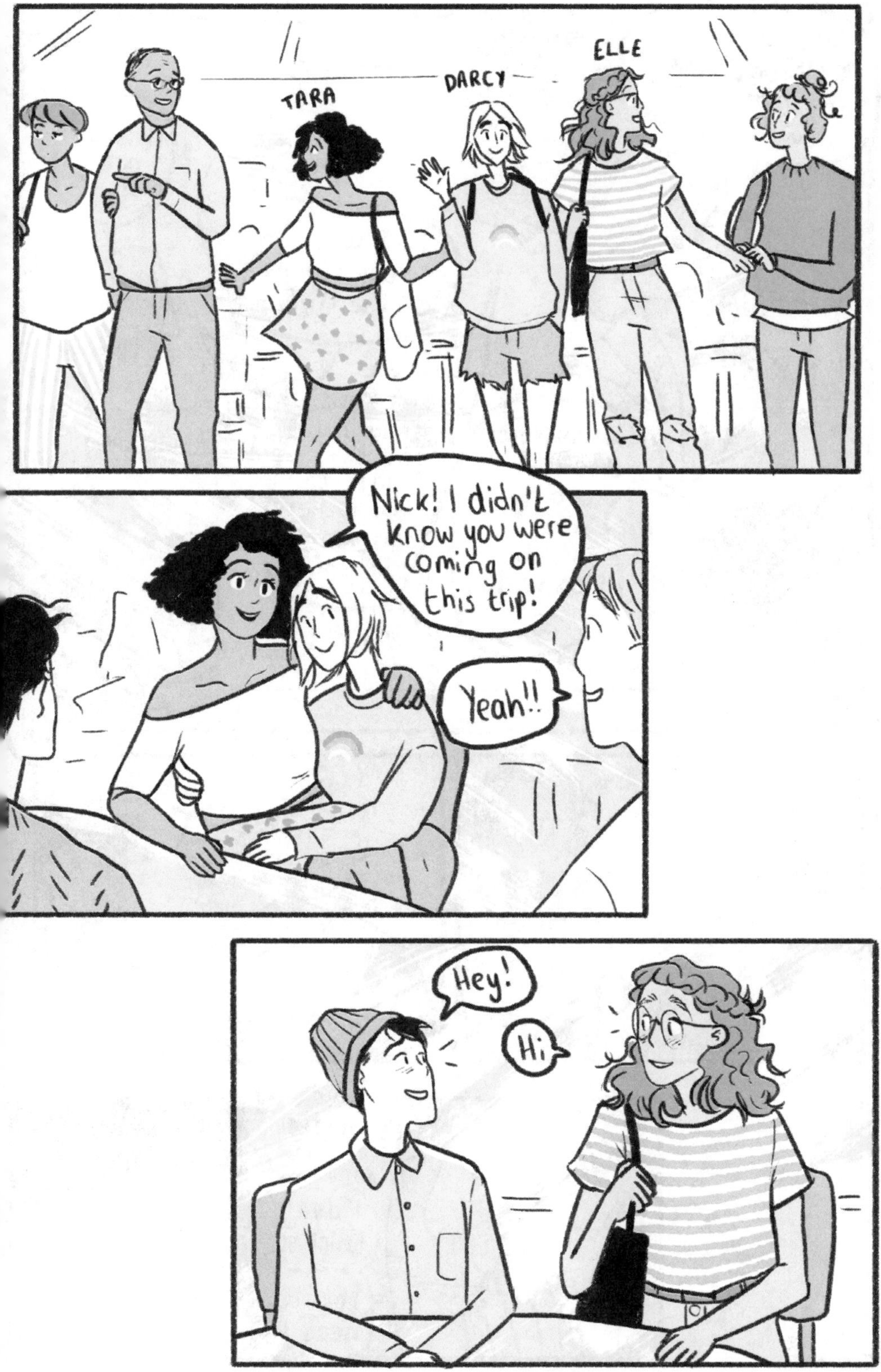
TARA
DARCY
ELLE
Nick! I didn't know you were coming on this trip!
Yeah!!
Hey!
Hi

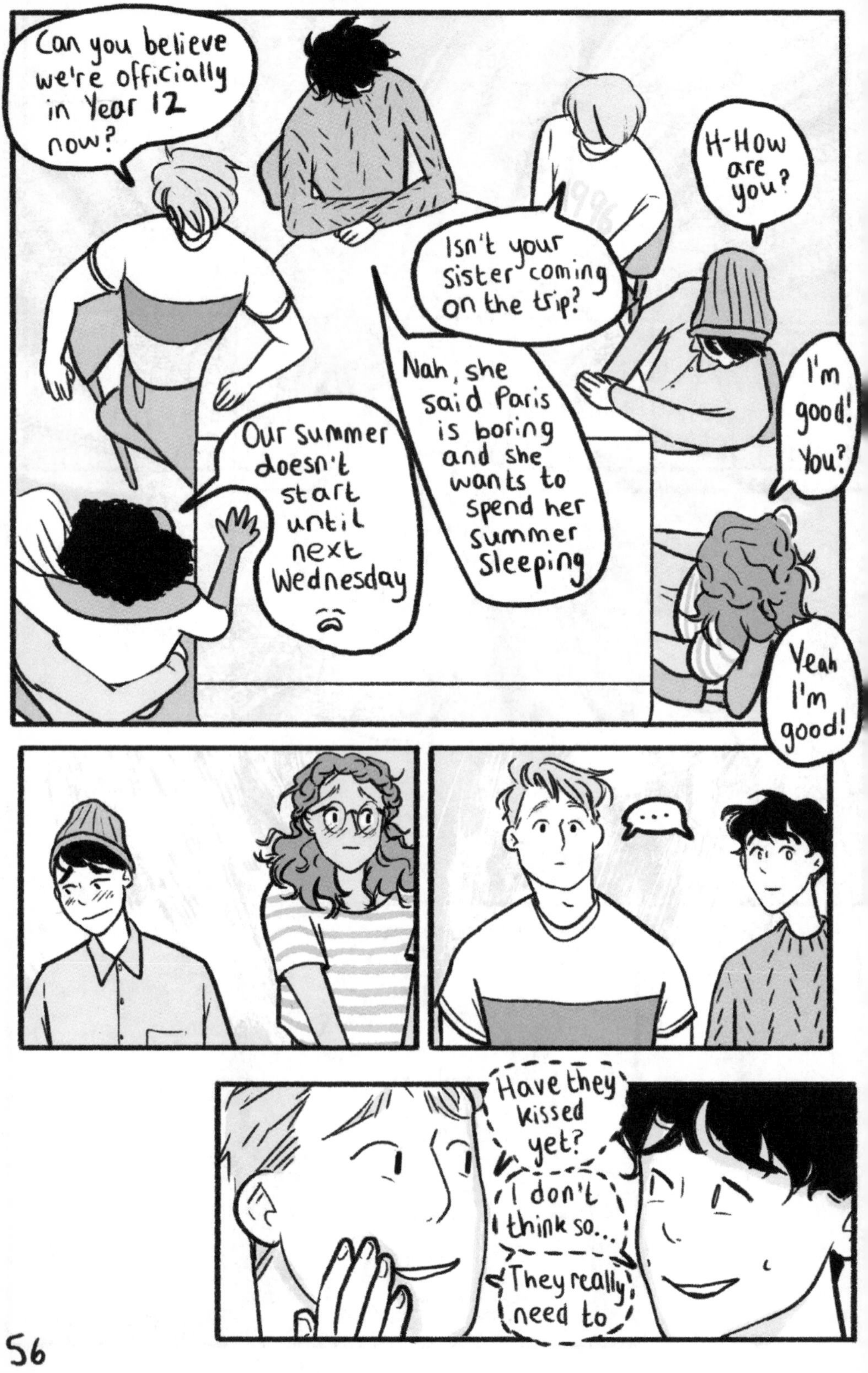
Can you believe we're officially in Year 12 now?
Isn't your sister coming on the trip?
H-How are you?
Nah, she said Paris is boring and she wants to spend her summer sleeping
I'm good! You?
Our summer doesn't start until next Wednesday
Yeah I'm good!
...
Have they kissed yet?
I don't think so...
They really need to

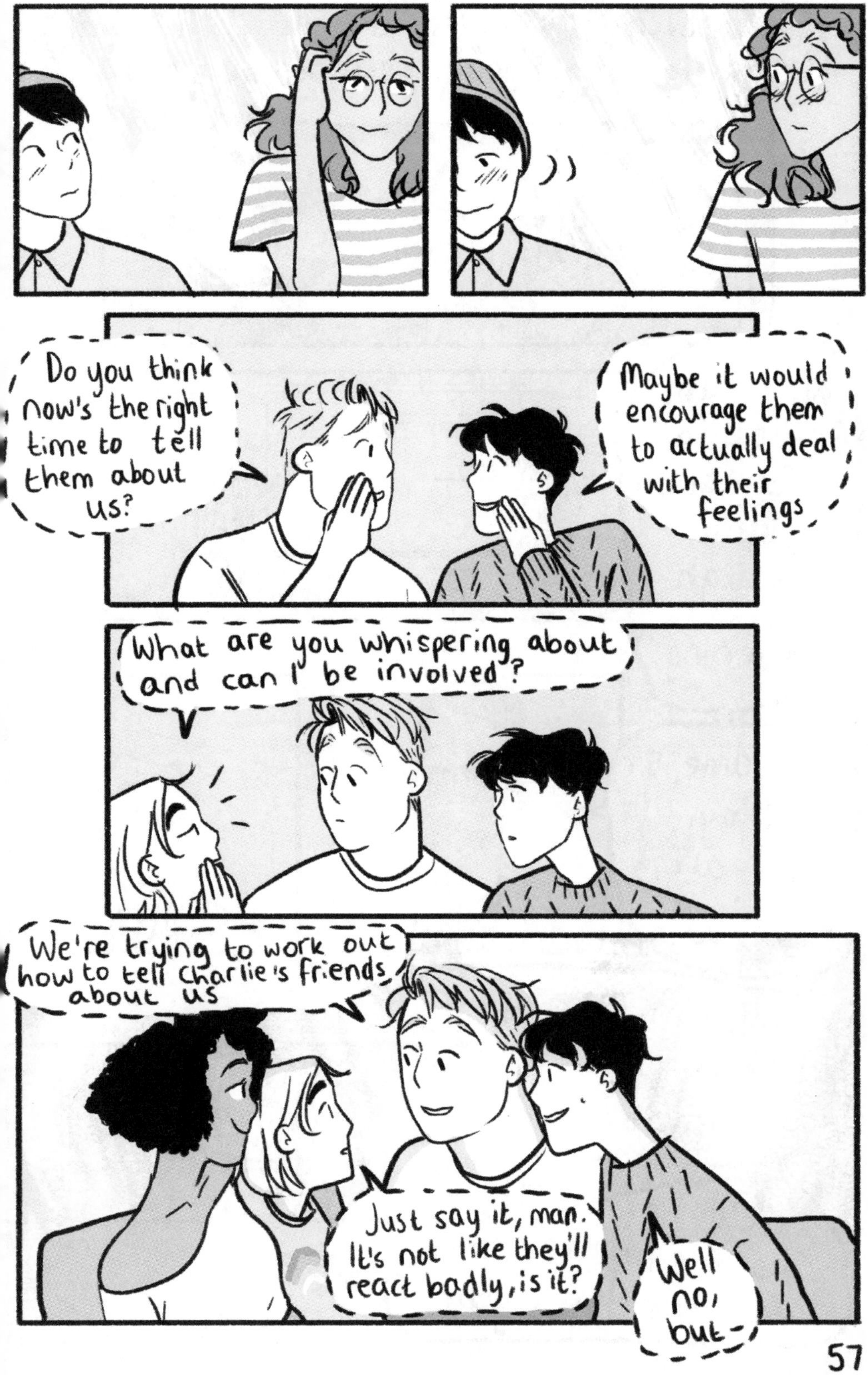
Do you think now's the right time to tell them about us?
Maybe it would encourage them to actually deal with their feelings
What are you whispering about and can I be involved?
We're trying to work out how to tell Charlie's friends about us
Just say it, man. It's not like they'll react badly, is it?
Well no, but-

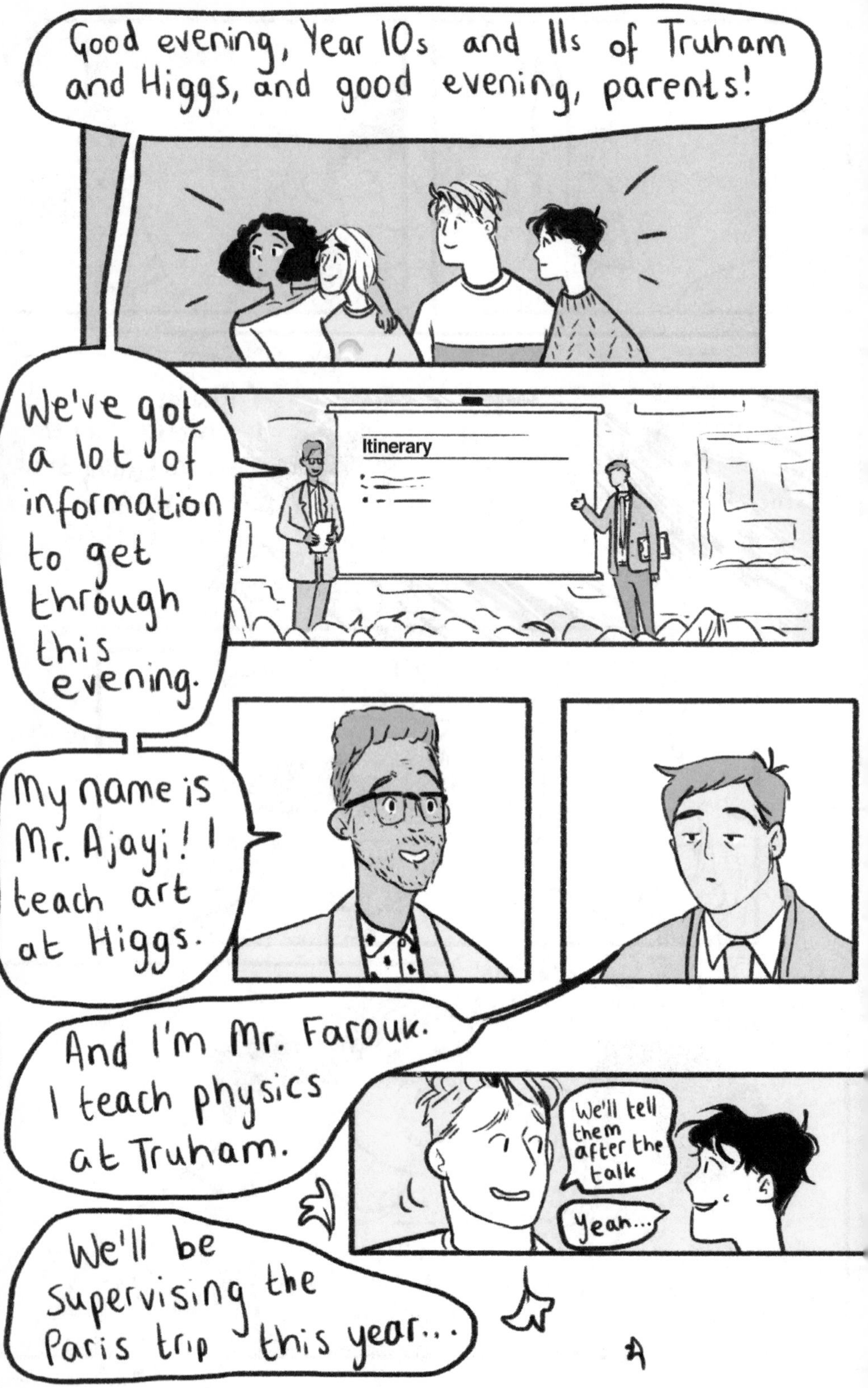
Good evening, Year 10s and 11s of Truham and Higgs, and good evening, parents!
We've got a lot of information to get through this evening.
Itinerary
My name is Mr. Ajayi! I teach art at Higgs.
And I'm Mr. Farouk. I teach physics at Truham.
We'll tell them after the talk
Yeah...
We'll be supervising the Paris trip this year...

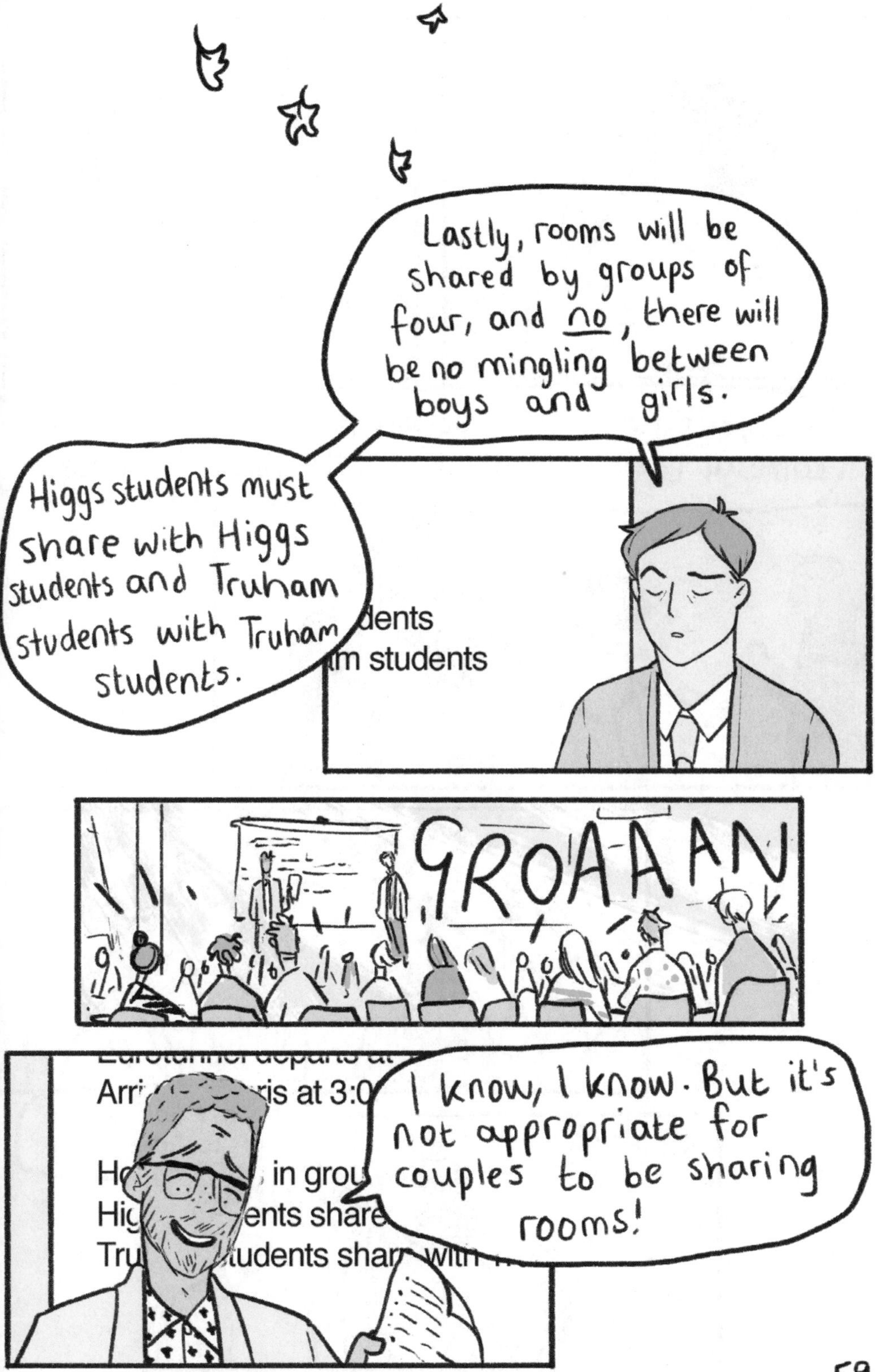
Lastly, rooms will be shared by groups of four, and no, there will be no mingling between boys and girls.
Higgs students must share with Higgs students and Truham students with Truham students.
GROAAAN
I know, I know. But it's not appropriate for couples to be sharing rooms!

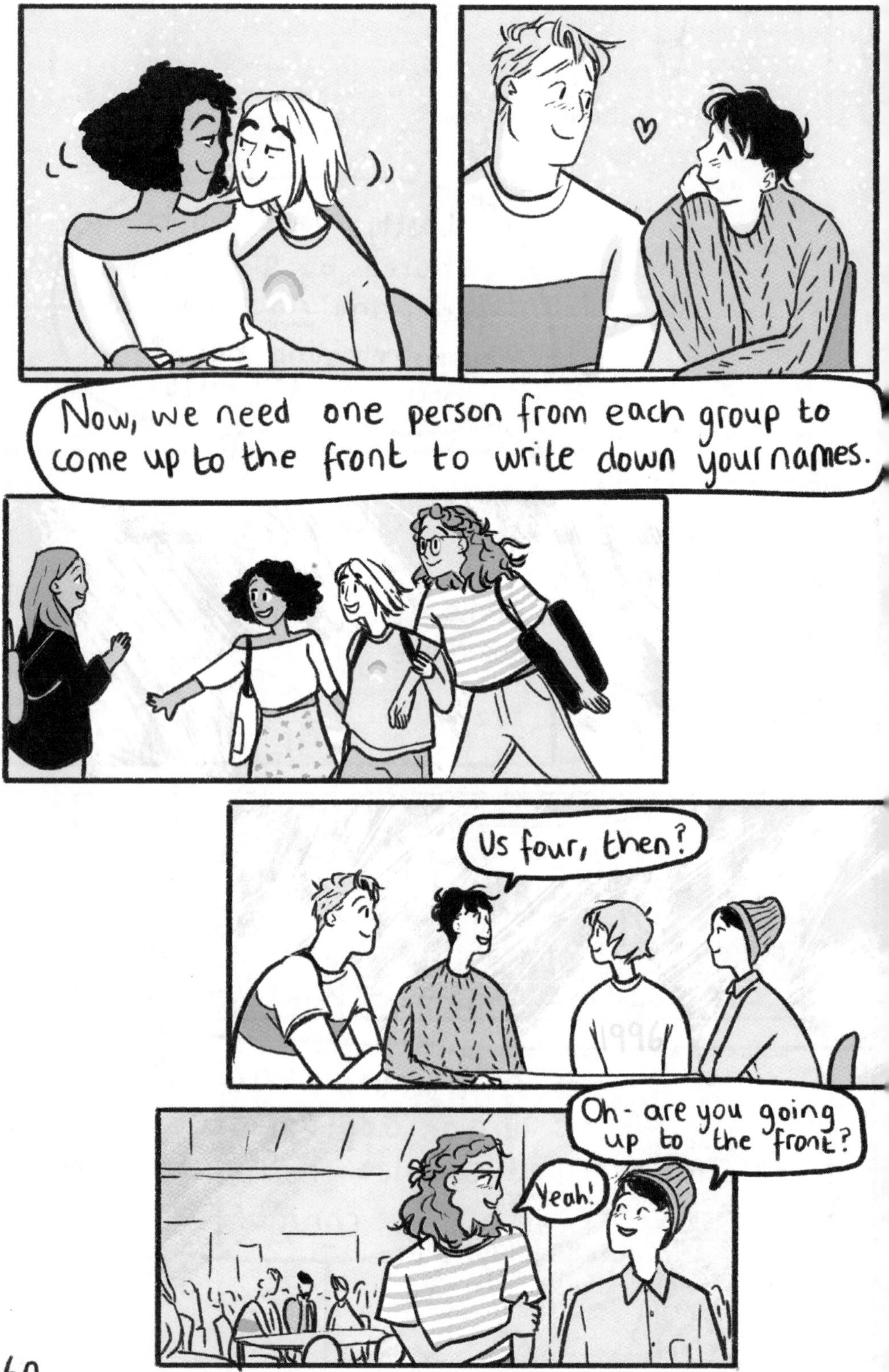
Now, we need one person from each group to come up to the front to write down your names.
Us four, then?
Oh- are you going up to the front?
Yeah!

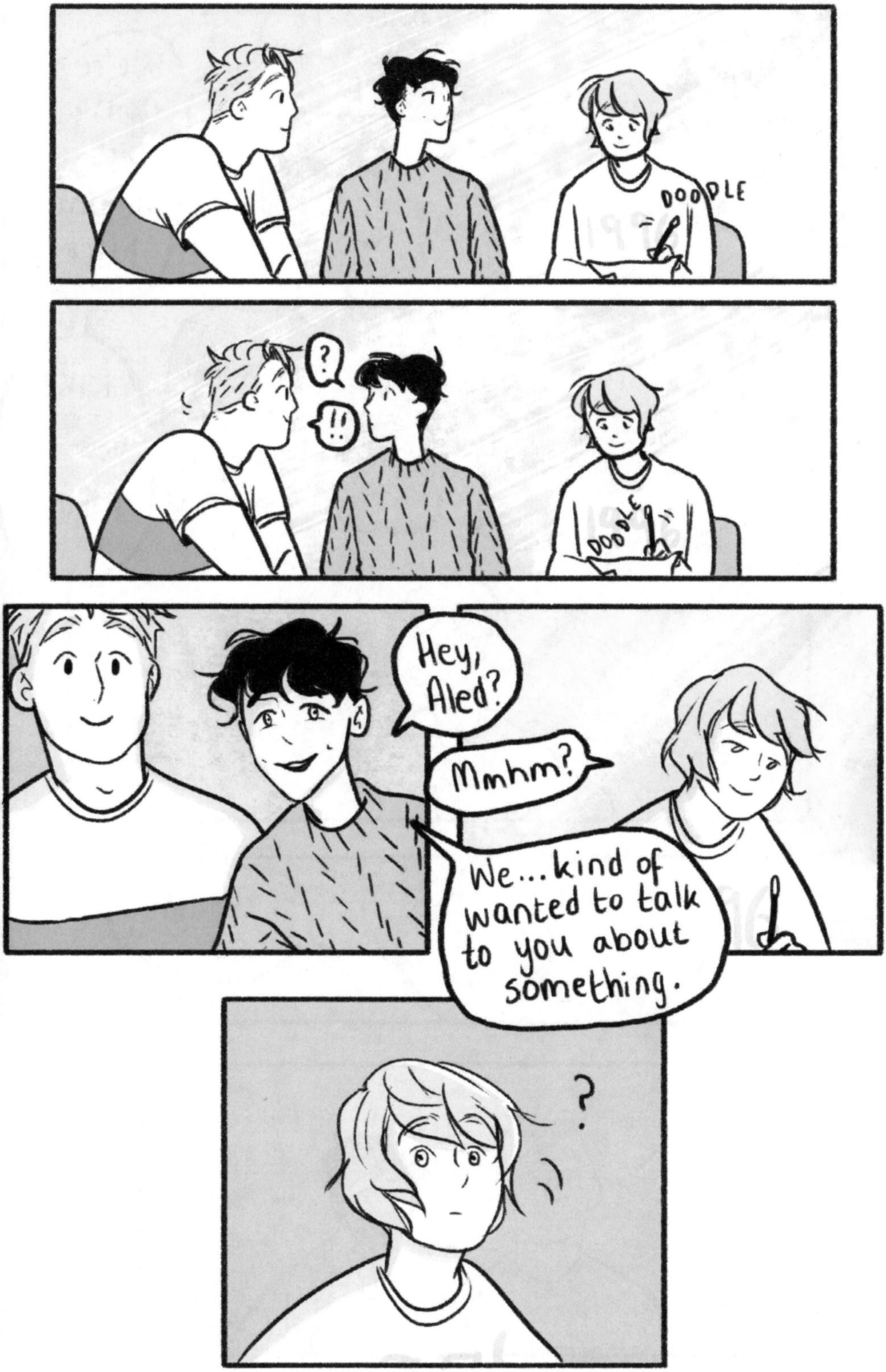
DOODLE
?
!!
DOODLE
Hey, Aled?
Mmhm?
We... kind of wanted to talk to you about something.
?

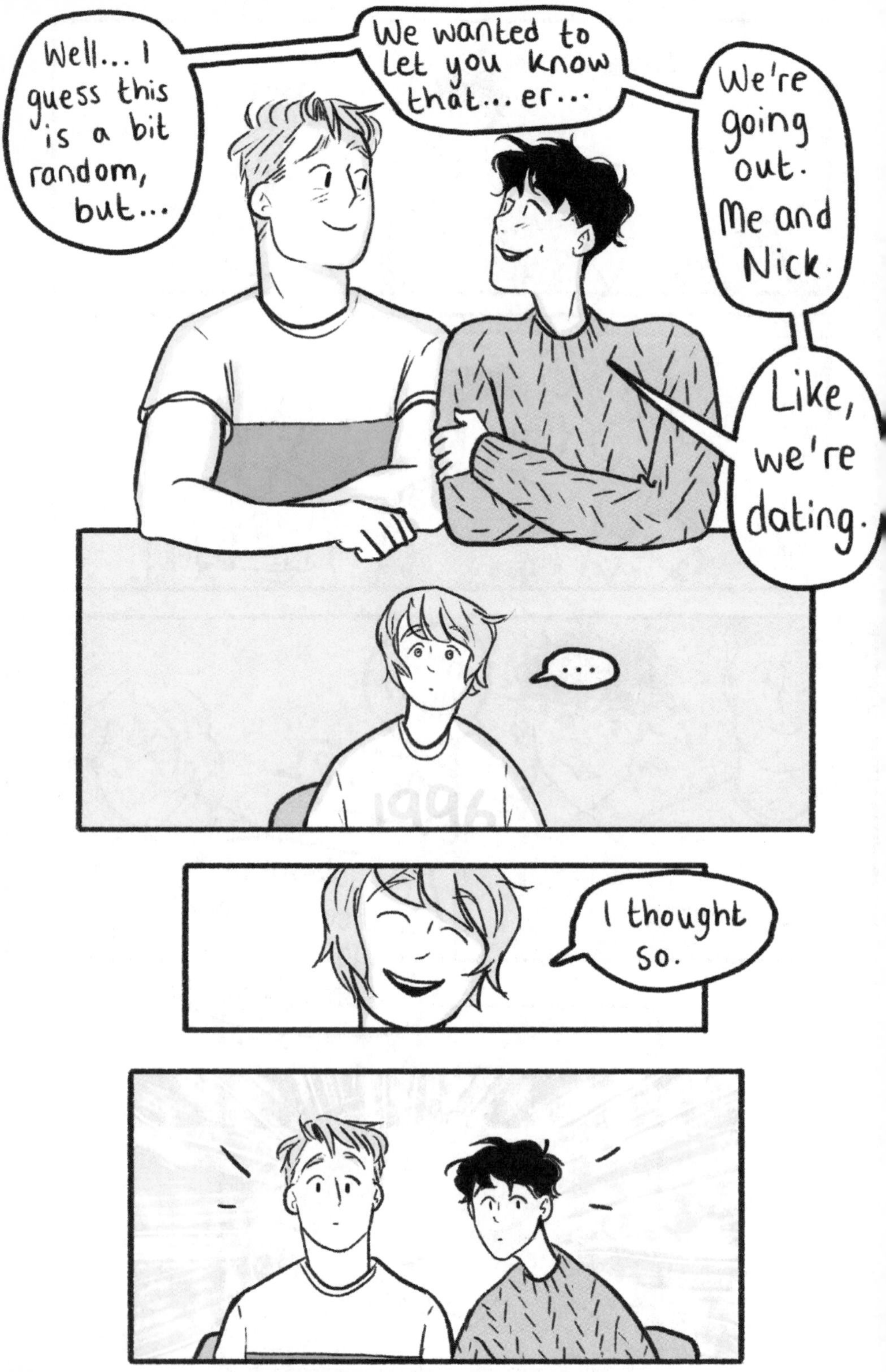

Well... I guess this is a bit random, but...
We wanted to let you know that... er...
We're going out. Me and Nick.
Like, we're dating.
...
I thought so.

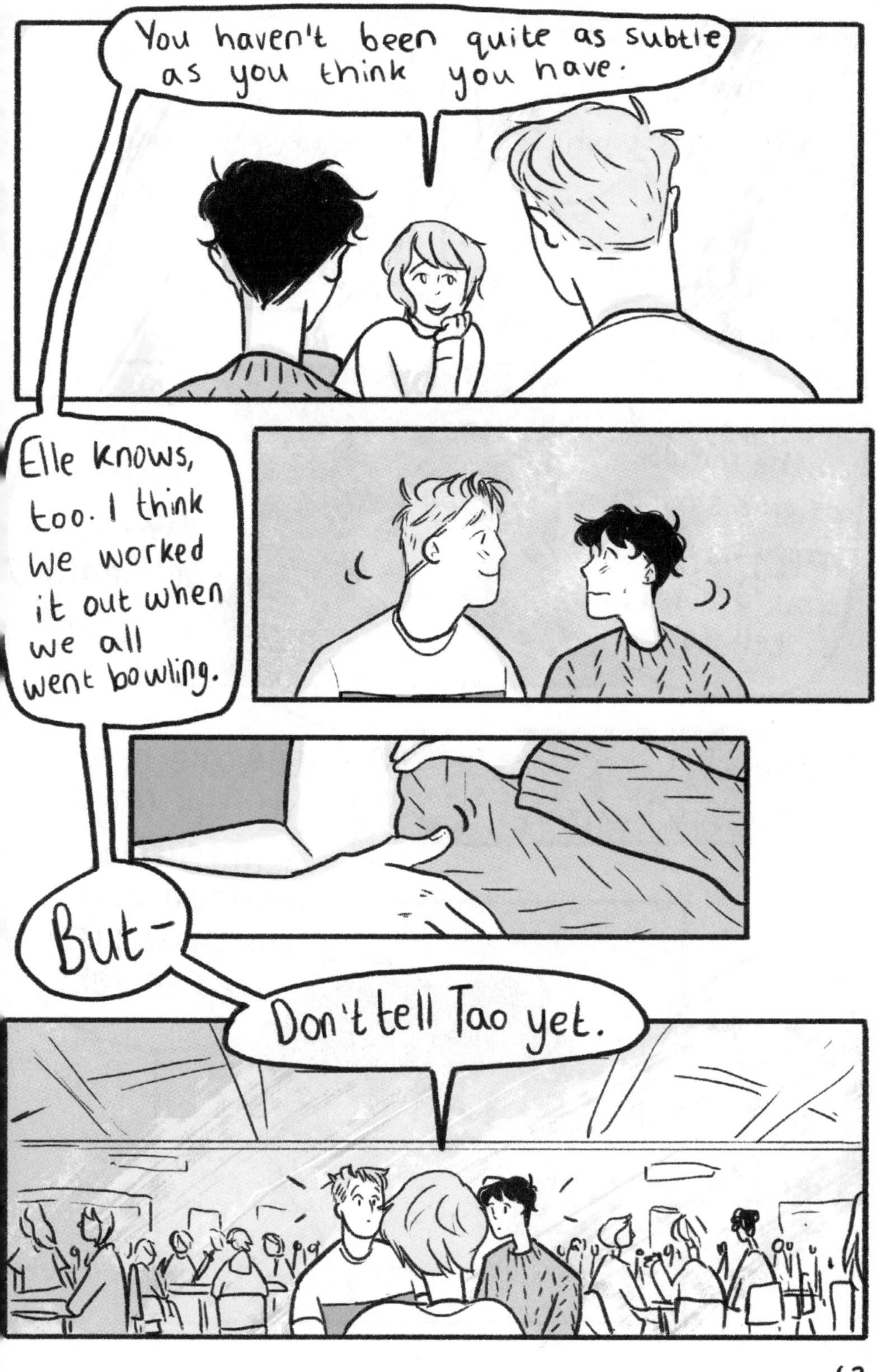
You haven't been quite as subtle as you think you have.
Elle knows, too. I think we worked it out when we all went bowling.
But-
Don't tell Tao yet.

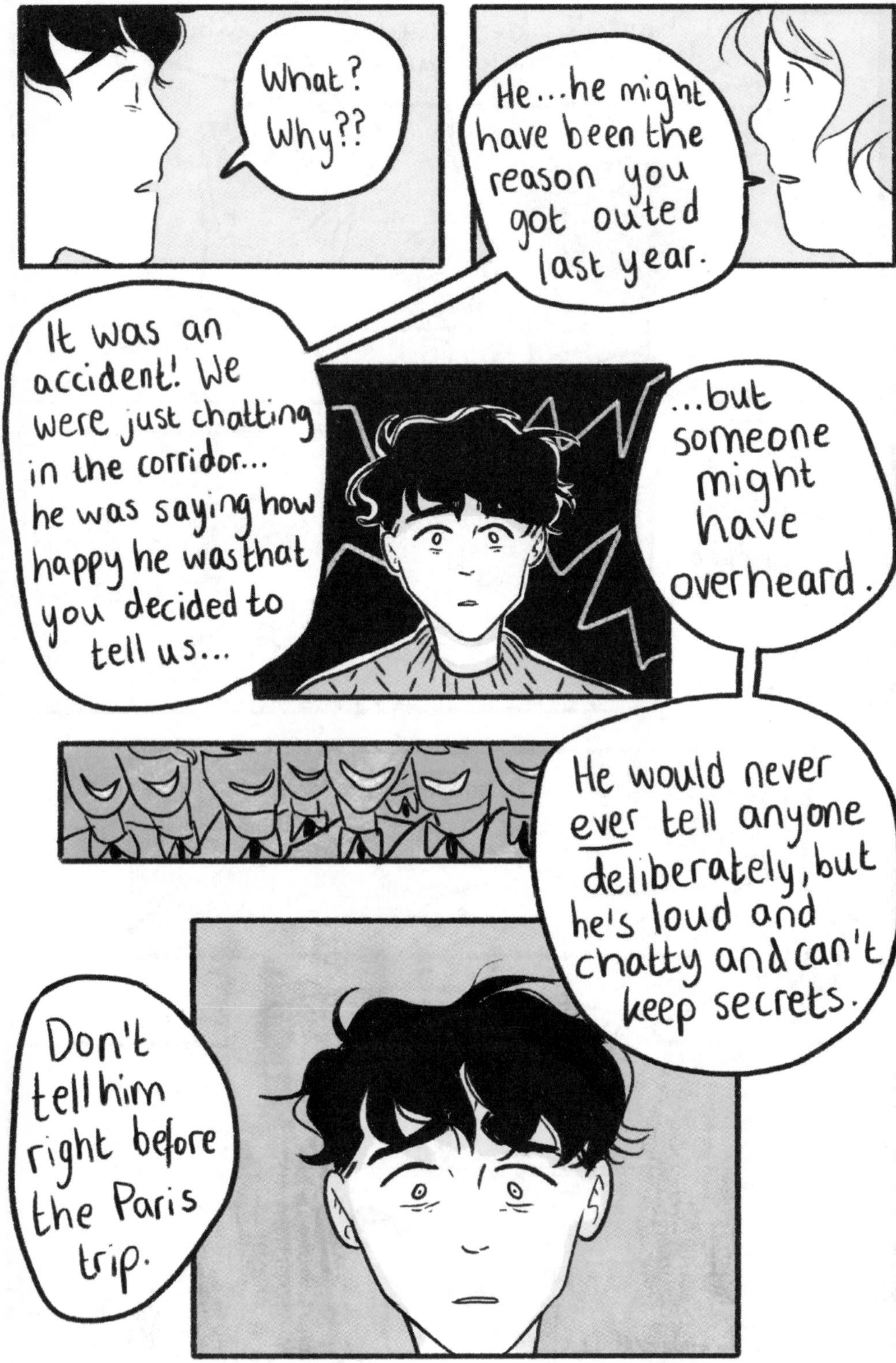
What? Why??
He...he might have been the reason you got outed last year.
It was an accident! We were just chatting in the corridor... he was saying how happy he was that you decided to tell us...
...but someone might have overheard.
He would never ever tell anyone deliberately, but he's loud and chatty and can't keep secrets.
Don't tell him right before the Paris trip.

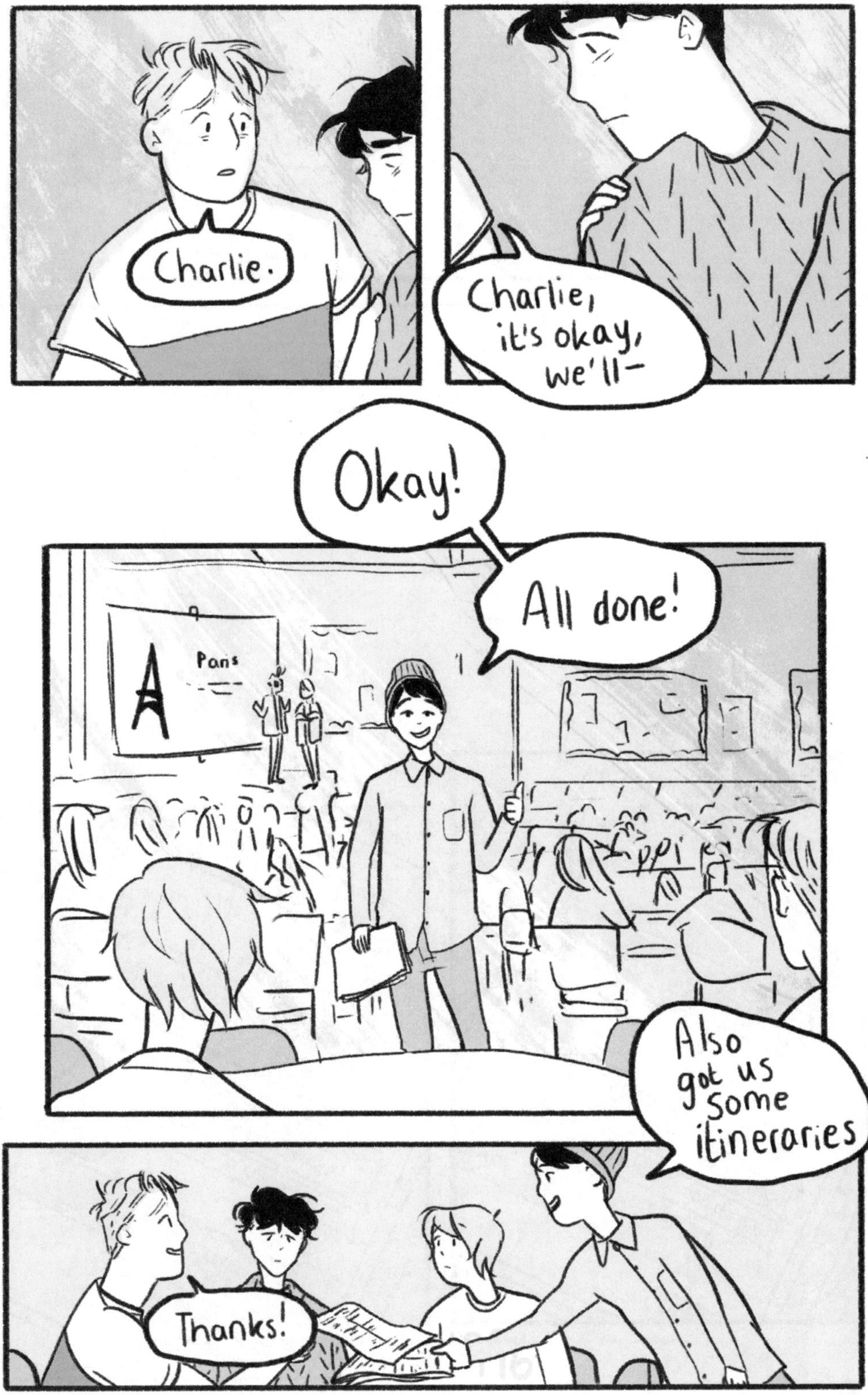
Charlie.
Charlie, it's okay, we'll–
Okay!
All done!
Also got us some itineraries
Thanks!

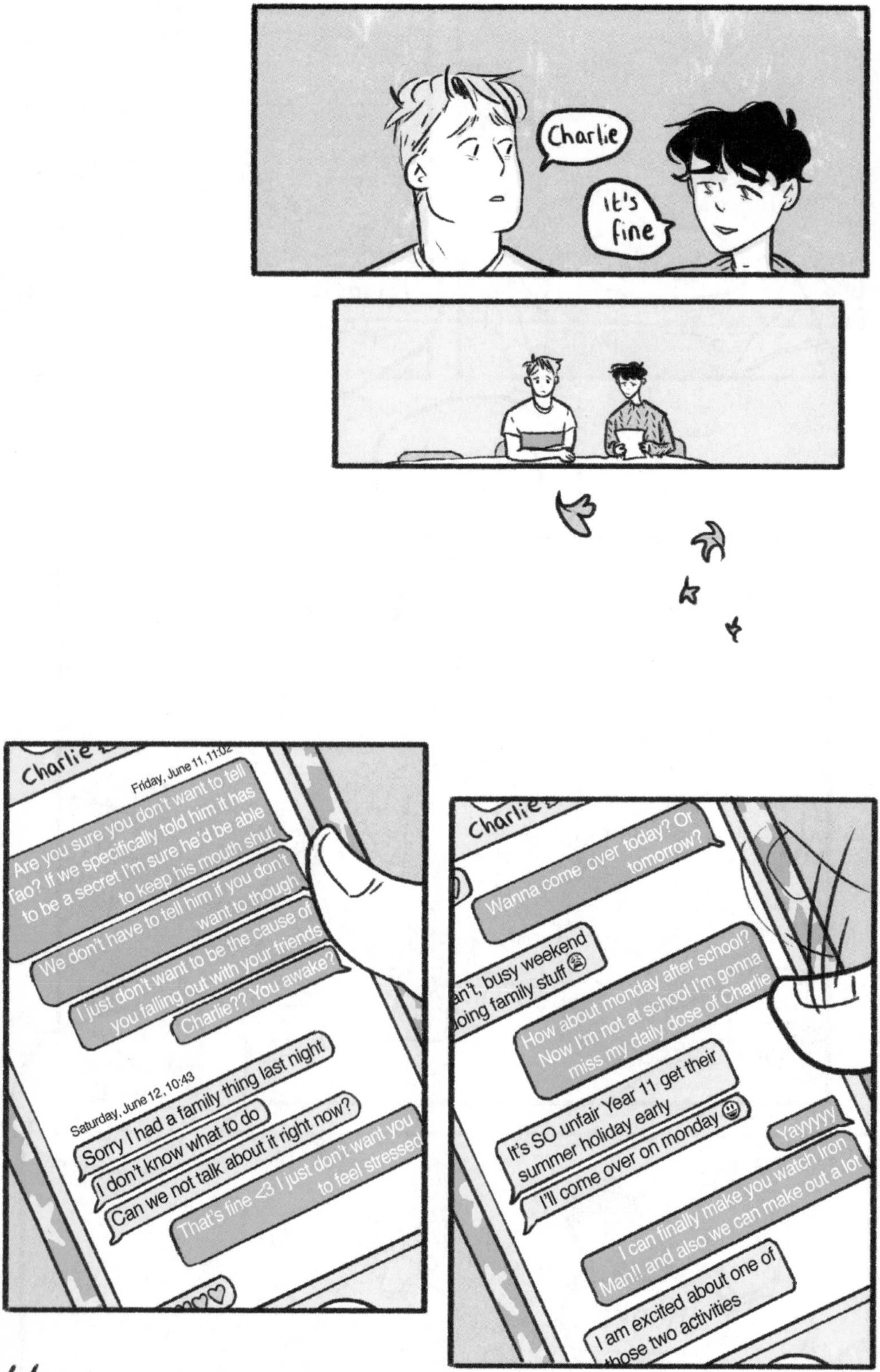

Charlie
It's fine
Charlie
Friday, June 11, 11:02
Are you sure you don't want to tell Tao? If we specifically told him it has to be a secret I'm sure he'd be able to keep his mouth shut
We don't have to tell him if you don't want to though
I just don't want to be the cause of you falling out with your friends
Charlie?? You awake?
Saturday, June 12, 10:43
Sorry I had a family thing last night
I don't know what to do
Can we not talk about it right now?
That's fine <3 I just don't want you to feel stressed
Charlie
Wanna come over today? Or tomorrow?
an't, busy weekend
oing family stuff
How about monday after school? Now I'm not at school I'm gonna miss my daily dose of Charlie
It's SO unfair Year 11 get their summer holiday early
I'll come over on monday
Yayyyy
I can finally make you watch Iron Man!! and also we can make out a lot
I am excited about one of those two activities

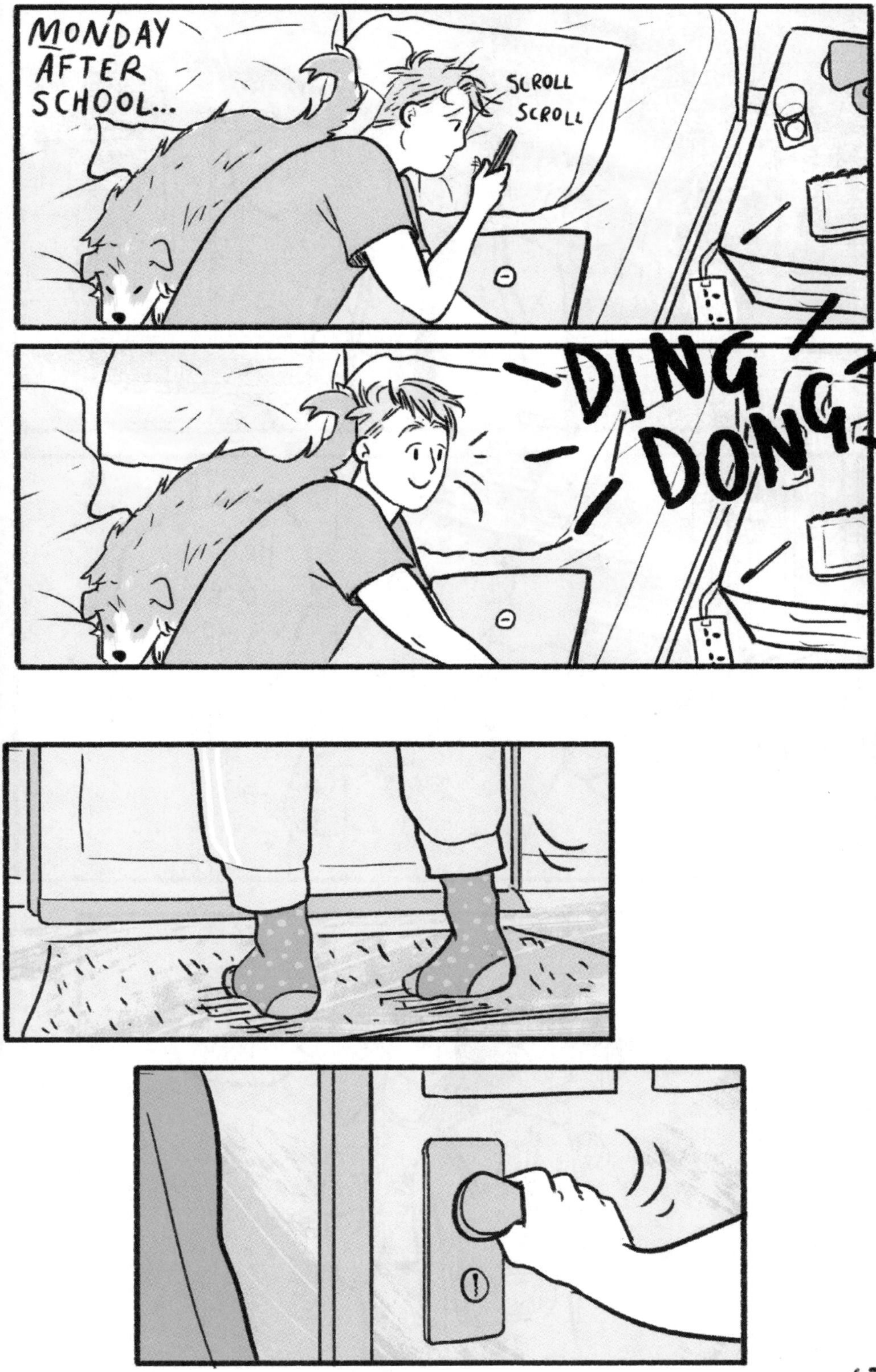
MONDAY AFTER SCHOOL...
SCROLL
SCROLL
DING
DONG

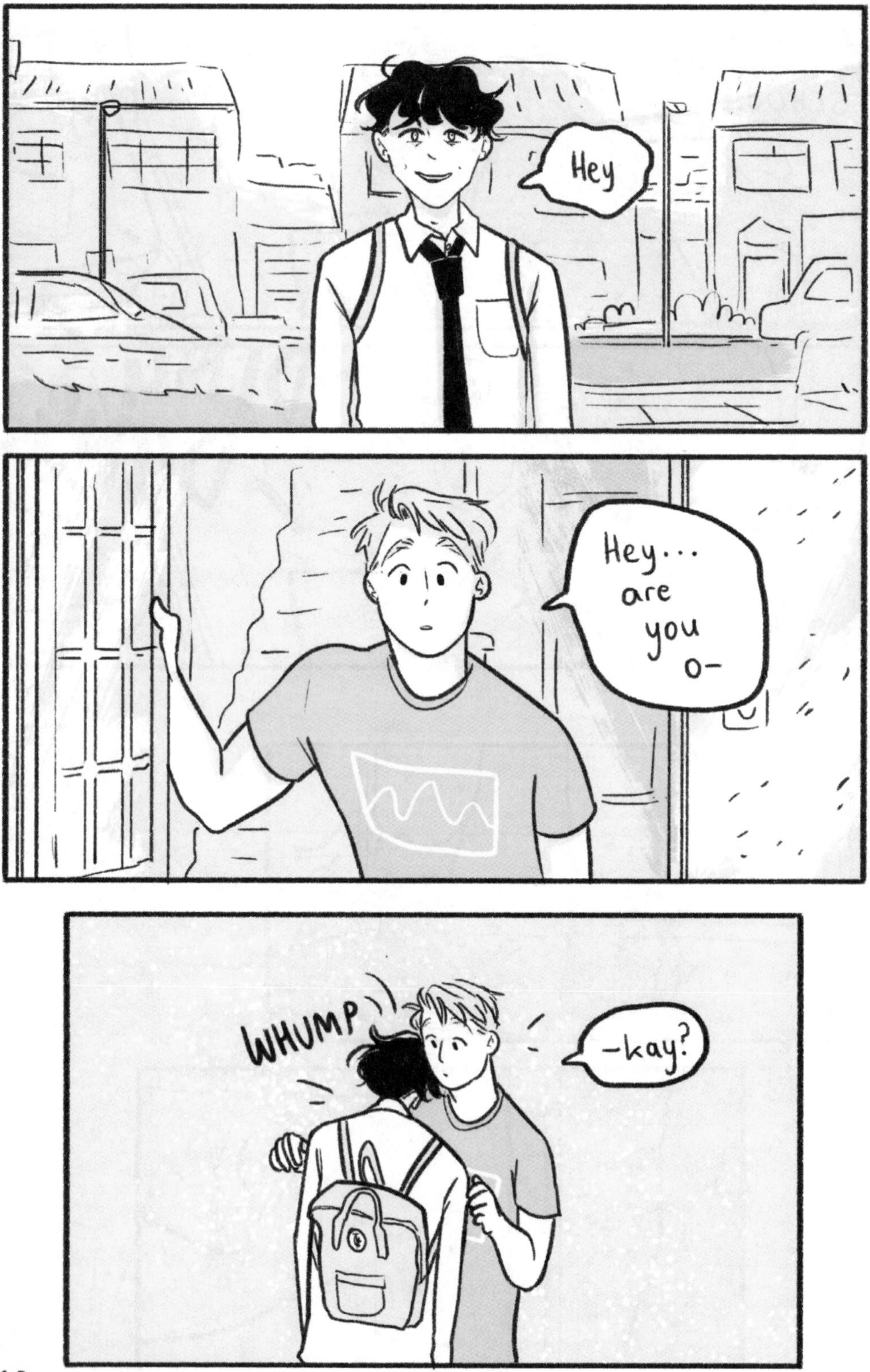
Hey
Hey... are you o-
WHUMP
-kay?

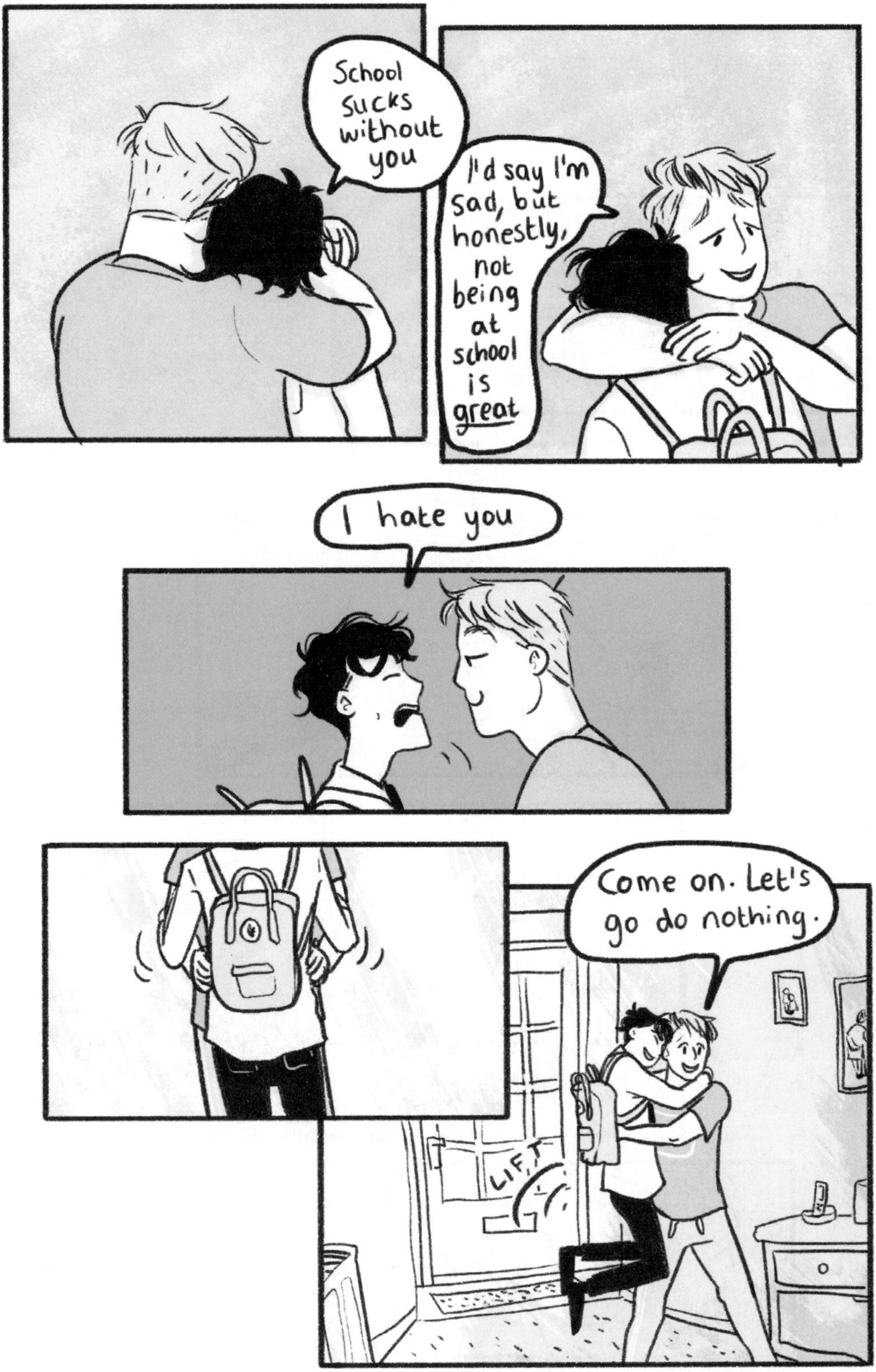
School sucks without you
I'd say I'm sad, but honestly, not being at school is great
I hate you
Come on. Let's go do nothing.
LIFT

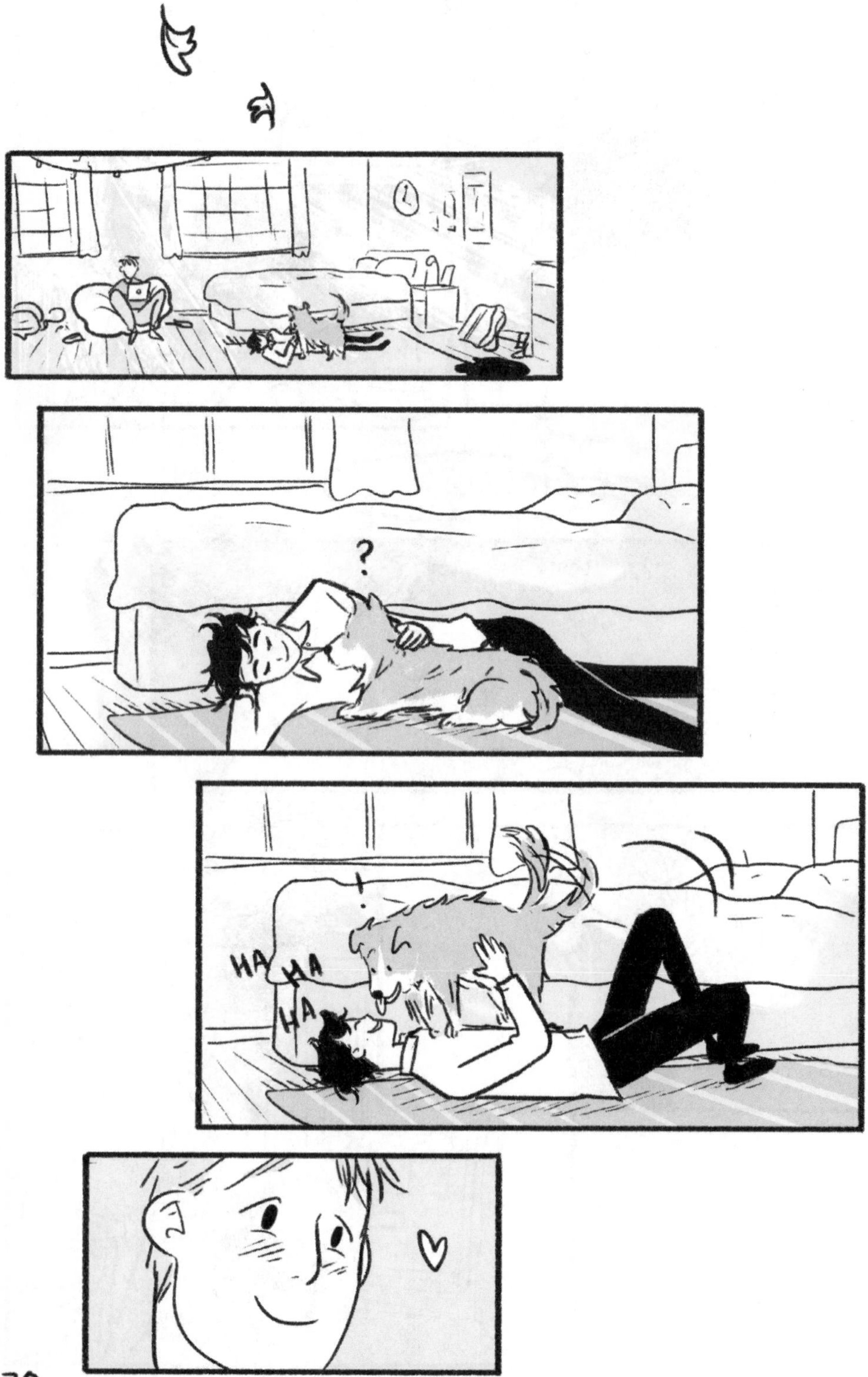
?
!
HA
HA
HA

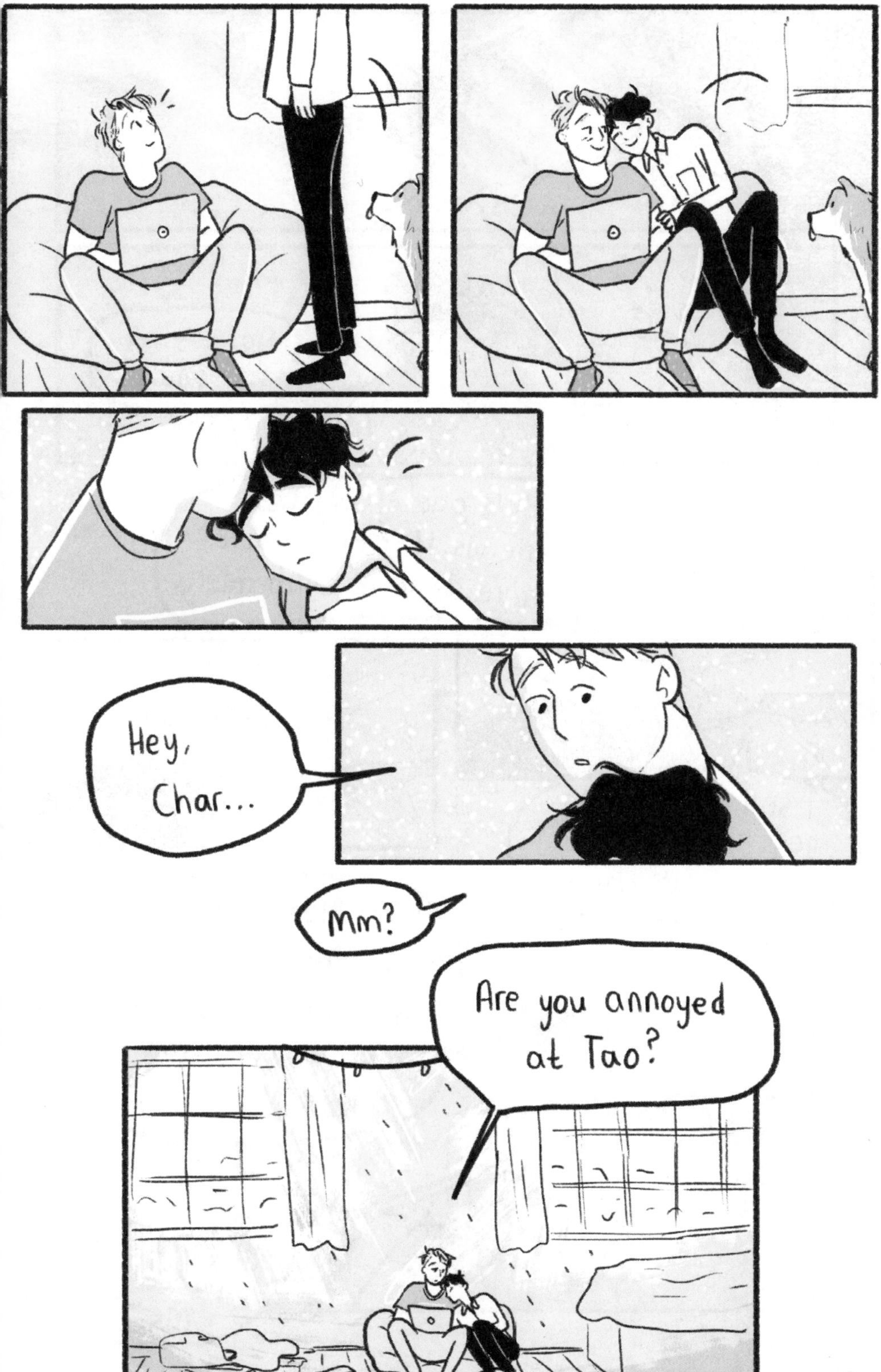
Hey,
Char...
Mm?
Are you annoyed at Tao?

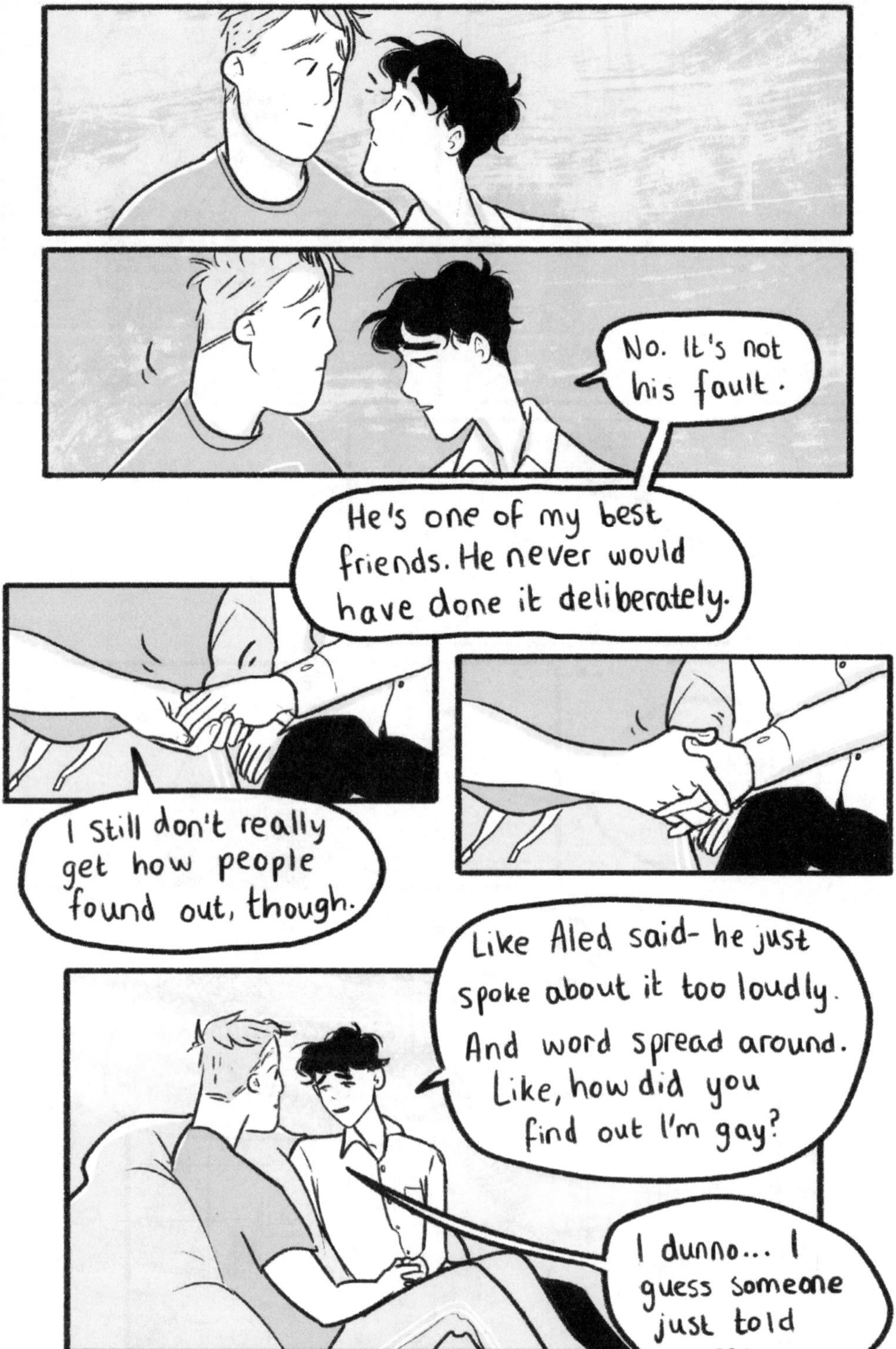
No. It's not his fault.
He's one of my best friends. He never would have done it deliberately.
I still don't really get how people found out, though.
Like Aled said- he just spoke about it too loudly.
And word spread around.
Like, how did you find out I'm gay?
I dunno... I guess someone just told me.

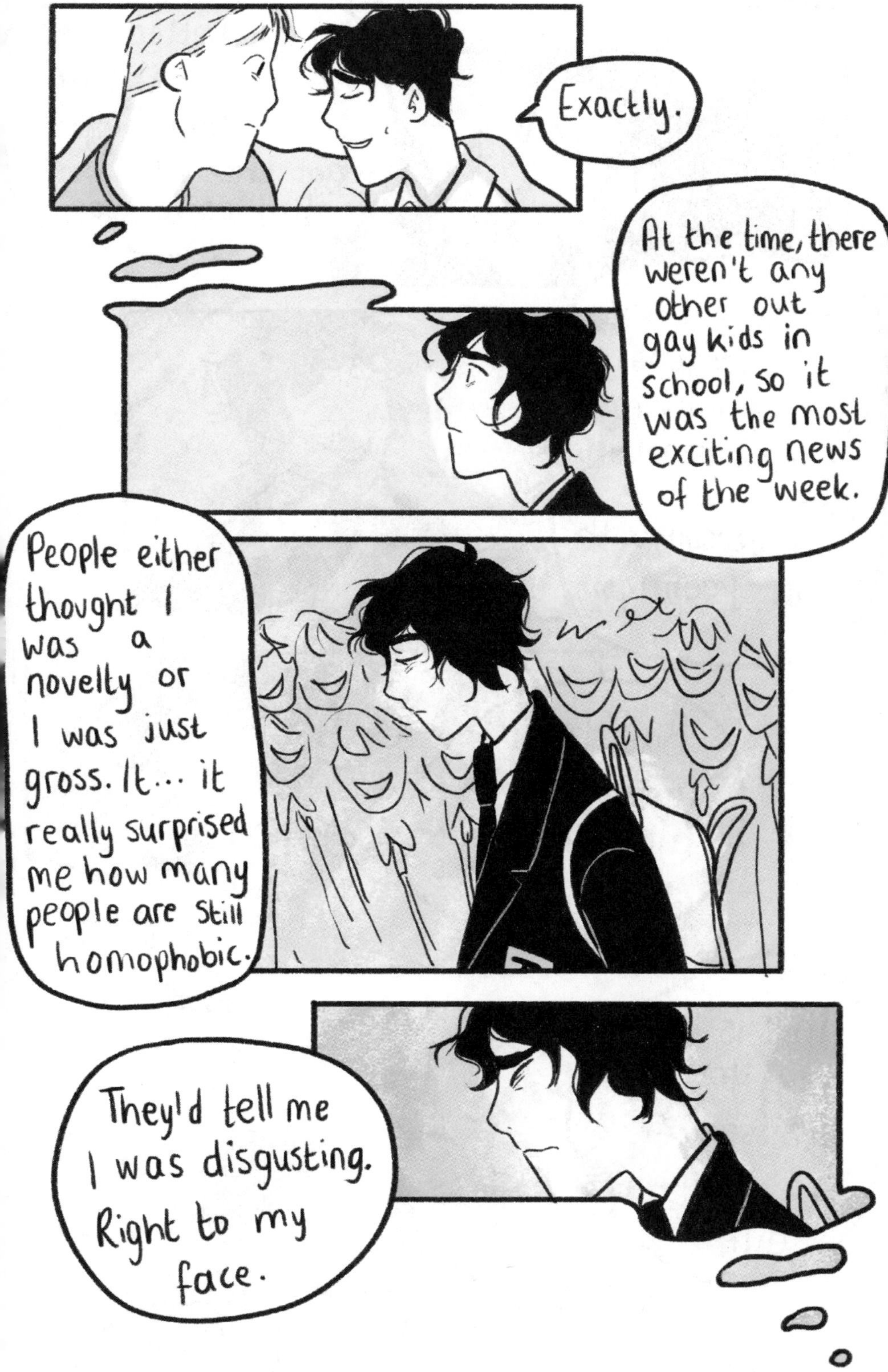
Exactly.
At the time, there weren't any other out gay kids in school, so it was the most exciting news of the week.
People either thought I was a novelty or I was just gross. It... it really surprised me how many people are still homophobic.
They'd tell me I was disgusting. Right to my face.

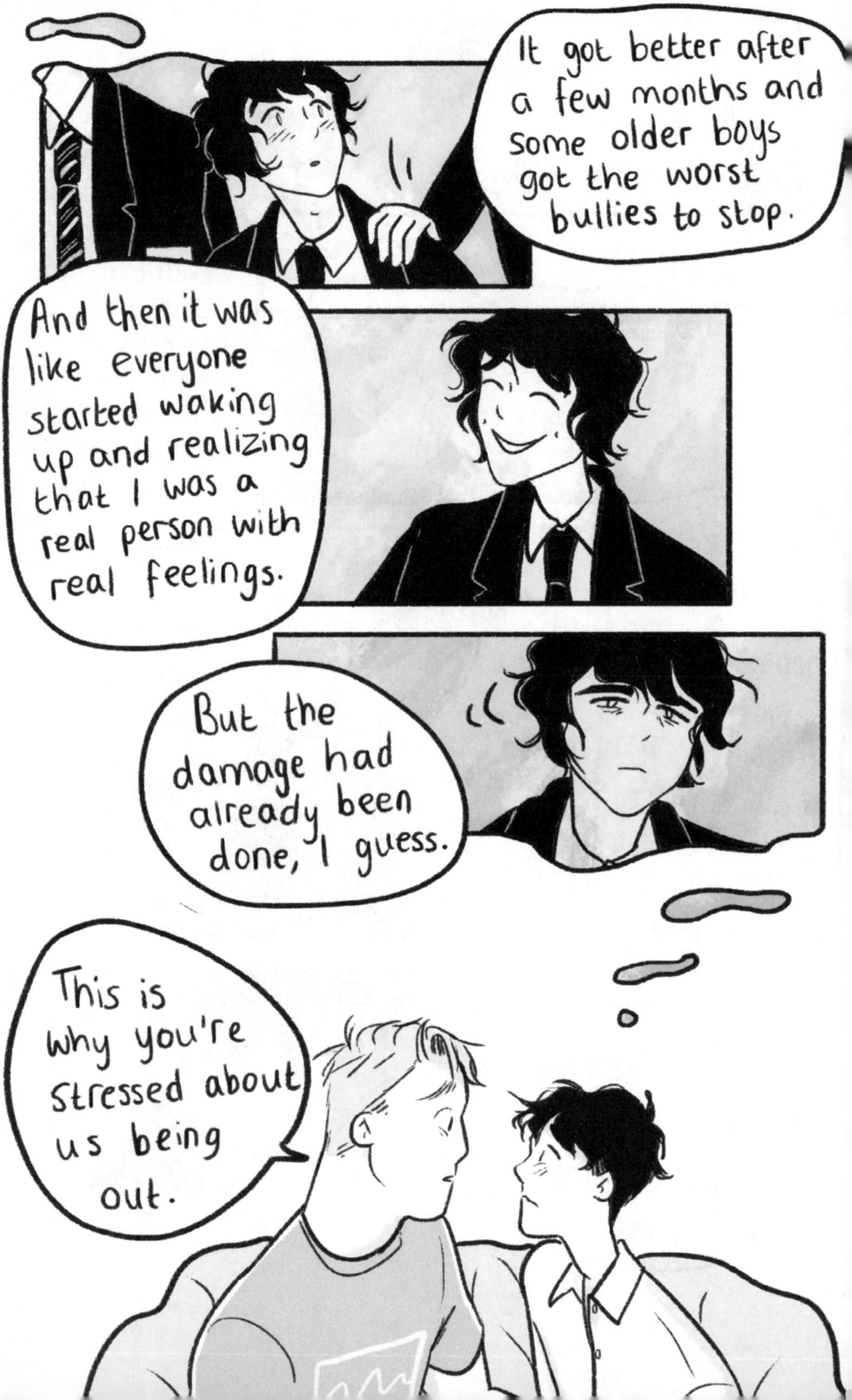
It got better after a few months and some older boys got the worst bullies to stop.
And then it was like everyone started waking up and realizing that I was a real person with real feelings.
But the damage had already been done, I guess.
This is why you're stressed about us being out.

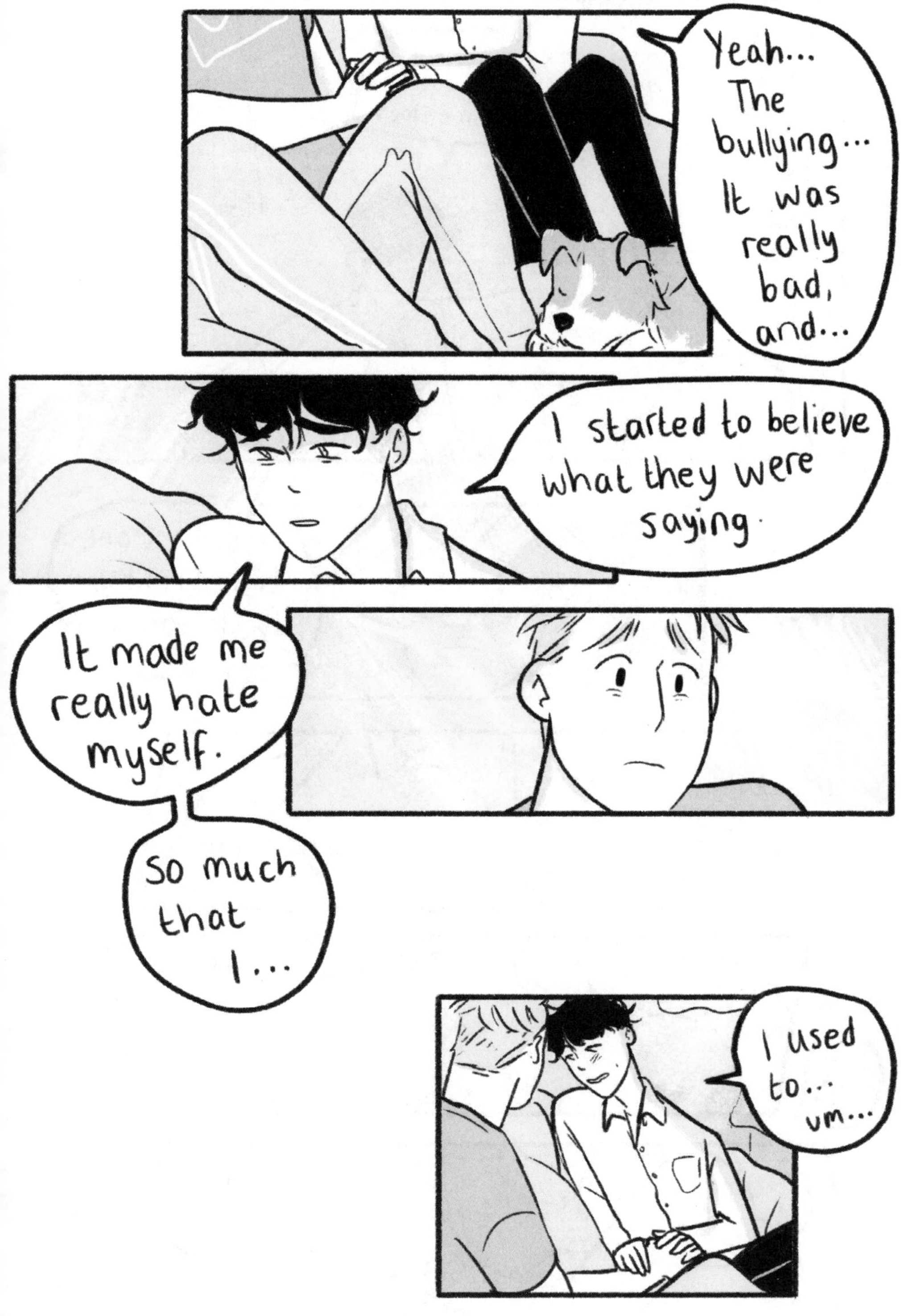
Yeah... The bullying... It was really bad, and...
I started to believe what they were saying.
It made me really hate myself.
So much that I...
I used to... um...

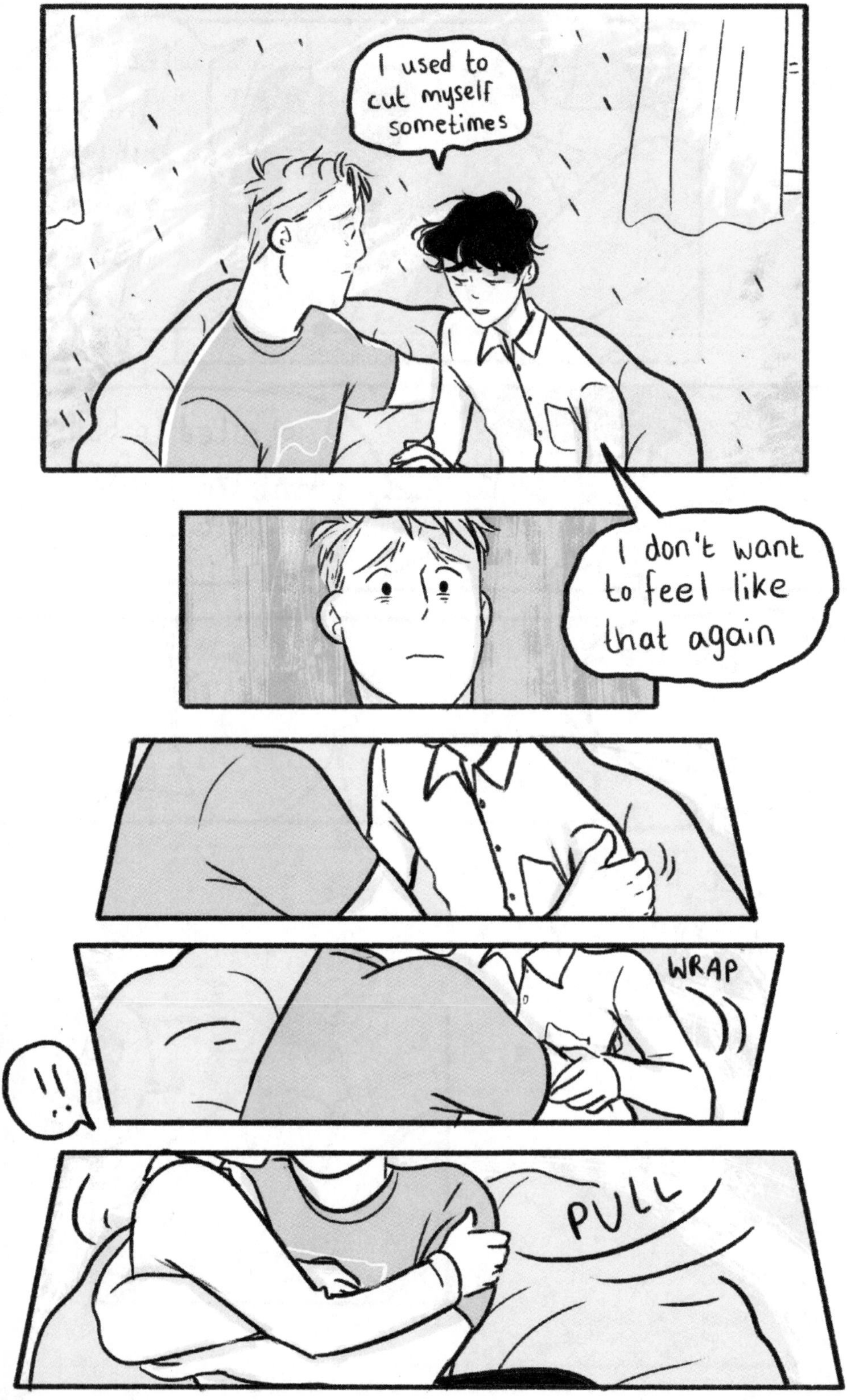
I used to cut myself sometimes
I don't want to feel like that again
WRAP
!!
PULL

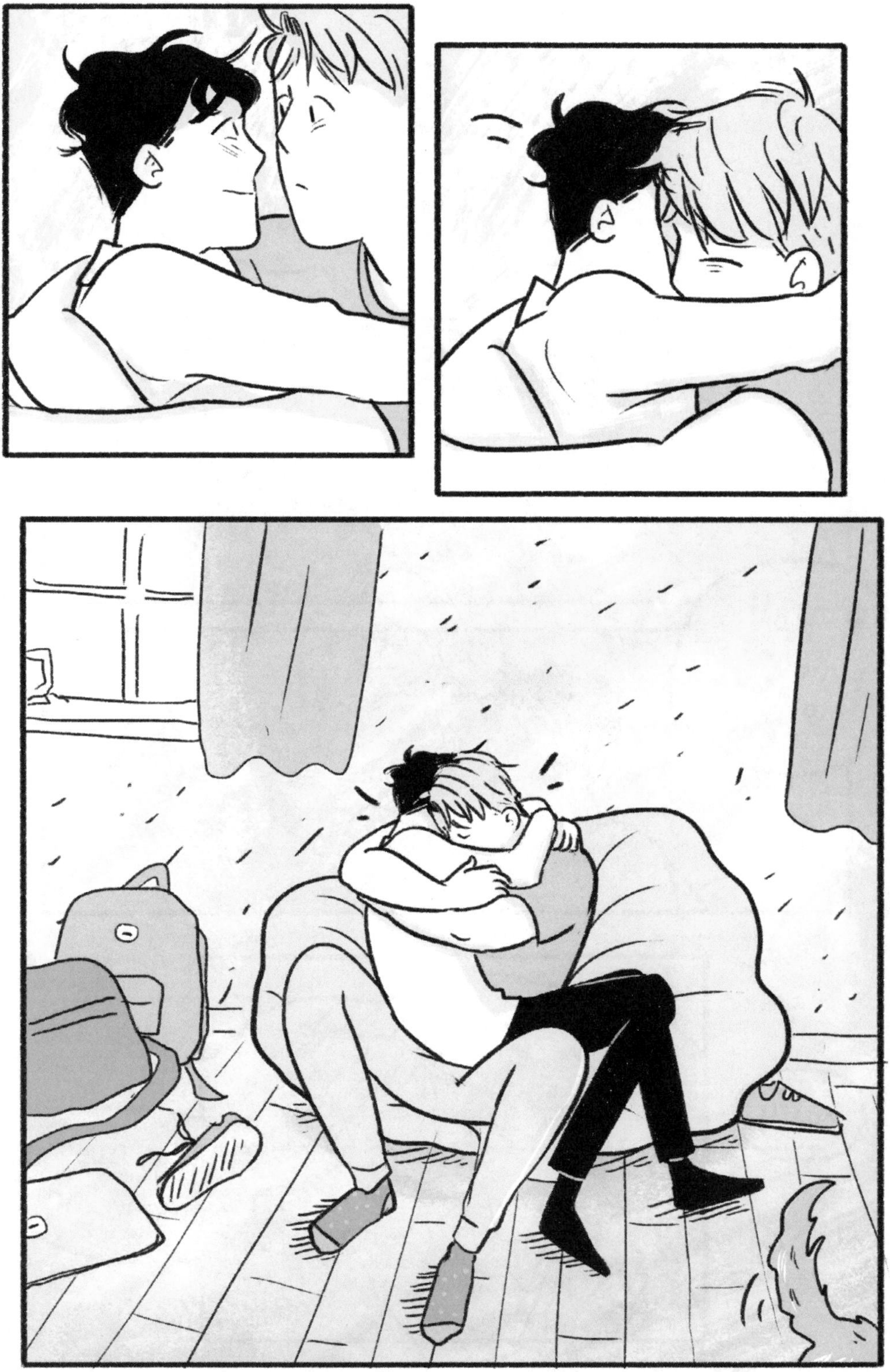

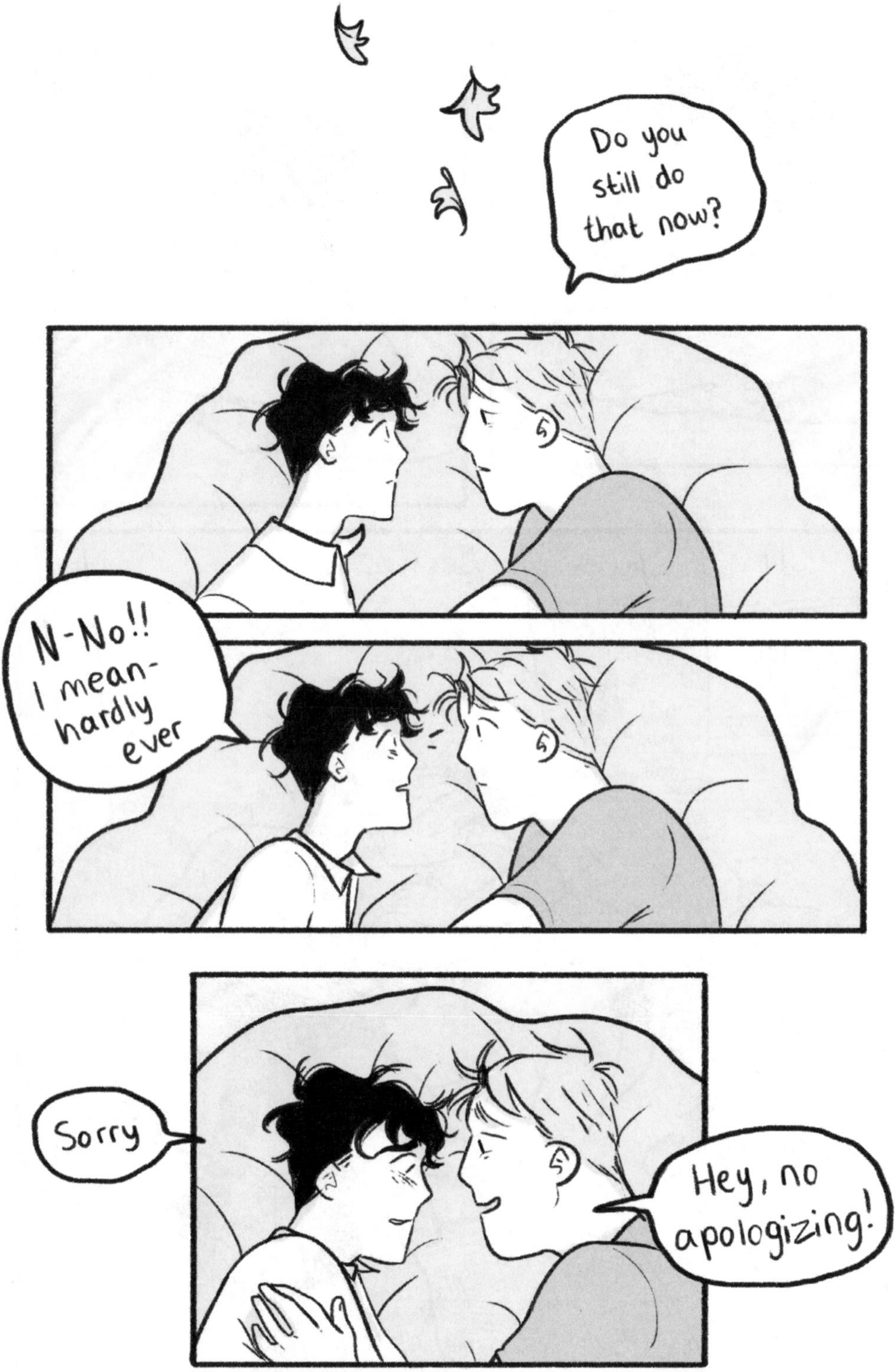
Do you still do that now?
N-No!! I mean- hardly ever
Sorry
Hey, no apologizing!

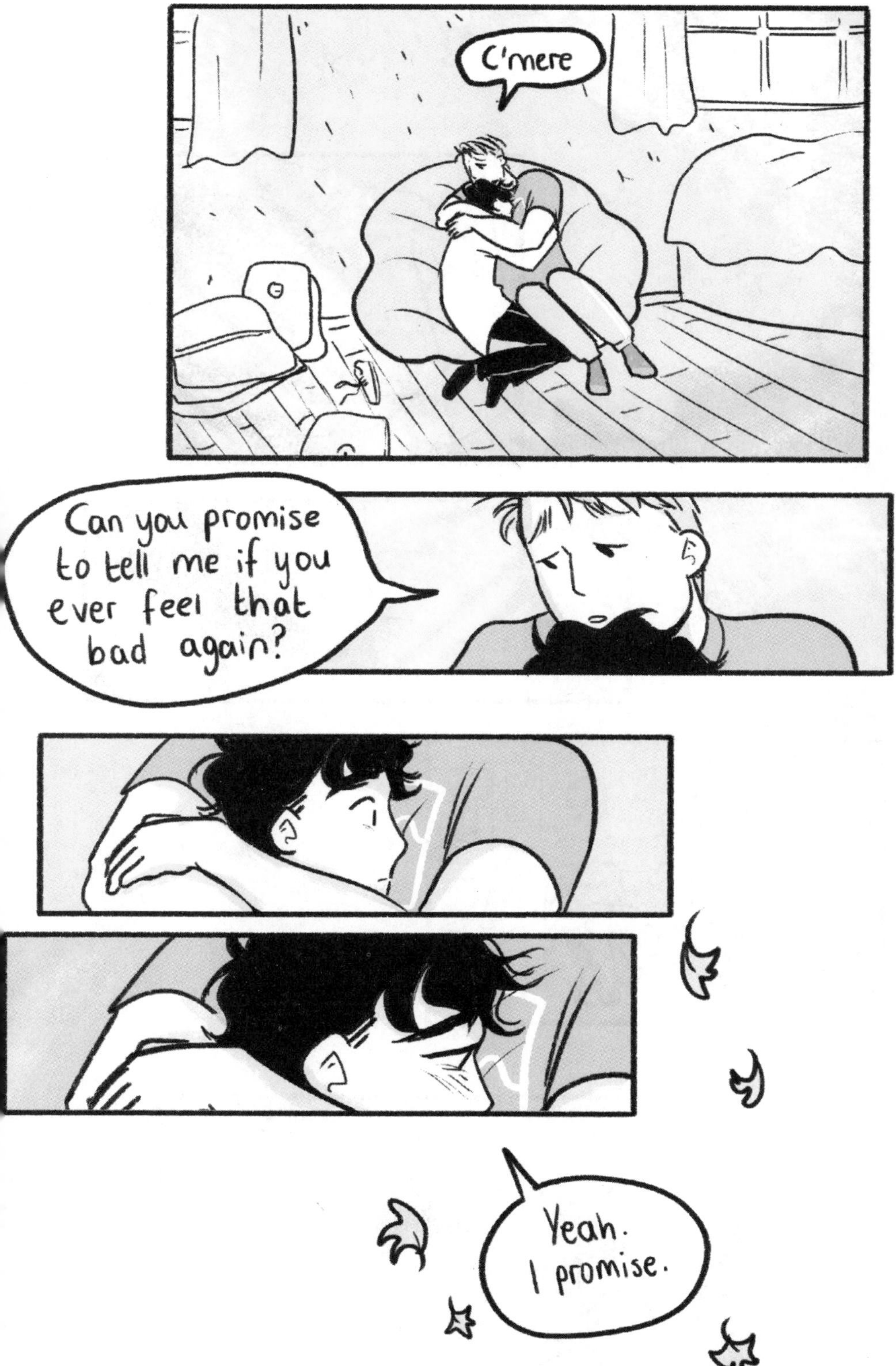
C'mere
Can you promise to tell me if you ever feel that bad again?
Yeah. I promise.

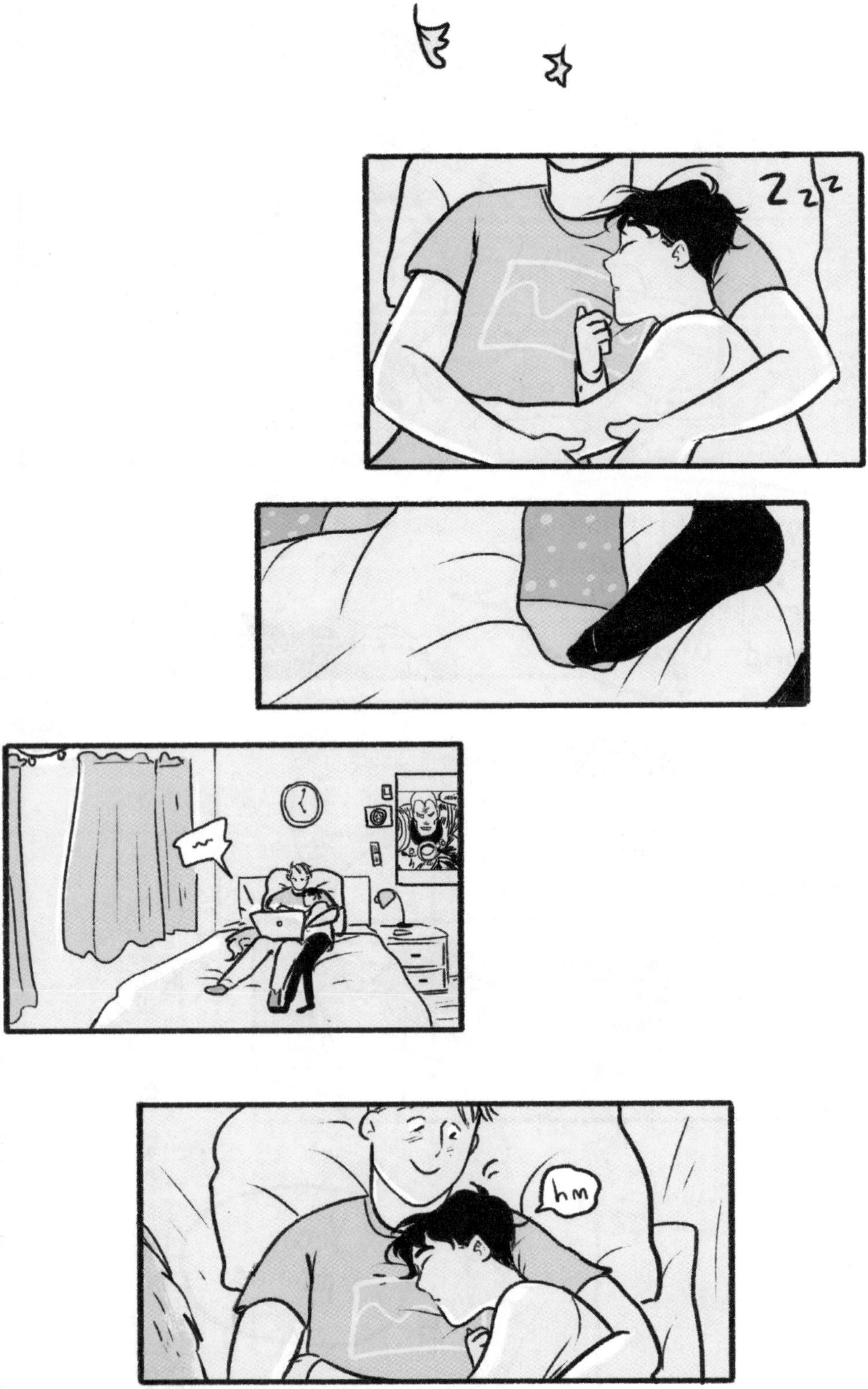
Zzz
hm

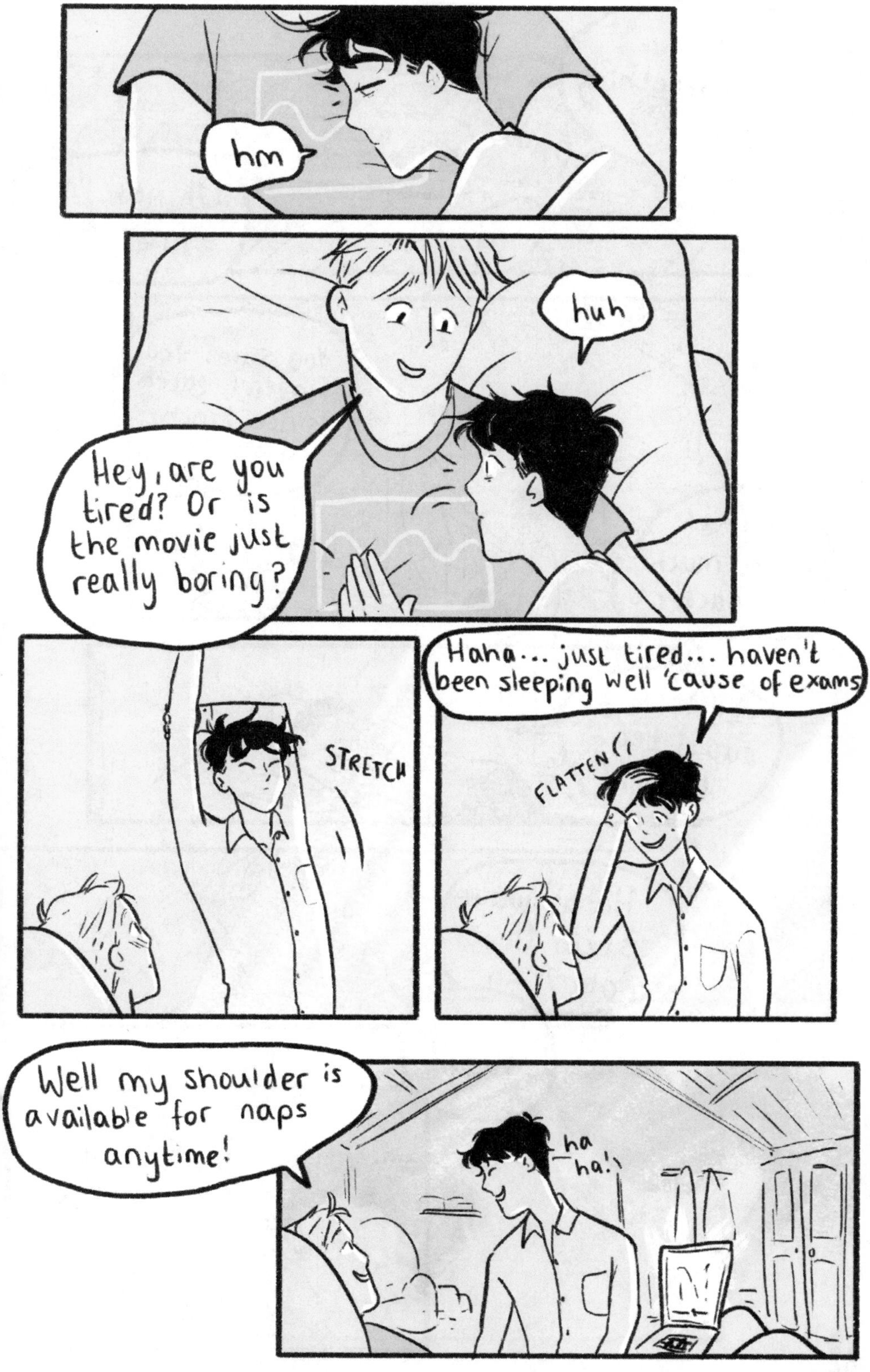
hm
huh
Hey, are you tired? Or is the movie just really boring?
STRETCH
Haha... just tired... haven't been sleeping well 'cause of exams
FLATTEN
Well my shoulder is available for naps anytime!
ha ha!

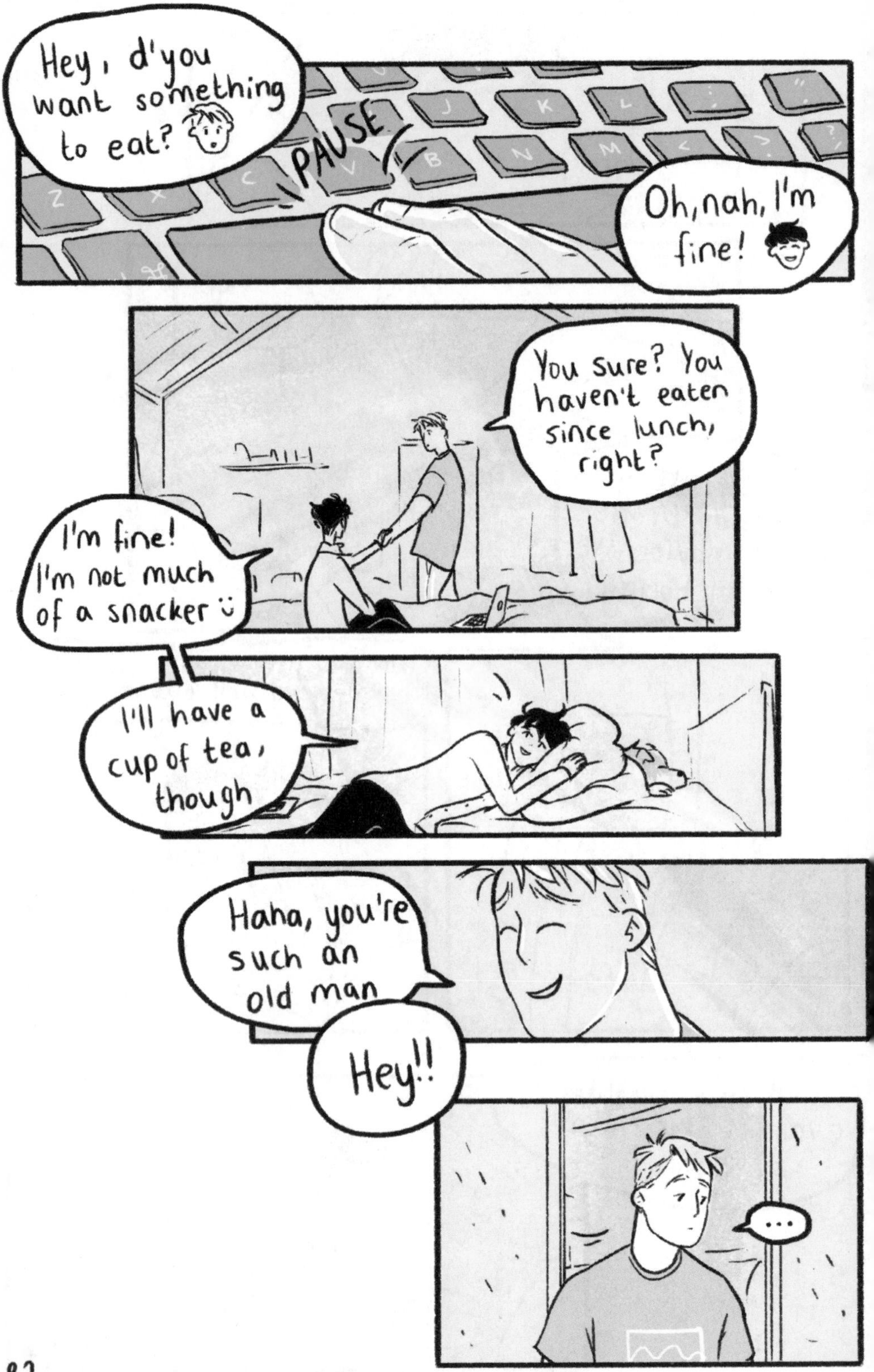
Hey, d'you want something to eat?
PAUSE
Oh, nah, I'm fine!
You sure? You haven't eaten since lunch, right?
I'm fine! I'm not much of a snacker
I'll have a cup of tea, though
Haha, you're such an old man
Hey!!
...

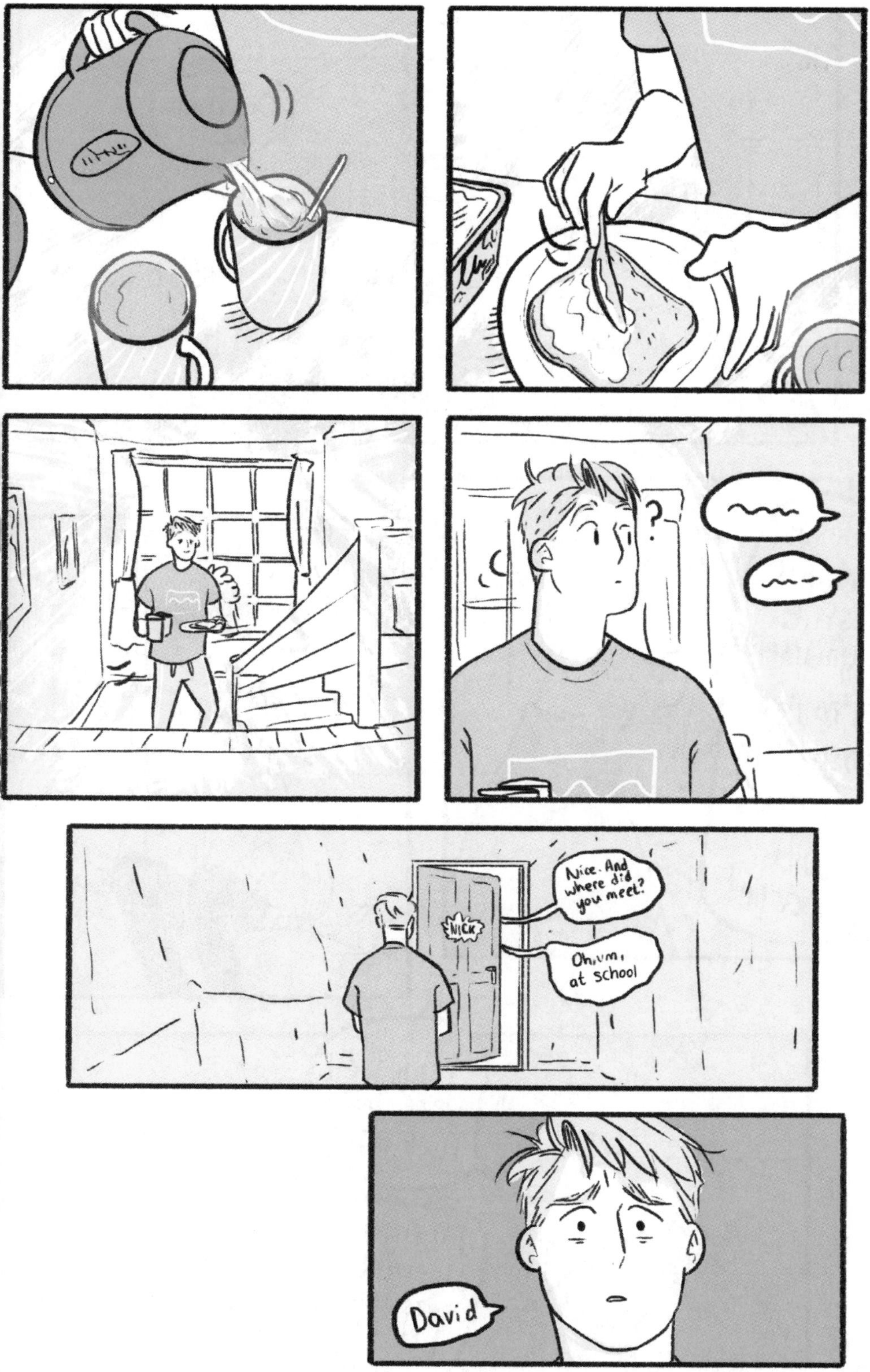
Nice. And where did you meet?
Oh, um, at school
David

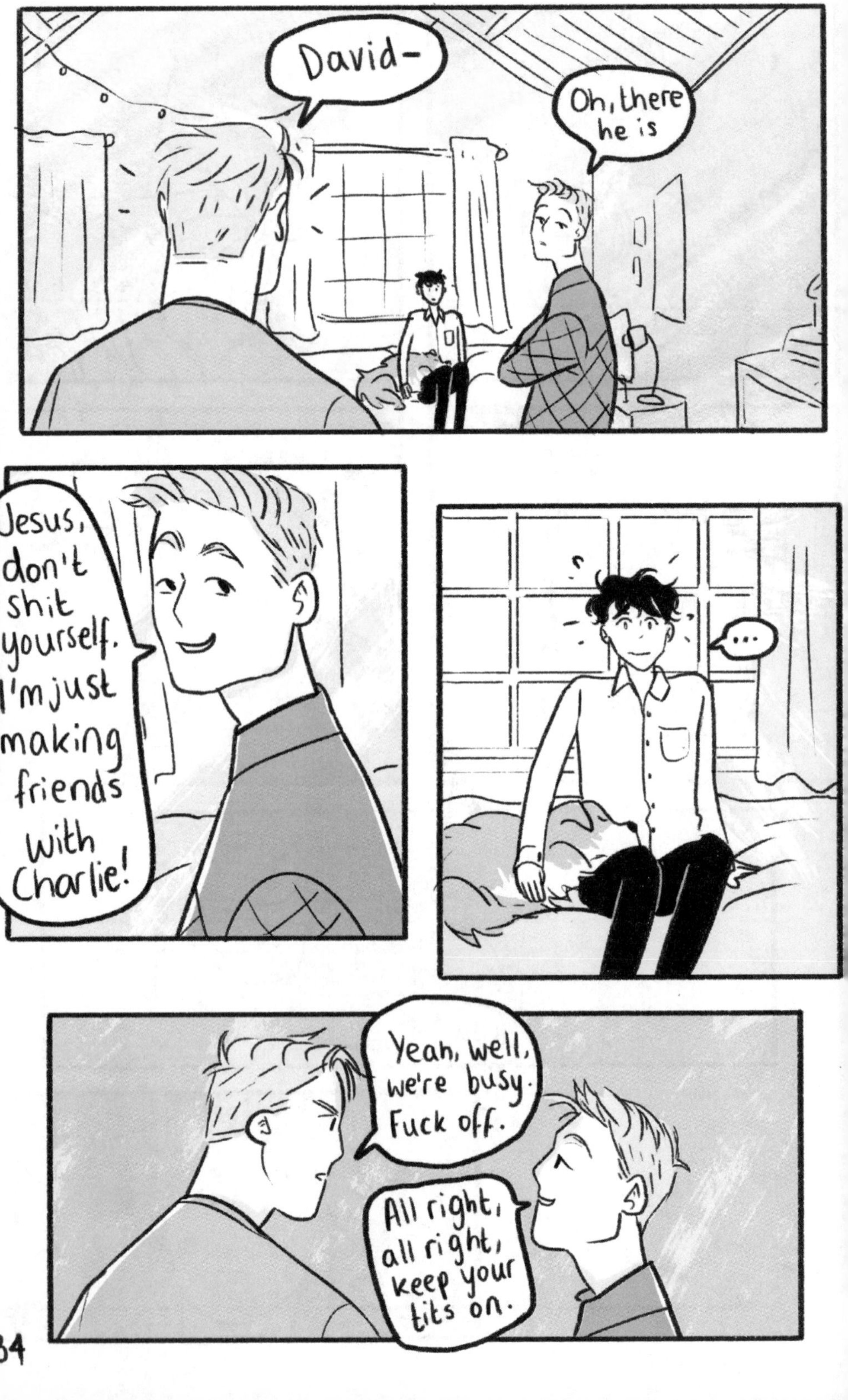
David-
Oh, there he is
Jesus, don't shit yourself. I'm just making friends with Charlie!
...
Yeah, well, we're busy. Fuck off.
All right, all right, keep your tits on.

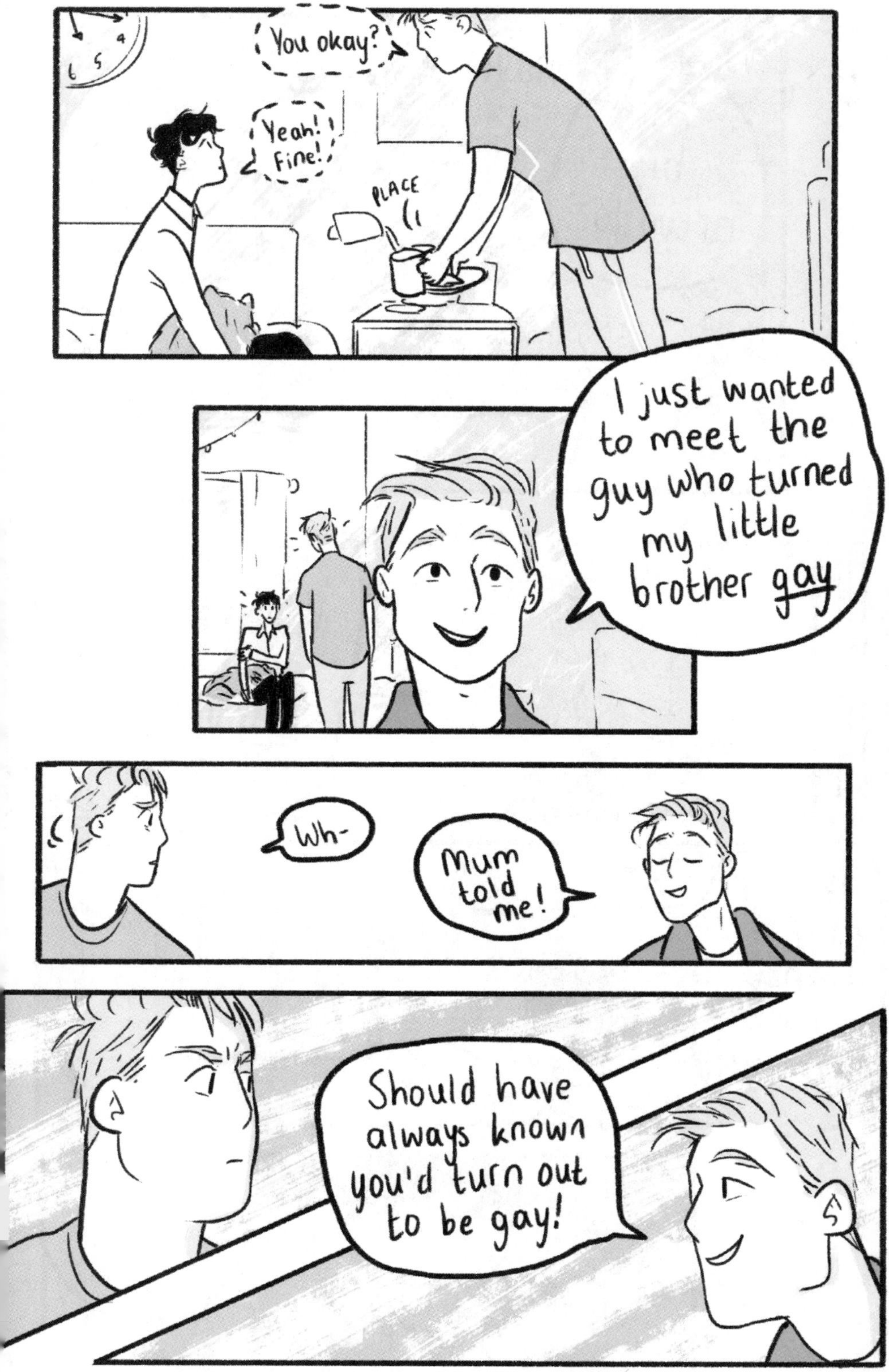
You okay?
Yeah! Fine!
PLACE
I just wanted to meet the guy who turned my little brother gay
Wh-
Mum told me!
Should have always known you'd turn out to be gay!

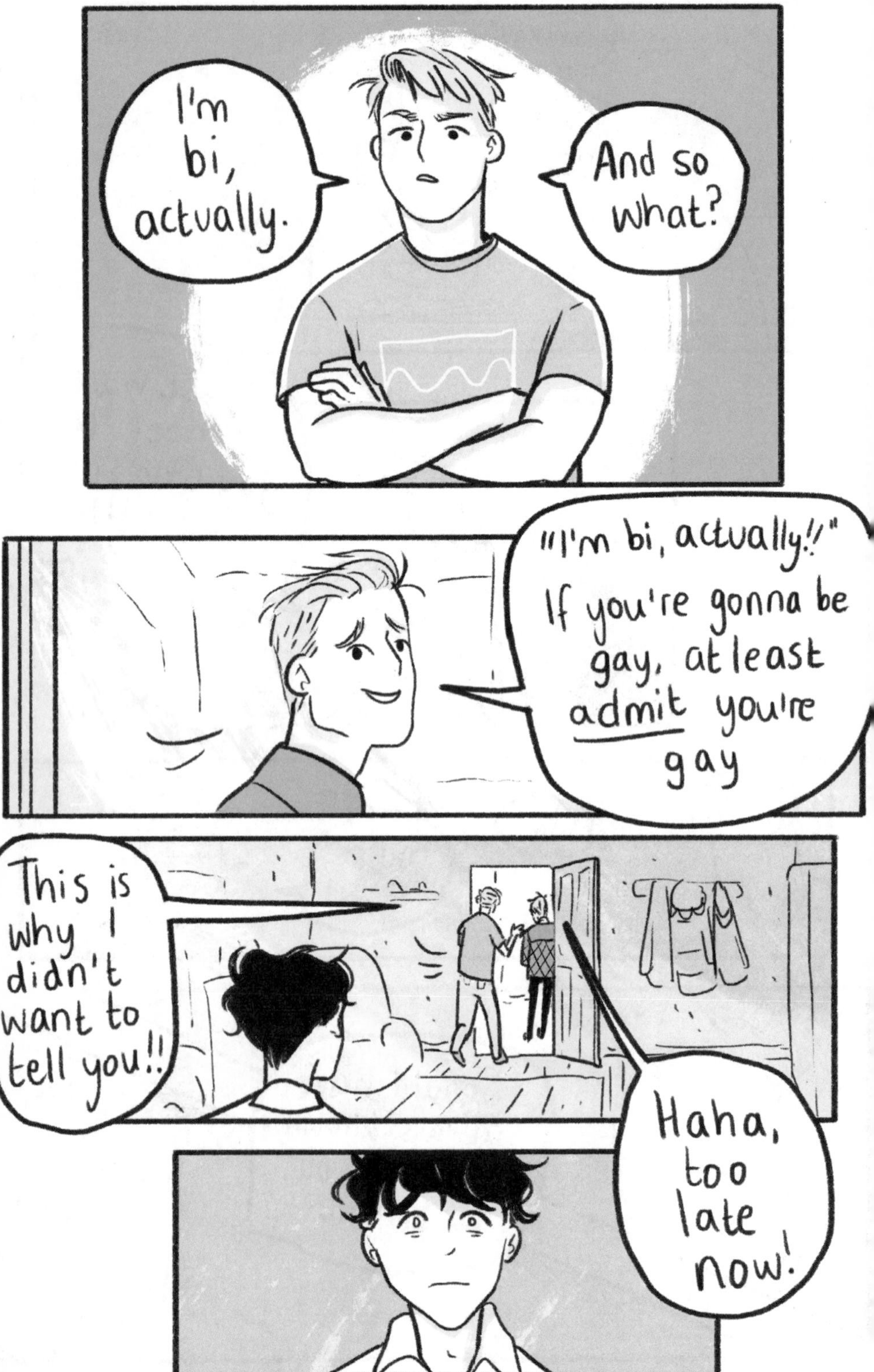
I'm bi, actually.
And so what?
"I'm bi, actually!!" If you're gonna be gay, at least admit you're gay
This is why I didn't want to tell you!!
Haha, too late now!

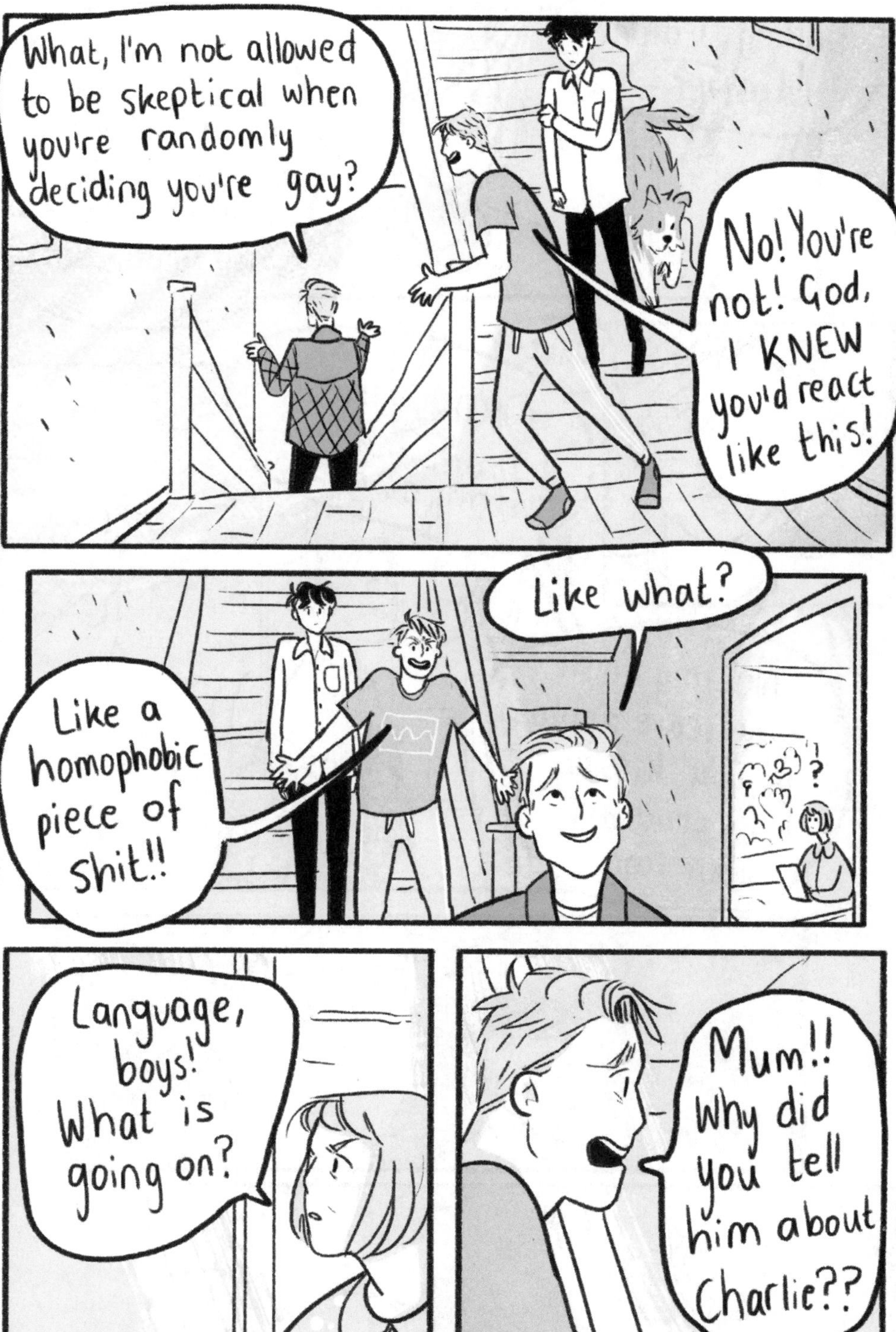
What, I'm not allowed to be skeptical when you're randomly deciding you're gay?
No! You're not! God, I KNEW you'd react like this!
Like what?
Like a homophobic piece of shit!!
Language, boys! What is going on?
Mum!! Why did you tell him about Charlie??

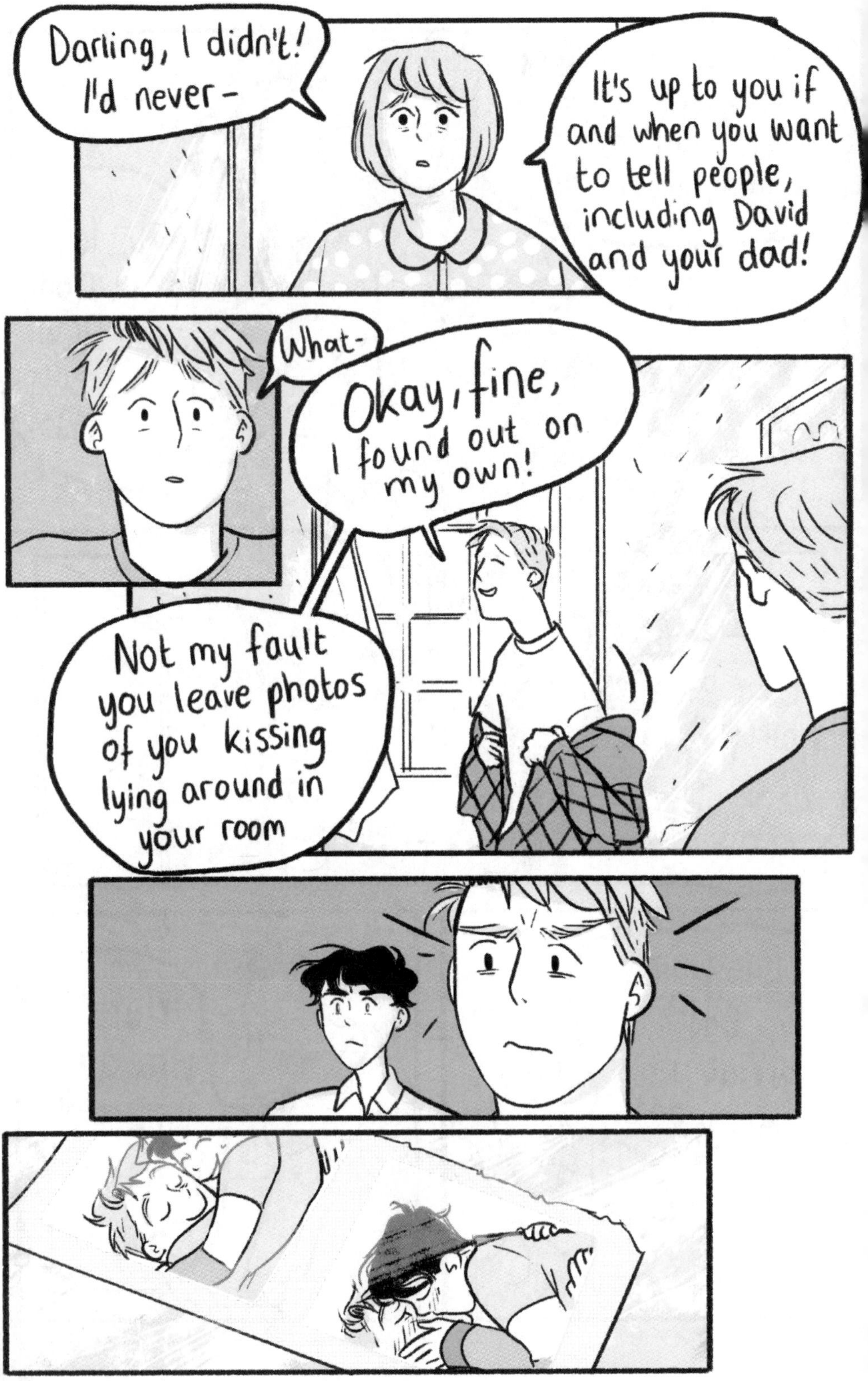
Darling, I didn't! I'd never-
It's up to you if and when you want to tell people, including David and your dad!
What-
Okay, fine, I found out on my own!
Not my fault you leave photos of you kissing lying around in your room

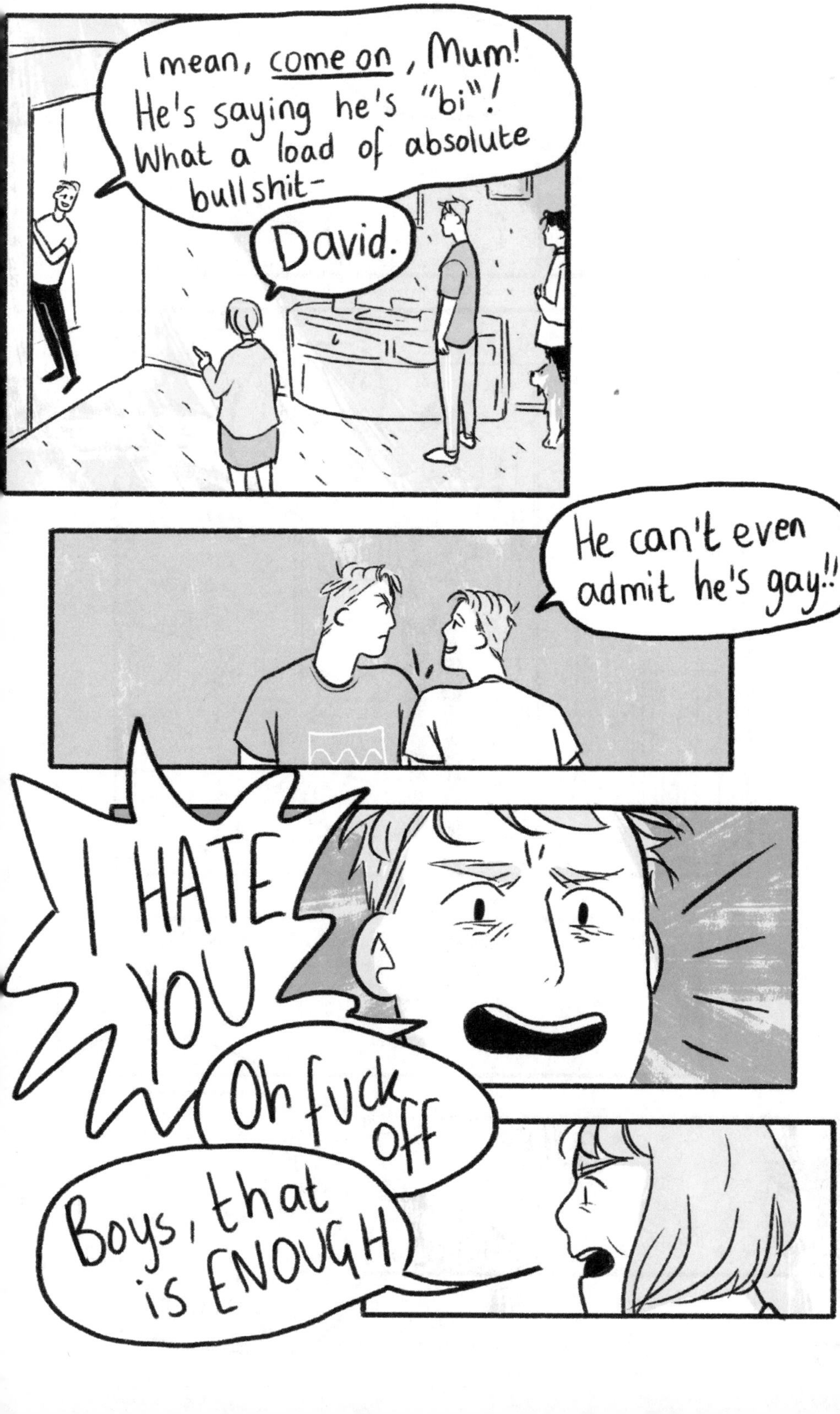
I mean, come on, Mum! He's saying he's "bi"! What a load of absolute bullshit-
David.
He can't even admit he's gay!!
I HATE YOU
Oh fuck off
Boys, that is ENOUGH

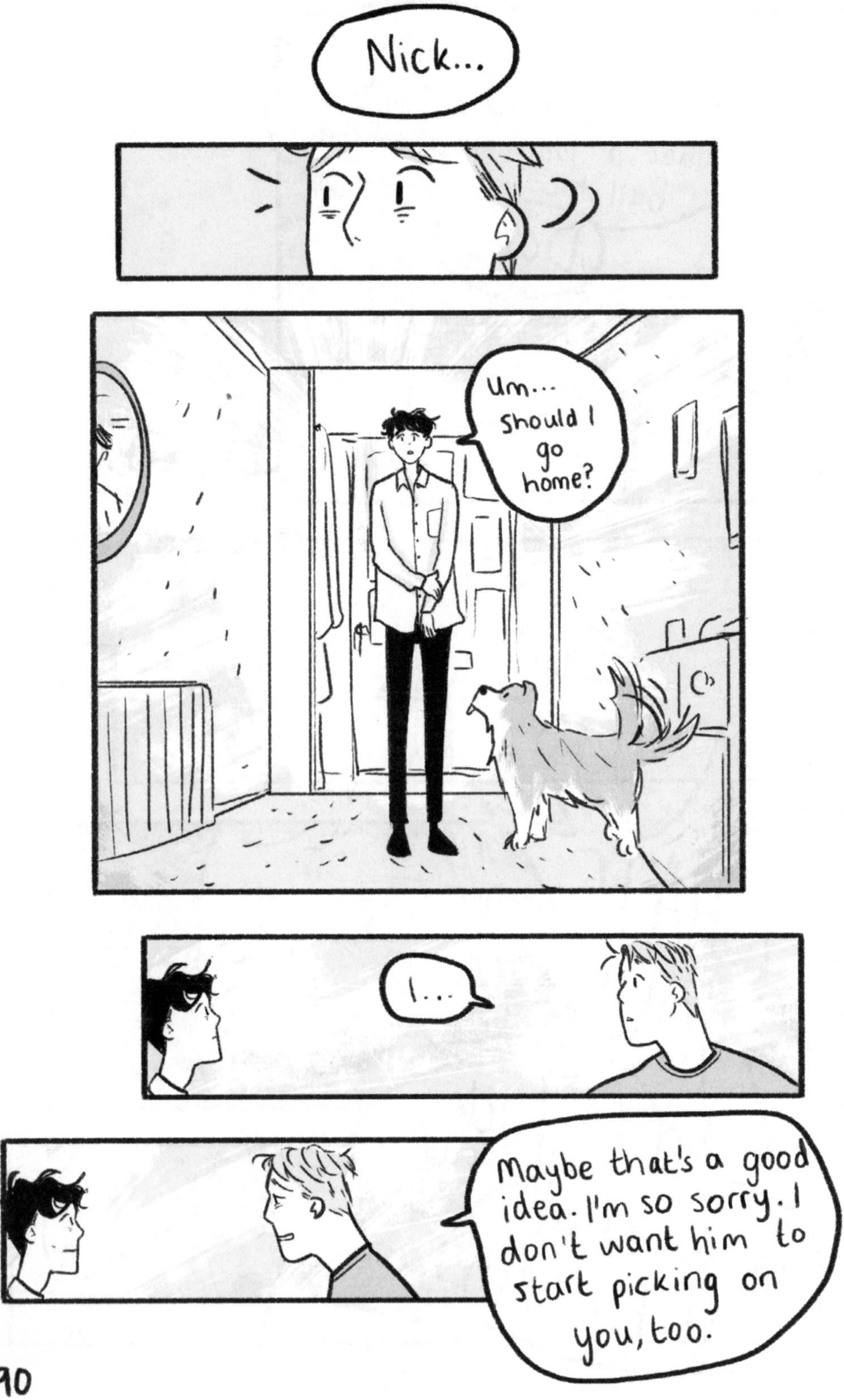
Nick...
Um... should I go home?
I...
Maybe that's a good idea. I'm so sorry. I don't want him to start picking on you, too.

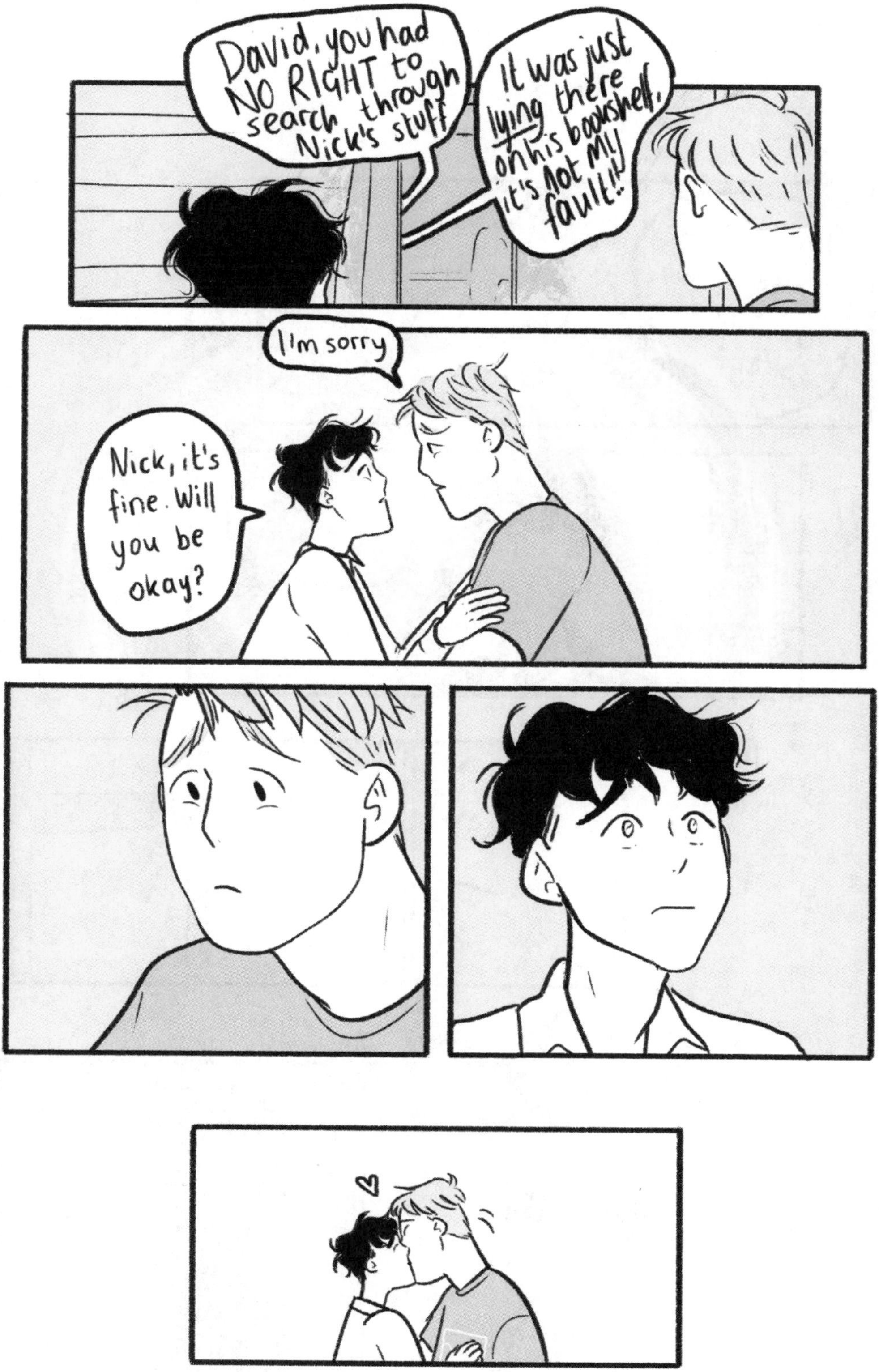
David, you had NO RIGHT to search through Nick's stuff
It was just lying there on his bookshelf, it's not my fault!!
I'm sorry
Nick, it's fine. Will you be okay?

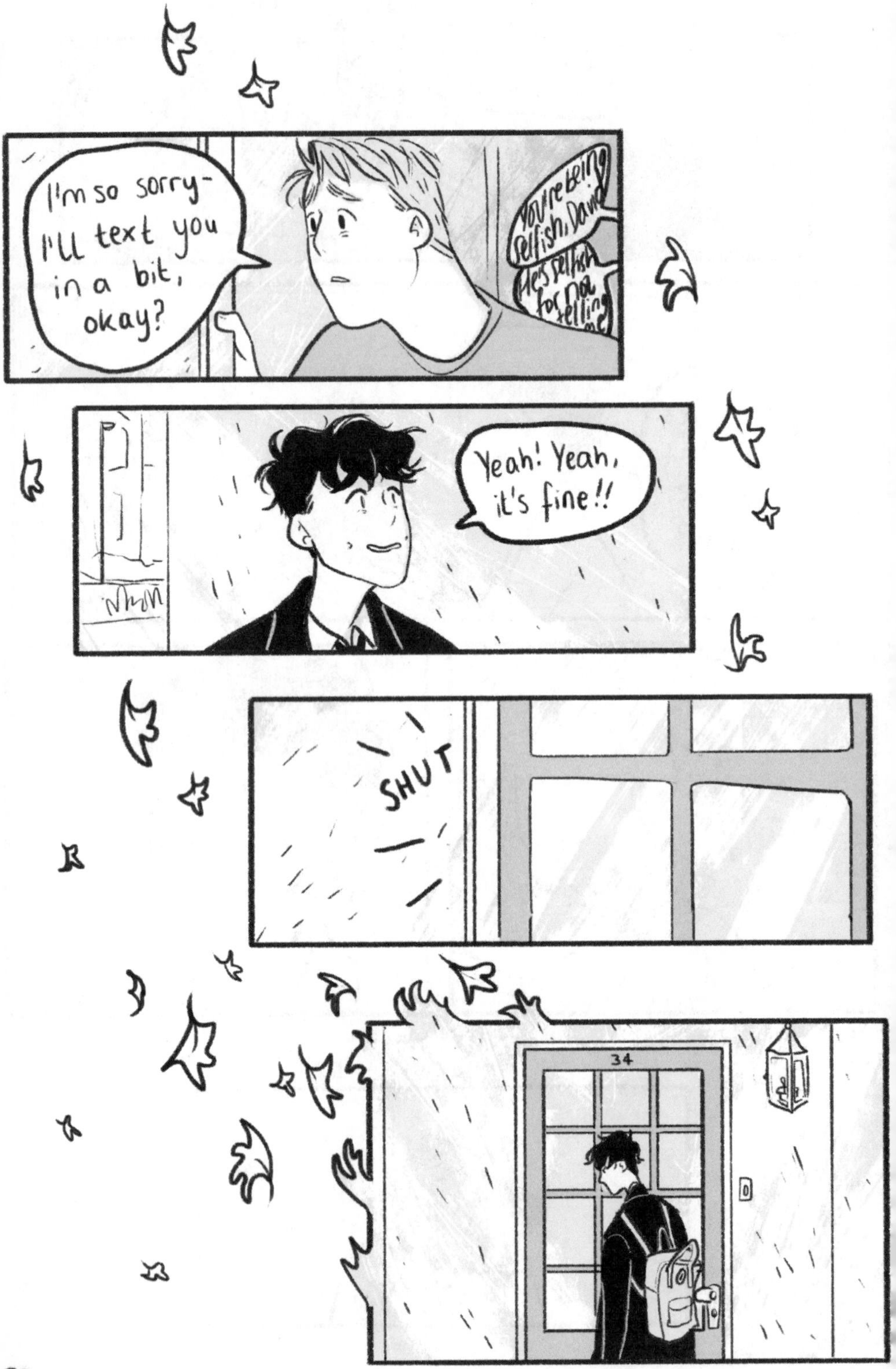
I'm so sorry- I'll text you in a bit, okay?
You're being selfish, Dav
He's selfish for not telling me
Yeah! Yeah, it's fine!!
SHUT
34

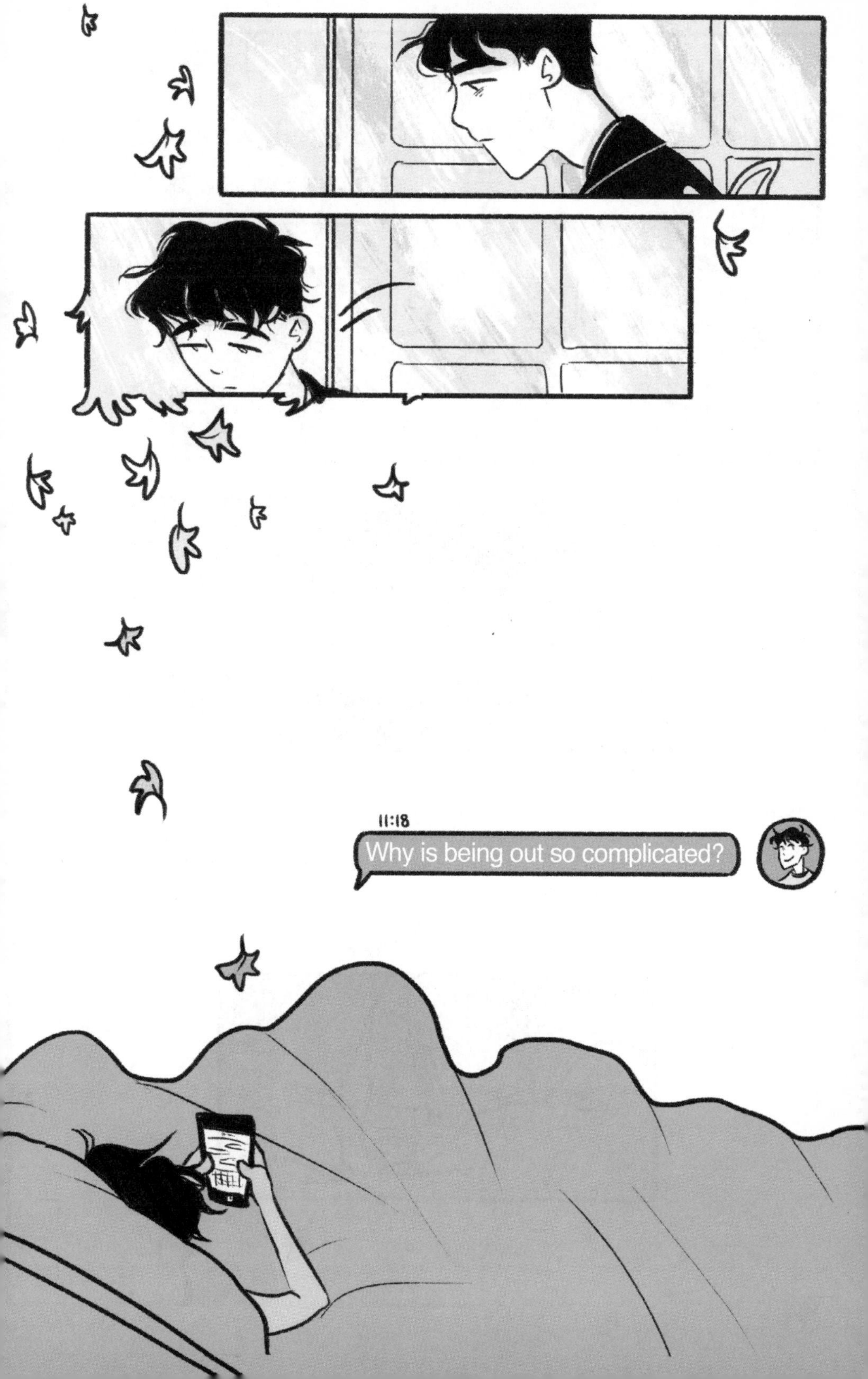
11:18
Why is being out so complicated?

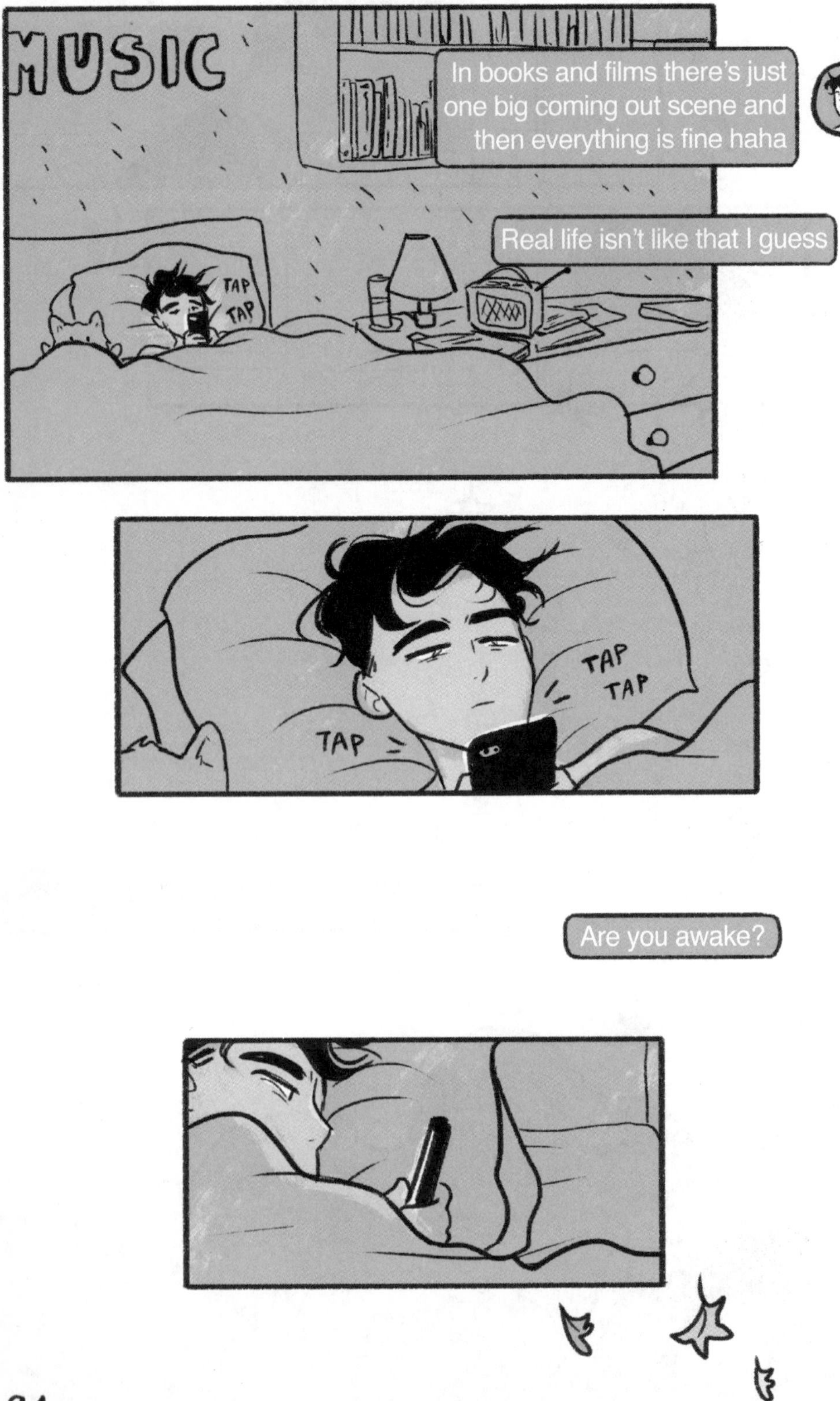
MUSIC
In books and films there's just one big coming out scene and then everything is fine haha
Real life isn't like that I guess
TAP TAP
TAP TAP
TAP
Are you awake?

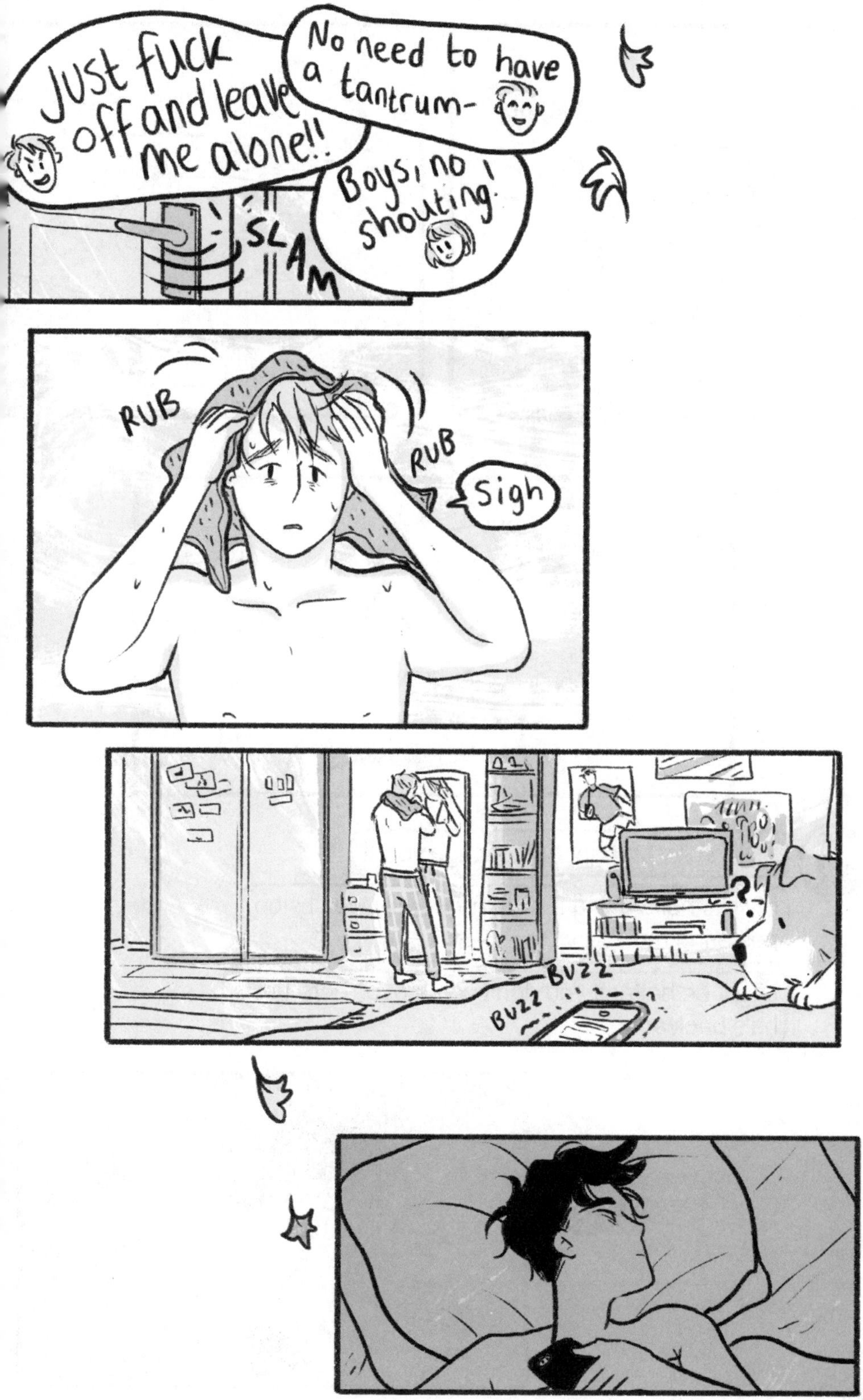
Just fuck off and leave me alone!!
No need to have a tantrum-
Boys, no shouting!
SLAM
RUB
RUB
Sigh
BUZZ
BUZZ

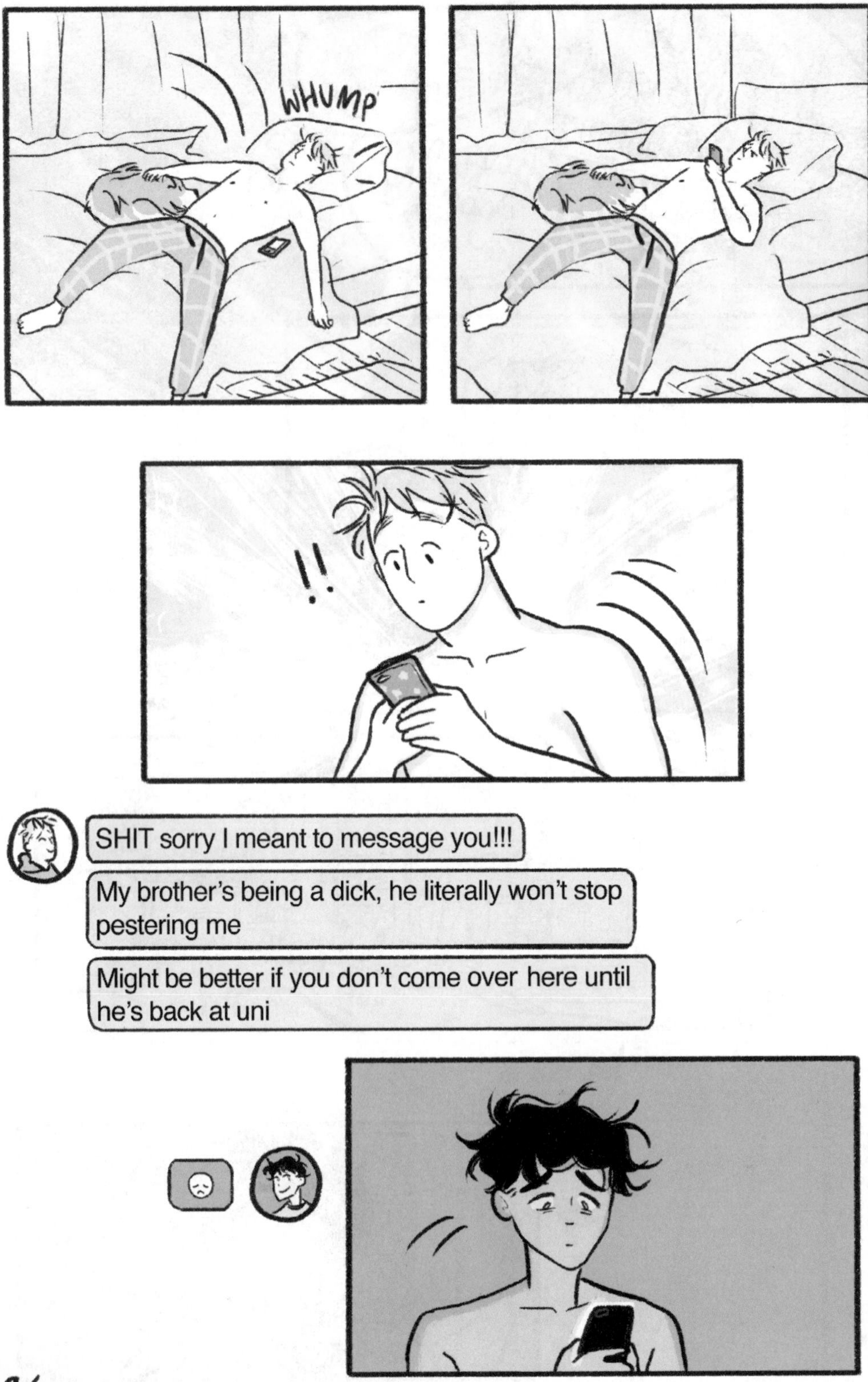
WHUMP
!!
SHIT sorry I meant to message you!!!
My brother's being a dick, he literally won't stop pestering me
Might be better if you don't come over here until he's back at uni

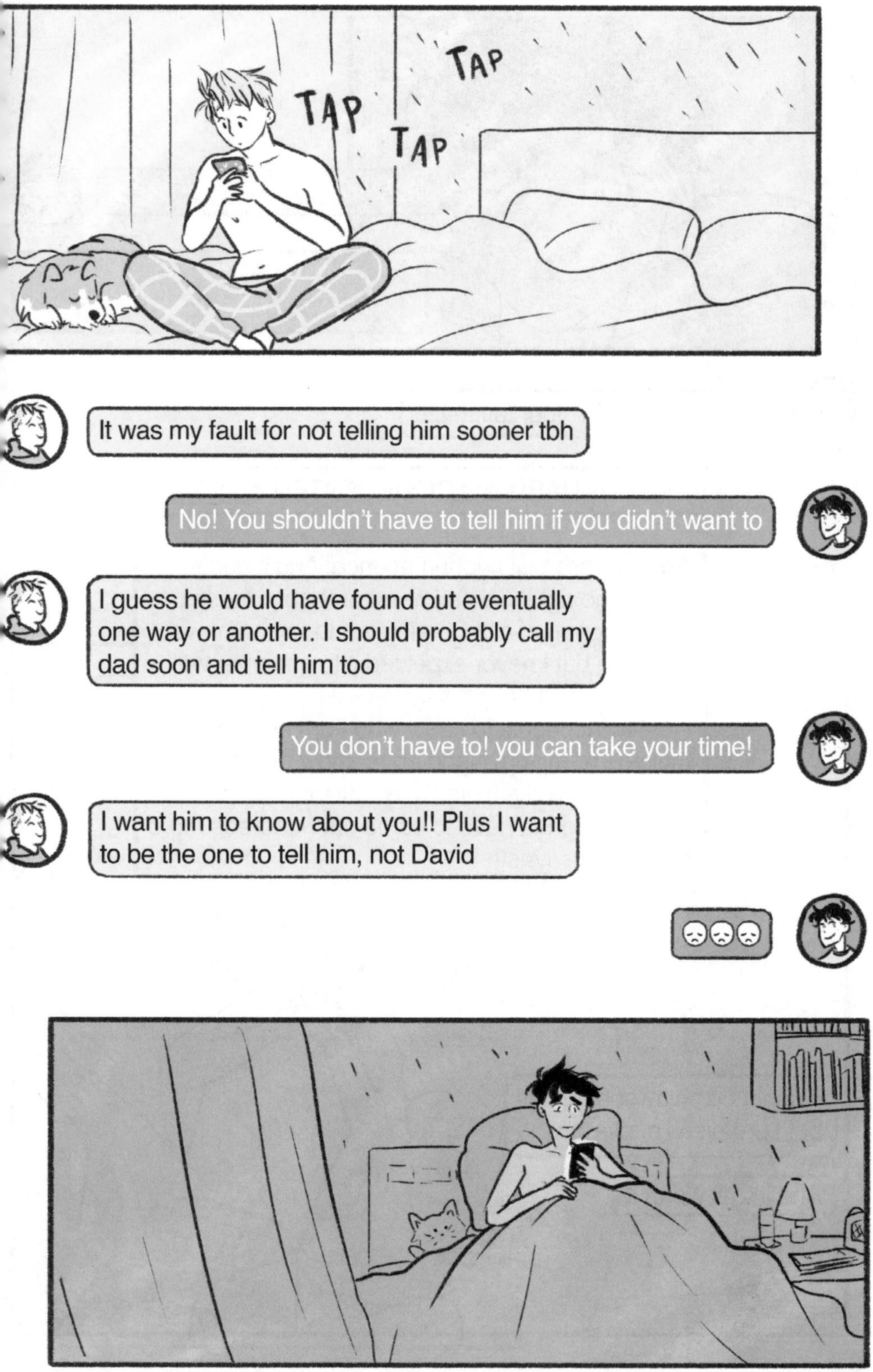

TAP
TAP
TAP
It was my fault for not telling him sooner tbh
No! You shouldn't have to tell him if you didn't want to
I guess he would have found out eventually one way or another. I should probably call my dad soon and tell him too
You don't have to! you can take your time!
I want him to know about you!! Plus I want to be the one to tell him, not David

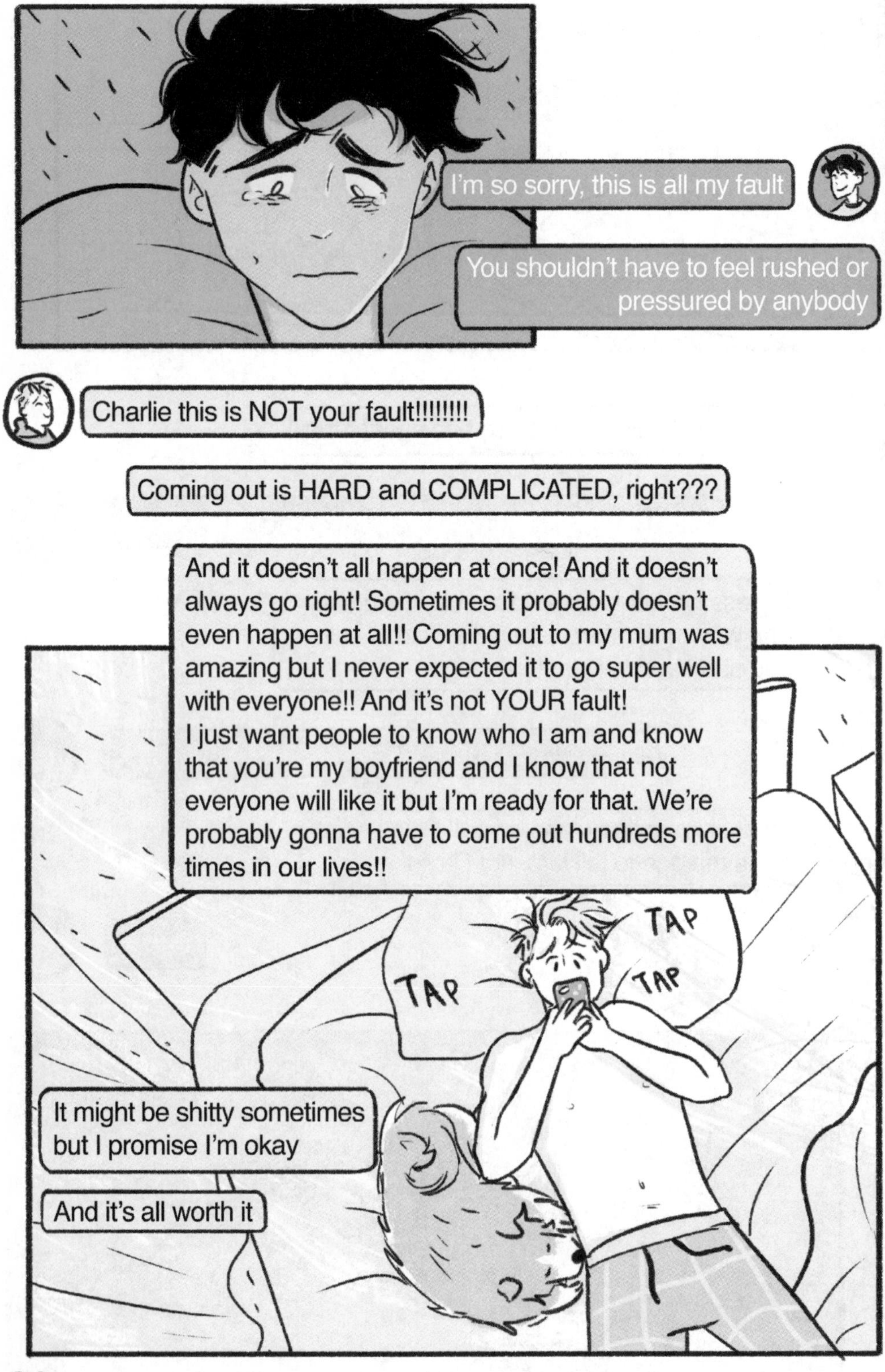
I'm so sorry, this is all my fault
You shouldn't have to feel rushed or pressured by anybody
Charlie this is NOT your fault!!!!!!!!
Coming out is HARD and COMPLICATED, right???
And it doesn't all happen at once! And it doesn't always go right! Sometimes it probably doesn't even happen at all!! Coming out to my mum was amazing but I never expected it to go super well with everyone!! And it's not YOUR fault!
I just want people to know who I am and know that you're my boyfriend and I know that not everyone will like it but I'm ready for that. We're probably gonna have to come out hundreds more times in our lives!!
TAP
TAP
TAP
It might be shitty sometimes but I promise I'm okay
And it's all worth it

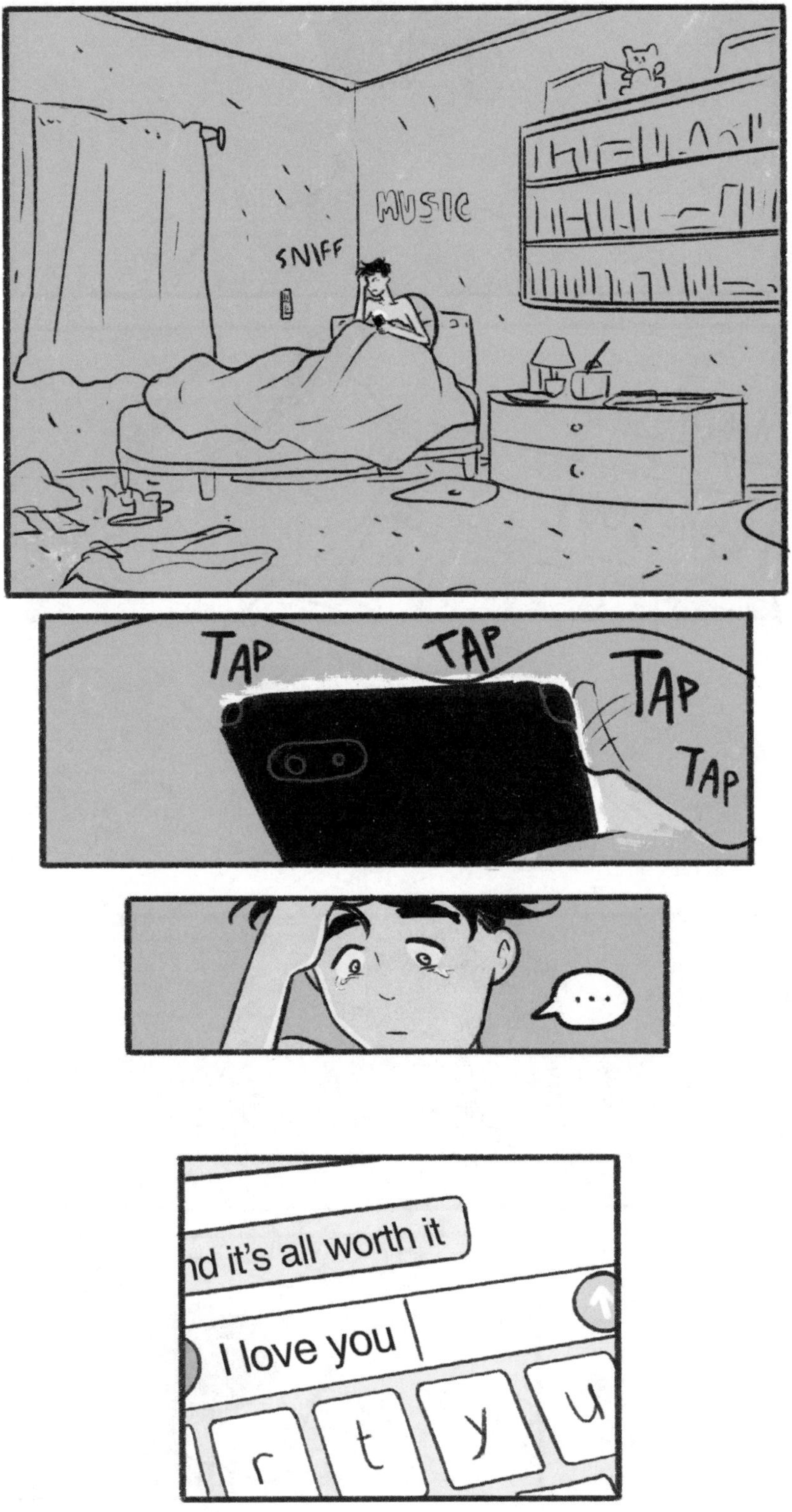
MUSIC
SNIFF
TAP
TAP
TAP
TAP
...
nd it's all worth it
I love you
r t y u

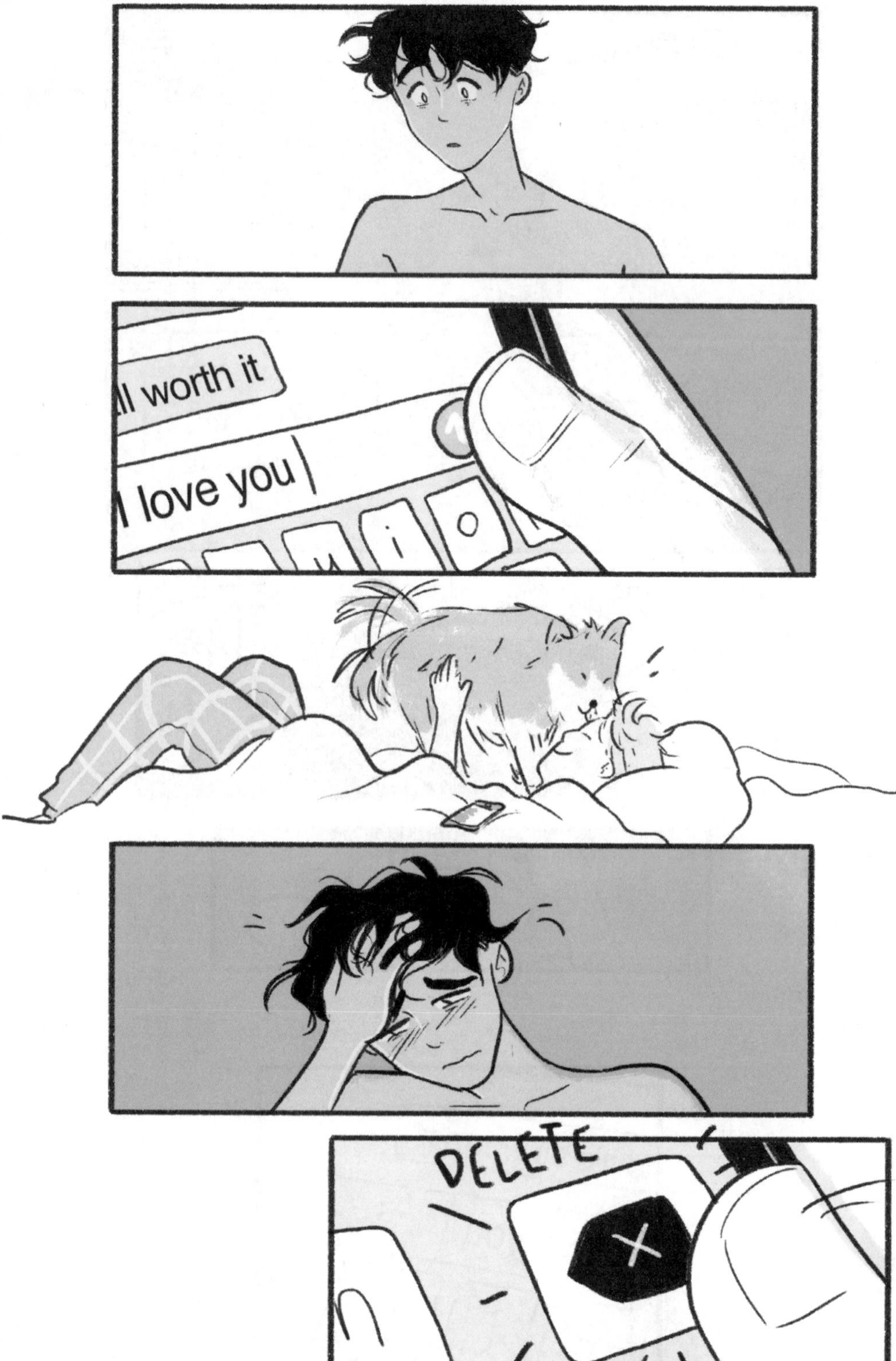
ll worth it
I love you
i o
DELETE

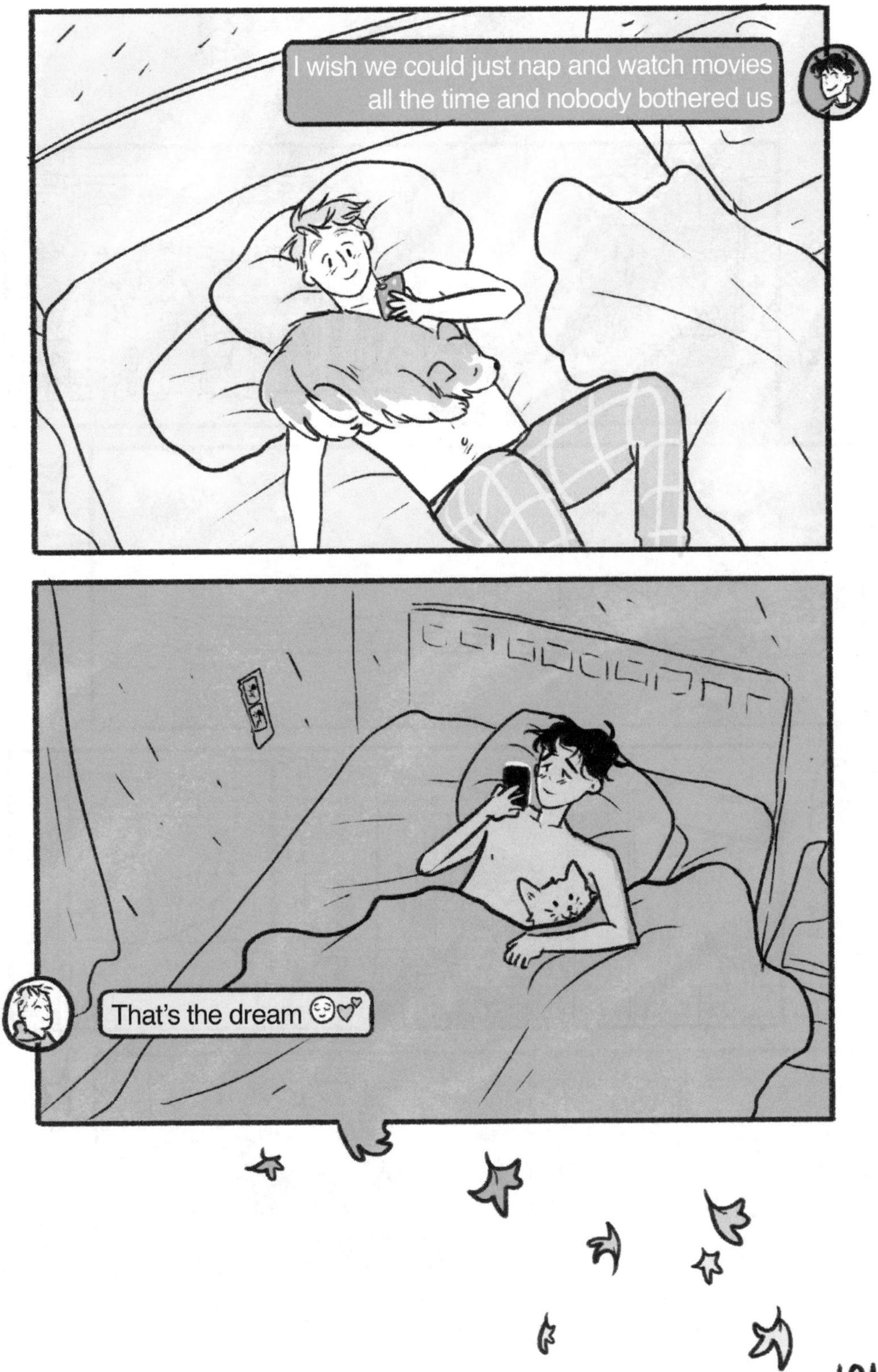
I wish we could just nap and watch movies all the time and nobody bothered us
That's the dream 😌💕

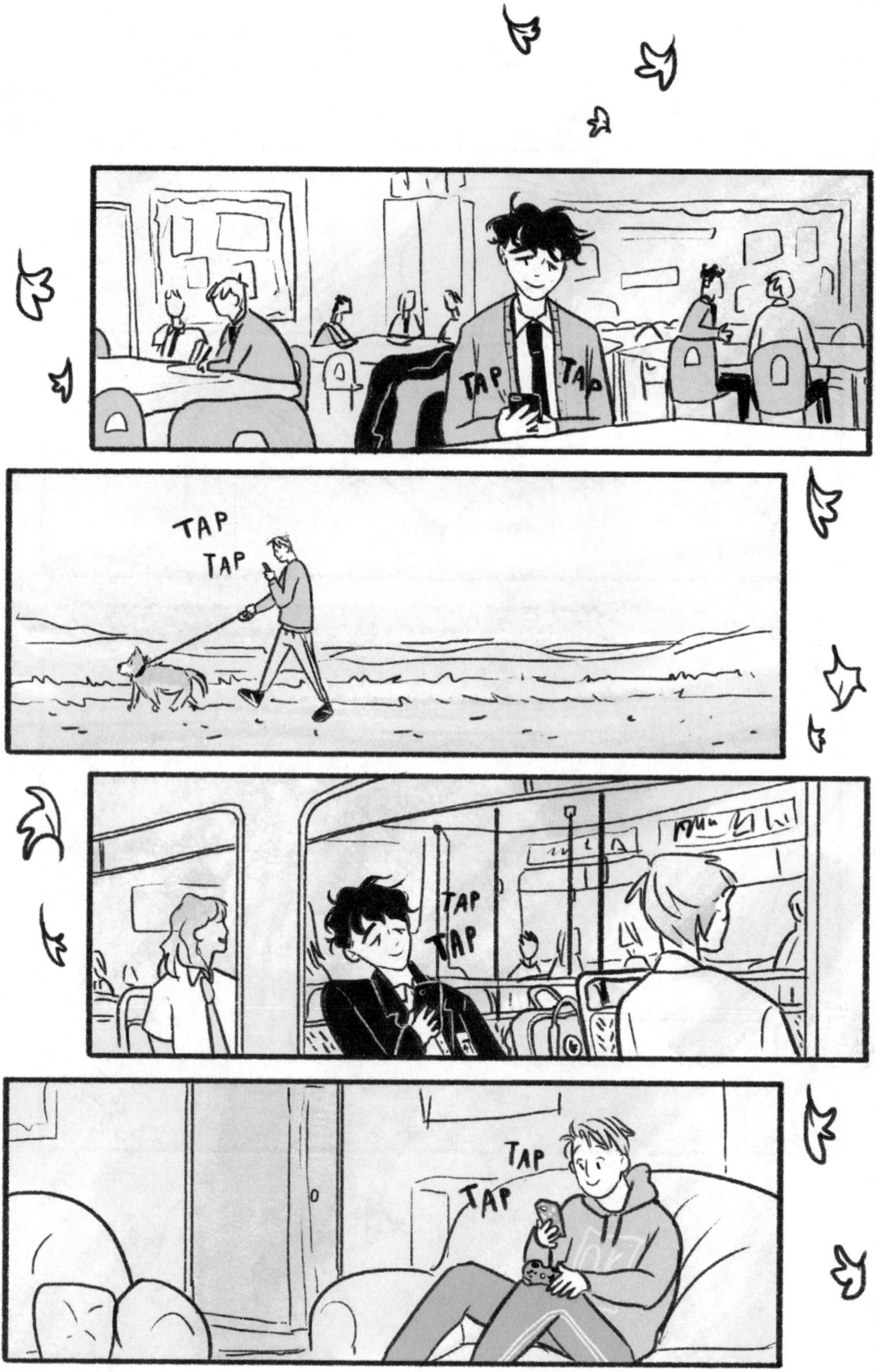
TAP TAP
TAP
TAP
TAP
TAP
TAP
TAP

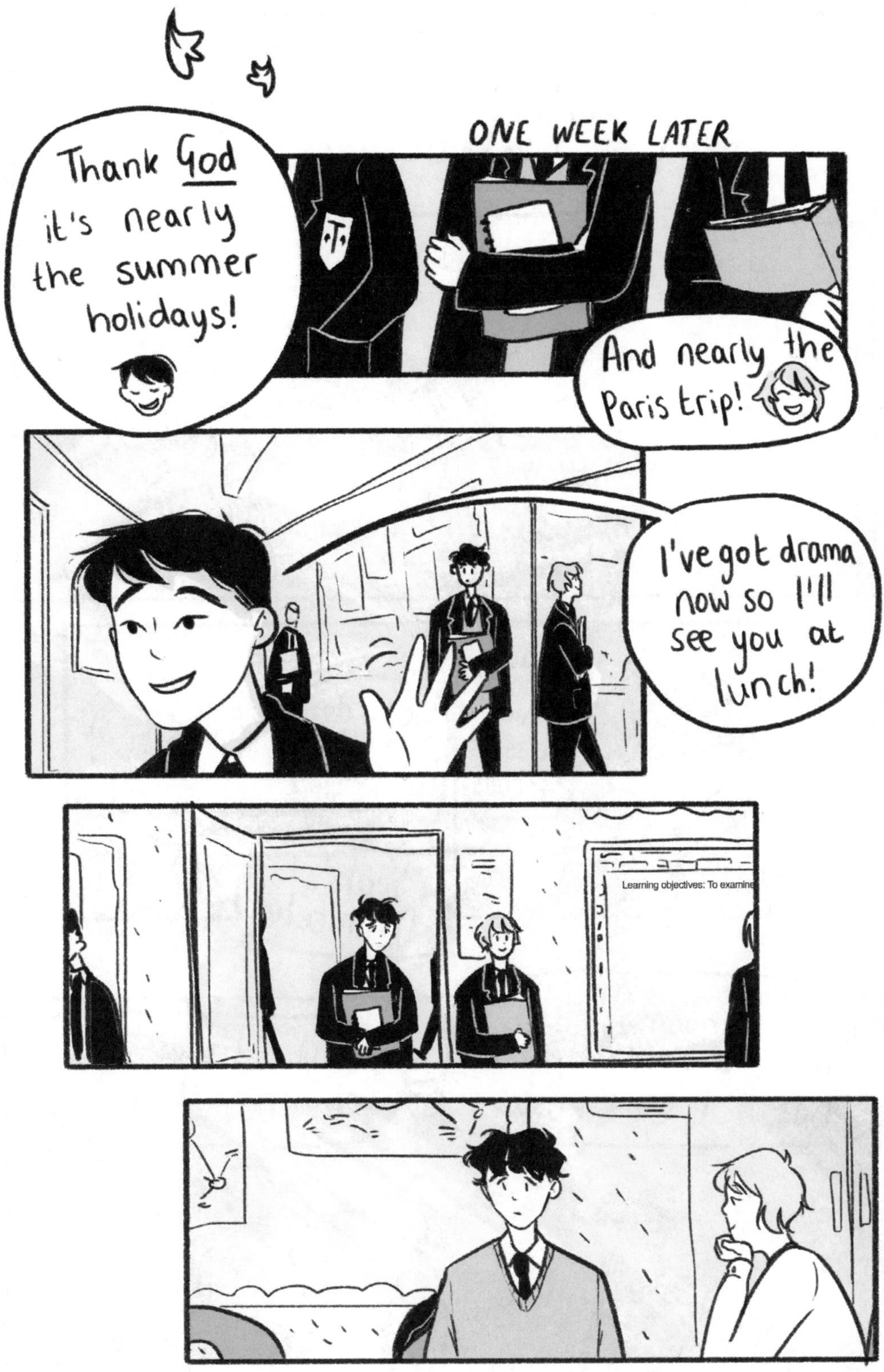
ONE WEEK LATER
Thank God it's nearly the summer holidays!
And nearly the Paris trip!
I've got drama now so I'll see you at lunch!
Learning objectives: To examine

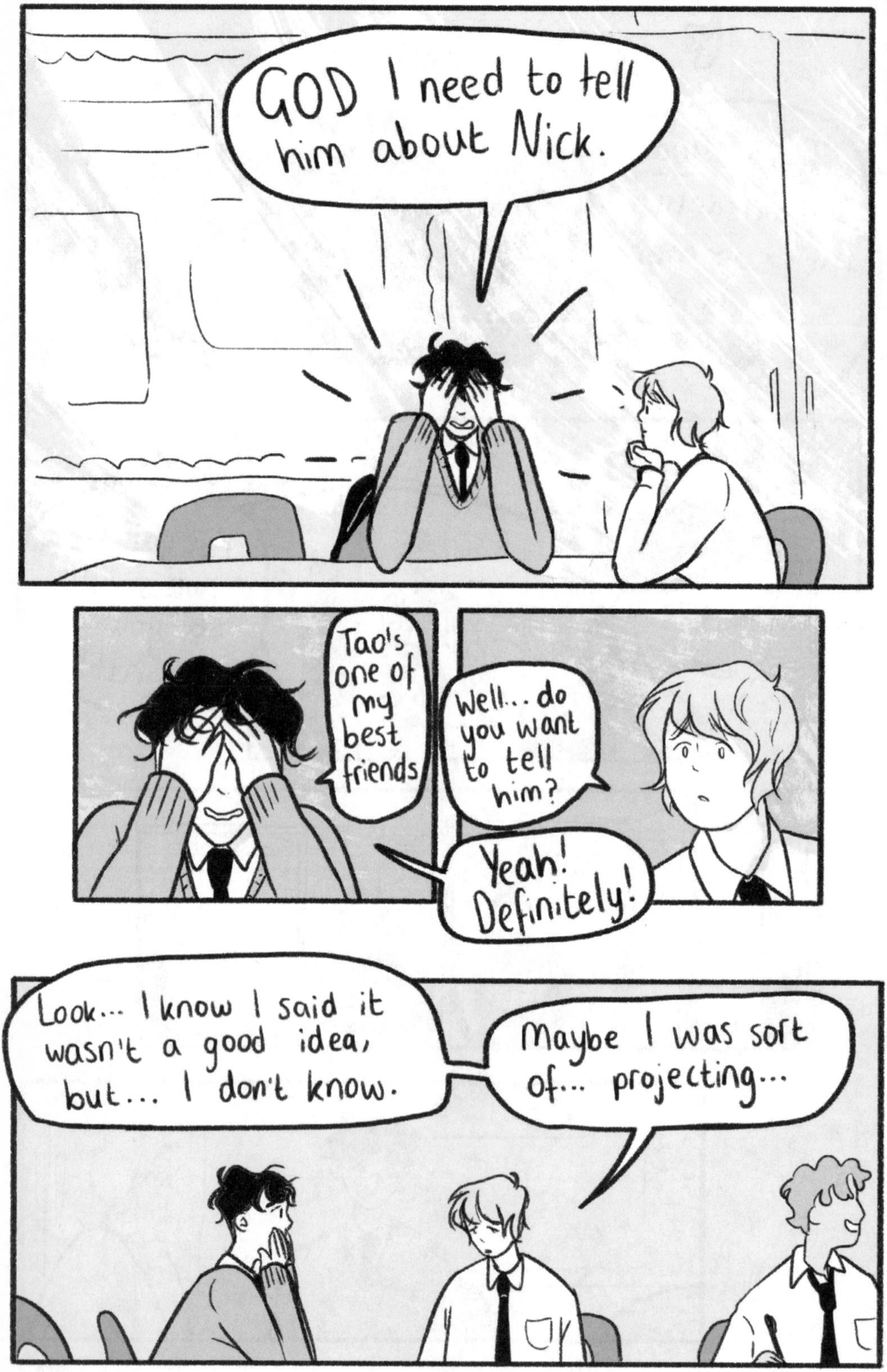

GOD I need to tell him about Nick.
Tao's one of my best friends
Well... do you want to tell him?
Yeah! Definitely!
Look... I know I said it wasn't a good idea, but... I don't know.
Maybe I was sort of... projecting...

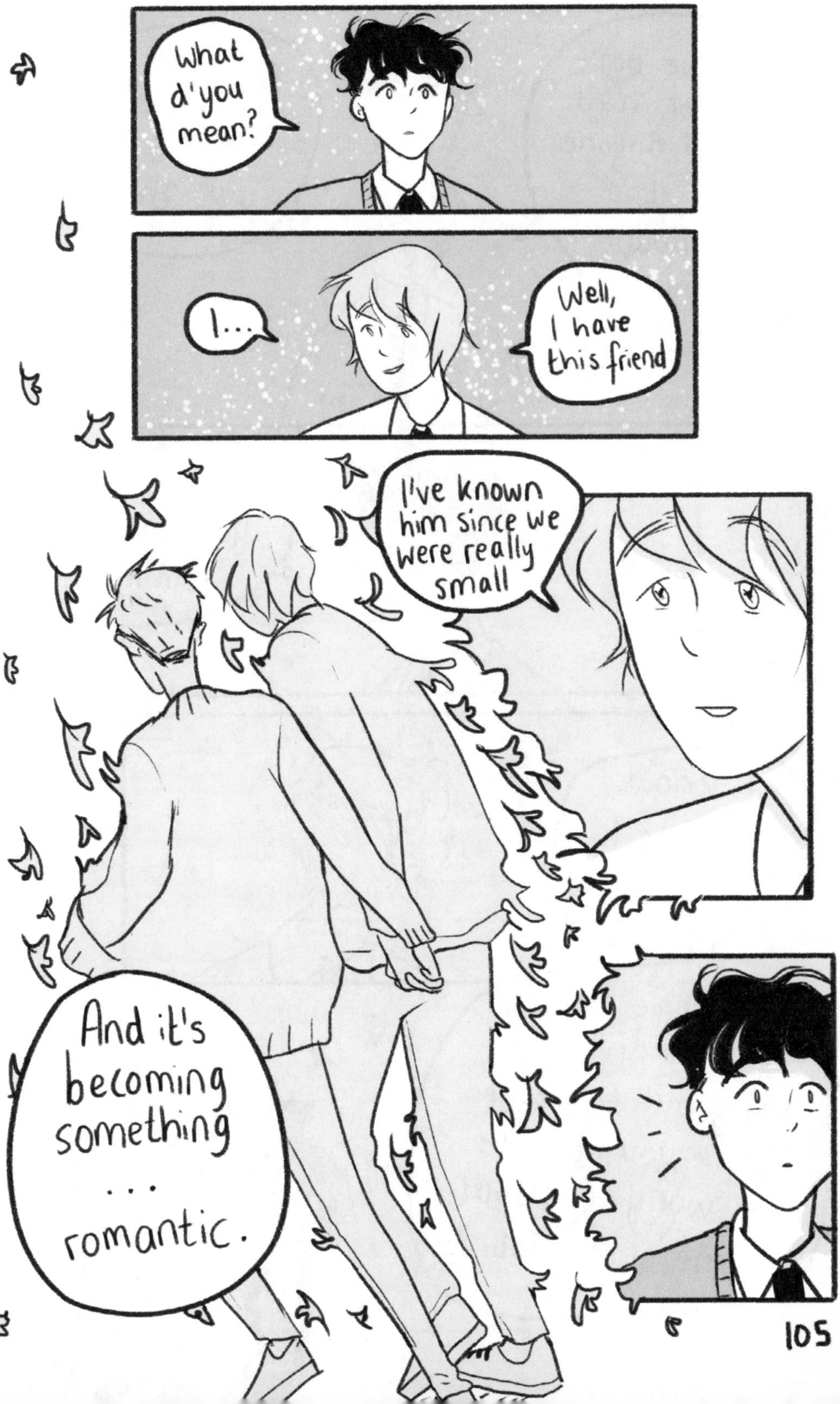
What d'you mean?
I...
Well, I have this friend
I've known him since we were really small
And it's becoming something ... romantic.

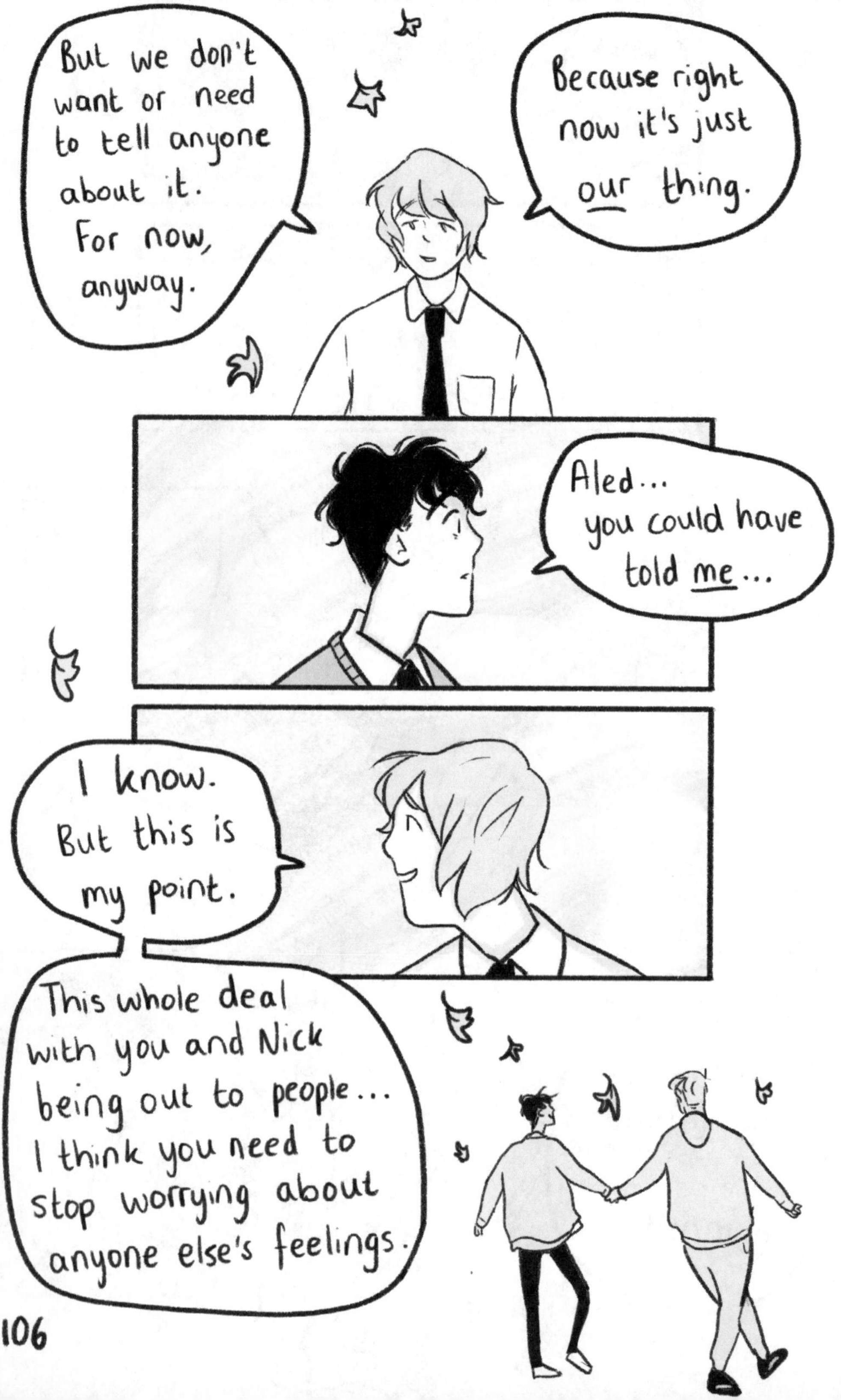
But we don't want or need to tell anyone about it. For now, anyway.
Because right now it's just our thing.
Aled... you could have told me...
I know. But this is my point.
This whole deal with you and Nick being out to people... I think you need to stop worrying about anyone else's feelings.

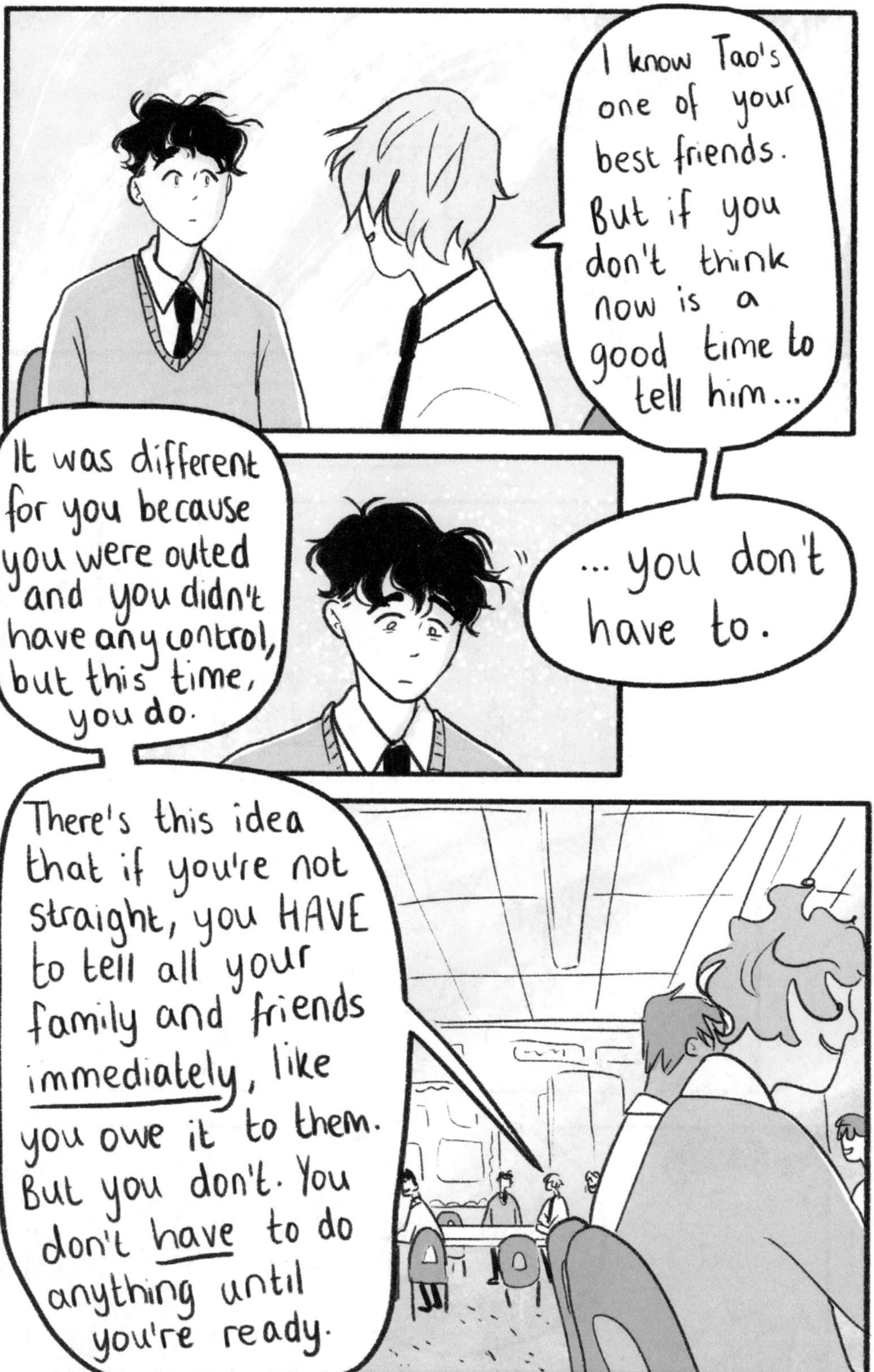
I know Tao's one of your best friends. But if you don't think now is a good time to tell him...
... you don't have to.
It was different for you because you were outed and you didn't have any control, but this time, you do.
There's this idea that if you're not straight, you HAVE to tell all your family and friends immediately, like you owe it to them. But you don't. You don't have to do anything until you're ready.

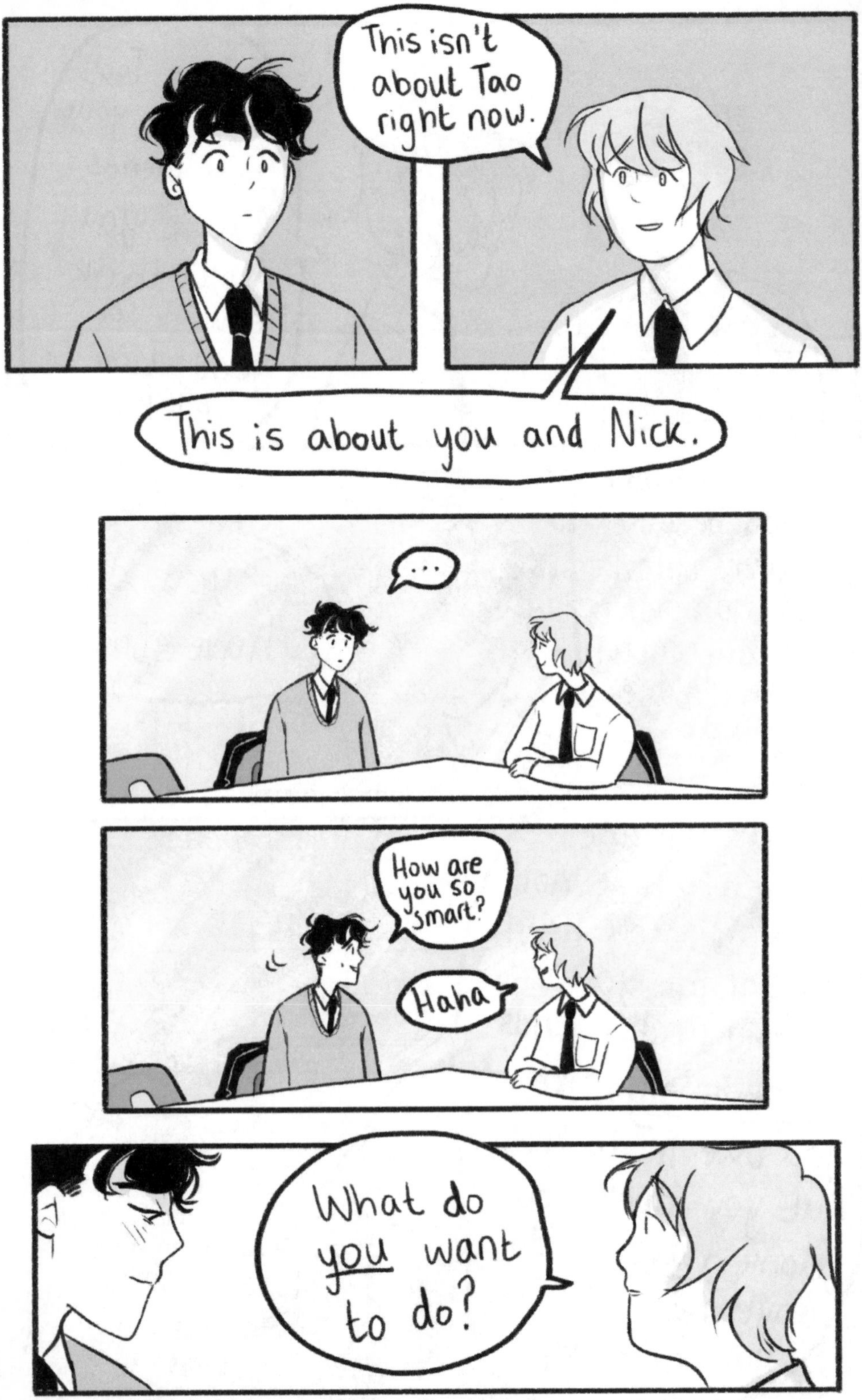
This isn't about Tao right now.
This is about you and Nick.
...
How are you so smart?
Haha
What do you want to do?

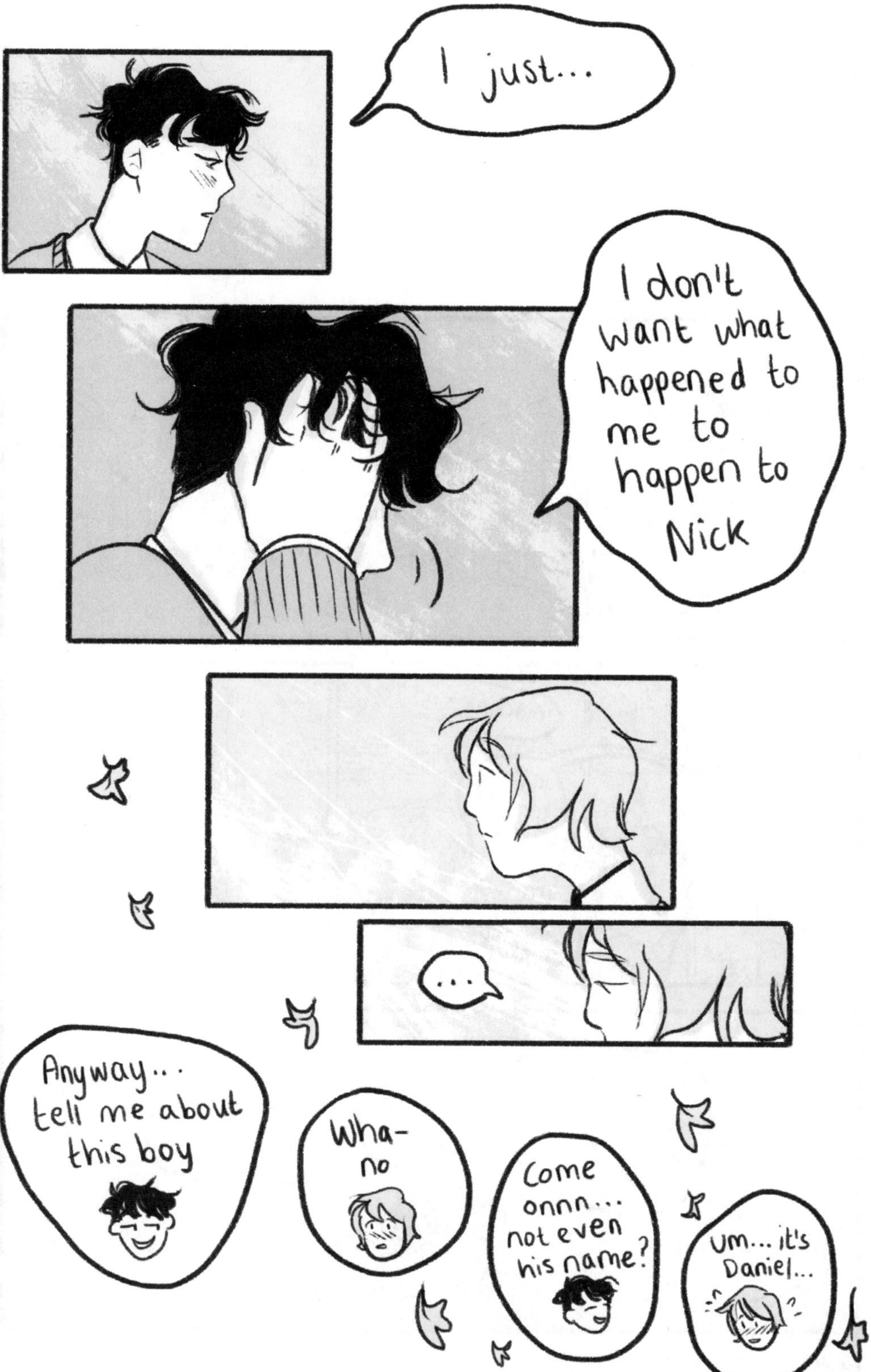
I just...
I don't want what happened to me to happen to Nick
...
Anyway... tell me about this boy
Wha- no
Come onnn... not even his name?
Um... it's Daniel...

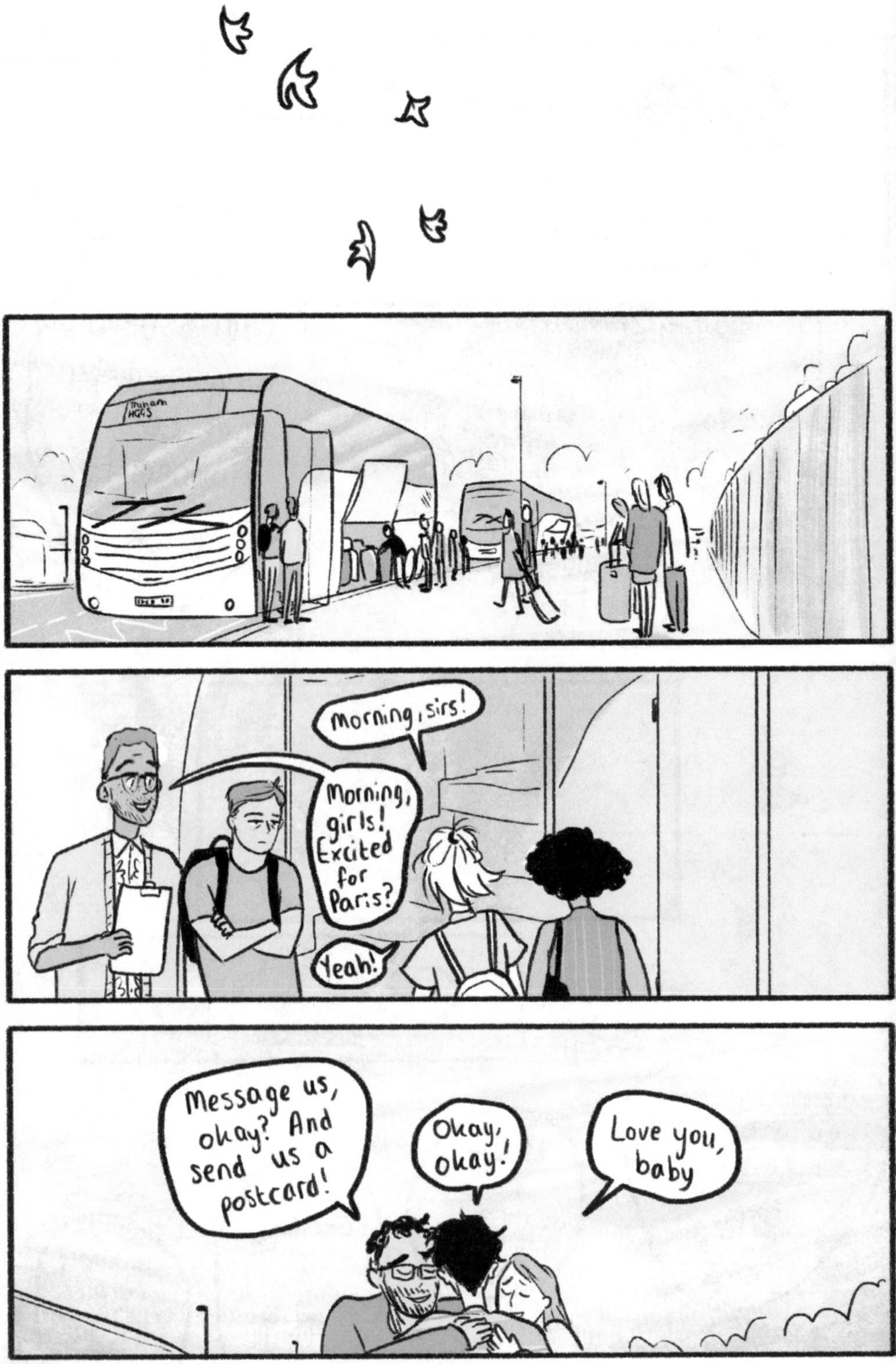
Morning, sirs!
Morning, girls! Excited for Paris?
Yeah!
Message us, okay? And send us a postcard!
Okay, okay!
Love you, baby

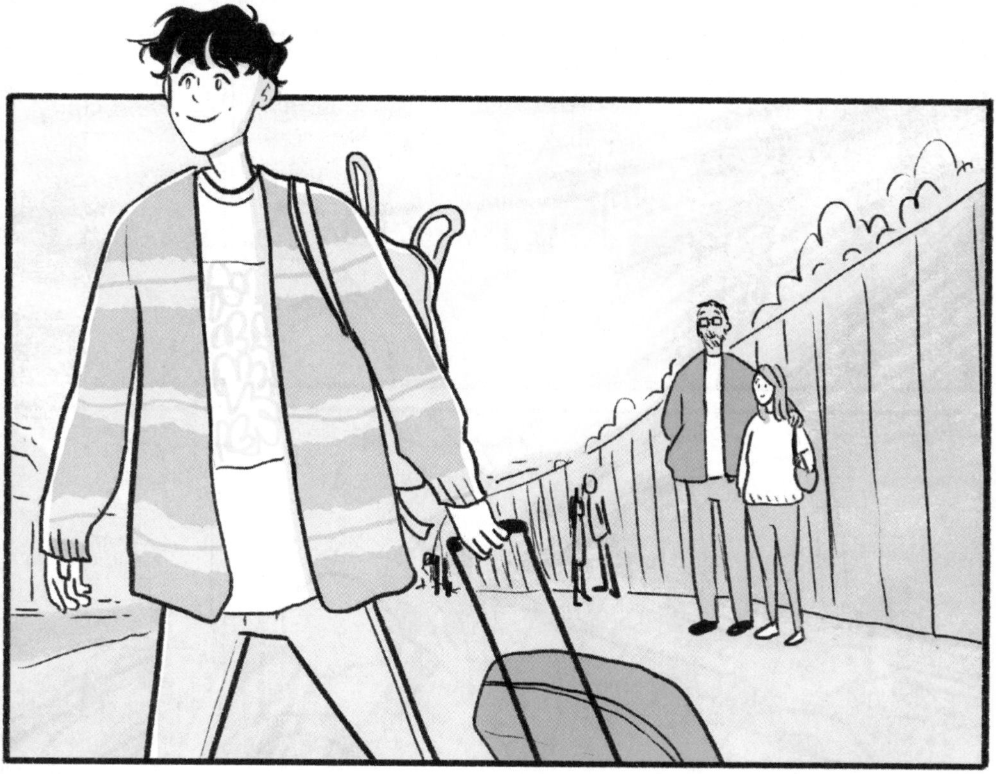

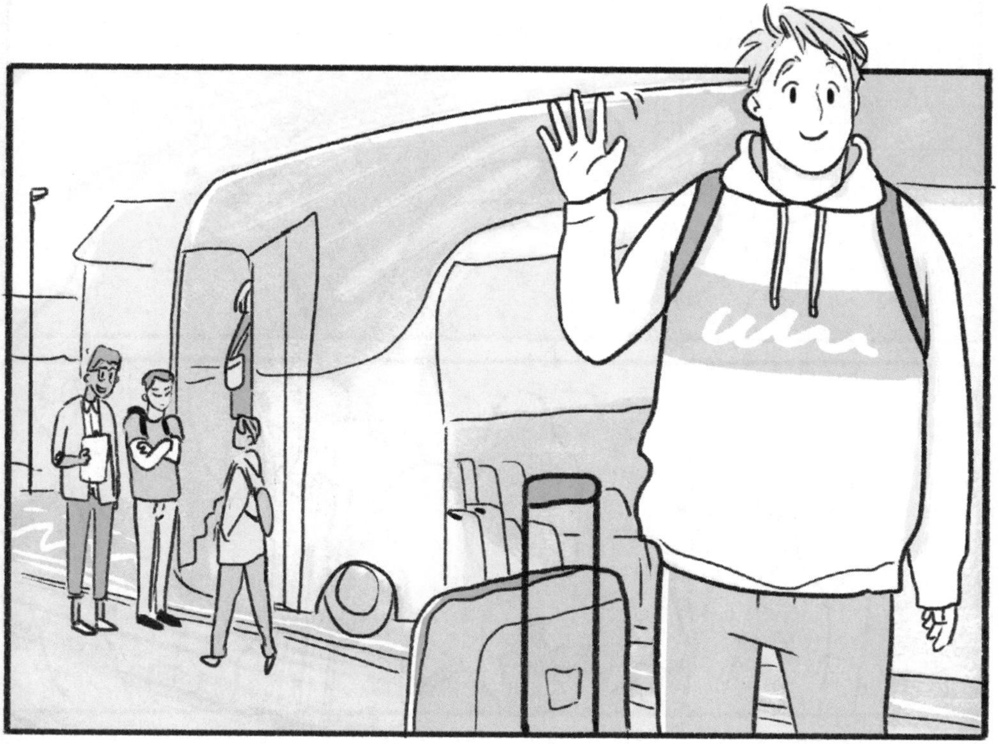

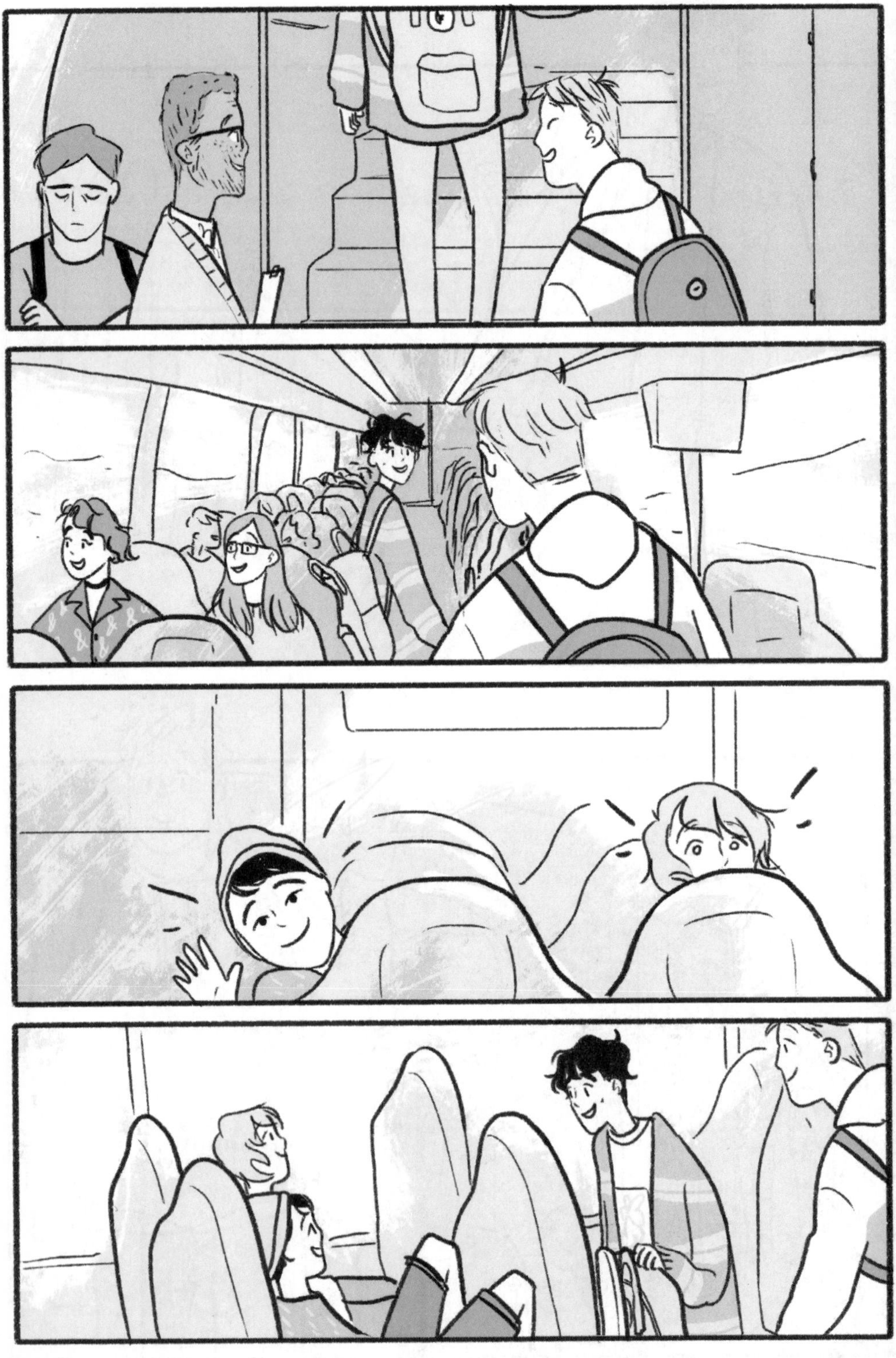

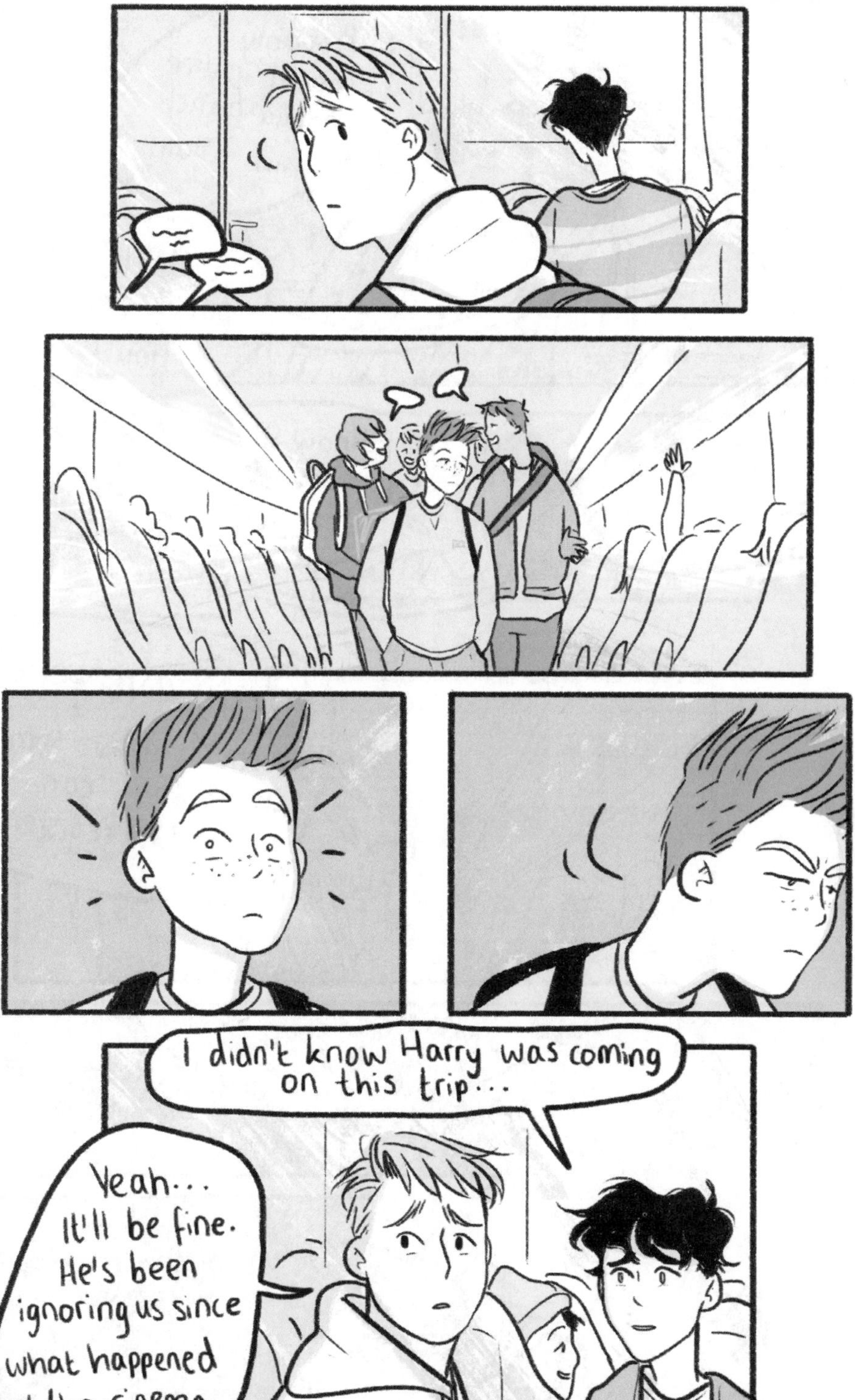
I didn't know Harry was coming on this trip...
Yeah... It'll be fine. He's been ignoring us since what happened at the cinema

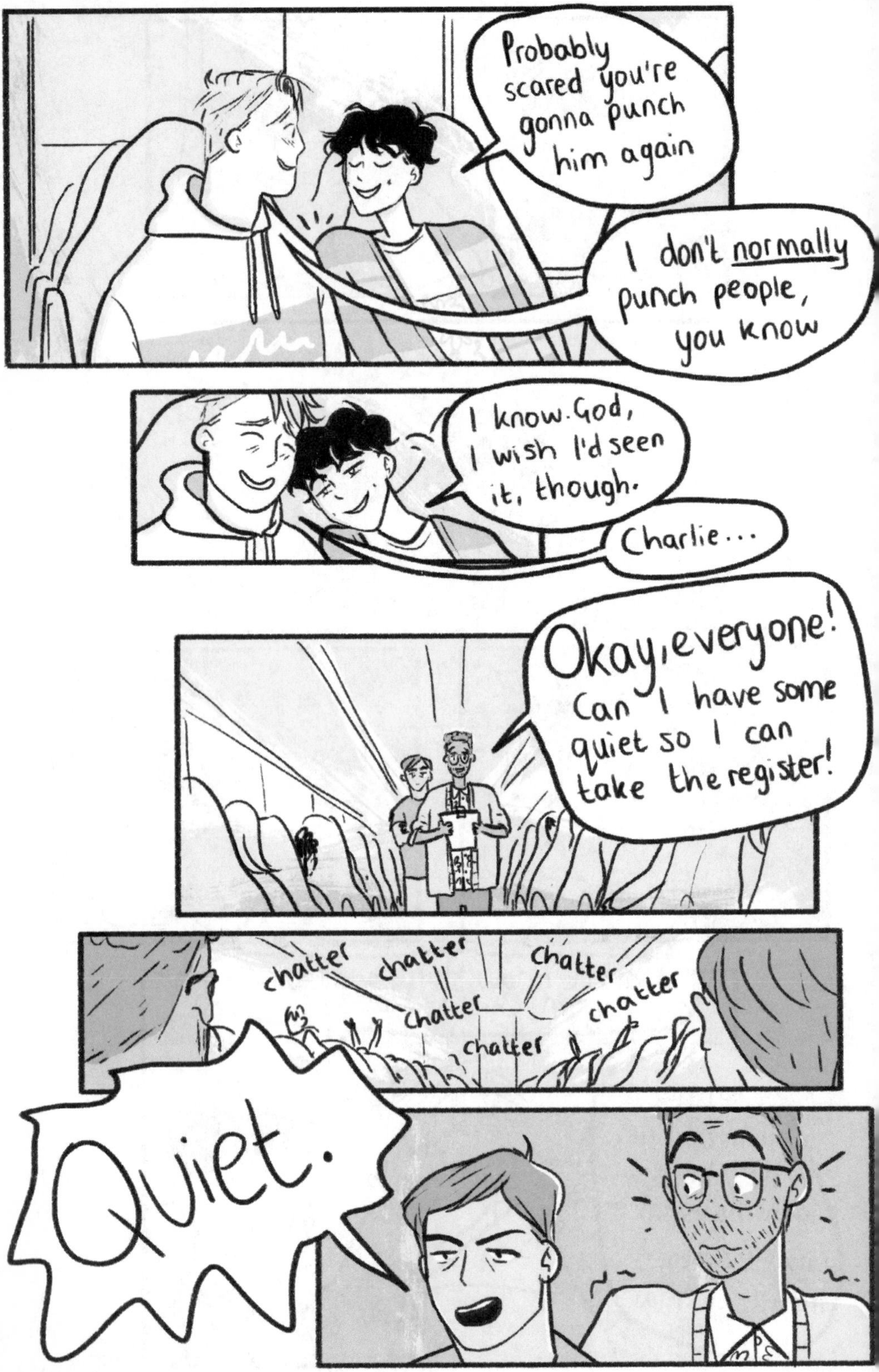

Probably scared you're gonna punch him again
I don't normally punch people, you know
I know. God, I wish I'd seen it, though.
Charlie...
Okay, everyone! Can I have some quiet so I can take the register!
chatter chatter chatter chatter chatter chatter
Quiet.

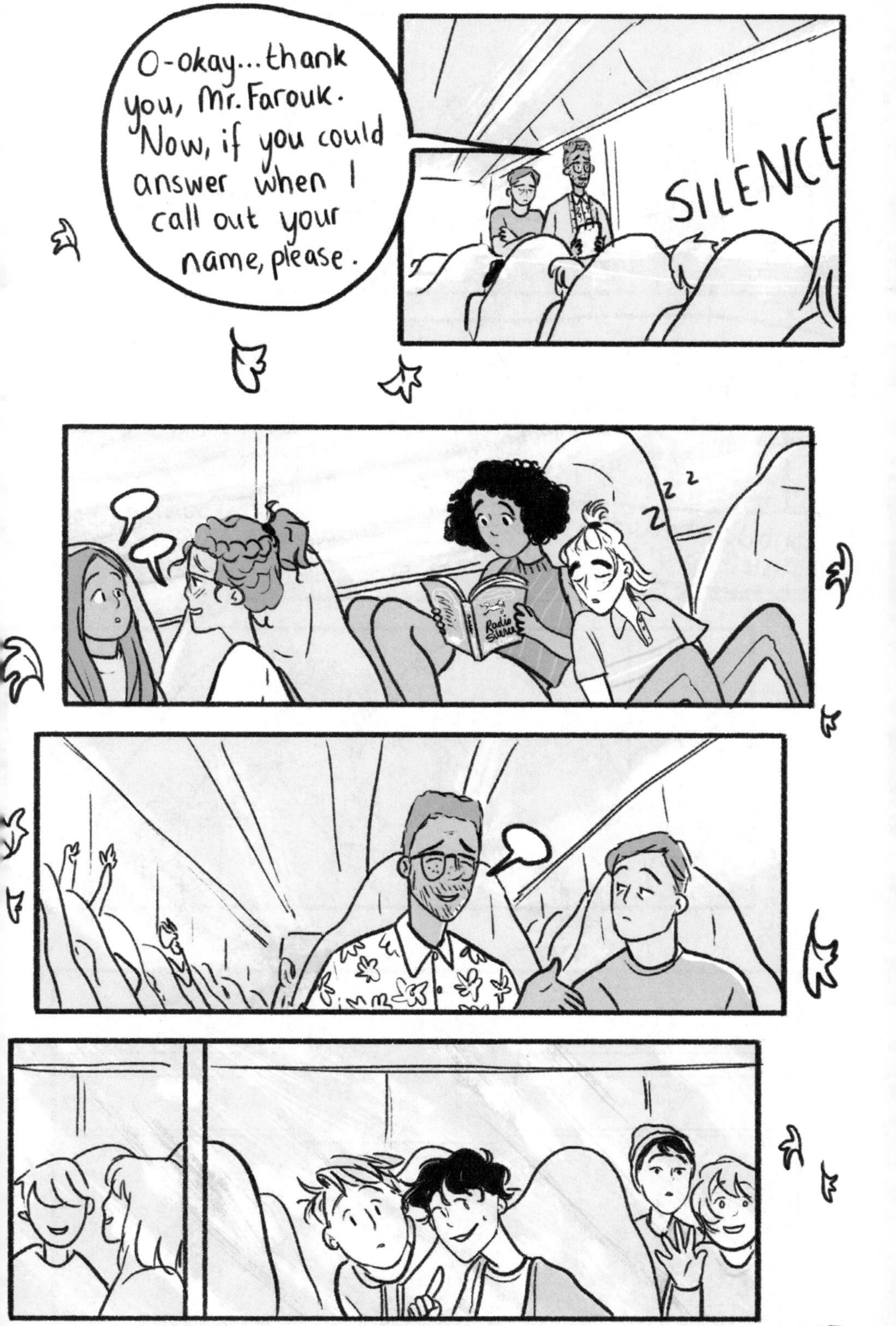
O-okay... thank you, Mr. Farouk. Now, if you could answer when I call out your name, please.
SILENCE
Z Z Z
Radio Silence

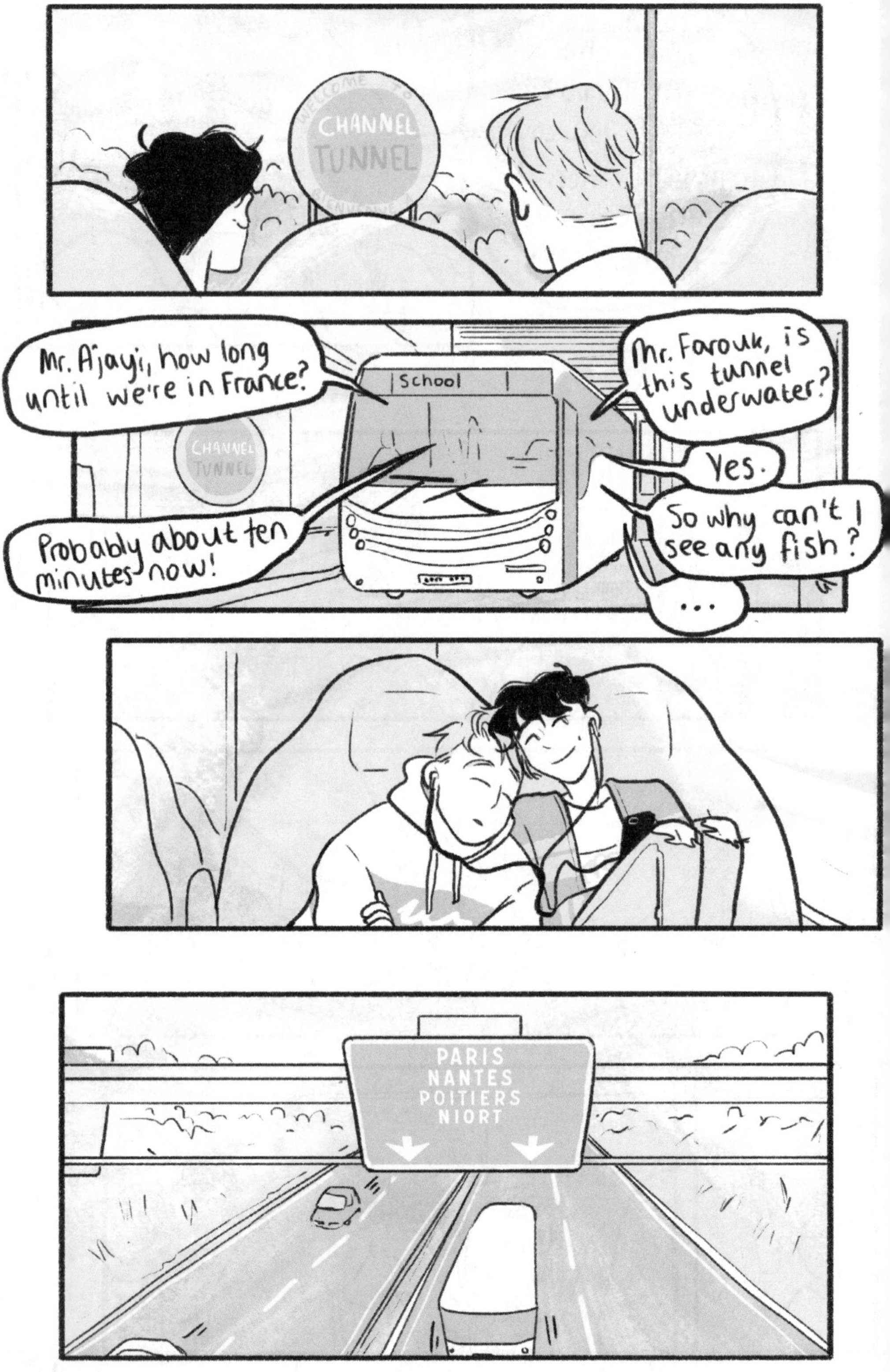
WELCOME TO
CHANNEL TUNNEL
Mr. Ajayi, how long until we're in France?
School
CHANNEL TUNNEL
Mr. Farouk, is this tunnel underwater?
Yes.
Probably about ten minutes now!
So why can't I see any fish?
...
PARIS
NANTES
POITIERS
NIORT

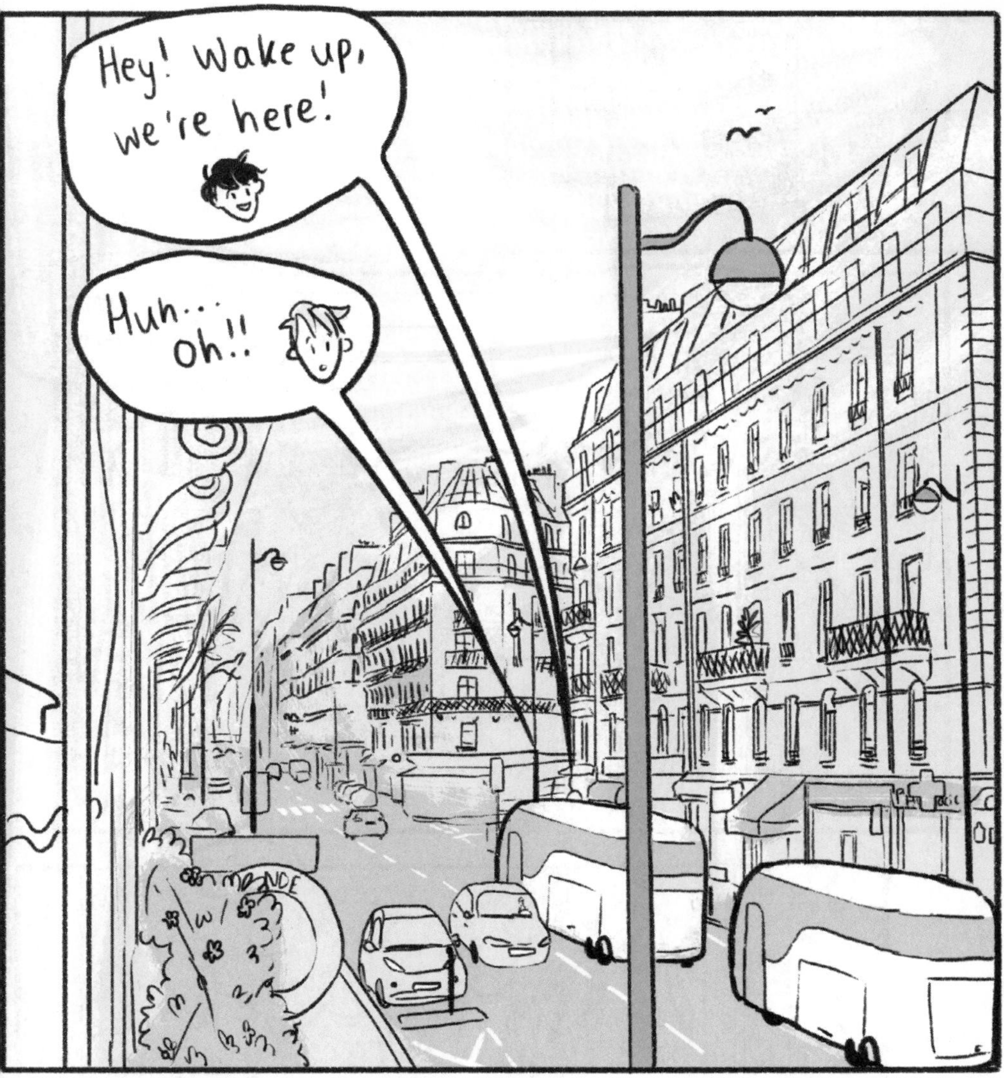
Hey! Wake up, we're here!
Huh... oh!!

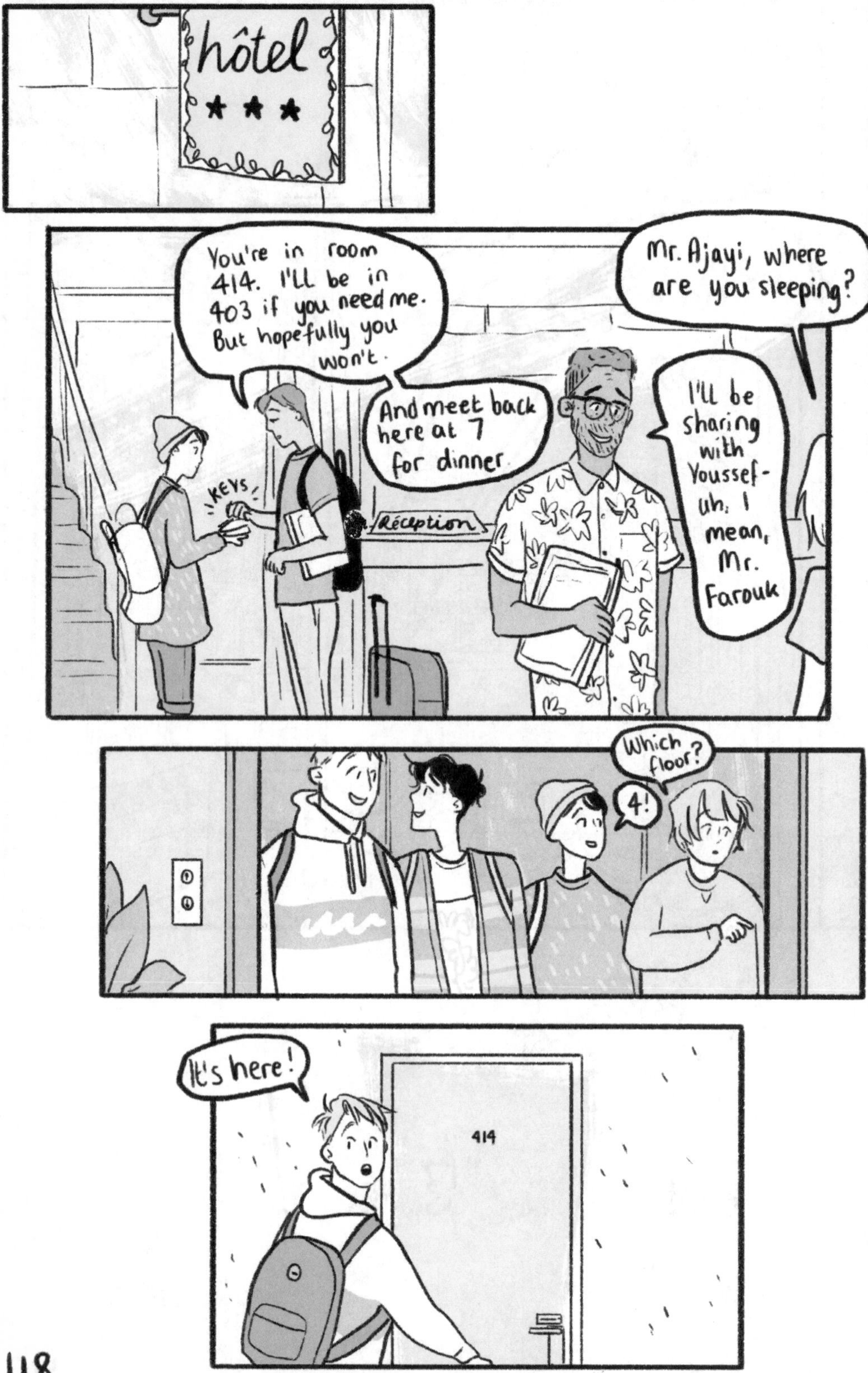
hôtel
You're in room 414. I'll be in 403 if you need me. But hopefully you won't.
And meet back here at 7 for dinner.
KEYS
Réception
Mr. Ajayi, where are you sleeping?
I'll be sharing with Youssef- uh, I mean, Mr. Farouk
Which floor?
4!
It's here!
414

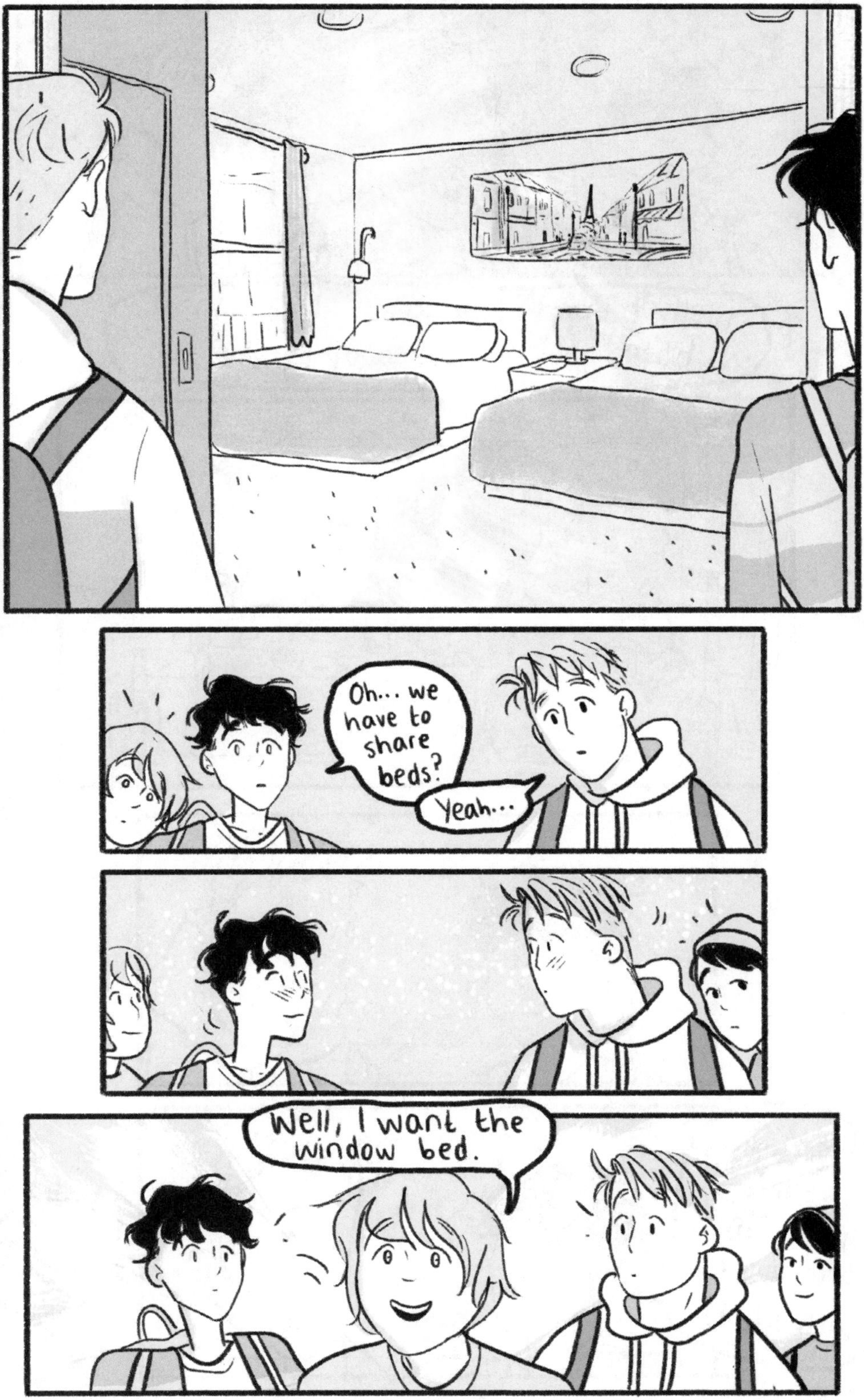
Oh... we have to share beds?
Yeah...
Well, I want the window bed.

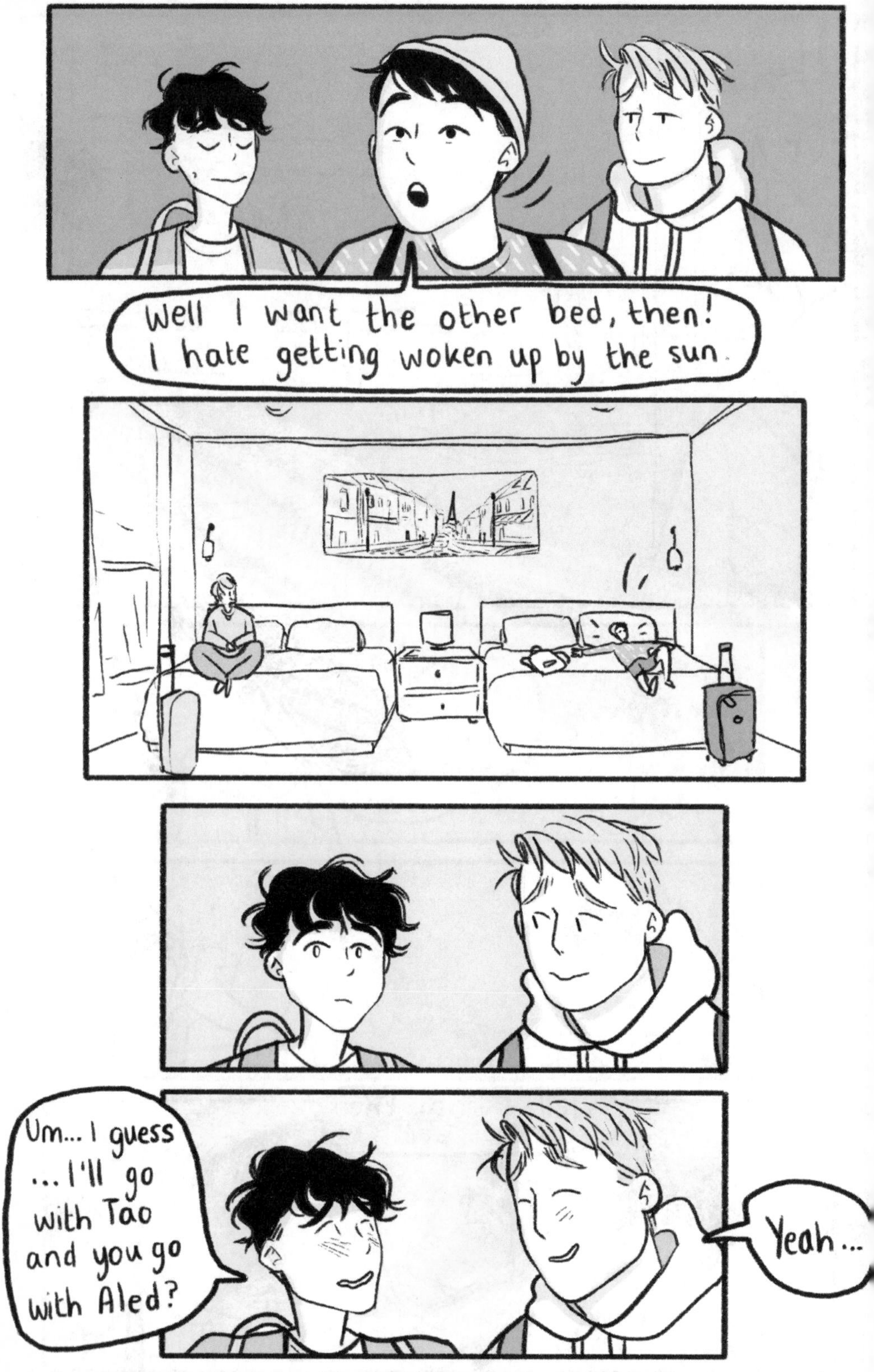
Well I want the other bed, then! I hate getting woken up by the sun.
Um... I guess ...I'll go with Tao and you go with Aled?
Yeah...

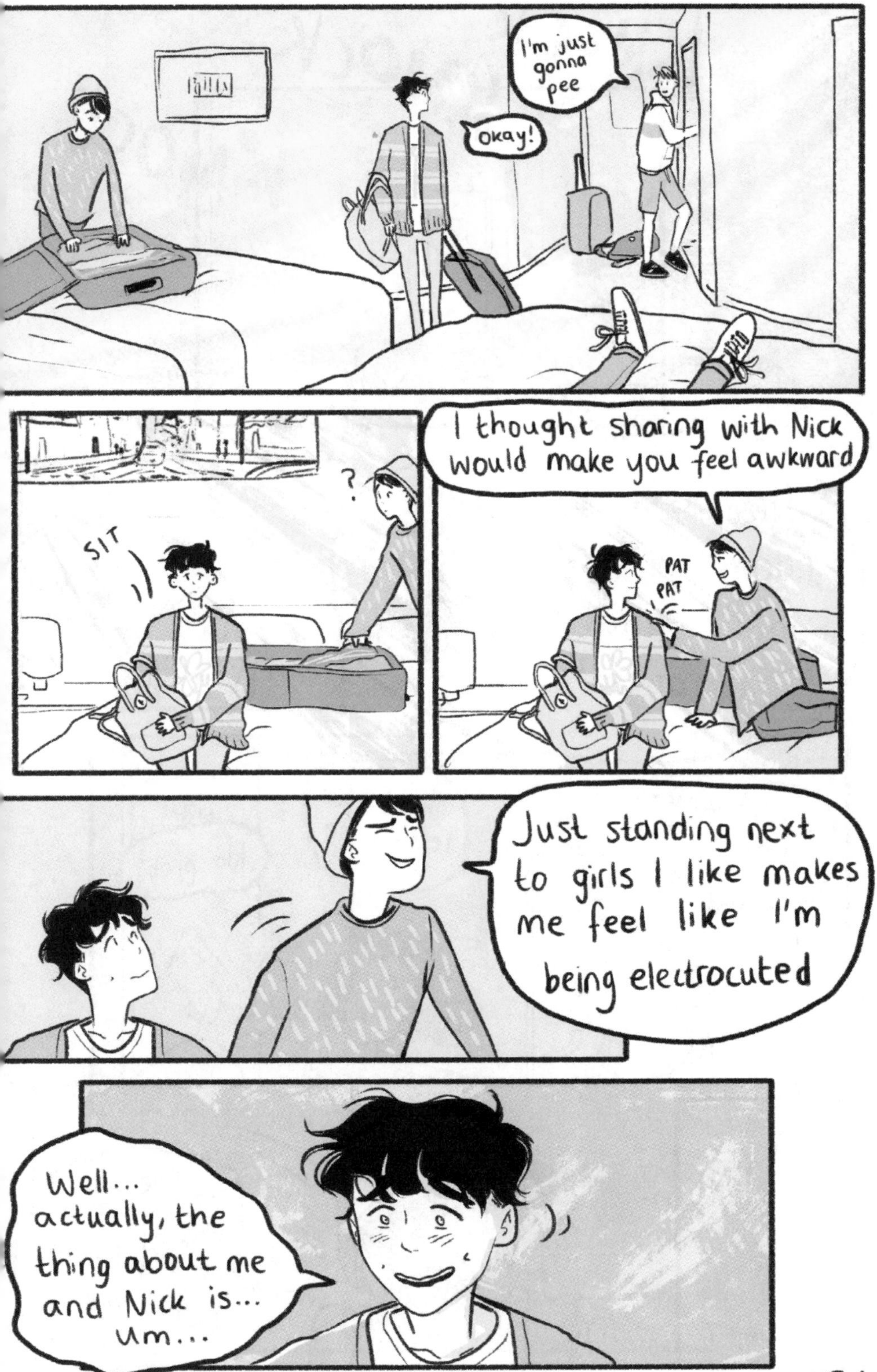
I'm just gonna pee
Okay!
SIT
?
I thought sharing with Nick would make you feel awkward
PAT PAT
Just standing next to girls I like makes me feel like I'm being electrocuted
Well... actually, the thing about me and Nick is... um...

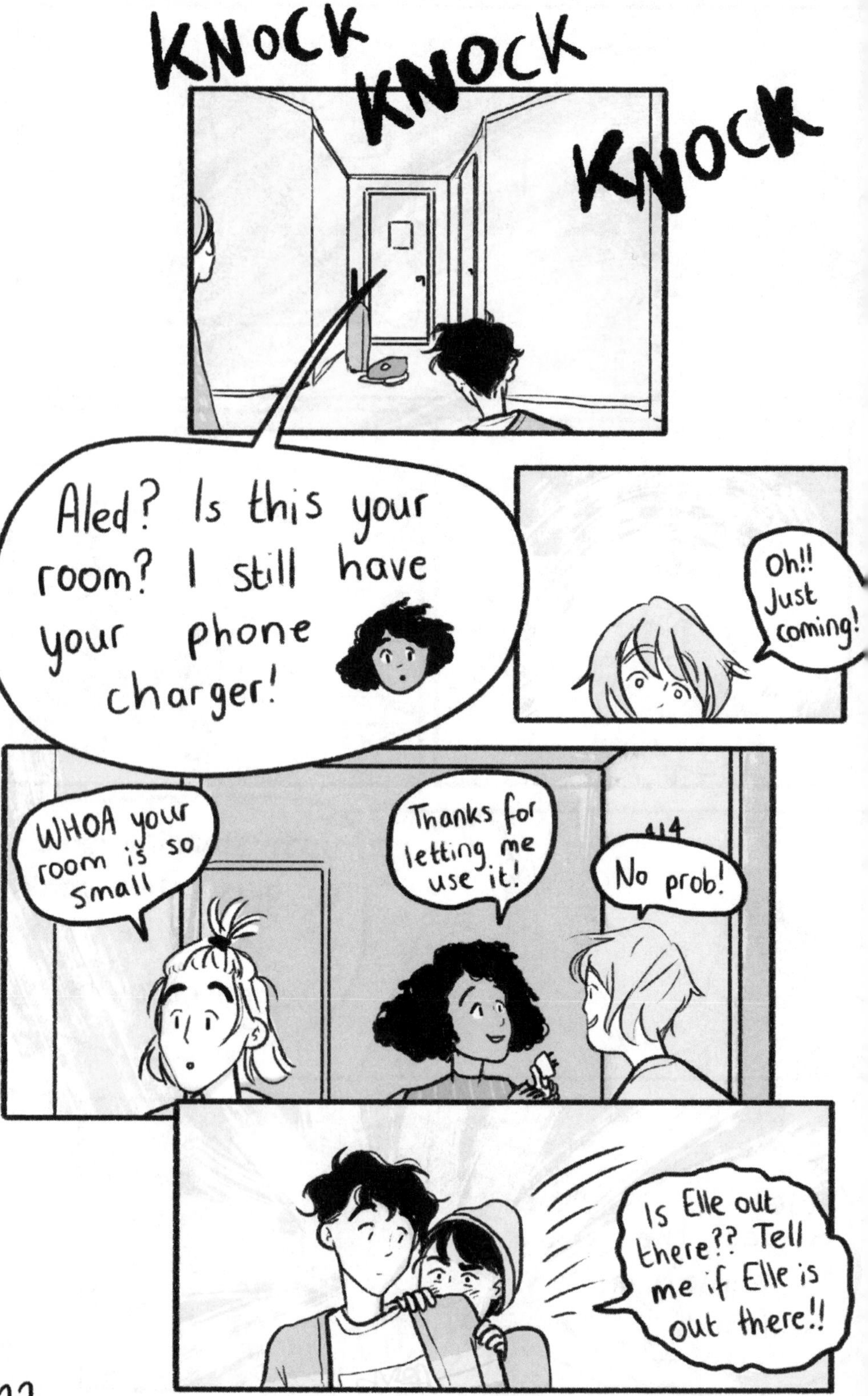
KNOCK
KNOCK
KNOCK
Aled? Is this your room? I still have your phone charger!
Oh!! Just coming!
WHOA your room is so small
Thanks for letting me use it!
No prob!
414
Is Elle out there?? Tell me if Elle is out there!!

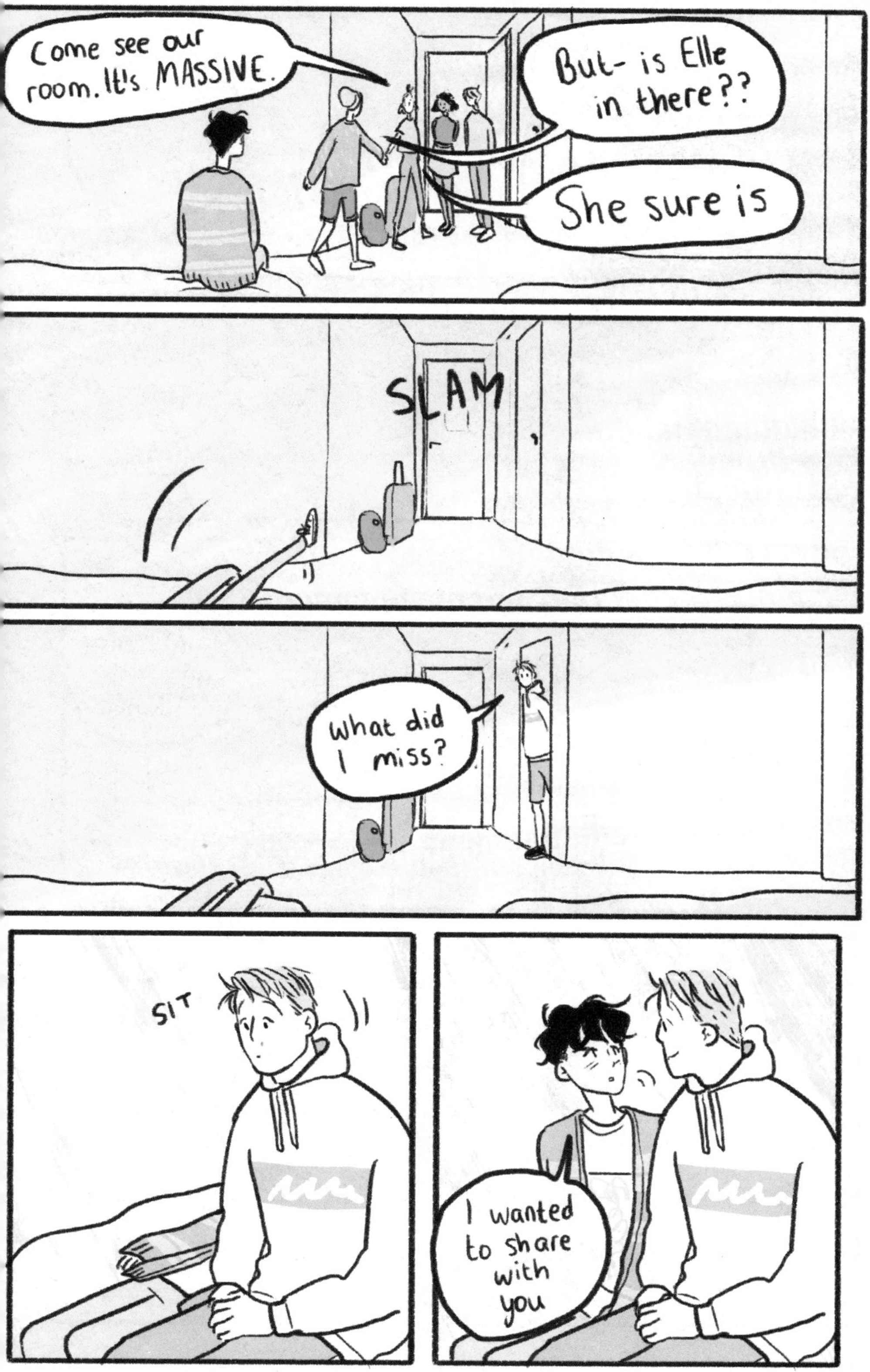
Come see our room. It's MASSIVE.
But- is Elle in there??
She sure is
SLAM
What did I miss?
SIT
I wanted to share with you

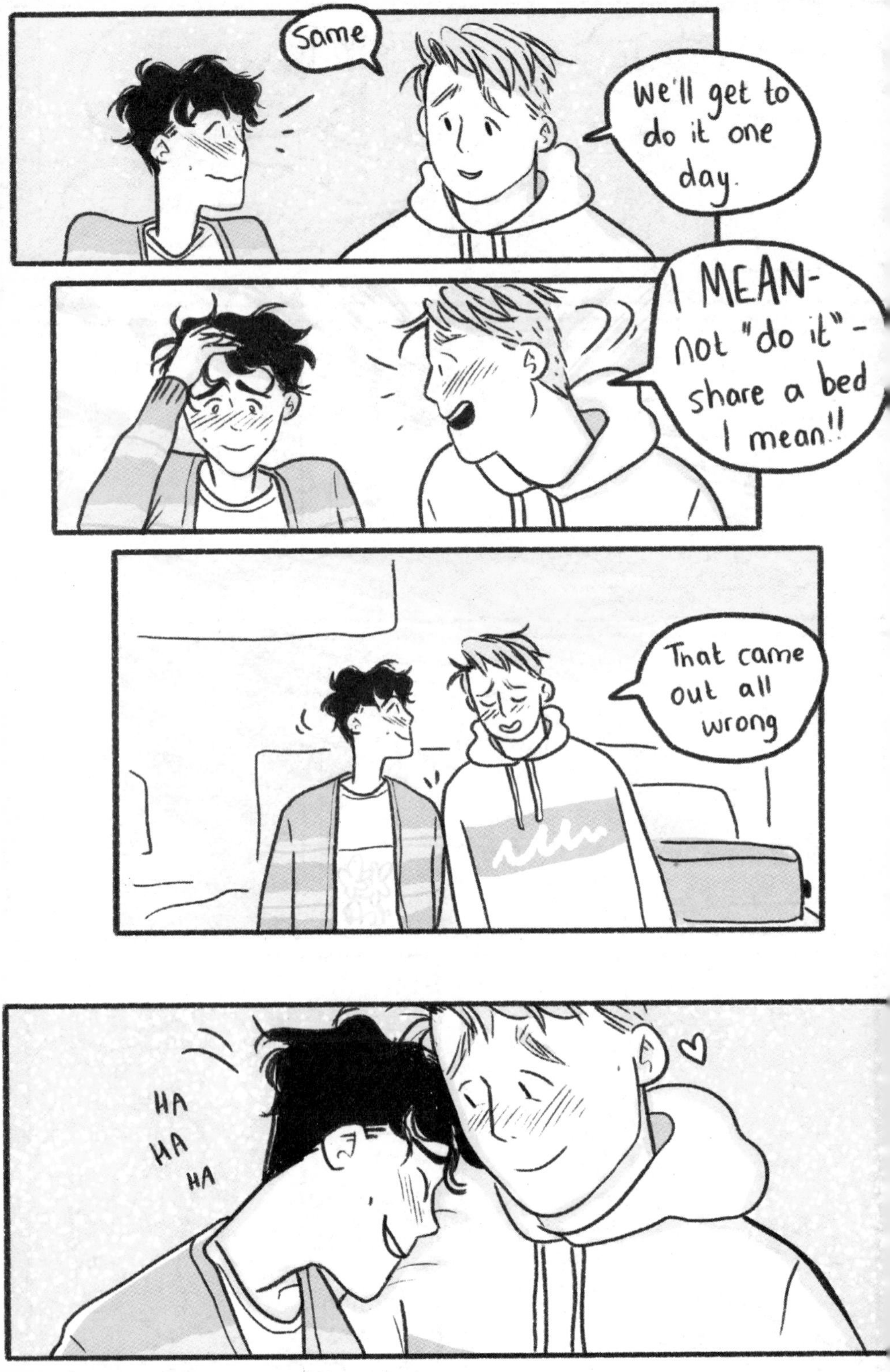
Same
We'll get to do it one day.
I MEAN- not "do it" - share a bed I mean!!
That came out all wrong
HA HA HA

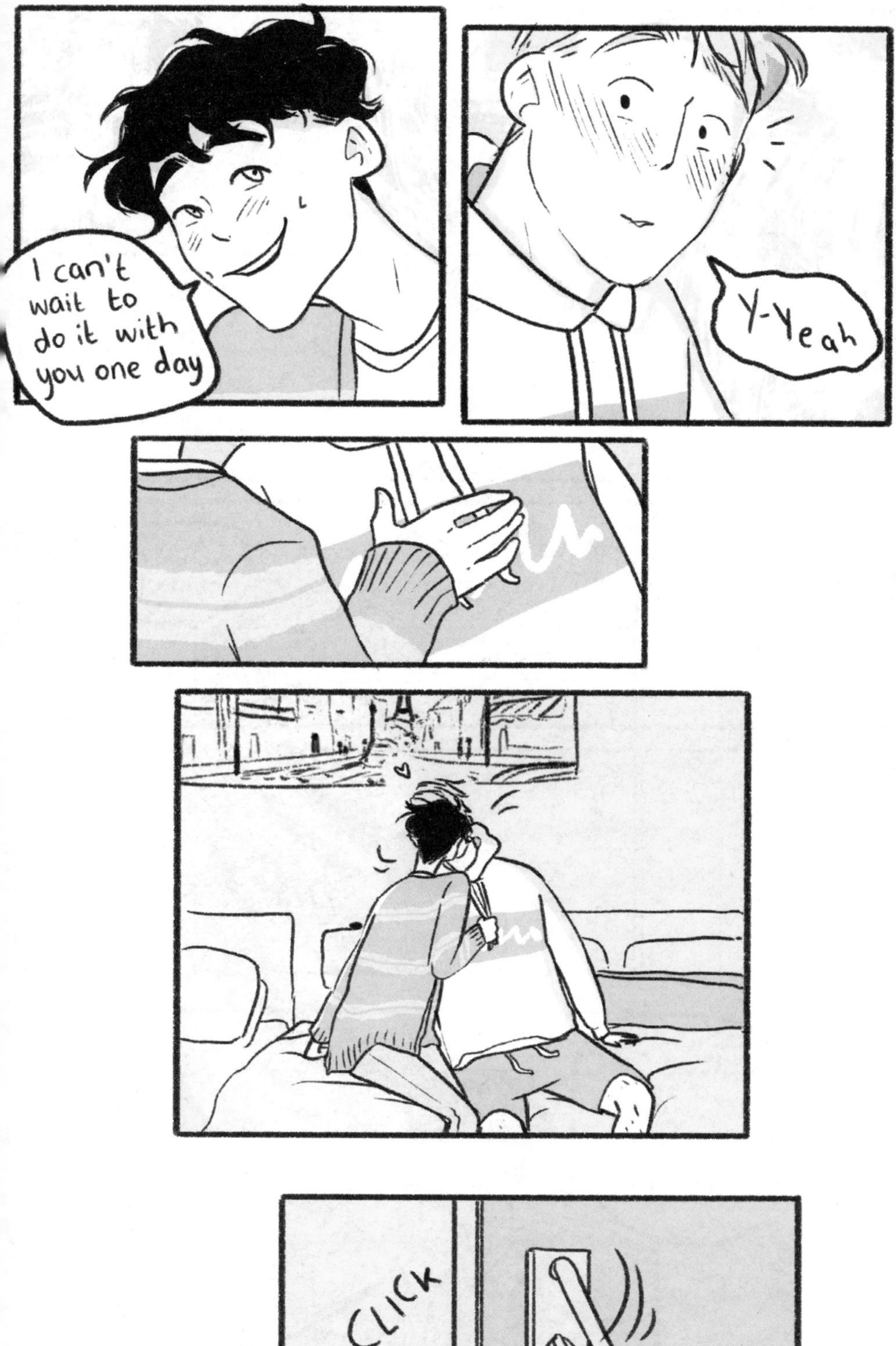
I can't wait to do it with you one day
Y-Yeah
CLICK

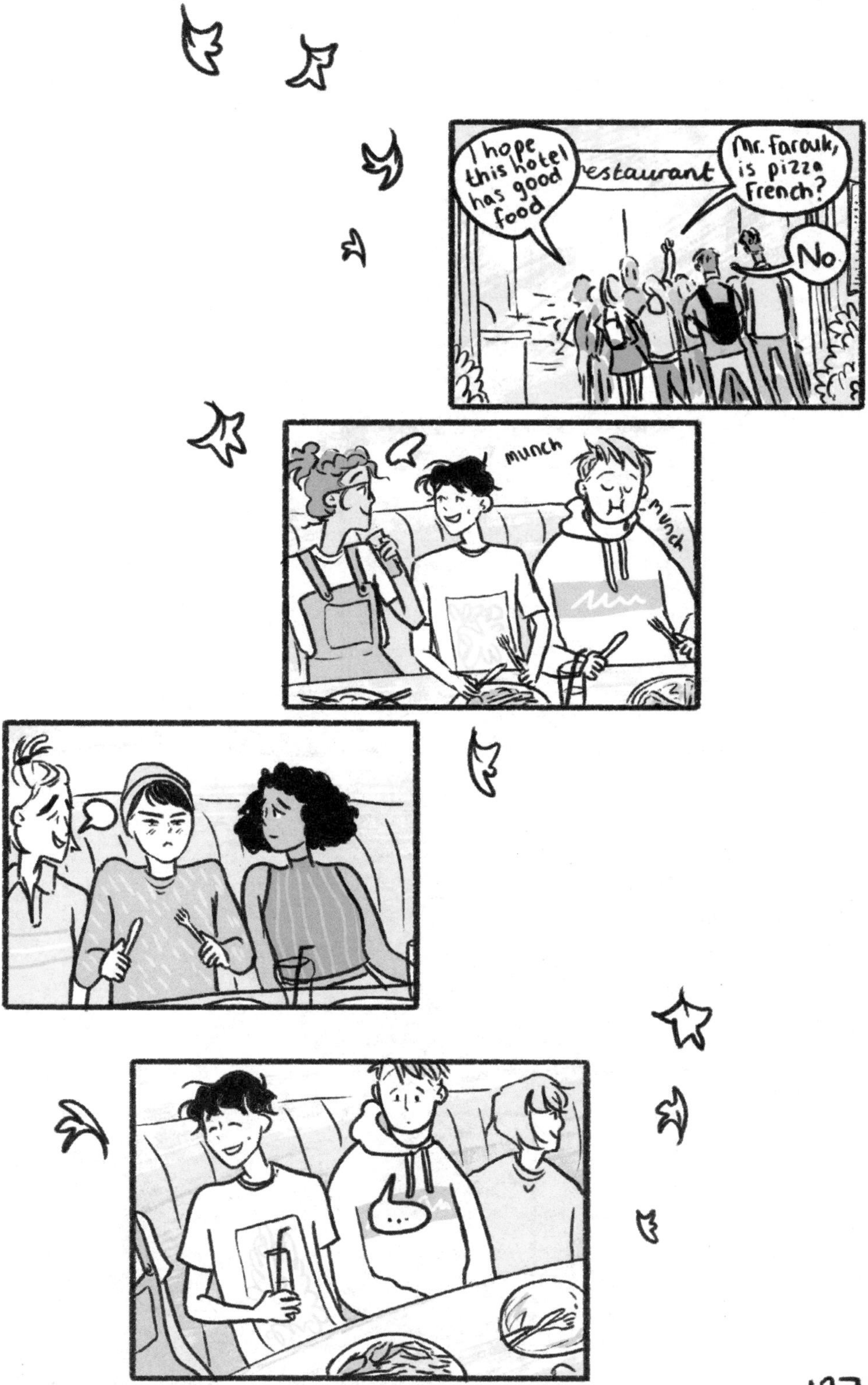
I hope this hotel has good food
estaurant
Mr. Farouk, is pizza French?
No.
munch
munch
...

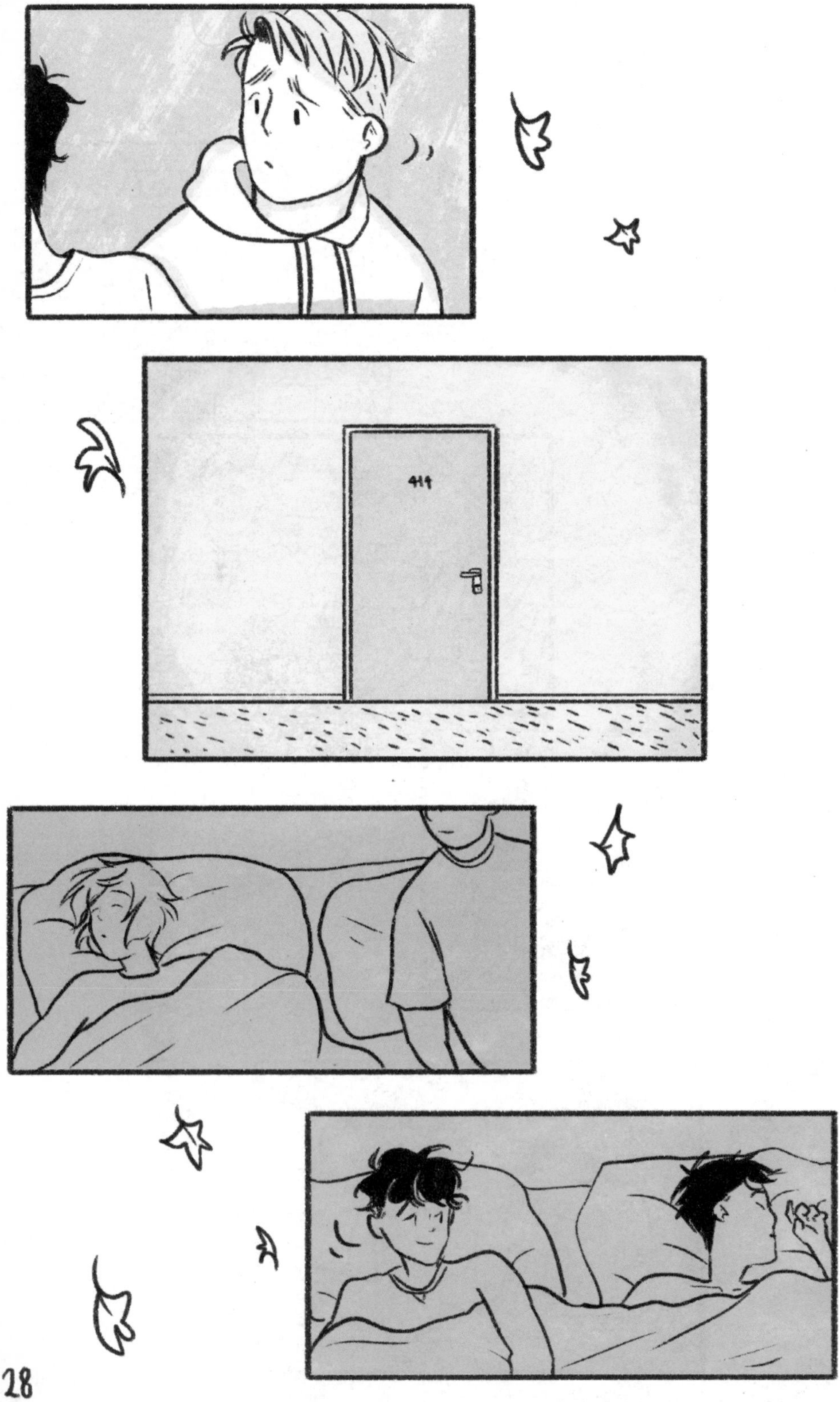
414

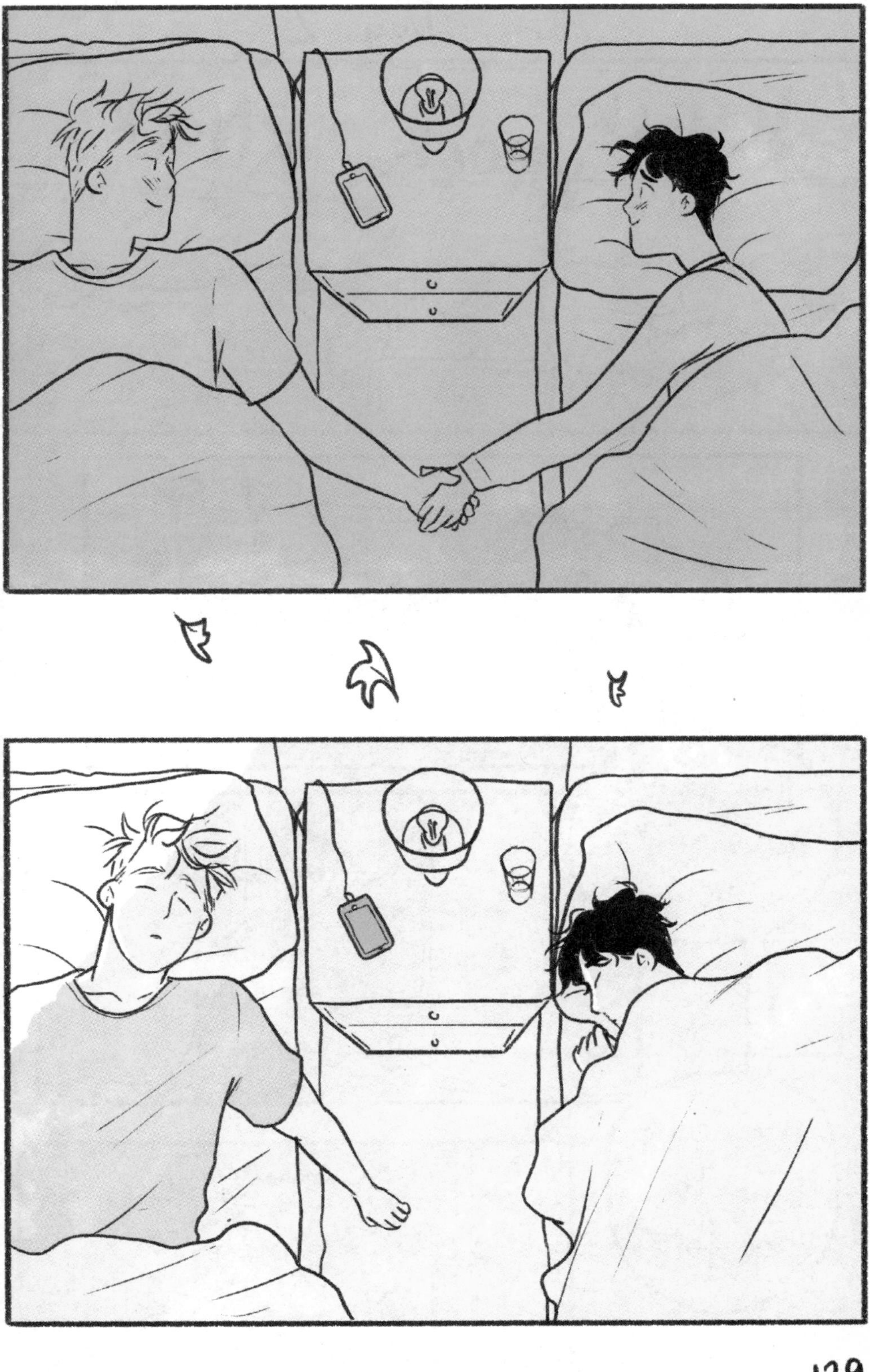

Paris - Day 2

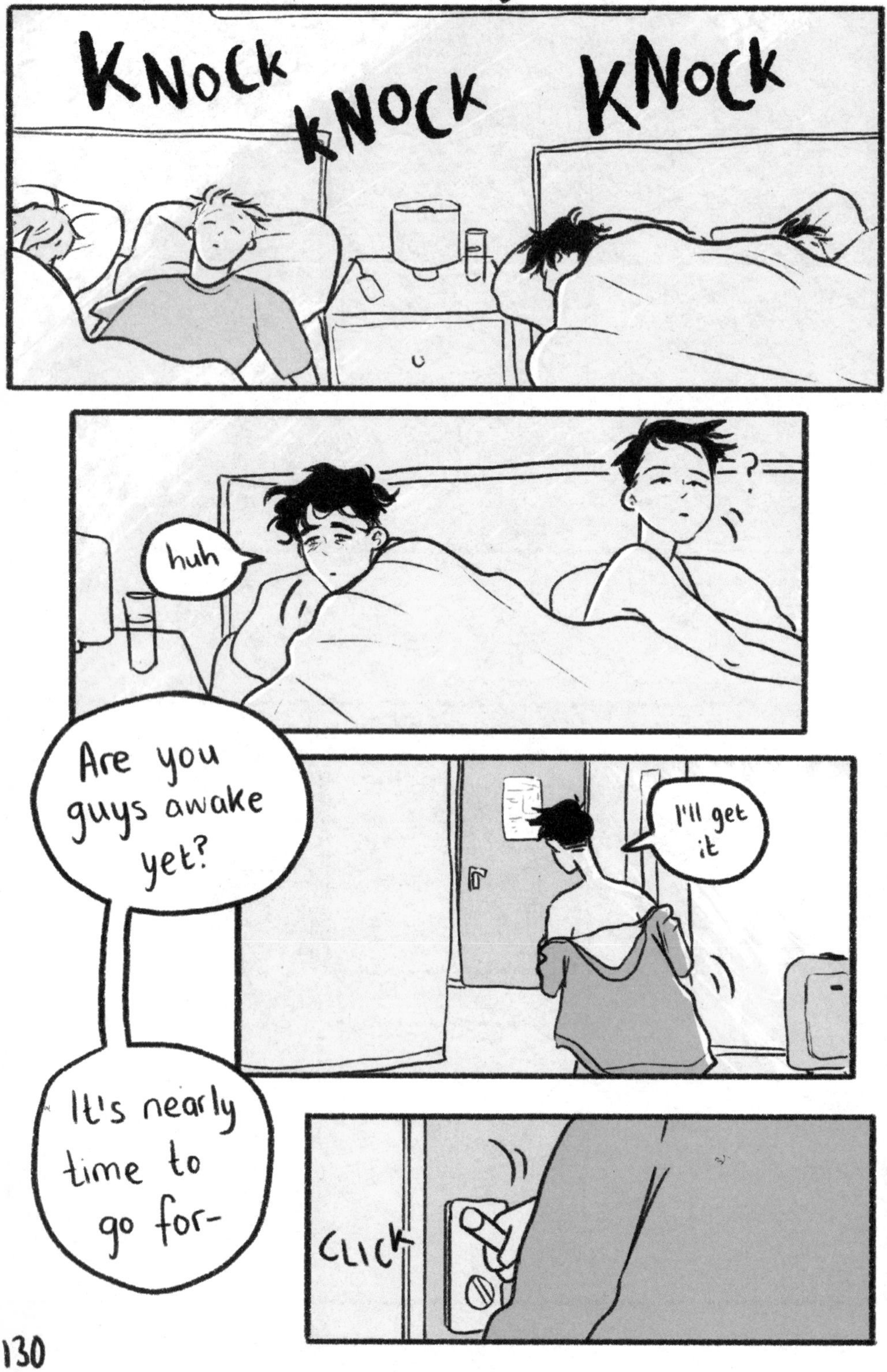
KNOCK
KNOCK
KNOCK
huh
?
Are you guys awake yet?
I'll get it
It's nearly time to go for-
CLICK

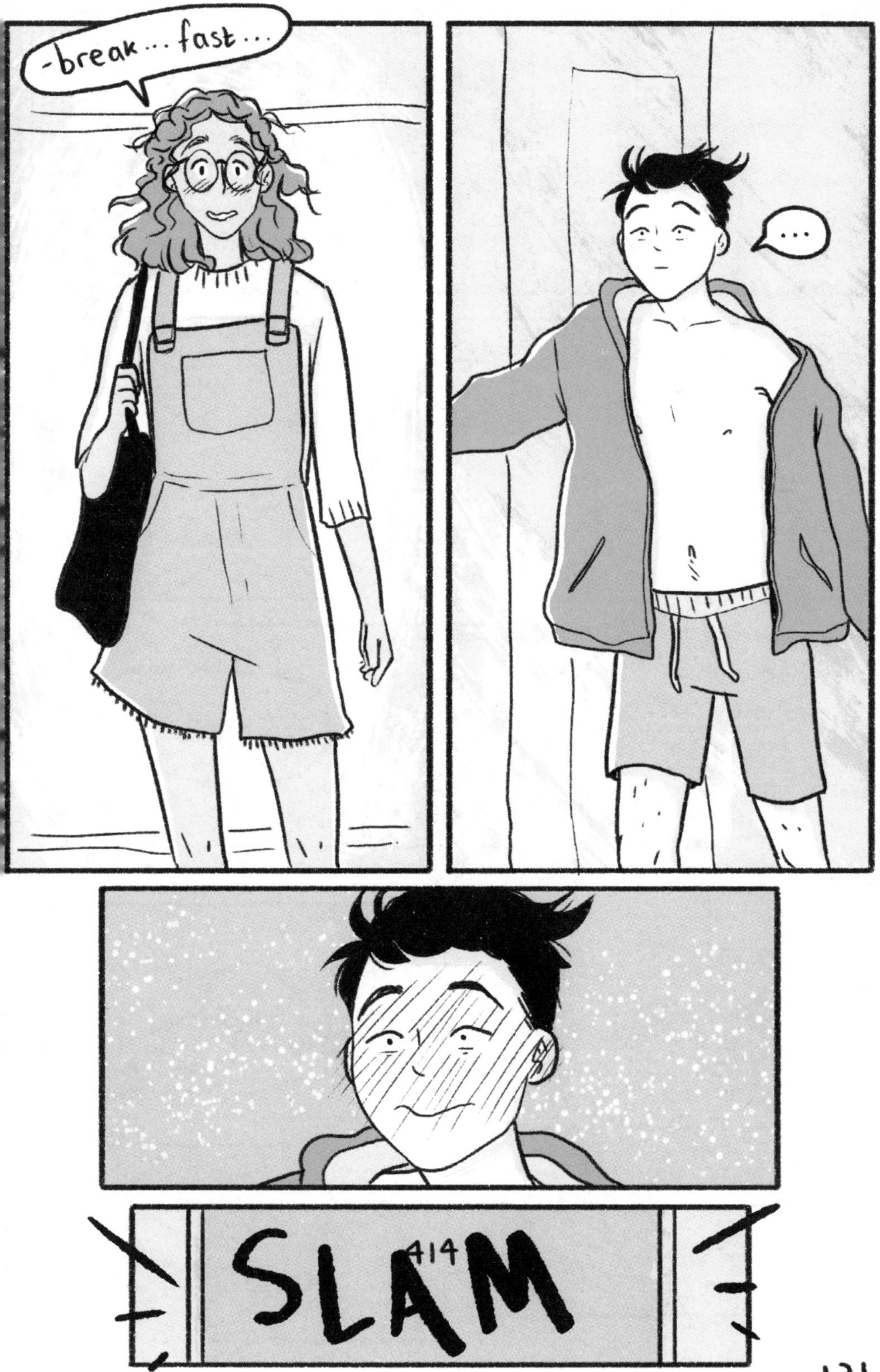
-break... fast...
...
414
SLAM

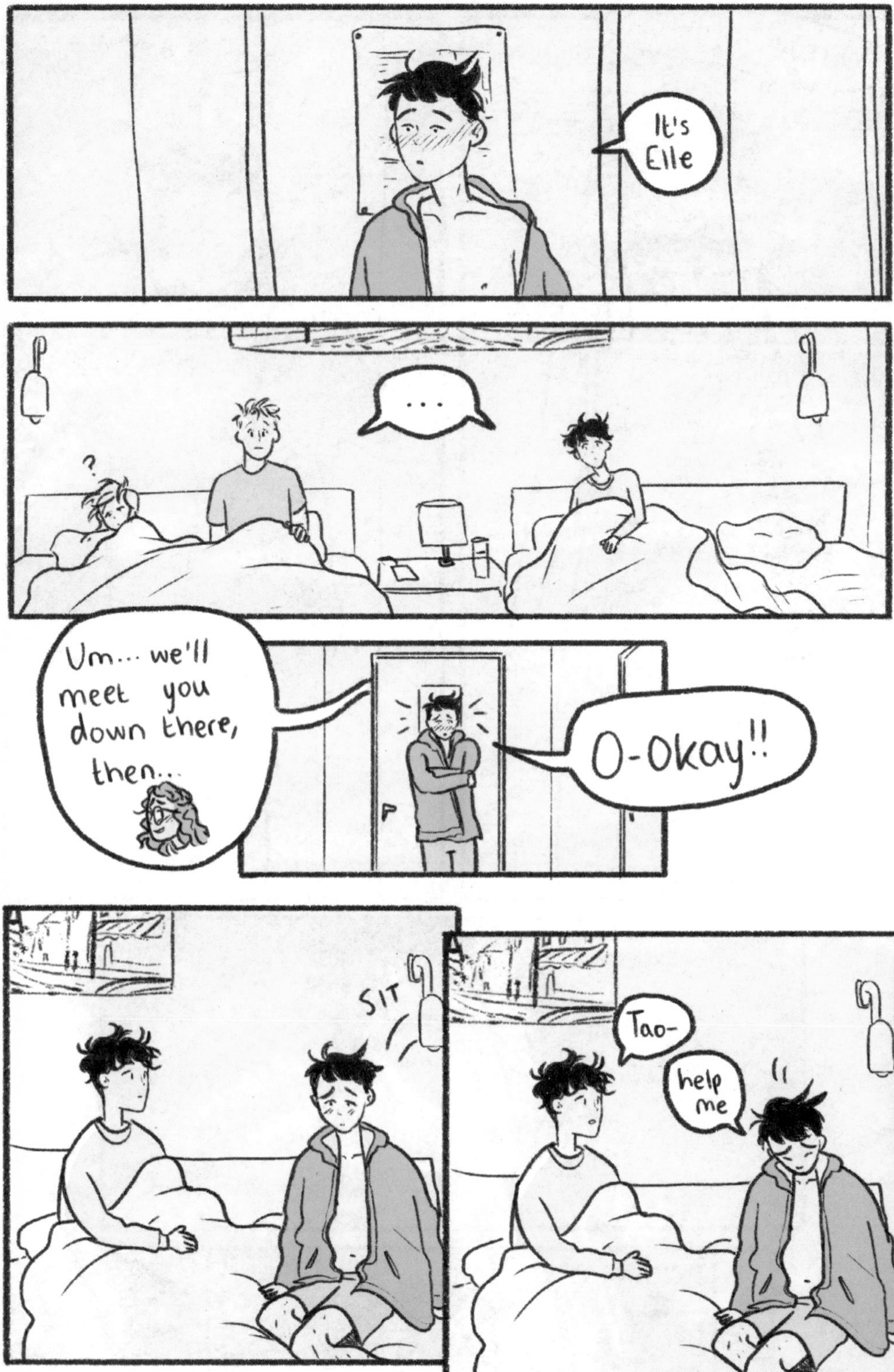
It's Elle
...
?
Um... we'll meet you down there, then...
O-Okay!!
SIT
Tao-
help me

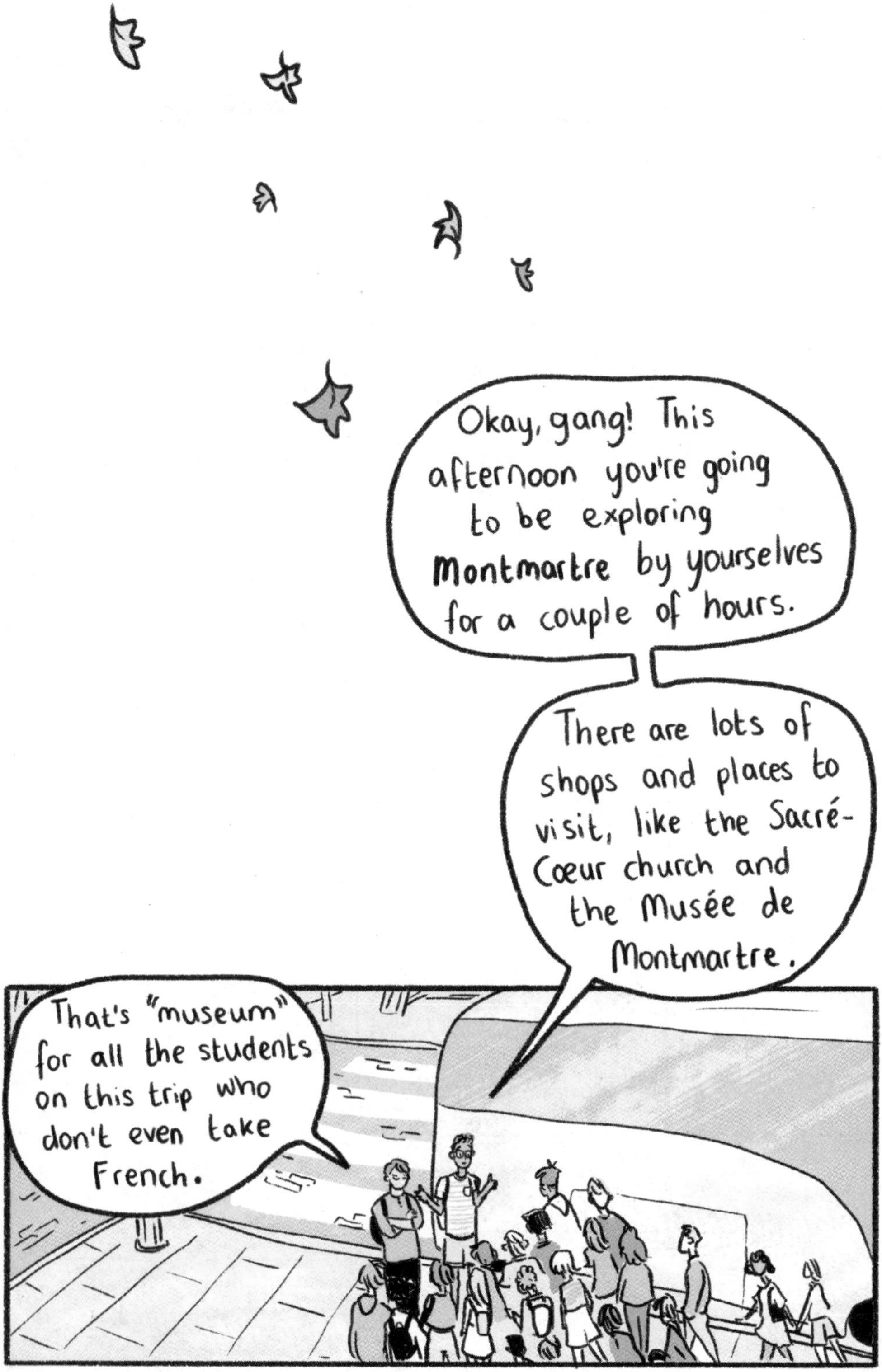

Okay, gang! This afternoon you're going to be exploring Montmartre by yourselves for a couple of hours.
There are lots of shops and places to visit, like the Sacré-Cœur church and the Musée de Montmartre.
That's "museum" for all the students on this trip who don't even take French.

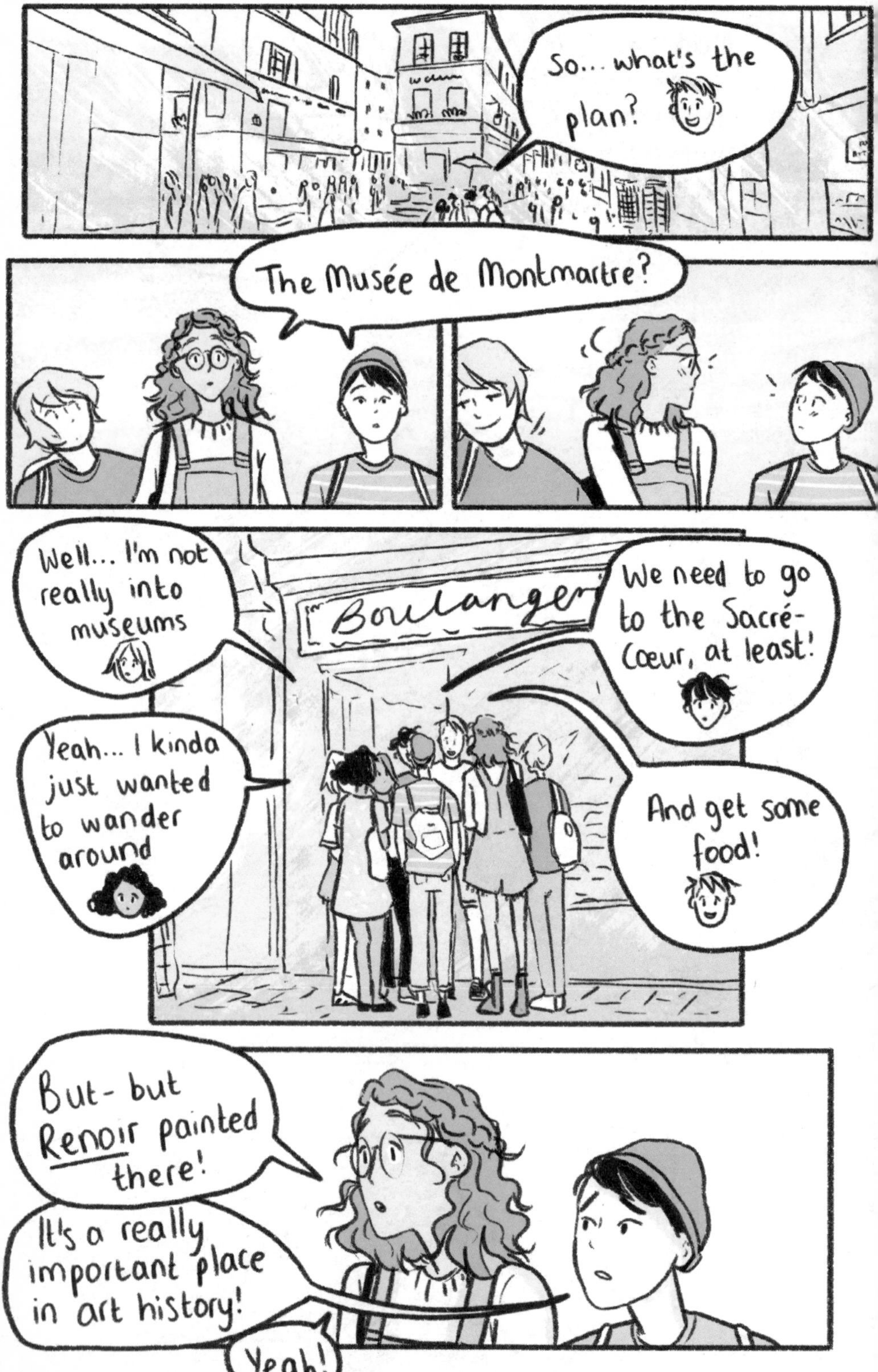
So... what's the plan?
The Musée de Montmartre?
Well... I'm not really into museums
Boulanger
We need to go to the Sacré-Cœur, at least!
Yeah... I kinda just wanted to wander around
And get some food!
But- but Renoir painted there!
It's a really important place in art history!
Yeah!

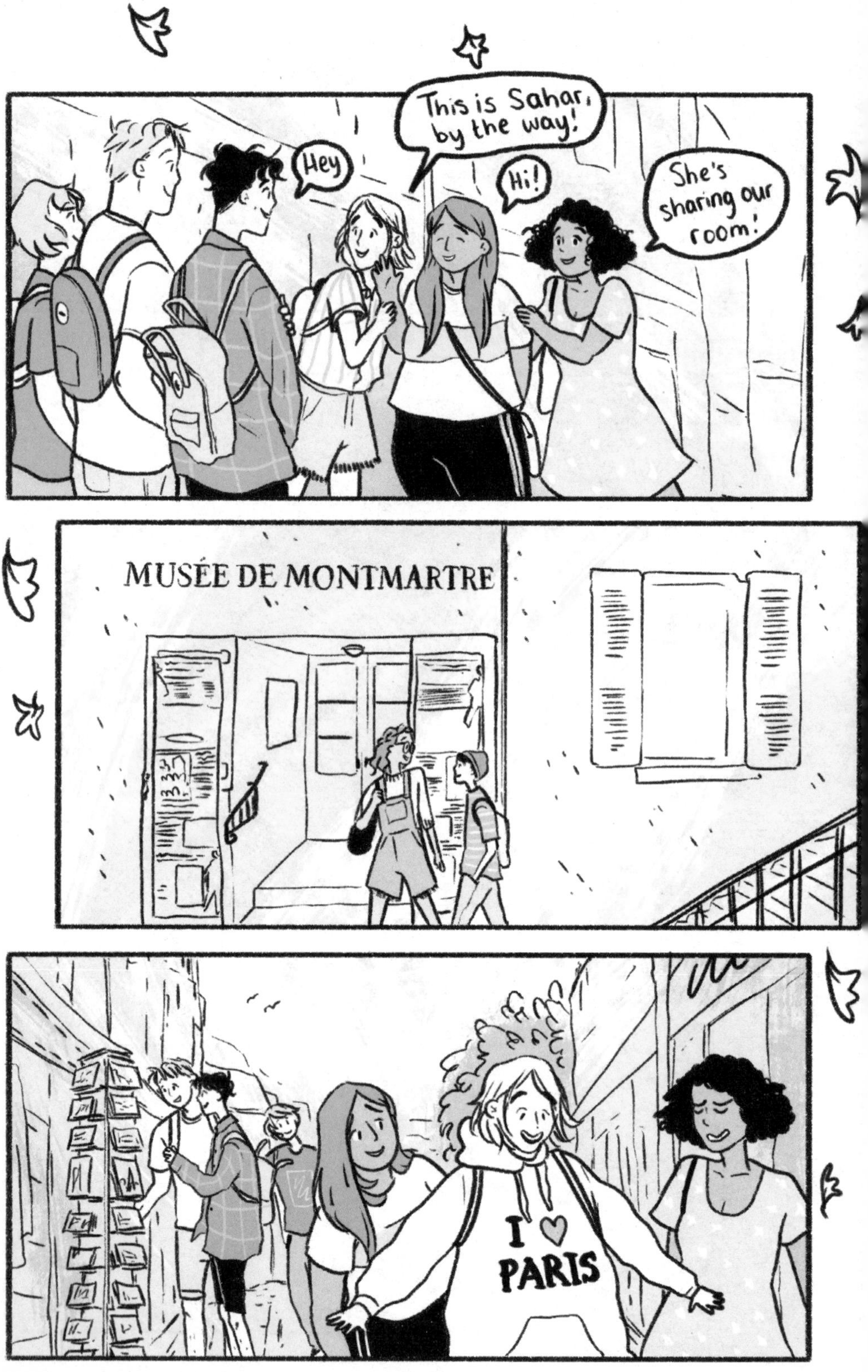
Hey
This is Sahar, by the way!
Hi!
She's sharing our room!
MUSÉE DE MONTMARTRE
I ♡ PARIS

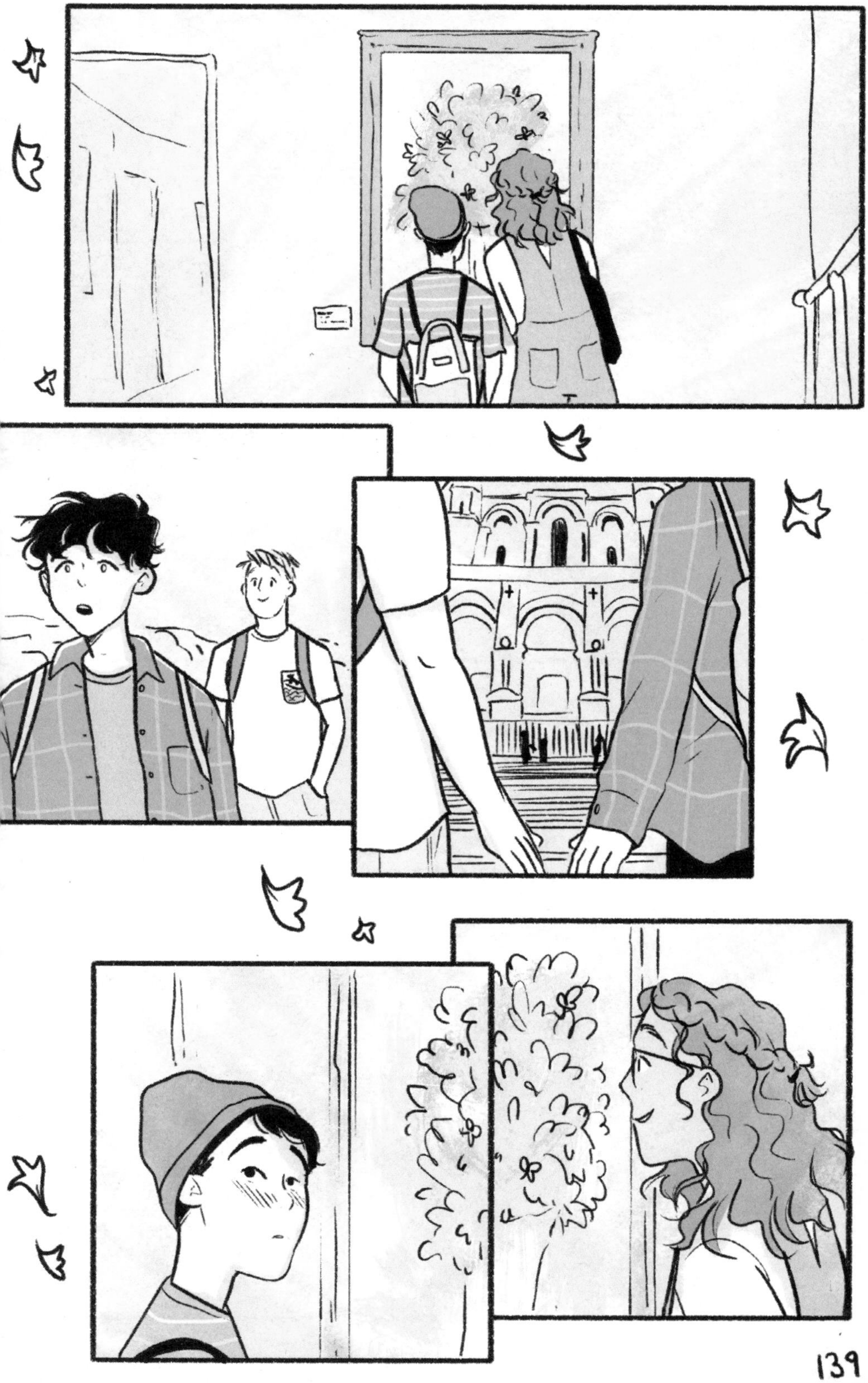

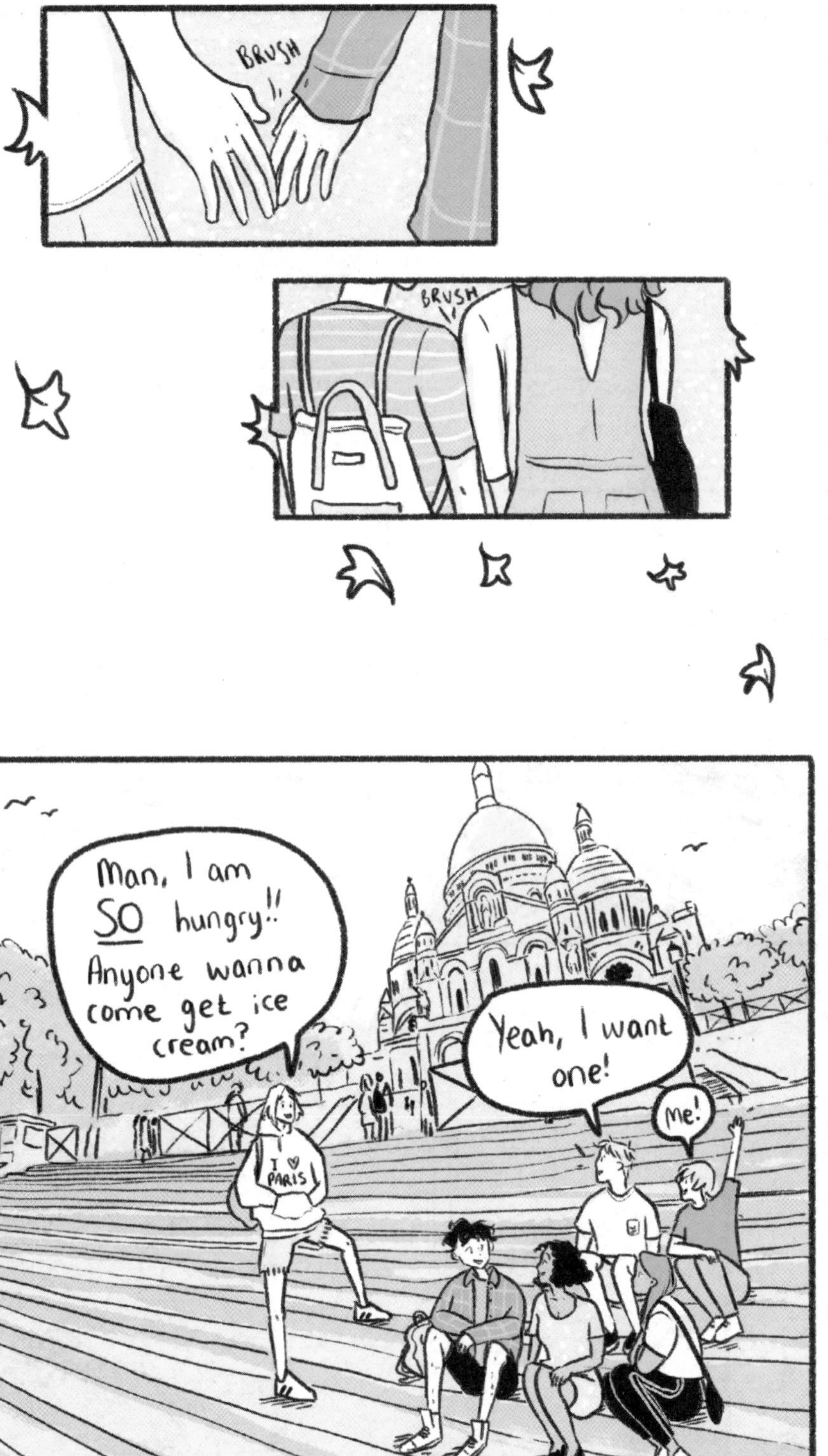
BRUSH
BRUSH
Man, I am SO hungry!! Anyone wanna come get ice cream?
I ♡ PARIS
Yeah, I want one!
Me!

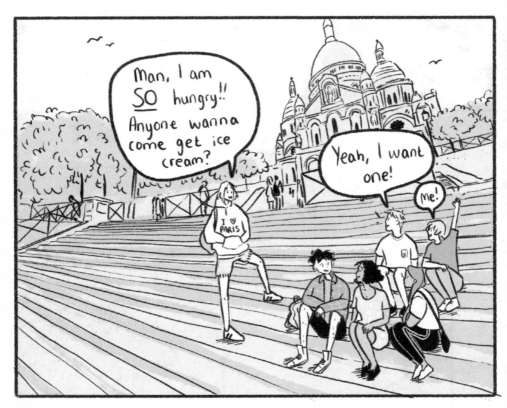

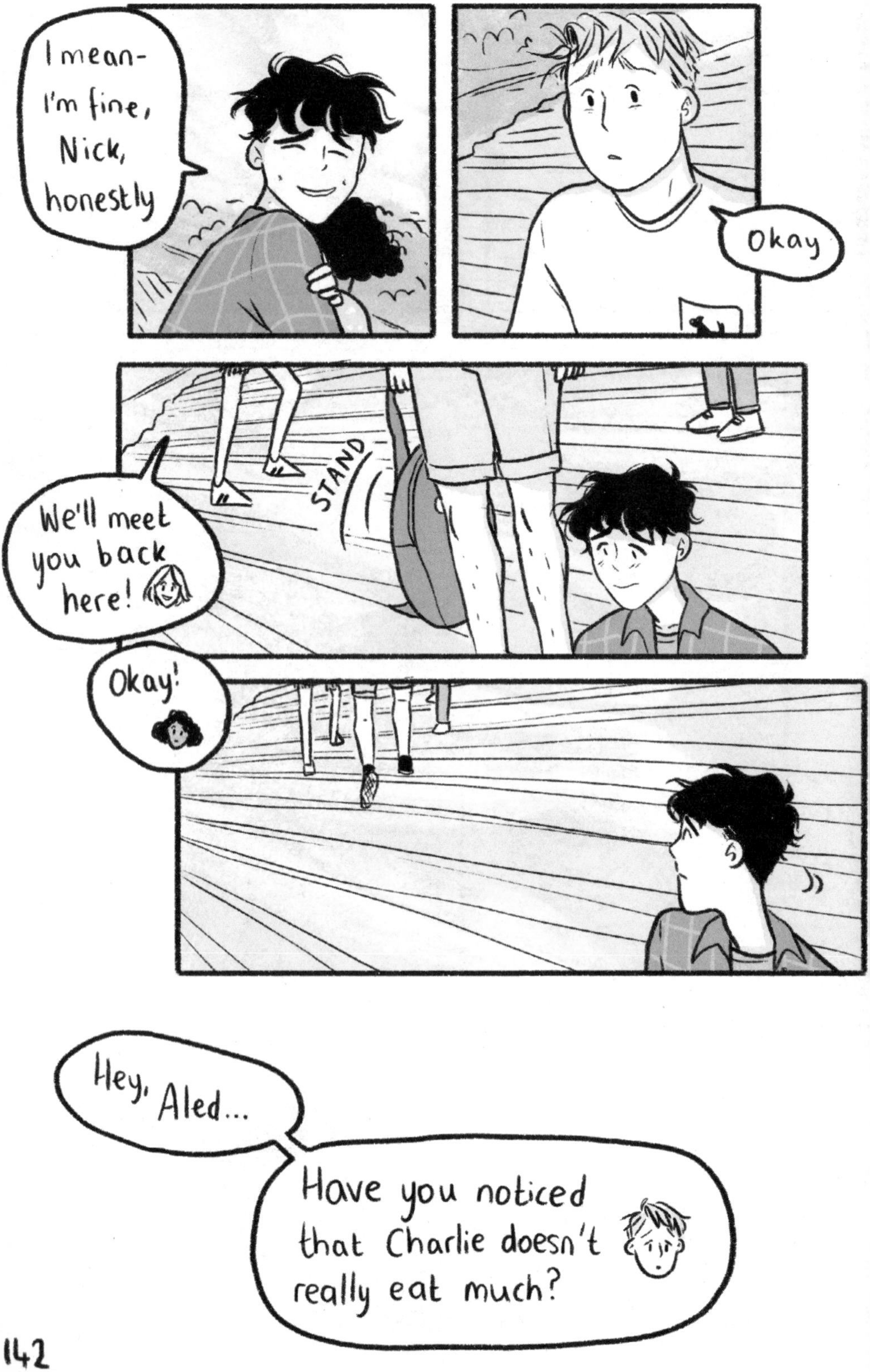
I mean- I'm fine, Nick, honestly
Okay
STAND
We'll meet you back here!
Okay!
Hey, Aled...
Have you noticed that Charlie doesn't really eat much?

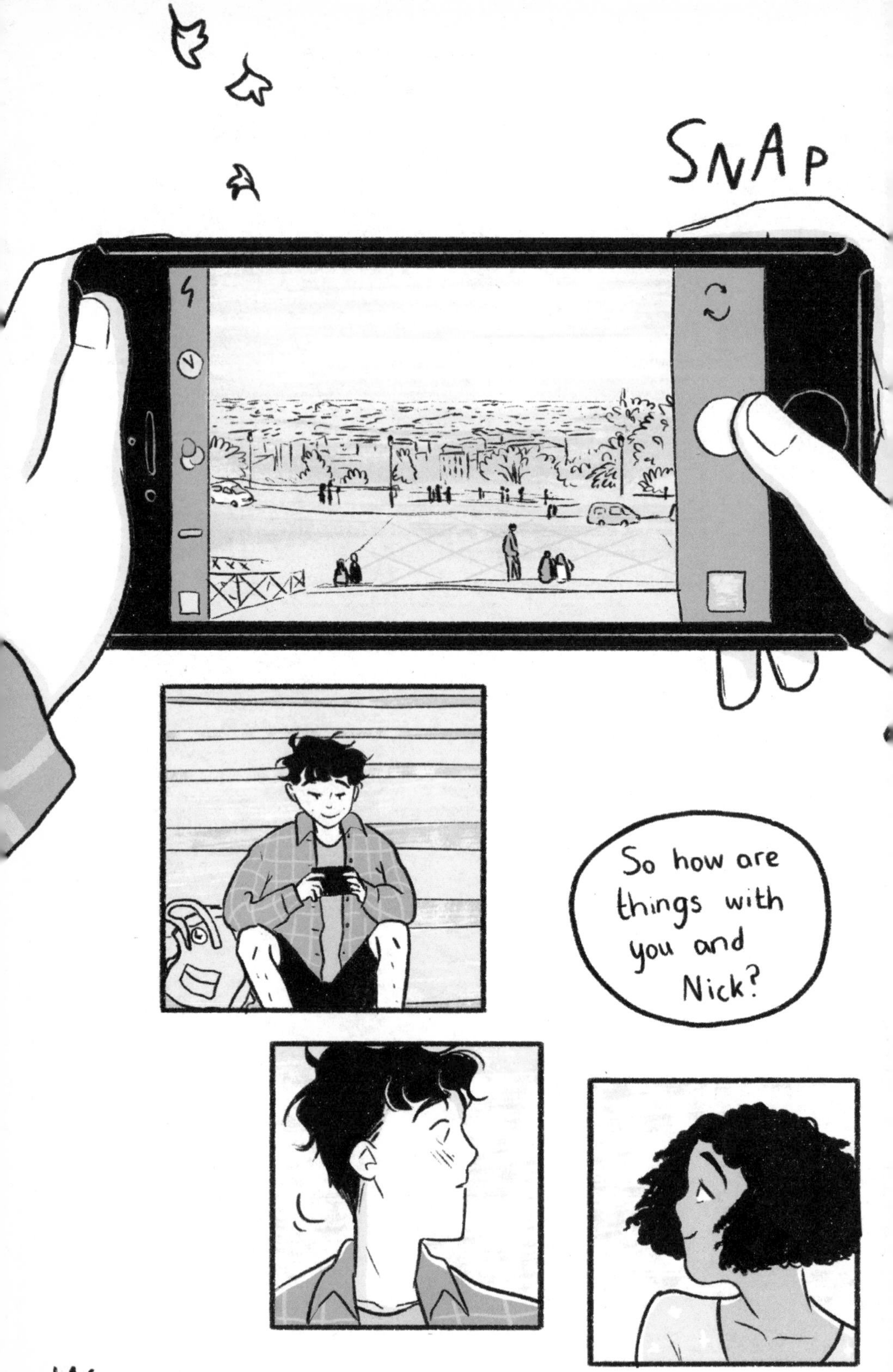
SNAP
So how are things with you and Nick?

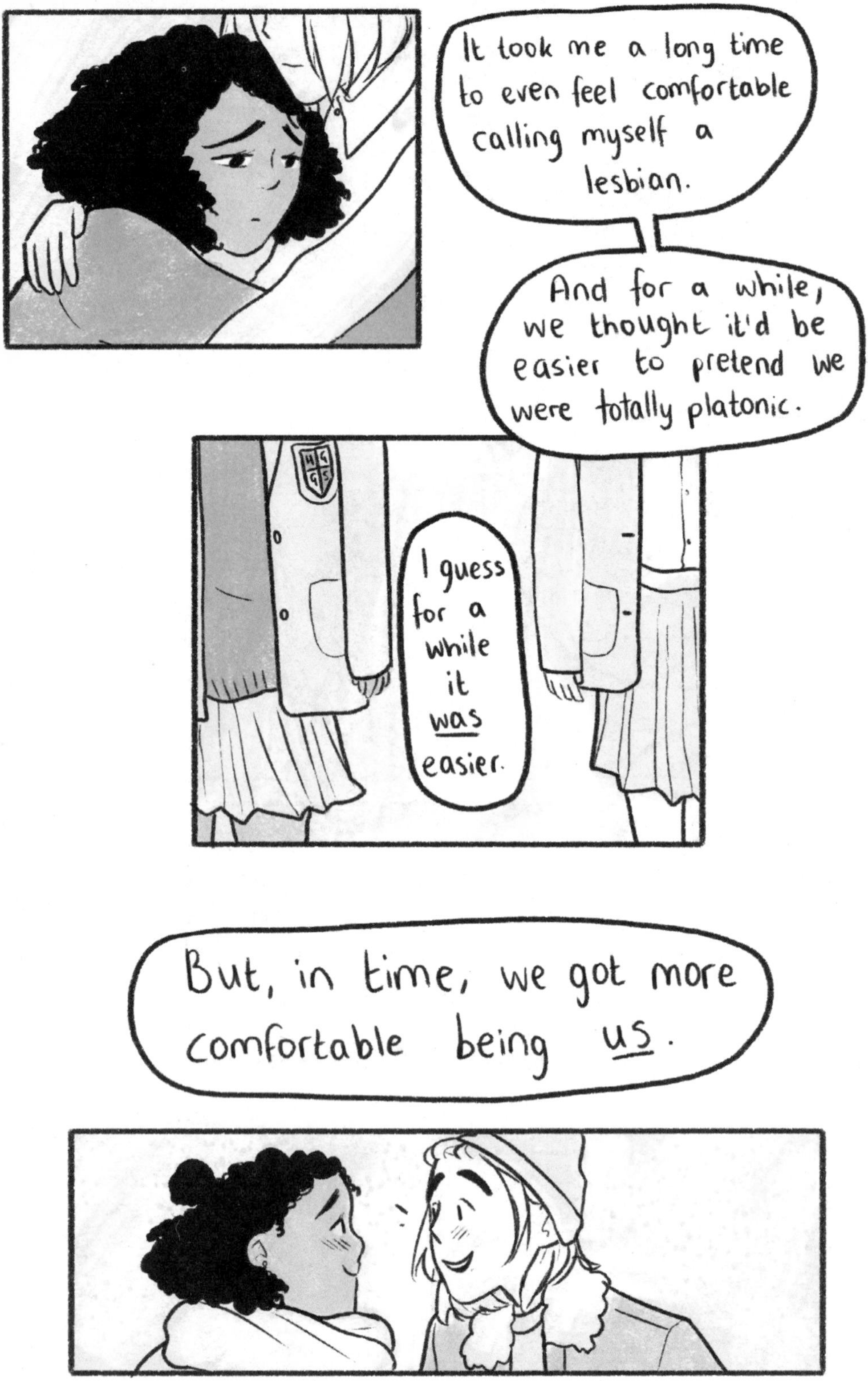
It took me a long time to even feel comfortable calling myself a lesbian.
And for a while, we thought it'd be easier to pretend we were totally platonic.
I guess for a while it was easier.
But, in time, we got more comfortable being us.

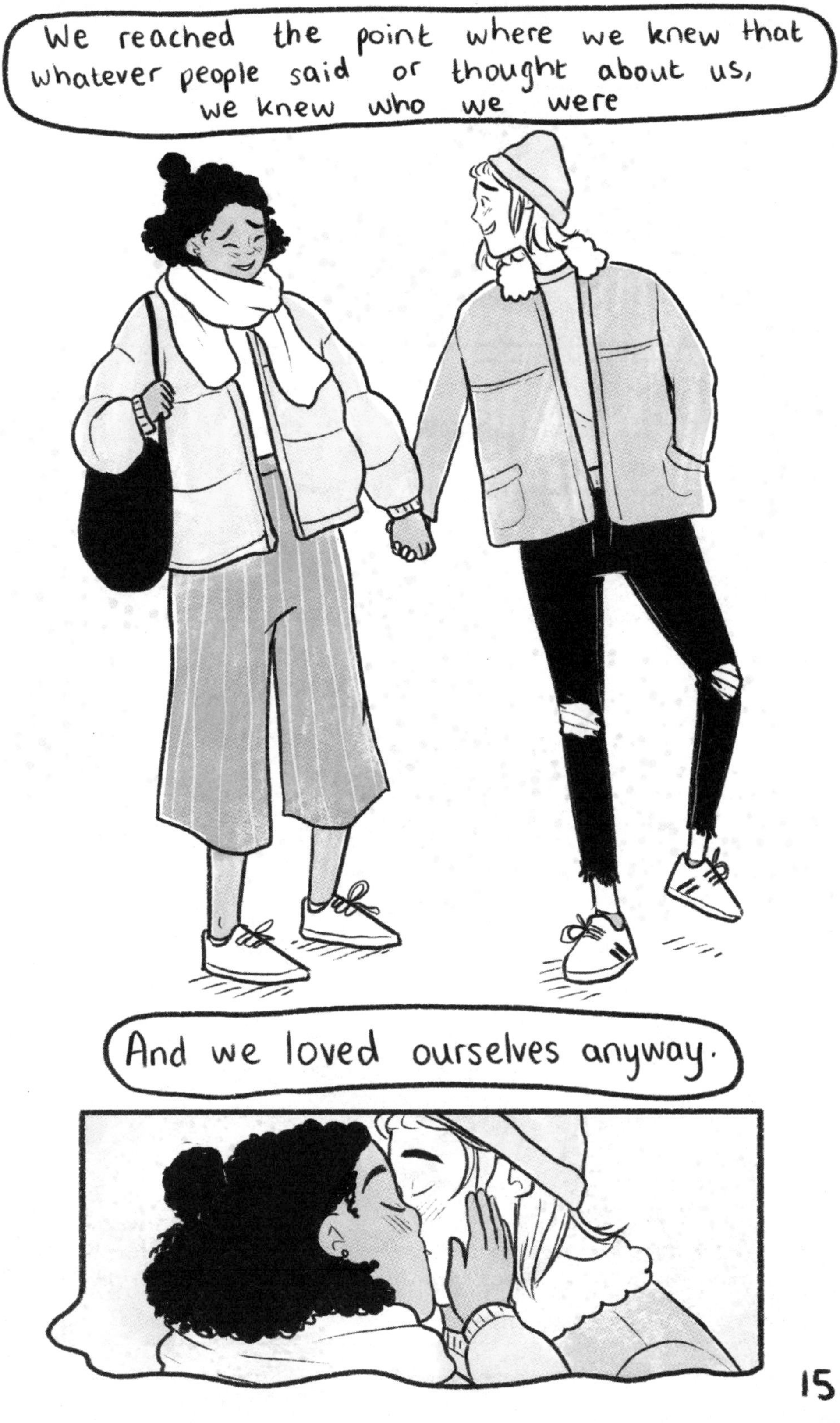
We reached the point where we knew that whatever people said or thought about us, we knew who we were
And we loved ourselves anyway.

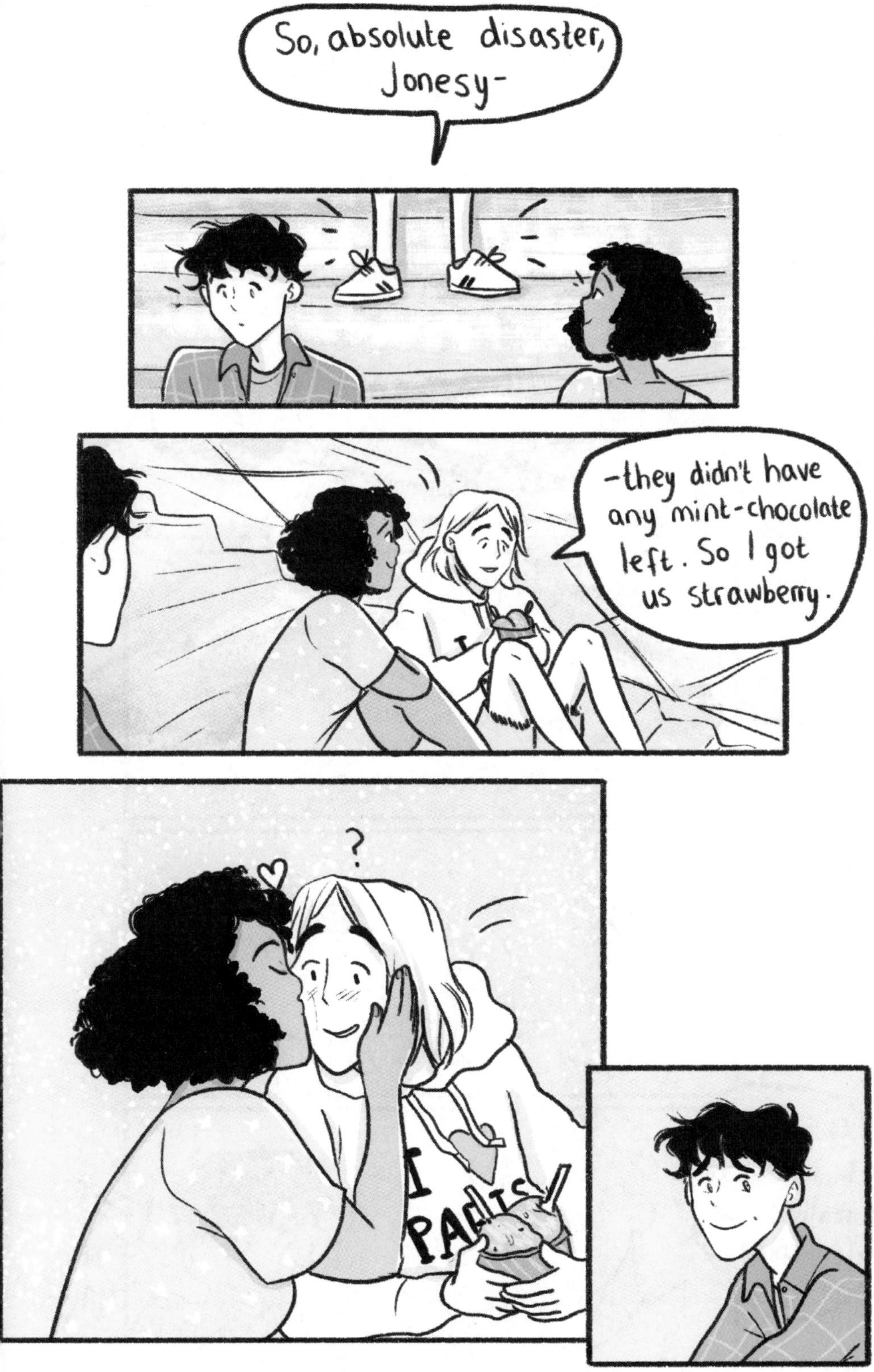
So, absolute disaster, Jonesy-
-they didn't have any mint-chocolate left. So I got us strawberry.

156

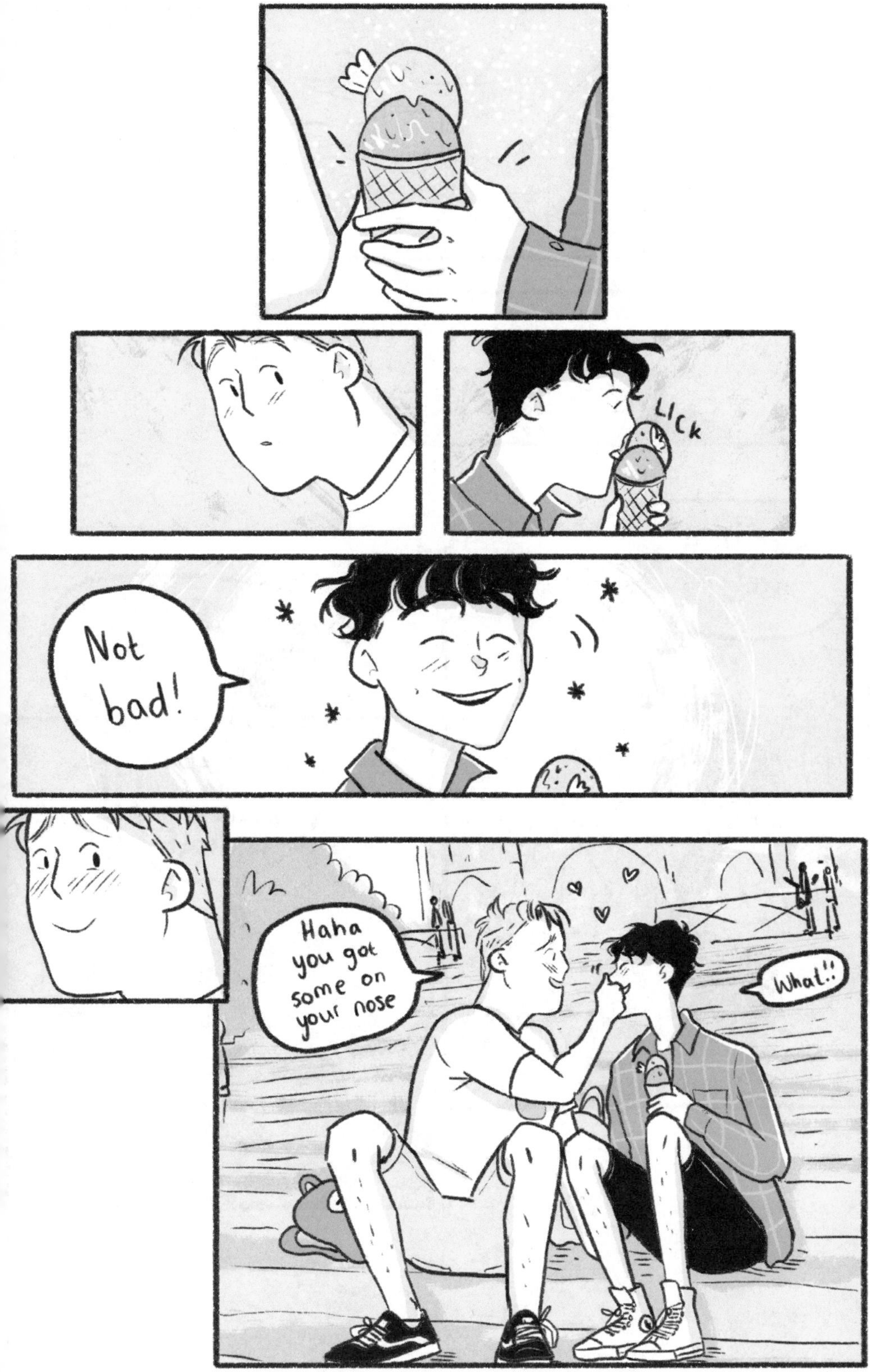
LICK
Not bad!
Haha you got some on your nose
What!!

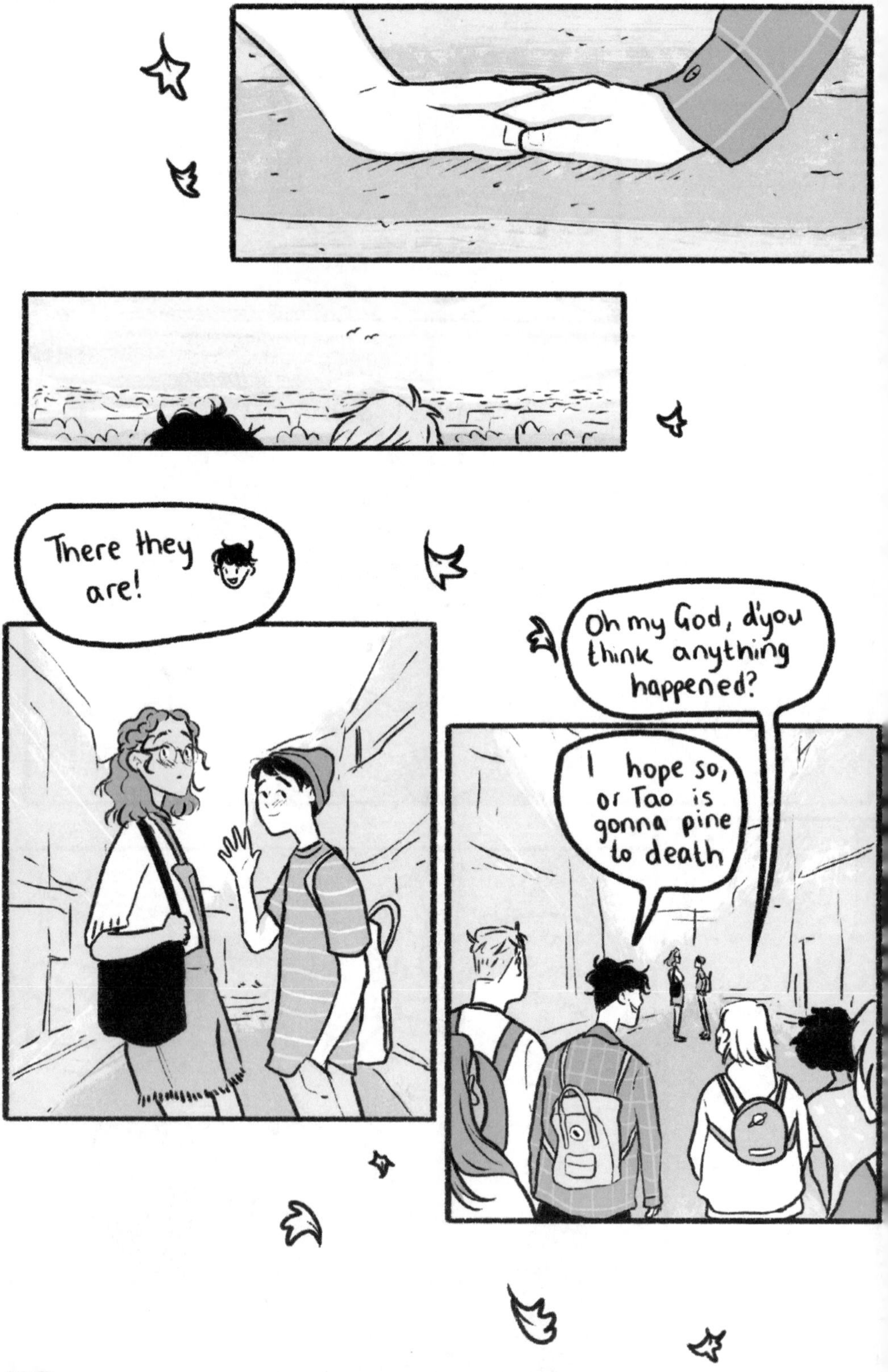
There they are!
Oh my God, d'you think anything happened?
I hope so, or Tao is gonna pine to death

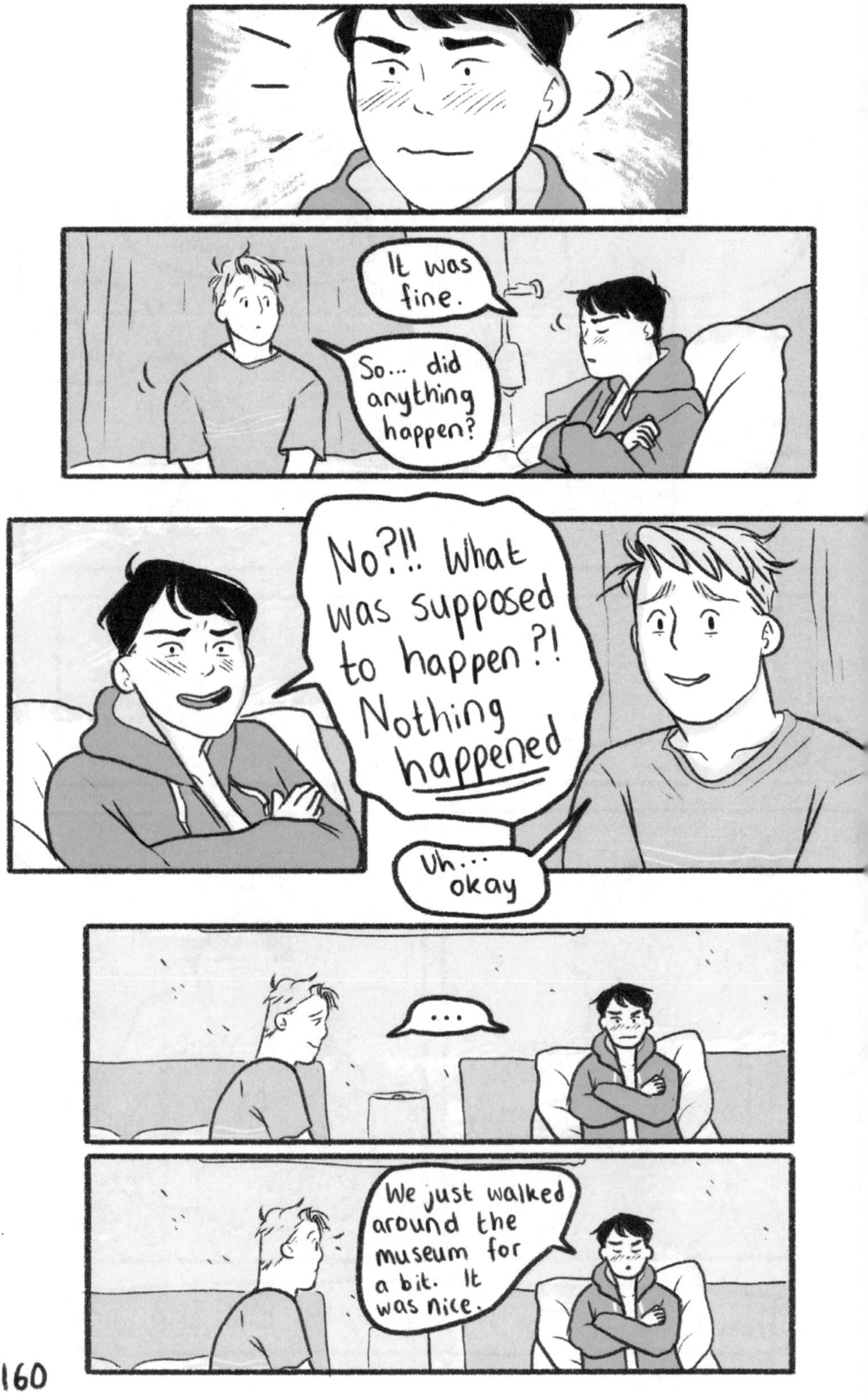
It was fine.
So... did anything happen?
No?!! What was supposed to happen?! Nothing happened
Uh... okay
...
We just walked around the museum for a bit. It was nice.

161

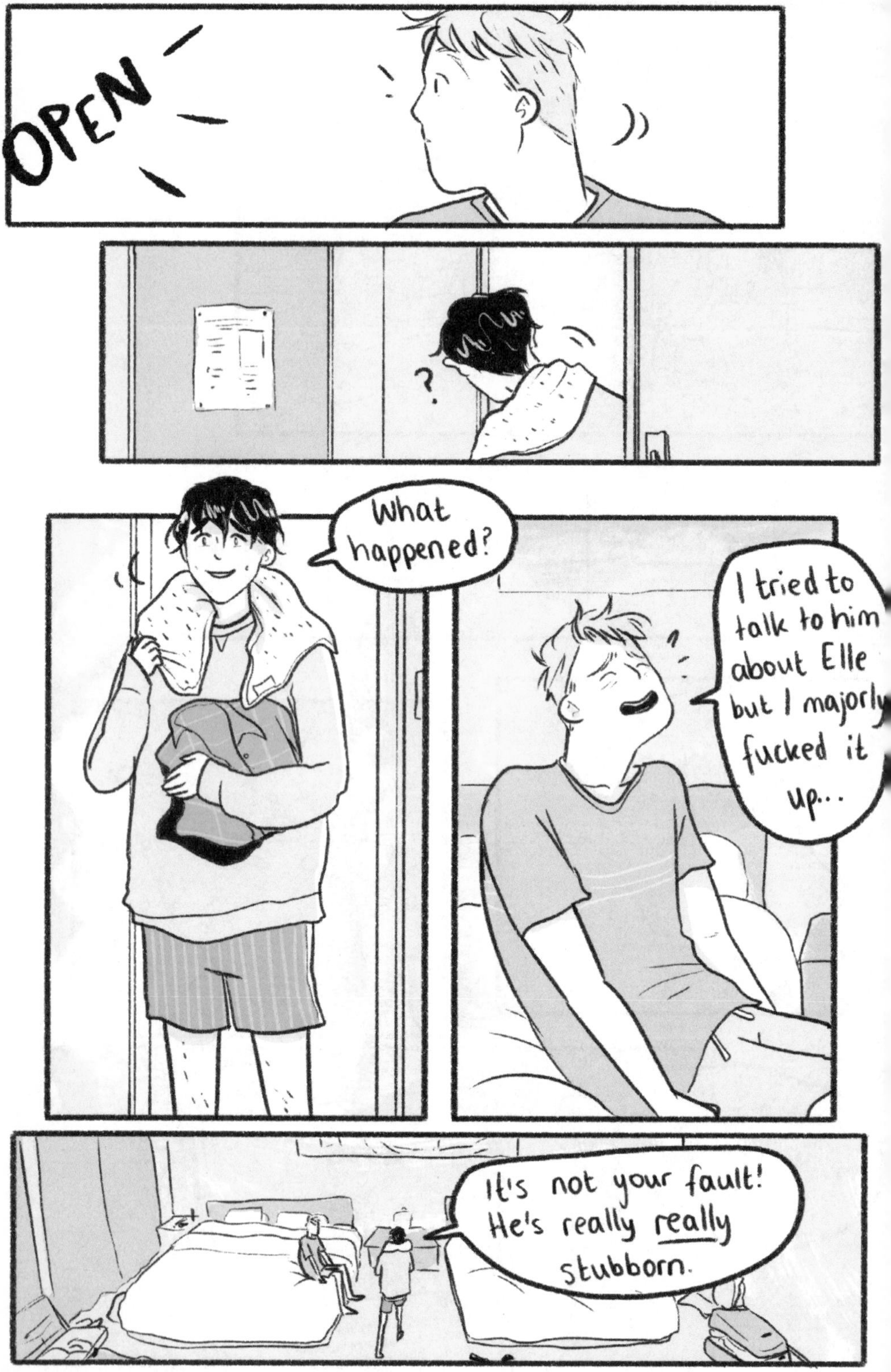
OPEN
What happened?
I tried to talk to him about Elle but I majorly fucked it up...
It's not your fault! He's really really stubborn.

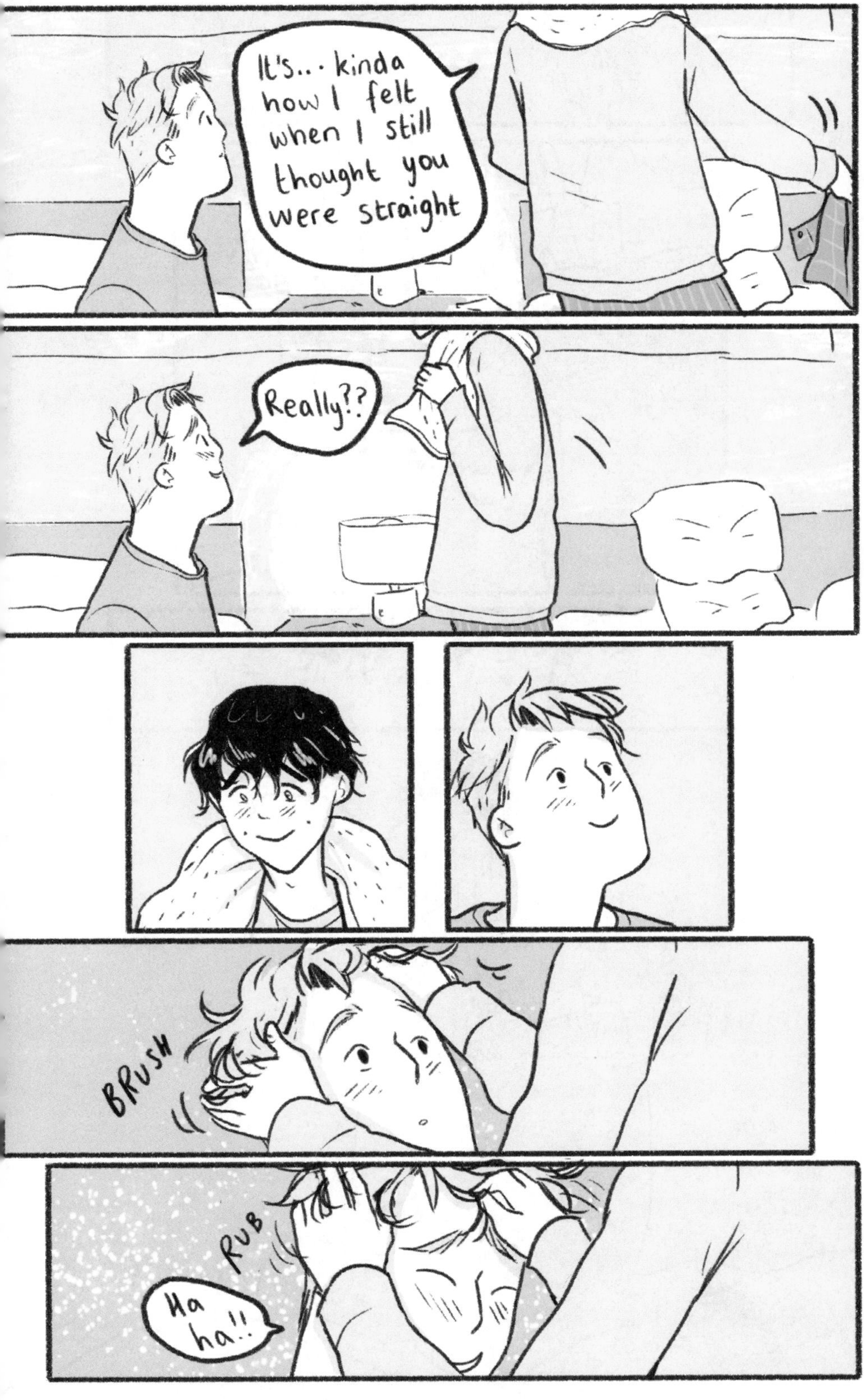
It's... kinda how I felt when I still thought you were straight
Really??
BRUSH
RUB
Ha ha!!

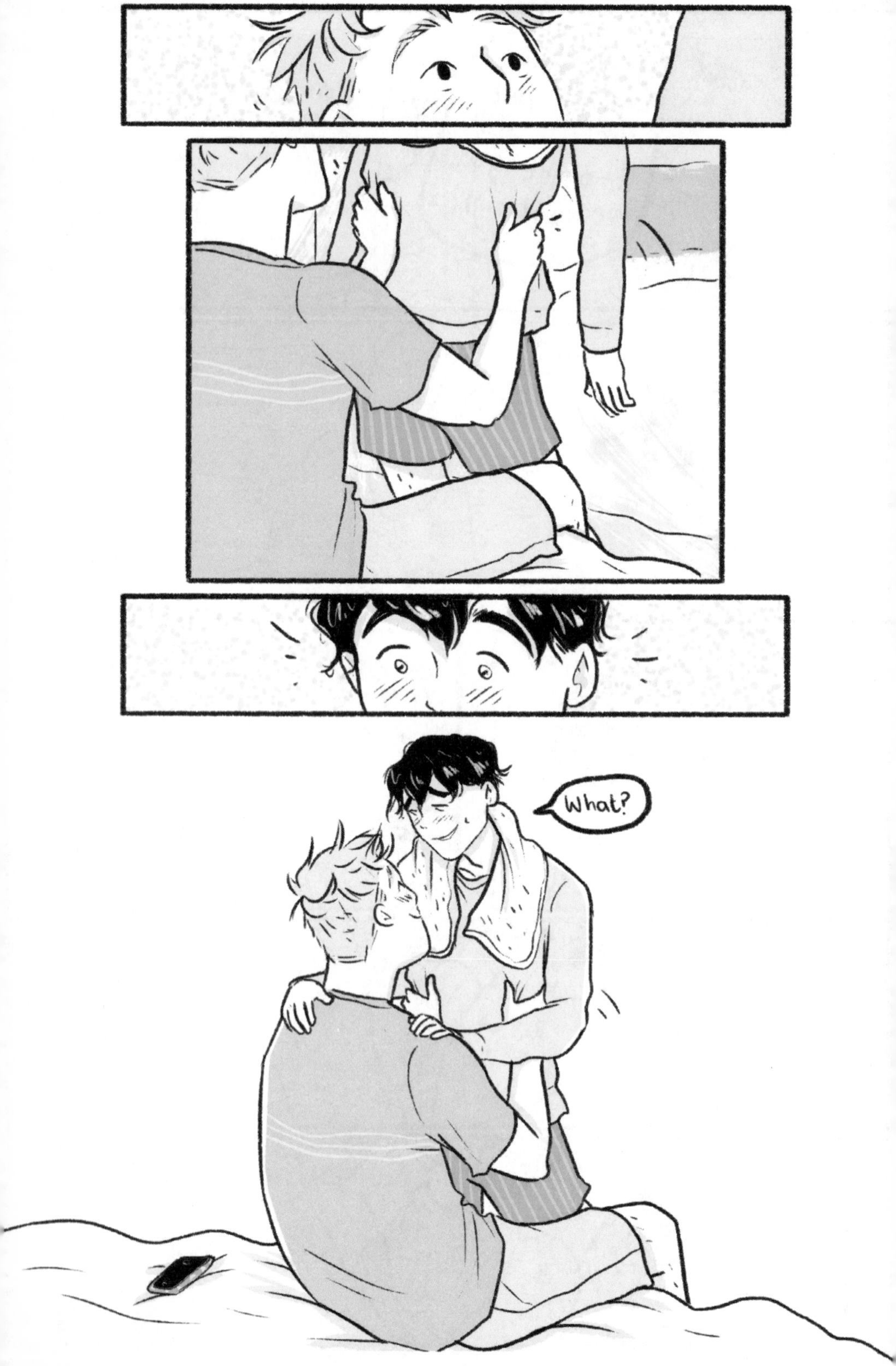
What?

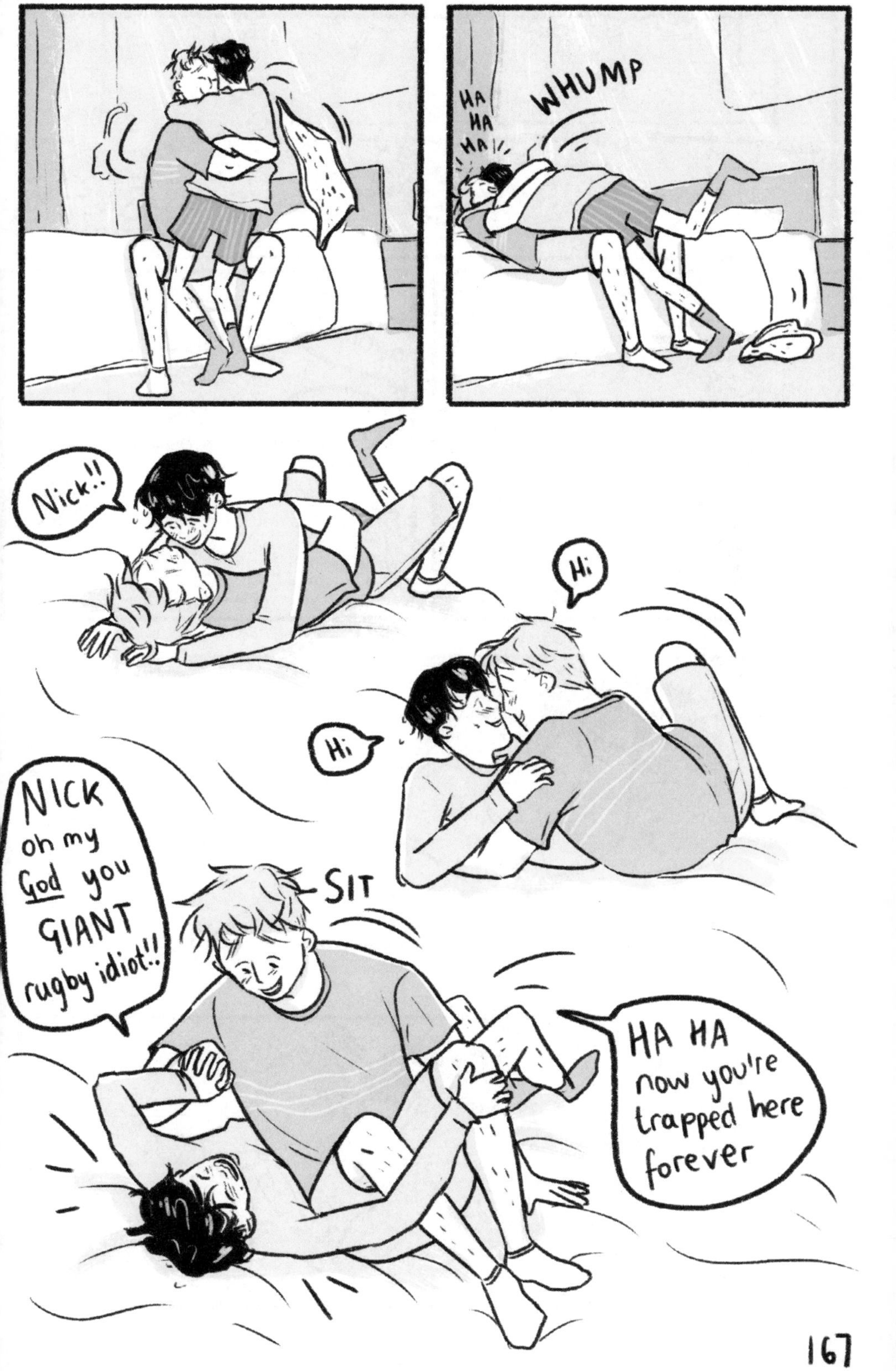
HA
HA
HA
WHUMP
Nick!!
Hi
Hi
NICK
oh my
God you
GIANT
rugby idiot!!
SIT
HA HA
now you're
trapped here
forever

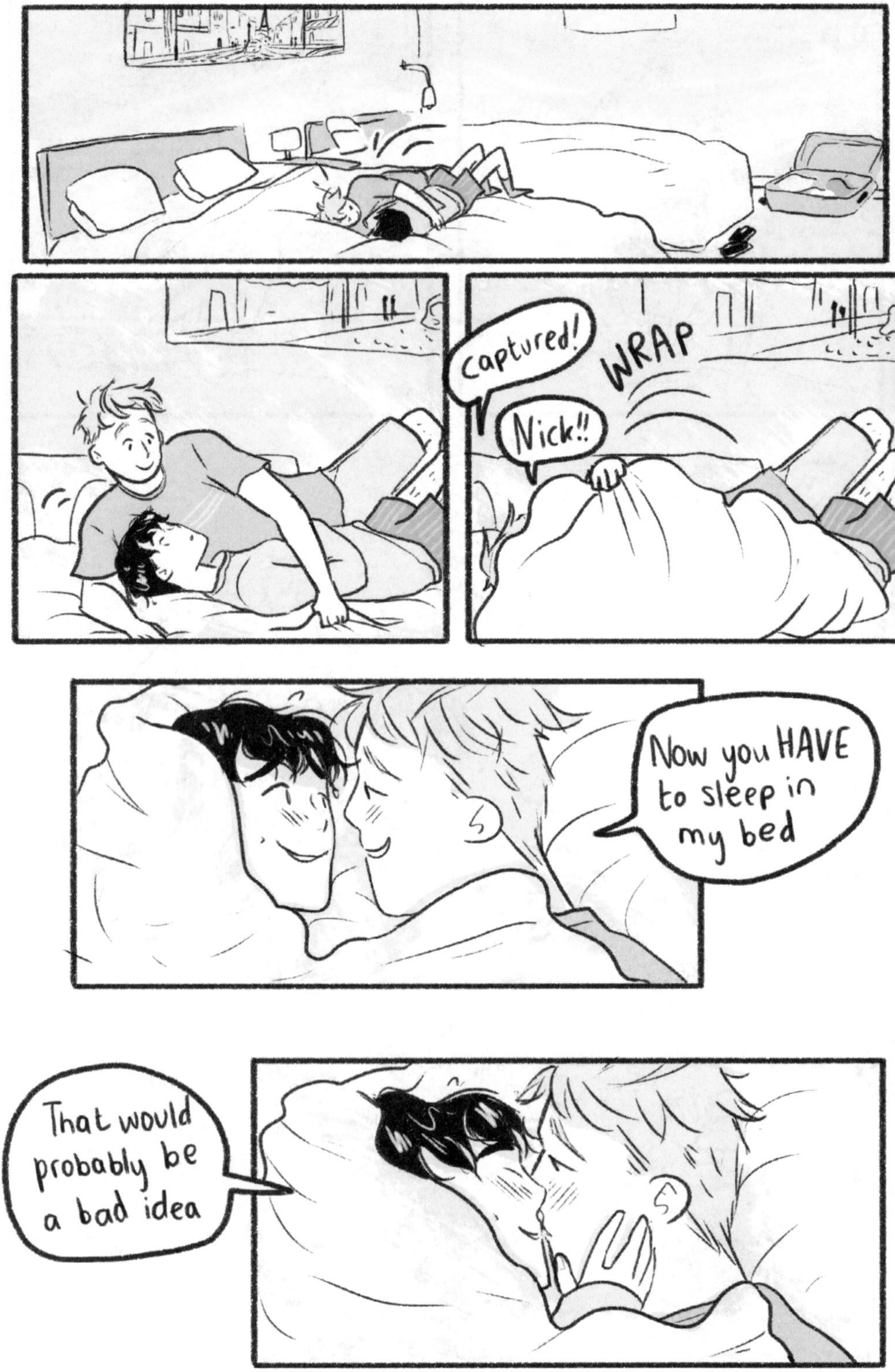
Captured!
WRAP
Nick!!
Now you HAVE to sleep in my bed
That would probably be a bad idea

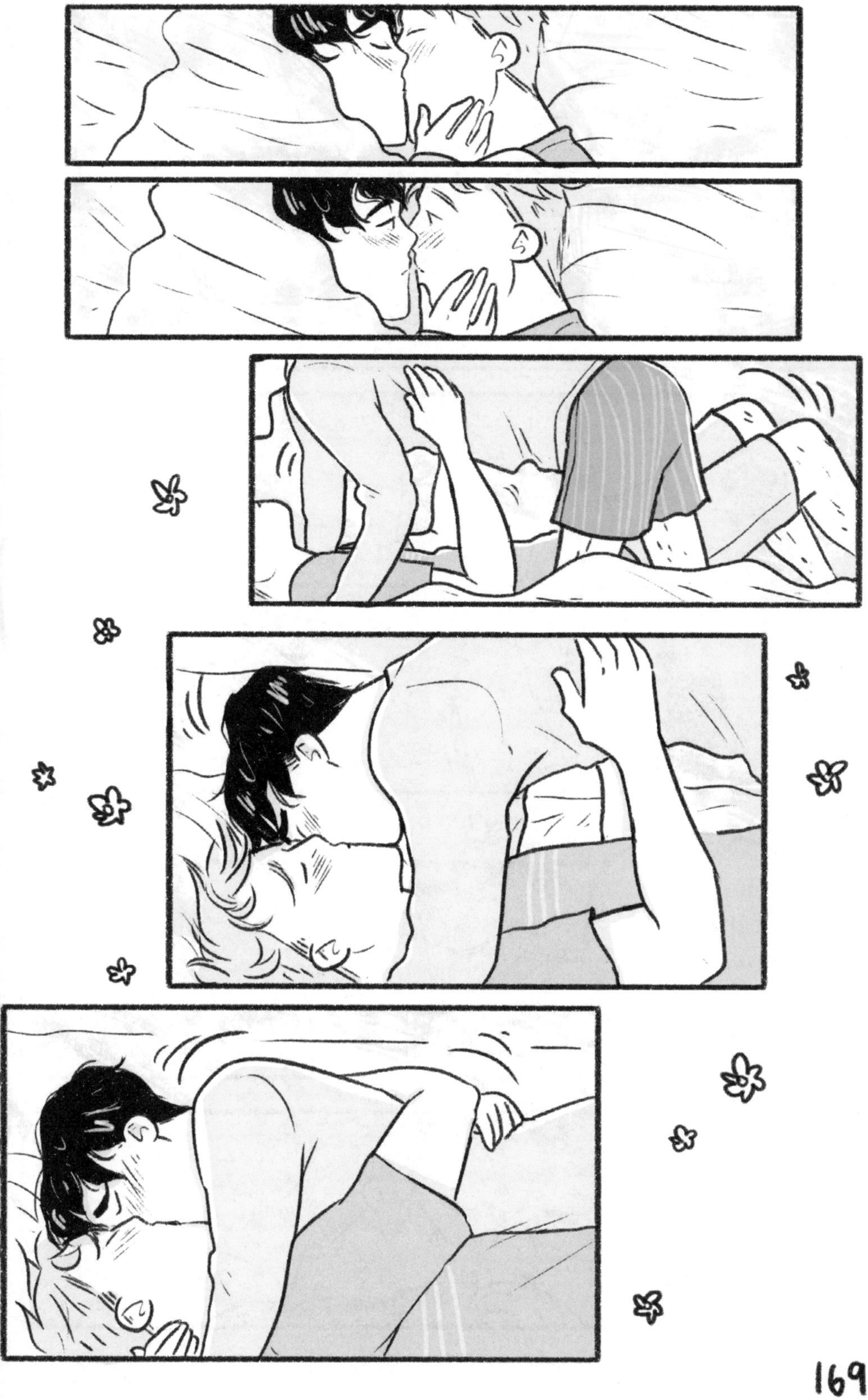

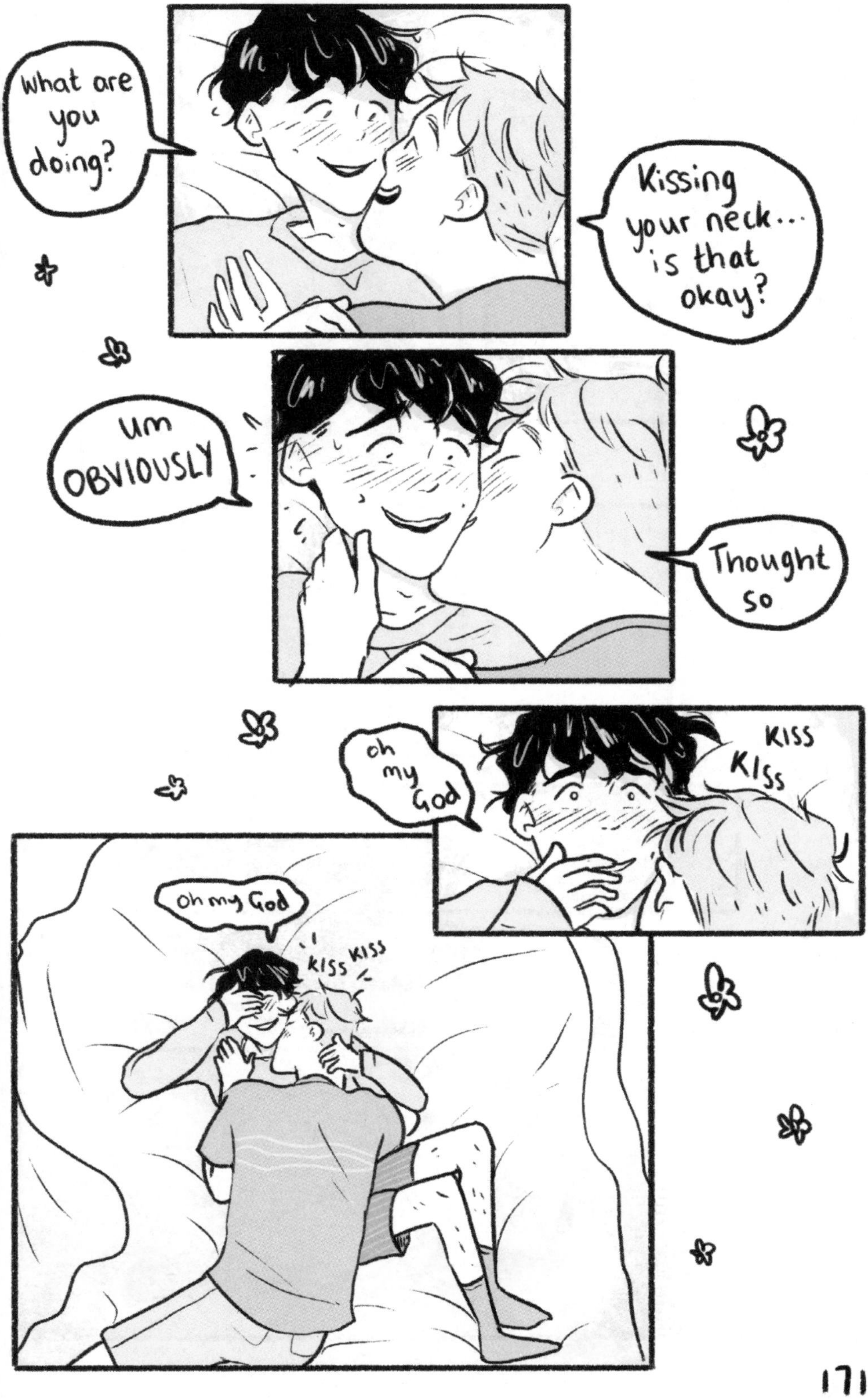

What are you doing?
Kissing your neck... is that okay?
Um OBVIOUSLY
Thought so
oh my God
KISS
KISS
Oh my God
KISS KISS

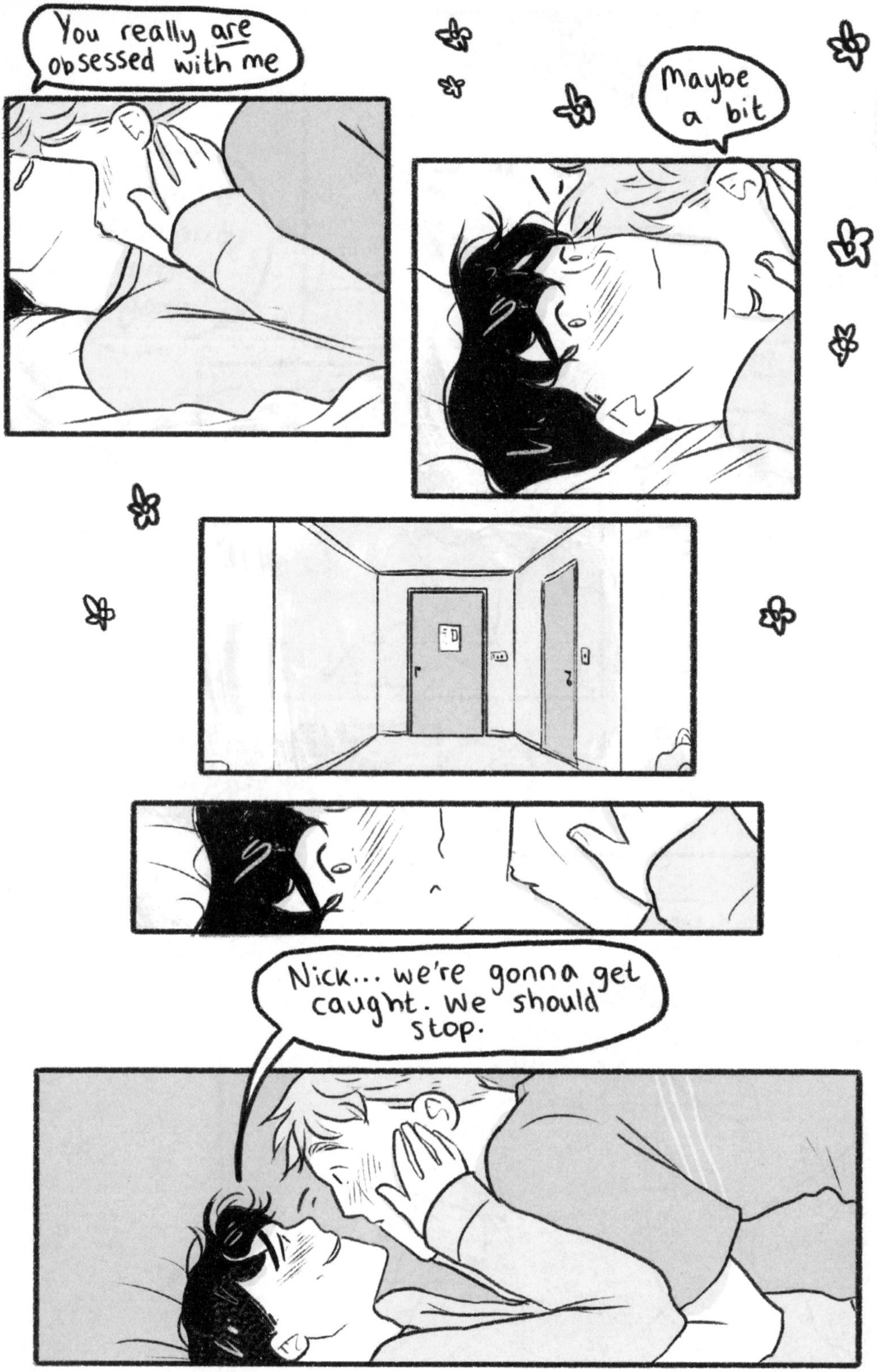

You really are obsessed with me
Maybe a bit
Nick... we're gonna get caught. We should stop.

173

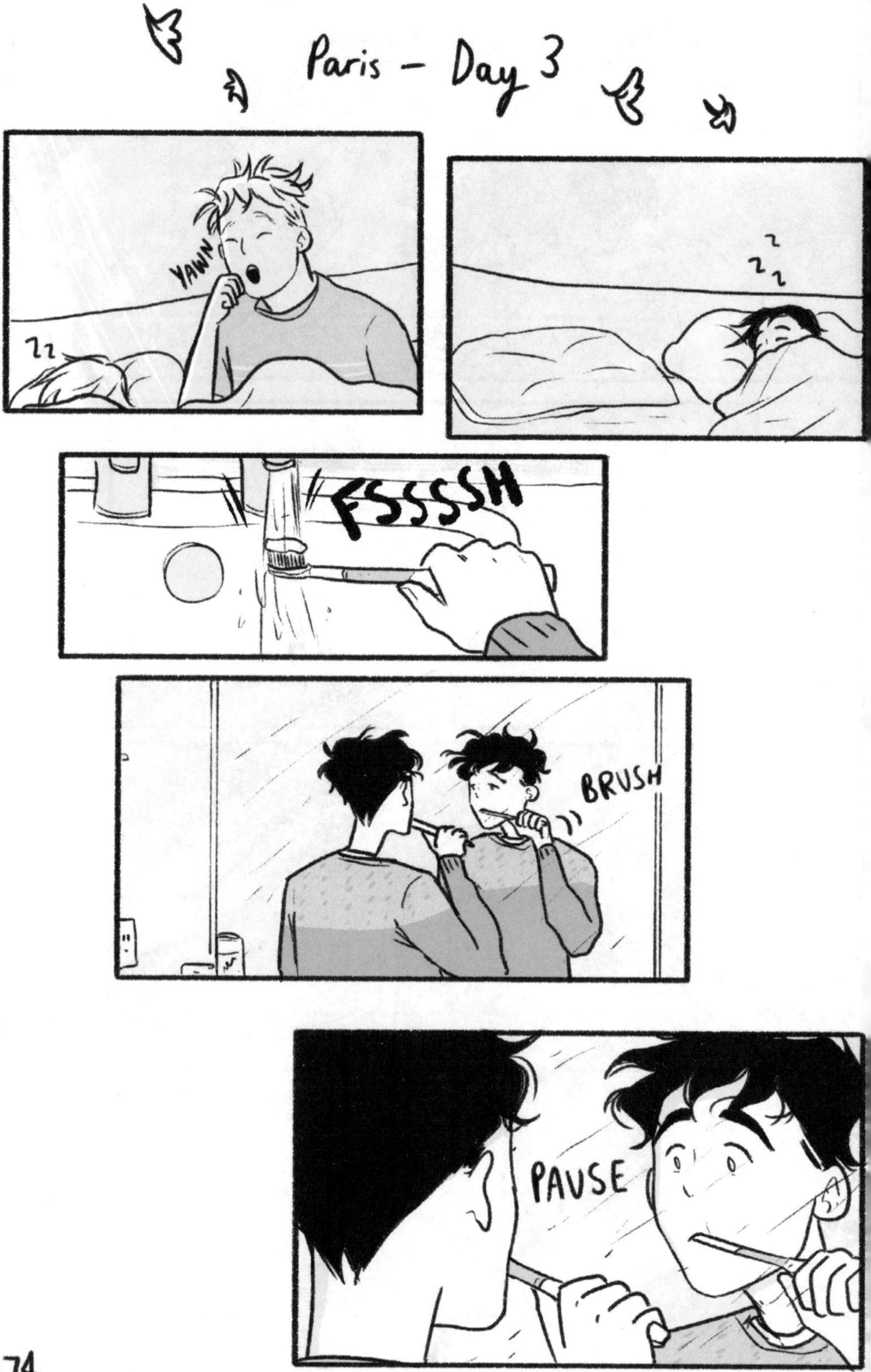
Paris - Day 3
YAWN
Zz
Z
Z
Z
FSSSSH
BRUSH
PAUSE

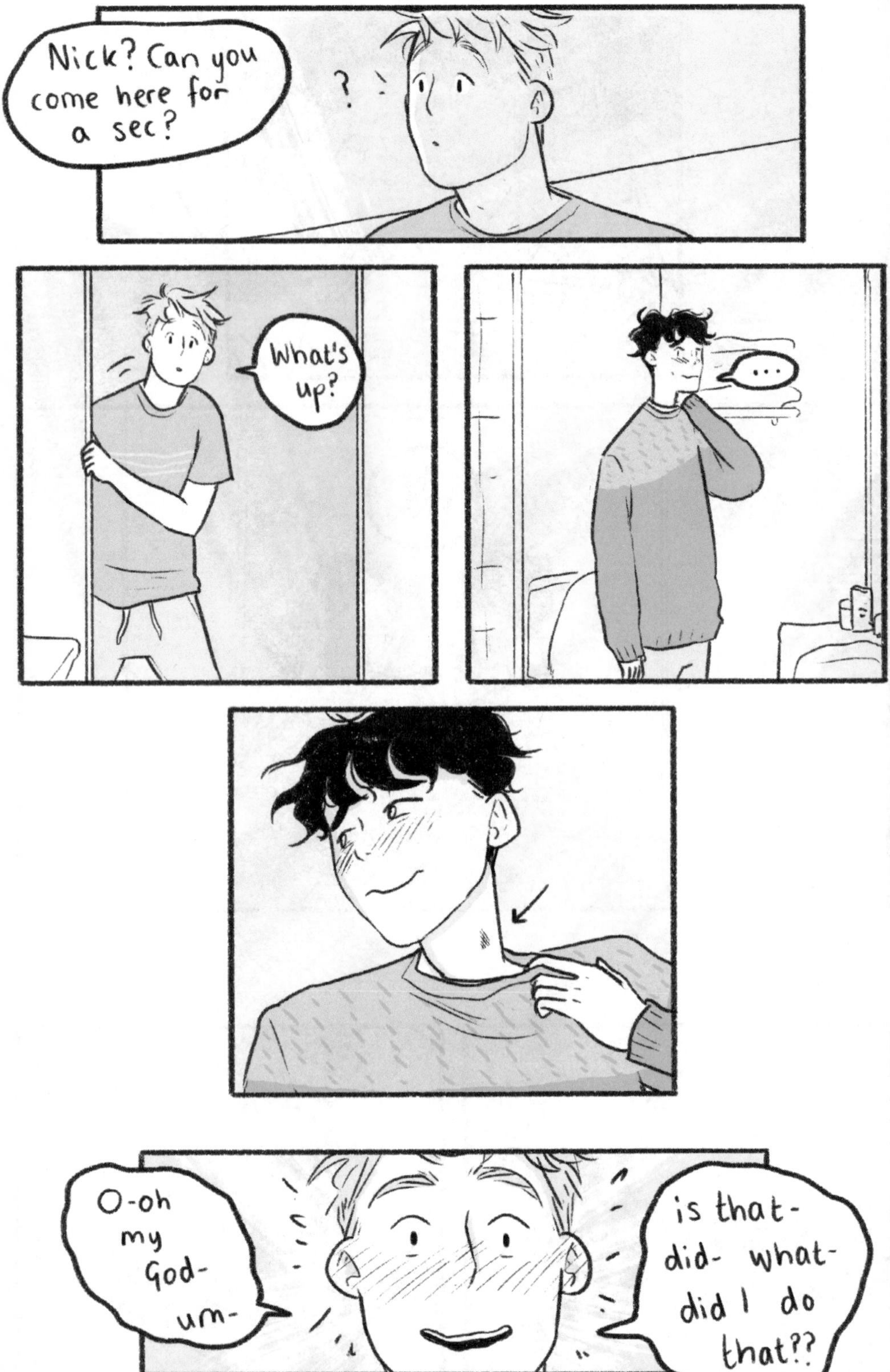
Nick? Can you come here for a sec?
?
What's up?
...
O-oh my God- um-
is that- did- what- did I do that??

177

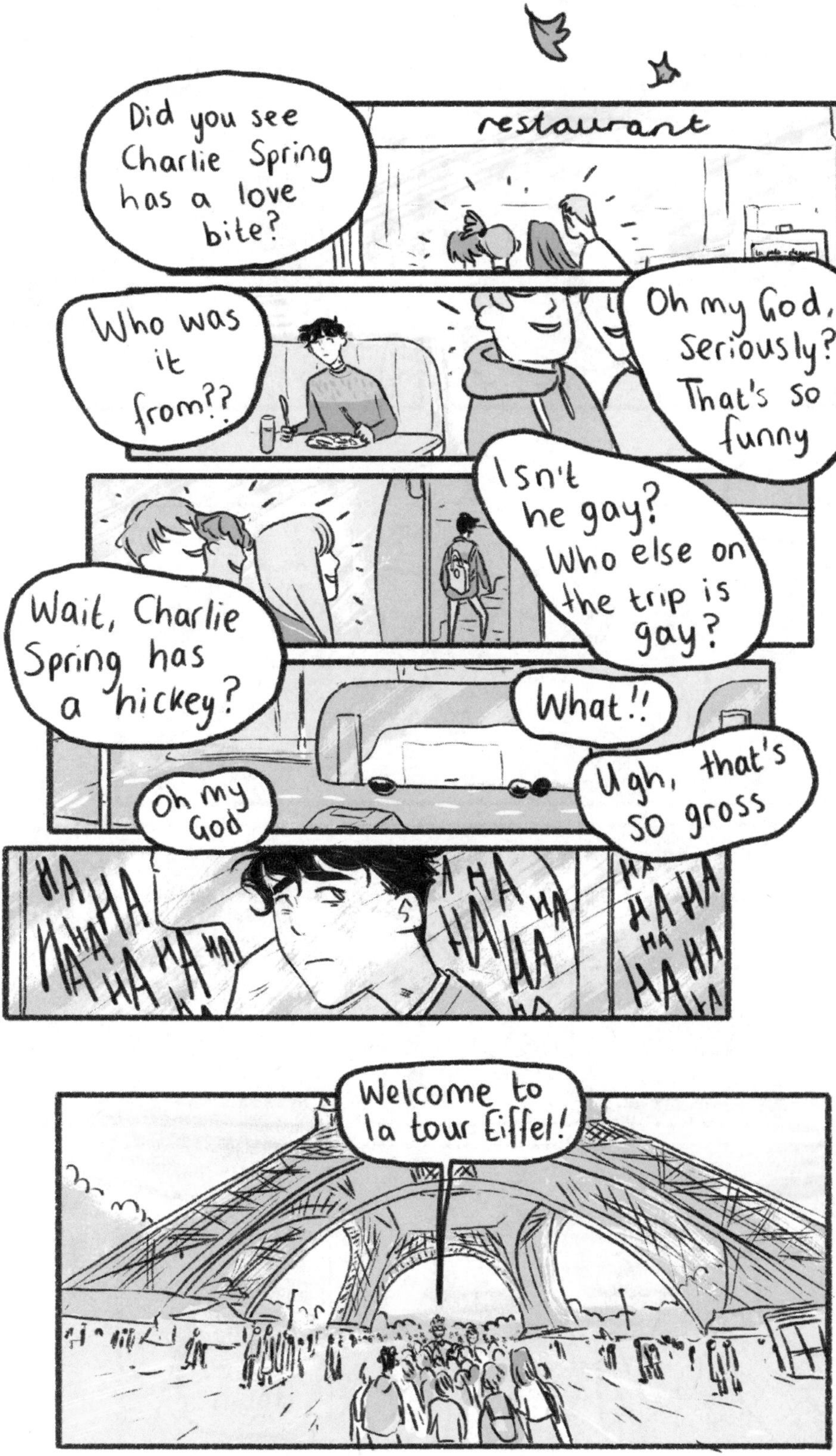
restaurant
Did you see Charlie Spring has a love bite?
Who was it from??
Oh my God, seriously? That's so funny
Isn't he gay? Who else on the trip is gay?
Wait, Charlie Spring has a hickey?
What!!
Oh my God
Ugh, that's so gross
HA HA HA HA HA HA HA HA HA
Welcome to la tour Eiffel!

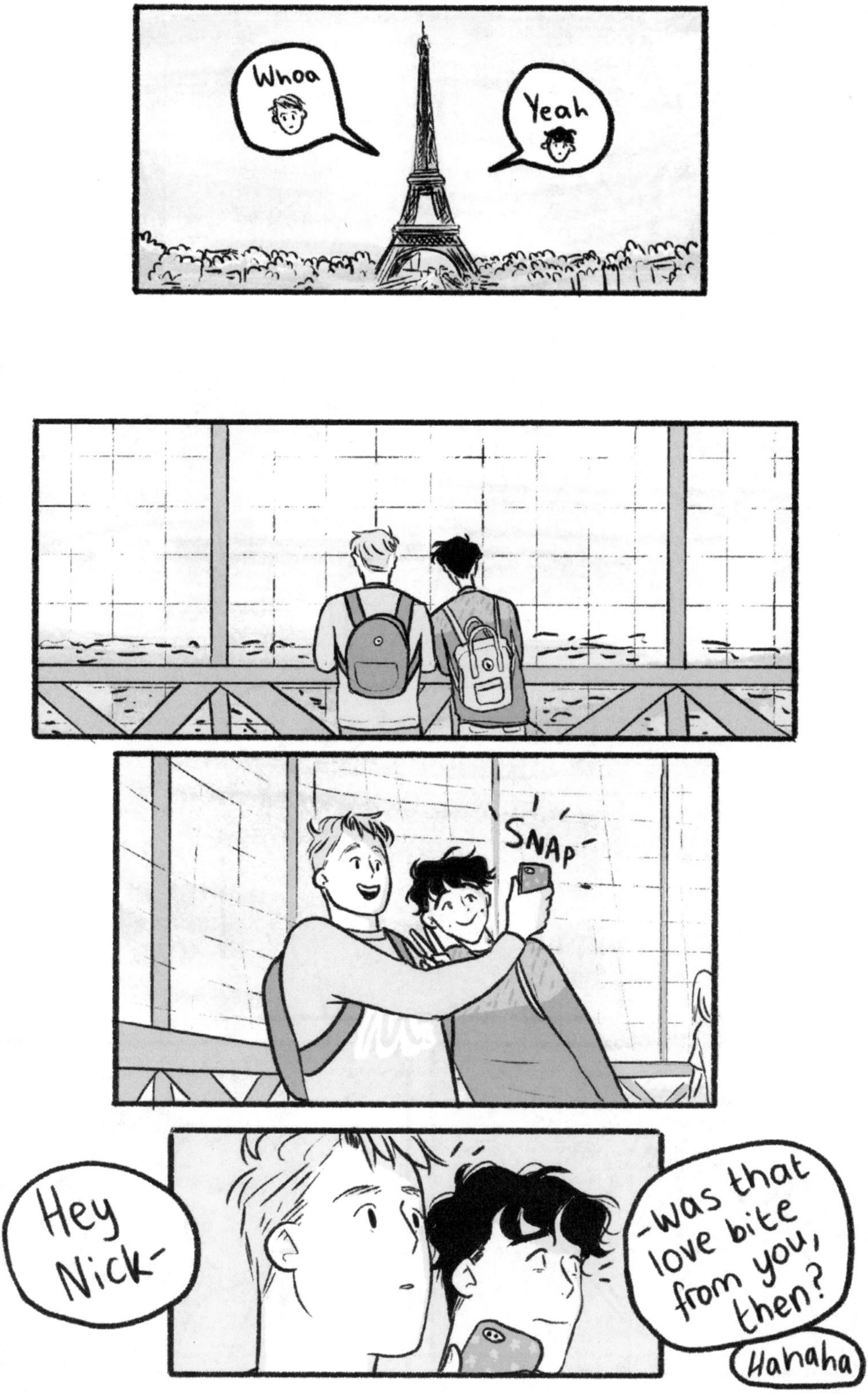
Whoa
Yeah
SNAP
Hey Nick-
-was that love bite from you, then?
Hahaha

185

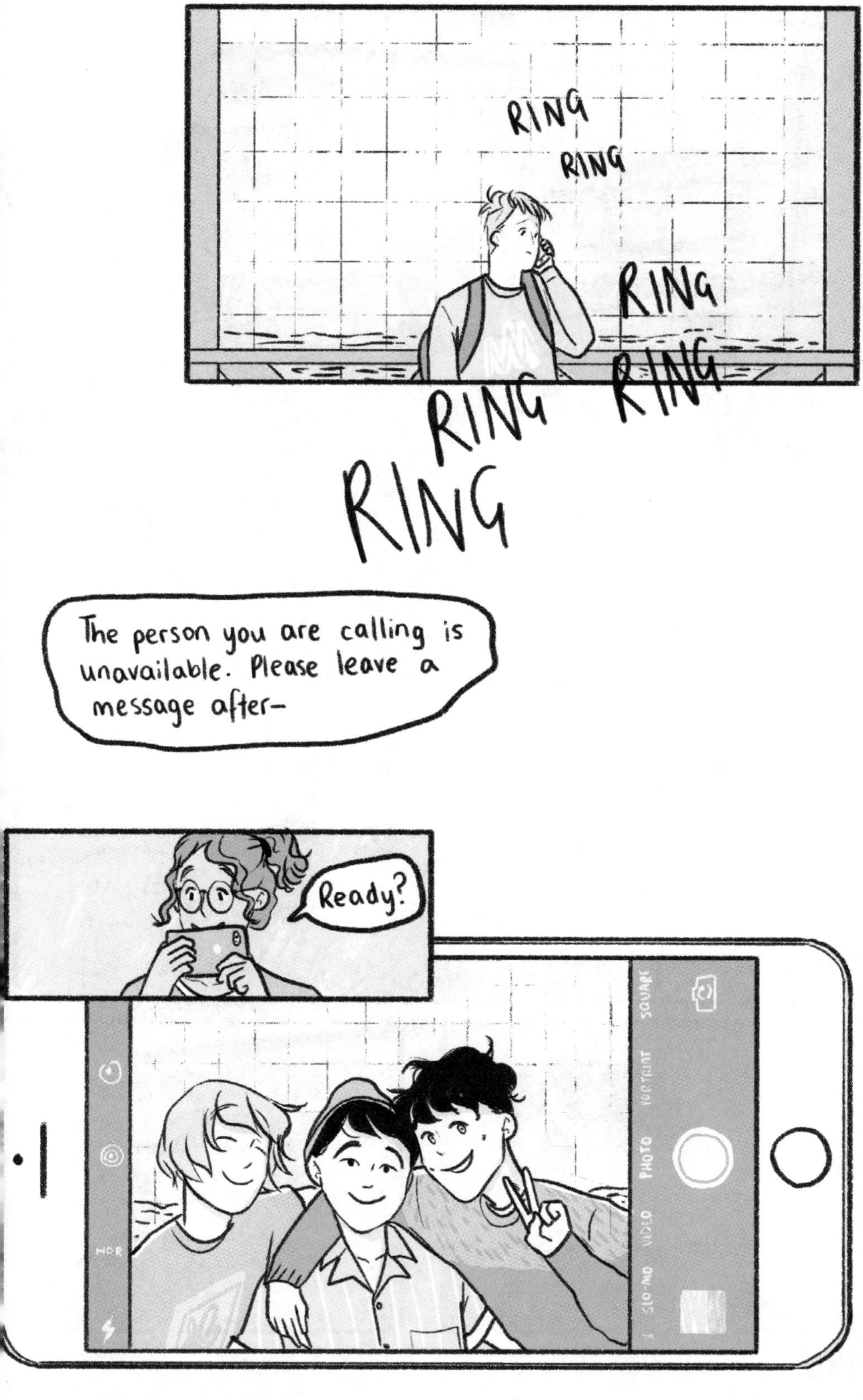
RING
RING
RING
RING
RING
RING
The person you are calling is unavailable. Please leave a message after—
Ready?
SQUARE
PORTRAIT
PHOTO
VIDEO
SLO-MO
HDR

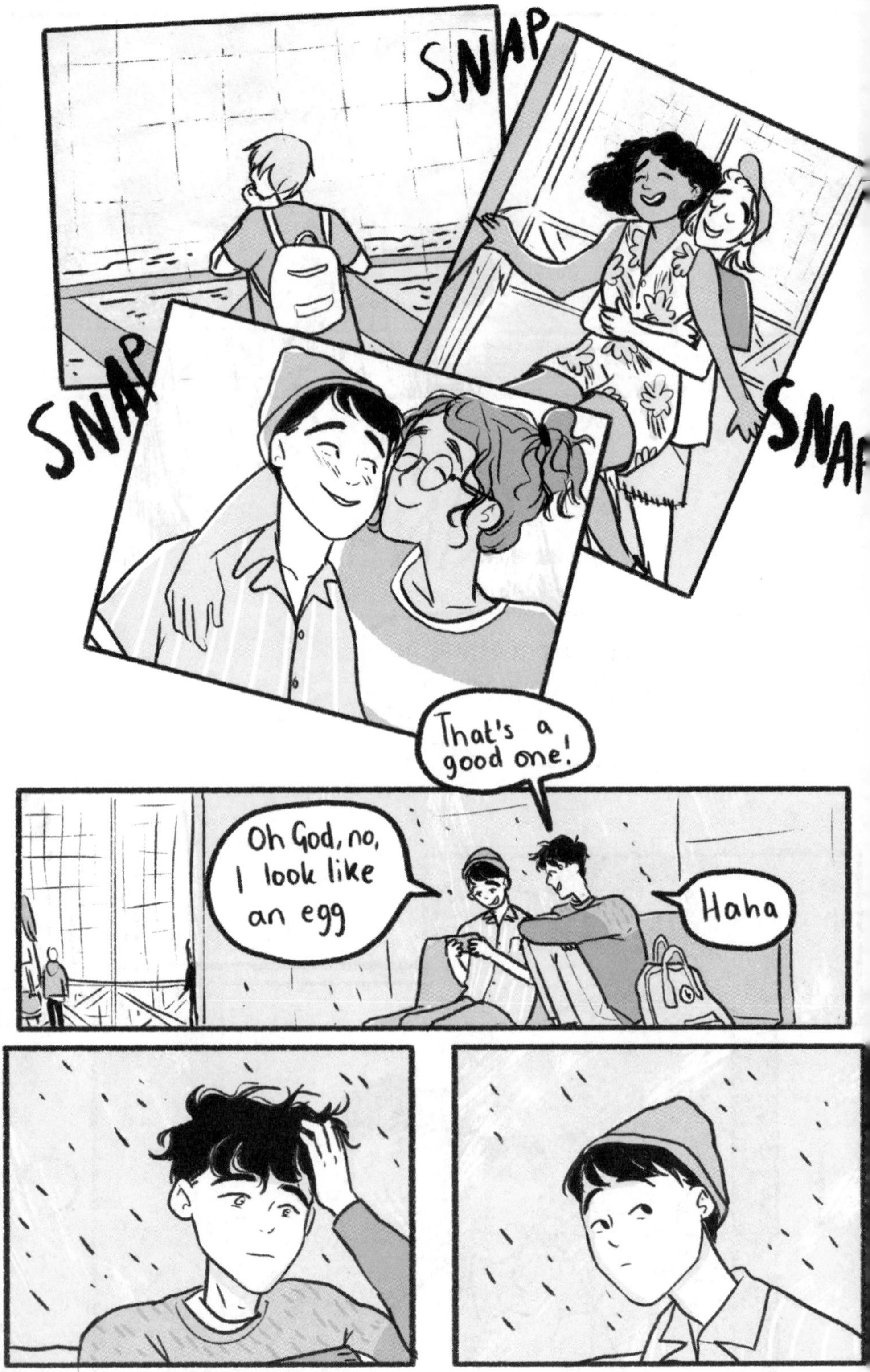
SNAP
SNAP
SNAP
SNAP
That's a good one!
Oh God, no, I look like an egg
Haha

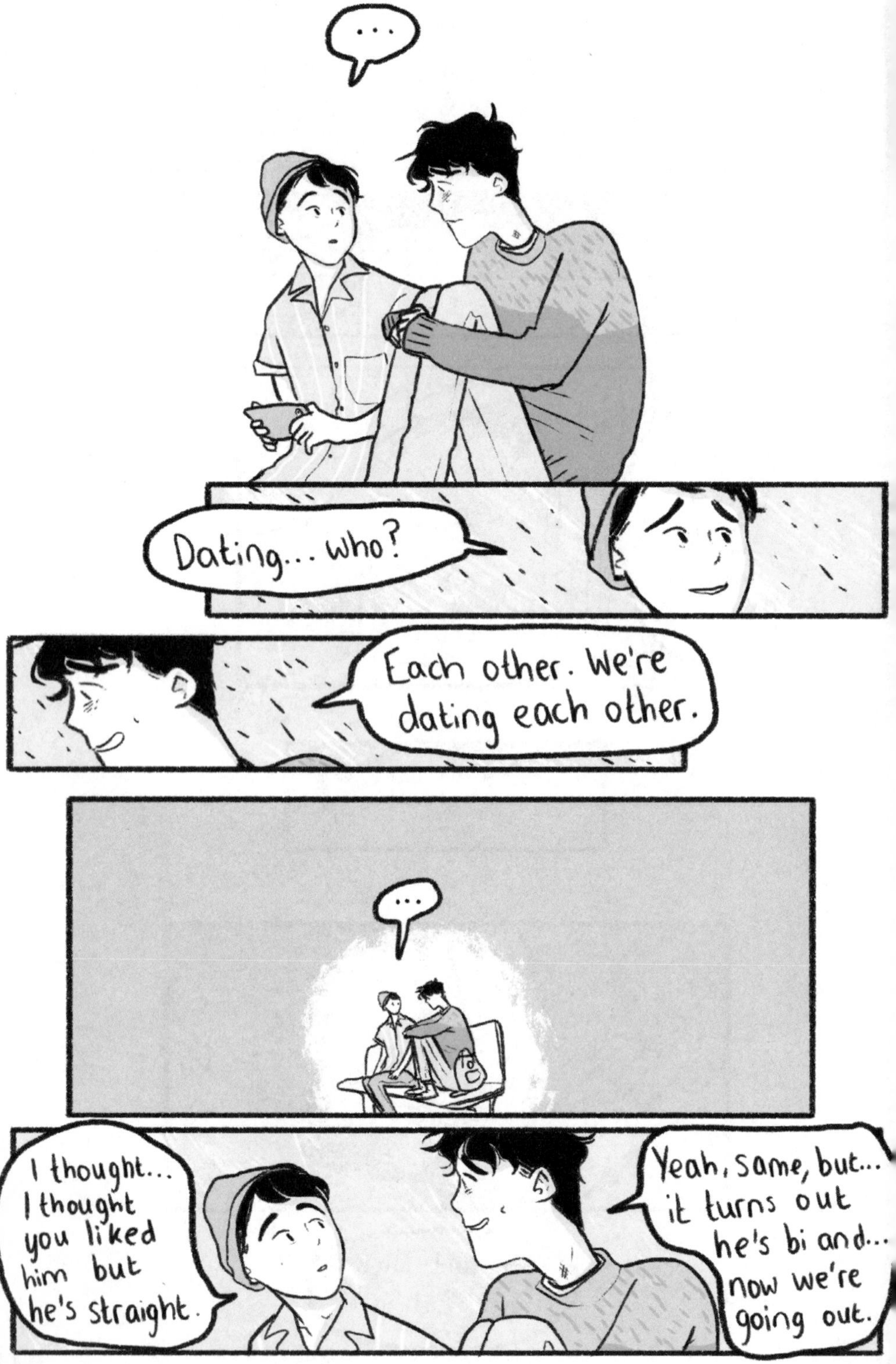
...
Dating... who?
Each other. We're dating each other.
...
I thought... I thought you liked him but he's straight.
Yeah, same, but... it turns out he's bi and... now we're going out.

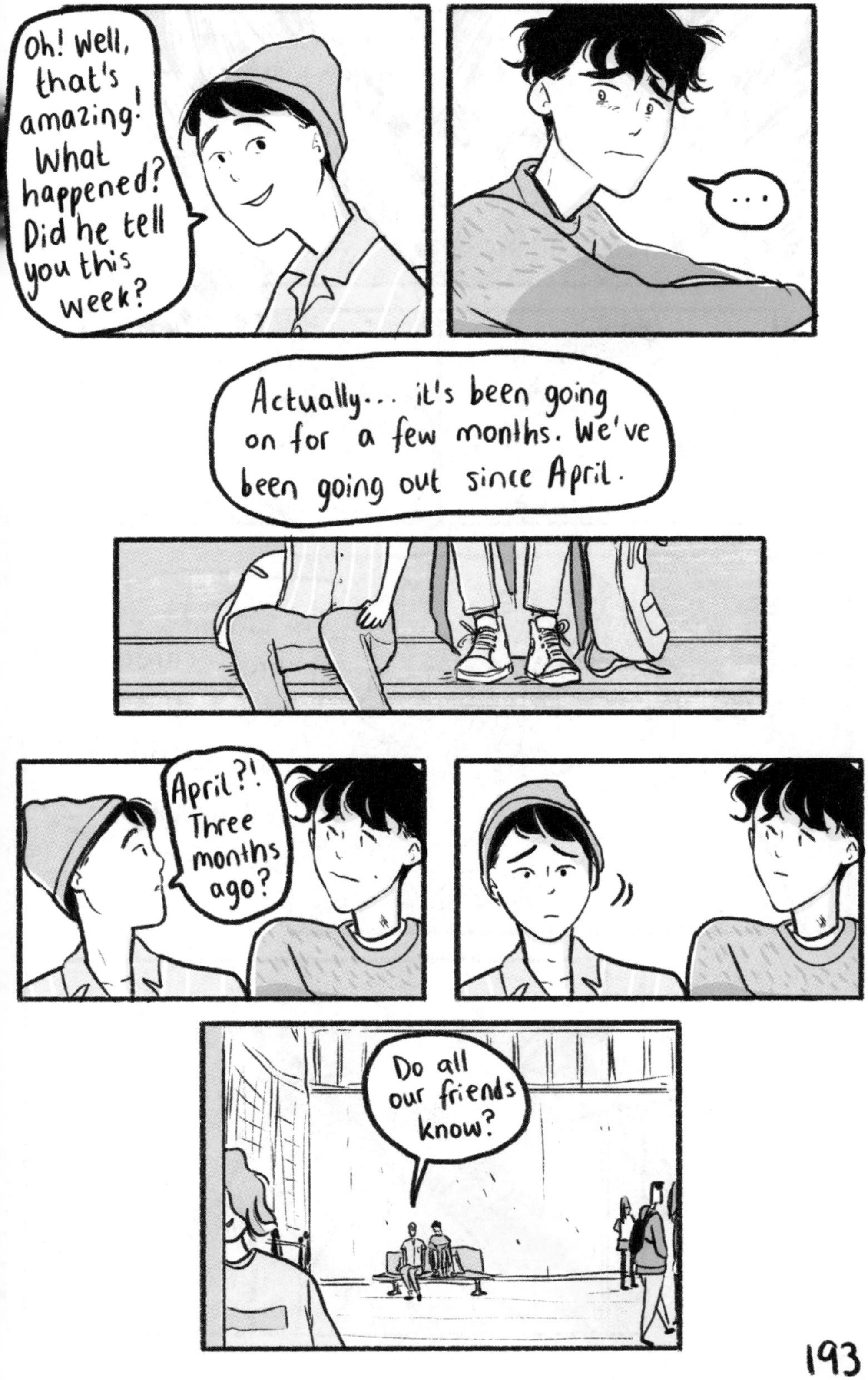
Oh! Well, that's amazing! What happened? Did he tell you this week?
...
Actually... it's been going on for a few months. We've been going out since April.
April?! Three months ago?
Do all our friends know?

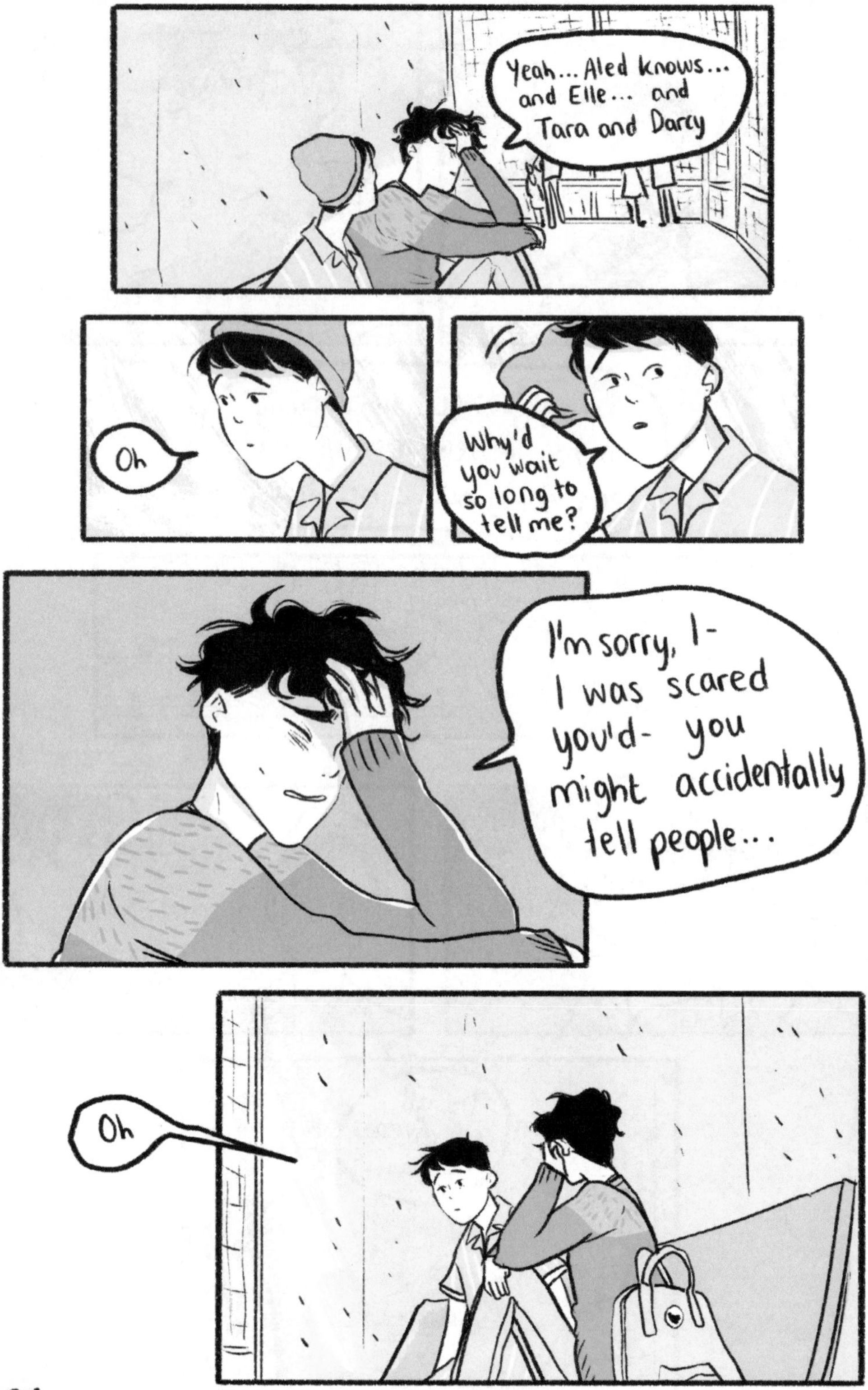
Yeah... Aled knows... and Elle... and Tara and Darcy
Oh
Why'd you wait so long to tell me?
I'm sorry, I- I was scared you'd- you might accidentally tell people...
Oh

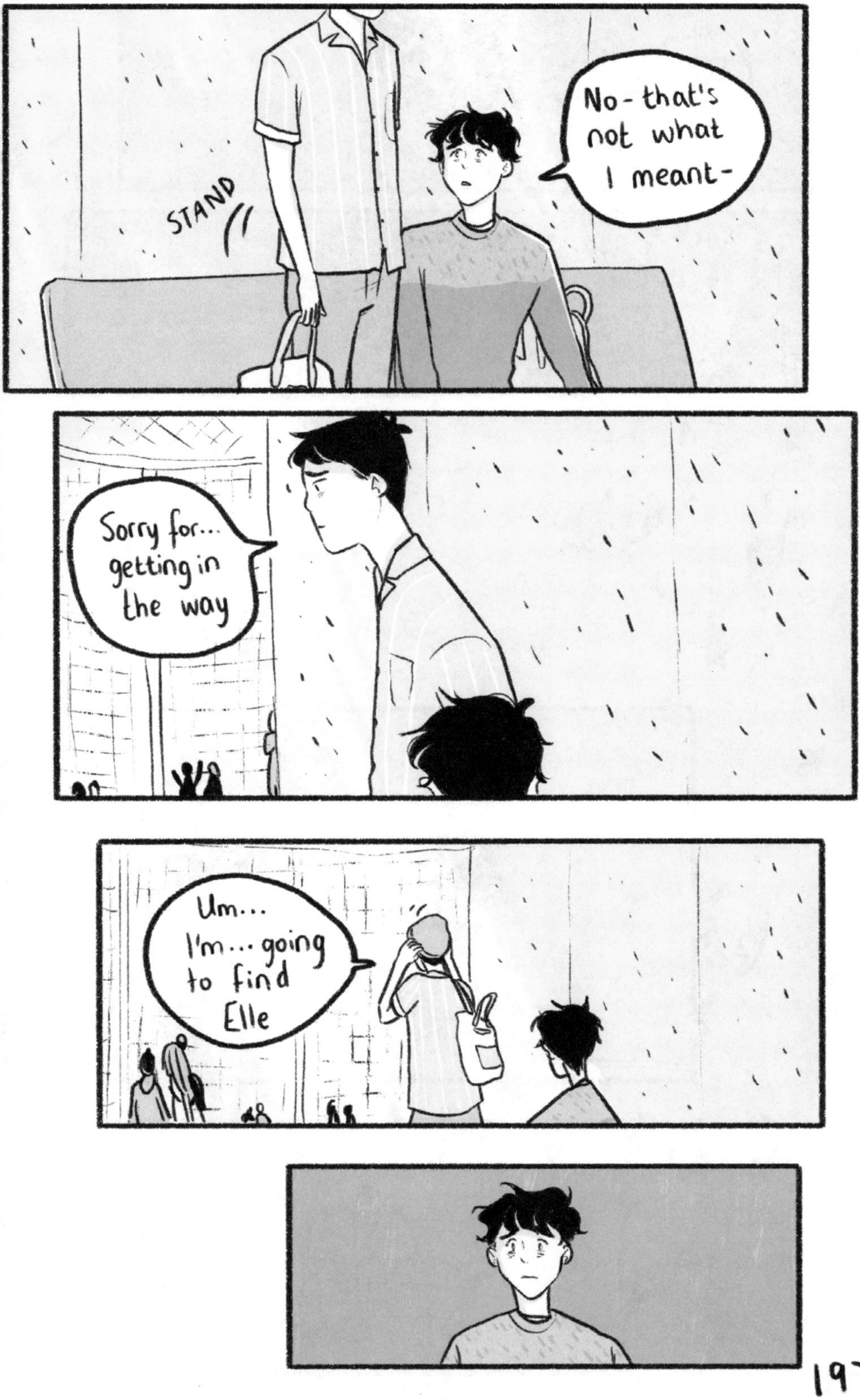
No- that's not what I meant-
STAND
Sorry for... getting in the way
Um... I'm... going to find Elle

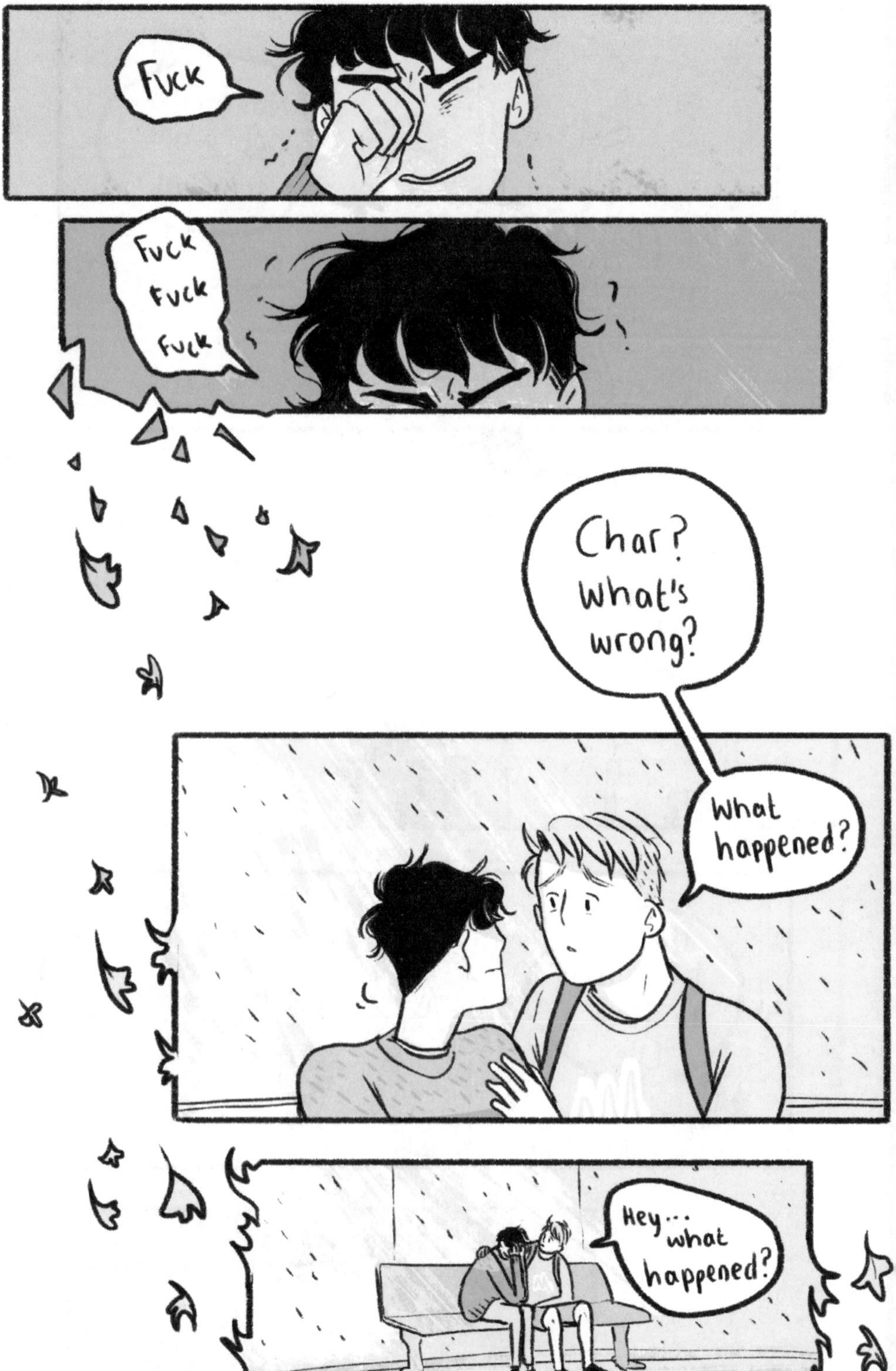
FUCK
FUCK FUCK FUCK
Char? what's wrong?
What happened?
Hey... what happened?

Paris - Day 4

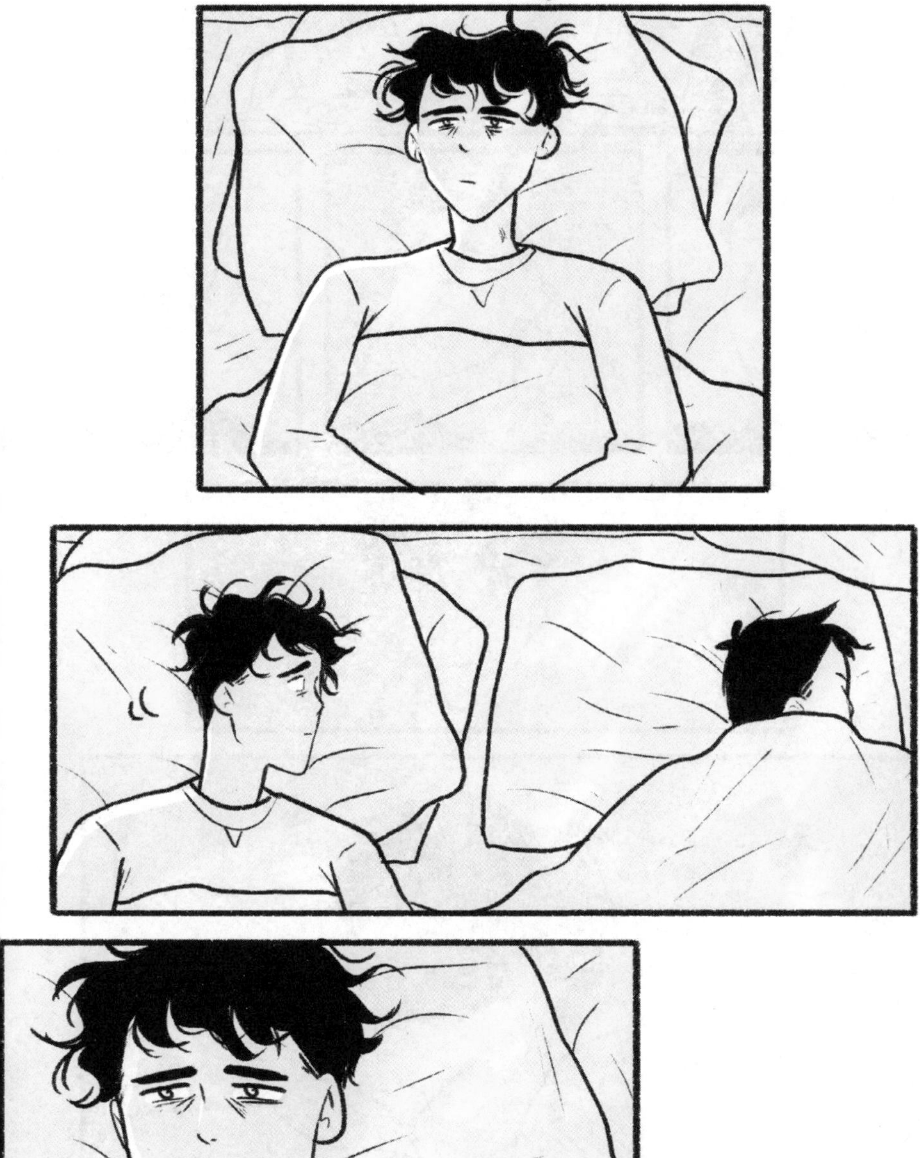

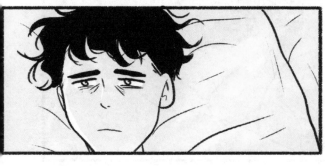

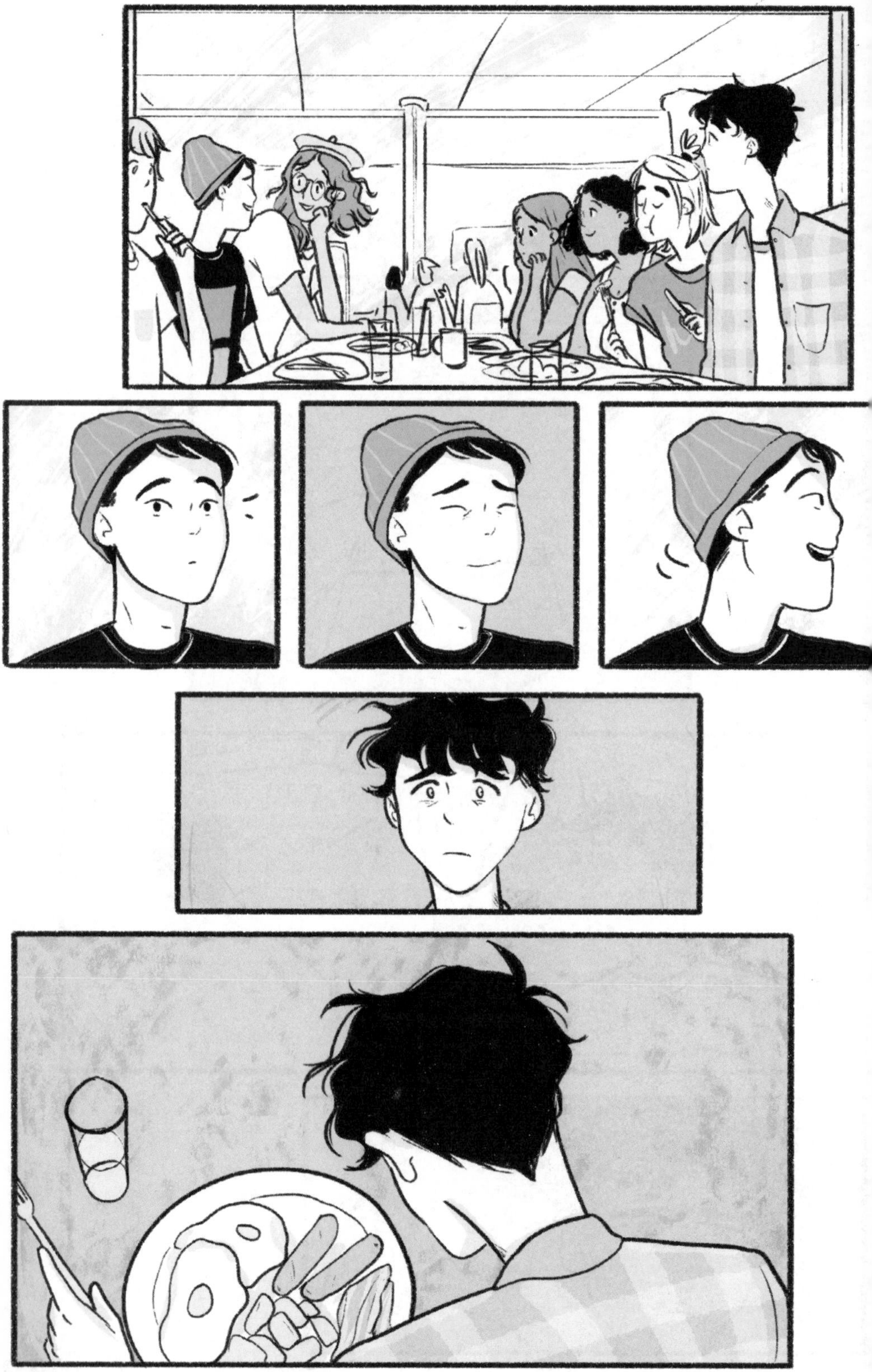

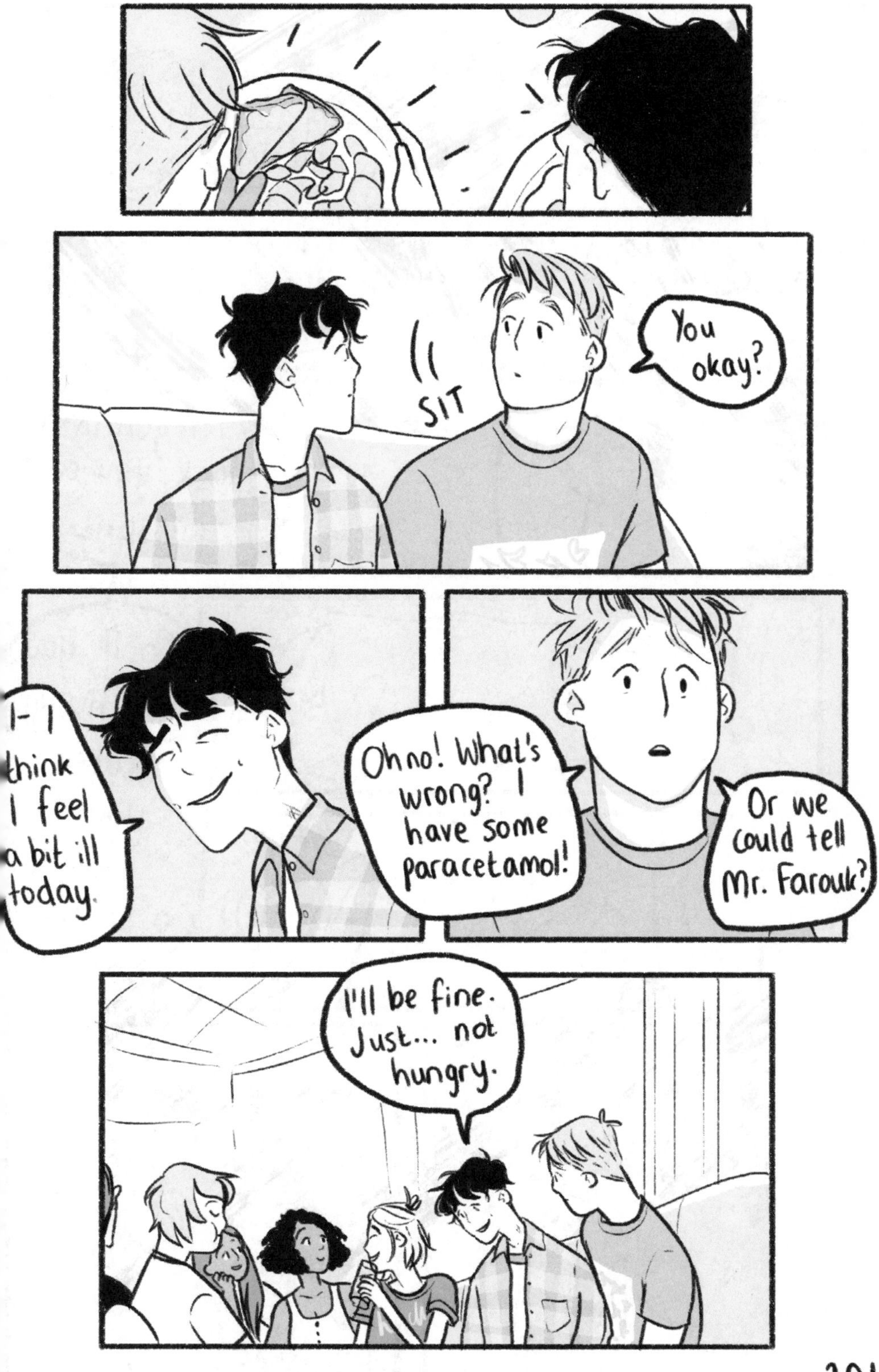
SIT
You okay?
I- I think I feel a bit ill today.
Oh no! What's wrong? I have some paracetamol!
Or we could tell Mr. Farouk?
I'll be fine. Just... not hungry.

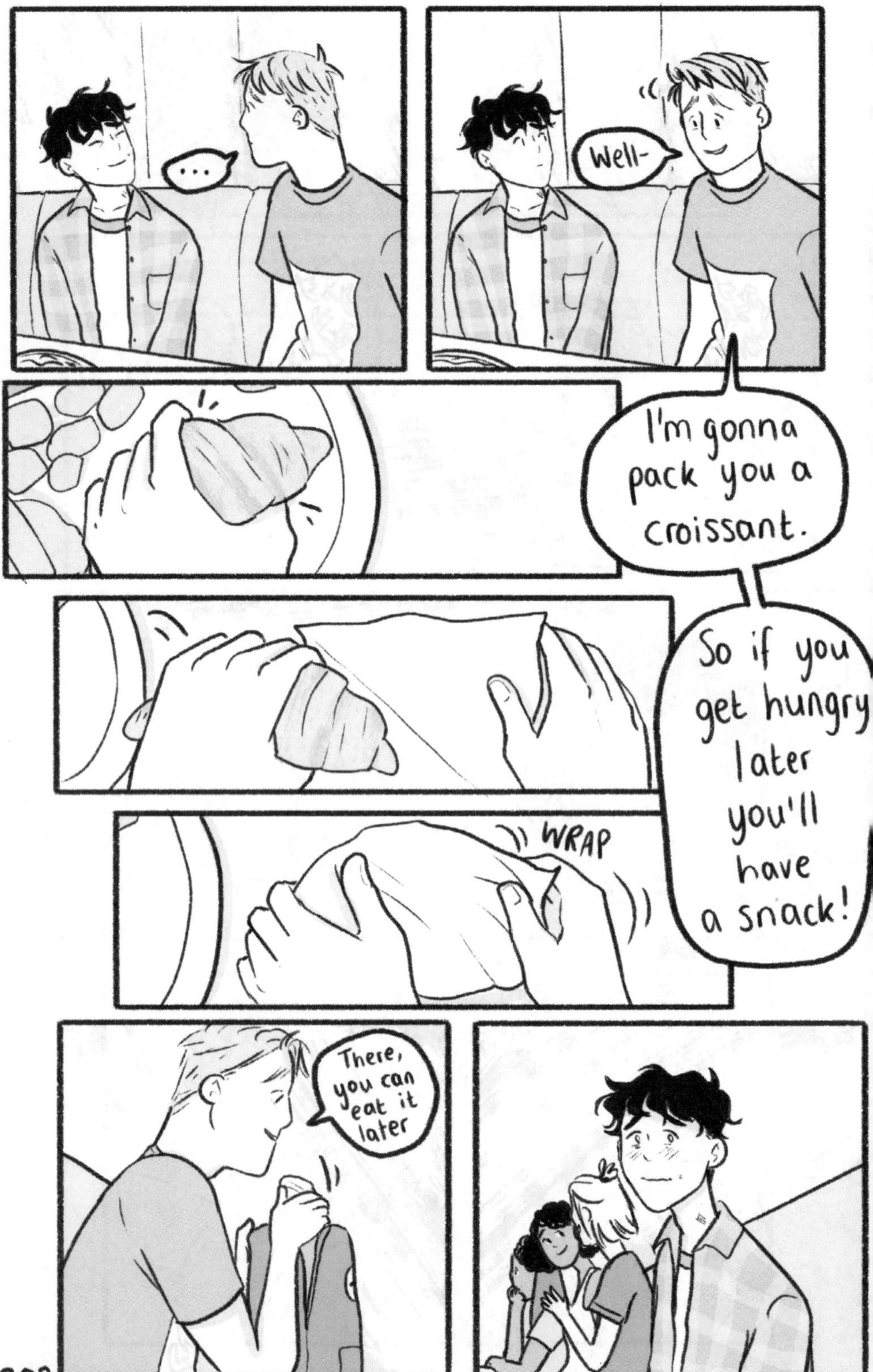
...
Well-
I'm gonna pack you a croissant.
So if you get hungry later you'll have a snack!
WRAP
There, you can eat it later

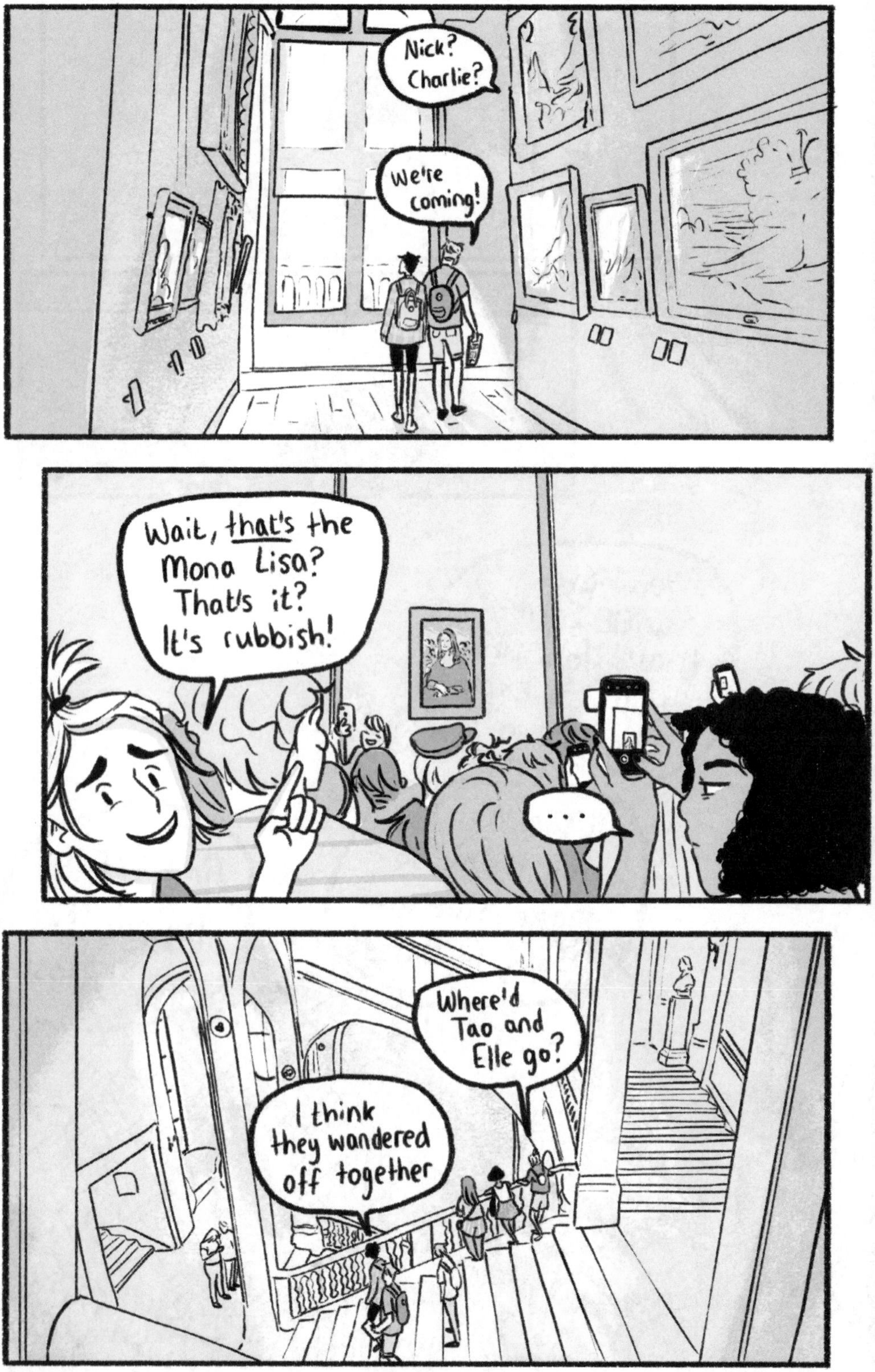
Nick? Charlie?
We're coming!
Wait, that's the Mona Lisa? That's it? It's rubbish!
...
Where'd Tao and Elle go?
I think they wandered off together

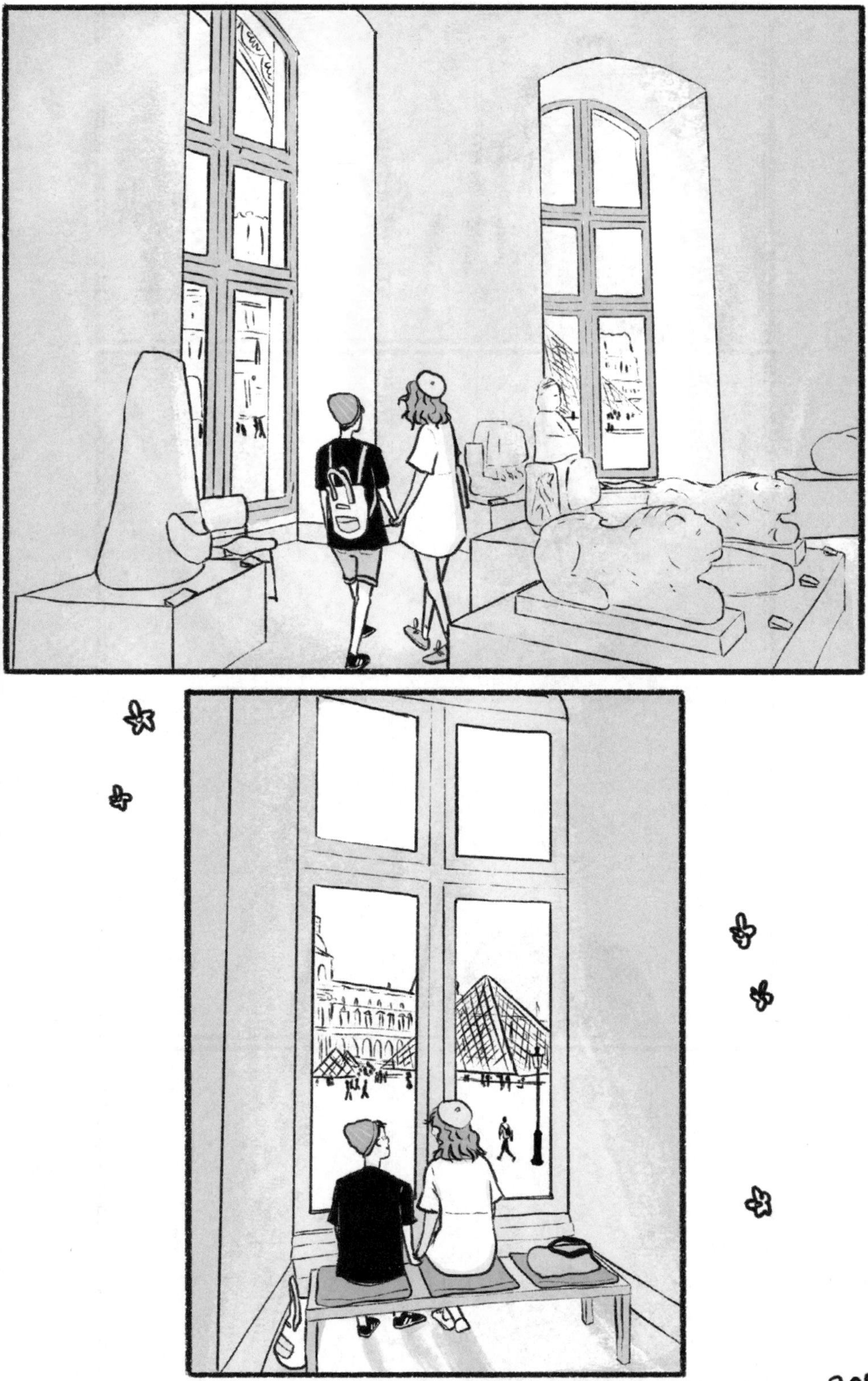

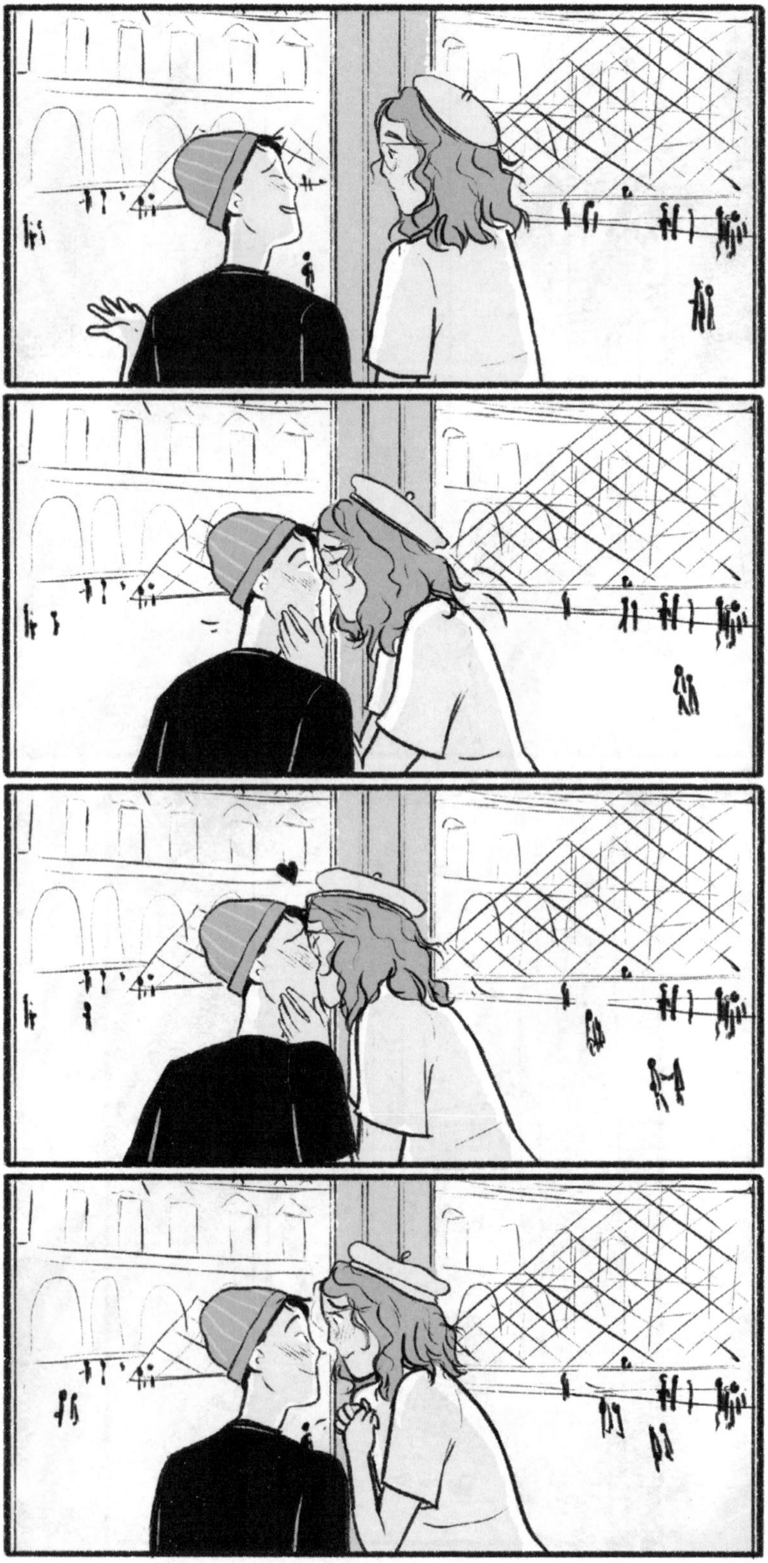

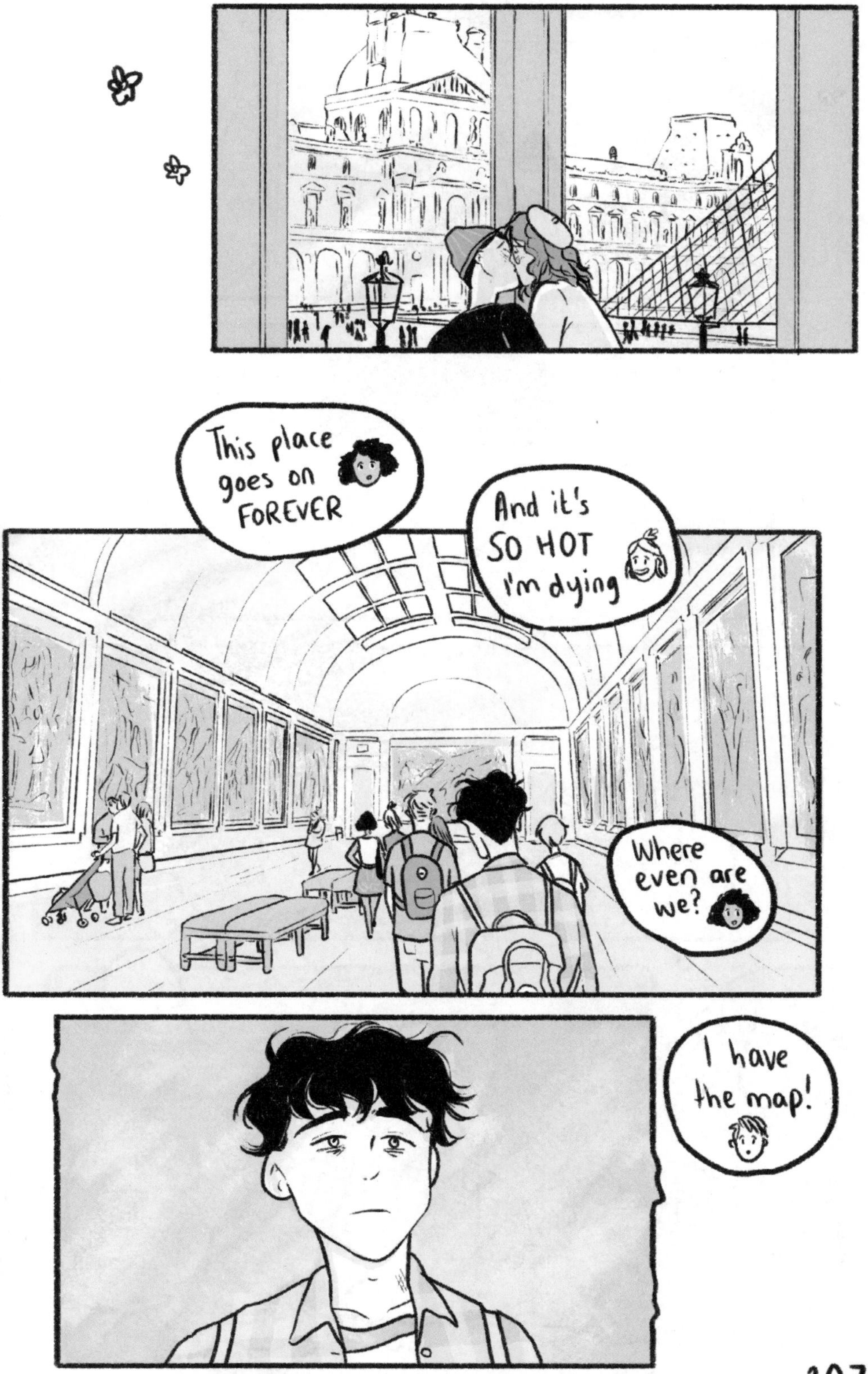
This place goes on FOREVER
And it's SO HOT I'm dying
Where even are we?
I have the map!

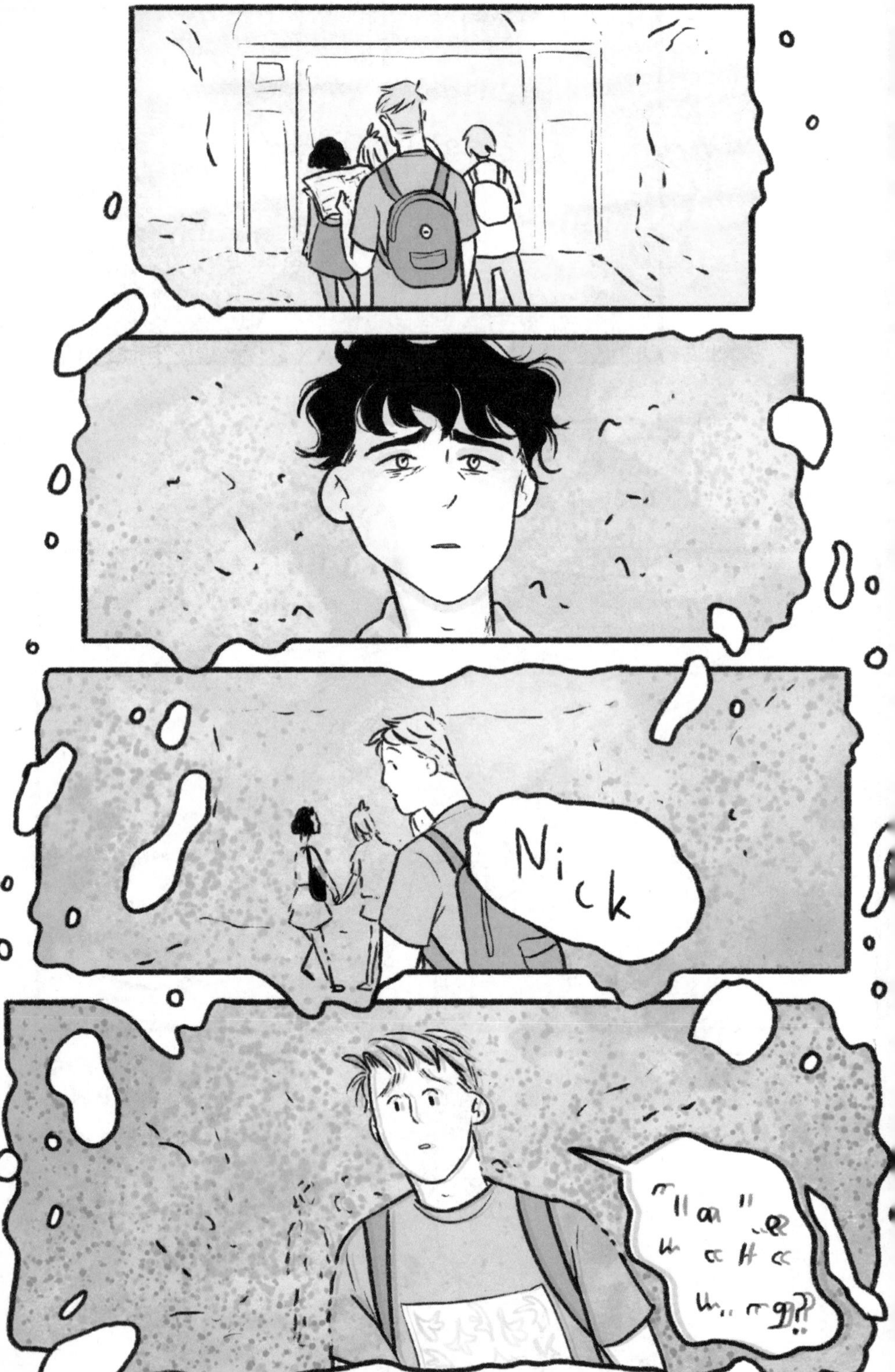
Nick

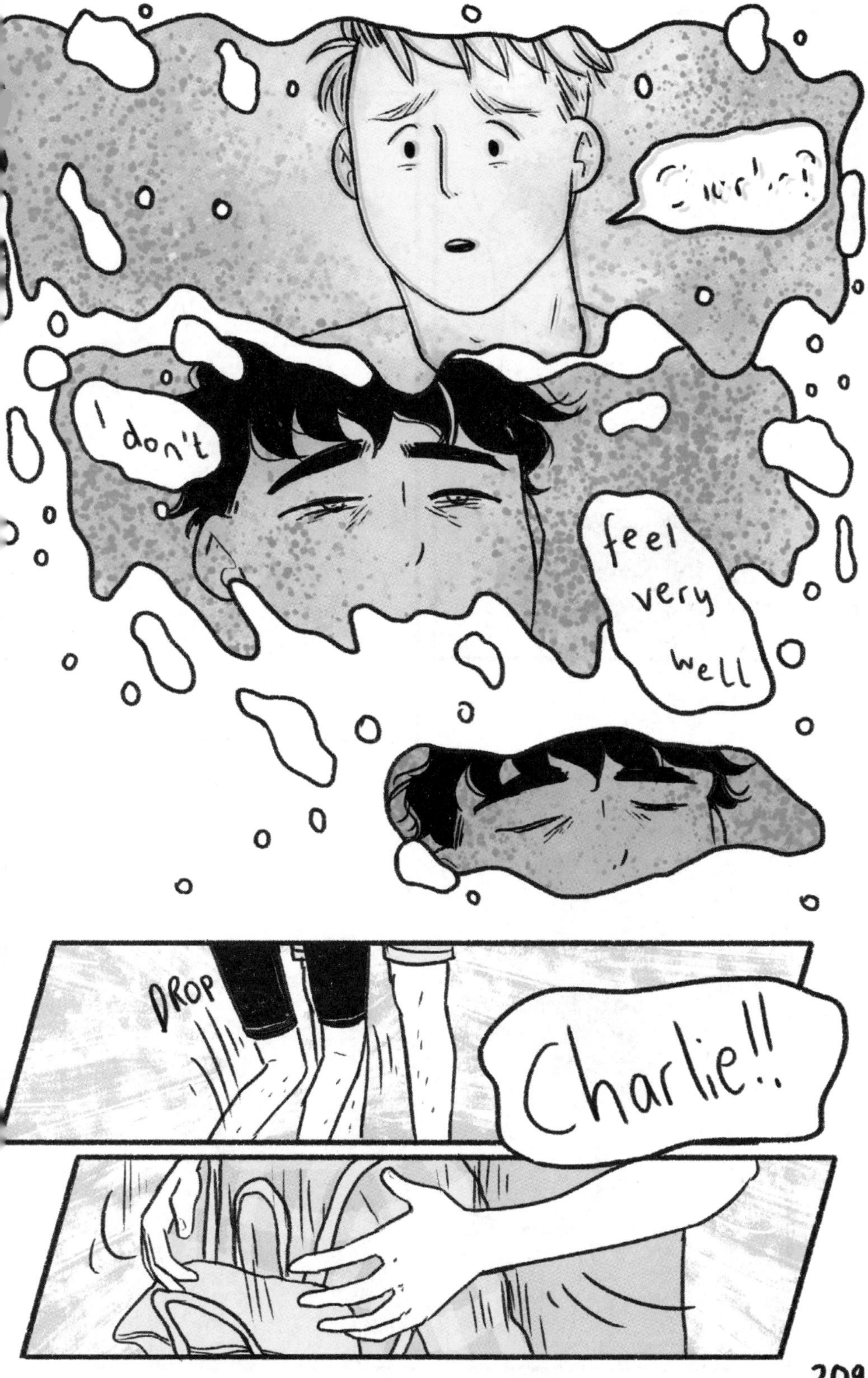
I don't
feel very well
DROP
Charlie!!

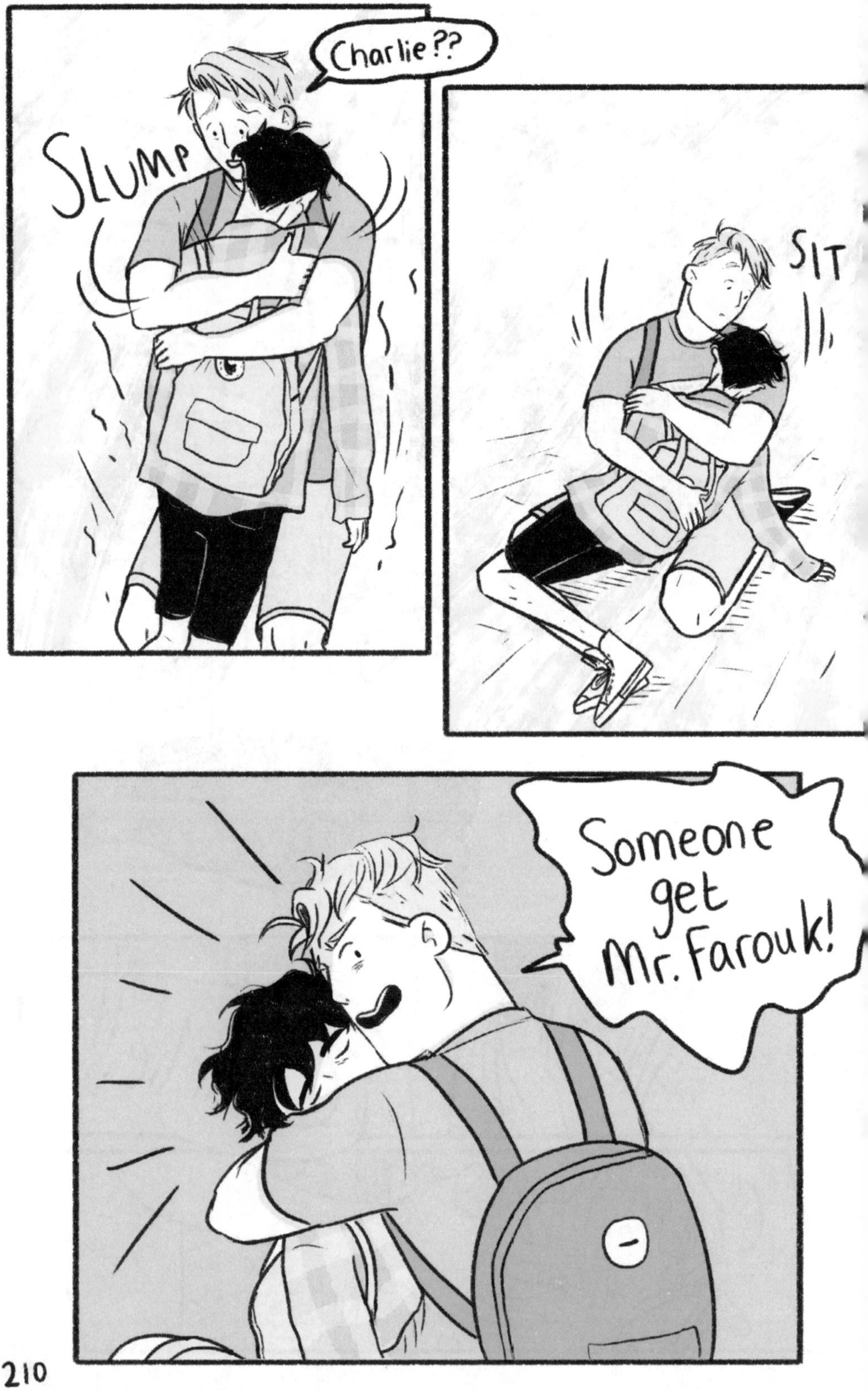
Charlie??
SLUMP
SIT
Someone get Mr. Farouk!

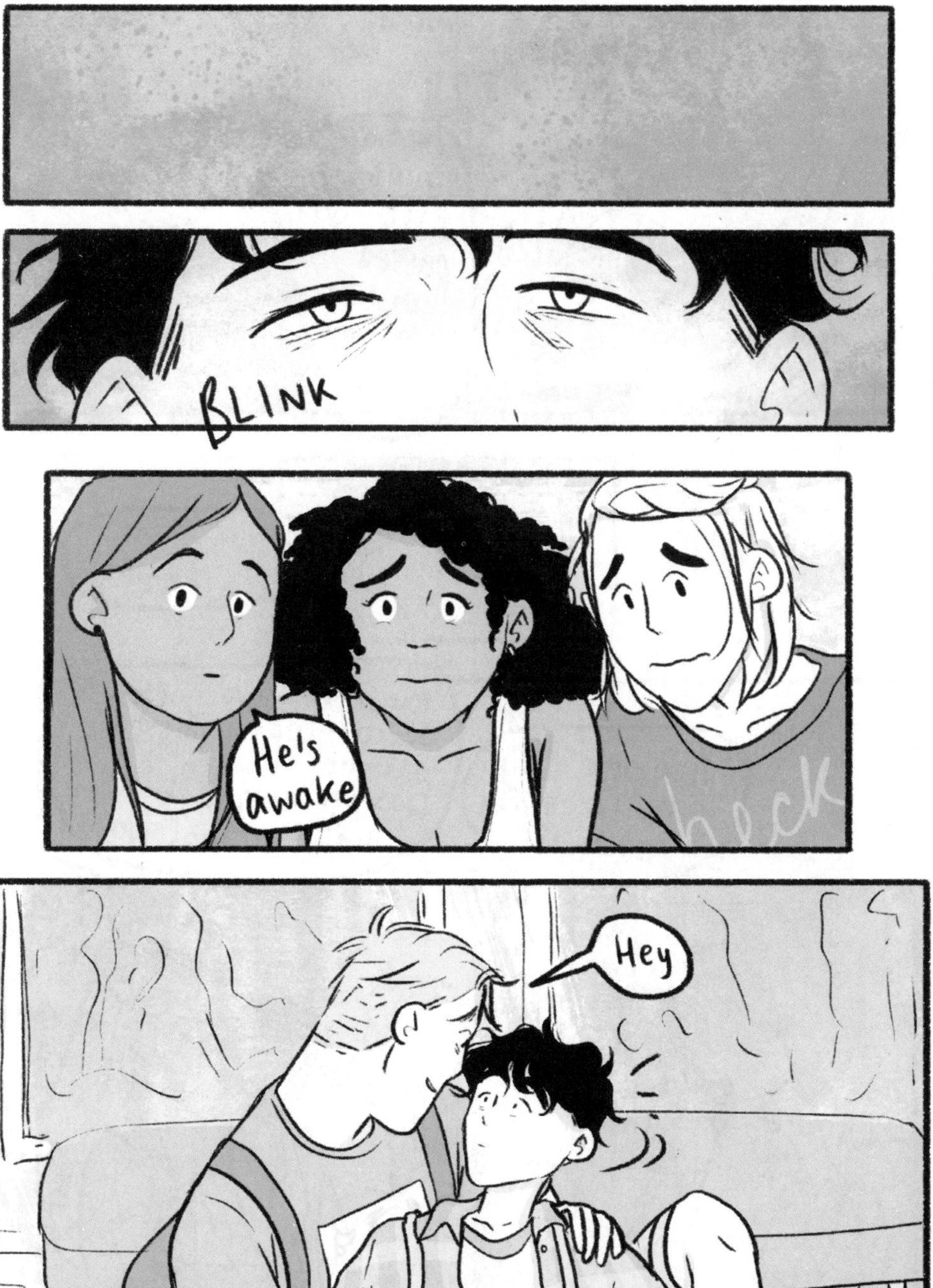
BLINK
He's awake
heck
Hey

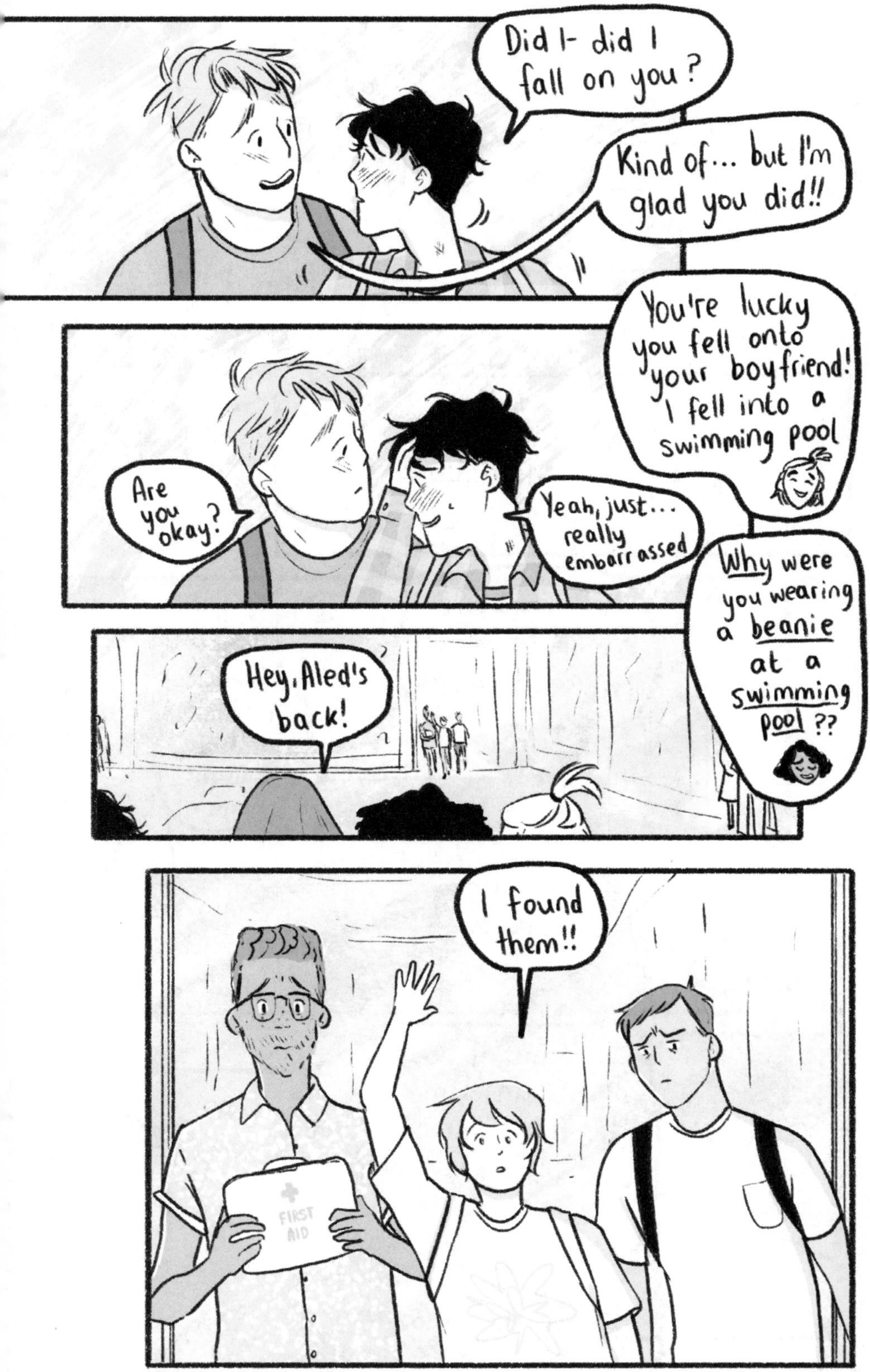
Did I- did I fall on you?
Kind of... but I'm glad you did!!
You're lucky you fell onto your boyfriend! I fell into a swimming pool
Are you okay?
Yeah, just... really embarrassed
Why were you wearing a beanie at a swimming pool??
Hey, Aled's back!
I found them!!
FIRST AID

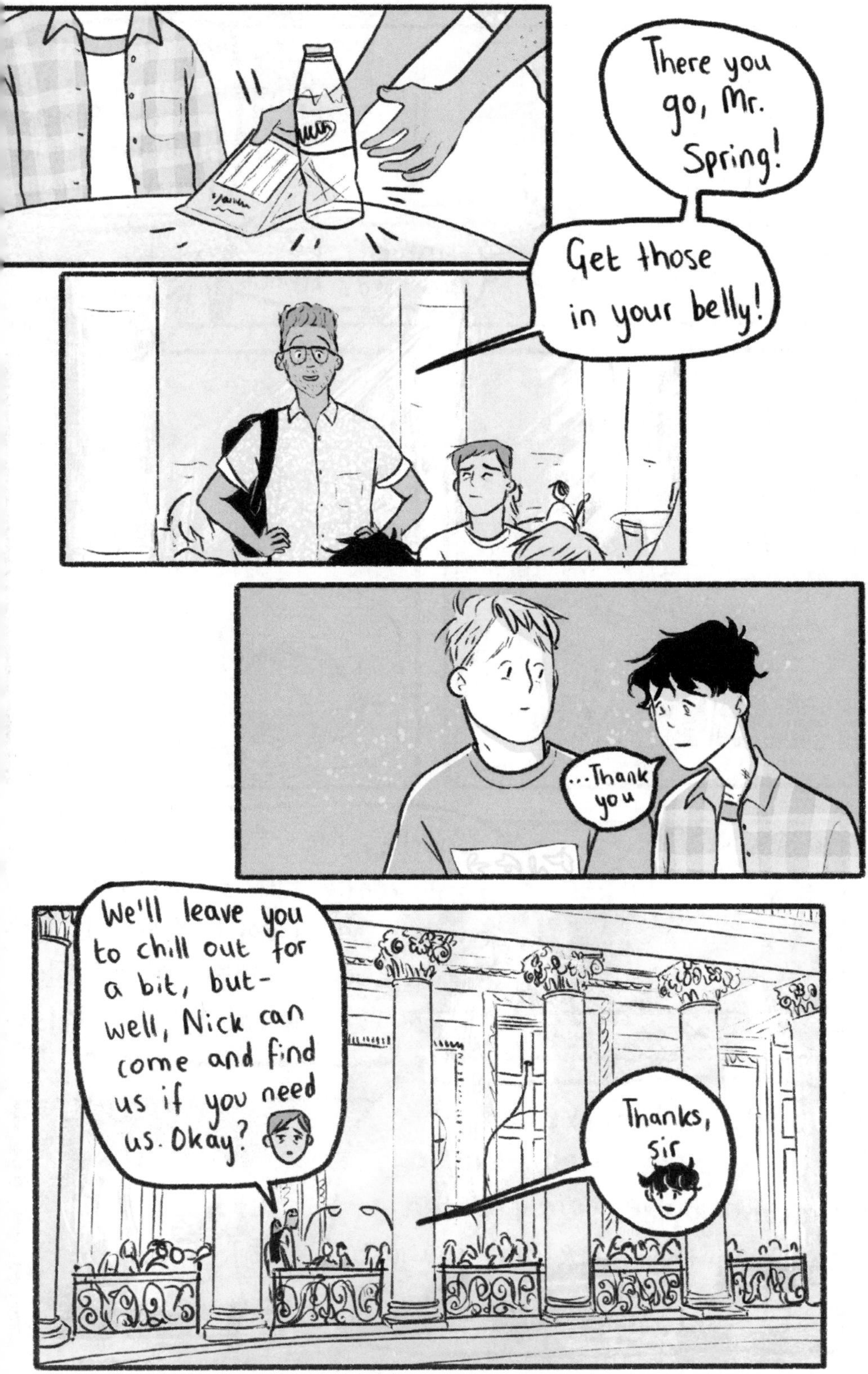
There you go, Mr. Spring!
Get those in your belly!
...Thank you
We'll leave you to chill out for a bit, but- well, Nick can come and find us if you need us. Okay?
Thanks, sir

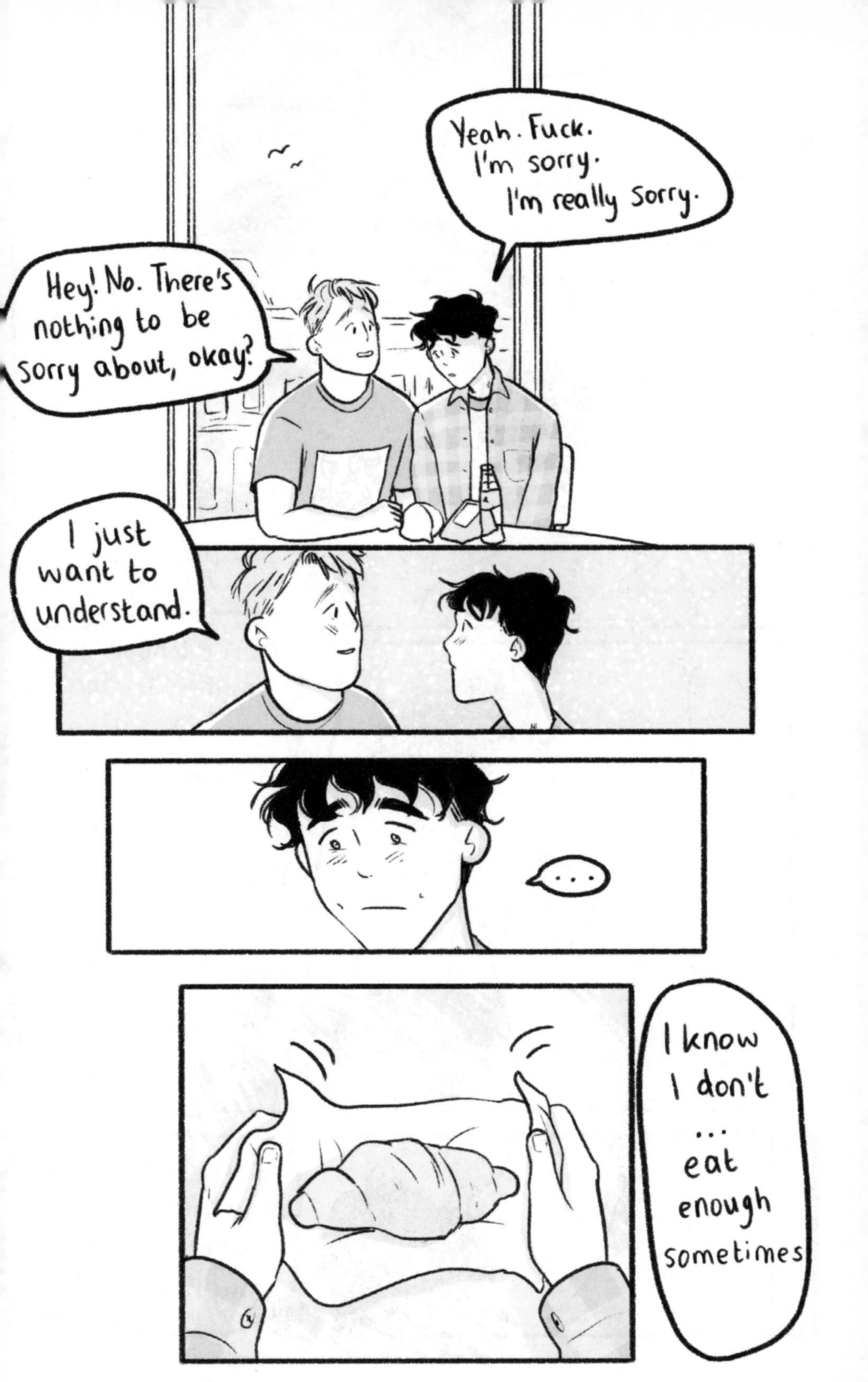
Yeah. Fuck. I'm sorry. I'm really sorry.
Hey! No. There's nothing to be sorry about, okay?
I just want to understand.
...
I know I don't ... eat enough sometimes

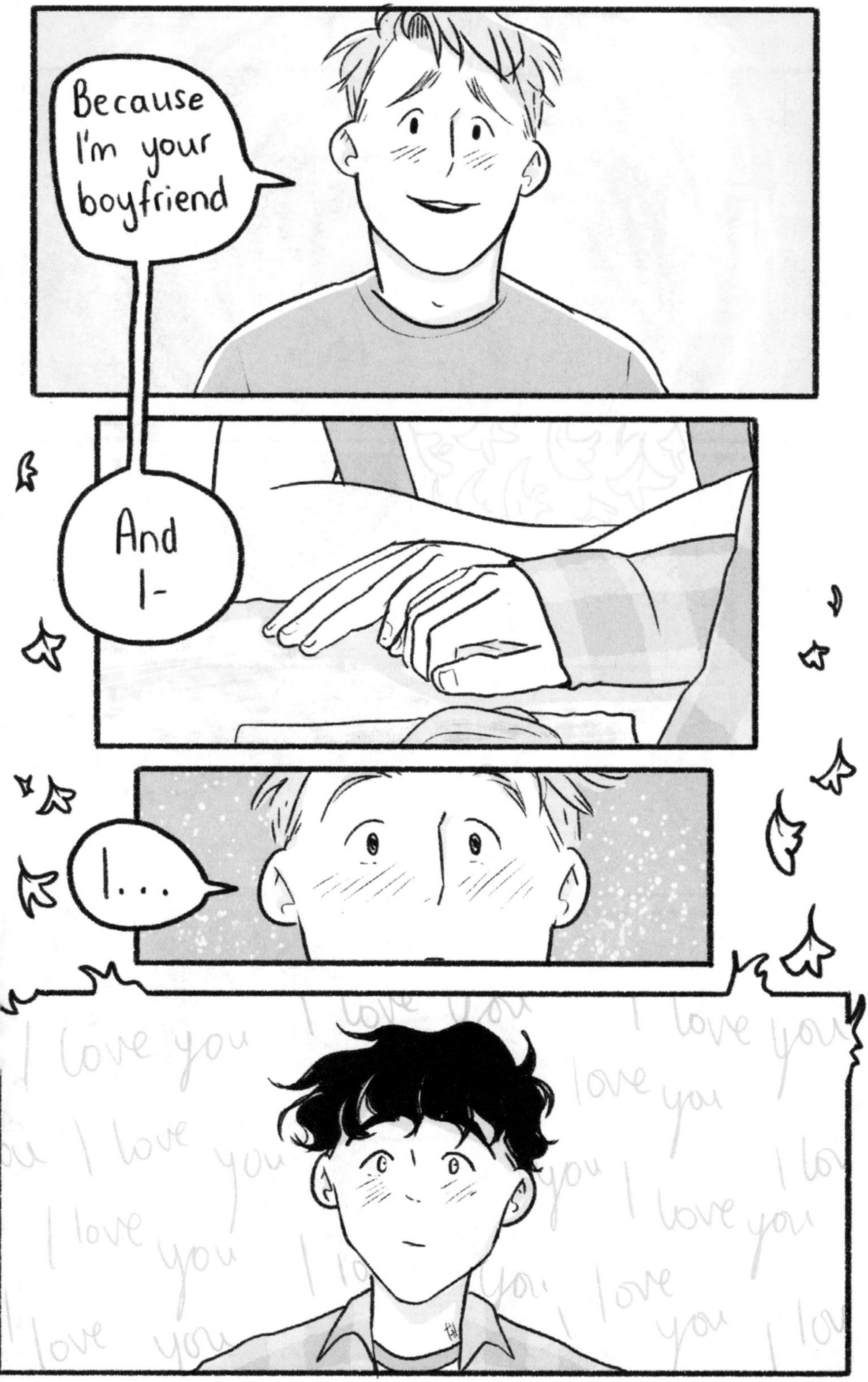
Because I'm your boyfriend
And I-
I...

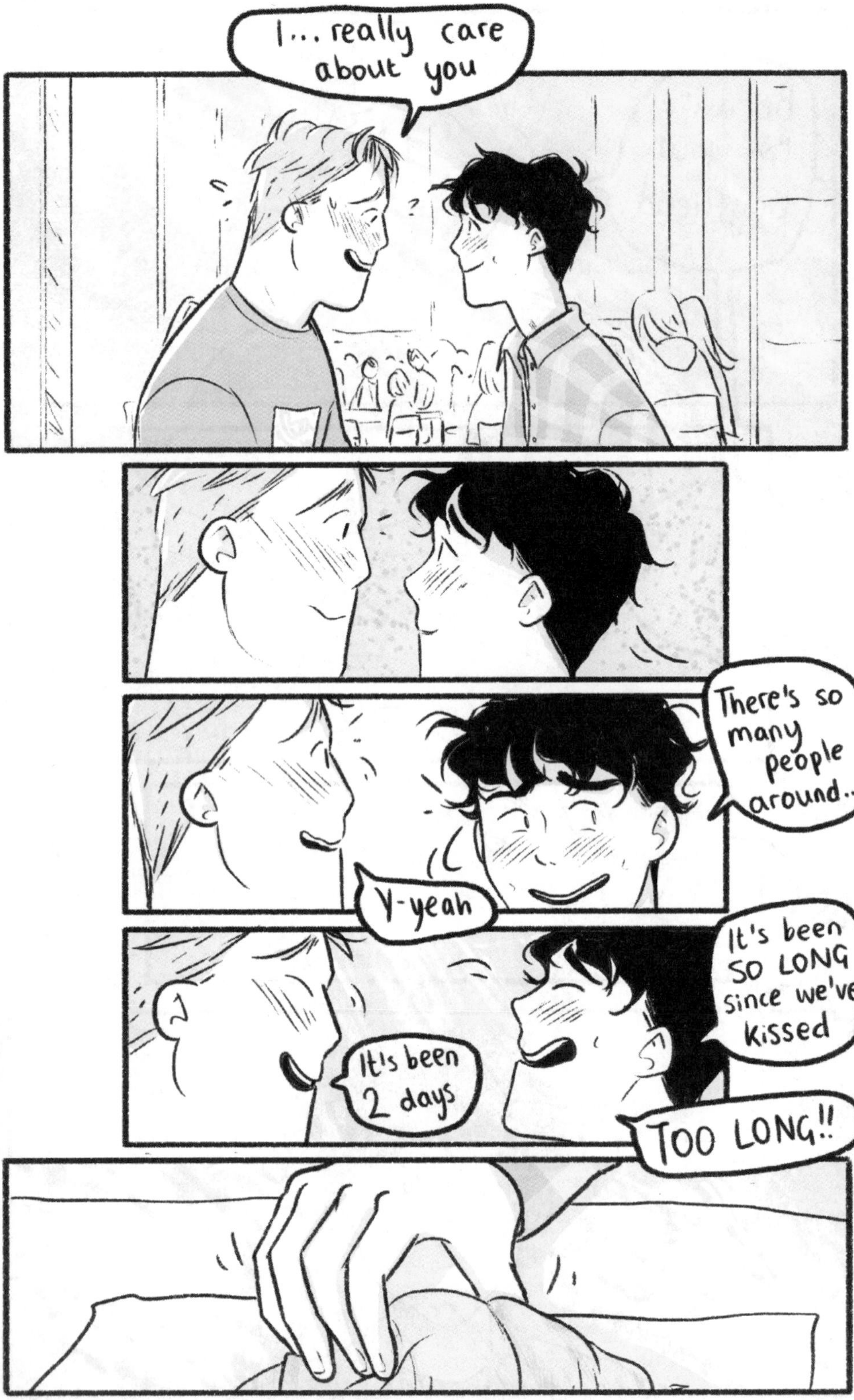
I... really care about you
There's so many people around...
Y-yeah
It's been SO LONG since we've kissed
It's been 2 days
TOO LONG!!

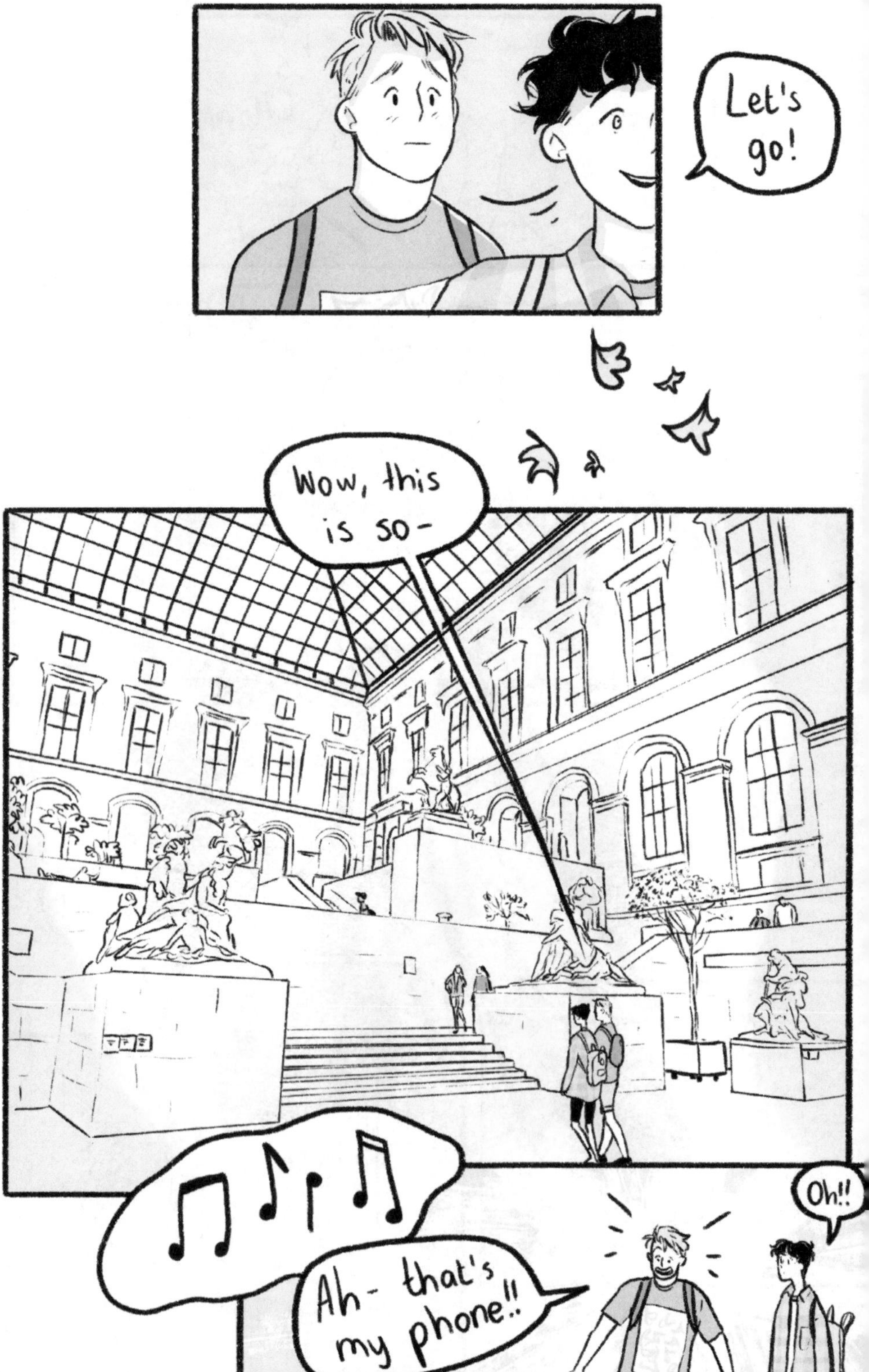
Let's go!
Wow, this is so-
Ah- that's my phone!!
Oh!!

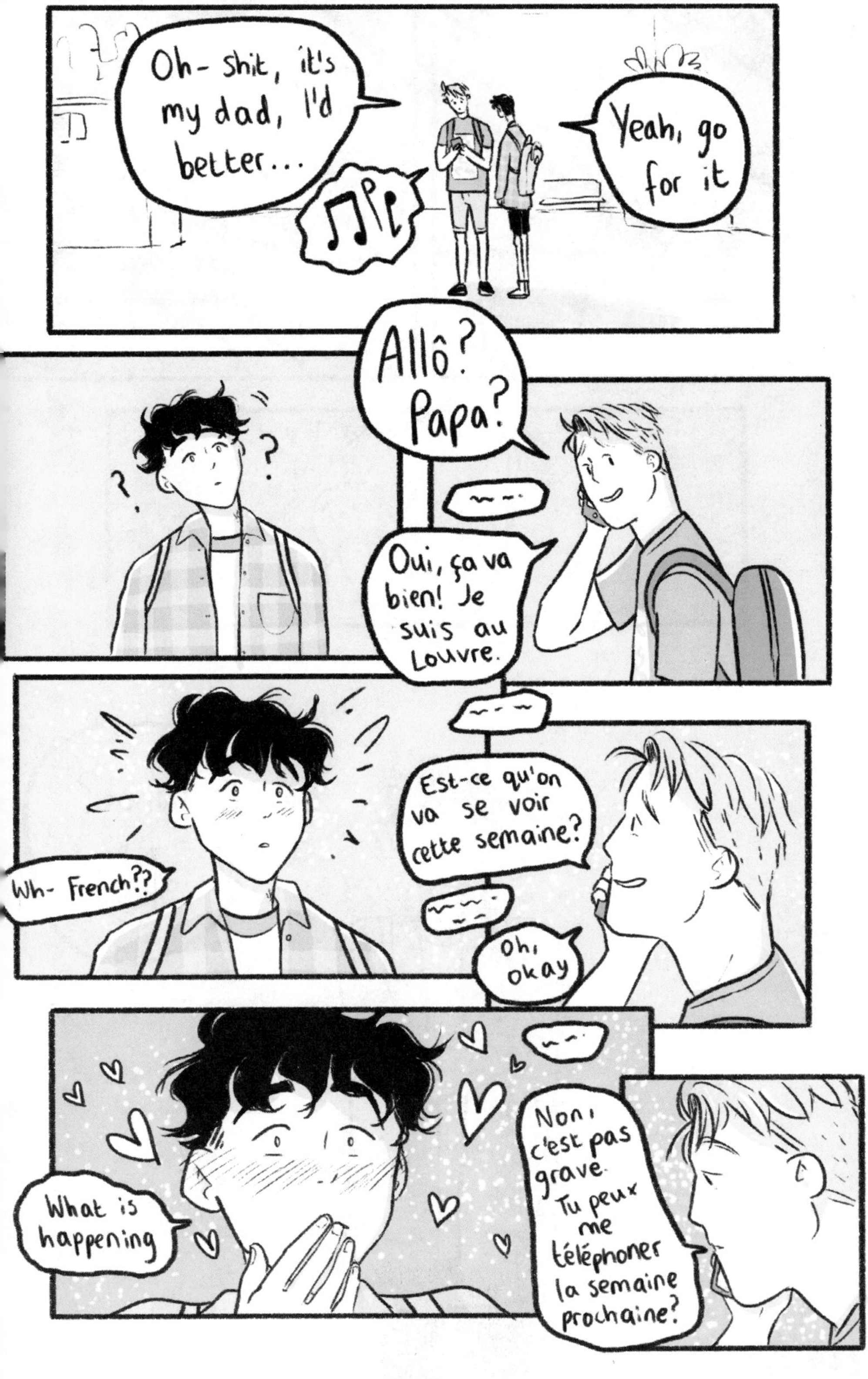
Oh- shit, it's my dad, I'd better...
Yeah, go for it
Allô? Papa?
Oui, ça va bien! Je suis au Louvre.
Est-ce qu'on va se voir cette semaine?
Wh- French??
Oh, okay
What is happening
Non, c'est pas grave. Tu peux me téléphoner la semaine prochaine?

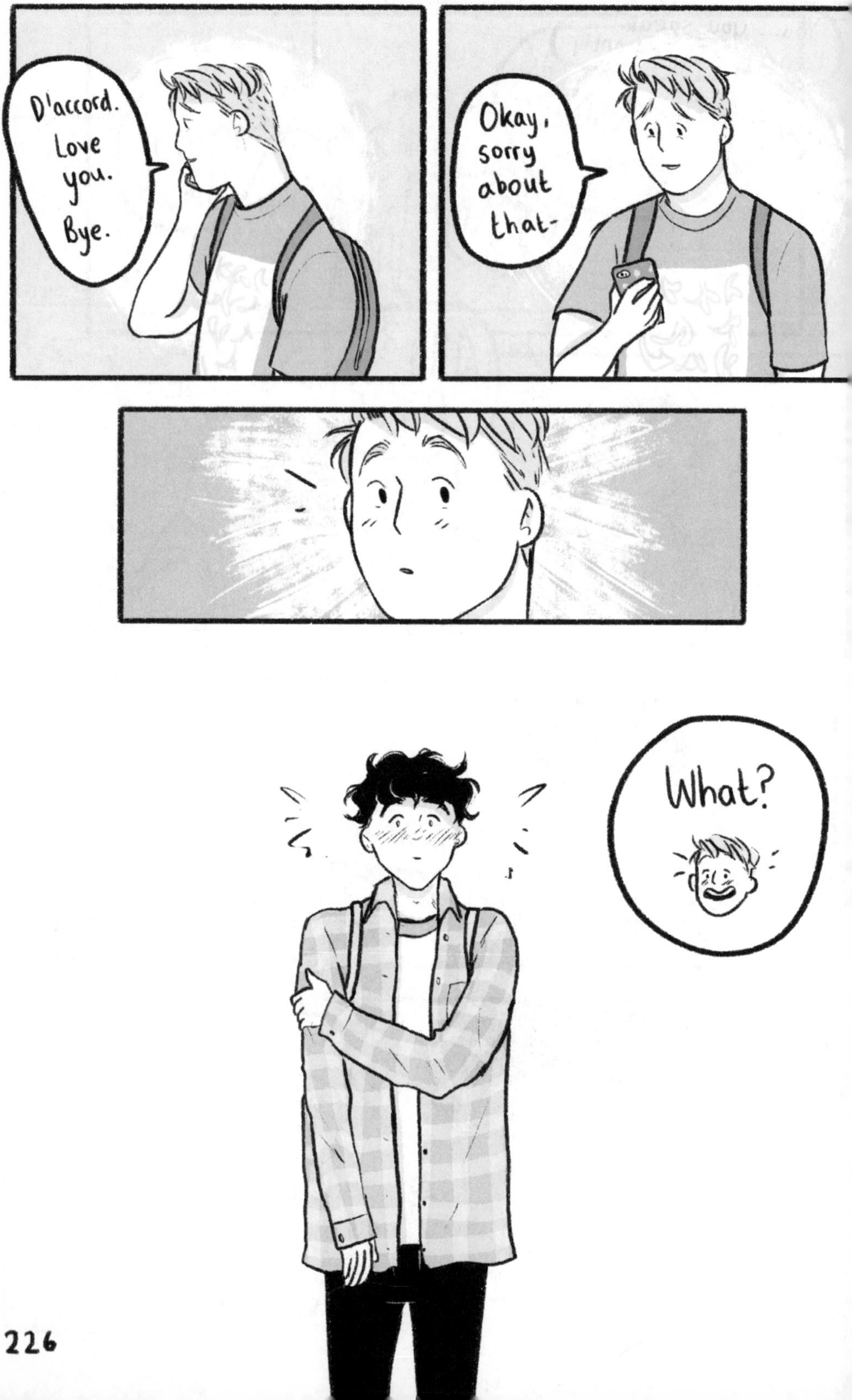
D'accord. Love you. Bye.
Okay, sorry about that-
What?

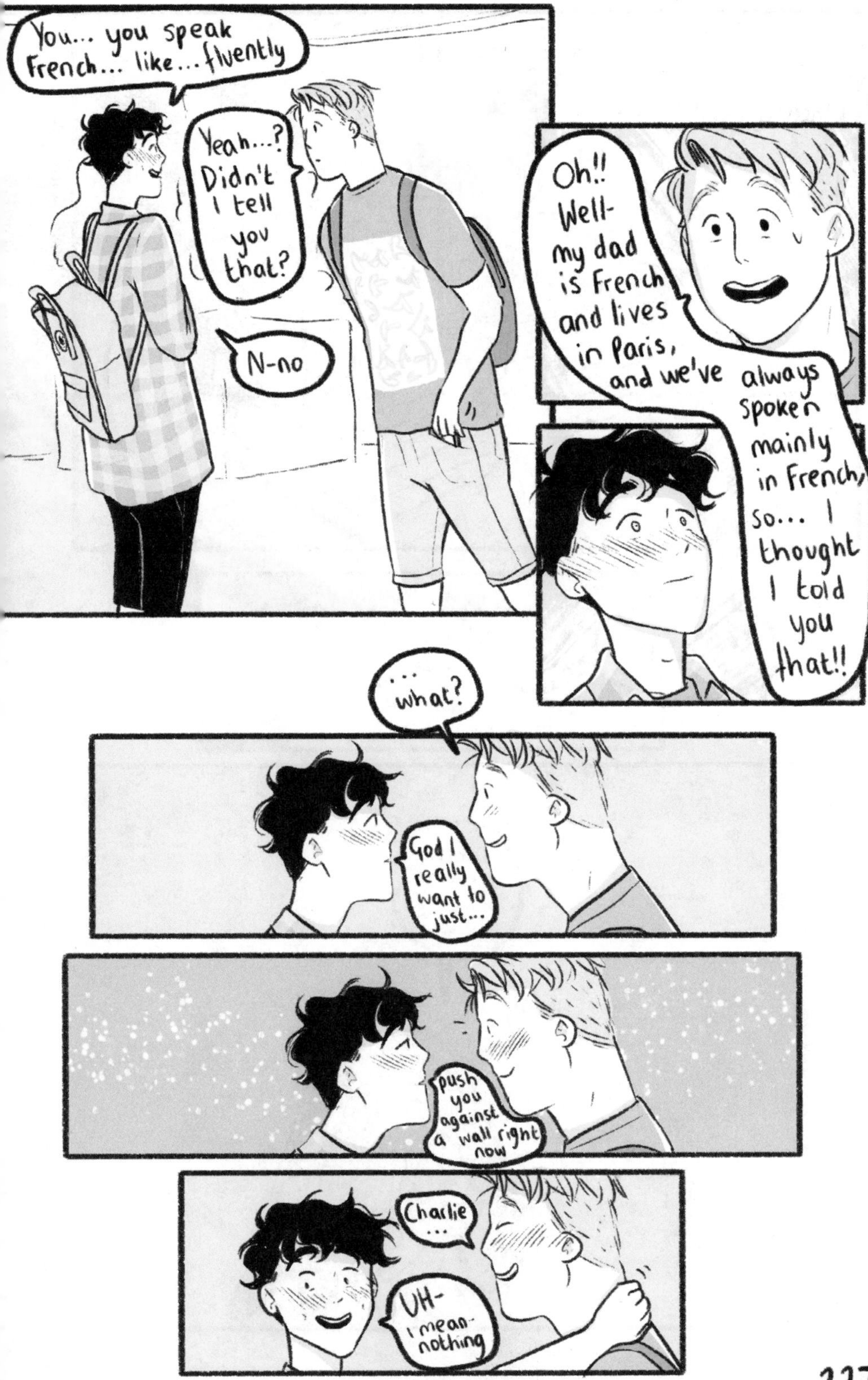
You... you speak French... like... fluently
Yeah...? Didn't I tell you that?
N-no
Oh!! Well- my dad is French and lives in Paris, and we've always spoken mainly in French, so... I thought I told you that!!
... what?
God I really want to just...
push you against a wall right now
Charlie ...
UH- I mean- nothing

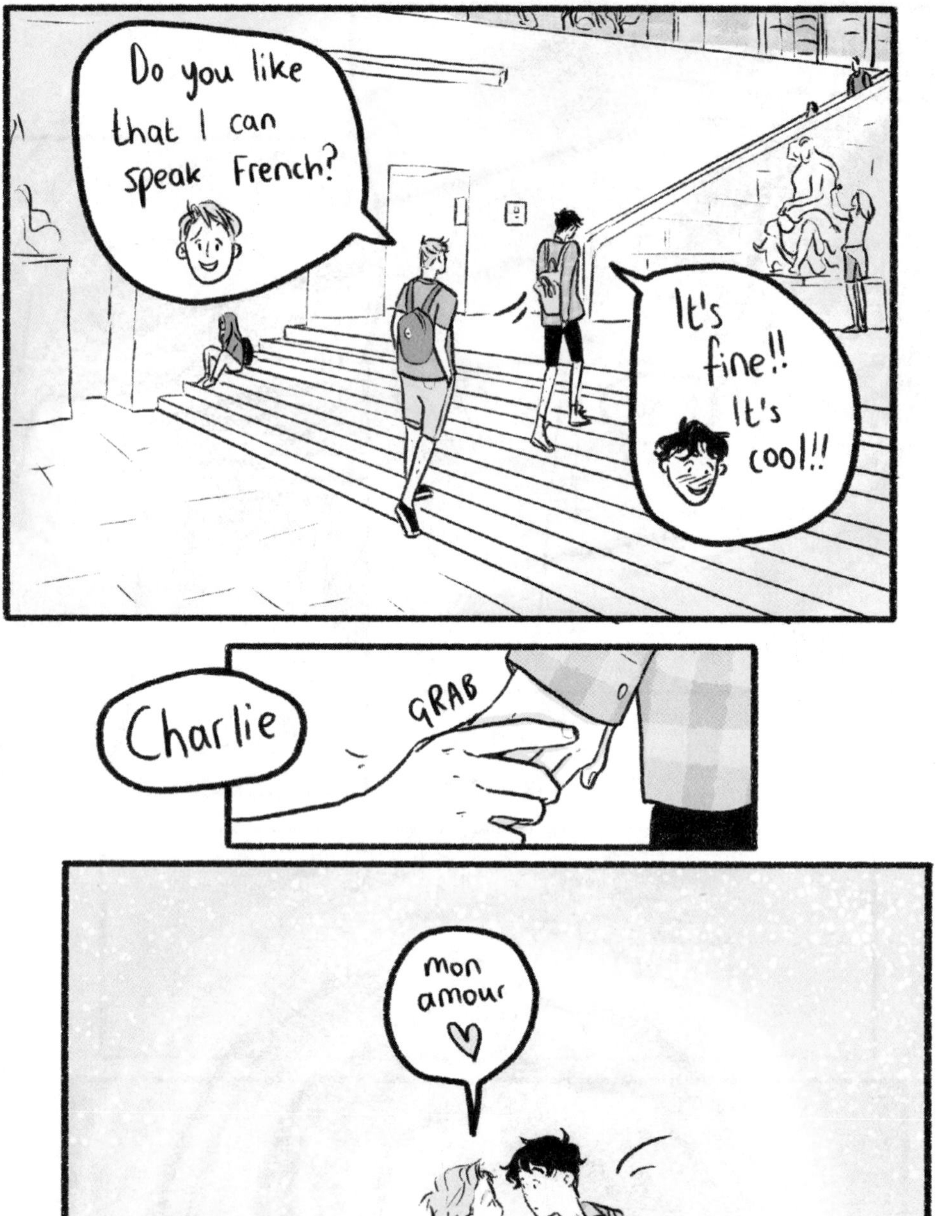
Do you like that I can speak French?
It's fine!! It's cool!!
Charlie
GRAB
mon amour

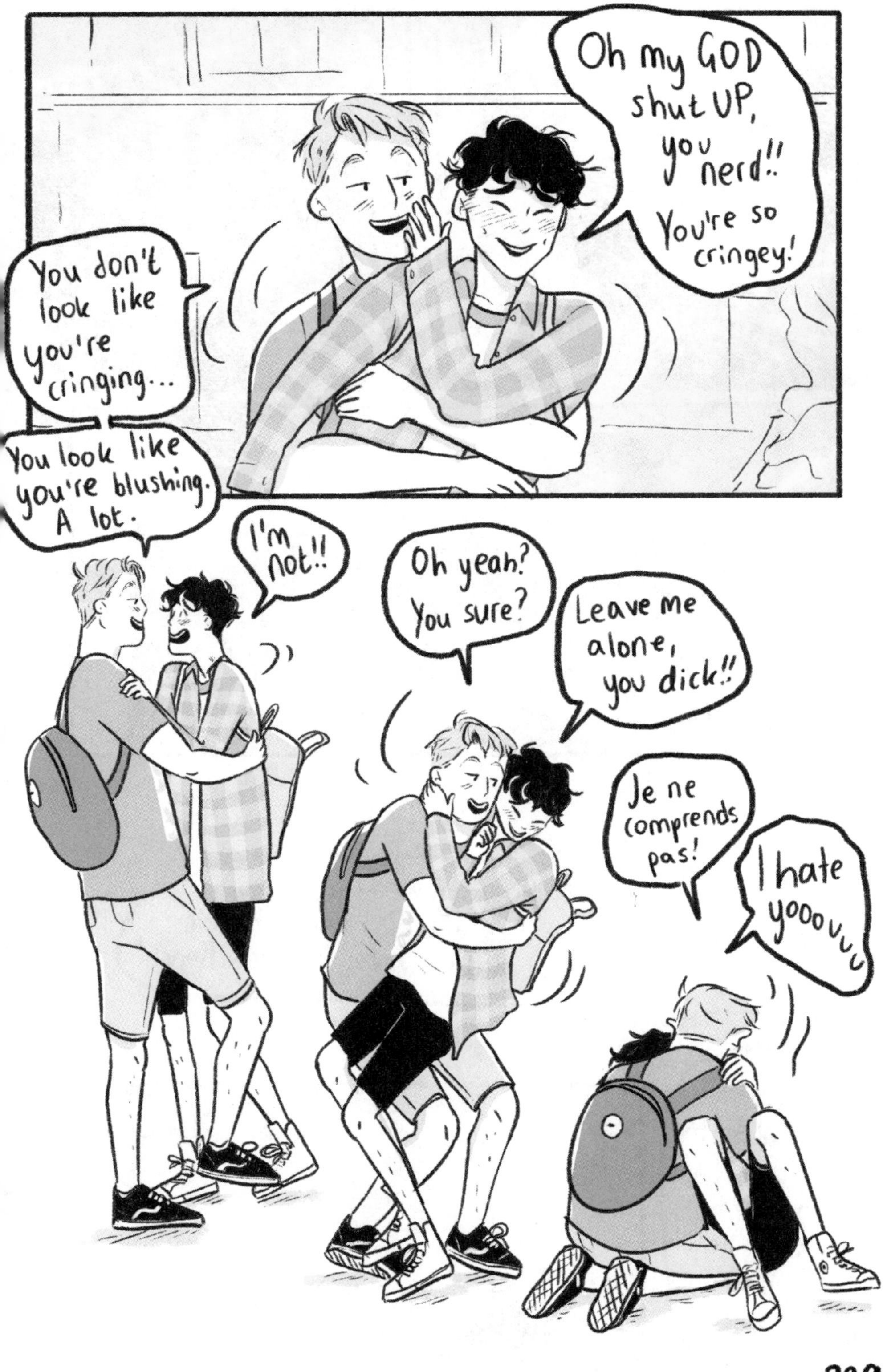
Oh my GOD shut UP, you nerd!!
You're so cringey!
You don't look like you're cringing...
You look like you're blushing. A lot.
I'm not!!
Oh yeah? You sure?
Leave me alone, you dick!!
Je ne comprends pas!
I hate yooouuu

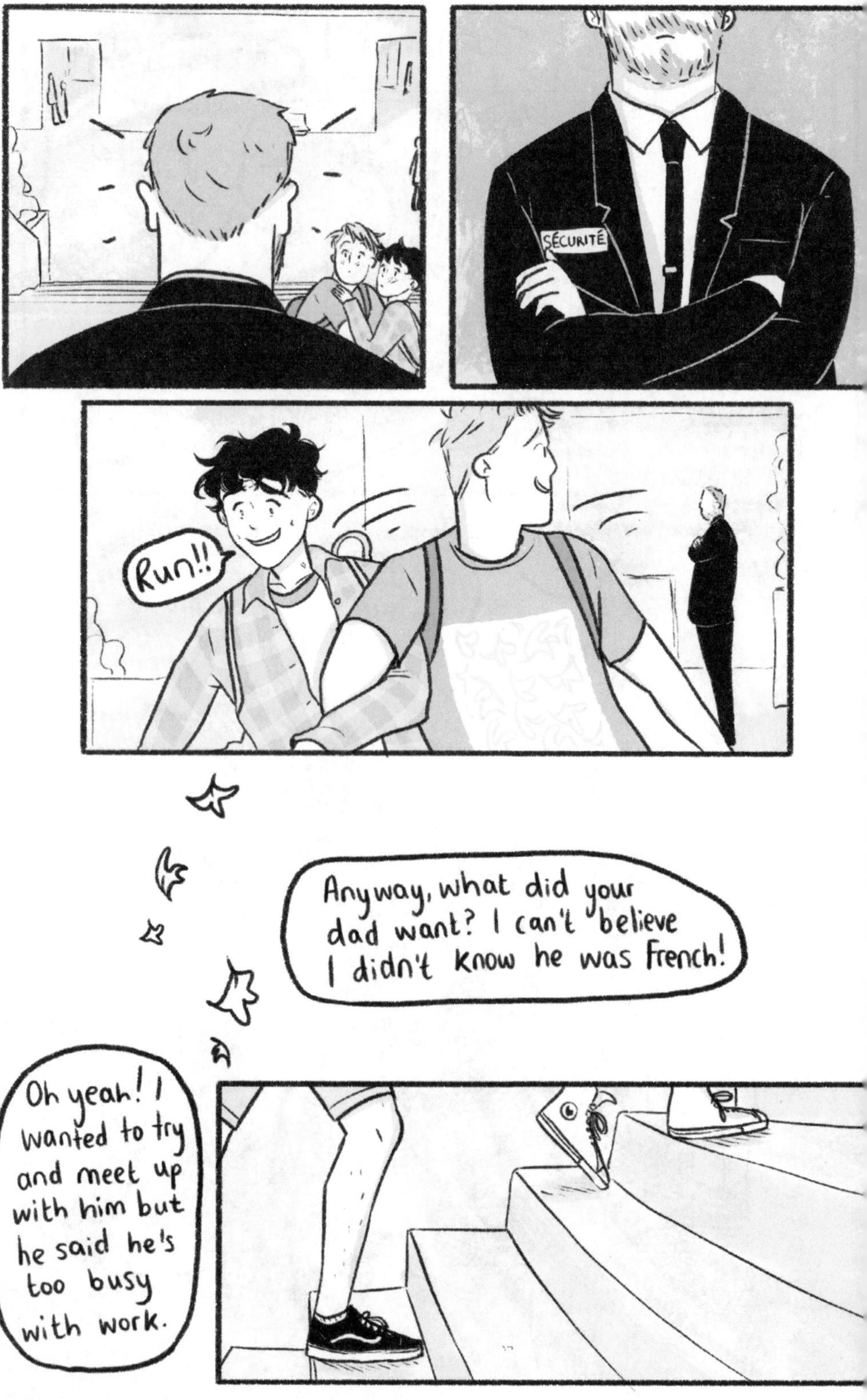
SÉCURITÉ
Run!!
Anyway, what did your dad want? I can't believe I didn't know he was French!
Oh yeah! I wanted to try and meet up with him but he said he's too busy with work.

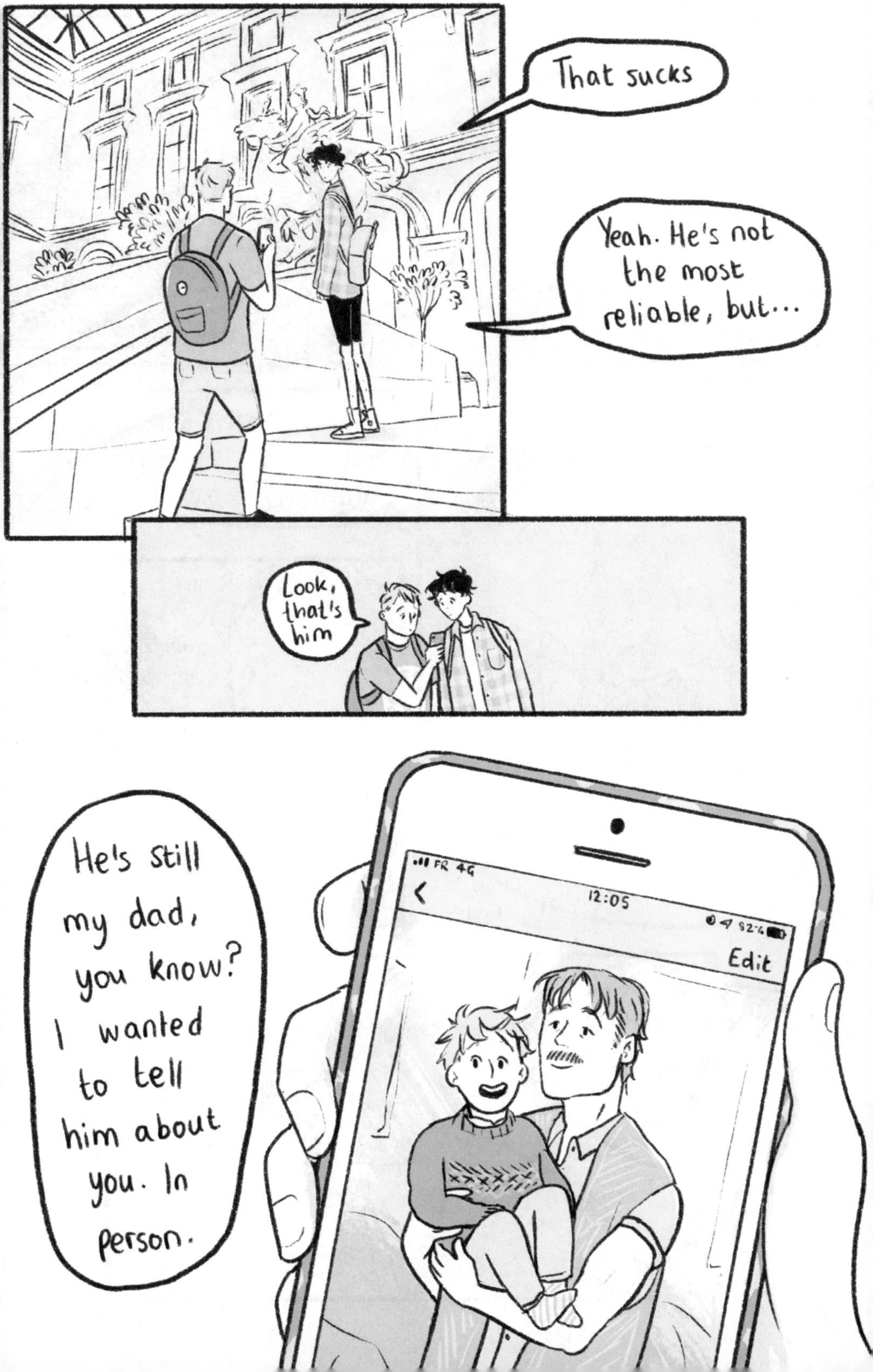
That sucks
Yeah. He's not the most reliable, but...
Look, that's him
He's still my dad, you know? I wanted to tell him about you. In person.
12:05
Edit

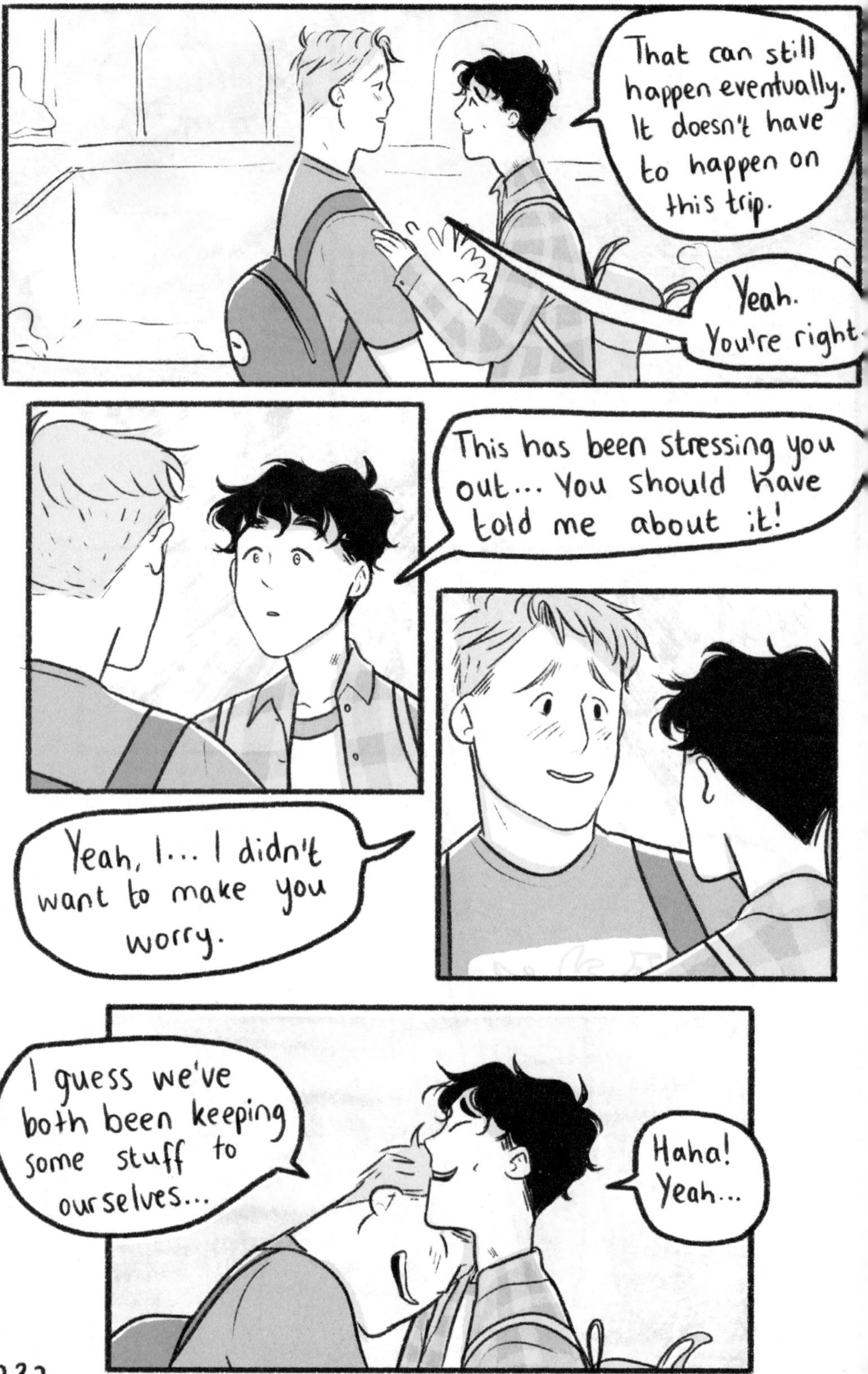
That can still happen eventually. It doesn't have to happen on this trip.
Yeah. You're right.
This has been stressing you out... You should have told me about it!
Yeah, I... I didn't want to make you worry.
I guess we've both been keeping some stuff to ourselves...
Haha! Yeah...

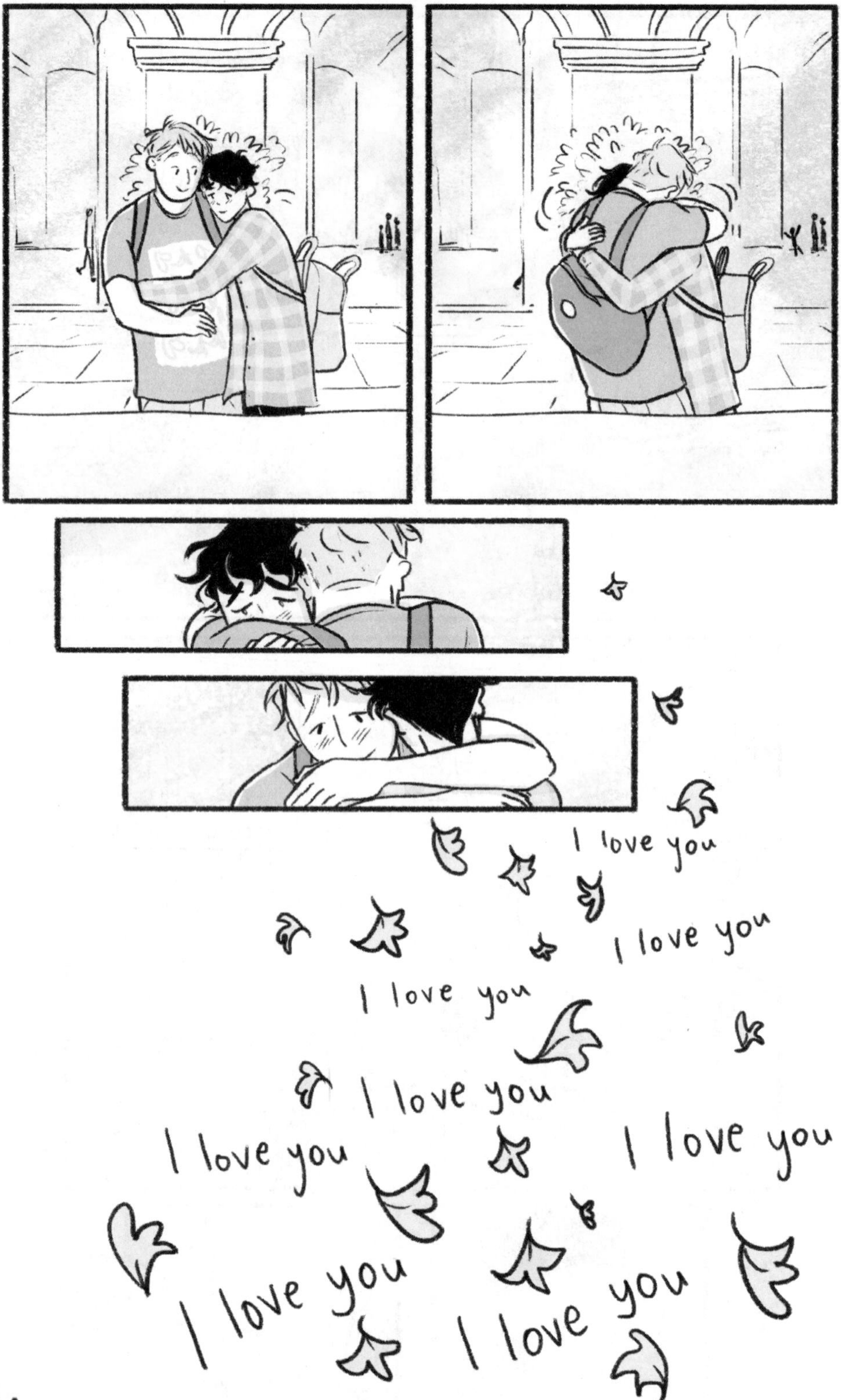
I love you
I love you
I love you
I love you
I love you
I love you
I love you
I love you

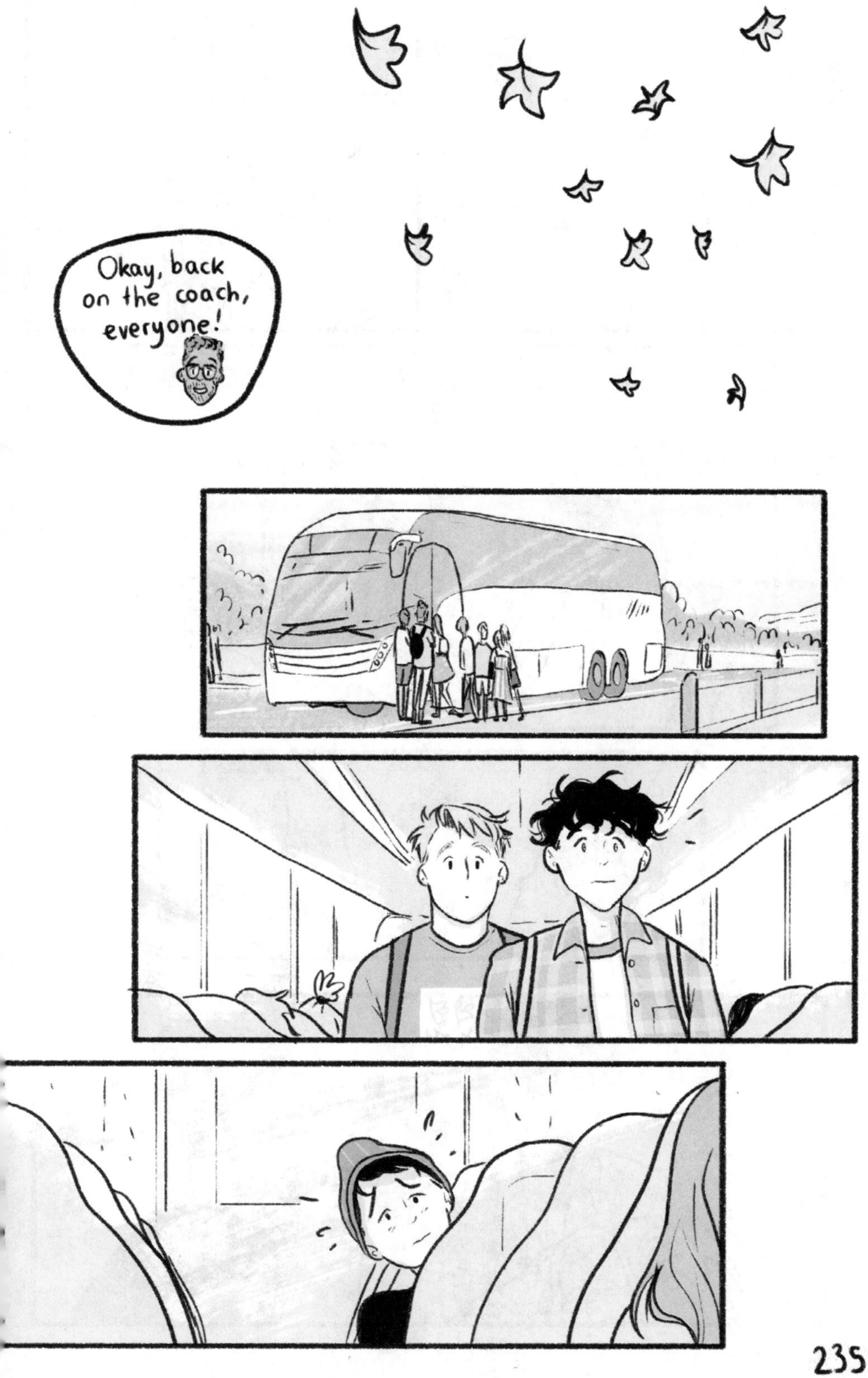
Okay, back on the coach, everyone!

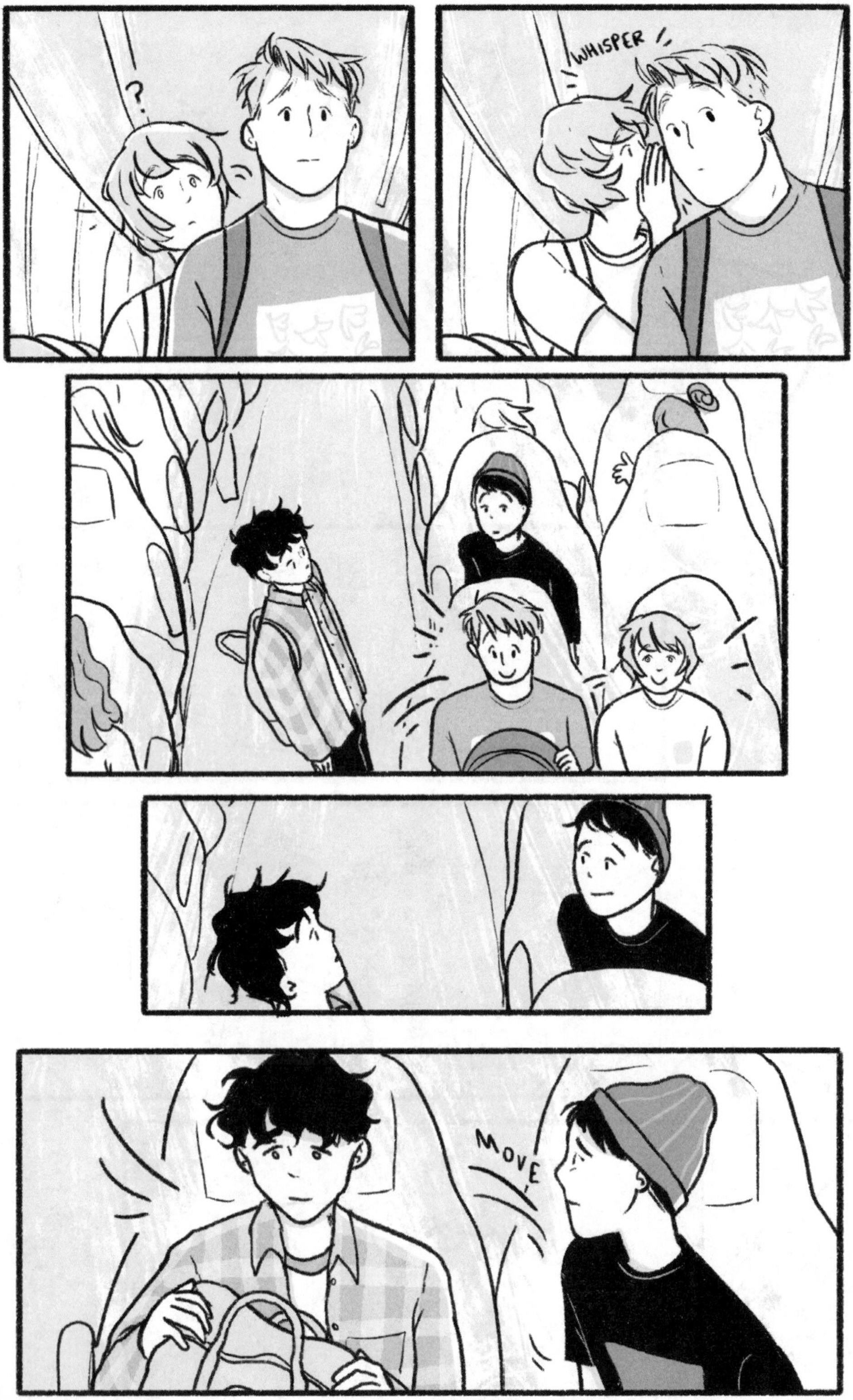
?
WHISPER
MOVE

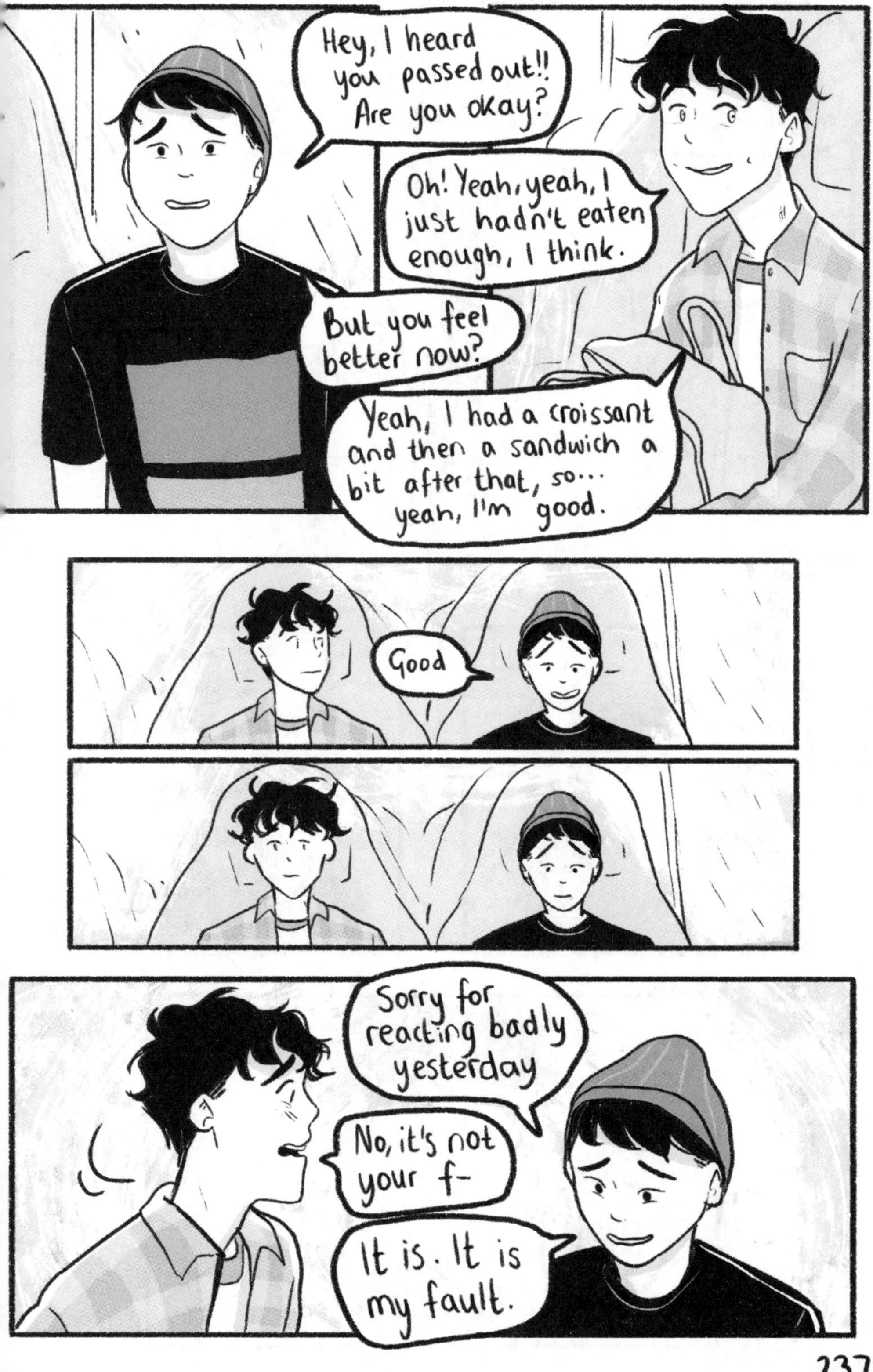
Hey, I heard you passed out!! Are you okay?
Oh! Yeah, yeah, I just hadn't eaten enough, I think.
But you feel better now?
Yeah, I had a croissant and then a sandwich a bit after that, so... yeah, I'm good.
Good
Sorry for reacting badly yesterday
No, it's not your f-
It is. It is my fault.

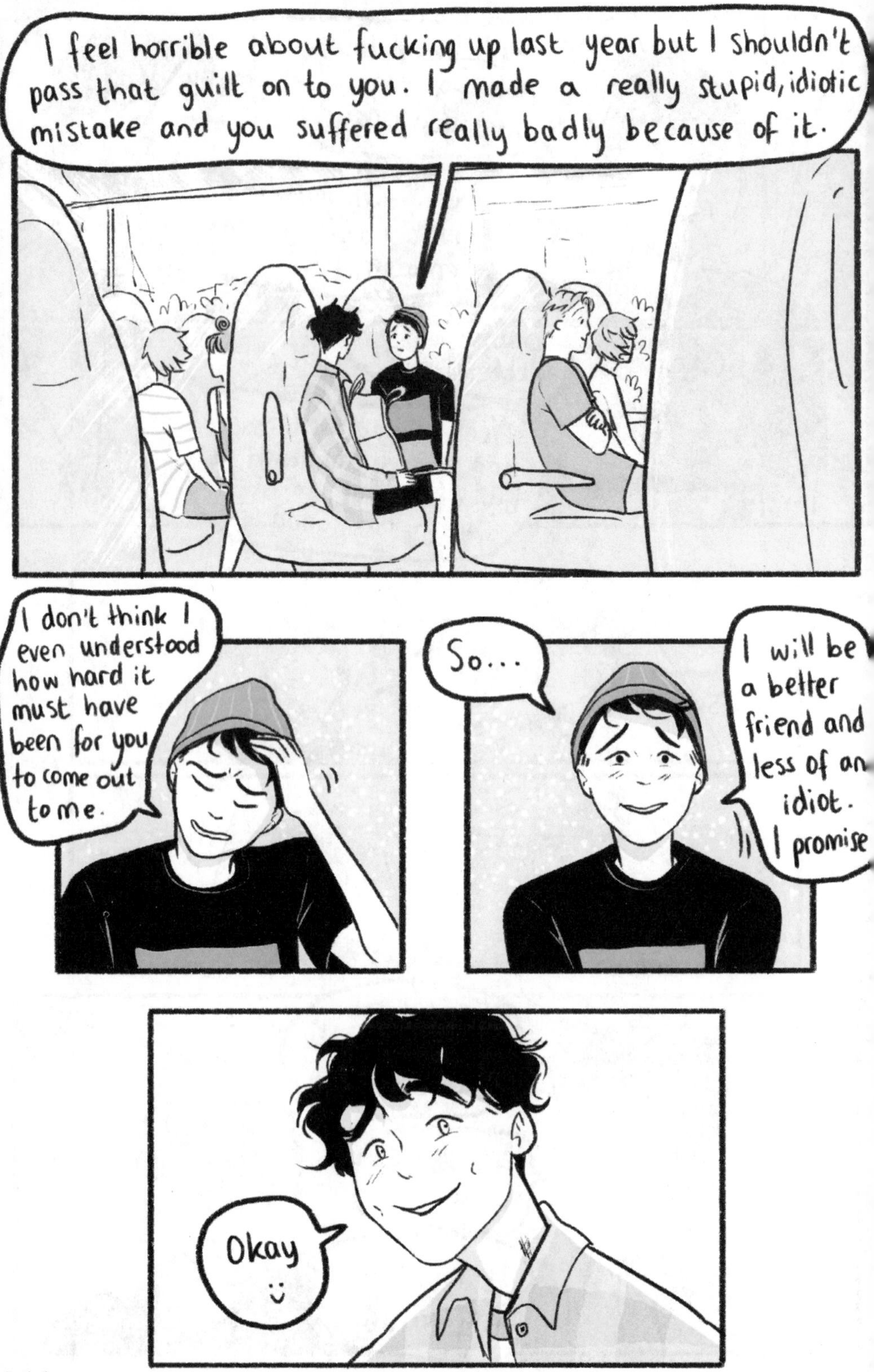
I feel horrible about fucking up last year but I shouldn't pass that guilt on to you. I made a really stupid, idiotic mistake and you suffered really badly because of it.
I don't think I even understood how hard it must have been for you to come out to me.
So...
I will be a better friend and less of an idiot. I promise
Okay

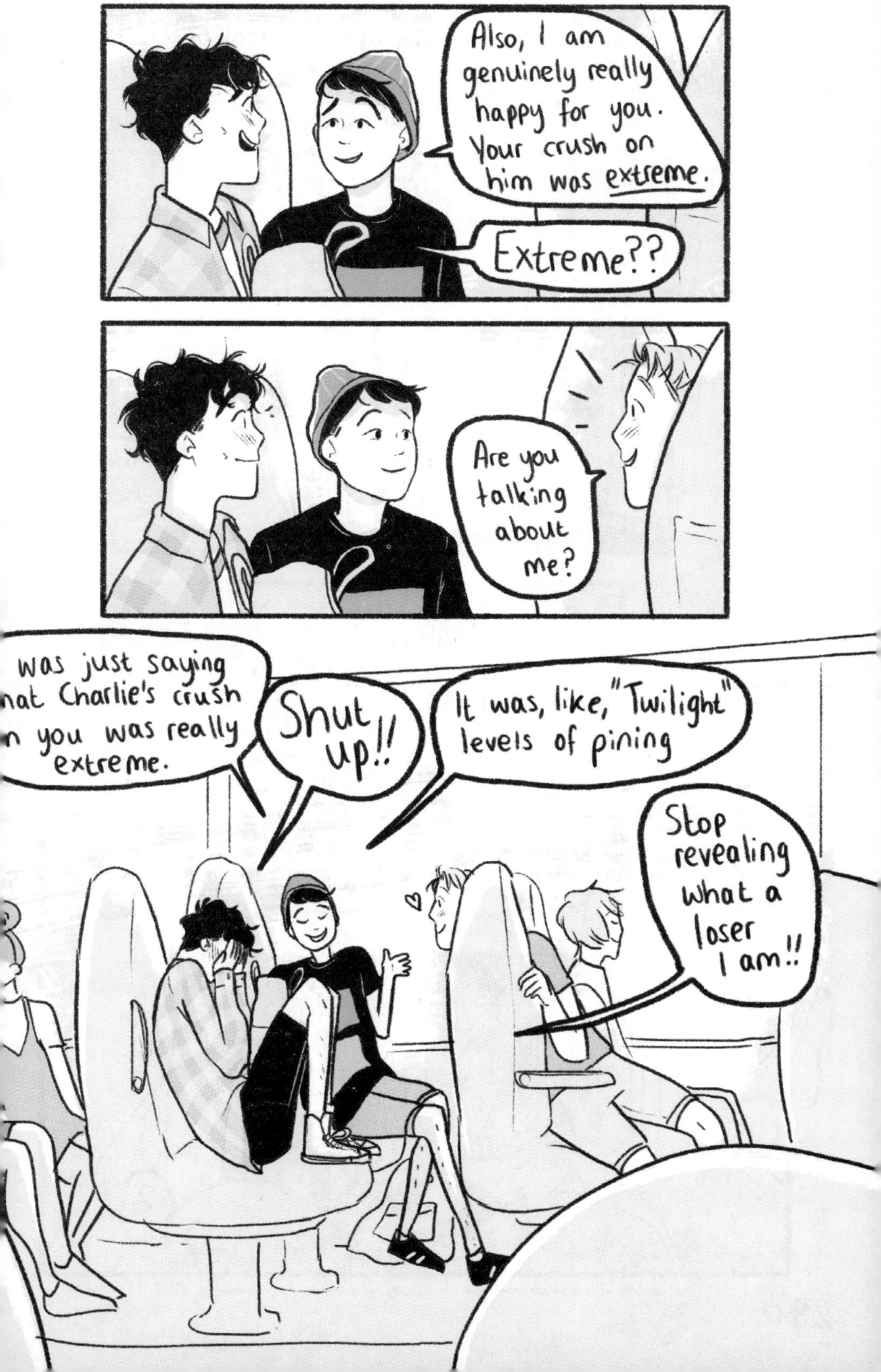
Also, I am genuinely really happy for you. Your crush on him was extreme.
Extreme??
Are you talking about me?
was just saying nat Charlie's crush n you was really extreme.
Shut up!!
It was, like, "Twilight" levels of pining
Stop revealing what a loser I am!!

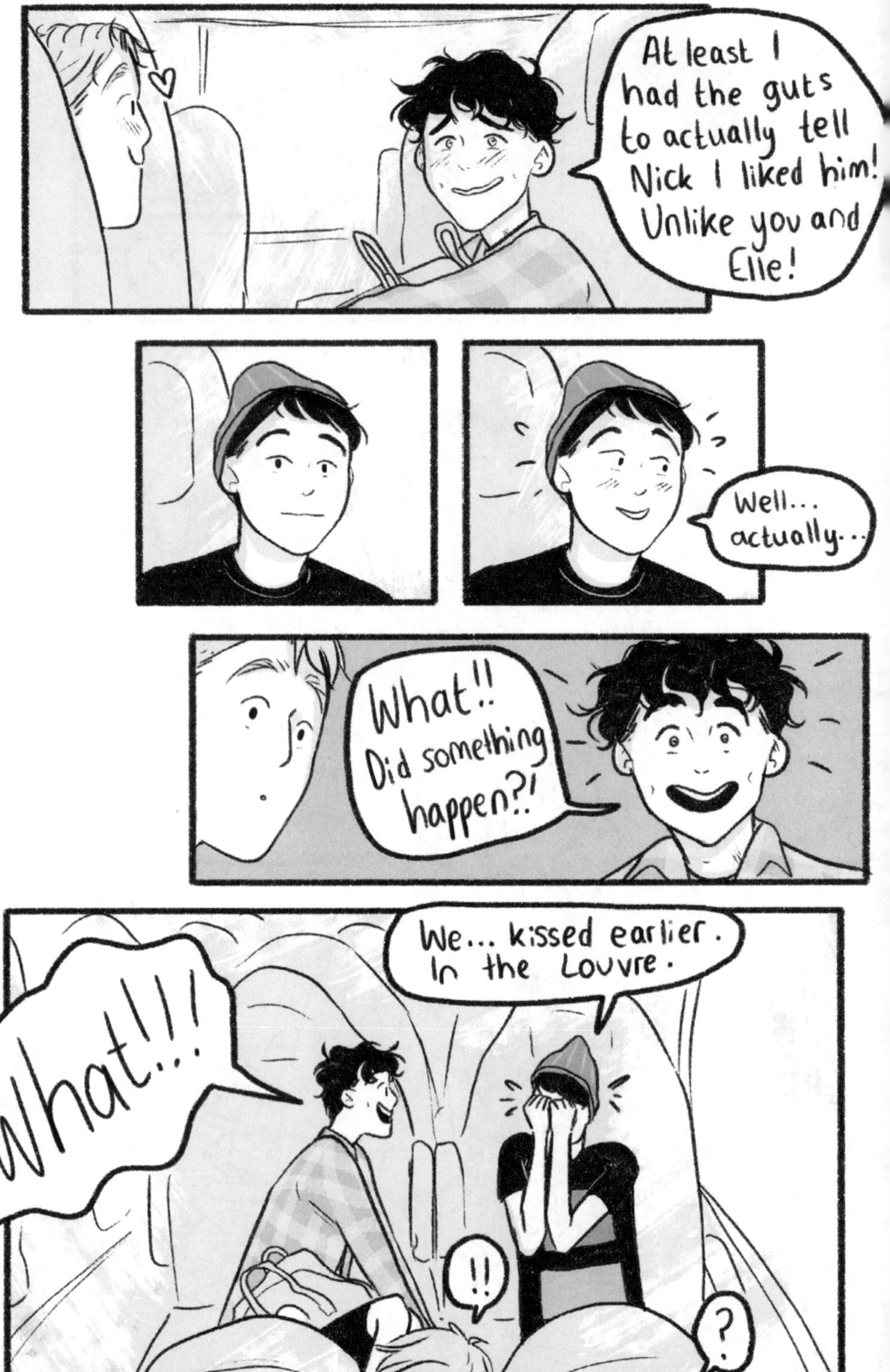
At least I had the guts to actually tell Nick I liked him! Unlike you and Elle!
Well... actually...
What!! Did something happen?!
What!!!
We... kissed earlier. In the Louvre.
!!
?

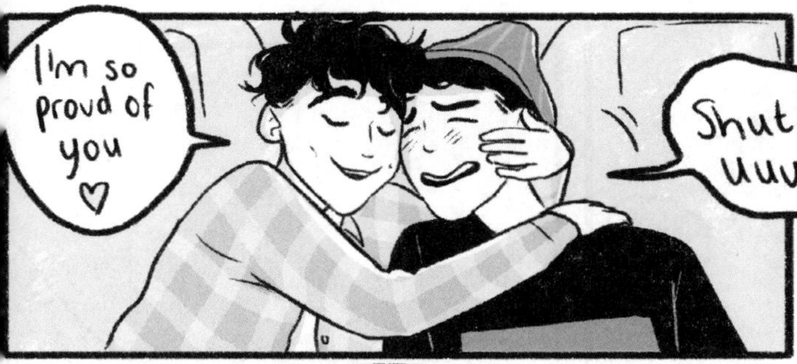
I'm so proud of you ♡
Shut uuuuup

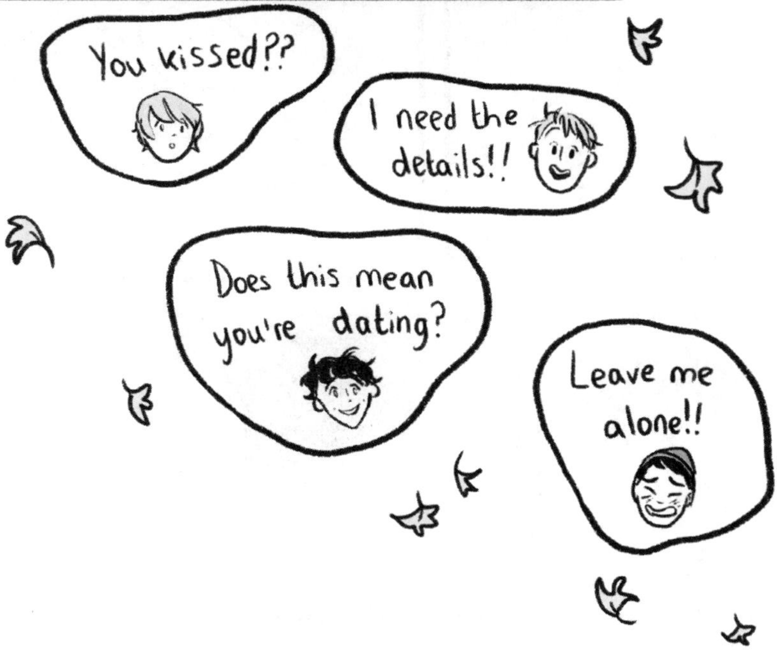
You kissed??
I need the details!!
Does this mean you're dating?
Leave me alone!!

Paris – Day 5

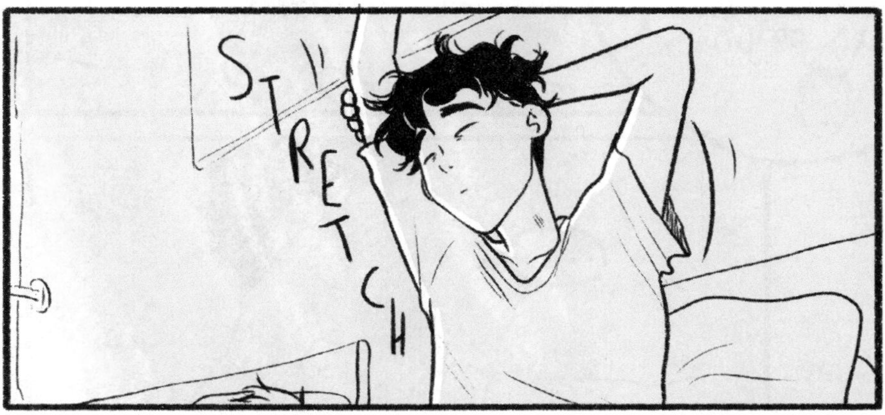
STRETCH

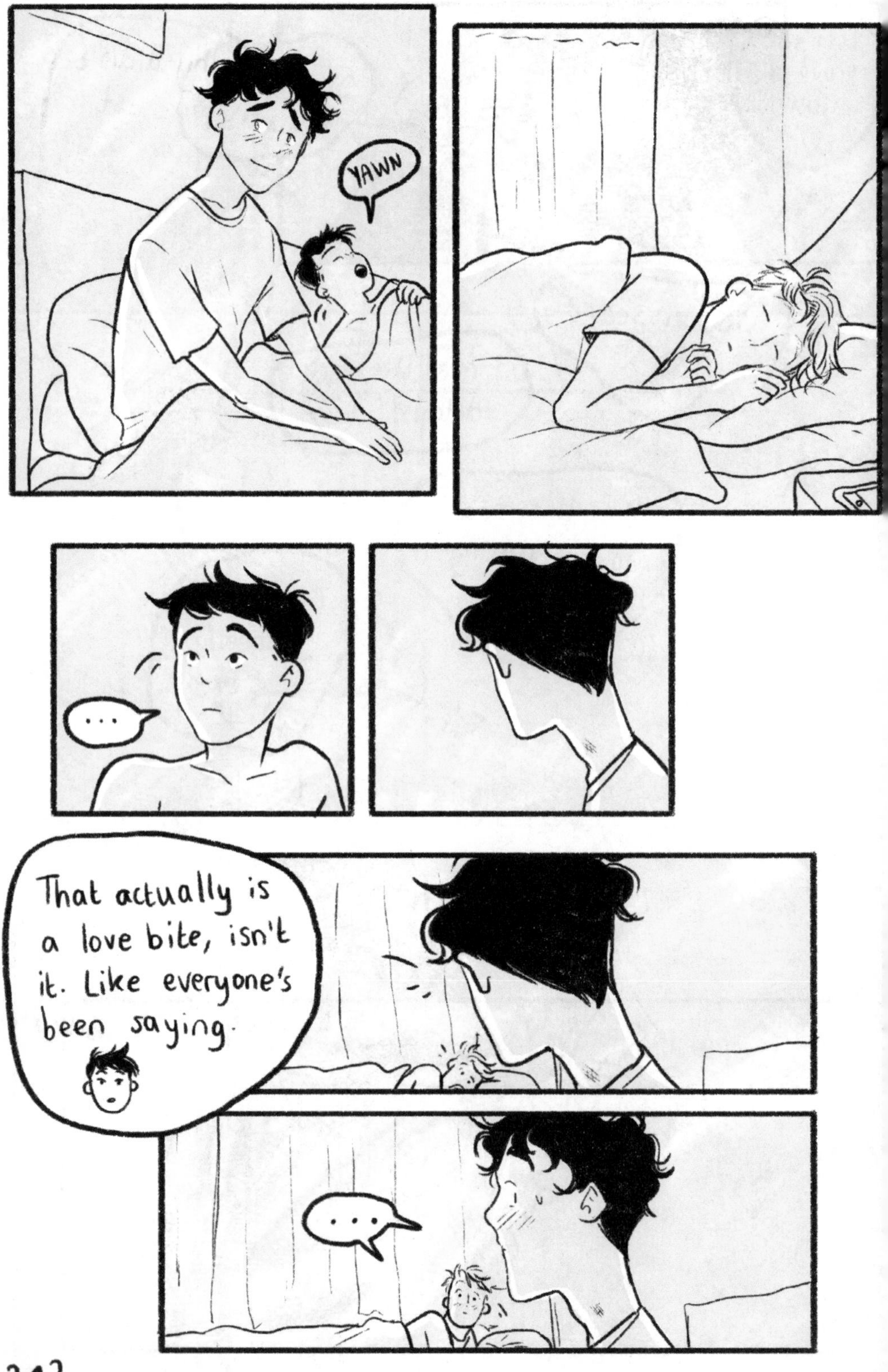
YAWN
...
That actually is a love bite, isn't it. Like everyone's been saying.
...

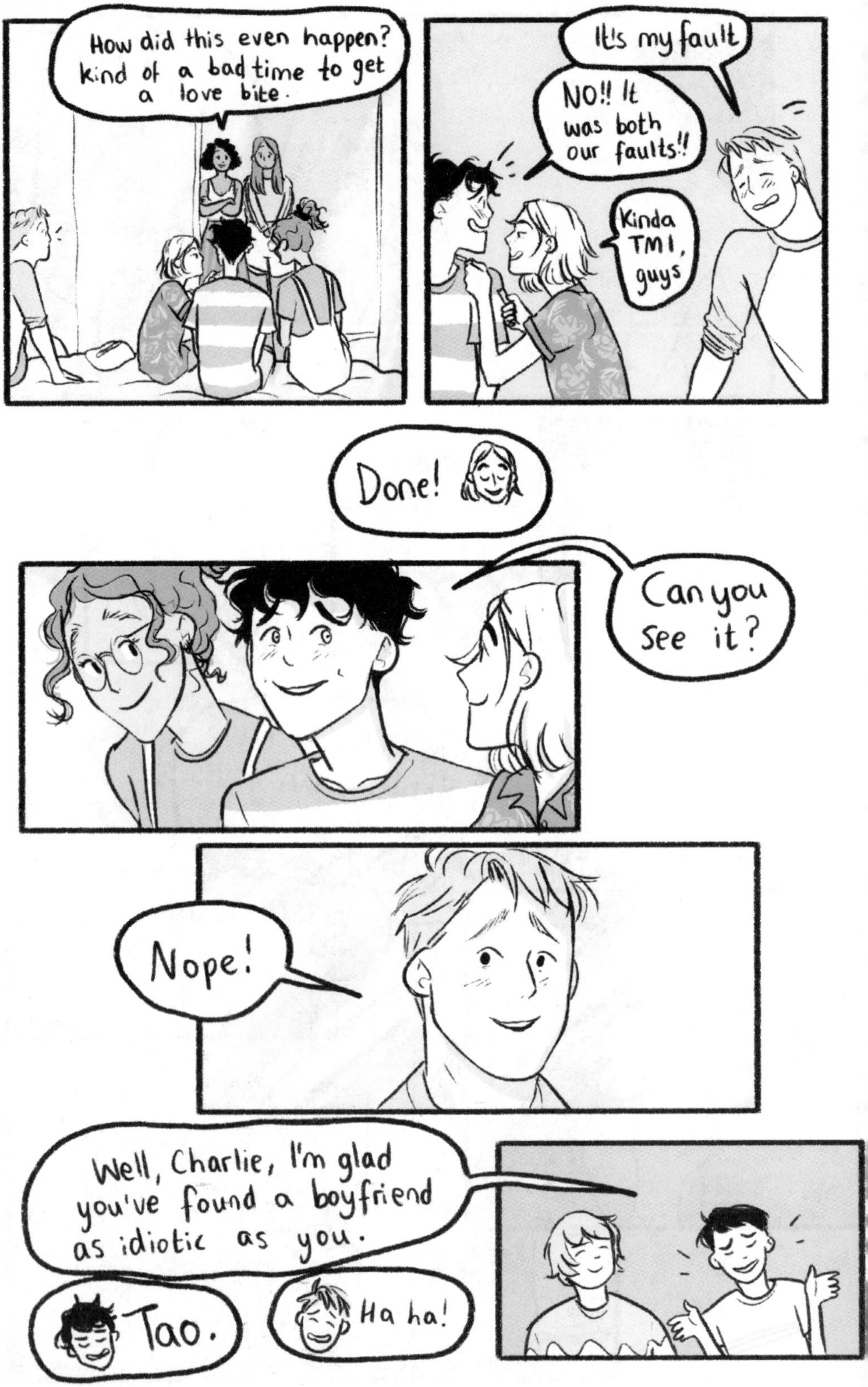
How did this even happen? kind of a bad time to get a love bite.
It's my fault
NO!! It was both our faults!!
Kinda TMI, guys
Done!
Can you see it?
Nope!
Well, Charlie, I'm glad you've found a boyfriend as idiotic as you.
Tao.
Ha ha!

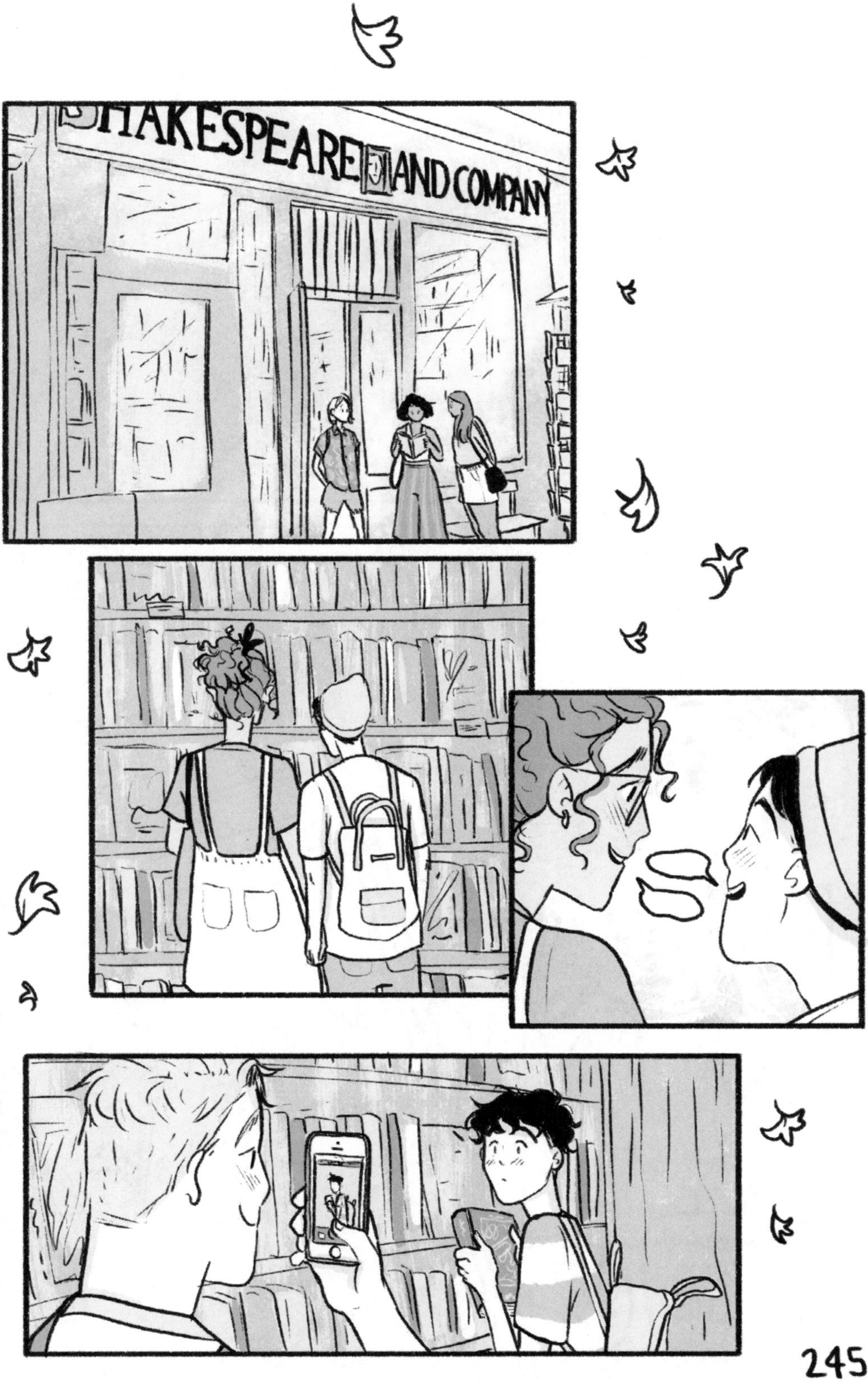
SHAKESPEARE AND COMPANY

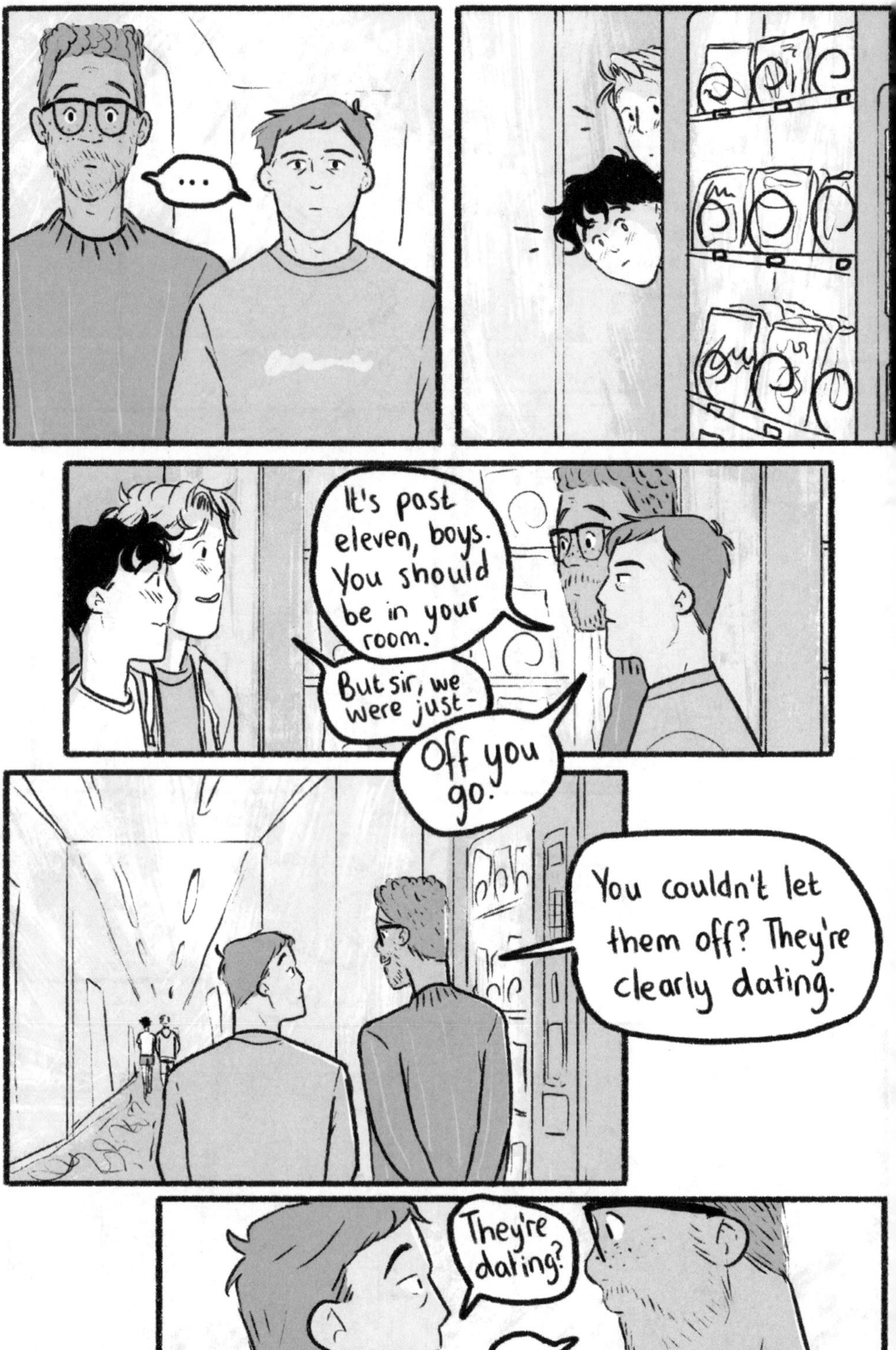
...
It's past eleven, boys. You should be in your room.
But sir, we were just-
Off you go.
You couldn't let them off? They're clearly dating.
They're dating?
...

251

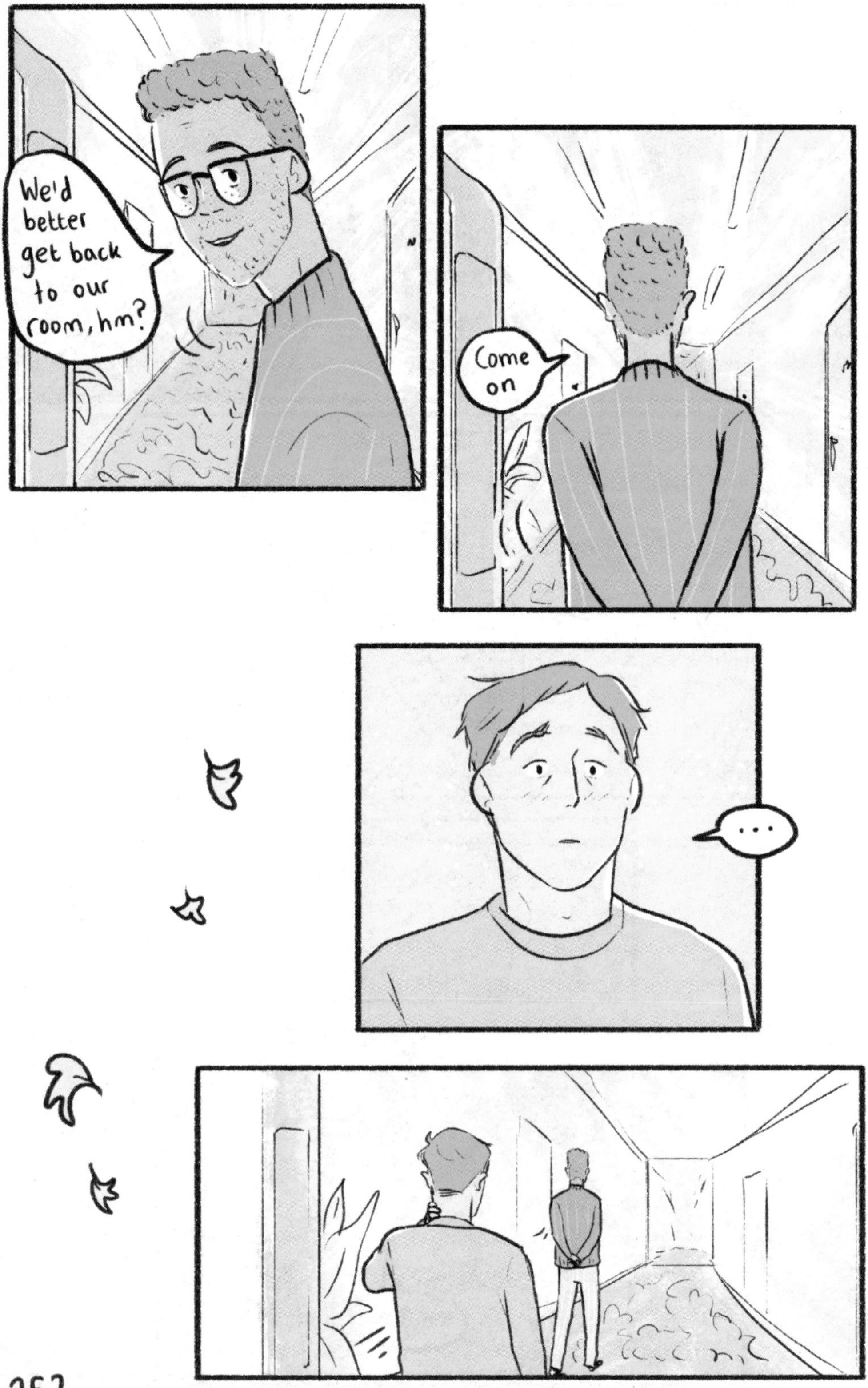
We'd better get back to our room, hm?
Come on
...

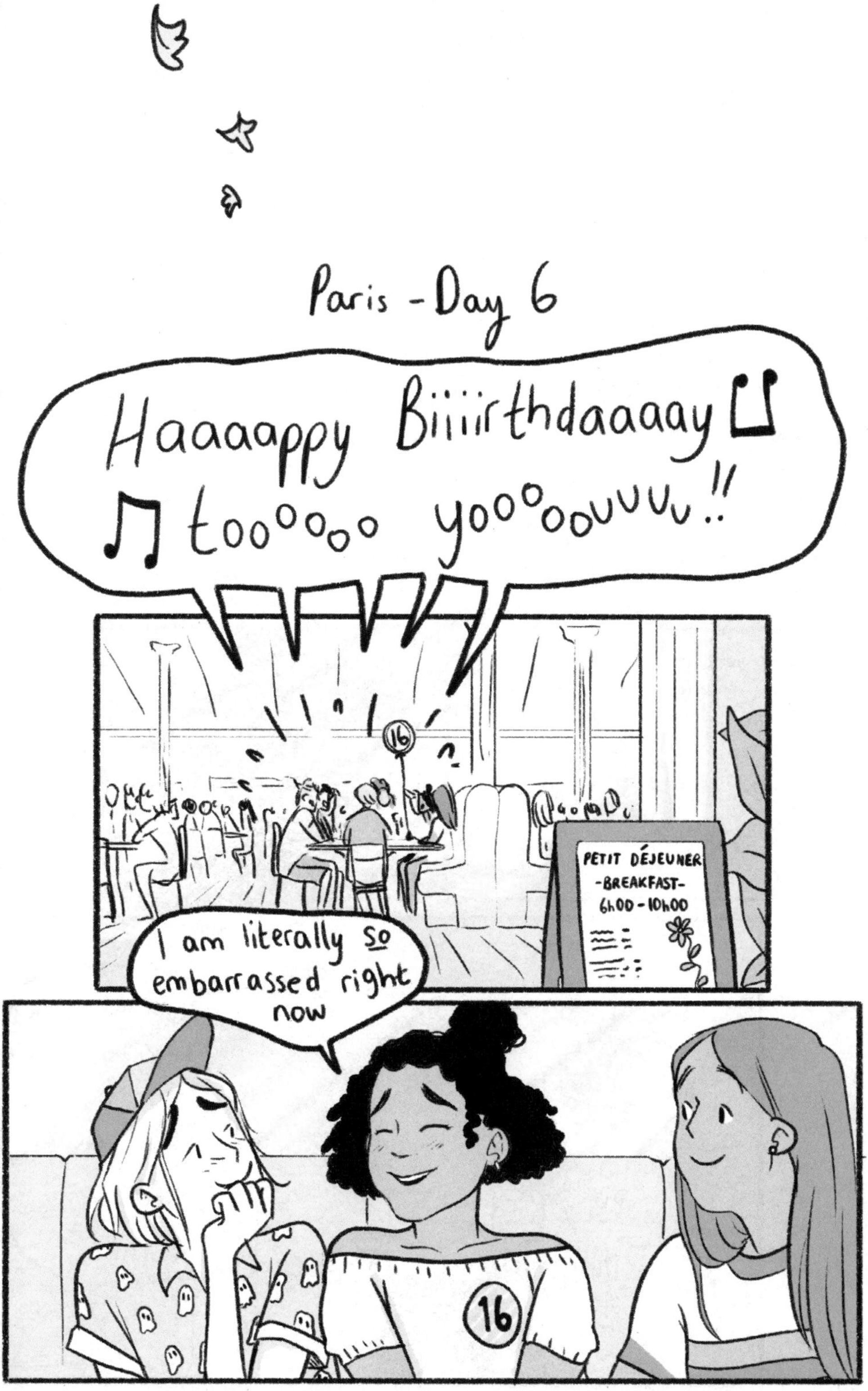
Paris - Day 6
Haaaappy Biiiirthdaaaay ♫ tooooooo yoooooouuuu!!
PETIT DÉJEUNER
-BREAKFAST-
6h00 - 10h00
I am literally so embarrassed right now
16

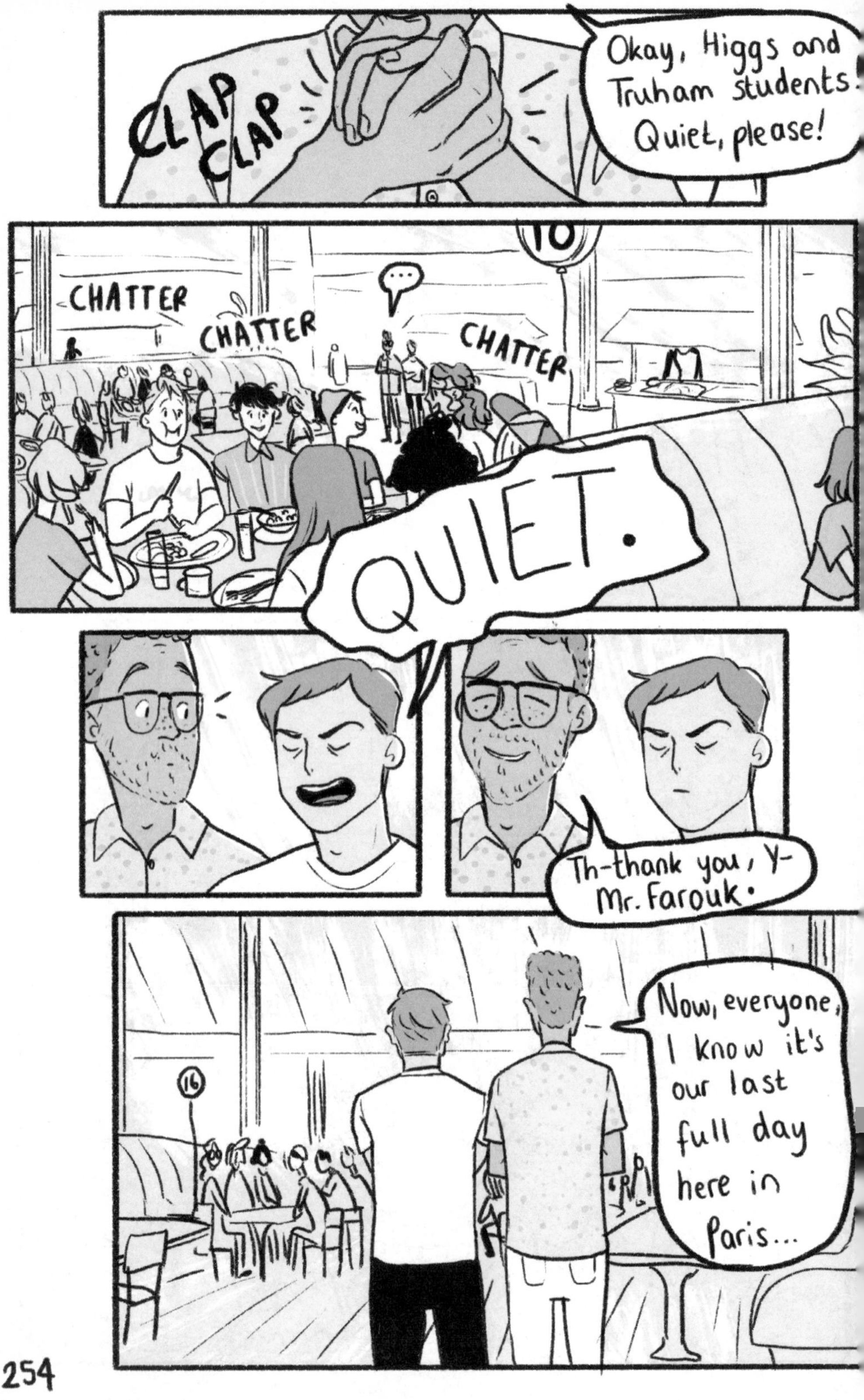
CLAP CLAP
Okay, Higgs and Truham students. Quiet, please!
CHATTER
CHATTER
...
CHATTER
16
QUIET.
Th-thank you, Y- Mr. Farouk.
16
Now, everyone, I know it's our last full day here in Paris...

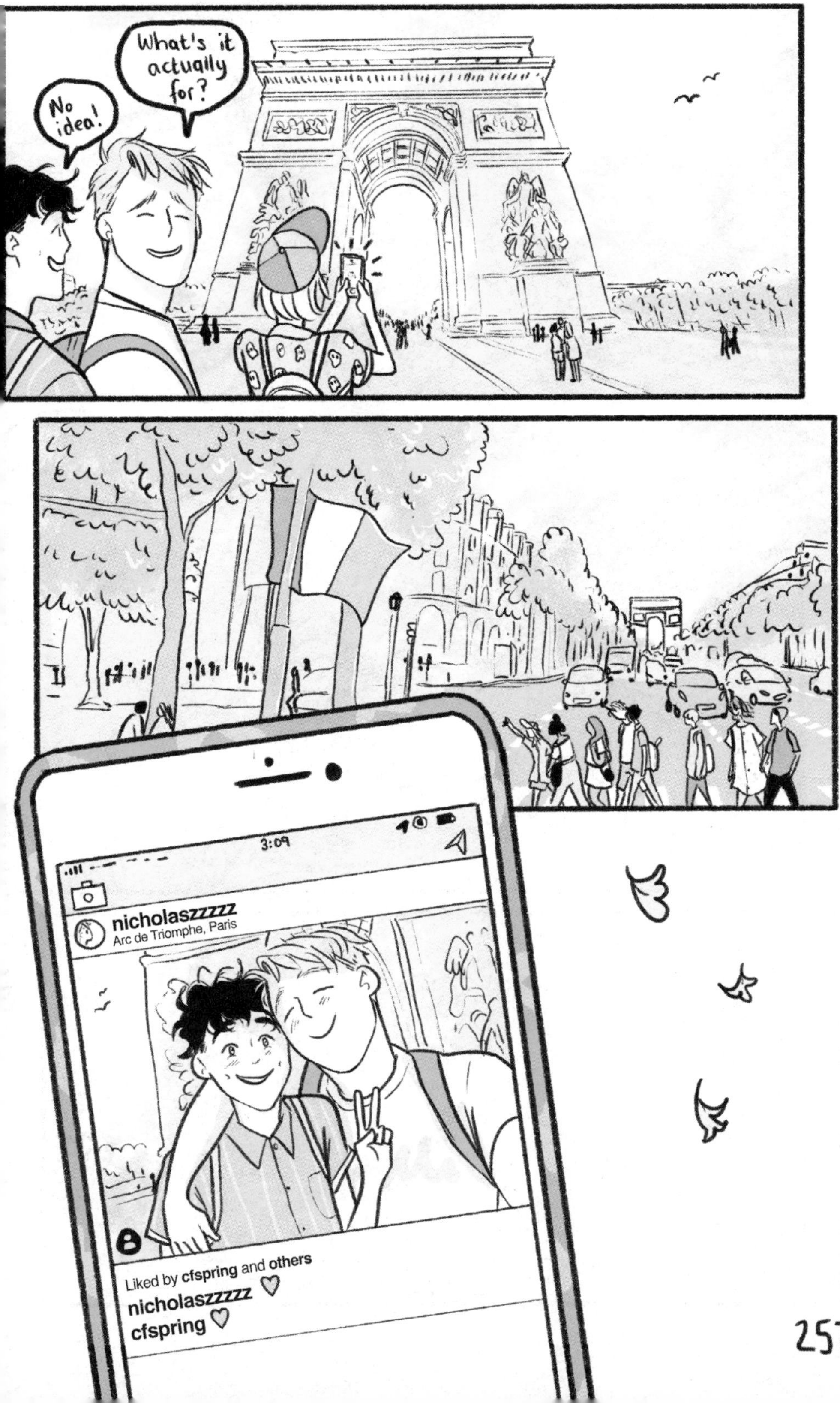
What's it actually for?
No idea!
nicholaszzzzz
Arc de Triomphe, Paris
Liked by cfspring and others
nicholaszzzzz
cfspring

Tara Jones + 39 others

Tara Jones
Casual party in my room at 9pm!!
Room 417!! Everyone's welcome 😊
and you can wear PJs!

Darcy Olsson
PLEASE BRING SNACKS IF YOU HAVE
ANY. ESPECIALLY IF YOU HAVE PRINGLES

also I have vodka 🤘

Katie Lee
Yassss we'll be there!

Tom Jaeger
CAN'T WAIT

Aleena Bukhsh
omg darcy how did you get vodka

Darcy Olsson
i have my ways

Jared Lambe
YEEEEE LET'S GET LIT

Charlie Spring
we'll be there!!!!!!

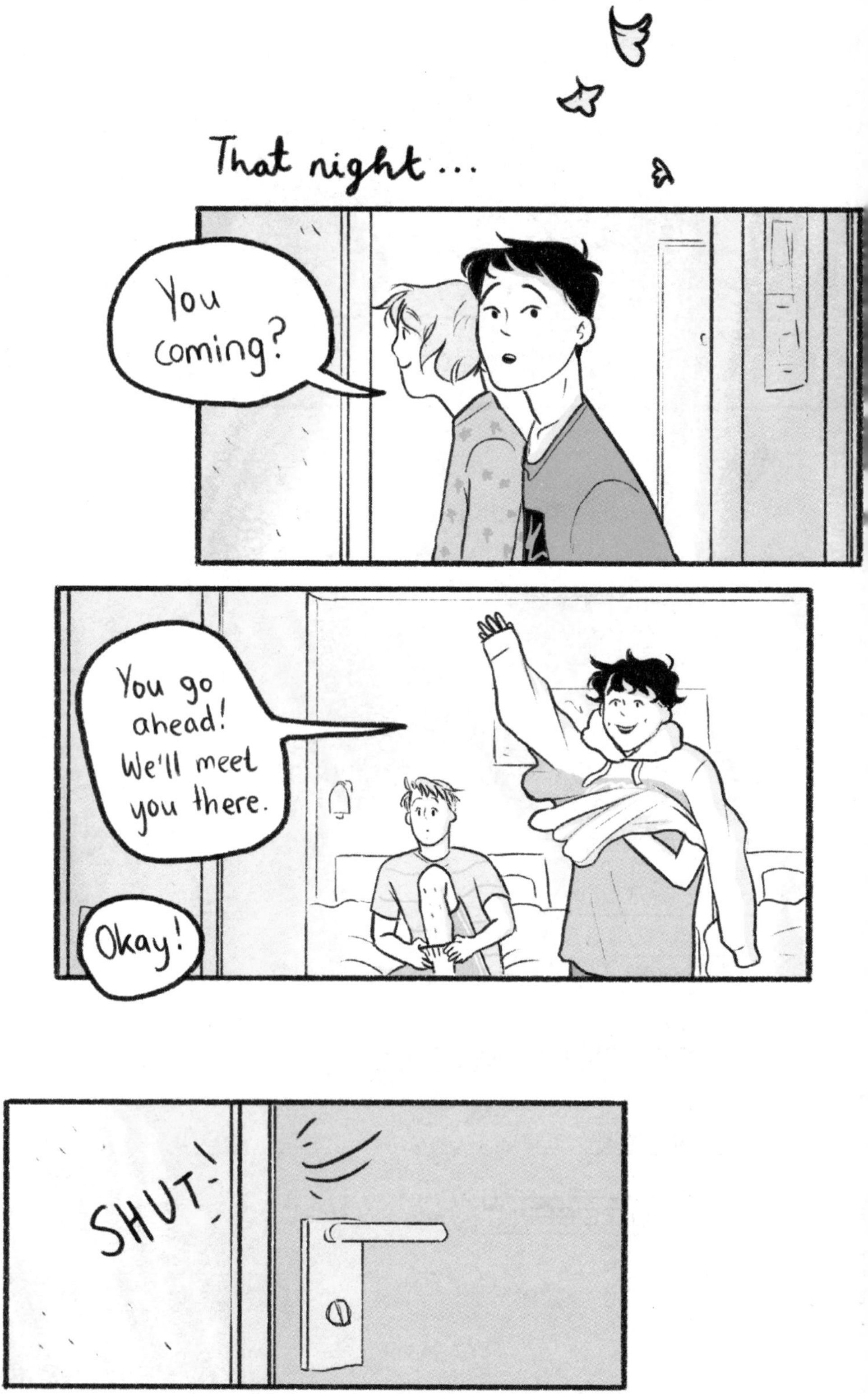
That night...
You coming?
You go ahead! We'll meet you there.
Okay!
SHUT!

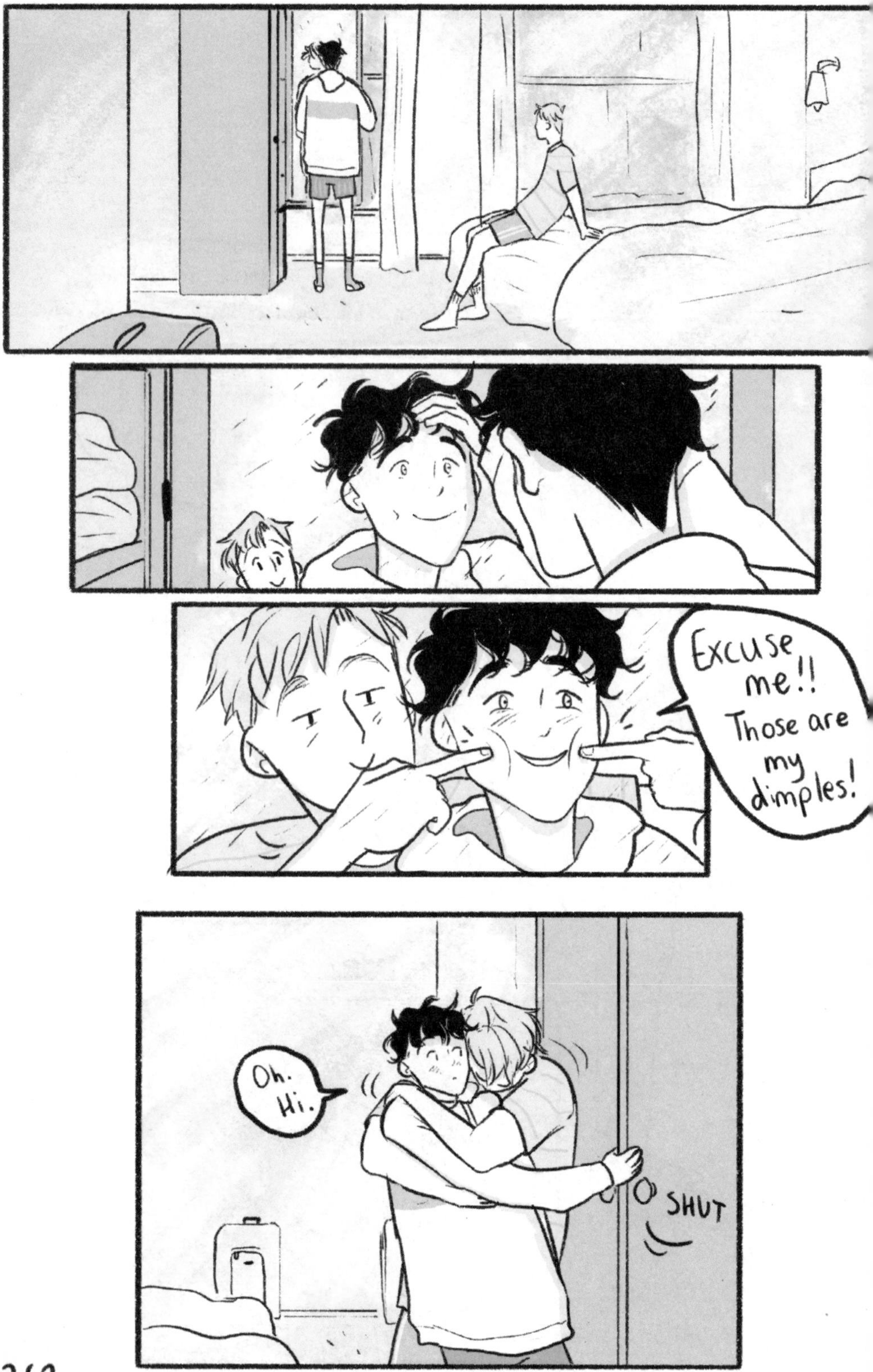
Excuse me!! Those are my dimples!
Oh. Hi.
SHUT

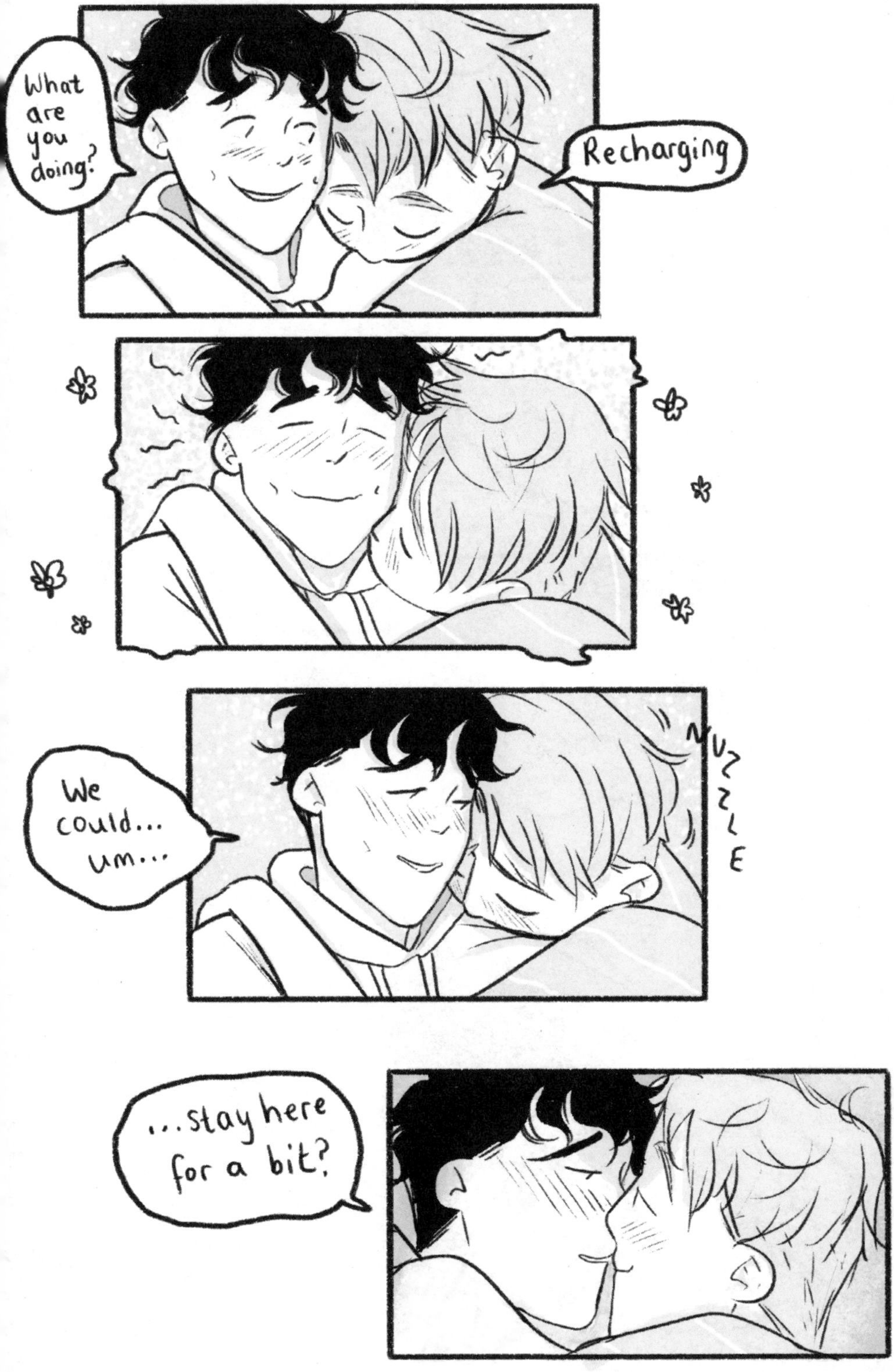
What are you doing?
Recharging
We could... um...
NUZZLE
...stay here for a bit?

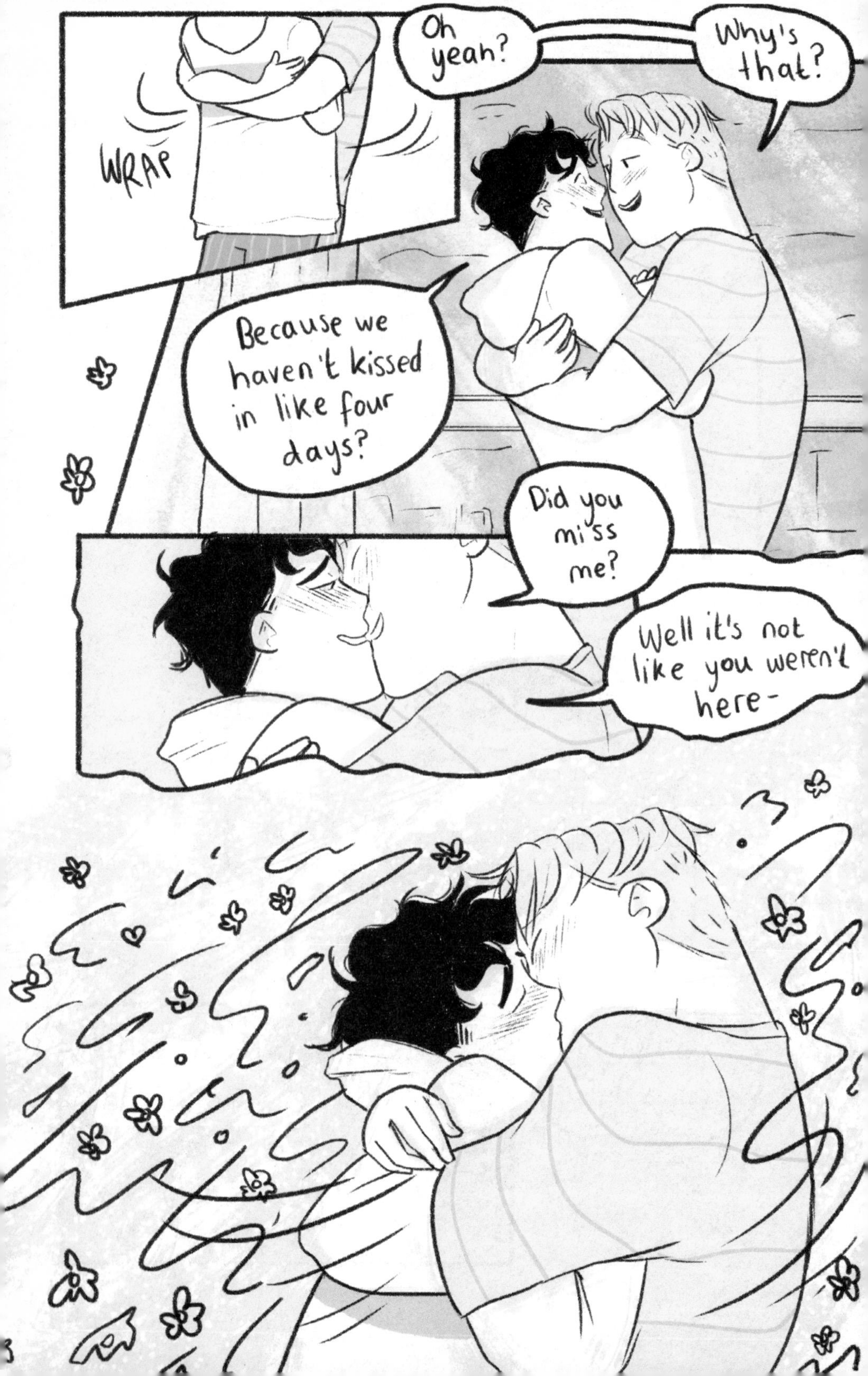
WRAP
Oh yeah?
Why's that?
Because we haven't kissed in like four days?
Did you miss me?
Well it's not like you weren't here-

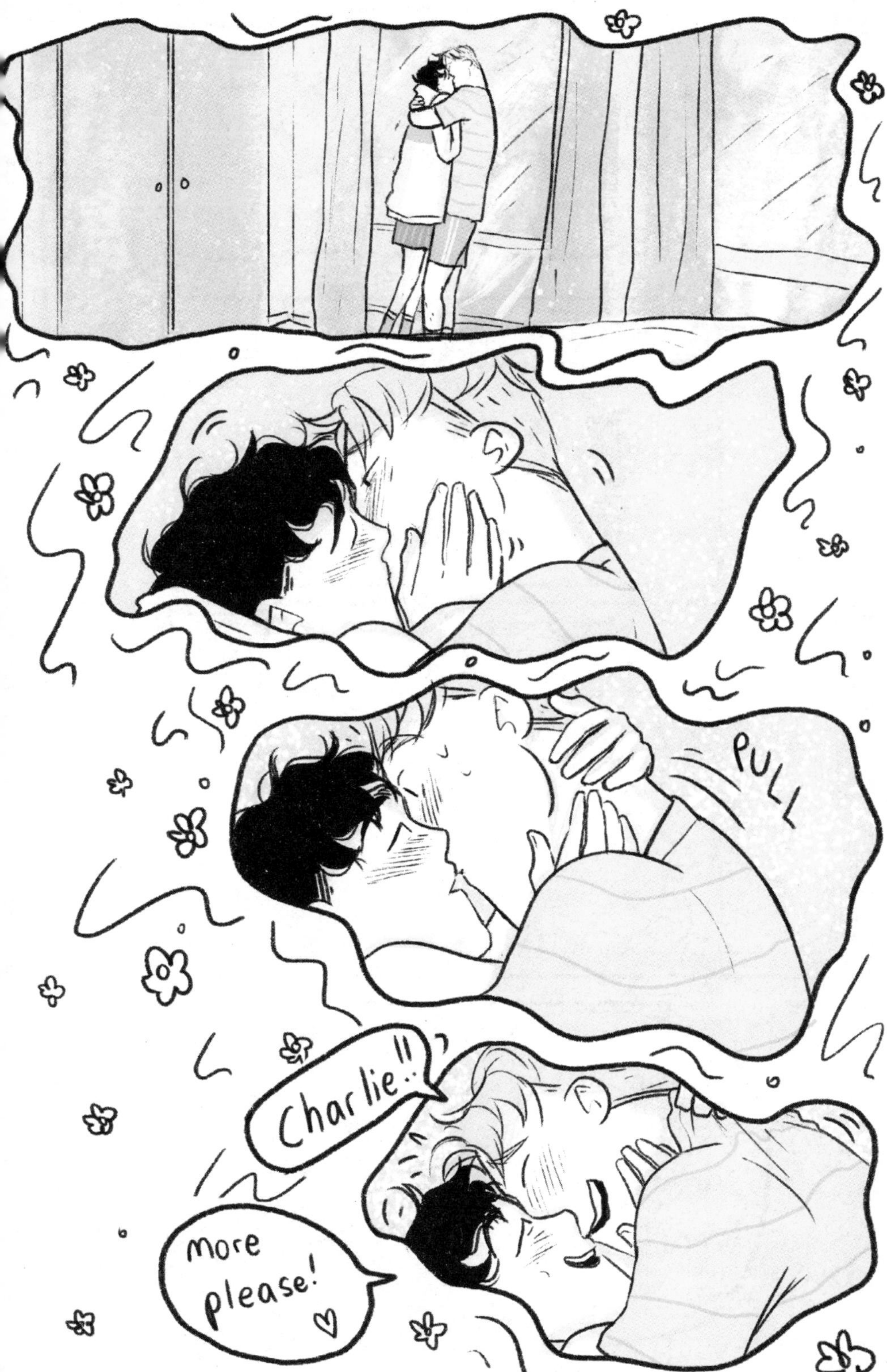
PULL
Charlie!!
more please!

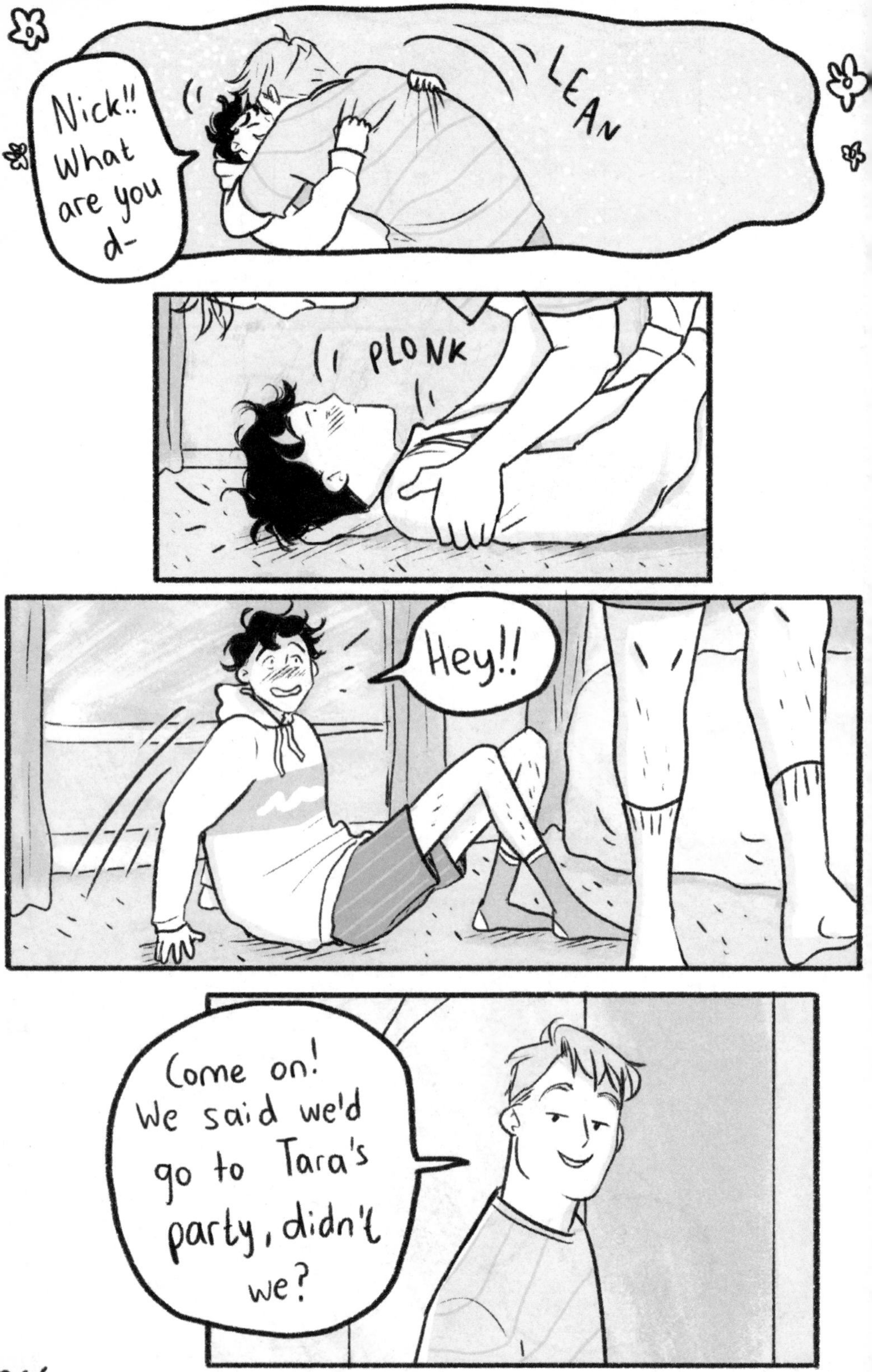
Nick!! What are you d-
LEAN
PLONK
Hey!!
Come on! We said we'd go to Tara's party, didn't we?

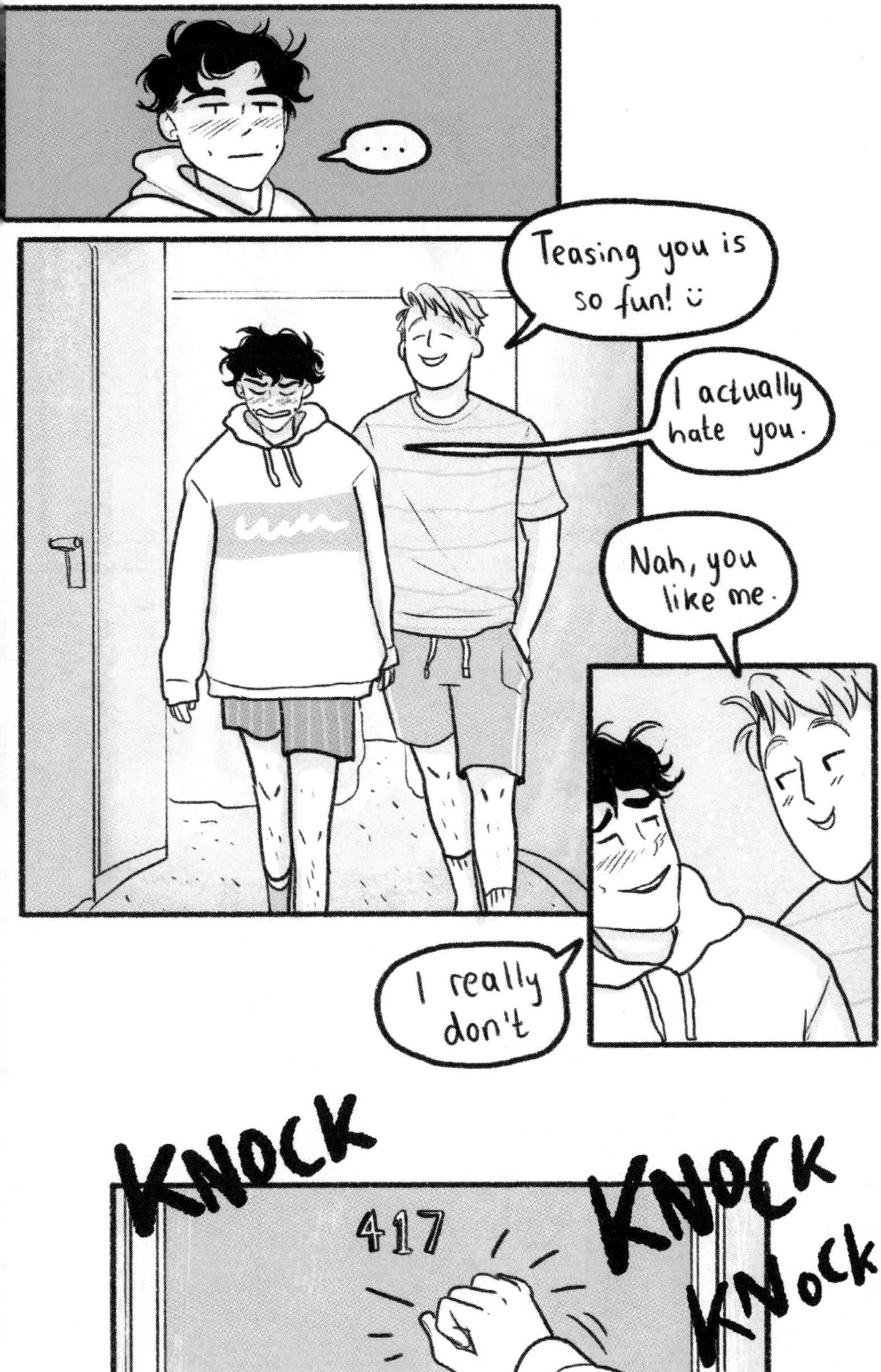
...
Teasing you is so fun! ᵕ
I actually hate you.
Nah, you like me.
I really don't
KNOCK
417
KNOCK
KNOCK

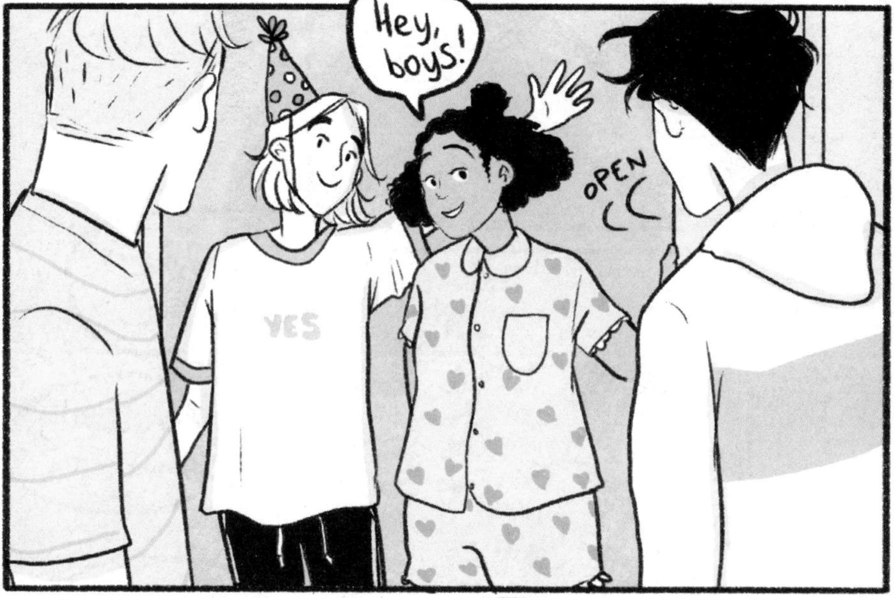
Hey, boys!
OPEN

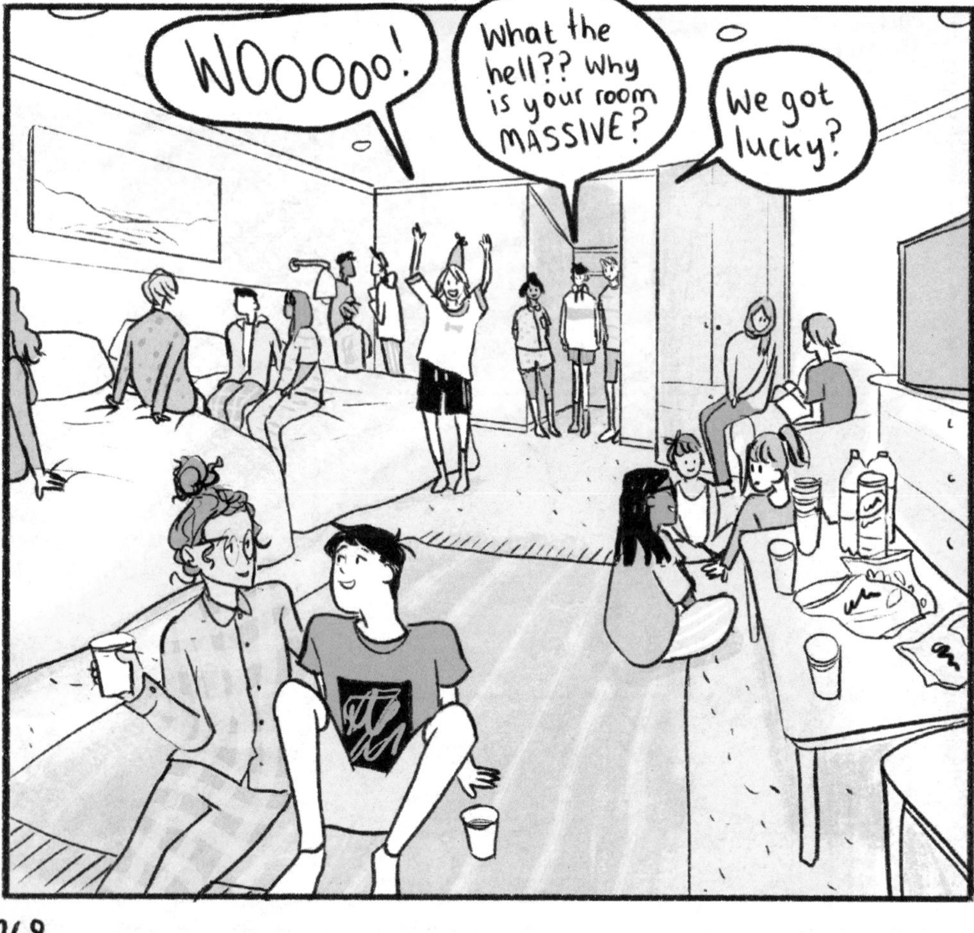
WOOOoo!
What the hell?? Why is your room MASSIVE?
We got lucky?

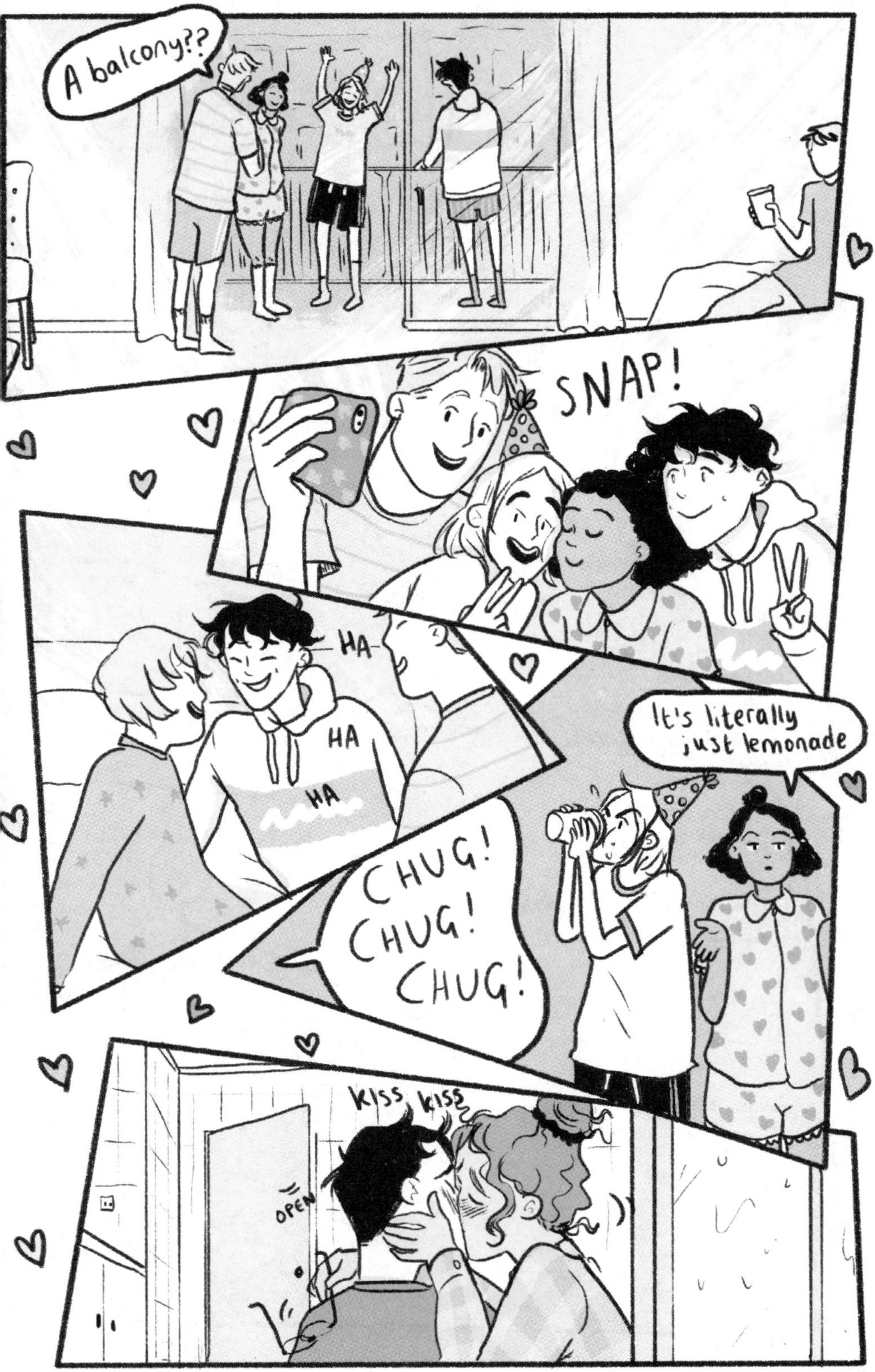
A balcony??
SNAP!
HA
HA
HA
It's literally just lemonade
CHUG! CHUG! CHUG!
KISS KISS
OPEN

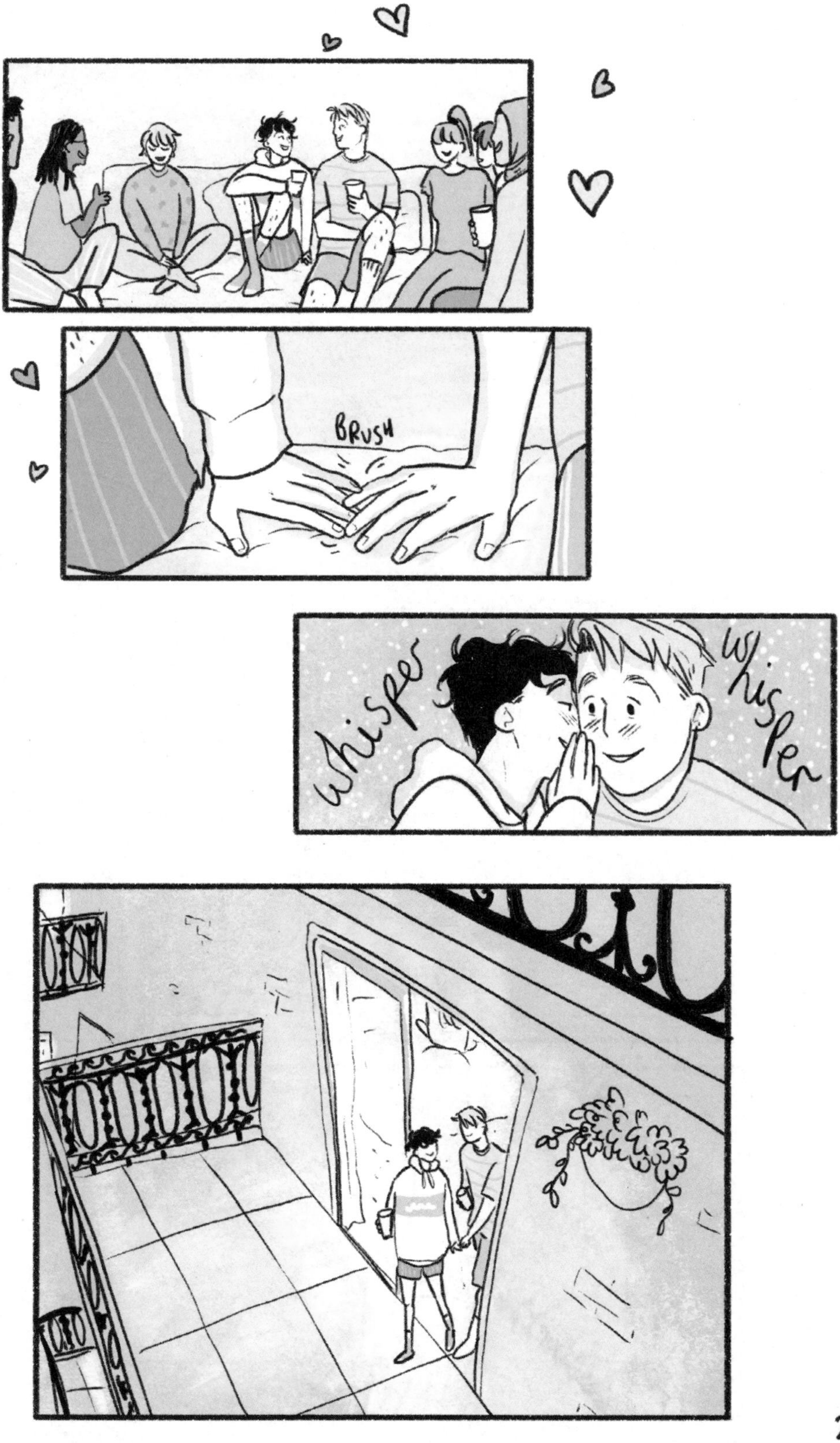
BRUSH
whisper
whisper

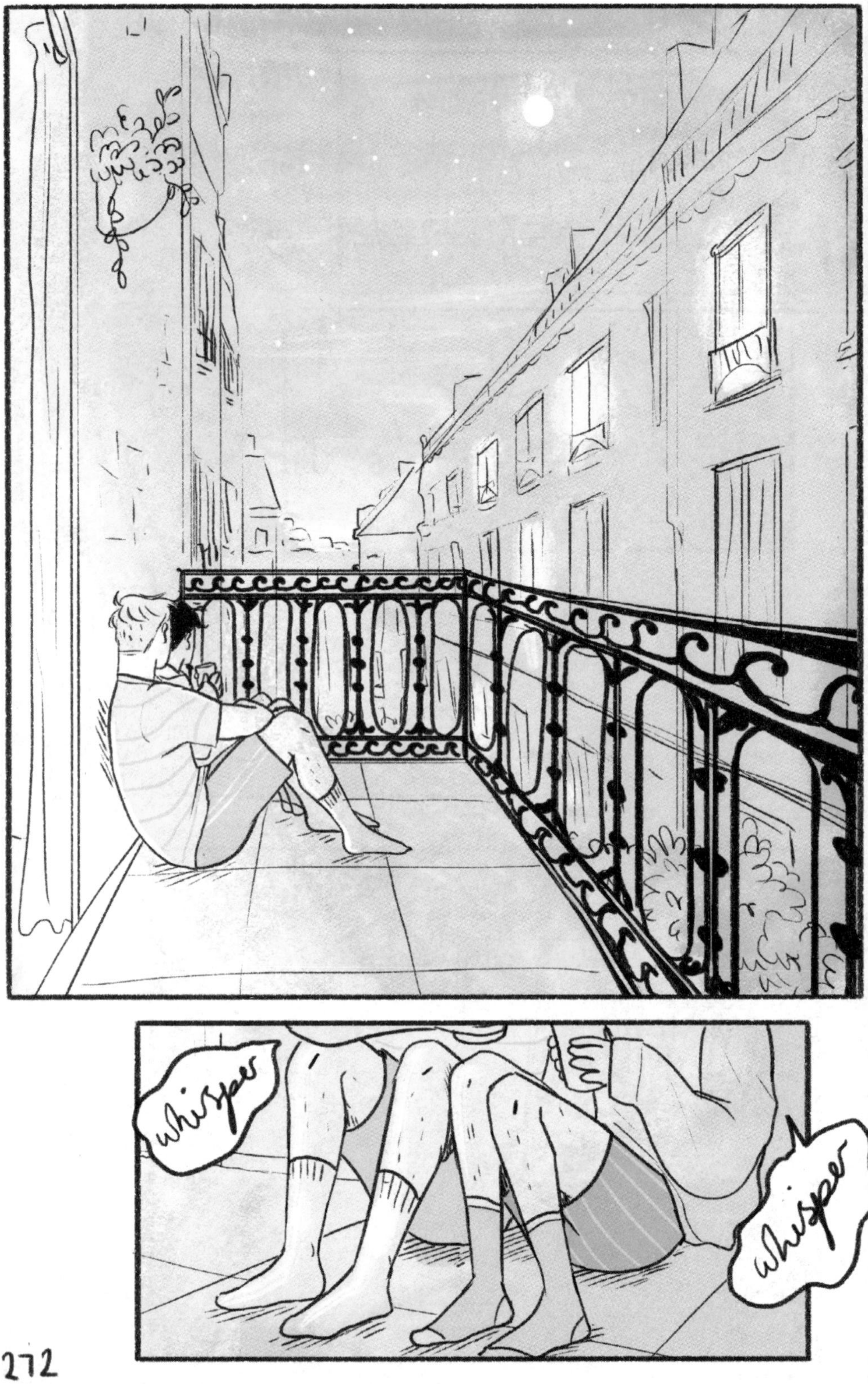
whisper
whisper

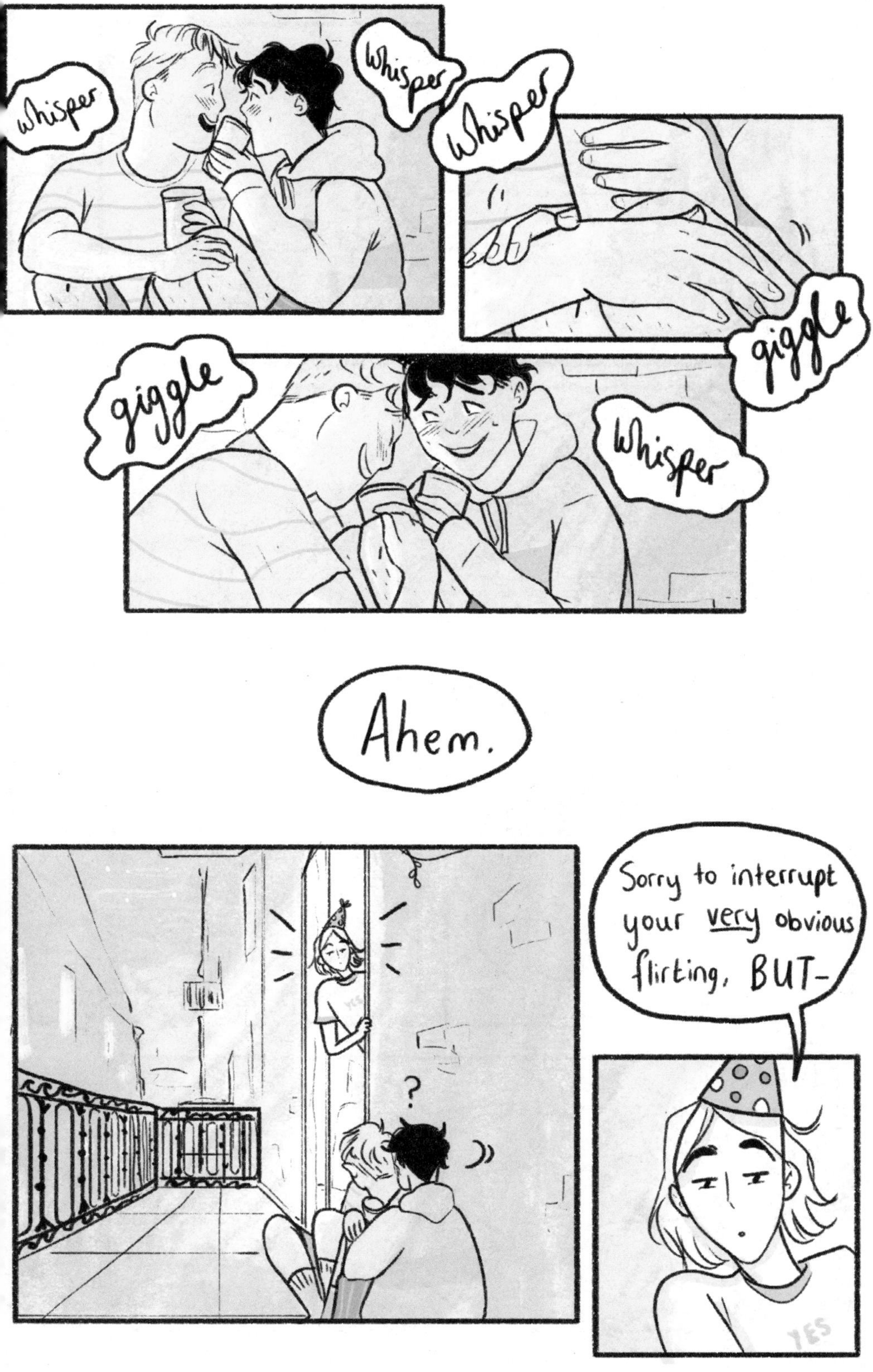

Whisper
Whisper
Whisper
giggle
giggle
Whisper
Ahem.
Sorry to interrupt your very obvious flirting, BUT-

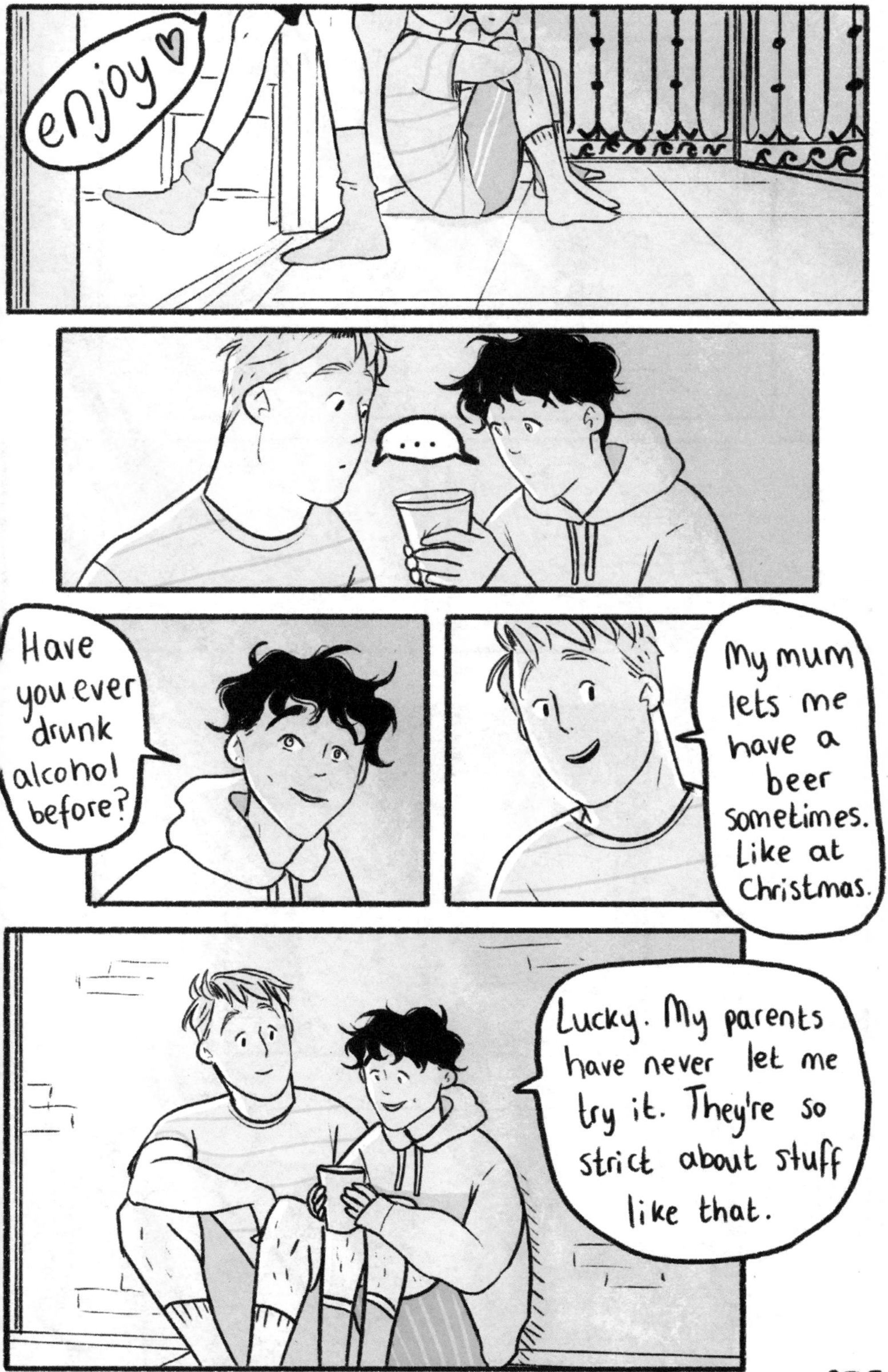
enjoy ♡
...
Have you ever drunk alcohol before?
My mum lets me have a beer sometimes. Like at Christmas.
Lucky. My parents have never let me try it. They're so strict about stuff like that.

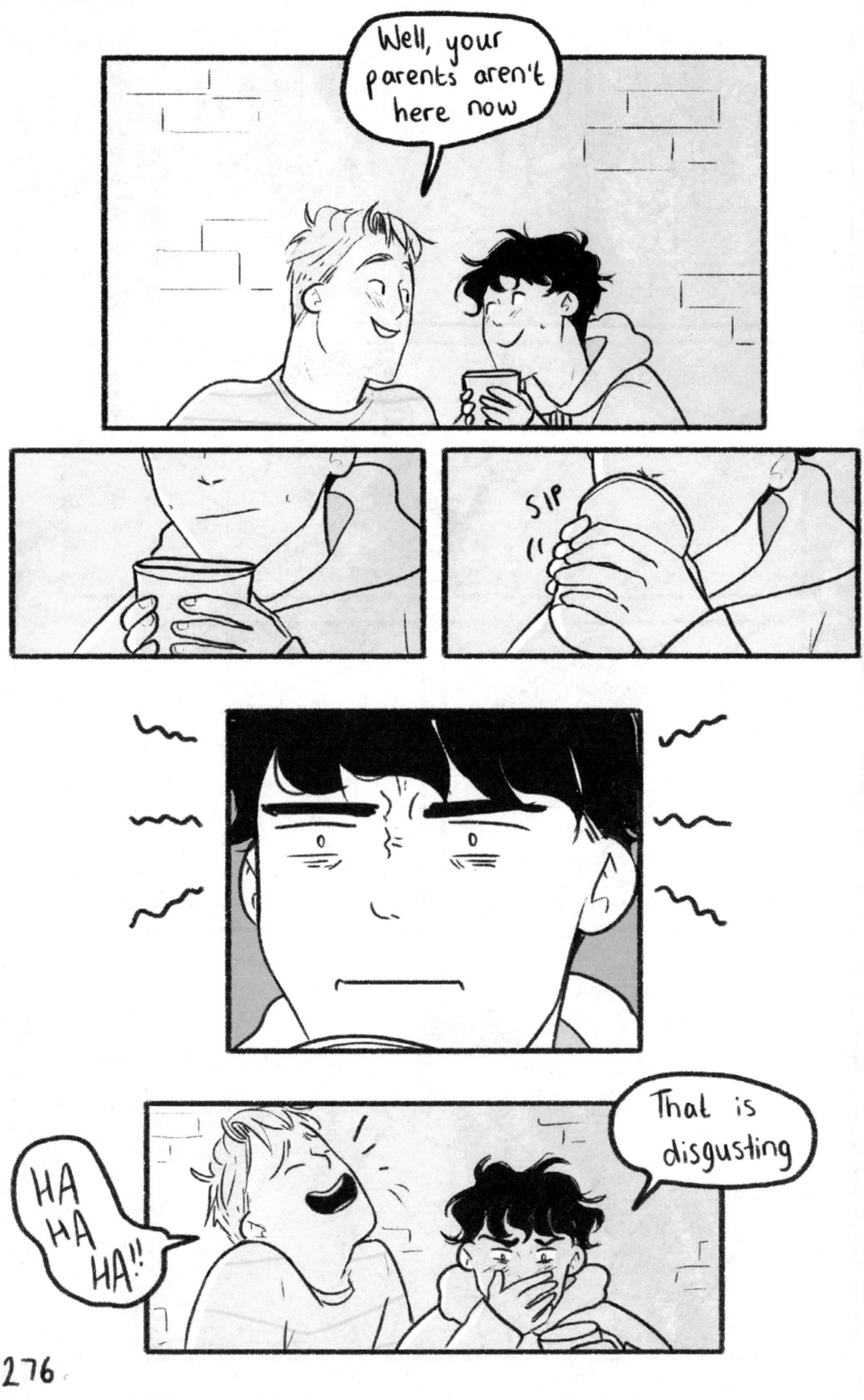
Well, your parents aren't here now
SIP
That is disgusting
HA HA HA!!

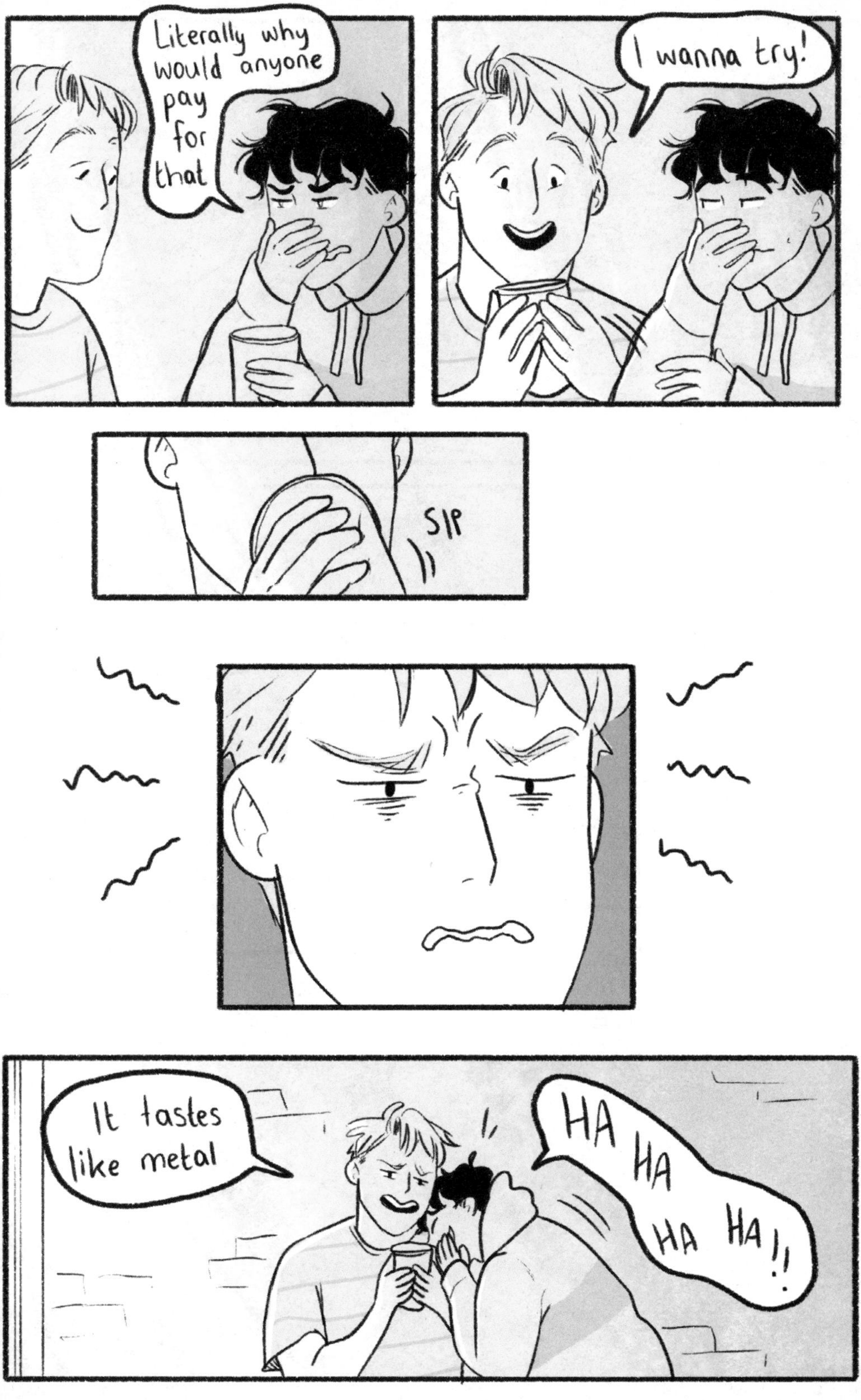
Literally why would anyone pay for that
I wanna try!
SIP
It tastes like metal
HA HA HA HA!!

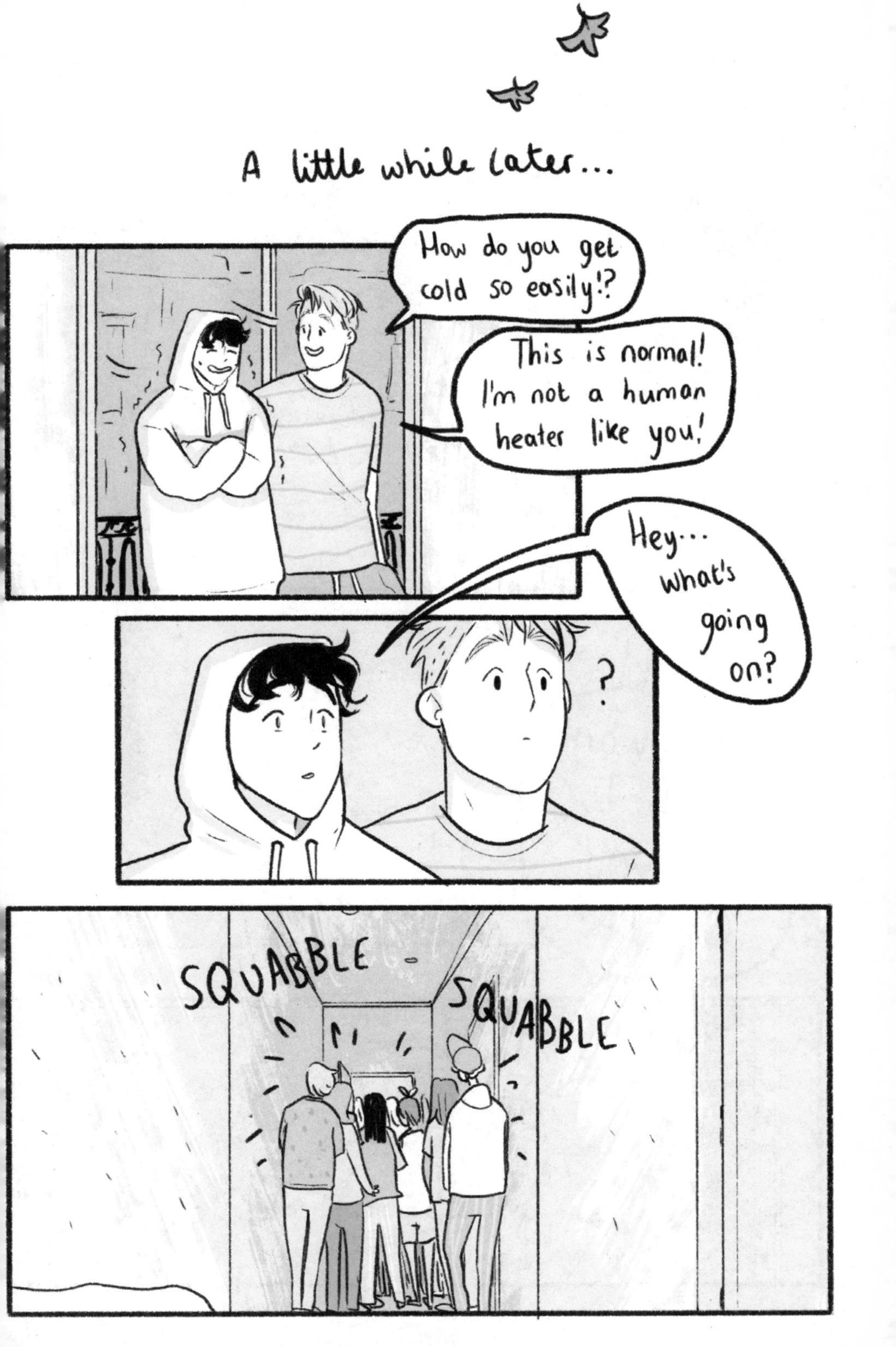
A little while later...
How do you get cold so easily!?
This is normal! I'm not a human heater like you!
Hey... what's going on?
?
SQUABBLE
SQUABBLE

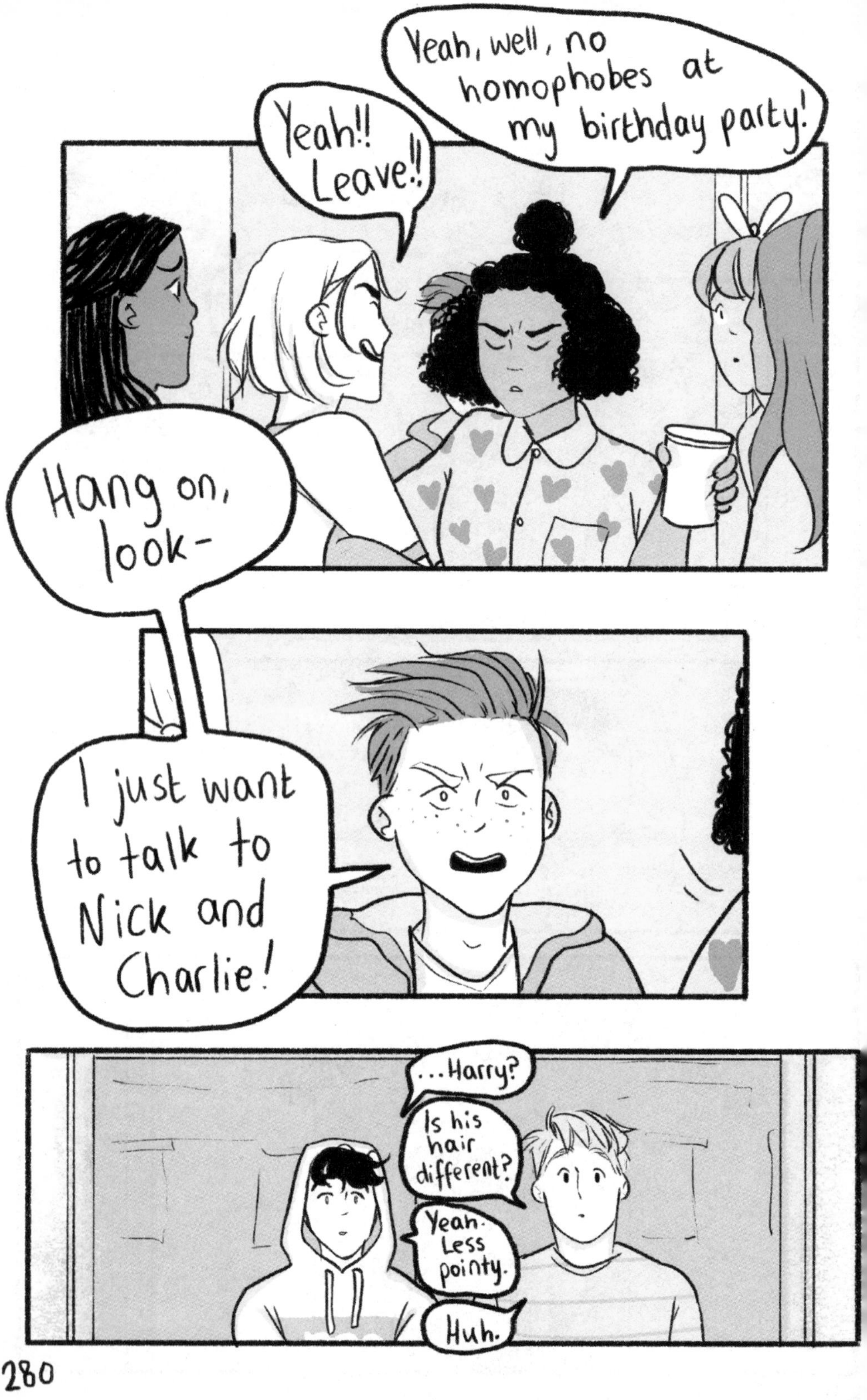
Yeah, well, no homophobes at my birthday party!
Yeah!! Leave!!
Hang on, look-
I just want to talk to Nick and Charlie!
...Harry?
Is his hair different?
Yeah. Less pointy.
Huh.

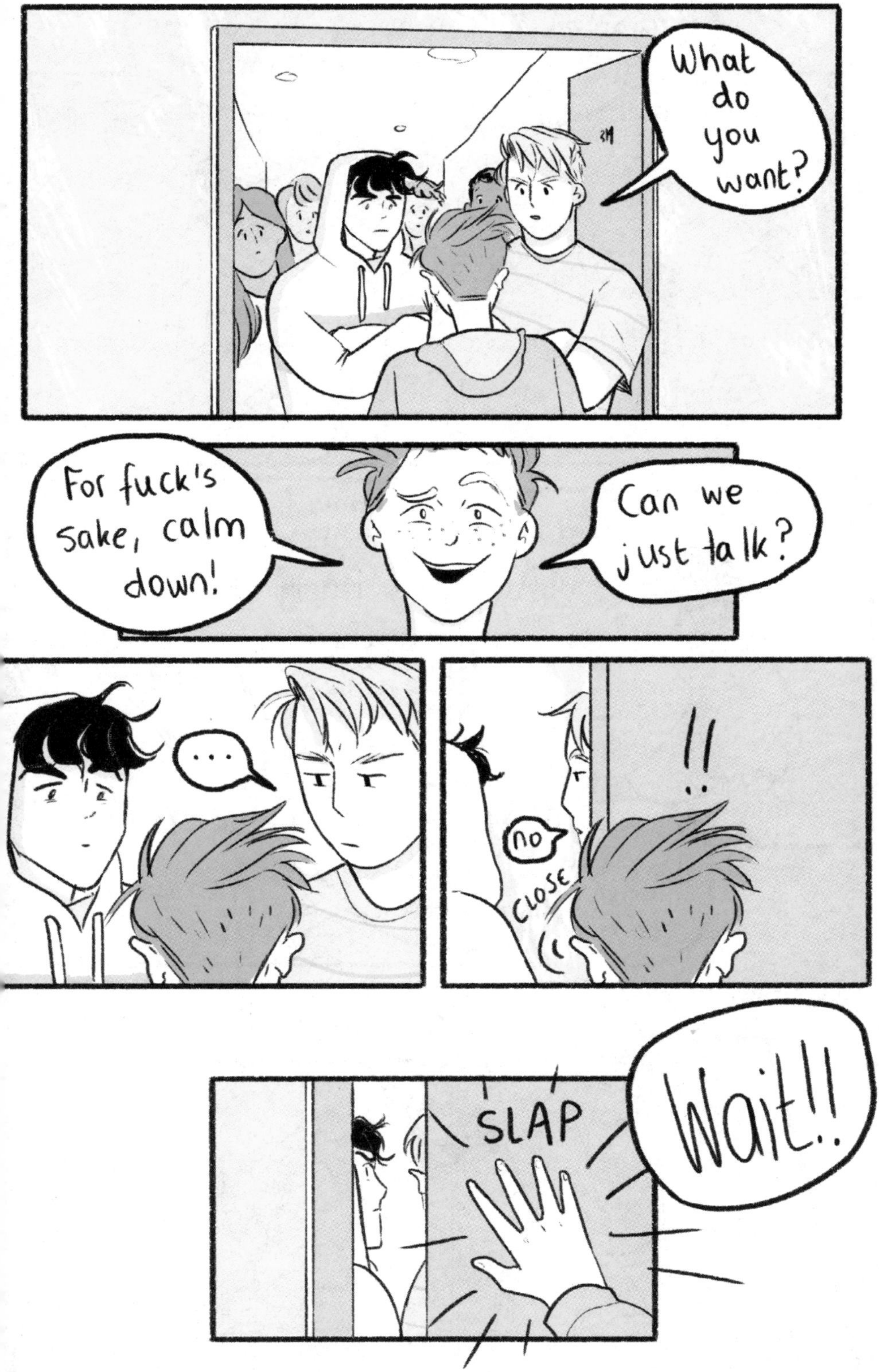
What do you want?
For fuck's sake, calm down!
Can we just talk?
...
!!
no
CLOSE
SLAP
Wait!!

284

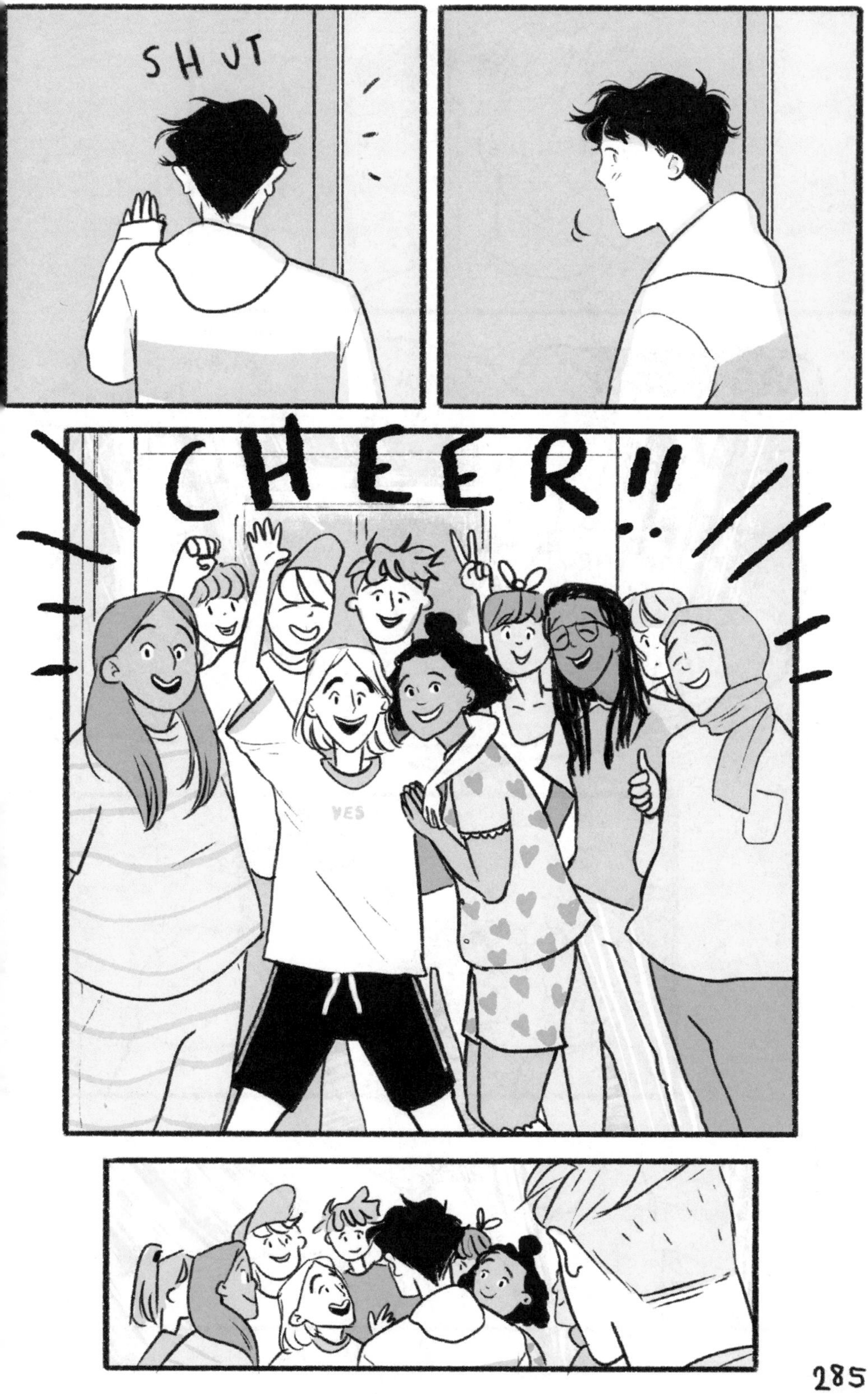
SHUT
CHEER!!
YES

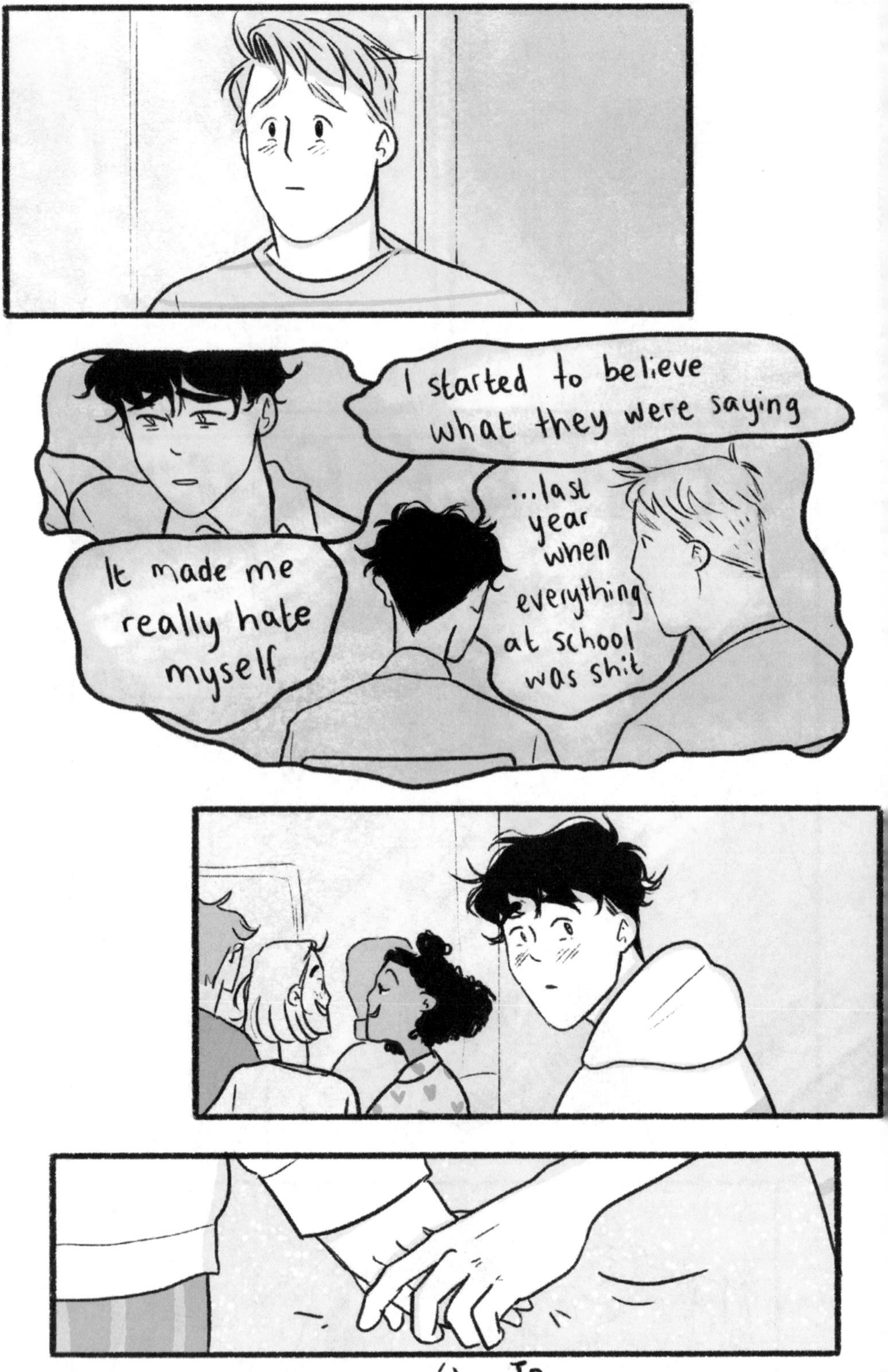
I started to believe what they were saying
It made me really hate myself
...last year when everything at school was shit
TOUCH

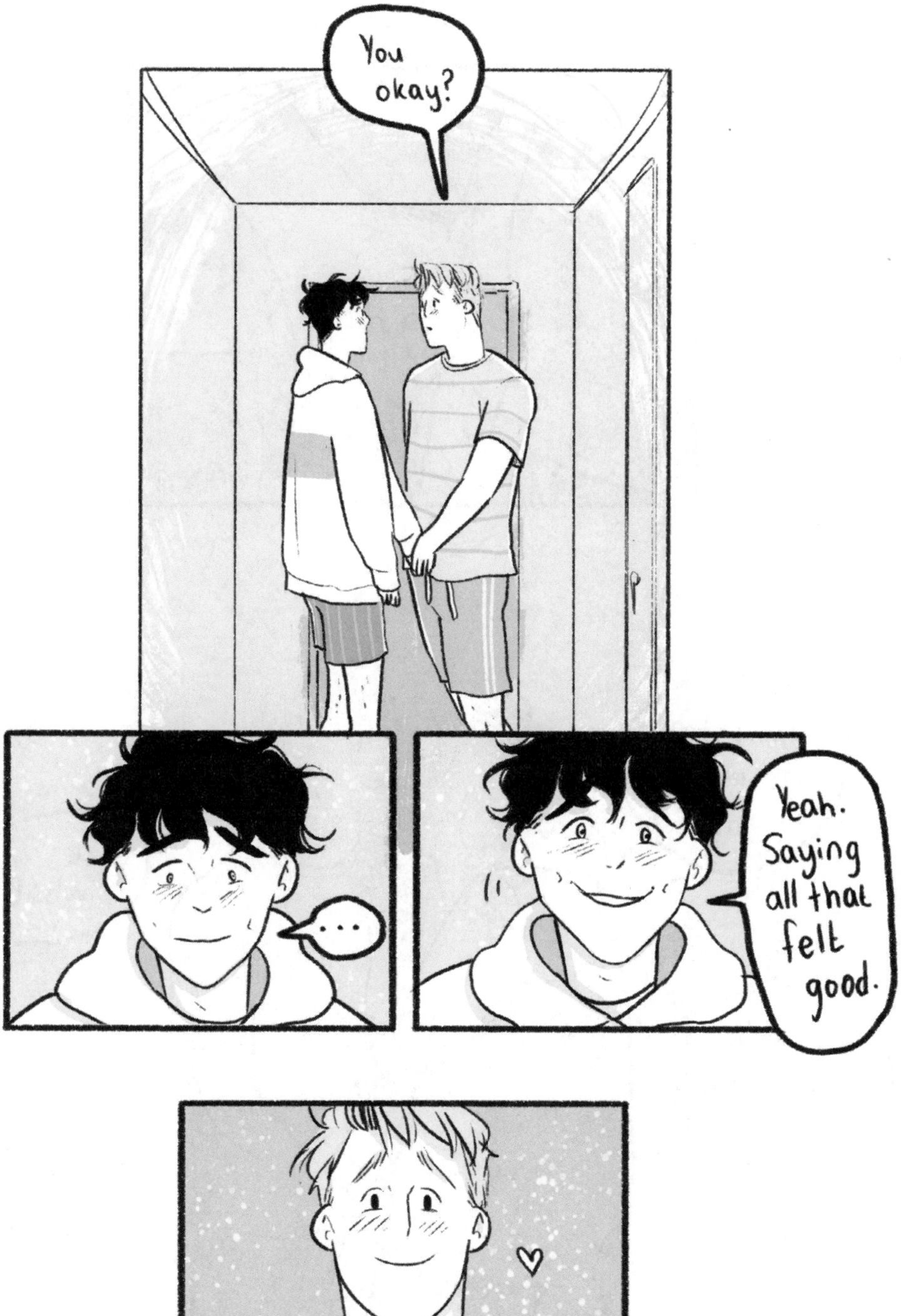
You okay?
...
Yeah. Saying all that felt good.

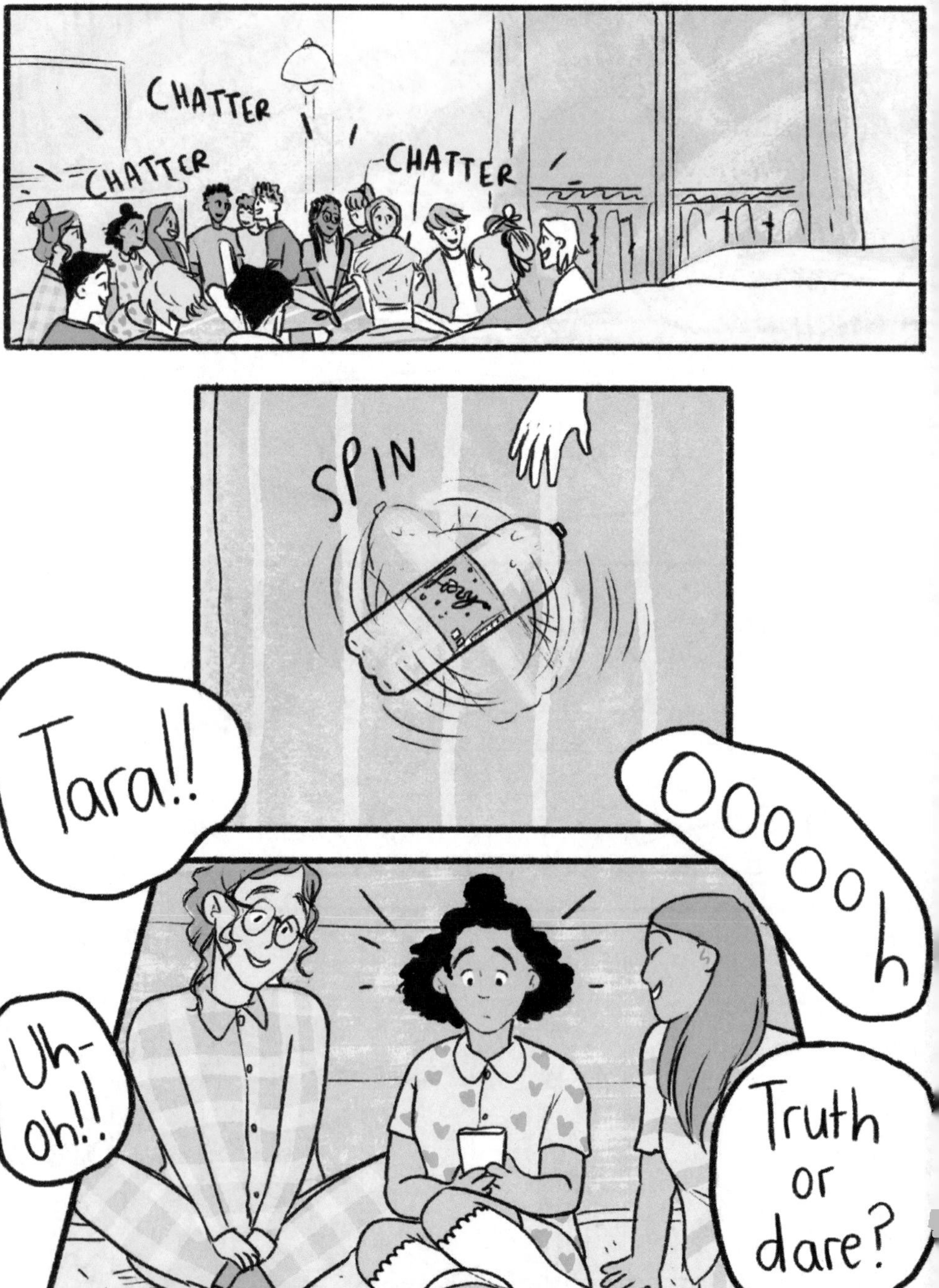
CHATTER
CHATTER
CHATTER
SPIN
Tara!!
Ooooooh
Uh-oh!!
Truth or dare?
STOP

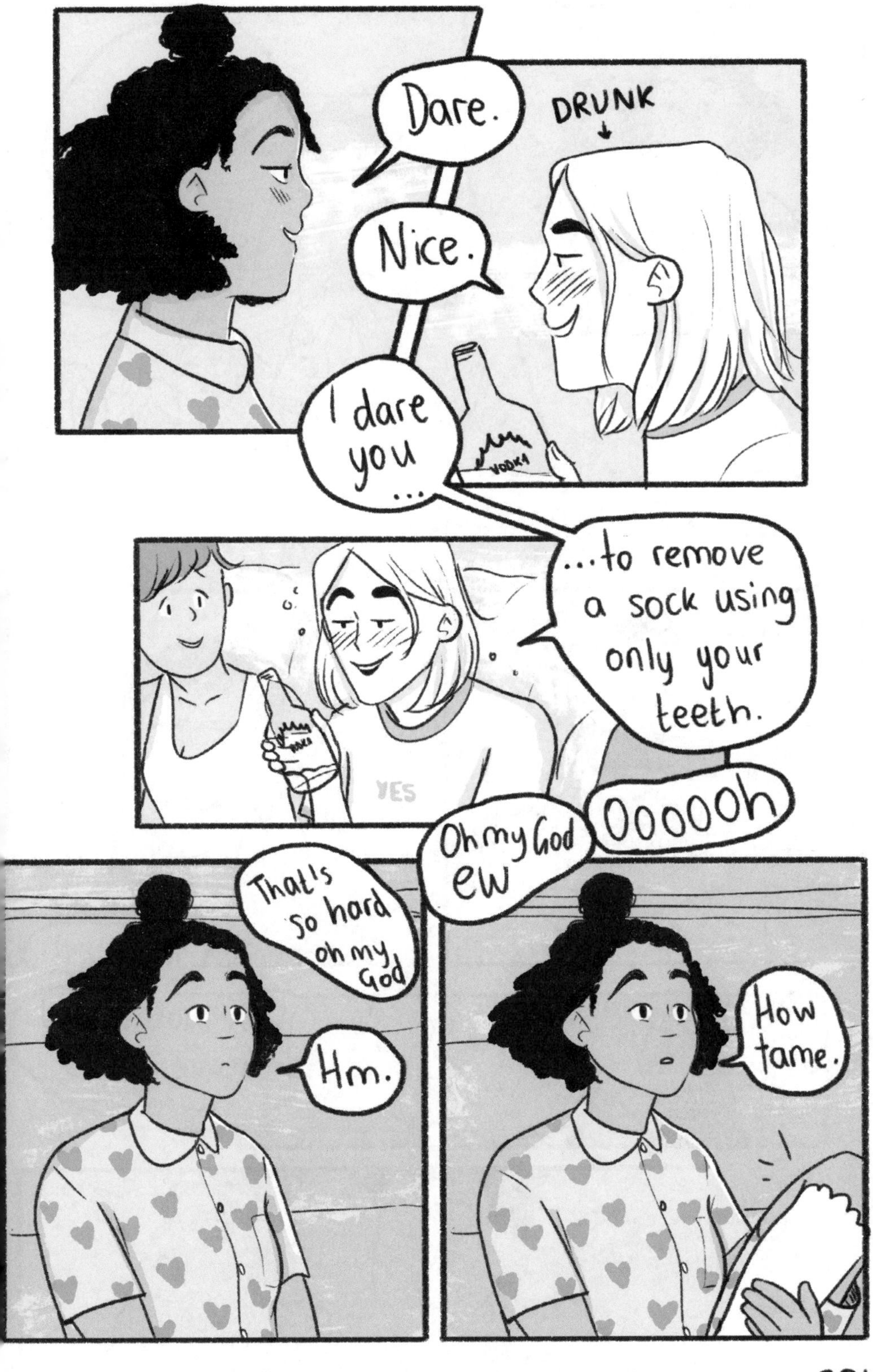
Dare.
DRUNK
Nice.
I dare you ...
VODKA
...to remove a sock using only your teeth.
YES
Oooooh
Oh my God ew
That's so hard oh my God
Hm.
How tame.

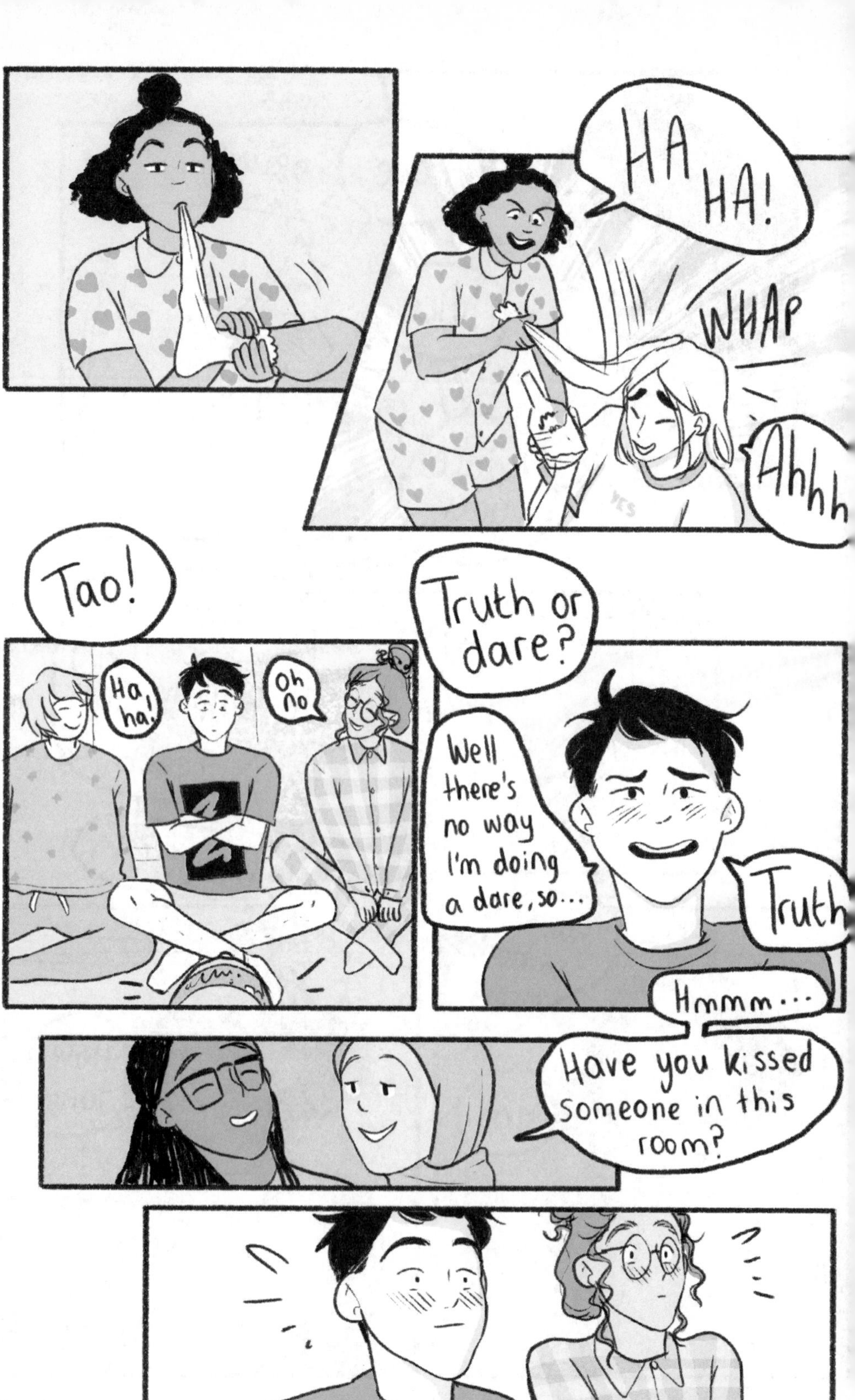
HA HA!
WHAP
Ahhh
Tao!
Ha ha!
Oh no
Truth or dare?
Well there's no way I'm doing a dare, so...
Truth
Hmmm...
Have you kissed someone in this room?

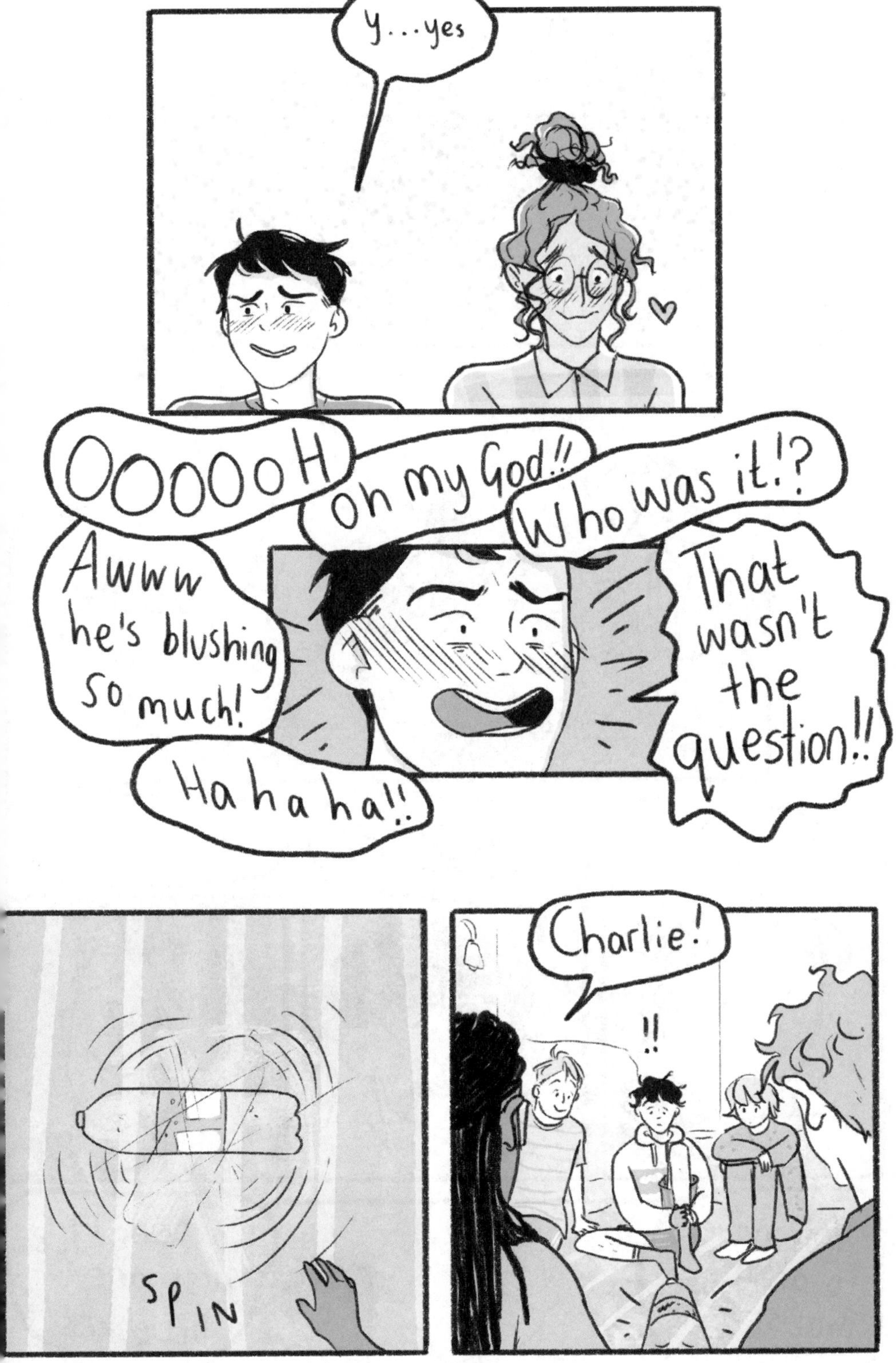
Y...yes
OOOOOH
Oh my God!!
Who was it!?
Awww he's blushing so much!
That wasn't the question!!
Ha ha ha ha!!
SPIN
Charlie!
!!

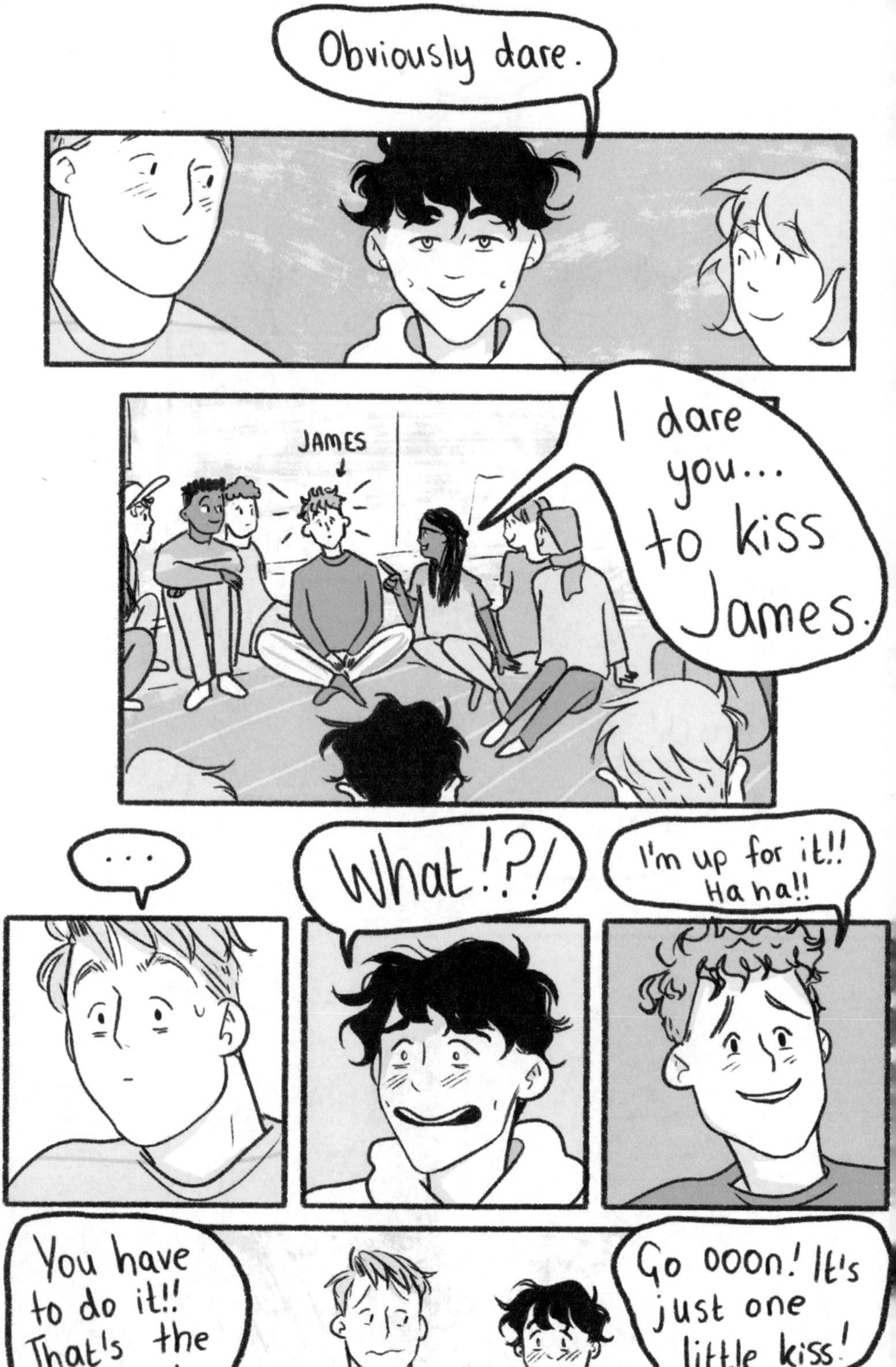
Obviously dare.
JAMES
I dare you... to kiss James.
. . .
What!?!
I'm up for it!! Ha ha!!
You have to do it!! That's the dare!
Go ooon! It's just one little kiss!

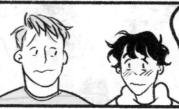

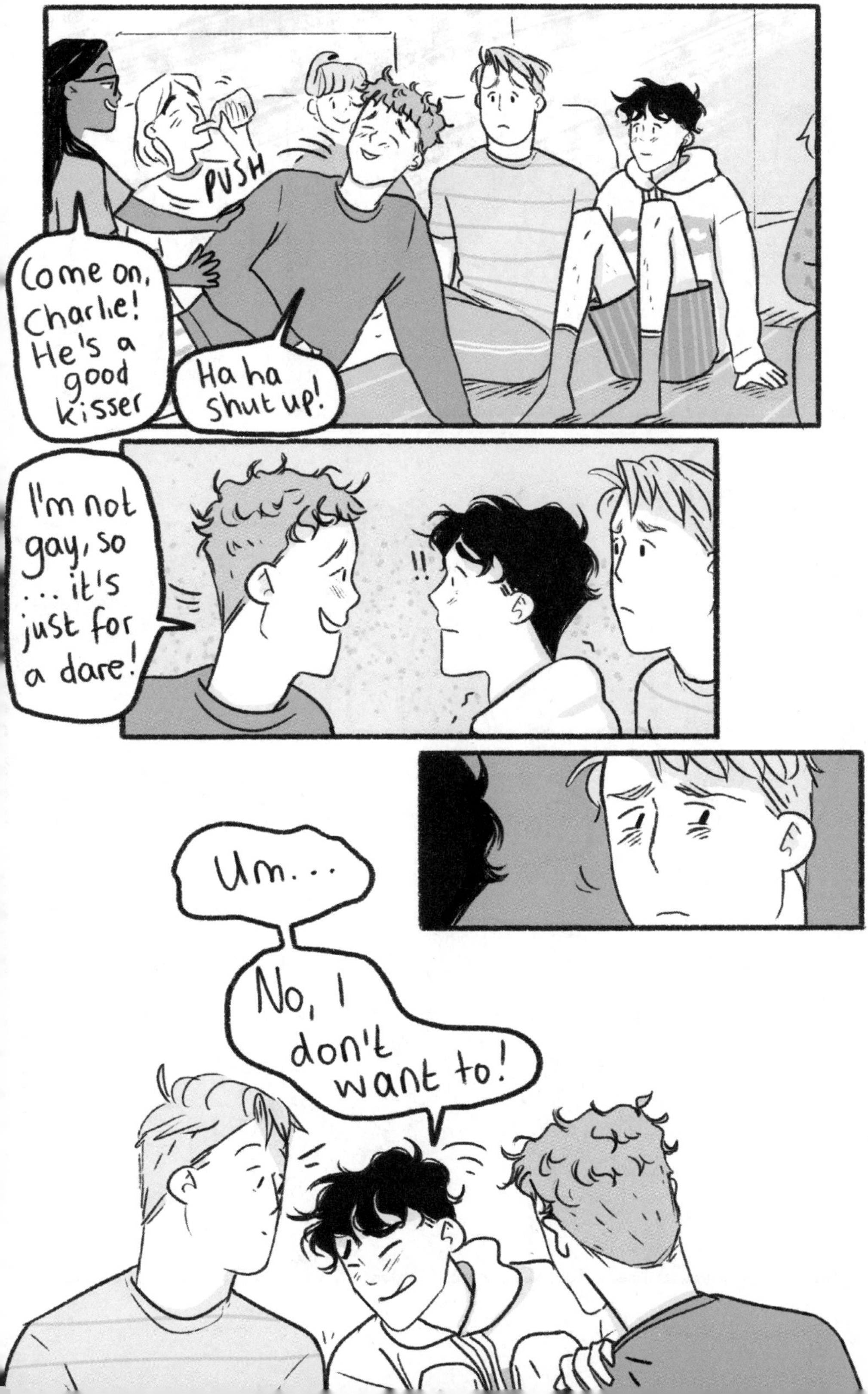
PUSH
Come on, Charlie! He's a good kisser
Ha ha shut up!
I'm not gay, so ... it's just for a dare!
!!
Um...
No, I don't want to!

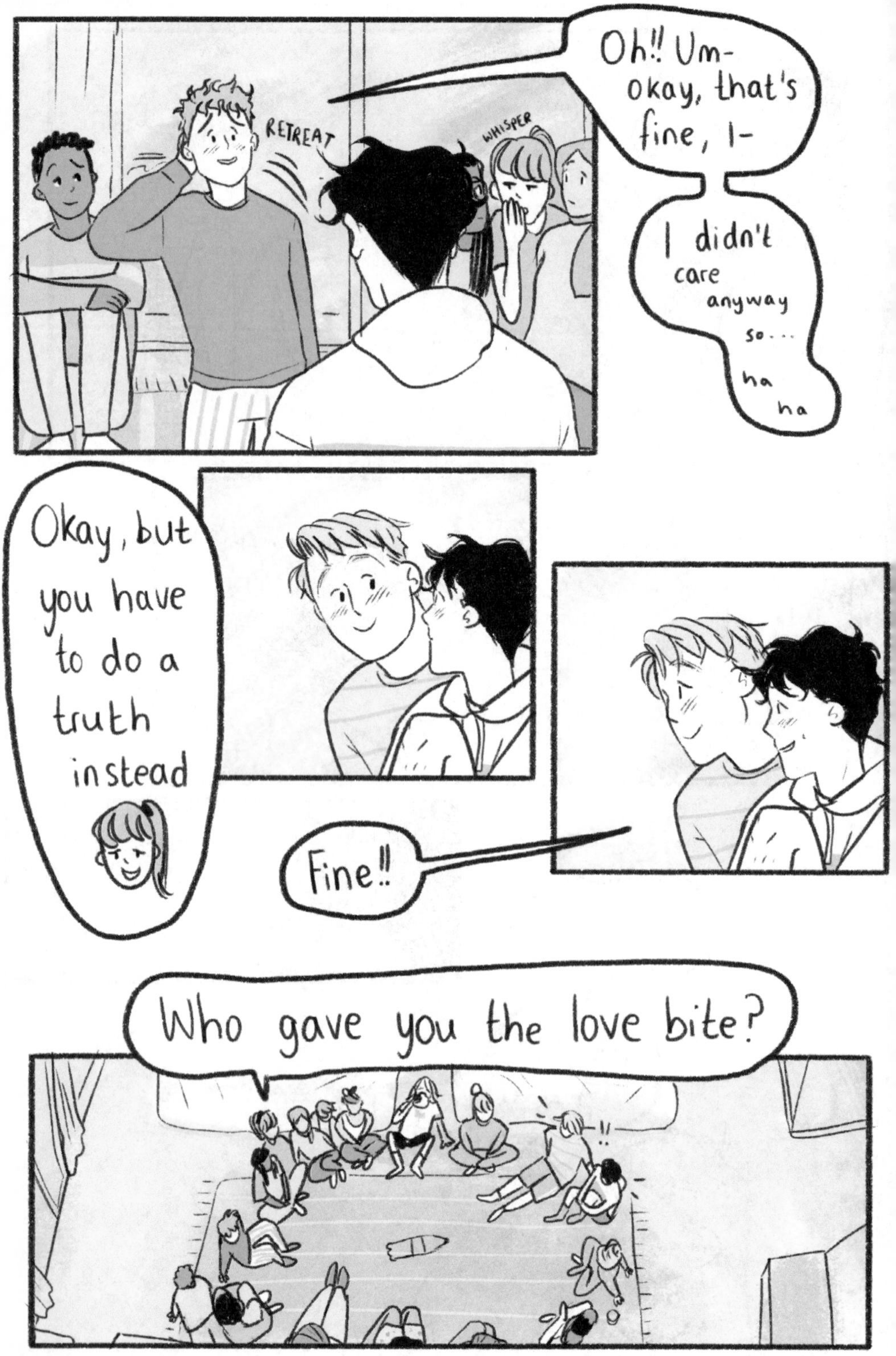
RETREAT
WHISPER
Oh!! Um- okay, that's fine, I-
I didn't care anyway so... ha ha
Okay, but you have to do a truth instead
Fine!!
Who gave you the love bite?
!!

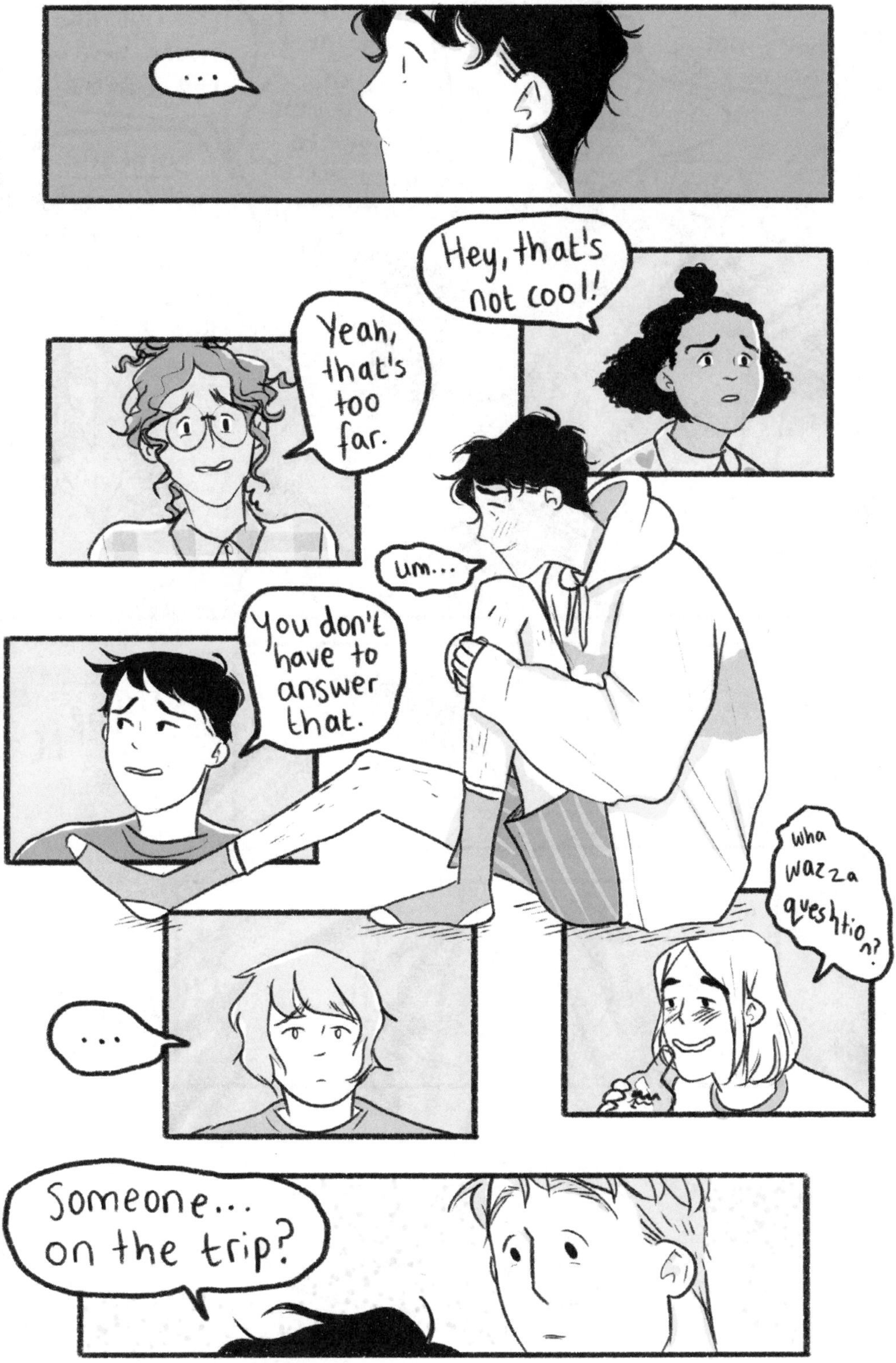
...
Hey, that's not cool!
Yeah, that's too far.
um...
You don't have to answer that.
wha wazza queshtion?
...
Someone... on the trip?

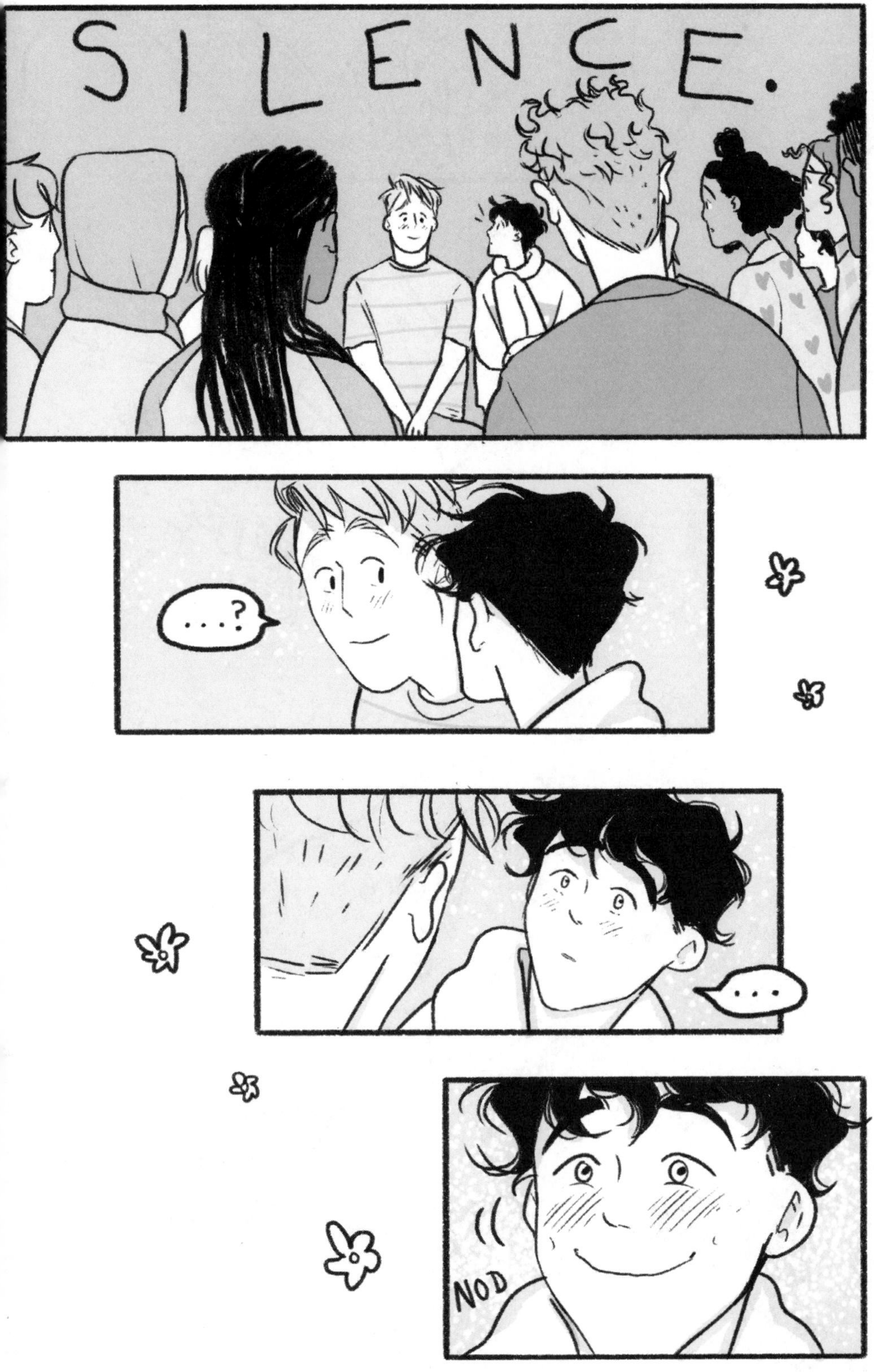
SILENCE.
...?
...
NOD

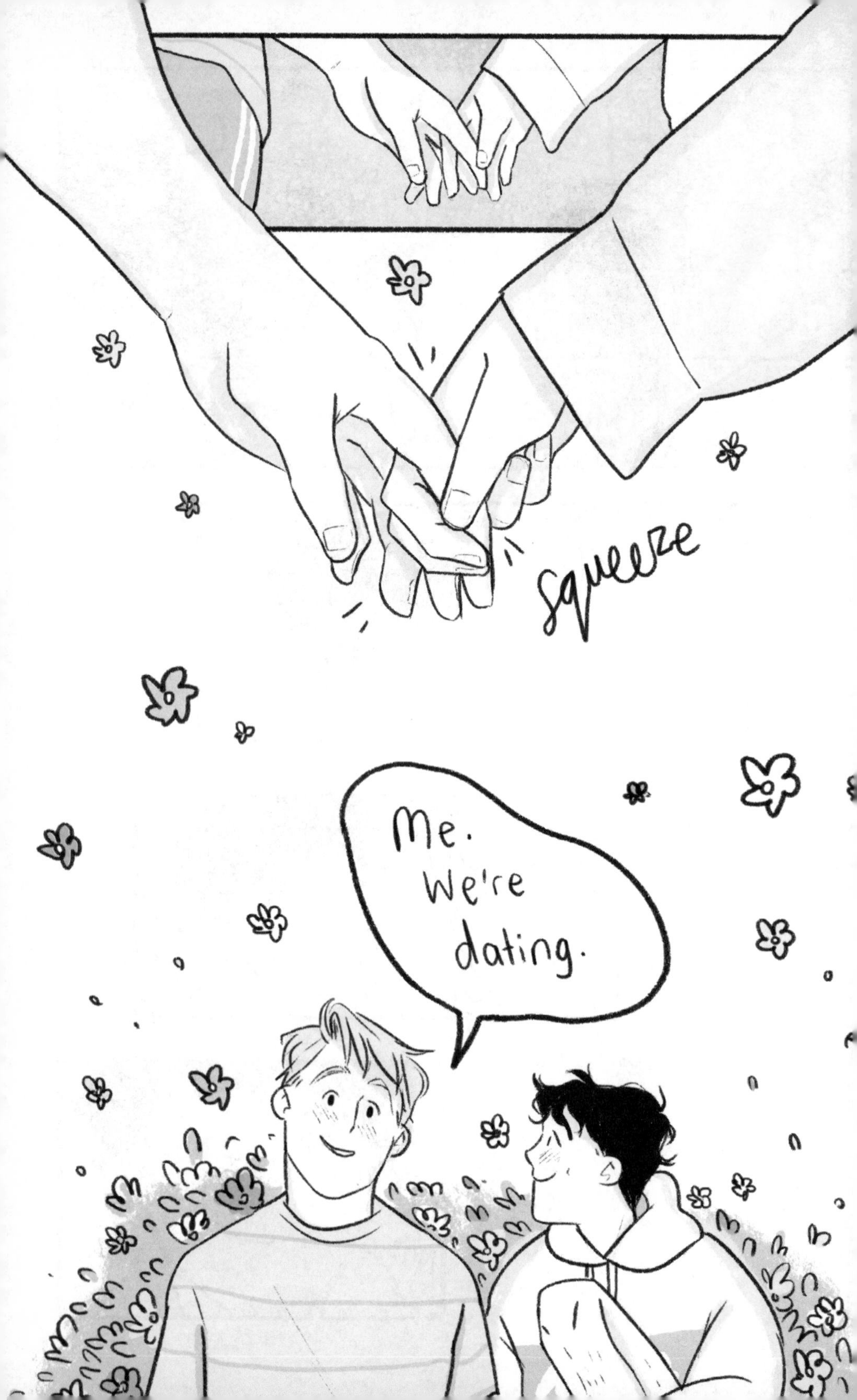
squeeze
Me.
We're
dating.

301

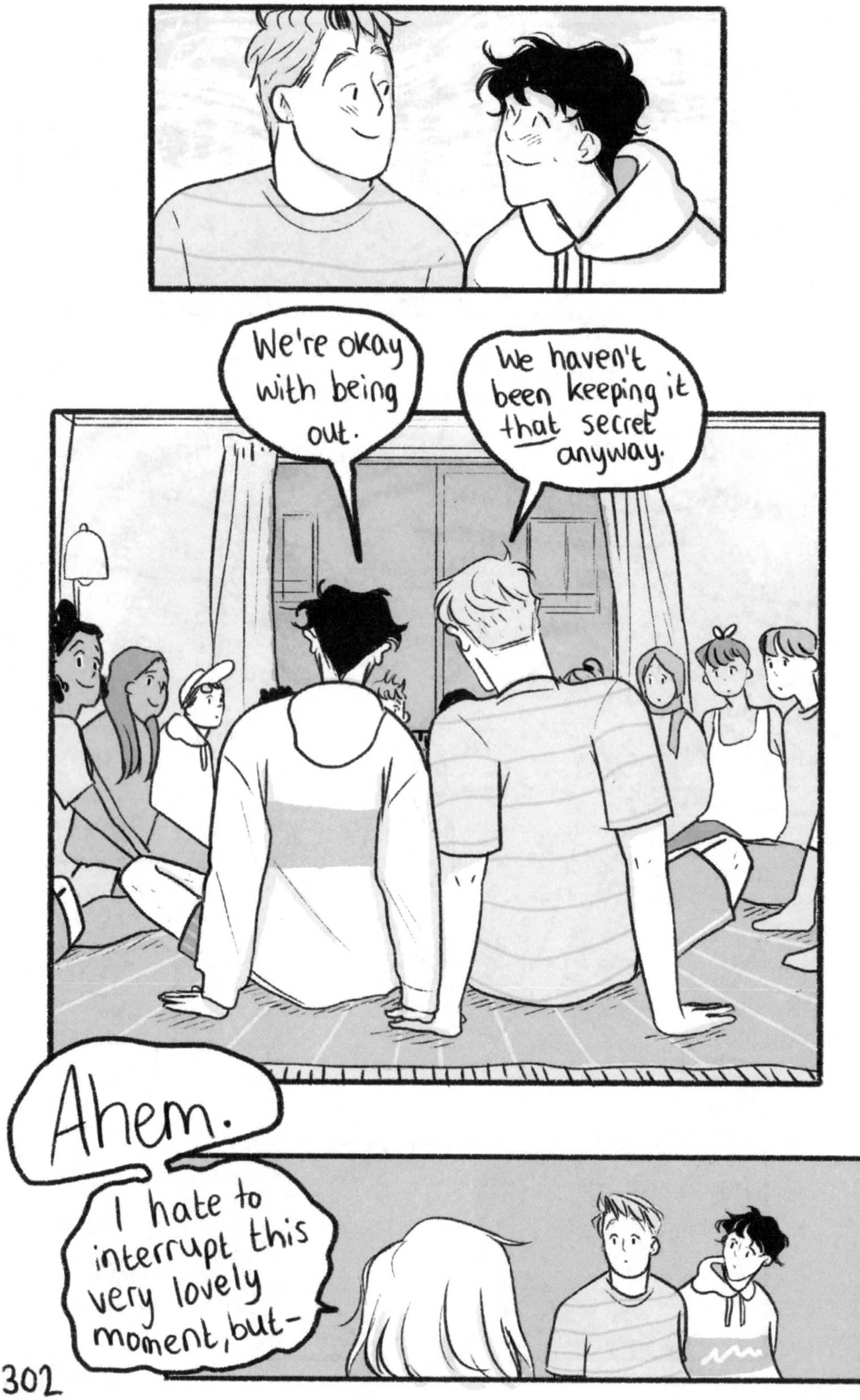
We're okay with being out.
We haven't been keeping it that secret anyway.
Ahem.
I hate to interrupt this very lovely moment, but-

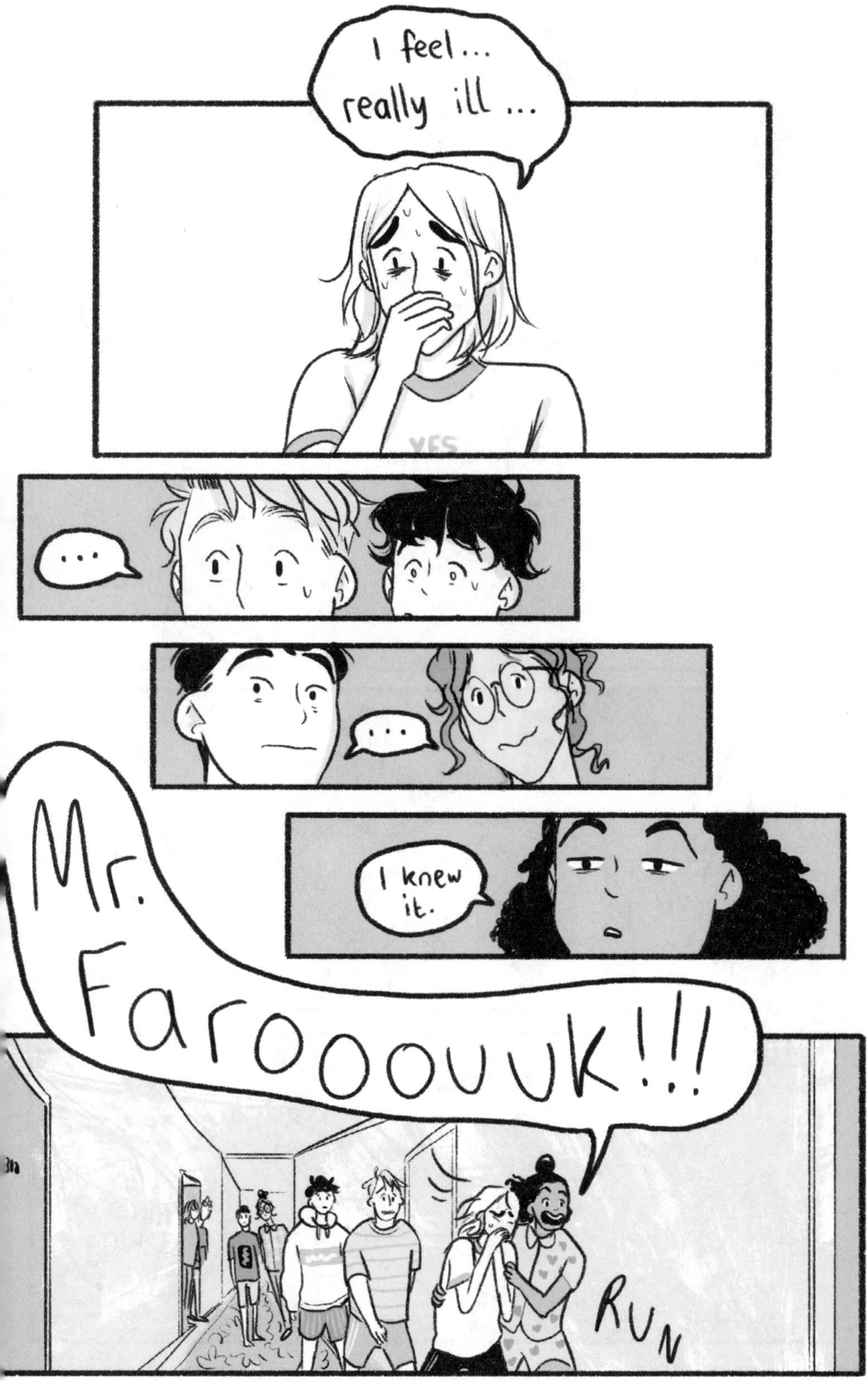
I feel...
really ill...
...
...
I knew it.
Mr. Faroooouk!!!
RUN

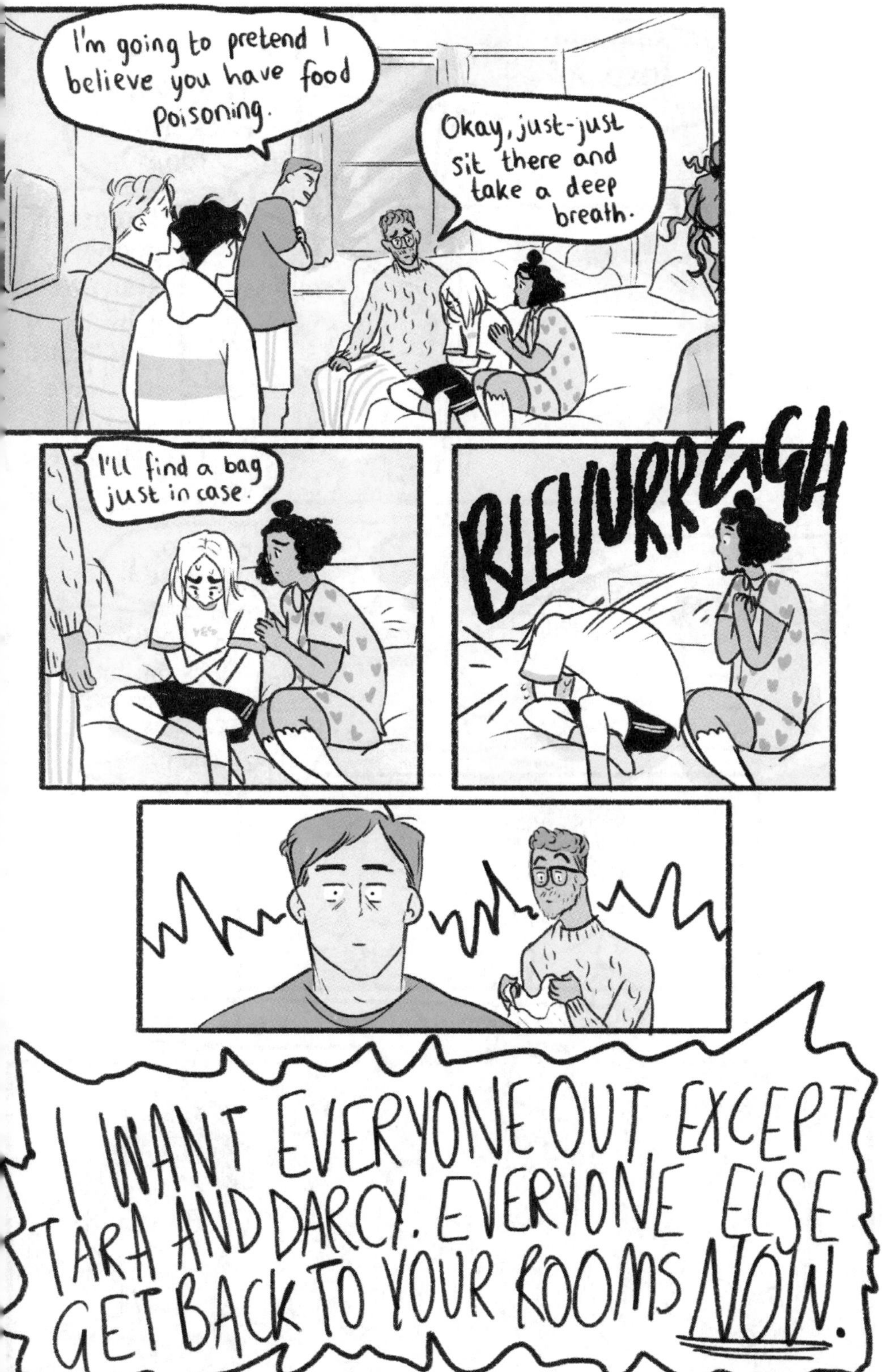
I'm going to pretend I believe you have food poisoning.
Okay, just-just sit there and take a deep breath.
I'll find a bag just in case.
BLEUURRGGH
I WANT EVERYONE OUT EXCEPT TARA AND DARCY. EVERYONE ELSE GET BACK TO YOUR ROOMS NOW.

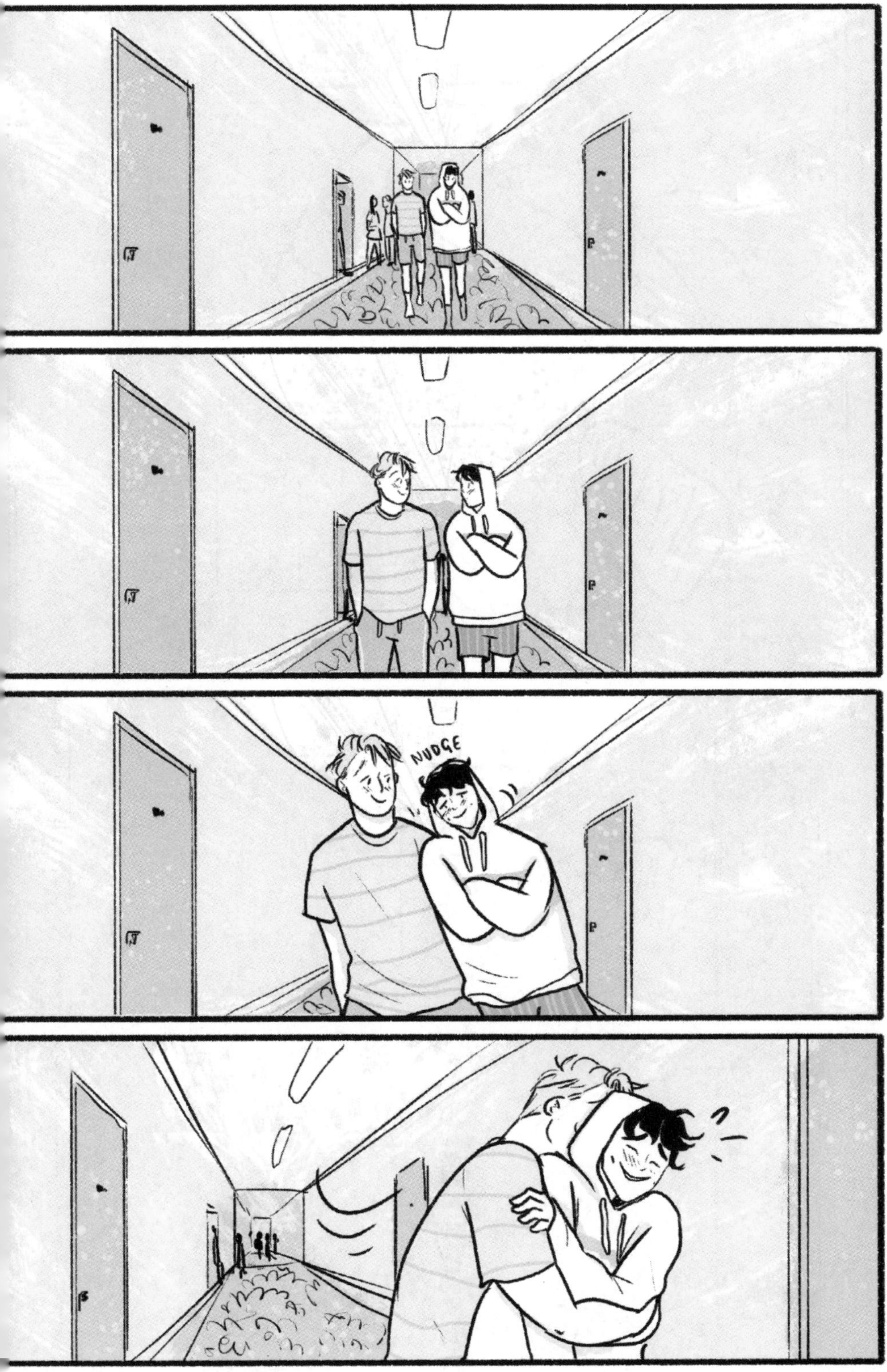
NUDGE

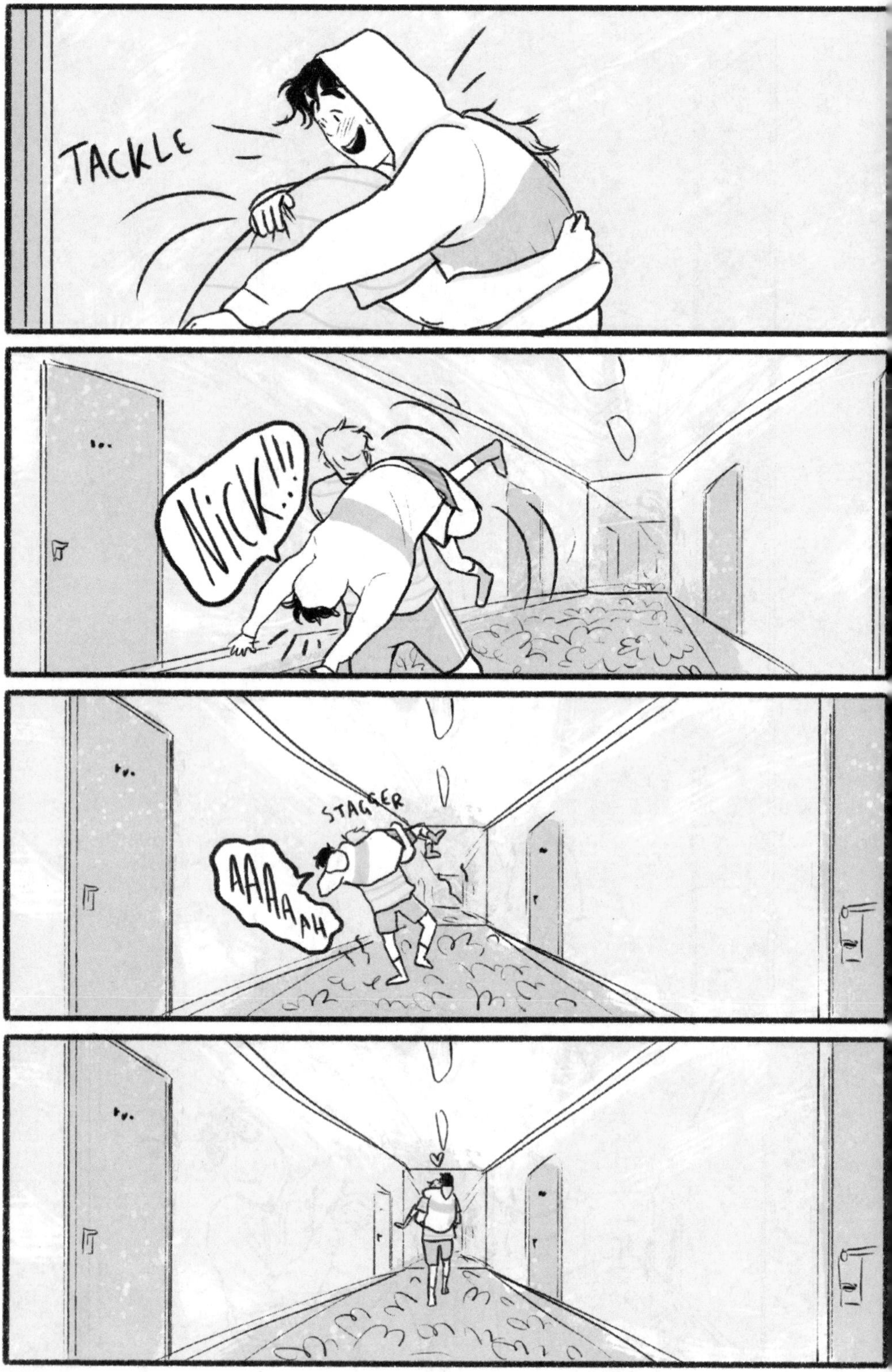
TACKLE
NICK!!!
STAGGER
AAAAAPH

SHUT

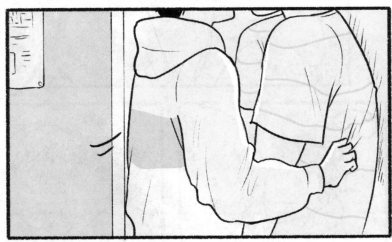

You came out to an entire room of people

Y-yeah, I guess I did.

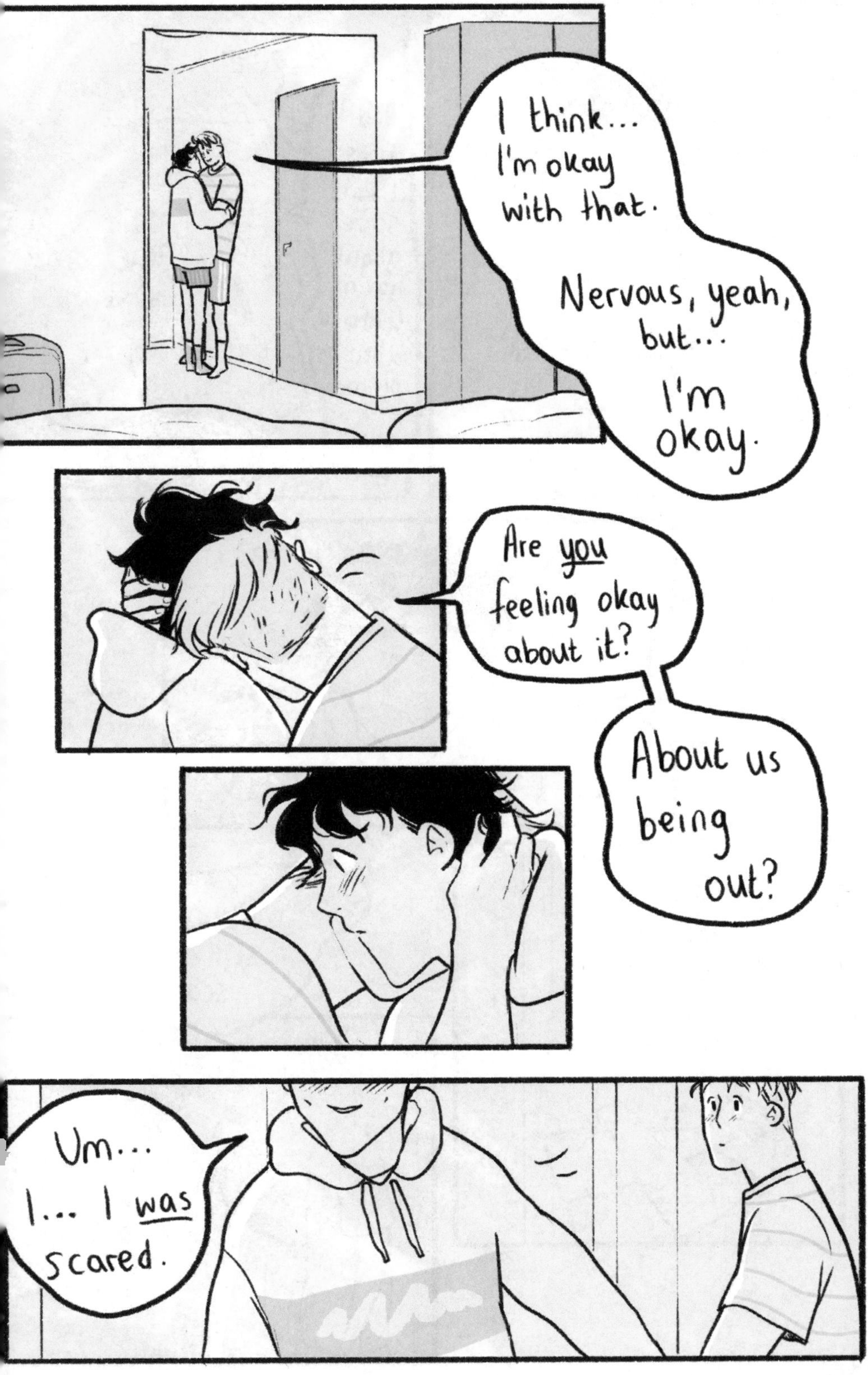
I think... I'm okay with that.
Nervous, yeah, but... I'm okay.
Are you feeling okay about it?
About us being out?
Um... I... I was scared.

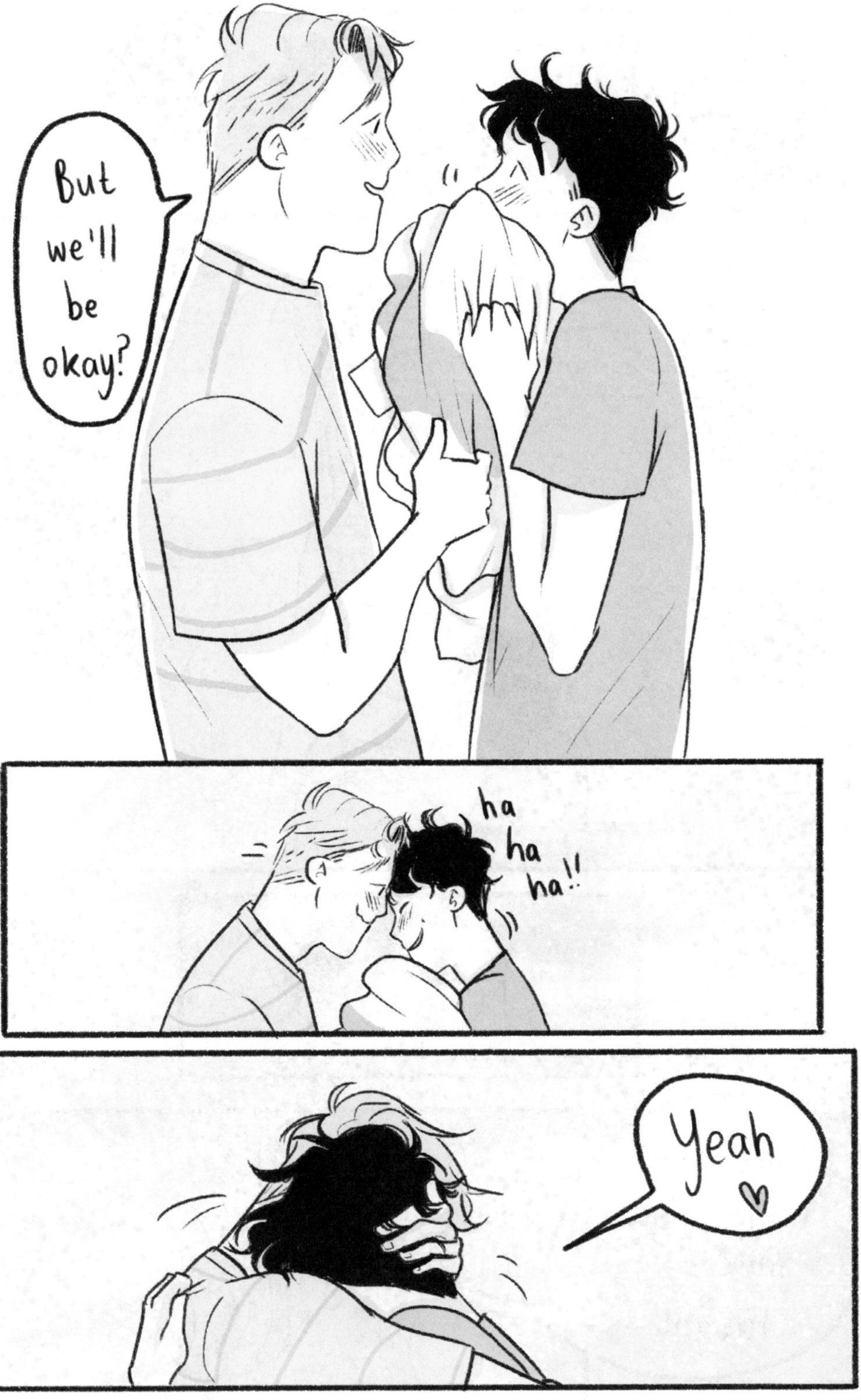
But we'll be okay?
ha ha ha!!
Yeah ♥

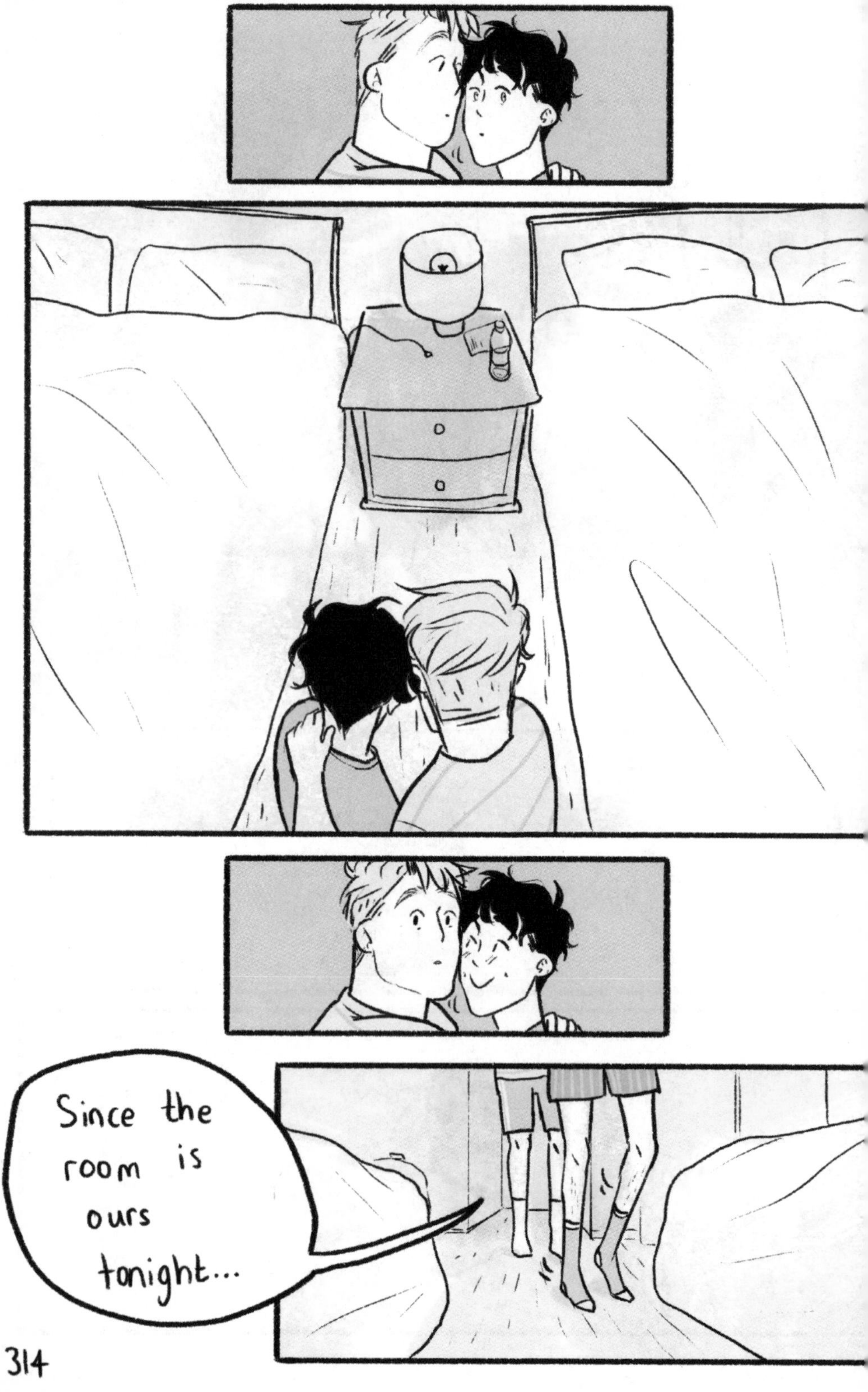
Since the room is ours tonight...

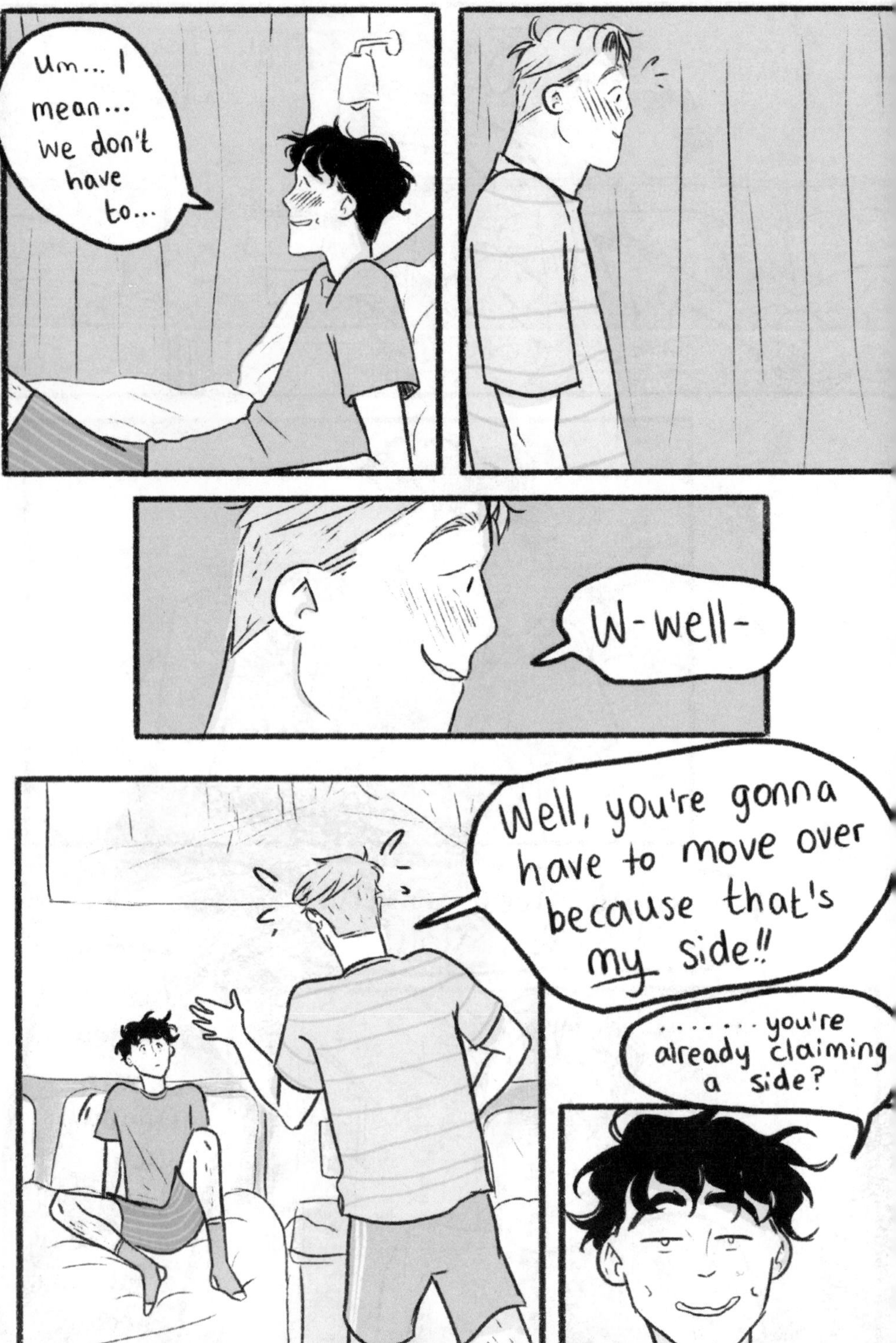
Um... I mean... we don't have to...
W-well-
Well, you're gonna have to move over because that's my side!!
.......you're already claiming a side?

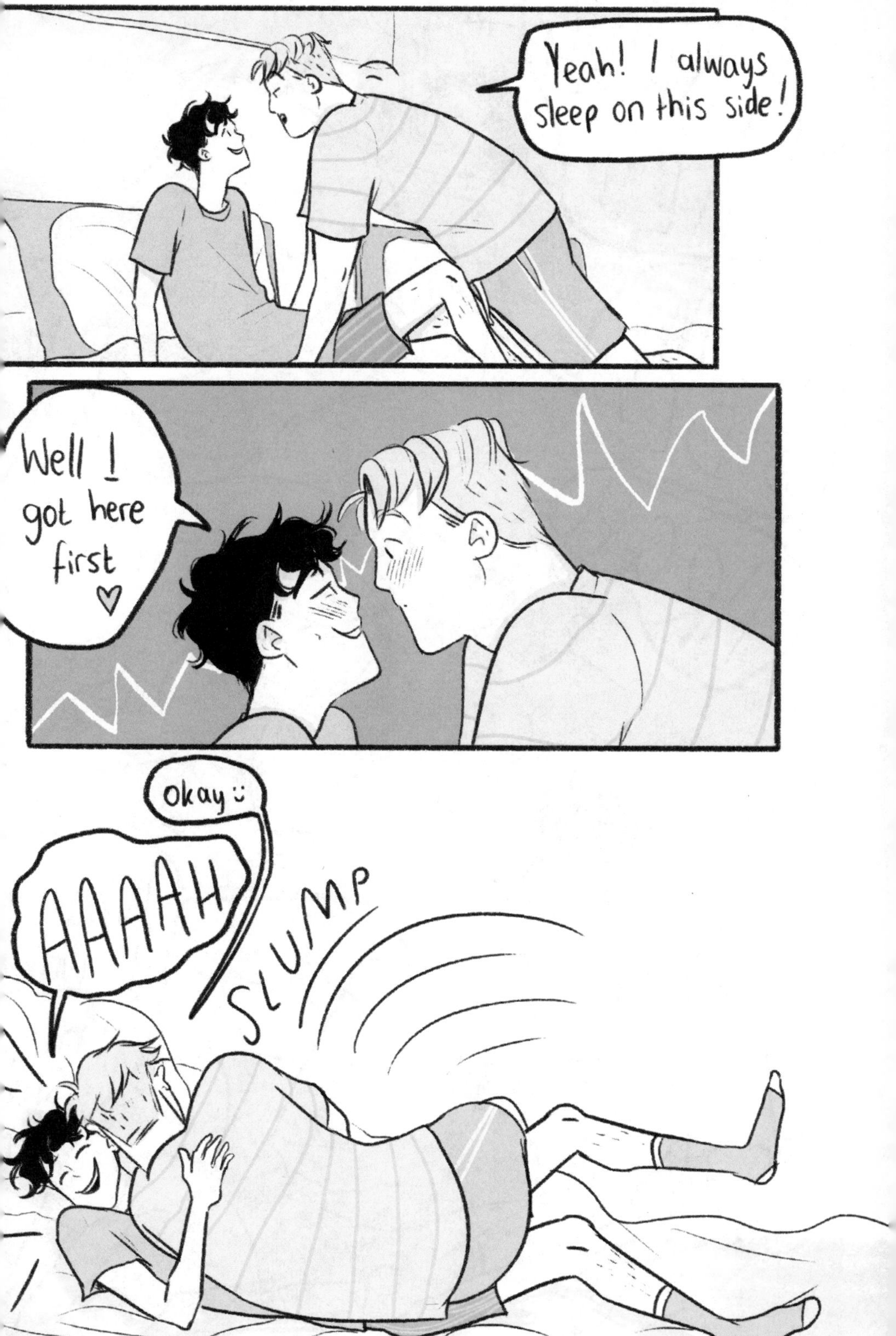
Yeah! I always sleep on this side!
Well I got here first ♡
okay ᵕ
AAAAH
SLUMP

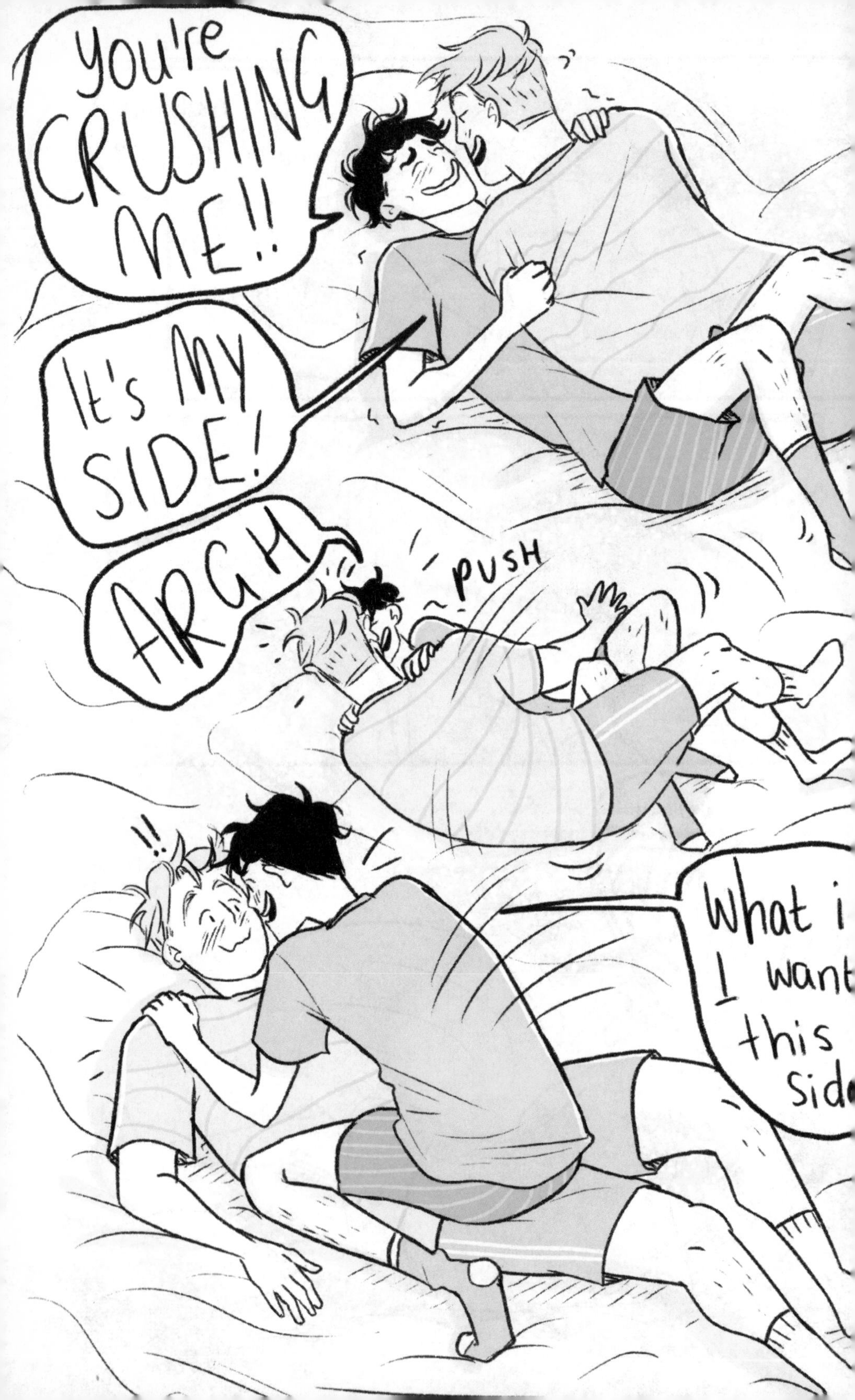
You're CRUSHING ME!!
It's MY SIDE!
ARGH
PUSH
What i
I want
this
sid

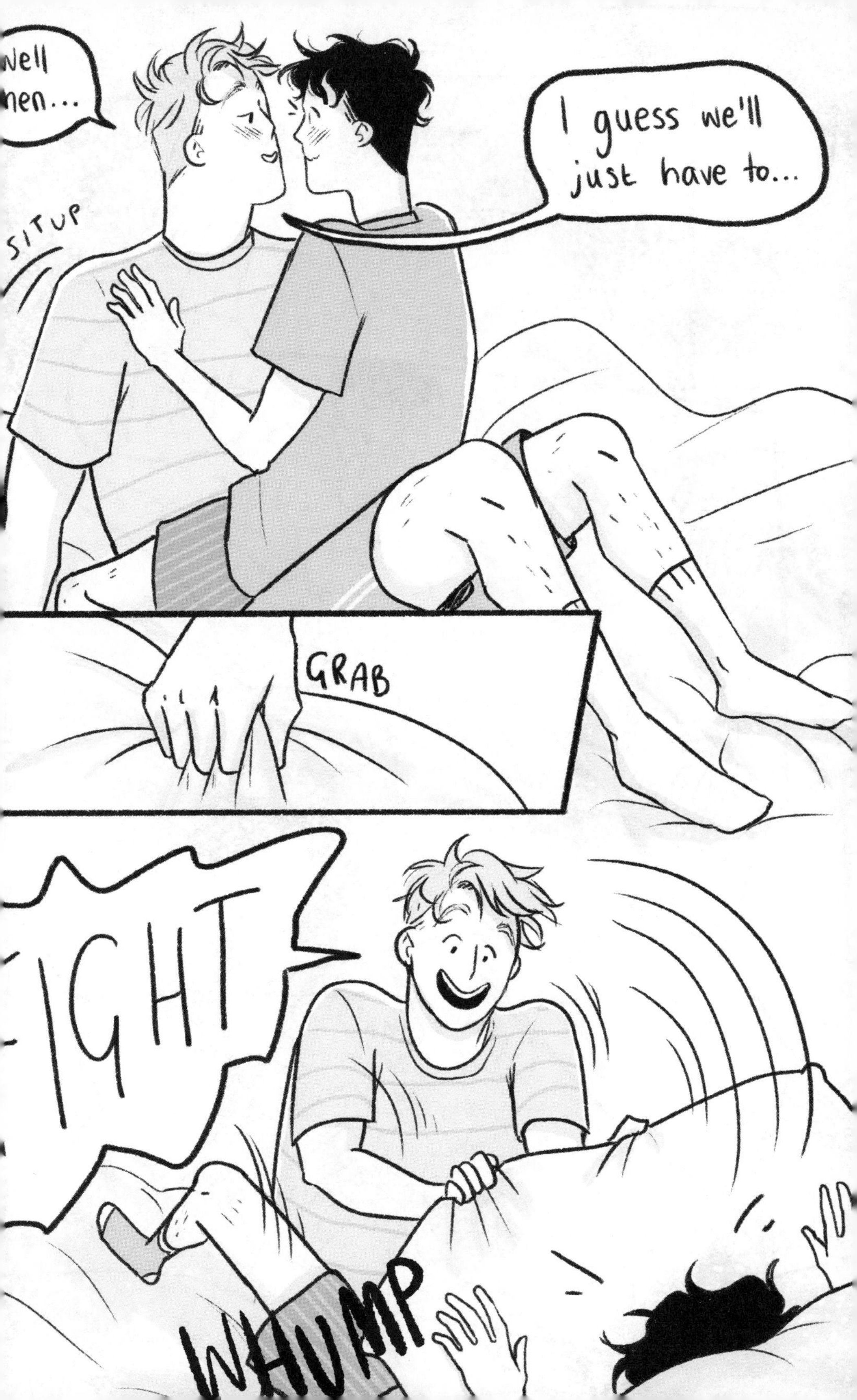
Well
hen...
I guess we'll just have to...
SITUP
GRAB
IGHT
WHUMP

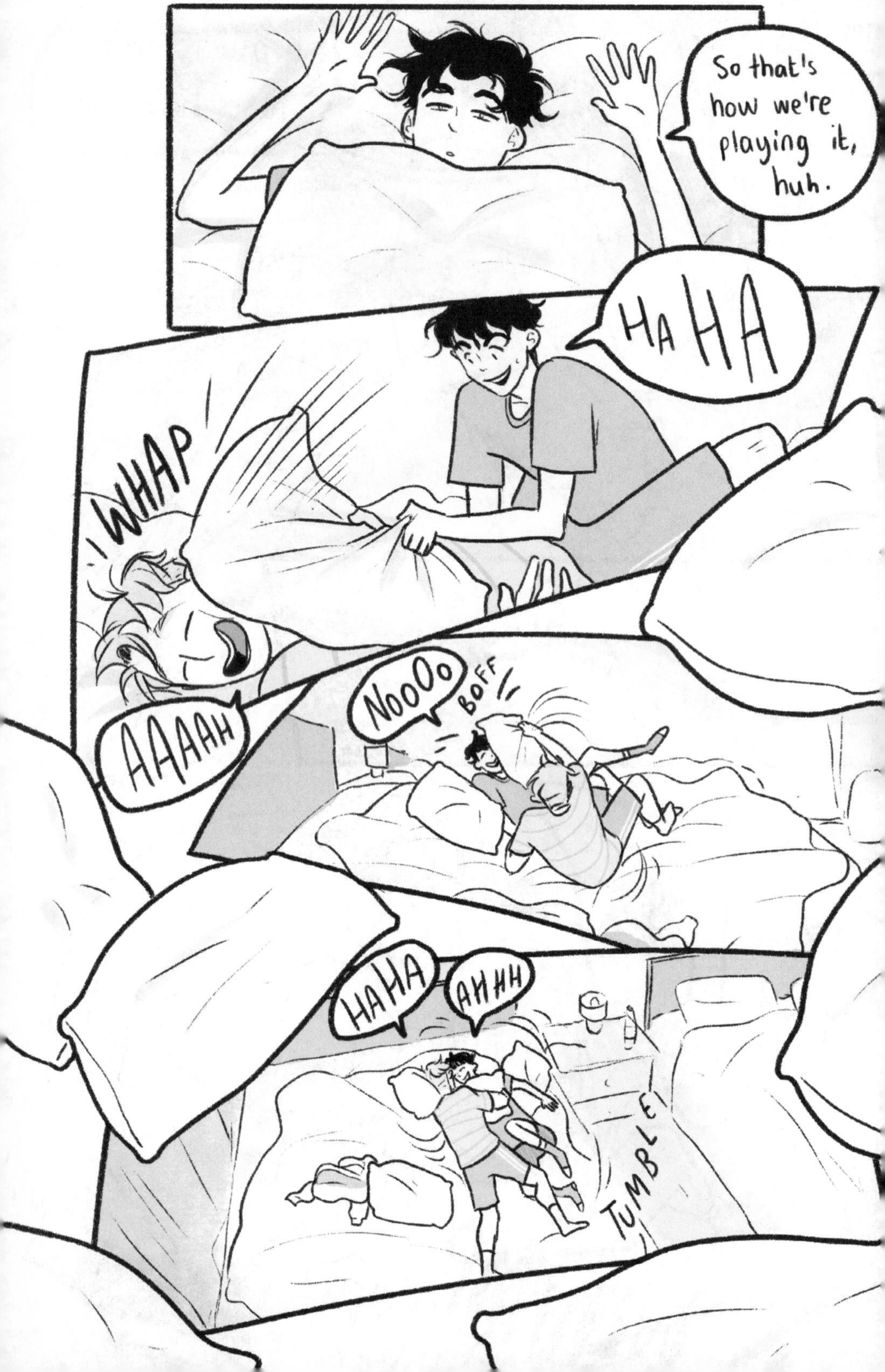
So that's how we're playing it, huh.
HaHA
WHAP
AAAAH
NooOo
BOFF
HAHA
AHHH
TUMBLE

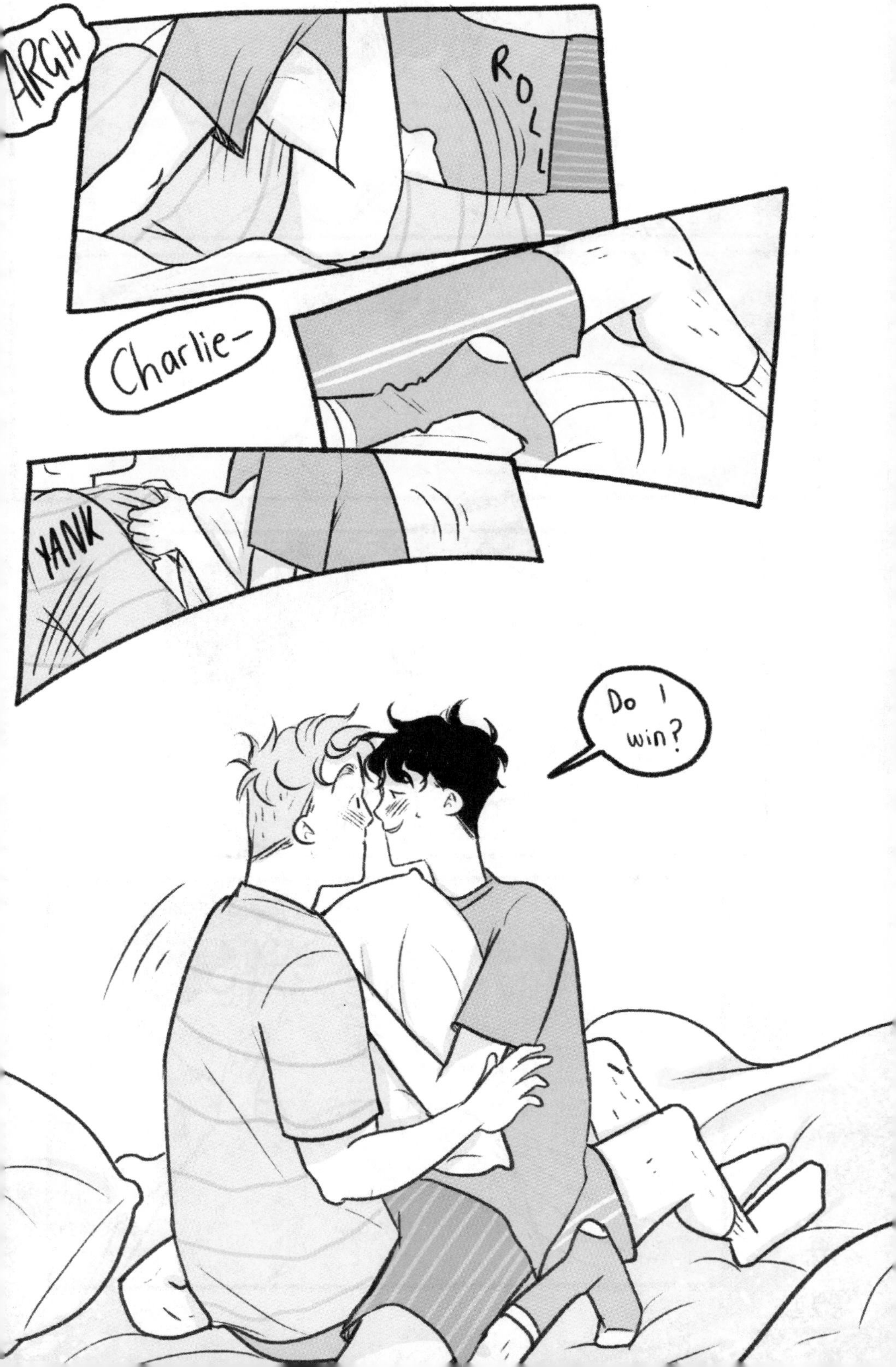
ARGH
ROLL
Charlie-
YANK
Do I win?

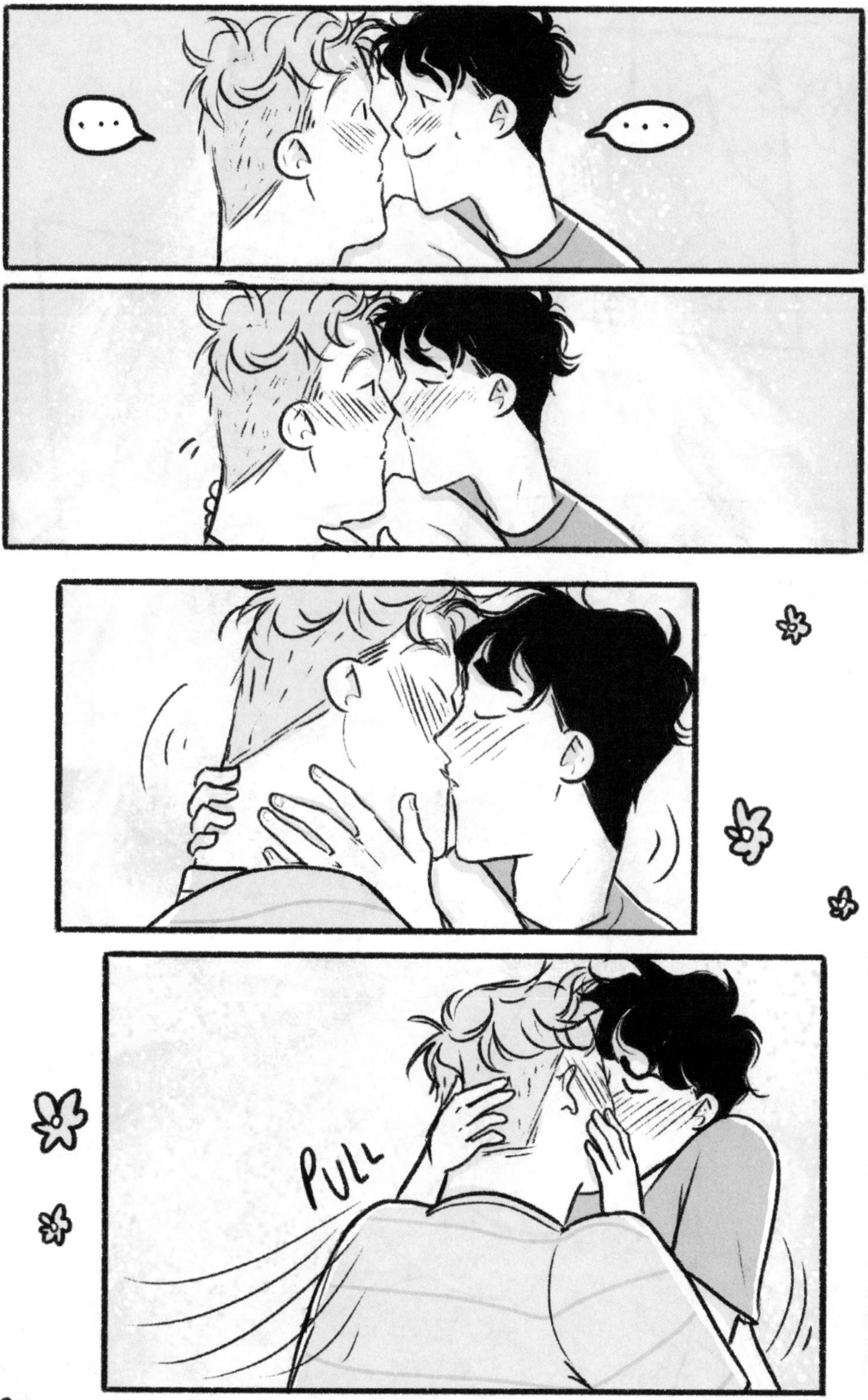
...
...
PULL

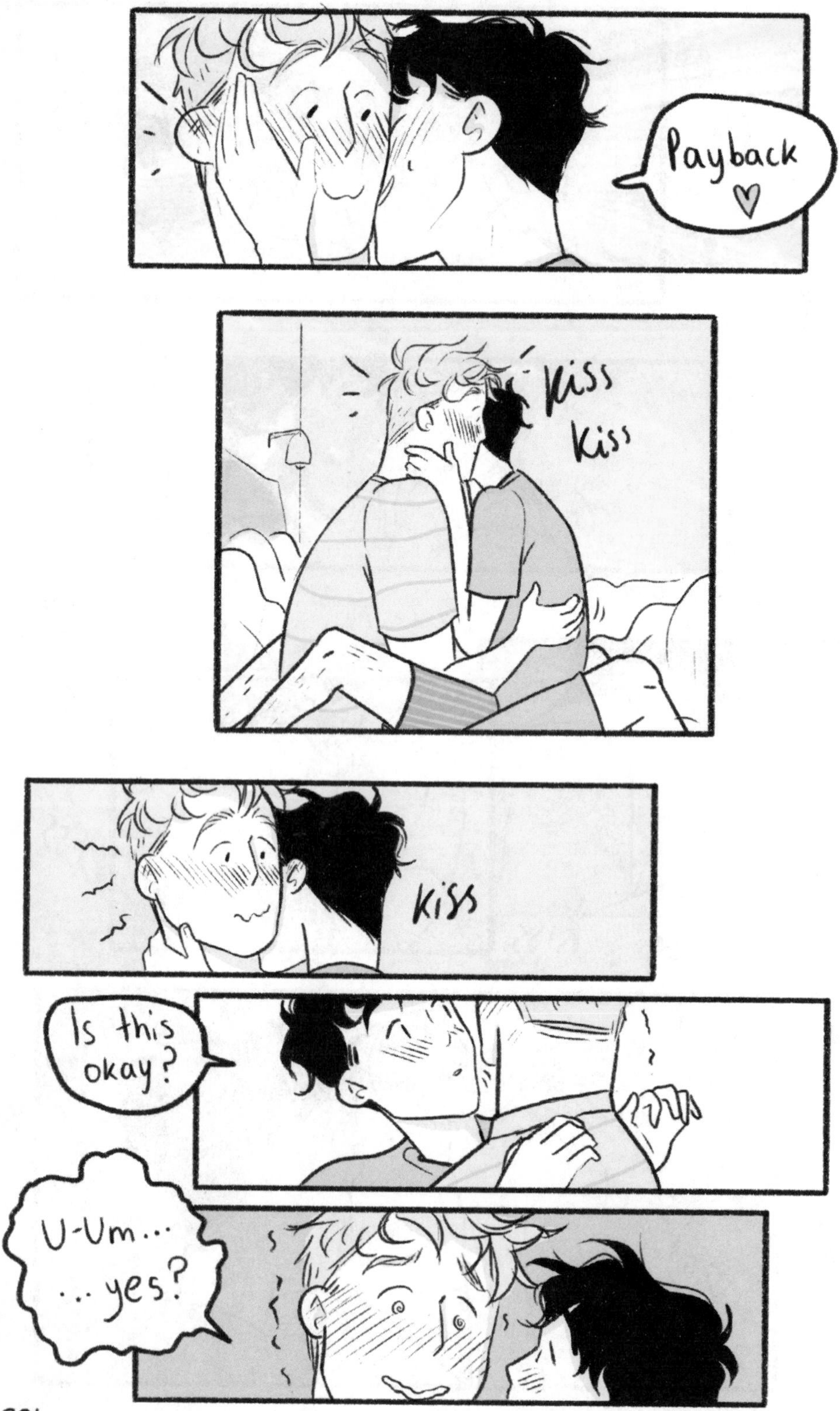
Payback ♥
kiss
kiss
kiss
Is this okay?
U-Um...
...yes?

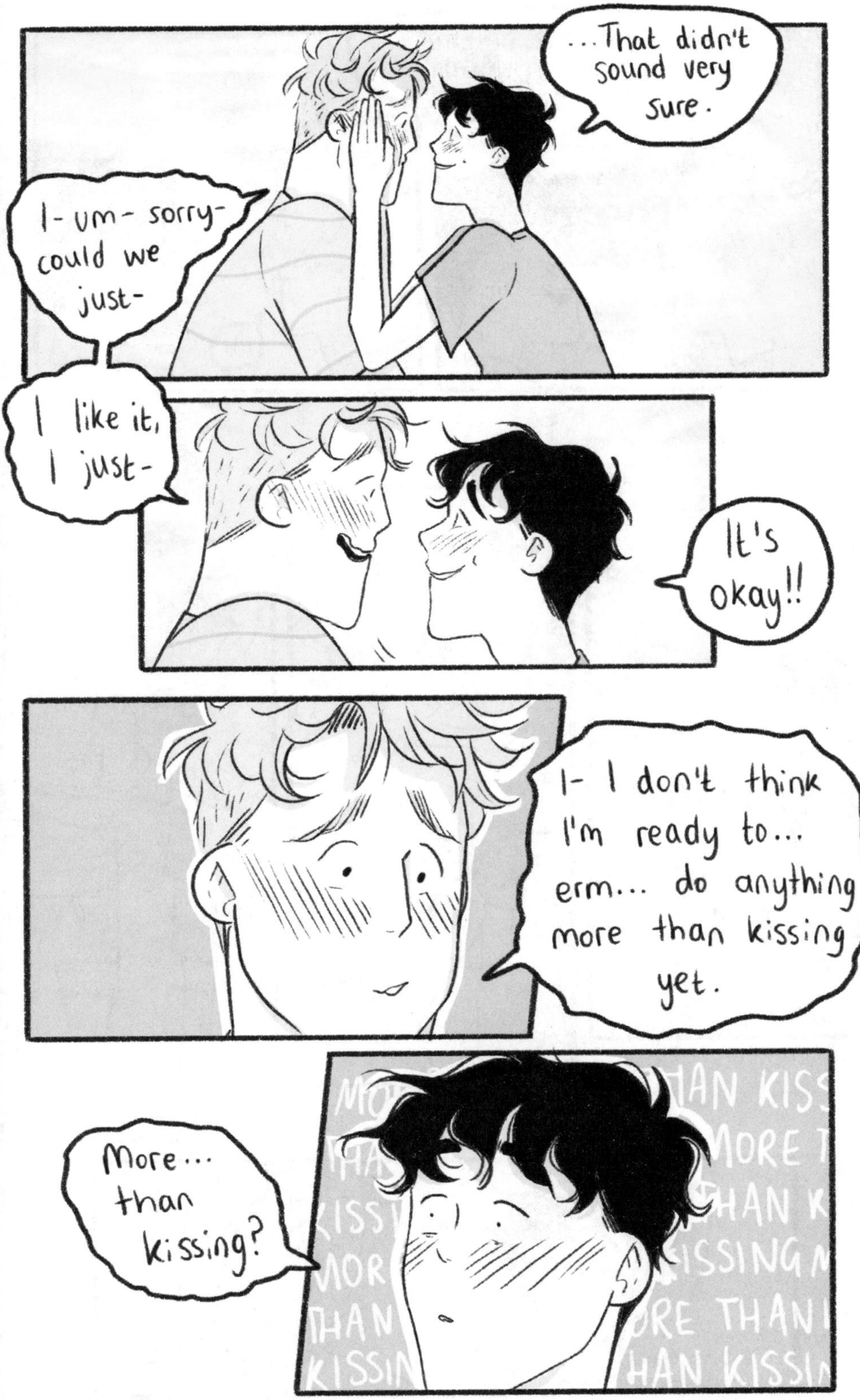
...That didn't sound very sure.
I- um- sorry- could we just-
I like it, I just-
It's okay!!
I- I don't think I'm ready to... erm... do anything more than kissing yet.
More... than kissing?
MORE THAN KISSING MORE THAN KISSING MORE THAN KISSING MORE THAN KISSING

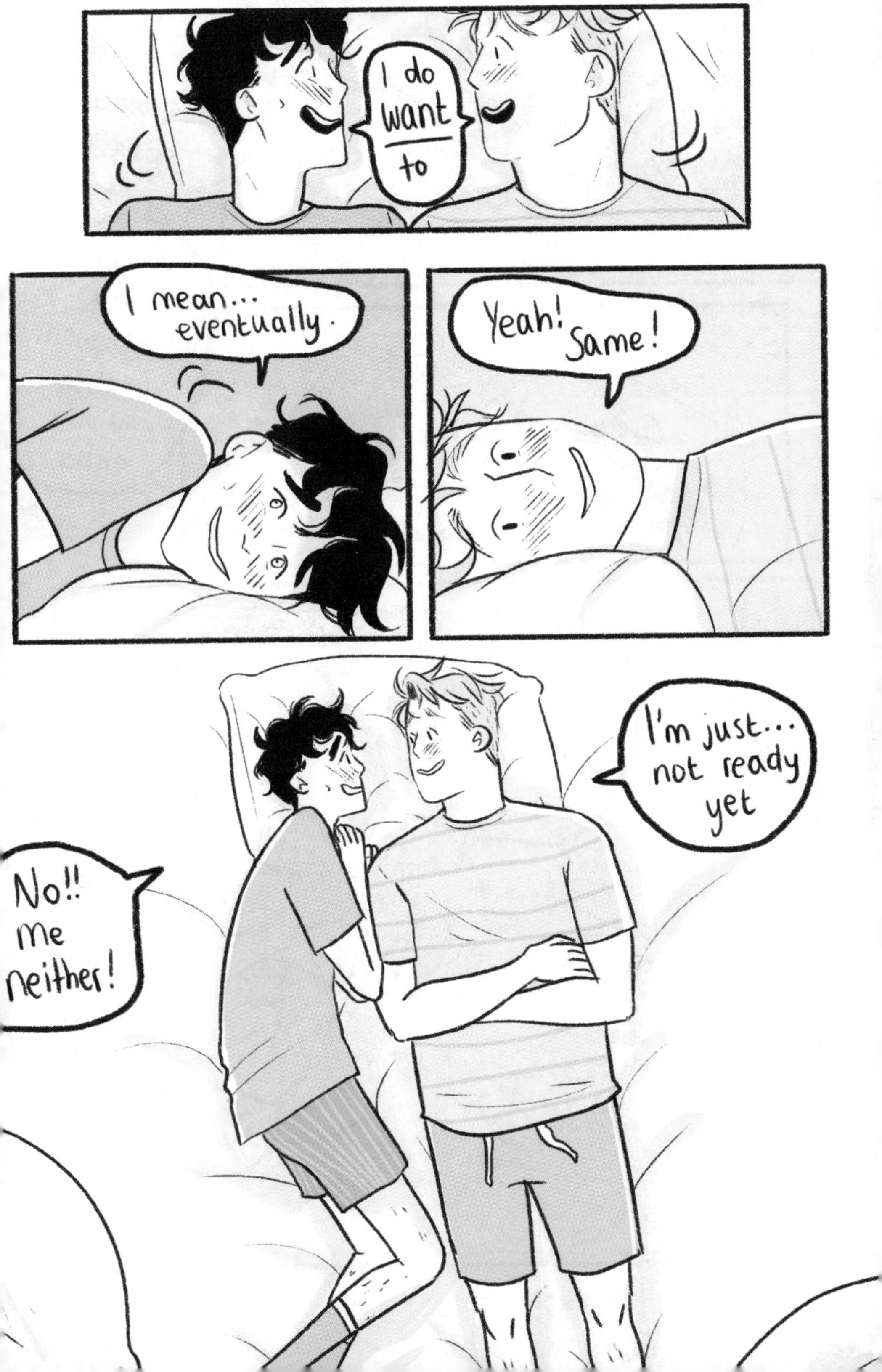
I do want to
I mean... eventually.
Yeah! Same!
I'm just... not ready yet
No!! me neither!

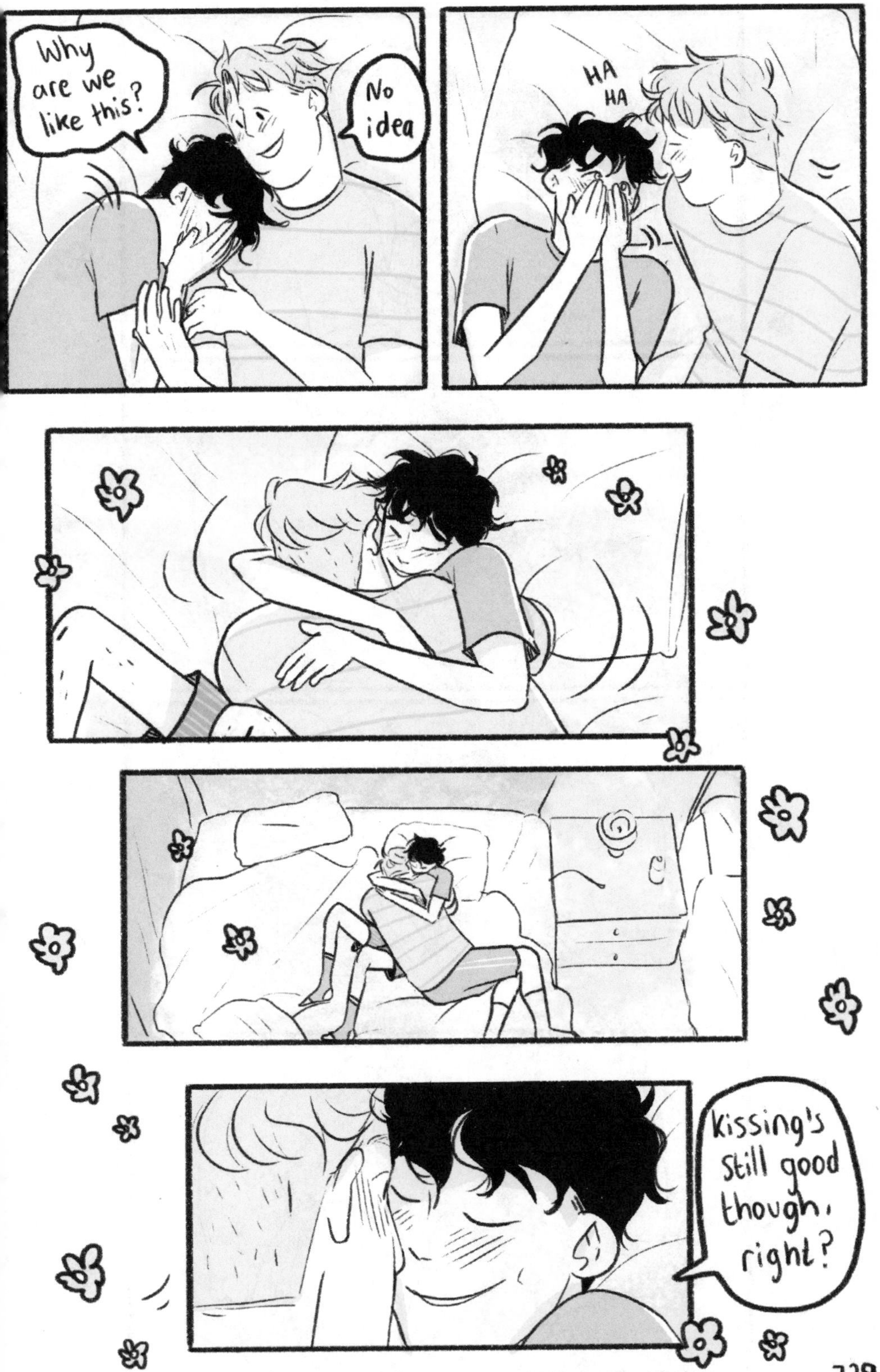
Why are we like this?
No idea
HA HA
Kissing's still good though, right?

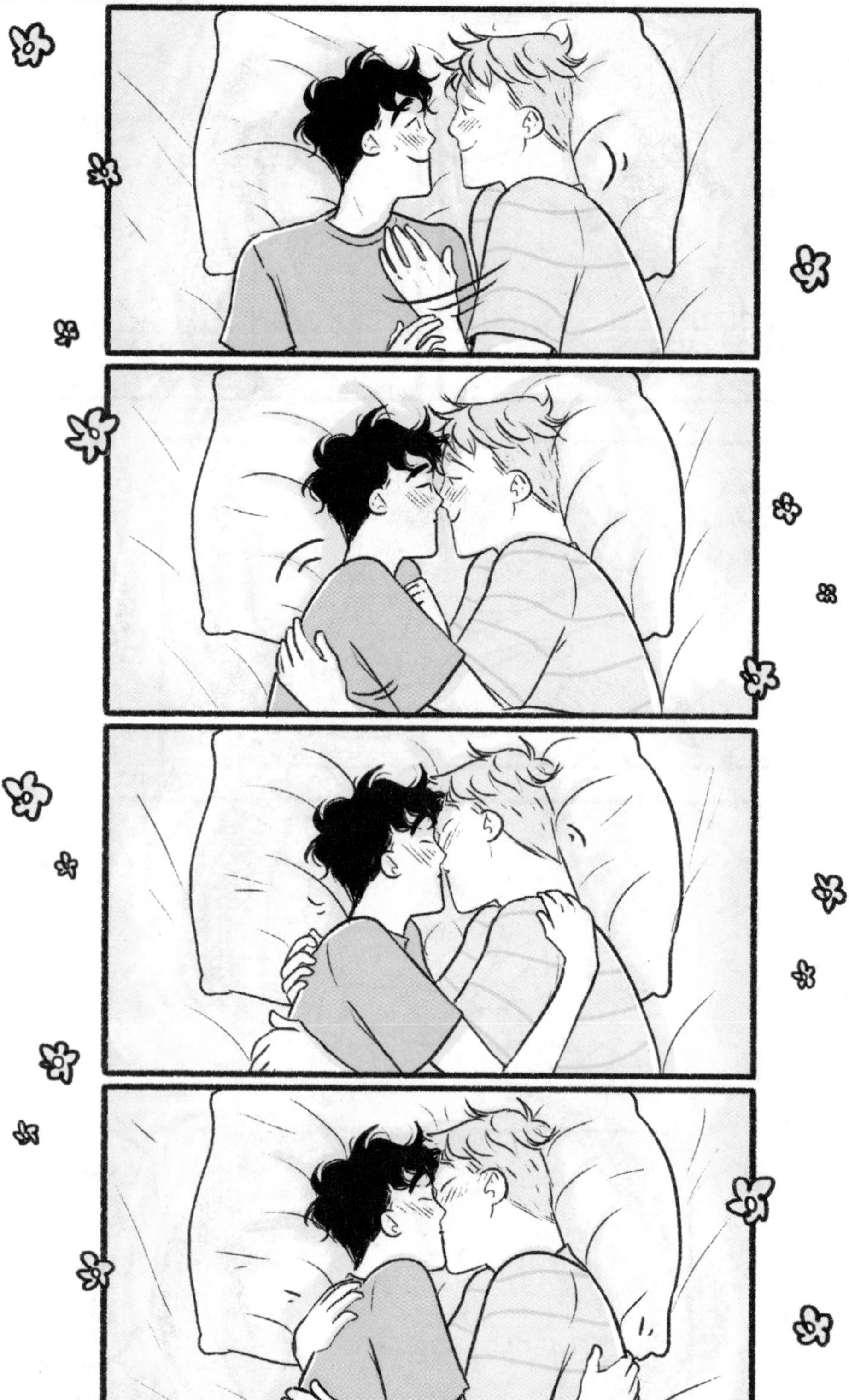

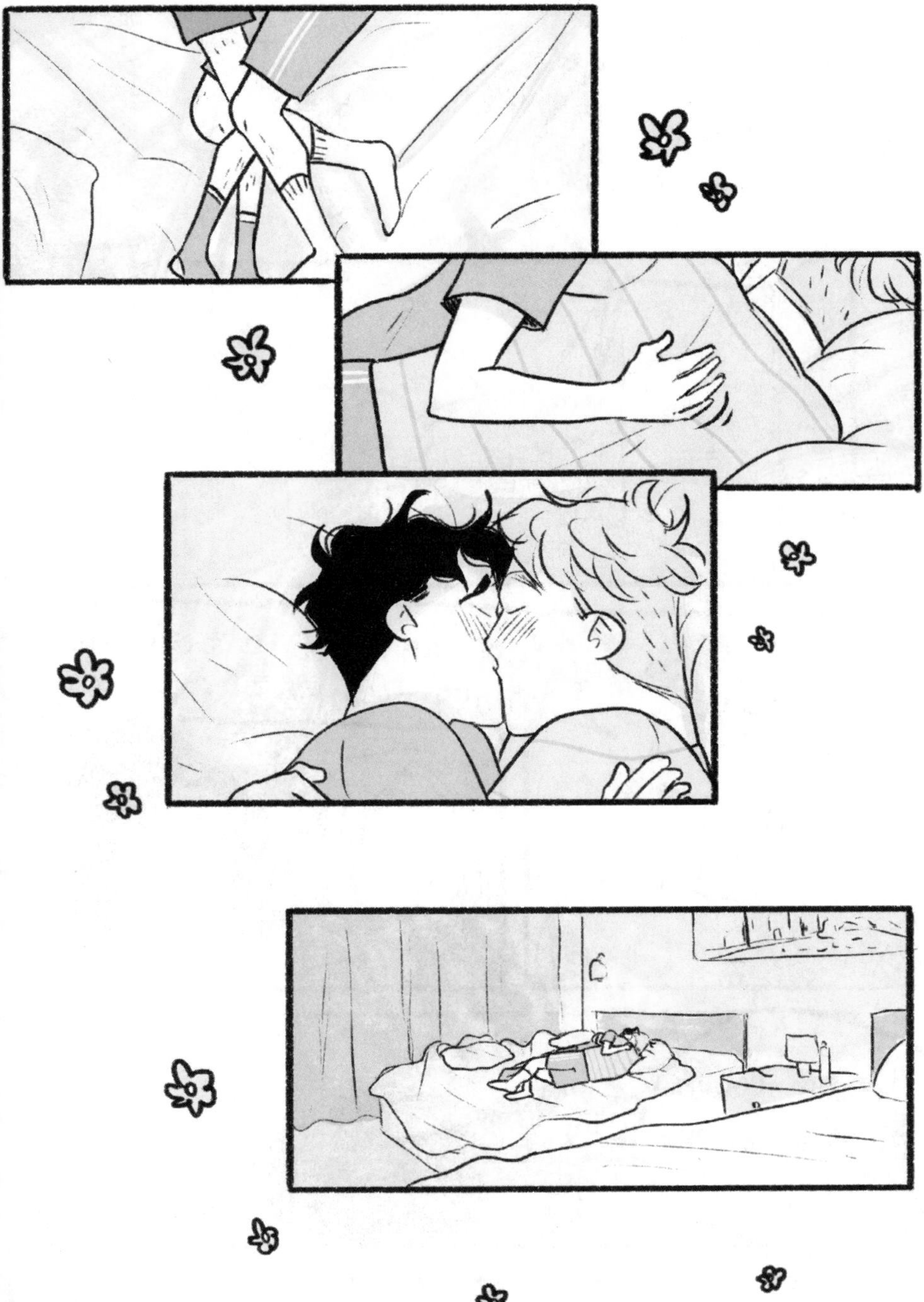

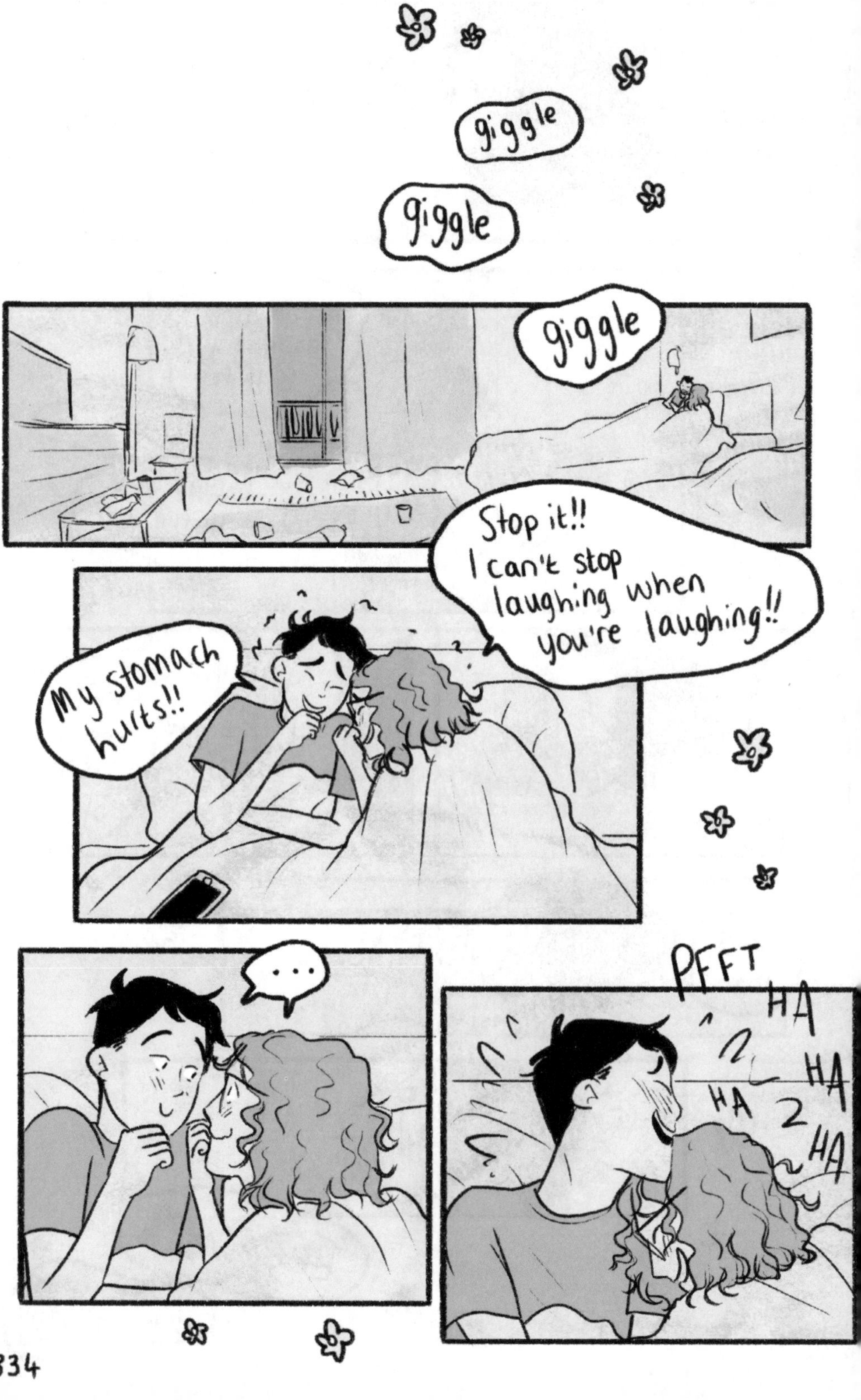
giggle
giggle
giggle
Stop it!! I can't stop laughing when you're laughing!!
My stomach hurts!!
...
PFFT
HA
HA
HA
HA

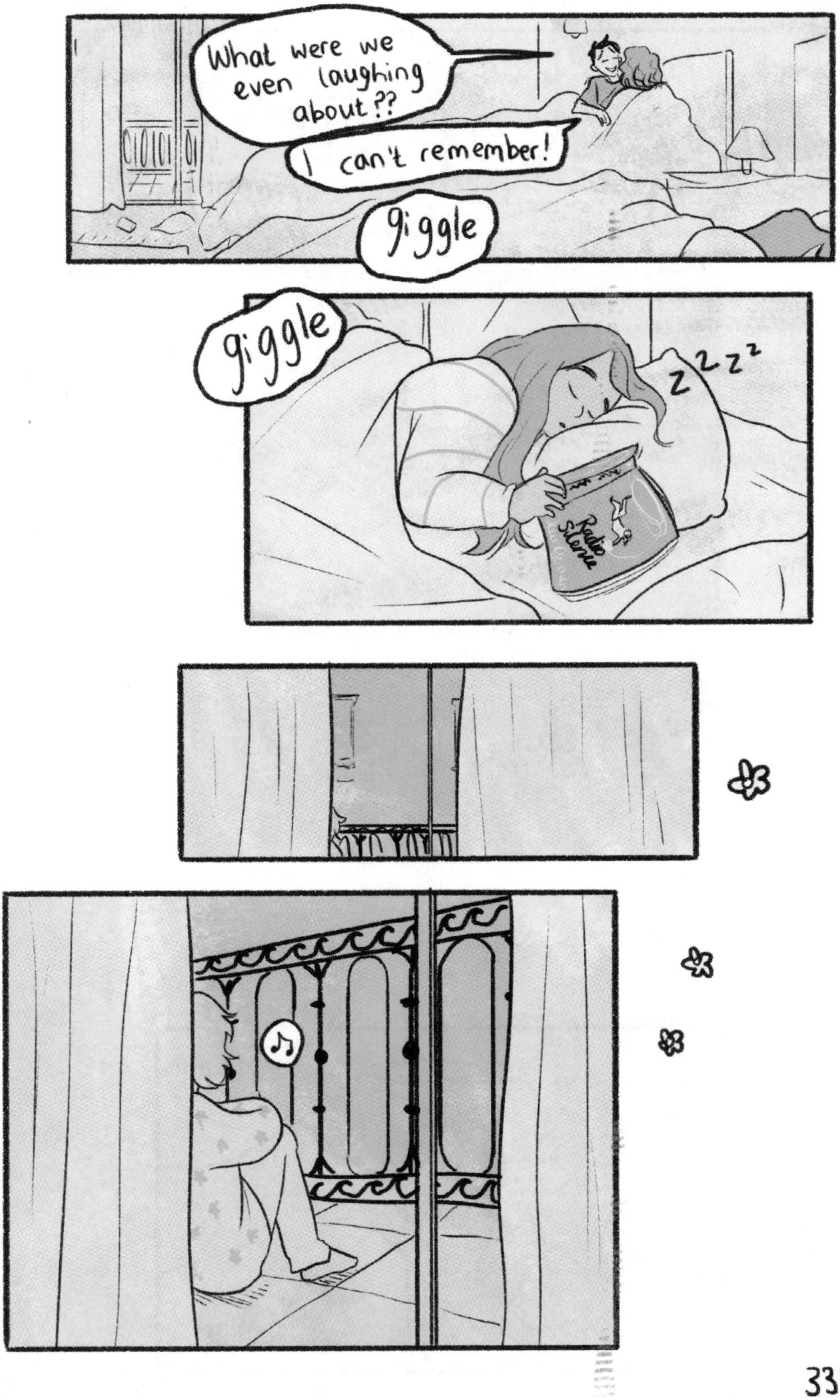
What were we even laughing about??
I can't remember!
giggle
giggle
Z z z z
Radio Silence

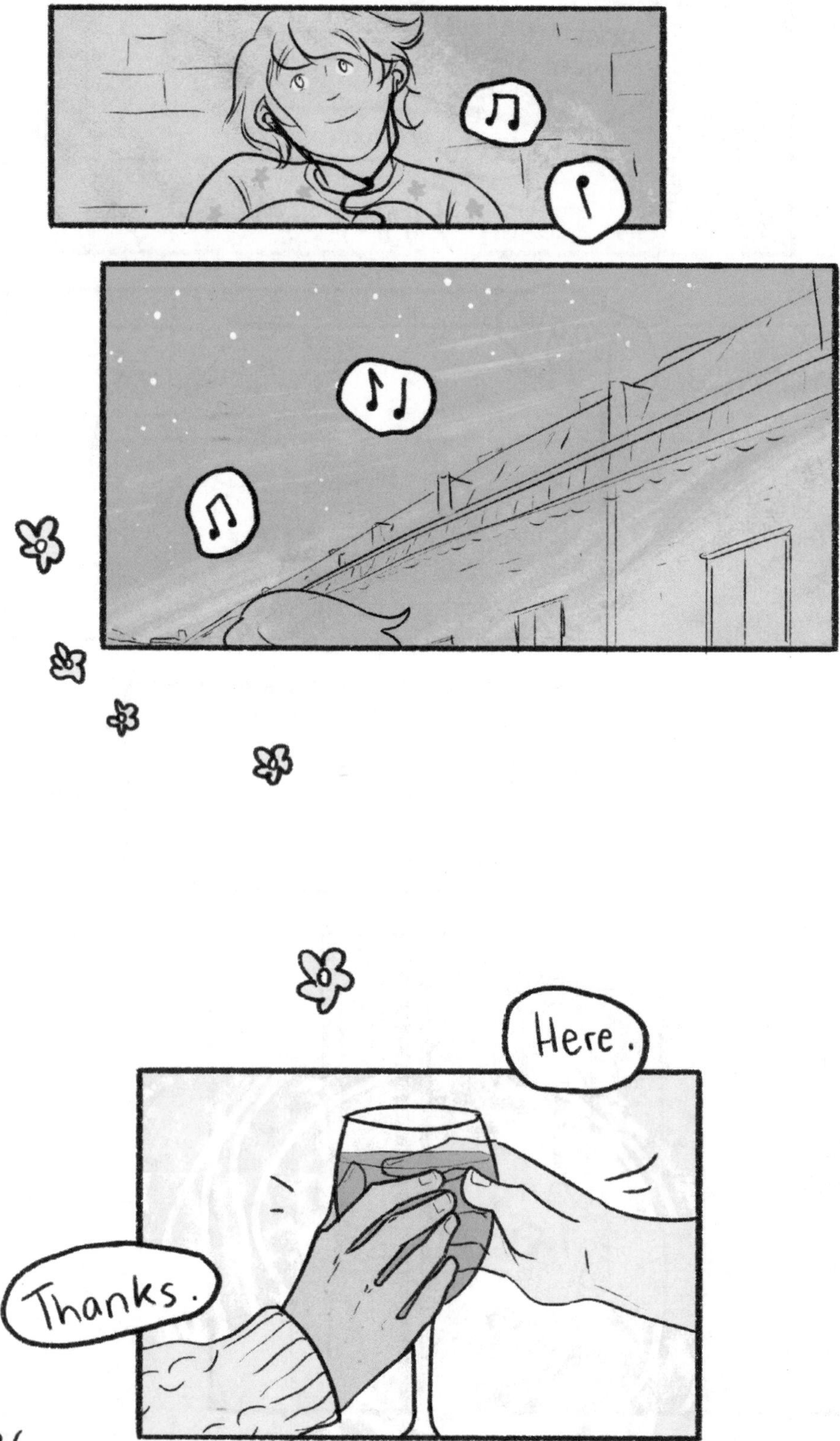
Here.
Thanks.

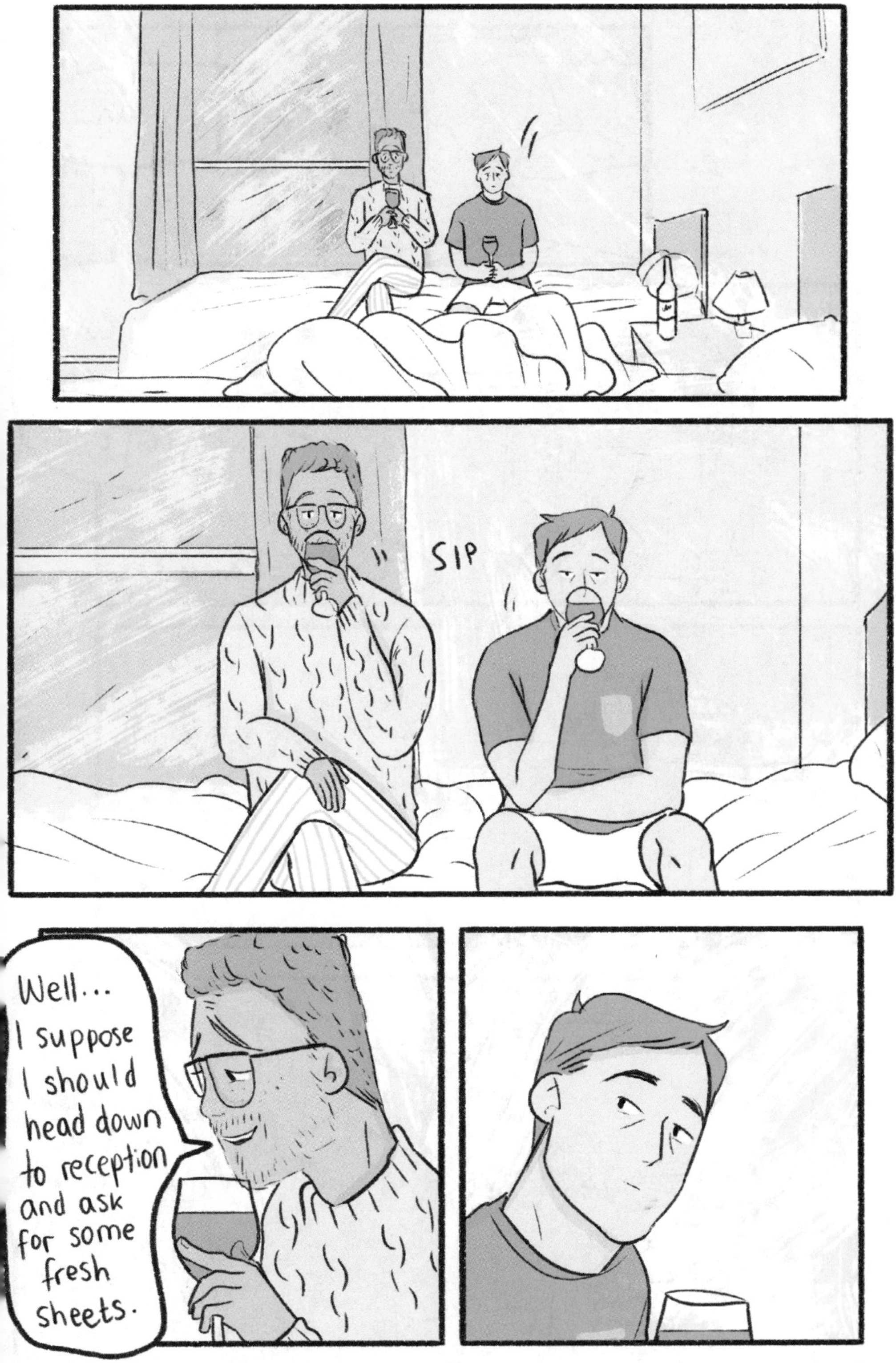
SIP
Well... I suppose I should head down to reception and ask for some fresh sheets.

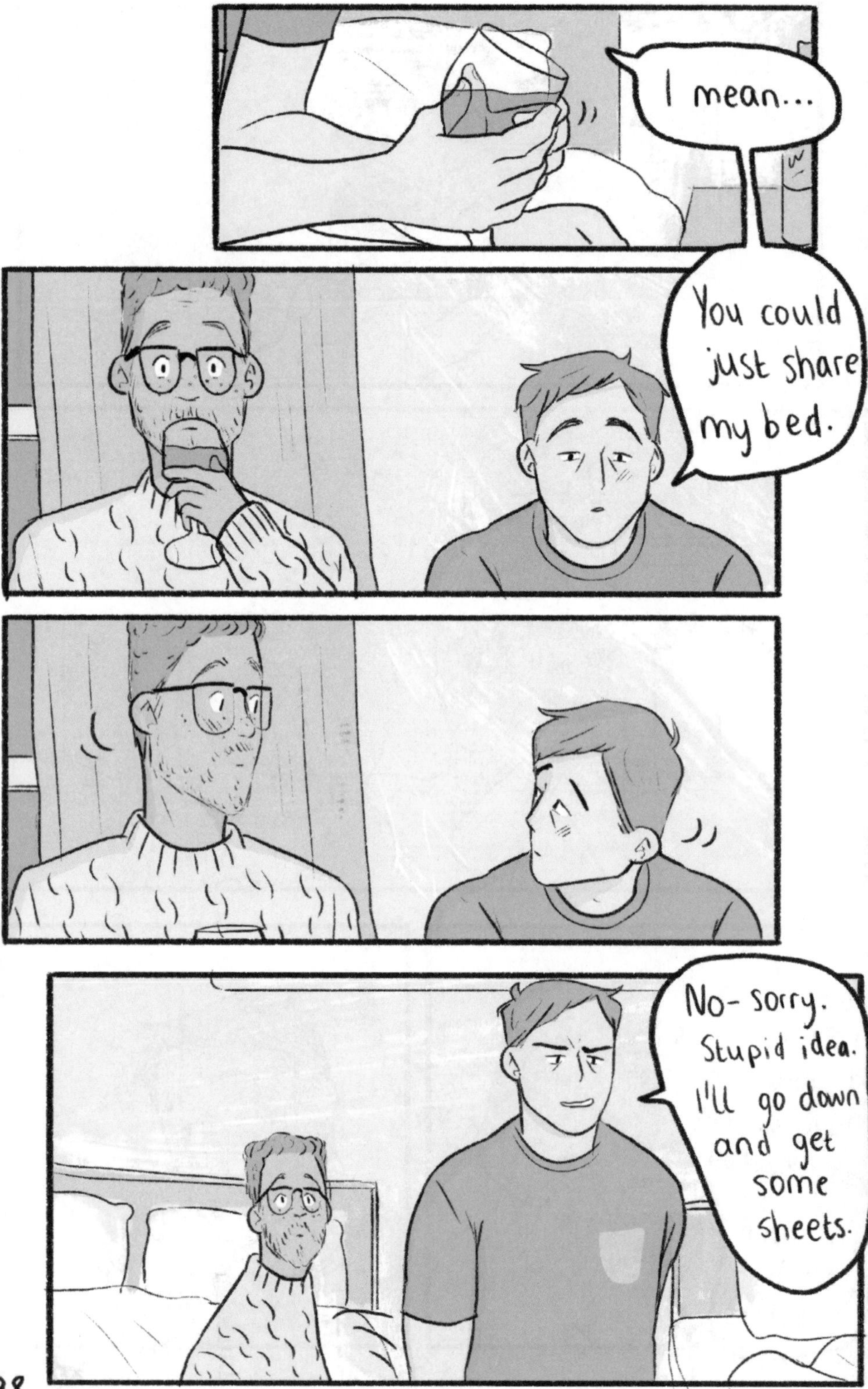
I mean...
You could just share my bed.
No- sorry. Stupid idea. I'll go down and get some sheets.

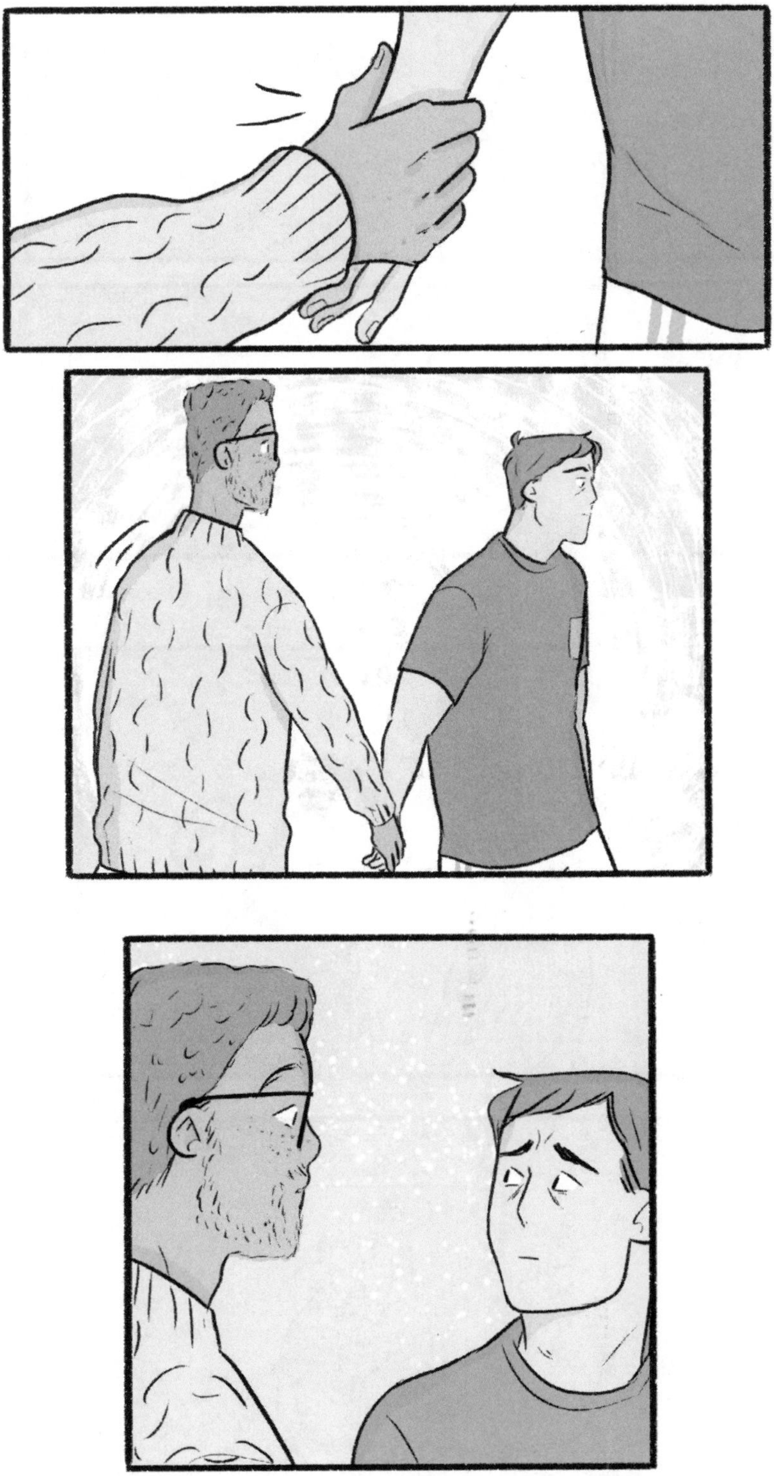

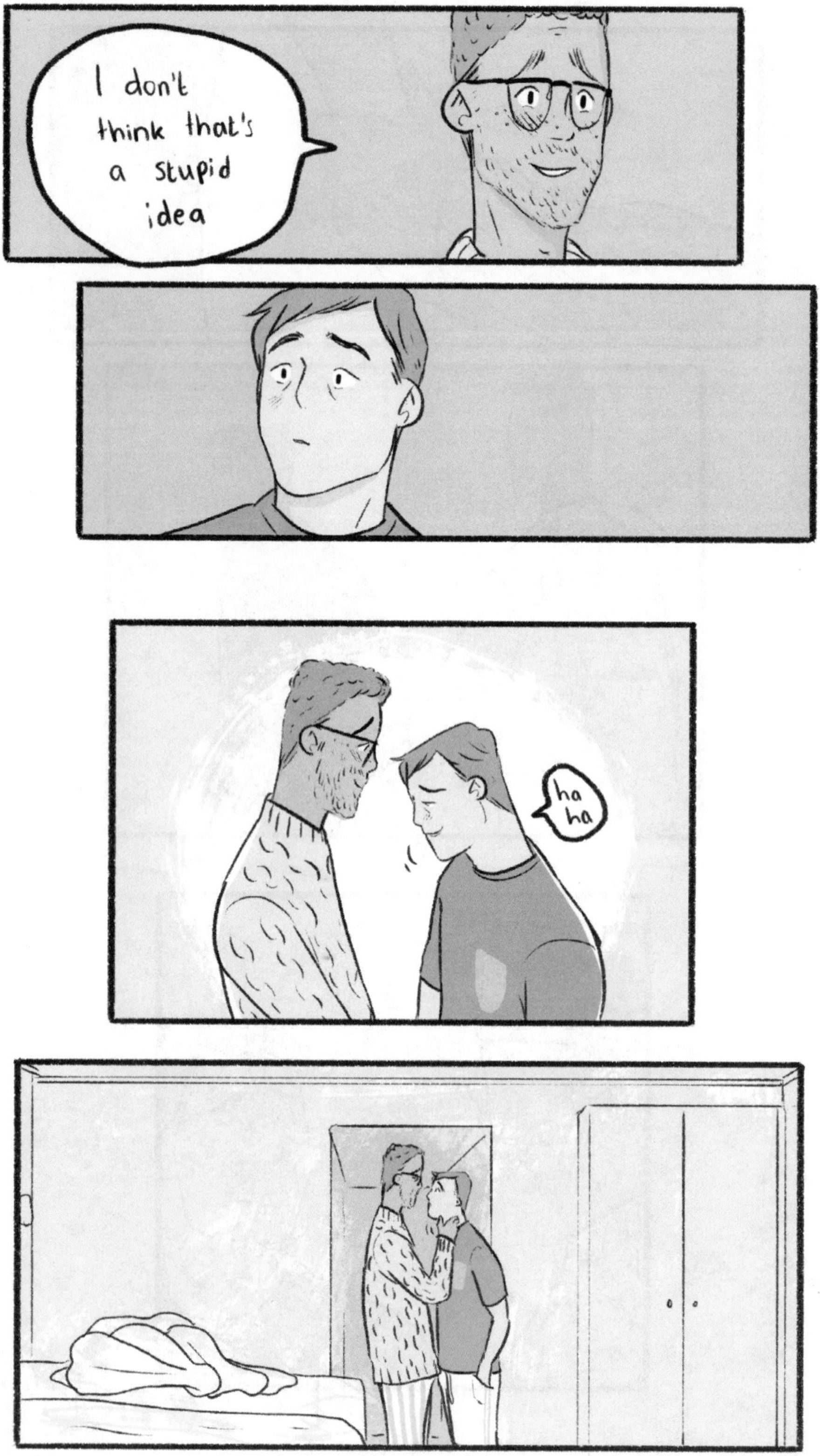
I don't think that's a stupid idea
ha ha

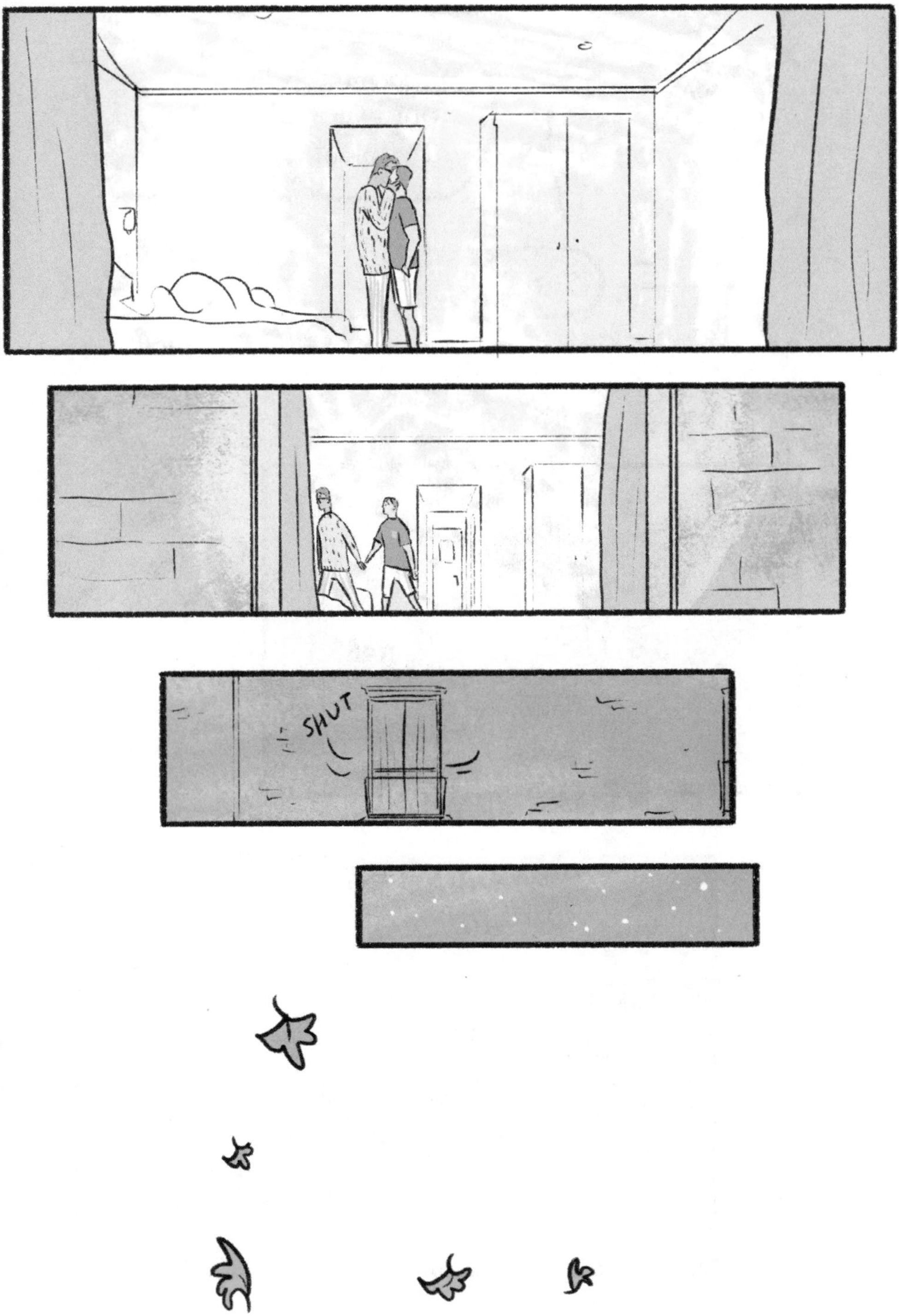
SHUT

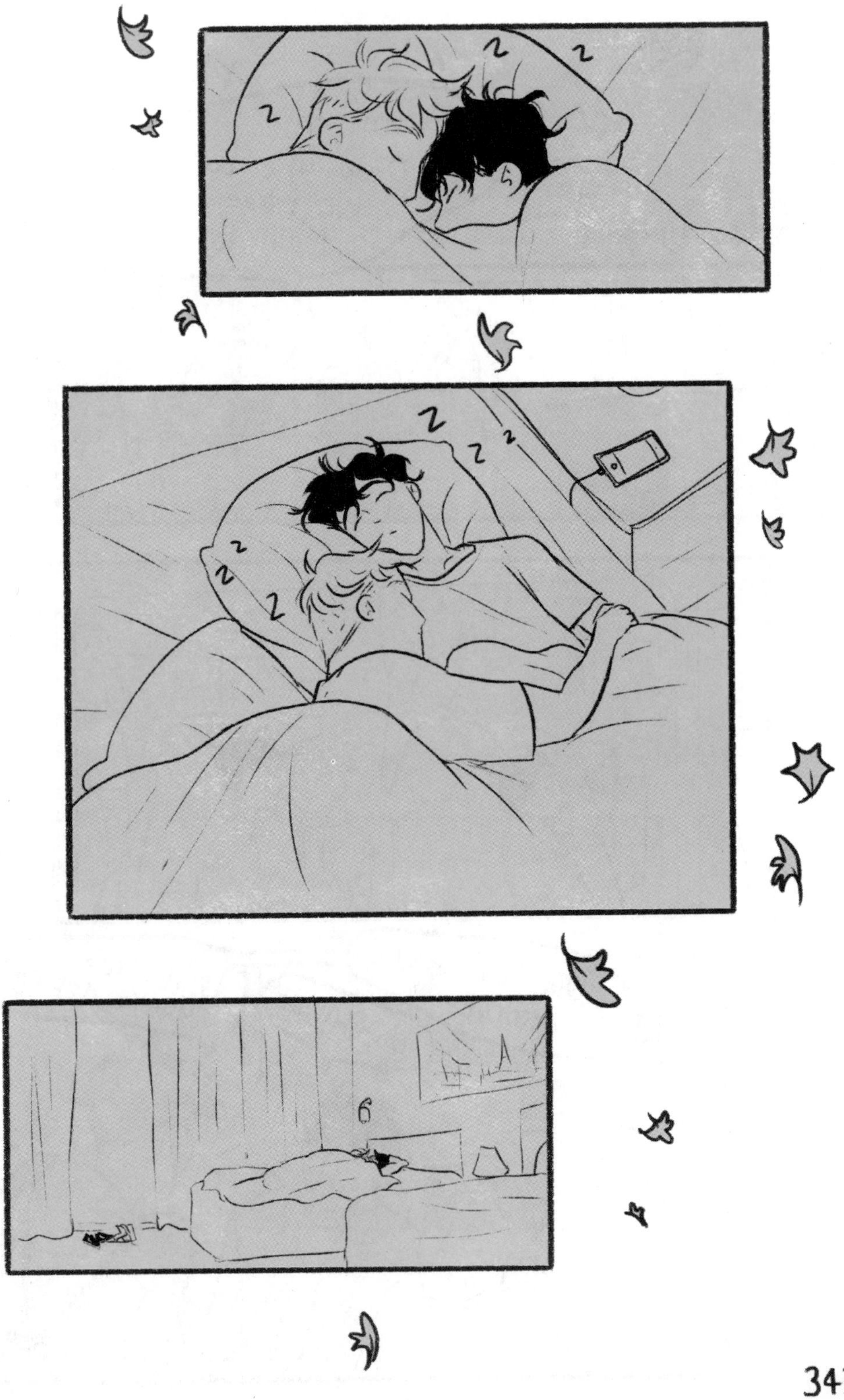

Z Z
Z
Z Z Z
Z Z
Z

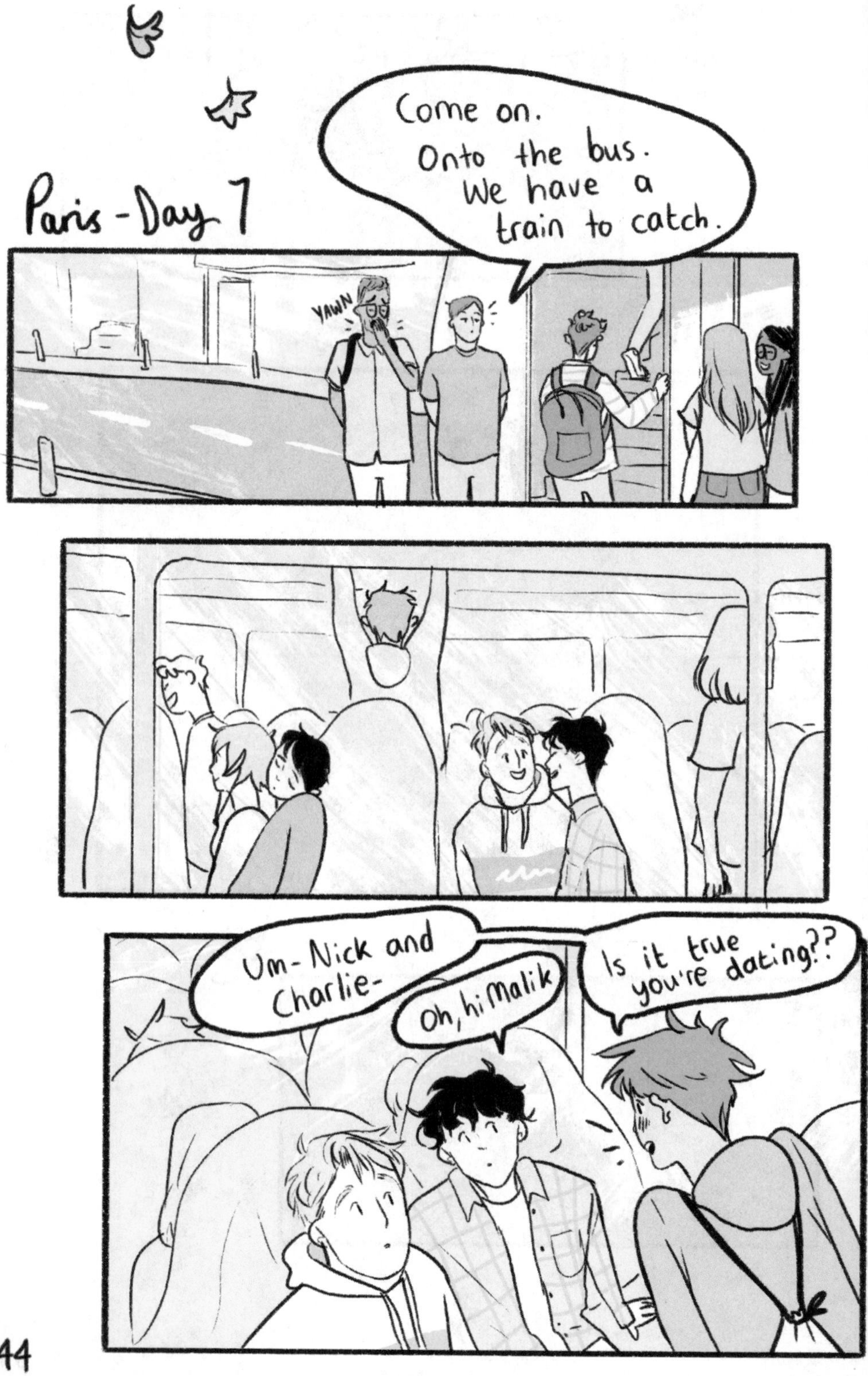
Paris - Day 7
Come on. Onto the bus. We have a train to catch.
YAWN
Um- Nick and Charlie-
Oh, hi Malik
Is it true you're dating??

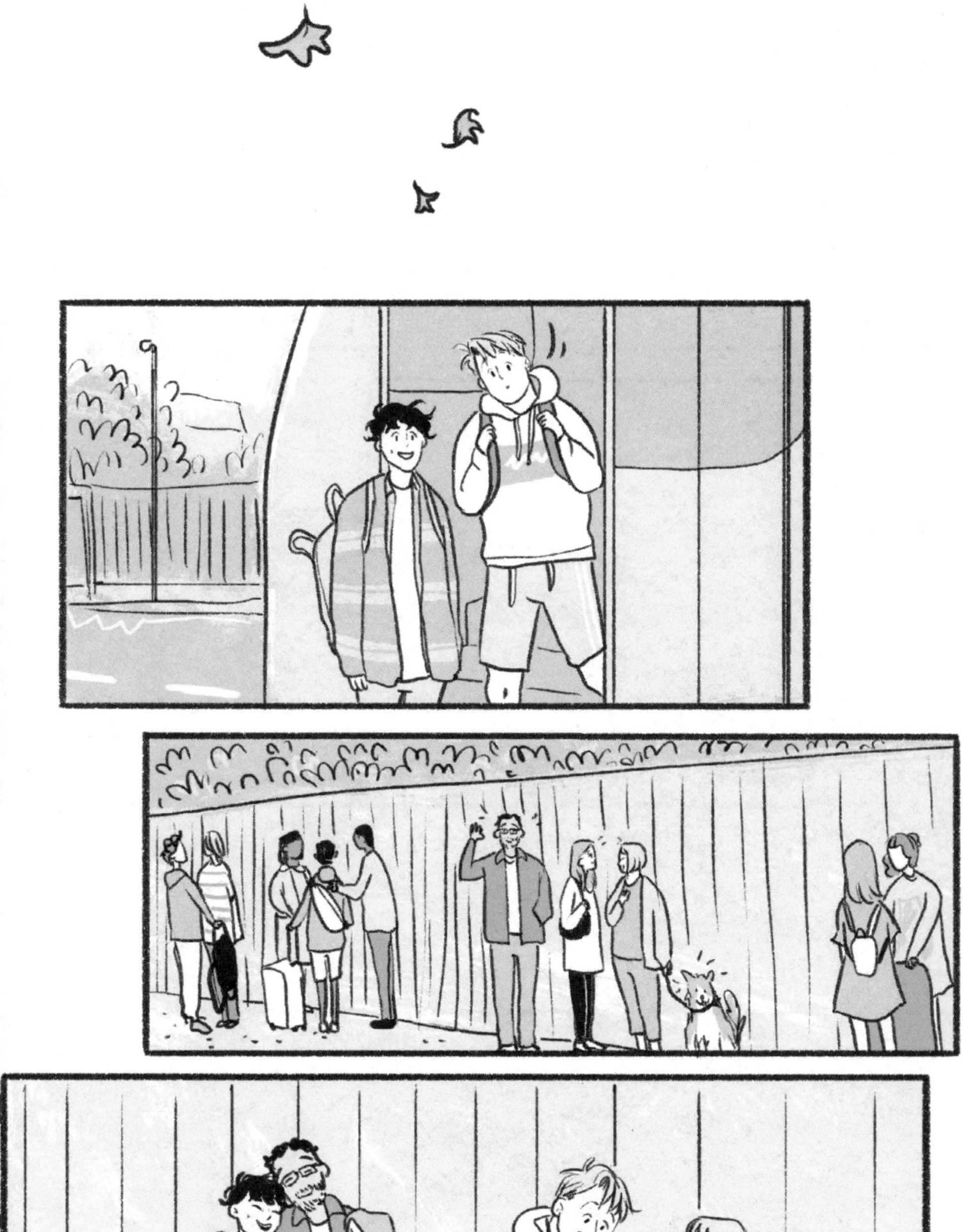

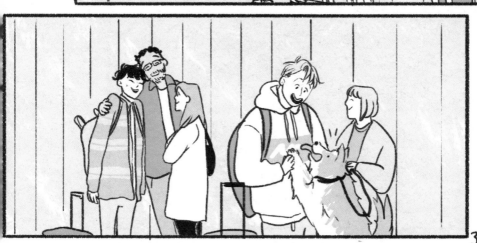

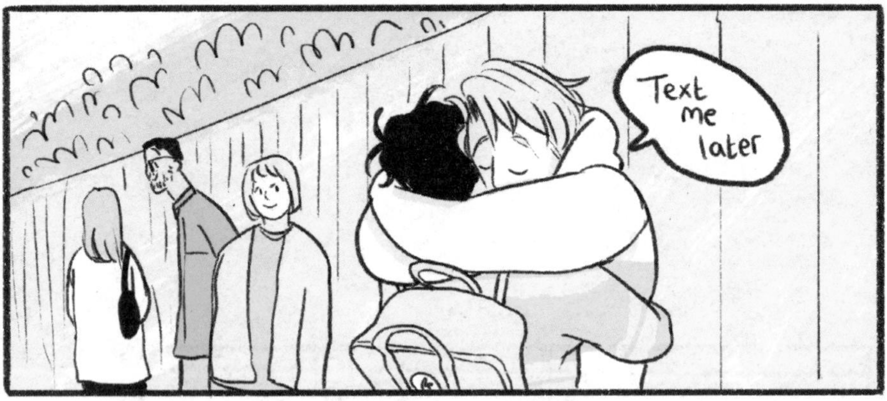
Text me later

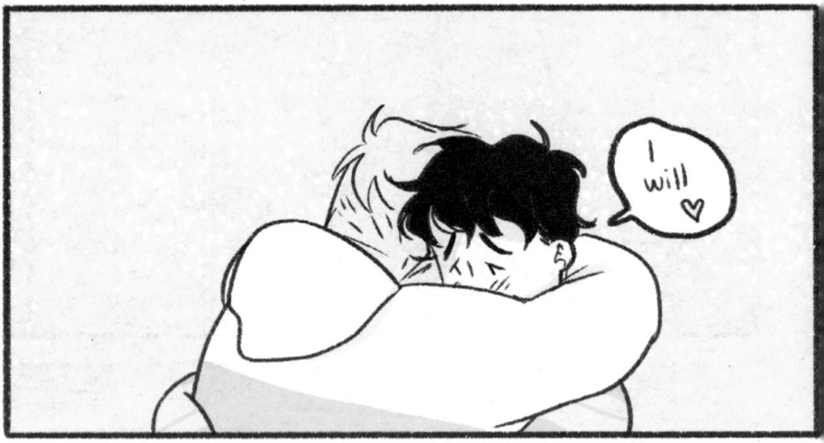
I will ♡

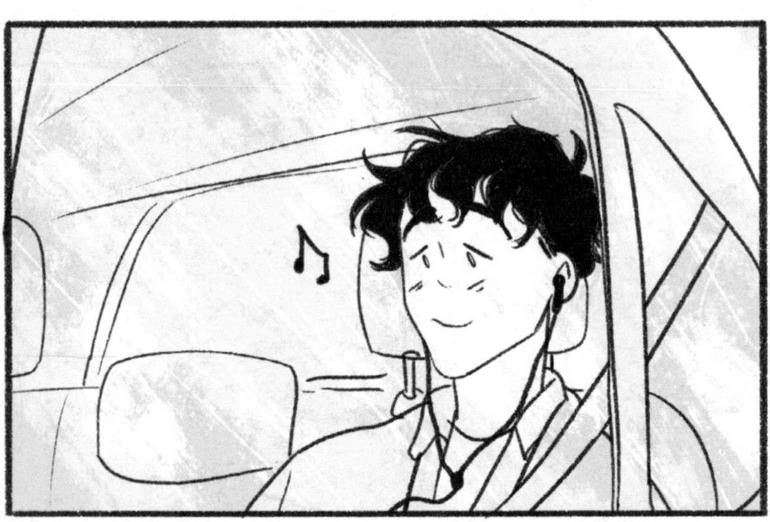

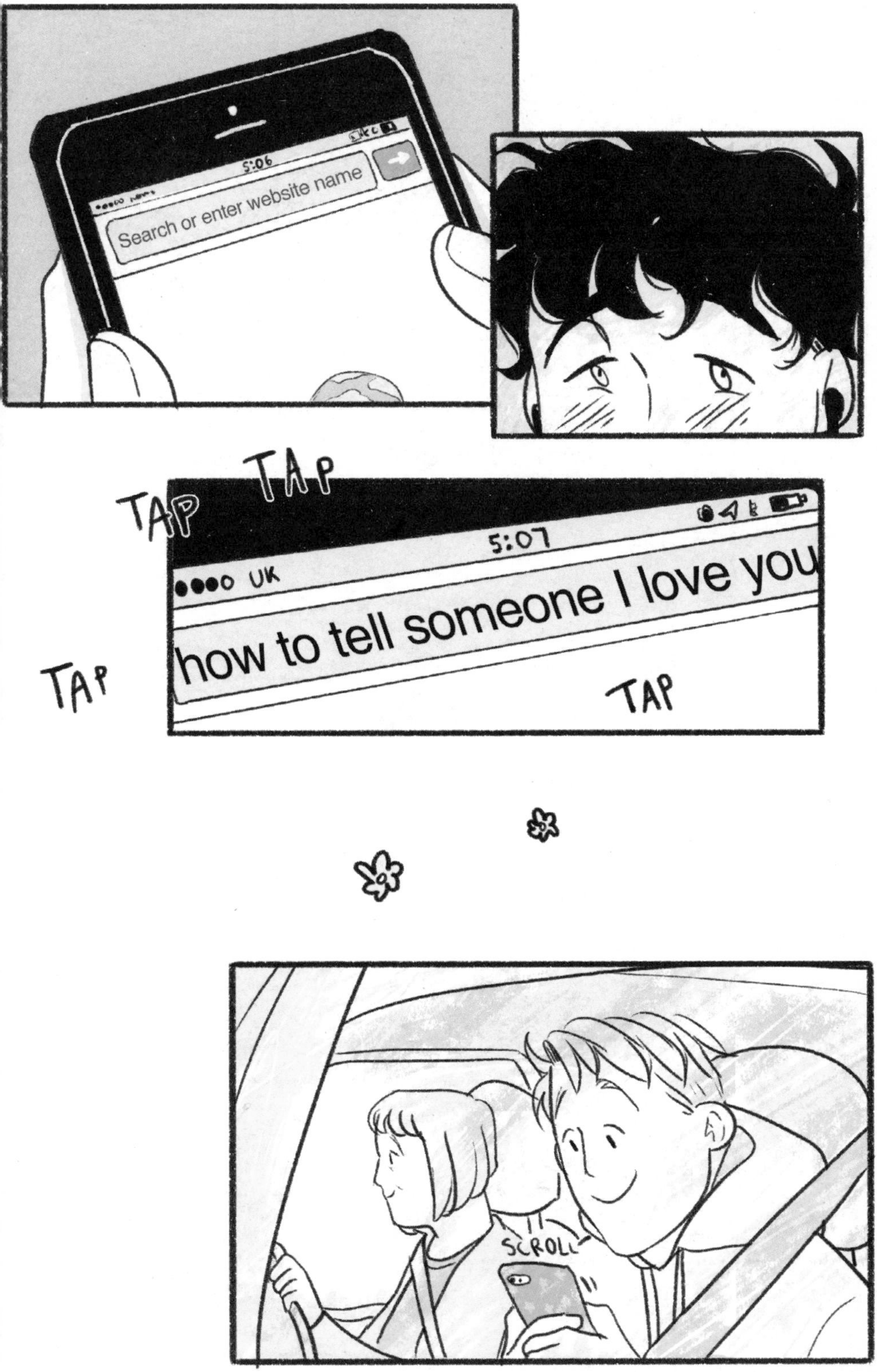
5:06
Search or enter website name
TAP
TAP
5:07
●●●○ UK
how to tell someone I love you
TAP
TAP
SCROLL

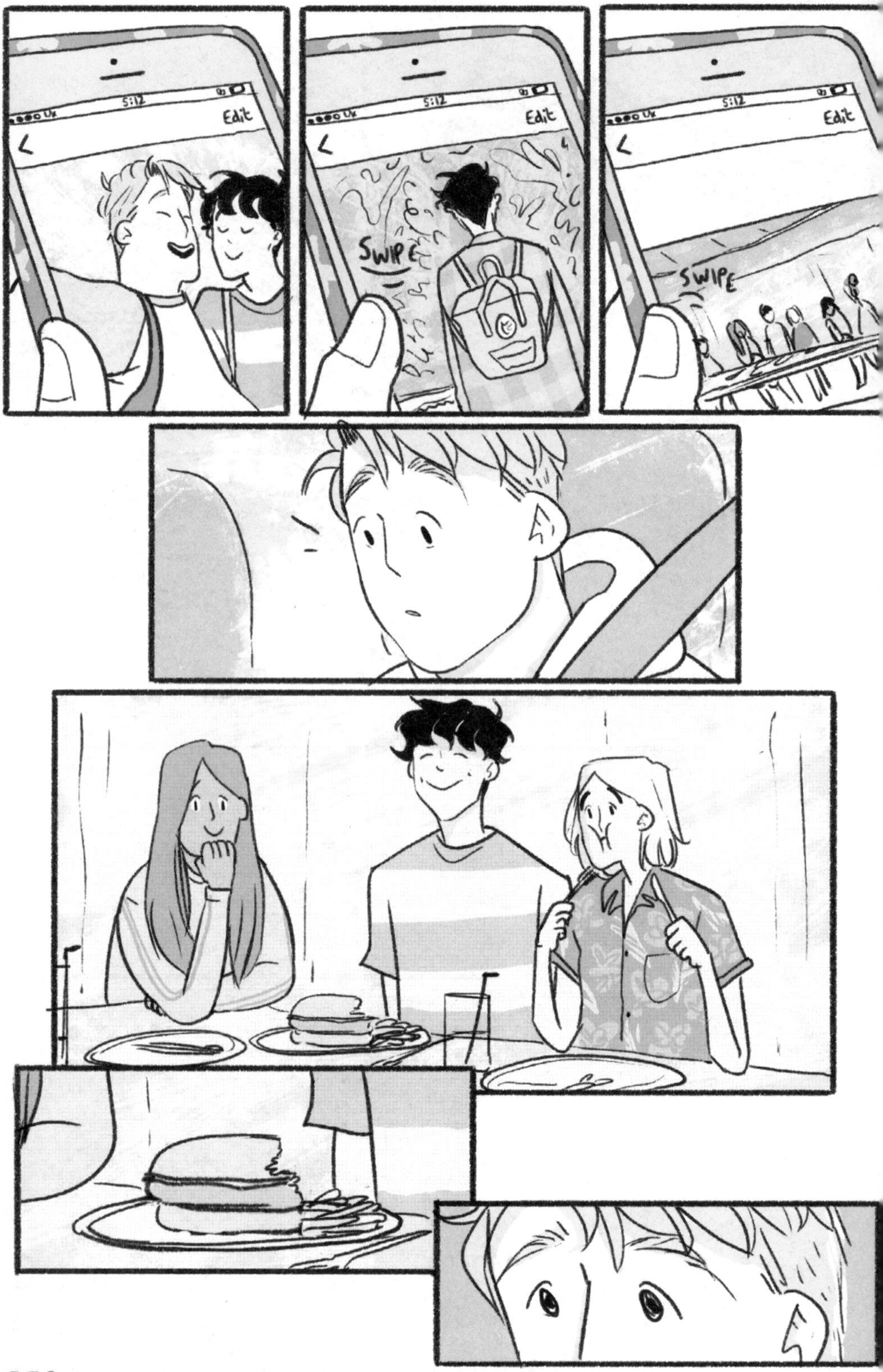
5:12
Edit
5:12
Edit
SWIPE
5:12
Edit
SWIPE

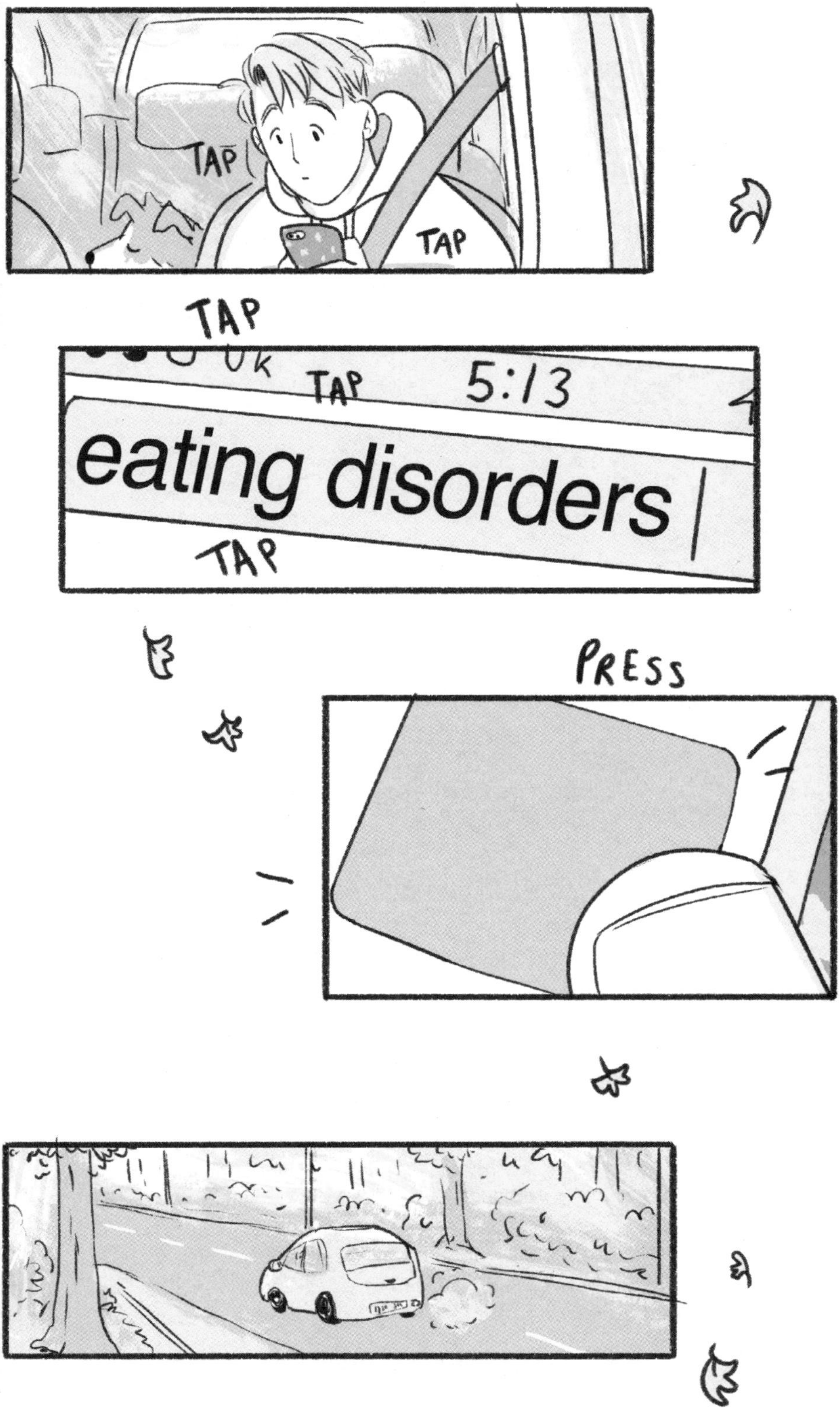
TAP
TAP
TAP
Ok
TAP
5:13
eating disorders
TAP
PRESS

Heartstopper will continue...

Sunday June 27th

So tomorrow I'll be going away for a whole week to PARIS.

♡ The city of love ♡

Okay that's dumb. But I'm very excited!!!

None of my Year 11 friends are going but I'll get to be with Charlie all day every day for a whole week, which is waaaaaaay better than being stuck at home now that my exams are over. And I really like Charlie's friends so I'd like to get to know them better.

I think I'm most looking forward to going up the Eiffel Tower. I always imagined it'd be super romantic to go up the Eiffel Tower with the person you ~~love~~ ~~like~~ love and take cheesy photos :)

very bad drawing of the Eiffel Tower →

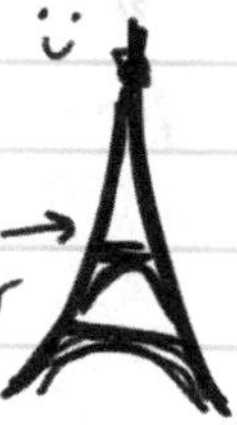

6/27

I've just finished packing for the Paris trip tomorrow!! I've been excited about it for sooooooo long— a whole week to just explore and have fun with my friends. YAY!

Plus, me and Nick are sleeping in the same room!! I know we won't really be able to kiss and be couple-y much because other people will be around, but I'm sorta hoping we get to sleep next to each other and just chat about silly random stuff all night...

And I WILL tell Tao about us. I want him to know. Even though he'll probably throw a fit about me not telling him.

I CAN DO THIS.

NAME: CHARLES "CHARLIE" SPRING

WHO ARE YOU: NICK'S BOYFRIEND

SCHOOL YEAR: YEAR 10   **AGE:** 15

BIRTHDAY: APRIL 27TH

FUN FACT: LOVES READING

NAME: Nicholas "Nick" Nelson

WHO ARE YOU: Charlie's boyfriend

SCHOOL YEAR: Year 11   **AGE:** 16

BIRTHDAY: September 4th

FUN FACT: Really good at cooking

NAME: Tao Xu

WHO ARE YOU: Charlie's friend

SCHOOL YEAR: Year 10   **AGE:** 15

BIRTHDAY: September 23rd

FUN FACT: Favorite movie is "Hunt for the Wilderpeople"

NAME: Victoria "Tori" Spring

WHO ARE YOU: Charlie's sister

SCHOOL YEAR: Year 11   **AGE:** 16

BIRTHDAY: April 5th

FUN FACT: HATES MOST THINGS

NAME: Elle Argent
WHO ARE YOU: Charlie's friend
SCHOOL YEAR: Year 11   **AGE:** 16
BIRTHDAY: May 4th
FUN FACT: makes many of her own clothes for fun

NAME: Tara Jones
WHO ARE YOU: Darcy's girlfriend
SCHOOL YEAR: Year 11   **AGE:** 16
BIRTHDAY: July 3rd
FUN FACT: used to attend a Majorettes class

NAME: Darcy Olsson
WHO ARE YOU: Tara's girlfriend
SCHOOL YEAR: Year 11   **AGE:** 16
BIRTHDAY: January 9th
FUN FACT: once ate a whole jar of mustard for a dare

NAME: Aled Last
WHO ARE YOU: Charlie's friend
SCHOOL YEAR: Year 10   **AGE:** 14
BIRTHDAY: August 15th
FUN FACT: wants to make a Podcast

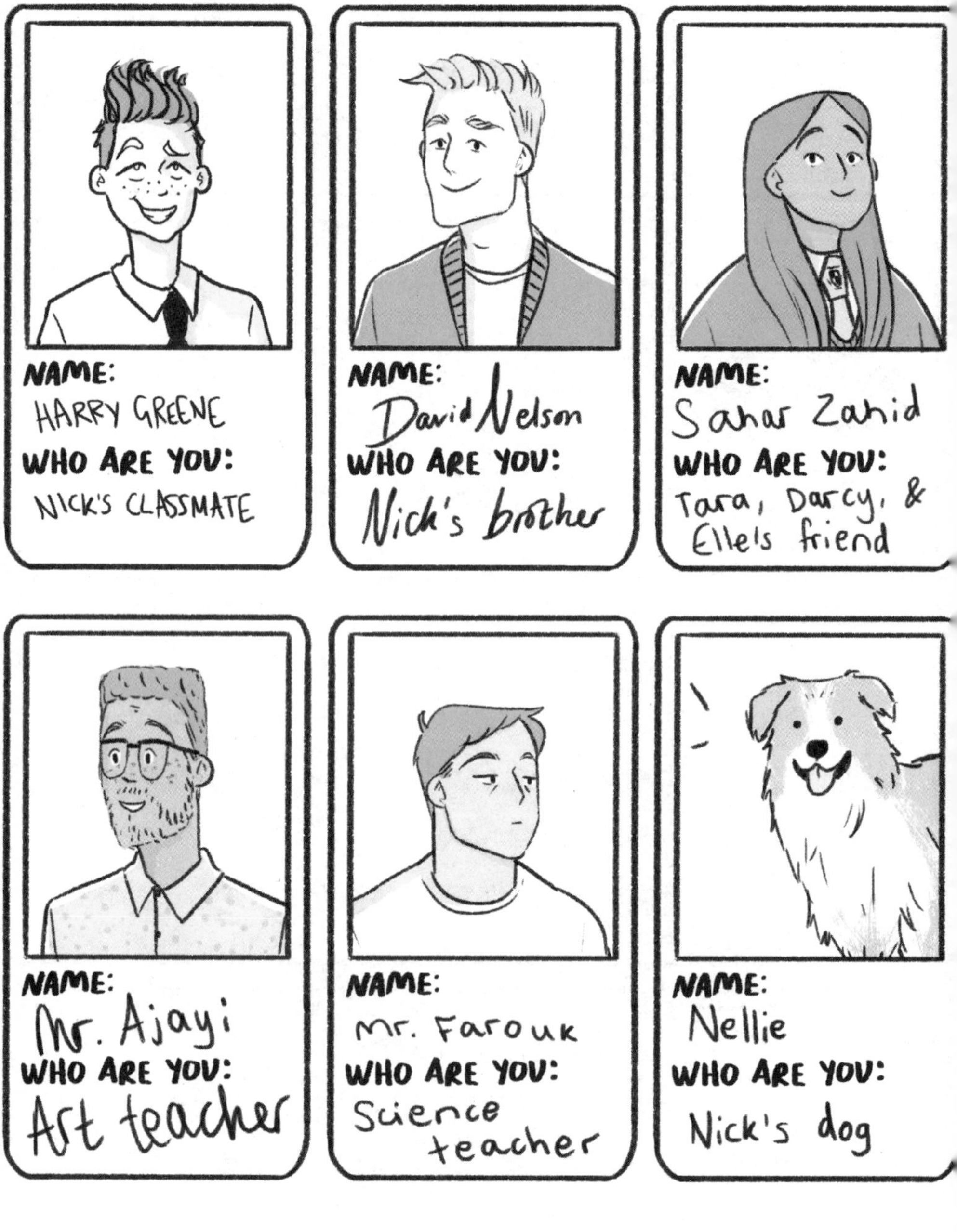
NAME:
HARRY GREENE
WHO ARE YOU:
NICK'S CLASSMATE
NAME:
David Nelson
WHO ARE YOU:
Nick's brother
NAME:
Sahar Zahid
WHO ARE YOU:
Tara, Darcy, & Elle's friend
NAME:
Mr. Ajayi
WHO ARE YOU:
Art teacher
NAME:
Mr. Farouk
WHO ARE YOU:
Science teacher
NAME:
Nellie
WHO ARE YOU:
Nick's dog

Nick's Room

view A

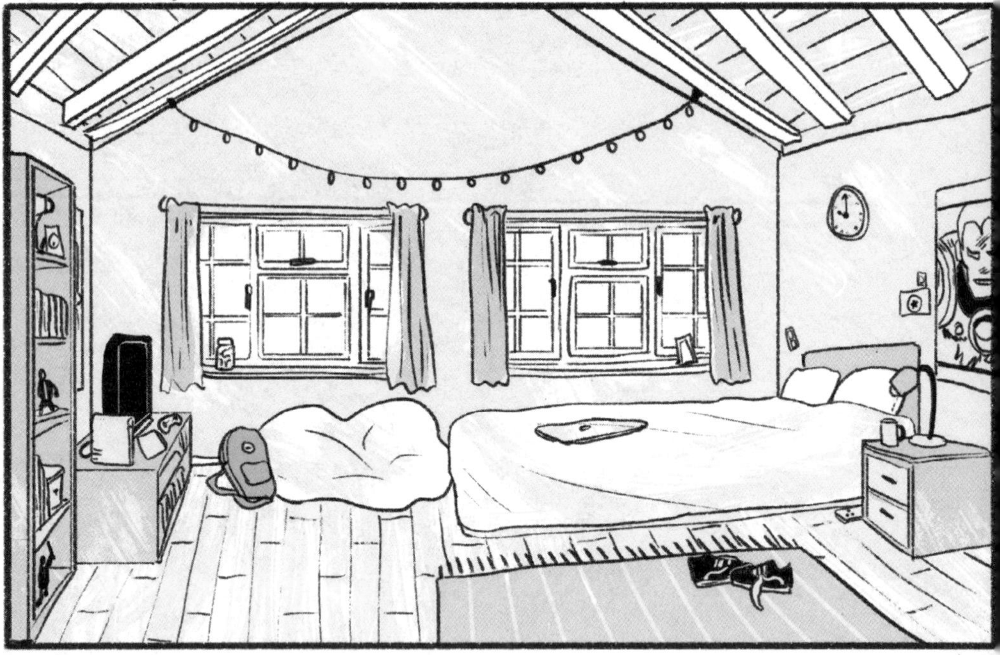

view B

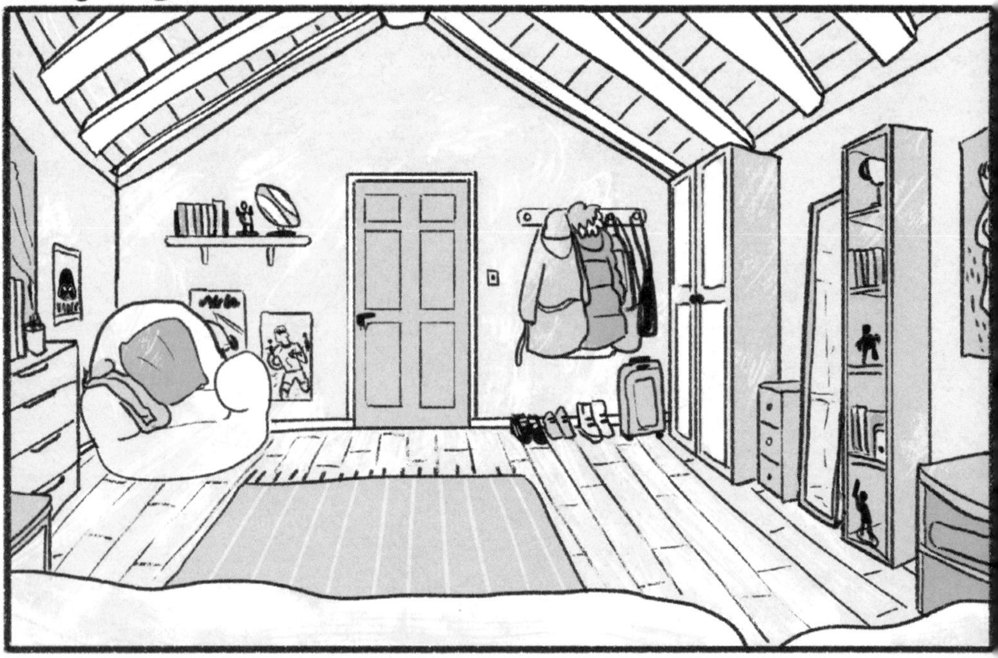

Key Features

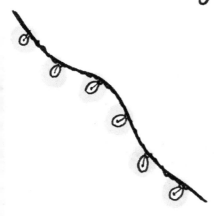

Fairy lights

Nick put up fairy lights in his bedroom one Christmas and forgot to take them down for three months. Eventually he decided he liked having them up all year round!

Beanbag

A comfy, cozy beanbag Nick's had for years. He ts in it sometimes, but mostly it's Nellie Nelson's favorite nap spot.

Posters

Along with posters of his favorite movies, Nick has some posters of his two favorite sports: rugby and motor racing.

Charlie's Room

View A

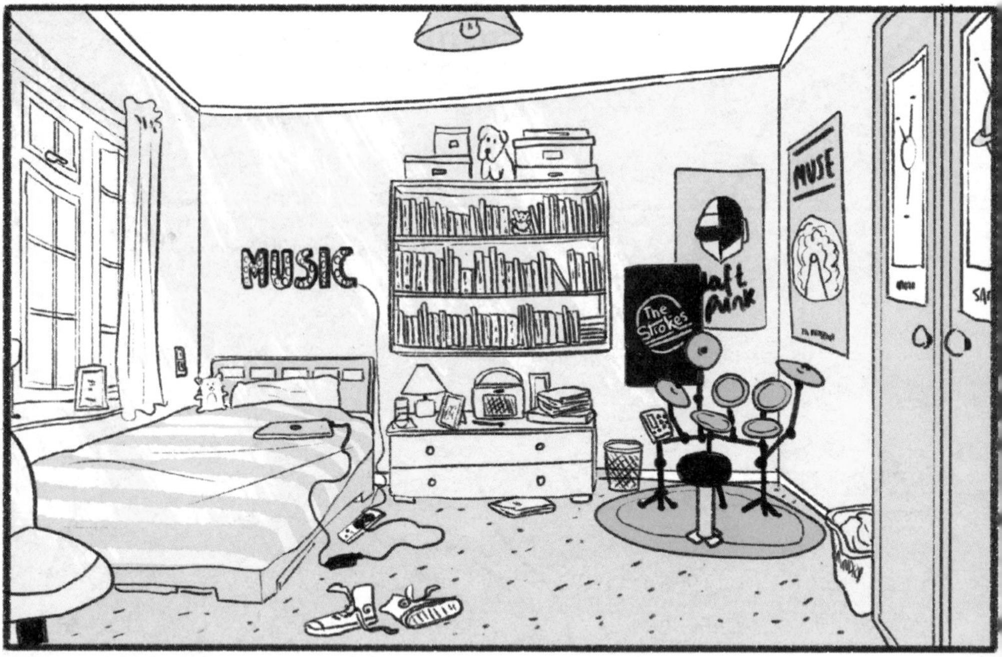
MUSIC
The Strokes
MUSE

View B

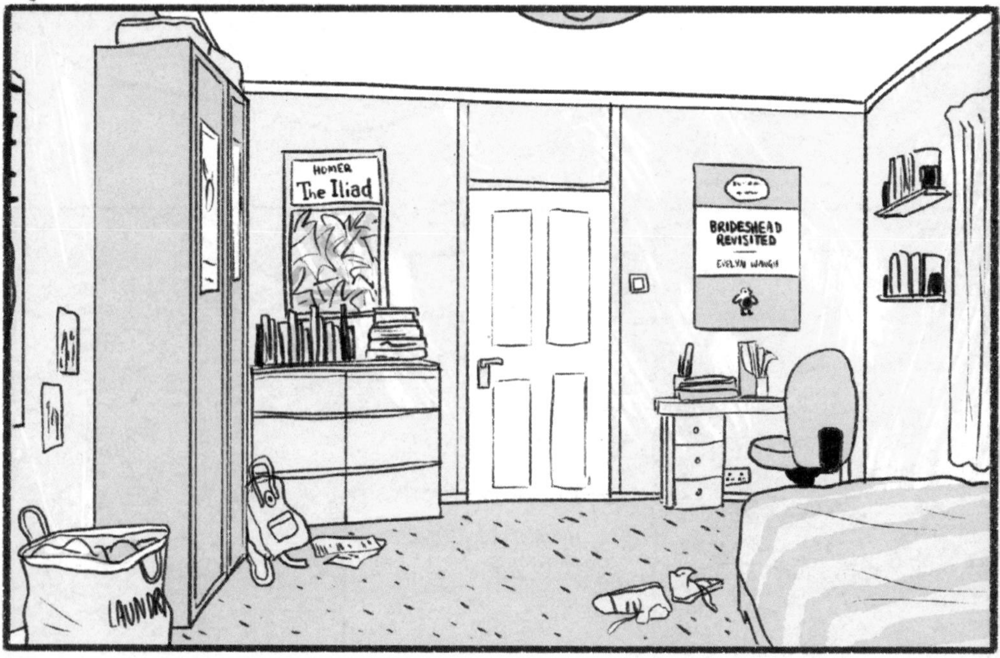
HOMER
The Iliad
BRIDESHEAD REVISITED
EVELYN WAUGH

Key Features

Electronic drum kit

Charlie started learning how to play the drums when he was nine. He doesn't have any particular aspirations to become a musician or be in a band, but he still really loves playing, especially to relieve stress!

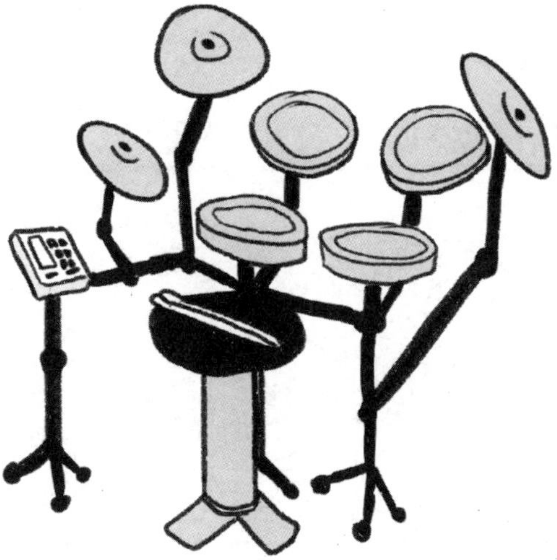

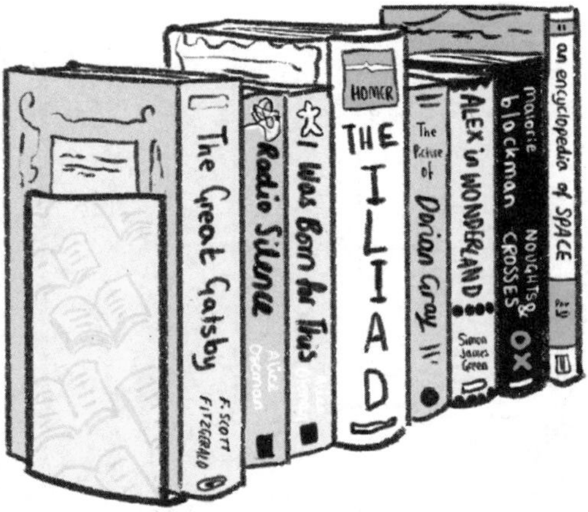
The Great Gatsby
F. SCOTT FITZGERALD
Radio Silence
Alice Oseman
I Was Born for This
HOMER
THE ILIAD
The Picture of Dorian Gray
ALEX in WONDERLAND
Simon James Green
malorie blackman
NOUGHTS & CROSSES
an encyclopedia of SPACE

Bookshelves

Charlie's favorite hobby is reading. He'll read any genre, especially if there are gay characters, but he finds Ancient Greek classical literature the most interesting.

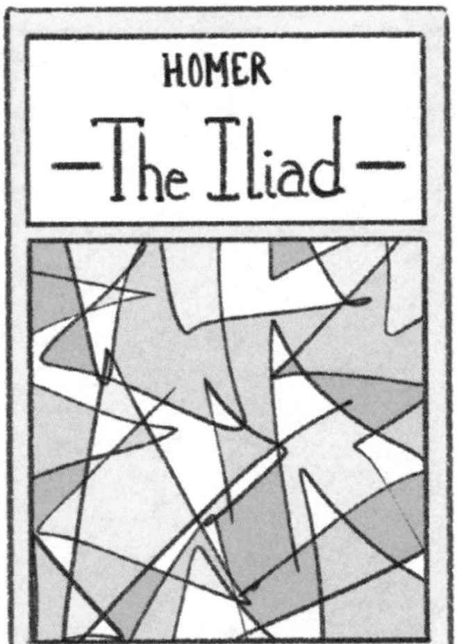
HOMER
—The Iliad—

Posters

Along with posters of his favorite bands, Charlie has posters of two of his favorite classic texts: *The Illiad* by Homer and *Brideshead Revisited* by Evelyn Waugh.

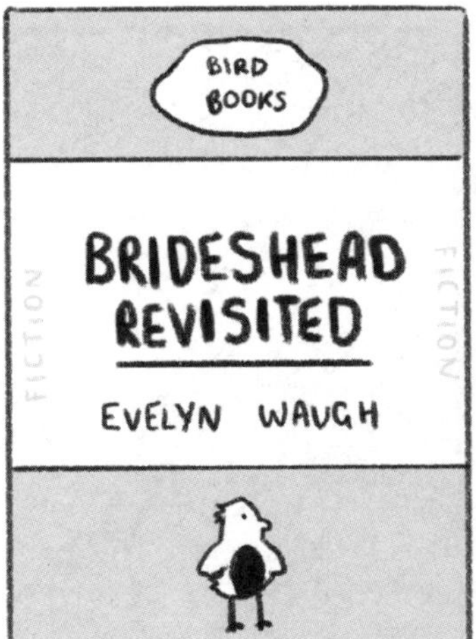
BIRD BOOKS
BRIDESHEAD REVISITED
EVELYN WAUGH
FICTION
FICTION

The First Day

a Heartstopper mini-comic

THE PREVIOUS SEPTEMBER...

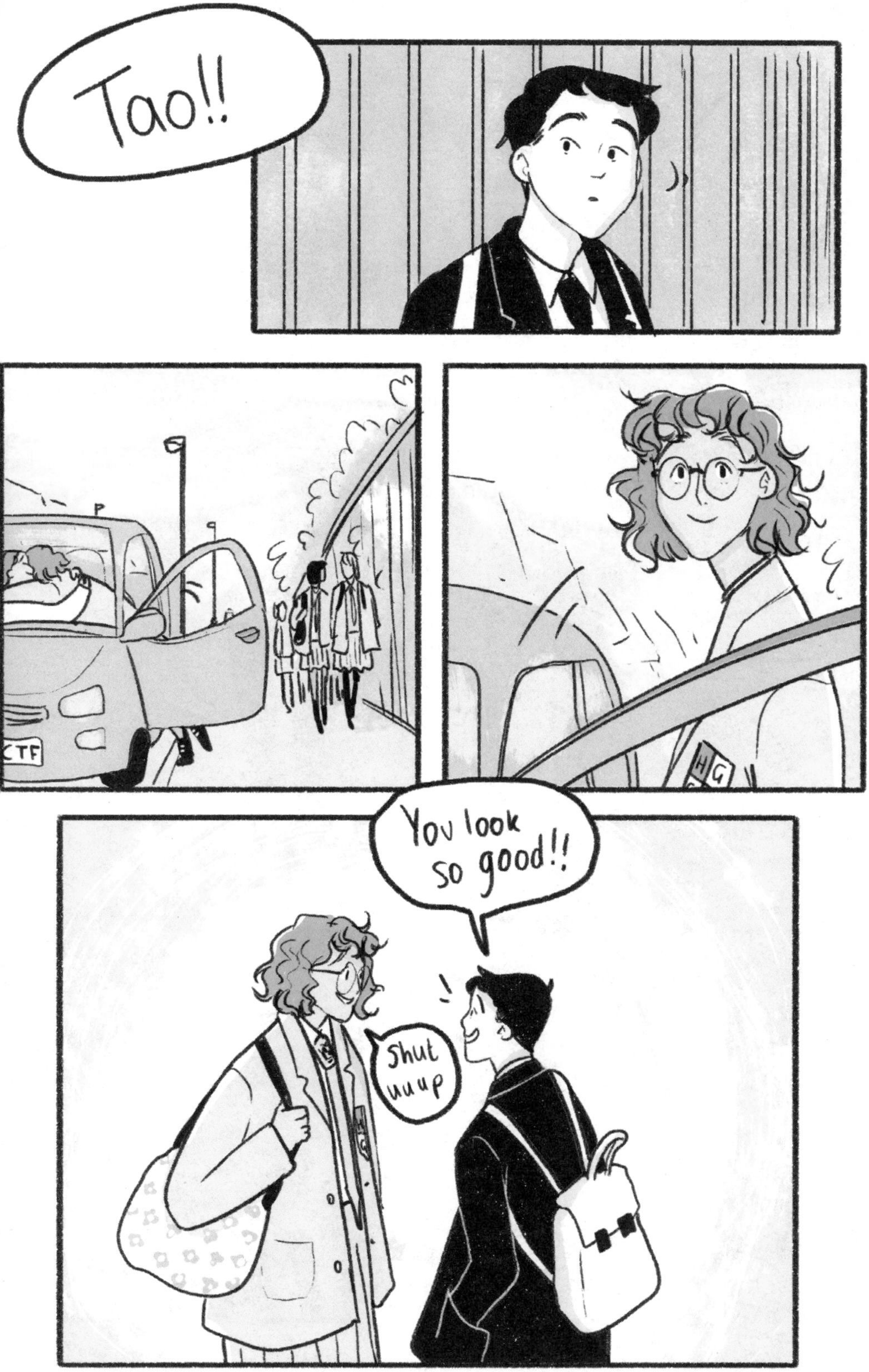
Tao!!
You look so good!!
Shut uuup

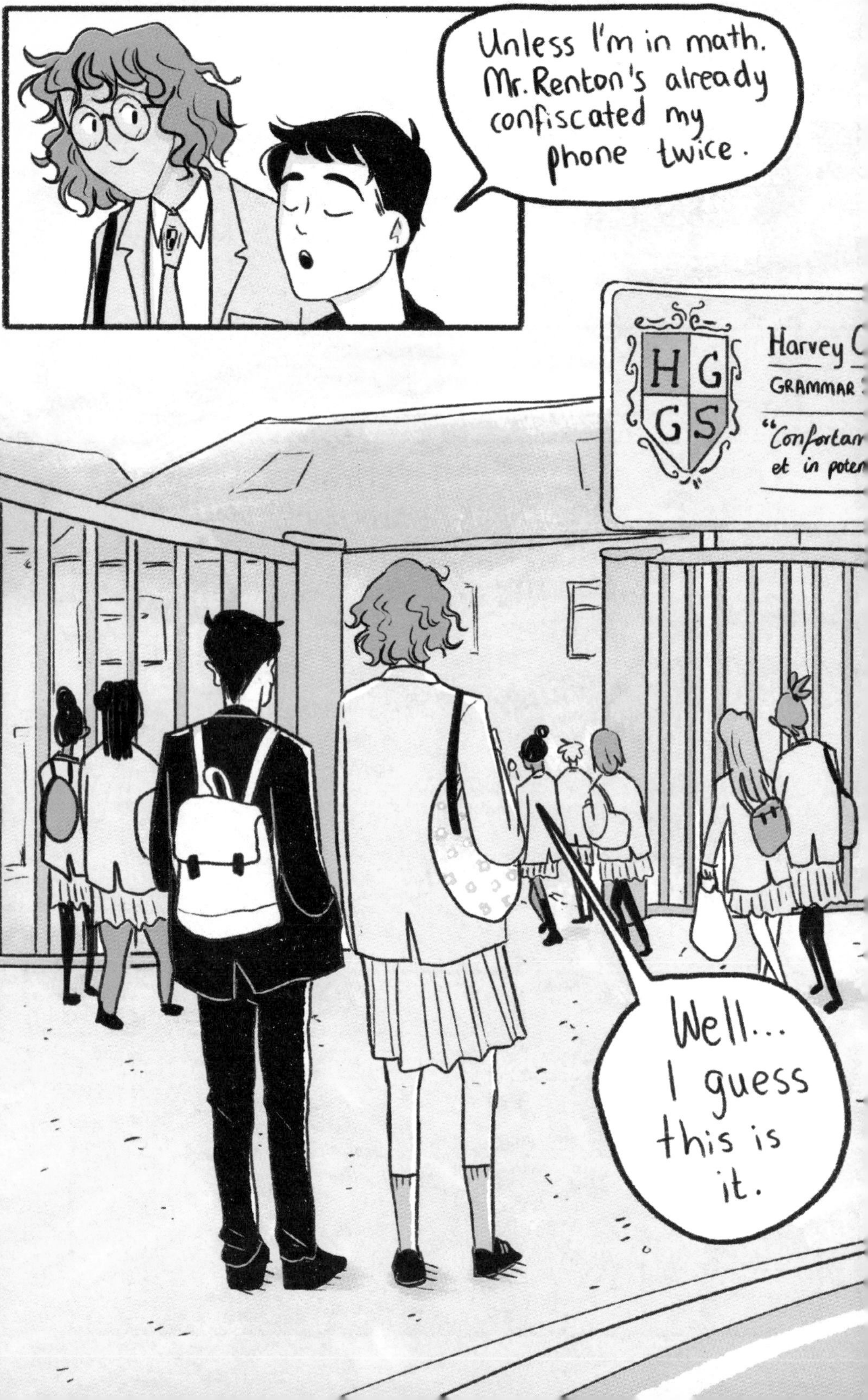
Unless I'm in math. Mr. Renton's already confiscated my phone twice.
HG
GS
Harvey
GRAMMAR
Well... I guess this is it.

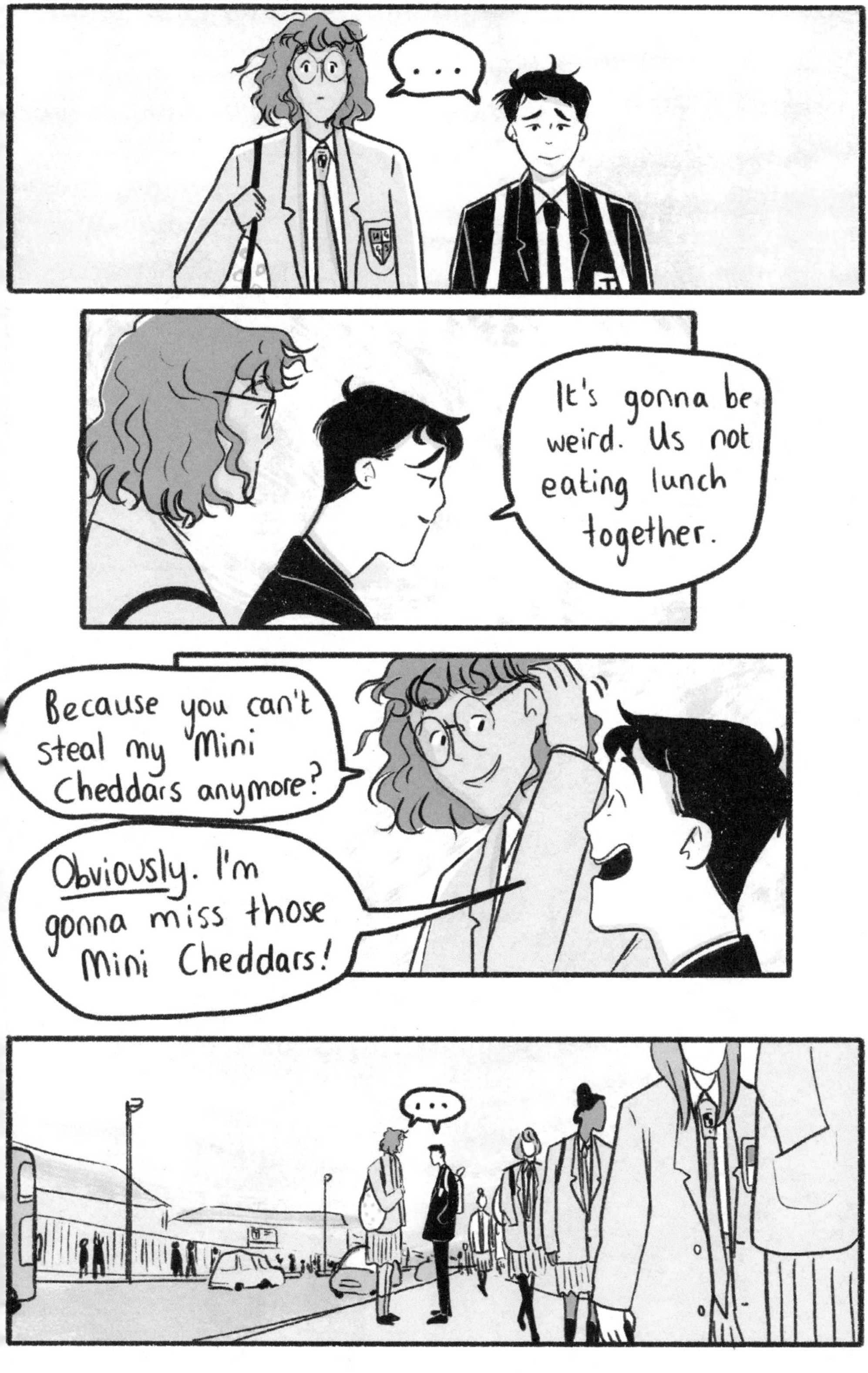
...
It's gonna be weird. Us not eating lunch together.
Because you can't steal my Mini Cheddars anymore?
Obviously. I'm gonna miss those Mini Cheddars!
...

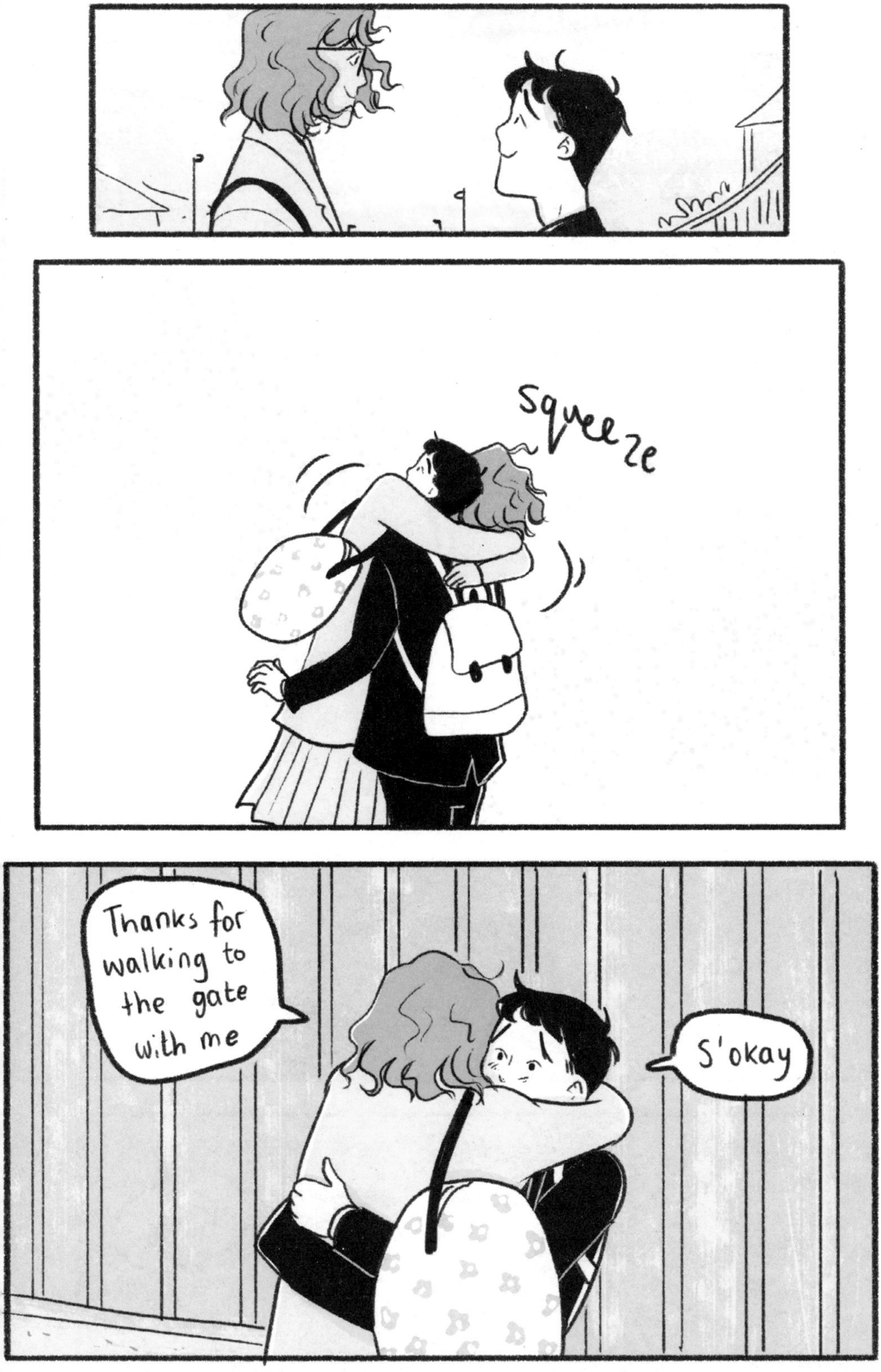
squeeze
Thanks for walking to the gate with me
S'okay

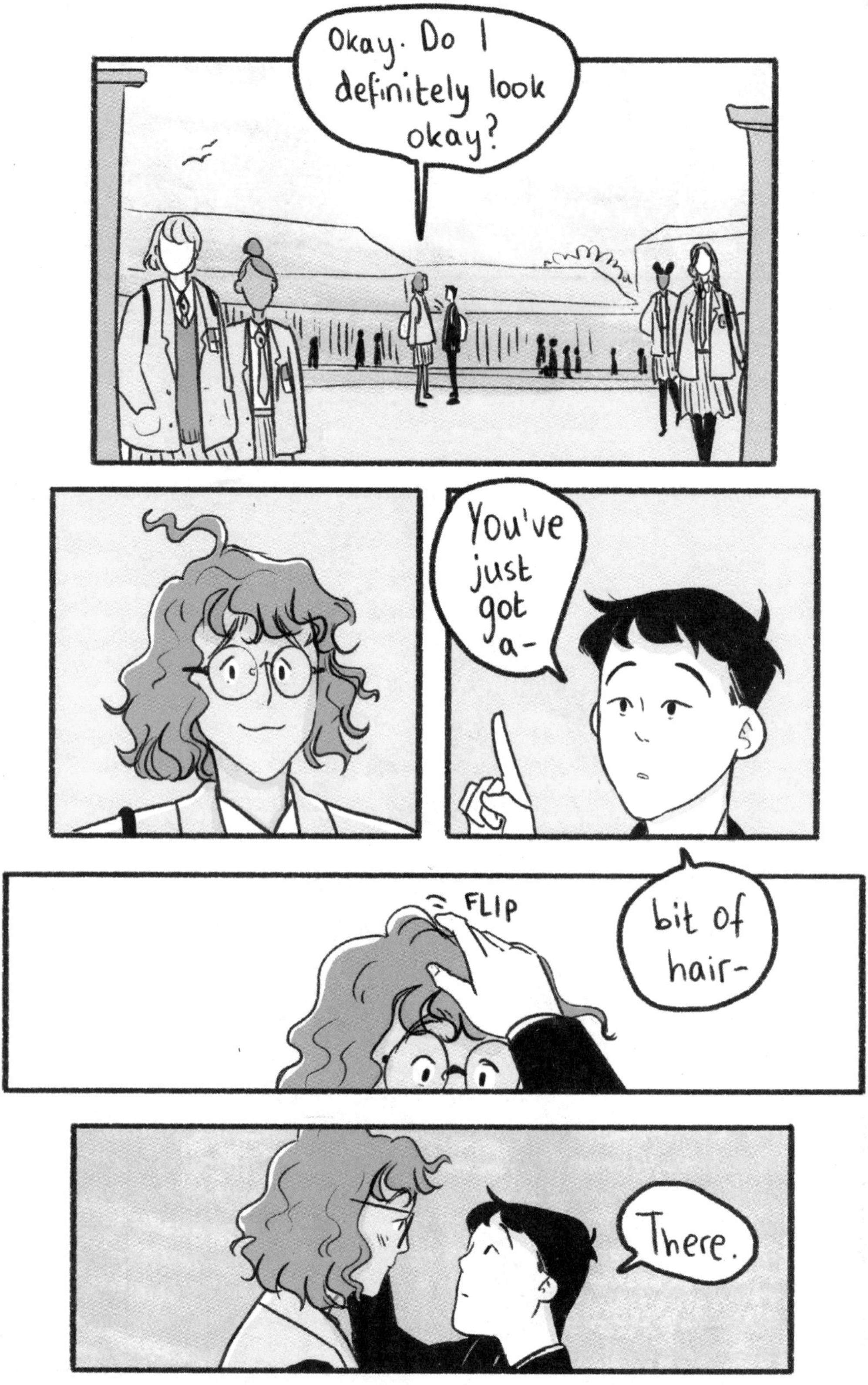
Okay. Do I definitely look okay?
You've just got a-
FLIP
bit of hair-
There.

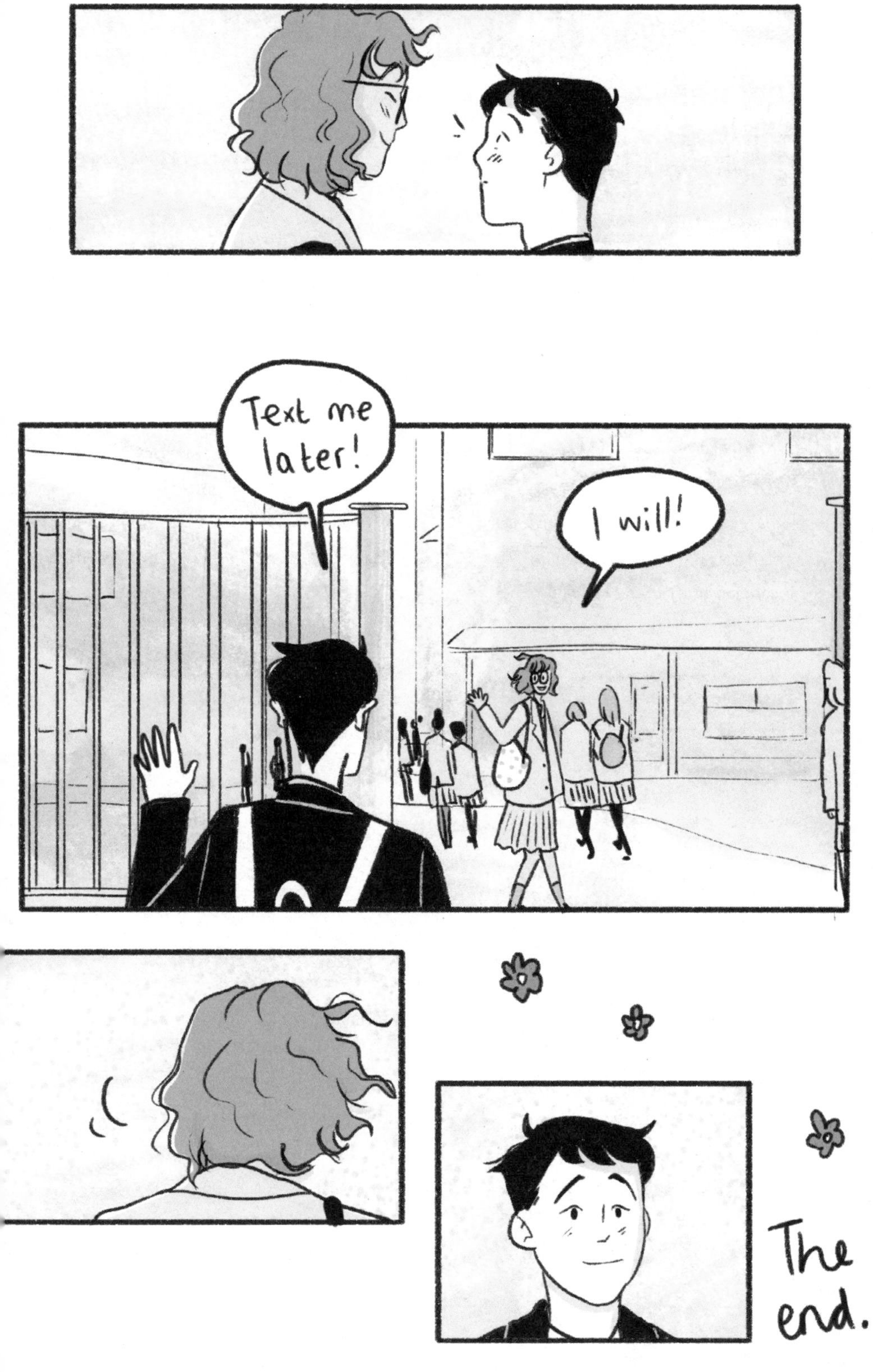
Text me later!
I will!
The end.

Author's Note

Here we are in the third volume of Heartstopper! It feels like only yesterday that I had two thousand books stacked in my house, ready to be shipped to my Kickstarter supporters. We've come so far since then!

This volume starts with Nick and Charlie solidly a couple but with a lot to learn about each other. I strongly believe that the "getting together" part of a romance is just the beginning and there's so much else to explore beyond that. Nick and Charlie spent much of this volume getting to know each other on a deeper level, which has been such a joy to write. It was also wonderful to get to know some of Heartstopper's side characters in this chapter! Tao, Elle, Tara, Darcy, and even Aled all have a bigger role to play, and I hope we continue to get to know them better in the next volume.

This volume also touched on the more serious topic of mental health; in particular self-harm and eating disorders. Mental health and mental illness are topics that are very close to me and I explore them in all my works, but here in Heartstopper I want the focus to always be on support, healing, and recovery. If you are struggling with any of the same issues, please do not hesitate to reach out to someone you love, just as Charlie has done, an adult you trust, and/or a medical professional. You could also seek help and advice from an online support network, such as:

The Heard Alliance: heardalliance.org
The Safe Zone Project: thesafezoneproject.com
The Trevor Project: thetrevorproject.org

Sending so much love and thanks to Heartstopper's online readers, my Patreon patrons, and the Kickstarter supporters! It's thanks to you that the series is able to continue.

To Rachel Wade, Alison Padley, Emily Thomas, Felicity Highet, and everyone else involved in Heartstopper at Hachette—thank you so much for making these books a reality! I'm so grateful to be working with such a passionate and dedicated team.

A huge thanks to my agent, Claire Wilson, who is my guiding light in the world of books!

And thank you, as always, to you, dear reader! I'll see you in the next one.

Alice
x

Alice Oseman was born in 1994 in Kent, England, and is a full-time writer and illustrator. She can usually be found staring aimlessly at computer screens, questioning the meaninglessness of existence, or doing anything and everything to avoid getting an office job.

As well as writing and illustrating Heartstopper, Alice is the author of three YA novels: *Solitaire*, *Radio Silence*, and *I Was Born for This*.

To find out more about Alice's work, visit her online:

aliceoseman.com
twitter.com/AliceOseman
instagram.com/aliceoseman

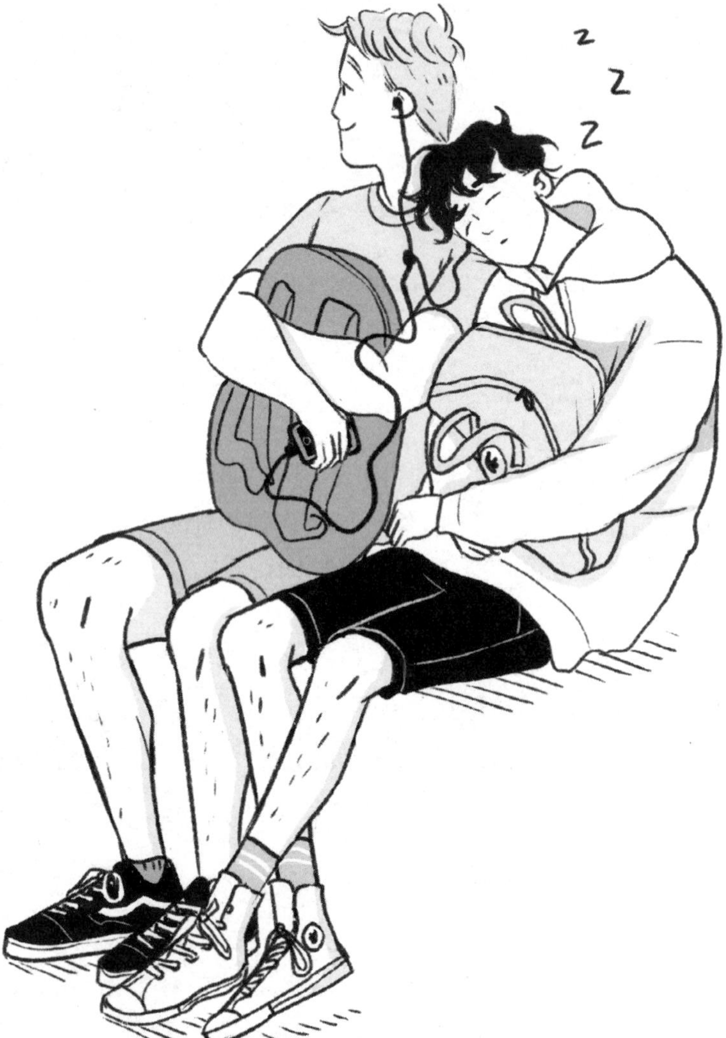
z
Z
Z